VIOLETTE MALAN'S
Spectacular Novels
Now Available from DAW Books:

THE MIRROR PRINCE
SHADOWLANDS

The Novels of Dhulyn and Parno:
THE SLEEPING GOD
THE SOLDIER KING
THE STORM WITCH
PATH OF THE SUN

VIOLETTE MALAN

THE DHULYN AND PARNO NOVELS:
VOLUME ONE

THE SLEEPING GOD

THE SOLDIER KING

DAW BOOKS, INC.
DONALD A. WOLLHEIM, FOUNDER
375 Hudson Street, New York, NY 10014

ELIZABETH R. WOLLHEIM
SHEILA E. GILBERT
PUBLISHERS
www.dawbooks.com

First Printing, February 2015
1 2 3 4 5 6 7 8 9

Author's Note

It's pronounced "Dillan," by the way. It's a variation on the Welsh spelling of Dylan, among other things, but it's mainly an homage to Fritz Leiber, and his incredible Fafhrd and Grey Mouser stories.

There were a number of things I wanted to do when I first came up with the idea for the Dhulyn and Parno universe, but the primary one was to write my own version of Fafhrd and the Grey Mouser. I'd loved those stories growing up—I still do—and I wanted to do something similar myself. Of course, I'm a woman, which meant that at least one of my duo had to be female. And I wanted to try my hand at a male/female pairing that didn't have any sexual tension—you know, something without the "do they/don't they; will they/won't they" that we associate with so much television programming.

I didn't want to copy Leiber, so my characters couldn't be thieves, but to retain the flavor of the old stories, they had to have a similar level of mobility, with similar opportunities to get into trouble. Looked at that way, making them mercenaries makes a lot of sense, doesn't it? However, as you've likely noticed, there are mercenaries and mercenaries. I thought it was too easy to have them on the despised "kill for money" end of the spectrum, so I decided to go to the opposite extreme.

Which brings us to another source of inspiration for me, Alexandre Dumas' *The Three Musketeers*. Though, when I think about it, the Mercenary Brotherhood that's home to Dhulyn Wolfshead and Parno Lionsmane is more like a cross between the Musketeers and the samurai. Greatly respected, superbly skilled, strict codes of conduct, and often able to settle an argument just by walking into a room.

Fafhrd and the Mouser frequently got themselves into just as much trouble following their own personal rules of conduct as they did by breaking society's rules, and that gave me the last thread I needed to complicate Dhulyn and Parno's lives.

I hope you enjoy these adventures. And as they say in the Brotherhood, "In battle, or in death."

Violette Malan
Ontario, Canada
2014

For Paul.

THE
SLEEPING GOD

Acknowledgments

Thanks go first to Joshua Bilmes and Sheila Gilbert for their hard work. Without their questions and input, and most especially their patience, this book could not have been finished. To my in-laws, Marj and Don Musselman, for their constant support; my friend Barb Wilson-Orange for her help with earlier versions; to Jay Ridler for his insights into military and social infrastructures; any errors are mine. Likewise thanks to Elizabeth Moon and Zdzislaw Sikora for a wonderful fencing demonstration and for answering my questions; again, any errors are mine. To Tanya Huff and Fiona Patton for their encouragement and example, and for reminding me to enjoy myself. Jenn Shannon and Brian and Marlene McCracken for their encouragement and support beyond the call. The Water Babes, the most courageous book club in the world.

The right to have a character named after her was bought at silent auction for Larissa Landon. Your mother said a bad guy, Larissa, so I hope you don't mind.

One

•

PARNO LIONSMANE STEPPED OFF the end of the ship's gangplank with deliberation. He and his Partner, Dhulyn Wolfshead, had only been aboard the *Catseye* for the four-day trip from the Isle of Cabrea, but it was enough for muscles to begin to adapt, and it wouldn't do for people to see a Mercenary Brother uncertain on his feet. Parno headed down the pier to where Dhulyn stood with the horses, his big gray gelding Warhammer and her own spotted mare Bloodbone, rubbing their faces and caressing their ears while they became accustomed once again to the feel of land underneath their hooves.

The horses showed every sign of putting their sea voyage behind them. As Parno walked up, Bloodbone was snuffling Dhulyn's shoulder, but both horses were alert, flicking their ears, bobbing their heads, and generally taking an interest in what was going on around them, as battle-trained mounts tended to do.

Dhulyn was doing the same, though in her own peculiar way. Still holding fast to the horses' bridles, she was watching a group of children play a skipping game farther along the pier, not far from where she stood. Having had no real childhood herself, it had always seemed to Parno natural that Dhulyn showed a great curiosity in the childhoods of others. She smiled as he neared her, her eyes still watching the children's game.

I'll tell her later, he decided. The news he'd just learned from the *Catseye*'s captain was disturbing; just how disturbing would have to wait until the comparative privacy of their inn. There was a surprising number of people about in Navra's harbor, considering most travelers were still waiting out the last of the winter storms.

"It's the same rhyme," Dhulyn said as he neared her. "That sweeping rhyme the children were singing in the street in Destila."

"You sure? Those kids were playing a game with blindfolds."

"Nevertheless, it's the same rhyme, same cadence, same consonance. How do these rhymes and games get transplanted from one place to another?"

Parno shrugged. Dhulyn had spent a year in a Scholars' Library before taking her final vows to the Mercenary Brotherhood, and she'd never lost the habit of making these scholarly observations. "Adults like you see them, I would suppose, and carry them home for their children, like new toys."

"It would be interesting to trace the songs and the games back, try to find the point of origin from which they spread."

"You think such a point could be found?" Parno said, smiling. His years with Dhulyn had taught him that many countries of the eastern continent told folktales and stories of amazing similarity.

"Unless it goes back to the time of the Caids, then it will appear to have sprung up everywhere at once." Dhulyn shrugged one shoulder. "Ah, well, a dissertation subject for some Scholar, no doubt. And, meanwhile, here we are back in the land of the Sleeping God."

"The Sleeping God's worshiped everywhere," Parno said, taking Warhammer's rein from her.

"But here, on the Letanian Peninsula, he is the first god, is he not?"

"The Brotherhood recognizes all gods," he reminded her.

"And all gods recognize the Brotherhood." She turned fully to look at him. "I told the first mate where to send our packs. Has the place changed very much? Do you remember the way to the inn you've been telling me about?"

"What do you think," he said, grinning as he took a firm grip on Warhammer's bridle.

"I think you got lost in our cabin last night."

Parno swung, Dhulyn ducked, and the children looked over from their game, excitement plain in their faces—as was the disappointment when no fight broke out. Dhulyn, grinning for the benefit of the children, tilted her chin toward the end of the pier.

They led the horses away from the *Catseye,* dodging seamen and dock workers loading and unloading from the ships and fishing boats tied up along the pier. Warhammer and Bloodbone were spoiling for exercise, but the streets close to the docks proved to be so uneven that Dhulyn suggested they continue afoot. Parno was just leading the way down a narrow lane when his Partner froze.

"Did you hear that?" she said, her rough voice unusually loud in the cold air.

"The market?" Parno said dryly, bracing his feet as Warhammer, not as well trained as Dhulyn's Bloodbone, shied slightly, pulling him forward.

Dhulyn held up one finger to silence him and listened again, eyes narrowed, head on an angle. Parno shrugged, wishing he'd worn his heavier cloak, and waited for Dhulyn to agree with him. The main market, if he remembered correctly, was off to the east, closer to the saltworks, but the barrows and stalls of the fish market, the one that served the docks and the ships, could be seen off to the other side of the pier they'd just left. Even this late in the afternoon, the buzz of the buyers and sellers, the calls of the merchants hawking their wares, even the sound of an optimistic flute, were still clear in the crisp air. But if Dhulyn thought she'd heard something else . . .

"There!" Dhulyn's head jerked up and she swung herself into the saddle, urging Bloodbone with her knees into an opening between two houses, turning away from the docks. Parno was mounted and only half a length behind his Partner before Bloodbone's tail disappeared from view.

The alleys between the houses and buildings in this quarter of Navra were none too clean, and the streets were not much better, Parno found as he followed Dhulyn out into a wider avenue. The freezing and thawing of early spring had heaved the cobbles and paving stones and left them slick underfoot. Even the dirt lanes were more than half slippery mud. Not the best conditions to be racing your horses, but Parno knew better than to argue with his Partner. He ducked an overhead sign with a swallowed curse. He was willing to wager practically anything he owned that it wouldn't be *her* horse that went down as she rode it much too fast around the next tight corner.

And he still had not heard anything out of the ordinary.

The laboring breath and clattering hooves of their horses made enough noise that the few people they encountered had plenty of time to get out of their way. Market day it might be, but away from the market itself and the busy areas around the docks, most townspeople finished their business early in weather like this; the day was turning cold, and the sky promised snow. One tall old man, well-wrapped in a red wool cloak, looked up in surprise as Dhulyn Wolfshead galloped past him and called out angrily, not noticing the tattoos of their Mercenary's badges, even though both she and Parno were bareheaded from habit.

They turned into a street of better-class houses, a few of them as much as four stories tall with the featureless lower walls that spoke of interior gardens or courtyards, or both. Not so fine as nobles' houses, to Parno's experienced eye these looked like the homes of well-to-do merchants. And suddenly Parno smelled smoke, and saw as they rounded yet another corner a three-story house with flames dancing in two upper windows that gave on the street.

Even now, he could not hear the sound of the fire, and he knew that Dhulyn—Outlander or no—could not possibly have heard it either. This burning house must have been some Vision she had Seen.

The usual crowd of people who gather out of nowhere at any sign of trouble were milling around in the irregular square in front of the burning building, but something was wrong—more wrong than just a house on fire. Parno frowned as he urged Warhammer forward. He'd seen many a mob in his time as a Mercenary, and this one wasn't behaving normally. Those closest to the fire acted as he would expect, some craning for a better view, others pointing and yelling—shock and excitement both apparent in faces and stances. As for those farther away, far too many were standing far too still, hands hanging limp, heads all, as he now realized, at the same angle. And aside from some shoving, and what looked like a fistfight breaking out on the far side of the crowd, no one was doing anything. Not putting out the fire, not bringing water, not even helping to drag out furniture. In fact, two men seemed to be preventing someone from coming out of the house. . . . Parno edged forward into the opening Dhulyn had made in the crowd just as a man put his hand on Warhammer's bridle. Parno bared his teeth as the man looked up. His eyes widened when he saw the red-and-gold tattoo reaching from Parno's temples to above his ears, and he backed away.

Closer now, Parno could hear the flames as they ate through the house wall, blistering the stucco to the right of the doorway. A woman at the front of the crowd threw a stone at the upper window on the left, screaming something Parno couldn't make out.

Flames or no, Dhulyn rode Bloodbone right through to the front of the house, swung her leg over the pommel of her saddle, and jumped off, knocking the two men who'd been blocking the doorway sprawling over one another. The darker of the two sprang to his feet, a cudgel ready in his fist. Dhulyn stepped in close to him, knocked his arm away with her left forearm, brought her booted heel down sharply on his instep, and drew her sword from the sheath that hung down her back.

All without taking her eyes from the doorway.

A young girl burst out of the now unguarded door, but was choking too much to actually speak.

"Children upstairs," Dhulyn called out to him as Parno drew rein beside her, using Warhammer's size and wickedly rolling eyes to push the crowding people farther back.

"I'll go," he said, tossing her his reins. *Demons and perverts,* he thought, not for the first time thankful that he didn't See what Dhulyn sometimes Saw. Children. He pulled his feet from the stirrups and, steadying himself with his hands on the pommel, hopped up on the saddle until he was balancing on Warhammer's back, wishing he was wearing something with more grip than his boots.

"Keep your eyes open." He didn't have to tell her to watch the crowd. She'd have noticed before he did that something was amiss.

Out of the corner of her eye Dhulyn Wolfshead watched Parno make the small jump that got his fingers hooked on the windowsill above them. The muscles in his arms bulged as he drew himself up, swung one leg over the sill, and was gone into the smoky darkness within the house.

"My lady." It was the young girl who had run out of the doorway. "My brothers—"

"I'm not your lady," Dhulyn said, "and my Brother's fetching yours." She glanced at the girl's soot-marked face. "Where's your people, then?" She'd known from her Vision the parents weren't alive inside the burning building, she'd Seen that much, but she hadn't been sure she and Parno wouldn't be stuck looking after a passel of orphaned children.

As the girl said something in which only the word "shop" was clear, Dhulyn whirled, her sword knocking aside another stone that came hurtling at them. She turned her head and smiled her wolf's smile at the thrower, an otherwise respectable-looking woman of middle years. The woman dropped the second rock—taken from her garden by the look of the dirt on it—and stepped back, pressing her lips together but lowering her eyes.

"Will none of you fetch water?" Surely there had to be some well or fountain nearby. Those closest to her shifted their feet, looking down and away from her searching eyes. Some drifted even farther off, one of them bumping into his neighbors in the crowd as if he couldn't see them.

Dhulyn again smiled her wolf's smile, and the people nearest her froze.

"I don't know what you have against this household," she called out, "but perhaps the neighbors might like to save *their* homes before they catch alight."

It was like tossing a snake into a hen coop. Sudden curses and determined scurrying, the quicker slapping the slower into movement. Dhulyn laughed aloud. "Blooded fools."

"It's bad luck to help the Marked, Mercenary," the stone thrower said, sharp nods punctuating her words. "Everyone knows that."

"Is it so?" Dhulyn looked and, sure enough, there was a sigil next to the door that showed the house belonged to a

Finder. She turned back to the woman, still smiling so that the scar on her lip pulled it back from her teeth. "If I find the one who helped them to this fire, they'll learn what bad luck is."

Bad enough they were going to Imrion in the first place, she thought, watching to make sure that the people moving through the crowd were bringing water and nothing else, if this was the kind of trouble she and Parno found before they even got there. For herself, she didn't care, one country was the same as another, and work was work. But Parno had wanted Imrion, reminiscing constantly about his childhood there—far too much for any Mercenary Brother, let alone a Partnered one—until finally she'd given in. Looking down at the Finder girl's tear-streaked face, Dhulyn hoped she wouldn't curse the day she'd done so.

And she didn't like the look of the crowd. She never thought much of town men—even country lordlings like Parno had once been showed more sense—but this bunch was stupider than usual. Why, half a dozen stood toward the back slack-jawed—one was even drooling—as if their wits had left them.

"Dhulyn!"

She looked up. Left-handed, she snatched a small bundle out of the air that turned out to be a little boy, continued the movement to lower him gently into his sister's waiting arms. Dhulyn looked up again to where Parno stood leaning out of the third-story window, a larger child dangling in his scarred hands. Dhulyn could see the flames close behind Parno's soot-streaked face. What was he waiting for? She took a breath to call to him, but something on his face stopped her from uttering a sound.

Even as he leaned out to drop the second child to safety, Parno froze, a finger of icy chill tickling up his back. He shivered despite the heat of the furniture burning in the room behind him. Every hair on his body stood up; even the tattoos on his temples seemed to itch. He resisted the urge to look around, feeling that someone was behind him, watching. He knew no one was there—no one *could* be there.

Only his eyes moving, Parno scanned the crowd. Many watched him, but there was nothing that should give him this feeling of . . . his stomach twisted. Someone, some *thing*, patting thieves' fingers through his thoughts, probing his mind and soul . . . leaving darkness and confusion in its wake. Parno shivered, blinking, forced himself to take a breath, and another. Forced his breathing into the pattern of the Turtle *Shora*. In. Out. Forcing his thoughts—

Movement caught his attention and he saw a man in red robes with a brown cloak on the edge of the crowd, his eyes so green Parno could see them even across the square. The fire cast the man's shadow over the wall of the house behind him. But it couldn't be his shadow, it didn't flicker in the fire glow like everyone else's. Rather it was as still as a pool of ink, looming over the man in red and brown like a smudge, far too large to have been cast by such a small man.

Too large and too dark.

Parno shivered again, trying to shake off the feeling that somehow it was the shadow that watched him, dissolving his thoughts. He wanted to look away, needed to look away.

"Sir?" the boy had hold of his sword harness and was pulling on it. "Sir, the fire."

Parno jerked and lowered his eyes to the child's tear-marked face, dragging in a ragged breath of smoke-tainted air. Though the boy was no great weight, his arms trembled, and the sweat on his face was not from the heat of the fire. Dhulyn still waited below, her face a pale oval in the darkening square. Parno shook himself, held the boy out, and dropped him into her waiting arms.

❈❈❈

It was harder for him to *use* the shape than to *be* it. Harder to merely look through the eyes than to inhabit. Especially at such a distance. Distance was shape, too. He shook, and pushed that thought away. To keep the human he now used whole, to keep its *shape*, he had to spread himself thin. Spread the undoing. Spread the NOT. The humans closest to him were fidgeting already, their eyes rolling and flicking from side to side, their heads beginning to twitch, their hands to clutch, to wring, to scratch.

A flicker of gold, high up on the wall, and with great effort he had the human whose eyes he used lift its head and look. Gathered his powers and felt. Sending his own essence like fingers tenuous as smoke, pushing into the human's eyes, probing into the flame he thought he had seen. He smelled it all over, tasted it, felt it begin to give way, then harden again, regain its shape. Yet it was not Marked. He withdrew. It was only a blue flame after all, not the gold one he sought.

But now the humans around him were crying out, some were striking their fellows, others falling to the ground weeping, tearing at their own skin and faces. He retreated again to the man whose eyes he used, resting a heartbeat or so before gathering his strength for the leap back to his host, the shape in which his essence now dwelt.

As he leaped, he saw again the gold flame, and he took one heartbeat more to look closer, to fix the flame's human shape and human coloring.

There.

She was the one he sought.

❧

By the time Parno stepped off the windowsill, landing neatly at her side, others in the crowd had begun to help douse the flames. The Finder's house couldn't be saved, Dhulyn thought, nor could the smaller structure to the south of it—attempts to put out the fire had started too late for that—and even now, less than two thirds of the people still in the small square were helping to douse the flames. Automatically, she shifted the angle of her sword and settled her feet firmly in a new position.

"Parno," she said, and felt him move to her left side.

"What's wrong with them?" he whispered.

She shook her head, voice freezing in her throat. The people not helping to put out the fire seemed confused, many as if they did not know where they were. Some were rolling on the ground slapping at themselves as if attacked by bees, others fought each other, clawing at each other's faces with stiffened fingers, seemingly unaware of the knives at their belts. Others were crying, rocking and holding themselves. One poor woman wandered as if blind, blood dripping from her nose and ears.

Some few of the unaffected were leaving the water brigade

and going to the aid of one or another of the afflicted, and some of those were calming down, a few looking around them, as if trying to remember where, and perhaps who, they were.

"Should we do anything?" Dhulyn said, her sword still raised.

"Leave," Parno said. "There's a Jaldean here. He'll see to them."

Dhulyn nodded, even as she pressed her lips together. Which was stranger, she wondered, the behavior that was even now dissipating like smoke blown away by a breeze, or that the Jaldean priest—bewildered looking but otherwise sane—was only now coming to help?

Parno was putting the older girl up on his horse, and passing the smallest child up to her when what could only be the Finder and his wife in identical dark green headgear came pushing through the line of people passing buckets. A few people muttered and pointed, and one man made as if to approach them, but Dhulyn discouraged him with a hard look.

"Why haven't you gone to the shrine, then?" the man called out, but he turned away, jaw and fists clenched, when Dhulyn jerked her head at him to be gone.

The wife went immediately to her children, but the Finder himself, after staring openmouthed, began to question those of his neighbors he found among the people passing the water. Dhulyn pulled him to one side and spoke, pitching her voice so only he could hear.

"Have you someplace else to go, Finder?"

The man focused his shocked gaze on her, responding to the touch of Dhulyn's hand on his arm much like a nervous horse responds to the trusted touch of its handler, calming automatically and without thought.

"I don't understand," he said to her, a countryman's accent under the polish of the Guild. "Why would they do this to me? I've always done my best to Find."

"You didn't Find my Jolda!" came a voice from a woman nearby.

Even in the uncertain light of the dying fire, Dhulyn could see that the Finder had gone pale. His lips moved, but in the suddenly increased noise she missed what he said. A stone came flying out of the crowd, and Dhulyn deflected it without a glance, stepping in front of the Finder, sword still raised. His wife took him by his arm and pulled him into the shelter of the horses, where Parno stood with the children.

"We can go to the shop," the woman whispered to Dhulyn. Dhulyn nodded and backed away, her sword still held out in front of her.

"Let the Brothers take them," someone else called out. "They'll know how to deal with them."

Dhulyn silently blessed the quick thinking of that particular person. So the Finder and his family had at least one friend in the mob. The slower wits in the crowd were happy enough to believe that she and Parno were taking the Finders under duress, and to let them leave with only jeers and sharp glances to send them on their way.

The Finder's shop was a small but comfortable space within easy walking distance of the house. Dhulyn settled Grenwen Finder into what was obviously his own chair behind a neat worktable while his wife, Mirandeth, took the children into a small kitchen room and set the older girl to making hot drinks for everyone before rejoining her husband. She made the Mercenaries take the clients' chairs and perched one hip on the edge of her husband's table.

Parno leaned forward, elbows on his knees. "Are you sure there's nothing . . . ?"

"Nothing, good Mercenary, I swear. I've always given full value, never charged more than the Guild recommends. And I've done all I can to follow the new restrictions," he said, rubbing his face with trembling hands. "The curfew was one thing," he said. "And the dress code." His gesture took in their headdresses. "That was bad enough, but this . . ."

"What was that the woman said about Jolda?" Dhulyn asked.

Mirandeth shook her head. "That was a sad thing, but a thing no one could have helped. And it's more than a year ago now. Mistress Fisher's child. Everyone thought the willful little thing was just hiding herself as usual after an argument with her sister. She'd done it before, and this time the parents—the Fishers, as I said, they own three boats and the salting sheds down by the point—thought they'd let the stubborn little mite sulk and come home on her own when she got hungry instead of chasing after her as they usually did."

"And so?" Parno asked when the wife fell silent.

"And so," Grenwen Finder said, "the child choked on a bit of fruit she'd had in her pocket, and by the time they came to me to Find her she was long dead. The Fishers didn't blame me—at least not then. How could they? I knew nothing of it 'fore they sent for me." The Finder pressed his lips together before continuing. "I Found the body."

"They didn't blame us then, as you say," Mirandeth said. "But it wasn't more than two moons later that Mistress Fisher didn't return my greeting in the market, and the stall holder told me that the Fishers were saying Grenwen hadn't really tried to Find the poor child until it was too late."

"Grief does strange things to people," Dhulyn said. The daughter came out of the kitchen area carrying a round wooden tray with two glasses and two clay mugs. The way she handed the tray to the Mercenaries made it clear they were meant to take the more expensive glasses. Dhulyn breathed in the rich scent of ganje. She could use a stimulant, she thought, and so could the Finders. "They'll blame themselves most of all, you see," she told them. "It's a hard day when an act of sensible discipline has the bad luck to result in such a tragedy, but they'd go mad if they blame themselves. Easier to blame you."

"But to set fire to my home?"

"The Fishers didn't fire the house, and you know it." Mirandeth put her mug down on the table. "At least not by themselves."

"Who then?" Parno said. "The Watch will want to know."

"The Watch? What point in telling the Watch? Where was the Watch when my own neighbors . . ." Mirandeth took a deep, steadying breath before going on. "You hear things, and you think 'well, away in Imrion, anything can happen.' But when my own friends and neighbors set fire to my house with my children inside. No," she turned to her husband, "you know who put the idea into Mistress Fisher's head that you were to blame for poor little Jolda, and who made sure the Watch knew nothing about the fire."

"Tell us, then, and we'll all know," said Dhulyn.

The husband and wife exchanged a look that was equal parts fear and determination. Finally, the Finder nodded.

"This has all been since the New Believers came out of Imrion last year, spreading their teachings. Did anyone see? Was there a Jaldean in the crowd?" he said.

Dhulyn was sure only she noticed the muscles in Parno's forearms twitch. His lips parted, but he closed them without saying a word.

"There was," Dhulyn said when it was clear Parno would not speak. "But what do the priests of the Sleeping God have to do with this?"

"Everything," Mirandeth said, nodding. "The New Believers have been preaching against the Marked for months now, and after the earthquake last summer, and the bad harvest . . ."

Dhulyn nodded, considering. The Marked had always made certain people nervous—those who were afraid of what they didn't understand and couldn't do themselves. In bad times, foolish talk in taverns wasn't unusual. But since when would sober, reasonable, law-abiding citizens turn against someone who could Heal or Find or Mend?

"What's different now?" she asked. "We've heard nothing of this, we've been away in the west, beyond Semlor, training with the armies of the Great King. The world's a different place out there."

"The world's a different place right here, Dhulyn Wolfshead, let me tell you." Mirandeth pressed her lips together and turned her head to the side, blinking.

"It seems it started," the Finder took up the tale, patting his wife on her hand, "when the Jaldeans found a new artifact of the Sleeping God. I don't know that anyone thought much of it. I certainly did not. They've found these things in the past, and for a while it makes people think a bit, reminds them the old gods are still with us, don't you know, for all that many are heeding the teachings coming from the west." The man swung his head from side to side. "When I first heard, I thought it a way to help the Jaldeans recruit more monks, to be honest. No harm in it."

"Then they started calling themselves the New Believers," Mirandeth said. "Started preaching on street corners instead of keeping to themselves in their hermitages and shrines in the old way. They came predicting danger and giving warning."

Dhulyn raised her eyebrows. *There* was a way to catch the attention, no doubt about it. But Mirandeth hadn't finished.

"They say the Marked are trying to awaken the Sleeping God before his time, and he'll destroy the world."

Parno fell back into his chair, his movement causing the ganje in his glass to slop out onto his knee. He didn't seem to notice.

"I don't understand," Dhulyn said. "Wouldn't the Marked be destroying themselves then?" None of the religions of townsfolk made any sense to her. There were three or four different sects that, as far as she could tell, called the same gods by different names—and she had respect for them all as often providing excellent reasons for war.

This time it was Parno who answered her. "The Marked have always been thought to have a special connection with the Sleeping God; maybe that's supposed to save them." He shook his head, "But—the Sleeping God's *supposed* to awaken, and come to our aid if he's needed. As indeed he's done in the past, according to the Jaldeans themselves."

"According to the Old Believers, yes," Grenwen Finder said. "But now that's all accounted heresy, and it's more than your life is worth to say so in public, whatever you might think to yourself in the safety of your own home."

The silence that fell lasted so long the Finders' daughter came to the door of the back room where she'd been distracting her brothers. Dhulyn knew what they were all thinking. The Finders' home had not turned out to be so very safe.

"Even so easily can people be turned against each other," she said.

"But they aren't . . ." Parno's voice trailed away, whatever argument he was marshaling collapsing unspoken.

"People believe what bad harvests and earthquakes tell them to believe," Dhulyn pointed out.

"They'll allow as how we might be innocent enough by

intent," Grenwen said. "At least some will. But that changes nothing. Somehow we've perverted the gifts the god gave us, and our actions are awakening him."

"So why did that man say you should go to the shrine?" Dhulyn asked.

"We're supposed to go and be blessed by the Jaldeans, any of us who wish to keep our homes and livelihoods."

"Willam Healer went, and no one's seen him since," Mirandeth said. "His family have sold off everything and disappeared, though I heard they have kin in Voyagin."

Grenwen's nod was slow and heavy. "I often helped him with his cases, Finding bad growths and infections for him, but now . . . I think Willam was one of the lucky ones. Of the few who've returned to their families, they're no longer . . ." the man swallowed, "they aren't *Marked* any longer."

Dhulyn thought of the blank faces she'd seen in the square.

"That's why the Watch didn't come," she said.

The Finder nodded. "I'll lodge a complaint, of course. And they'll listen to me, for now, even if they do nothing. There's still plenty that don't hold by the new beliefs. But many of *them* are starting to look the other way. It's only a matter of time, until they'll do more than that." He blinked slowly, his brow furrowed as if an idea had just come to him. "I was contracted to Find a new salt deposit before winter set in, and the project was postponed. It's past the time I should have heard, but surely they wouldn't—" he looked up at the Mercenaries. "The good of the town . . ."

Dhulyn glanced at Parno and looked away. Surely they would, and both she and her Partner knew it. Common sense and the good of the town flew out the window when what a god wanted came in the door.

"And Zendra Mender's gone—took ship for Berdana last week before the port closed to us—so you won't be inspecting the aqueduct together as you always did. It wasn't so bad before the Marked started coming here from Imrion, drawing attention to us—and I can't believe I just said that." Mirandeth covered her eyes with her hands. "We're all Marked, there's no Imrion and no Navra in this." She let her hands fall to her lap. "But it does mean the Prince has closed the port to us, as a favor to Imrion. The last of many favors." Her hand went up to touch her dark green head-dress.

"So what then?" Parno asked. "Have you no other recourse? What says your Guild?"

Grenwen Finder shook his head. "There's been no word from the Guildhall since the passes closed."

The silence around the table acknowledged what they all knew. The Guildhall of the Marked was in Gotterang, Imrion's capital.

"There's always the Cloud People." The daughter's voice made her parents jump; she'd been quiet so long they'd forgotten she was still there. "The Clouds don't believe any of this nonsense. They value the Marked."

Dhulyn exchanged another look with her Partner. Normally, the Finders would be considered safe enough with the Clouds. Neither the Tarkins of Imrion nor the Princes of Navra had found any profit in trying to pull the Clouds out of the mountain range that lay between the two countries, and that the Cloud People considered their home. But when religious fanatics became part of the game, sensible policies were often thrown from the board.

Mirandeth was shaking her head. "Child. Can we go to live in a cave in the mountains like a pack of wolves or Outlanders? No offense, Dhulyn Wolfshead."

"None taken," Dhulyn said, carefully not smiling. "But if you don't mind a bit of advice *from* an Outlander, consider what your daughter has said. Better to be a valued member of the wolf pack than the target and prey of civilized men."

The Finder nodded. "There's sense in that." His face showing more color now, he turned to his wife. "My bowl, Mira, if you please."

Mirandeth, a new light shining in her eyes, sprang to her feet and excused herself, returning from the kitchen in a moment with a small porcelain bowl. As wide as her two hands, its glaze was so pure a white that it seemed to glow in the fading light of the workroom. Grenwen Finder leaned back in his chair and allowed her to place the bowl directly in front of him on the tabletop. The daughter came close behind her mother, a pitcher of water in her hands. Fresh spring water, Dhulyn knew, poured three times through clean silk. She cocked an eyebrow at Parno and leaned forward in interest. Grenwen Finder was a skilled Mark, indeed, if he could Find something as abstract as a safe place for his family.

The Finder poured a small amount of water into the bowl, handed the jug back to his daughter, and placed his hands so that his fingers rested lightly on the bowl's edge. Back straight, he sat forward enough to be able to look directly into the depth of white porcelain. His breathing almost immediately became deep and steady, and the room grew so silent Dhulyn could hear the footsteps of a passerby in the street and the blood beating in her own ears. Then she could not hear even that, and it seemed that the world and everything in it had fallen still, stopped in its dance.

The Finder raised his head, and the world resumed.

"There *is* sanctuary," he said, his voice a whisper as if the Finding had taken all his strength. "It is in the mountains. But the passes—"

"Should be clear enough for determined people on horseback," Parno cut in. "And empty of everyone else. Have you beasts? Then fetch them and begin packing," he added when Grenwen Finder nodded.

Dhulyn stood, placed her empty glass carefully on the table. "The first thing you should do," she said, "is take those headdresses off."

Without a word, Mirandeth reached up and unfastened the pin in the carefully folded dark green cloth around her head. She pulled the headdress off and revealed her hairless and tattooed scalp.

Two

PARNO WATCHED AS DHULYN carried two cups of steaming ganje back to their table close to the fire at the Hoofbeat Inn. No one could tell by looking at her face, or watching the smooth way she moved, that they'd been up most of the night, sneaking the Finders out of Navra by an old way Parno remembered. The Hoofbeat hadn't changed much since he'd seen it last. There were a few more cracks in the dark ceramic tiles of the floor, and the small bricks making up the ceilings that arched between stubby pillars were more worn and crumbling than he recalled, but the pillars themselves, and the walls for that matter, were solid and had been recently whitewashed.

"Your friend the innkeeper has heard tell of something like it," Dhulyn said, putting down the cups and sliding in next to him. "He says it's happened a few times at Jaldean shrines, during meditations." Dhulyn shrugged, and lifted her cup. Parno knew perfectly well what she thought of townsmen's religious practices.

"Anyway, Linkon Grey tells me that this falling into a fit, this . . ." Dhulyn shivered, "whatever we want to call it, that's where it's happened before. Sometimes there are miracles, Healings and the like, and when that happens, the Jaldeans tell people they've touched the dreams of the Sleeping God." She took a swallow of her ganje. "Most come out of the fits all right. Not all."

"All that time in the Great King's court I was wishing we

were here, and now that we are, I'd give my best sword to be back with the Western Horde," Parno said.

"Always supposing we'd be welcomed back." The smile in Dhulyn's voice matched the one on her lips as she threw him a sparkling glance. Parno grinned back at her.

"What was it you so carefully didn't say, back there at the Finders?" she said, watching him over the rim of her cup. "When the wife asked was there a Jaldean in the crowd, you froze like a man caught in his neighbor's bed."

Parno's throat closed like a fist, his smile melting away. He couldn't tell her. She'd laugh at him. But she was his Partner. Who else could he tell? It would sit like a lump of poison in his gut if he didn't tell someone.

"Spit it out, you blooded effete," she advised him, her grin softening her words. "Stop trying to spare your dainty feelings."

"While I was standing in the window with the second boy," he began, his voice sharp as he pushed it past the tightness in his throat, "I had the oddest feeling of being watched."

"Of course you were being watched." Dhulyn's blood-red brows made a small vee above her eyes.

He pressed his lips together and shook his head. "Not like that, it was like . . . when you're all alone in the woods, but you feel you're not alone, and you look around and see nothing, but later you find a print and you know some beast's been watching you."

Dhulyn's nod was slow. "There was no animal in with the mob—not *that* kind anyway."

Parno shook his head. "I think it was that Jaldean New Believer. Or maybe, maybe something that was with him. I felt . . . there was something I couldn't see. Something that seemed to comb through my mind and thoughts and I couldn't stop it." Parno took a sip of his ganje to cover the trembling of his lips. "It made me feel . . . unmanned." He couldn't look up.

"Well, *that's* saying quite a lot." Dhulyn looked at him with eyes widened in pretended innocence.

"Demons and perverts! I should have known I'd get no sympathy from you."

"It isn't sympathy you want, you blooded fool, and you know it."

The tightness in his chest began to dissolve. "But you believe me?"

"It made you sweat to tell me," she said, reaching behind her to rub the small of her back with her fist. "I don't need any other proof. Of course I believe you."

Parno nodded, taking a swallow of ganje to hide his relief. He'd expected her to laugh, really laugh that is, not just tease him. Showed you that you never knew what an Outlander would do or say. And that seven years of Partnership doesn't always tell you everything about your Partner.

There was something else, something he'd better mention now, while he still could. "Did you see what color his eyes were?"

Dhulyn closed her own eyes a moment as she searched through the images of memory until she could light upon the one detail—

"Brown," she said.

That matched what he thought himself. "They were green when he looked at me," he told her. "Glowing green like slices of jade stone with the sun behind them."

Dhulyn raised her cup to her lips, made a face when she found it empty. Parno signaled the waiter, waited quietly while their cups were refilled. Dhulyn suddenly sat up straight, her eyes narrowing.

"Did you feel like crying?" she said. "Or striking yourself?"

"Ah." He drummed his fingers on the tabletop. "You're saying it *was* the Jaldean, *all* of it." He picked up his fresh ganje and set it back down again without tasting it.

"Or whatever it was made his eyes glow green." Dhulyn frowned, the fingers of her right hand braiding to form the sign against ill luck. "Some drug perhaps?"

"When did you See the fire?" he asked, using his night-watch voice, soundless and almost breathless. When she raised her eyebrows at him without answering, he added, "You knew which alley to go down."

She looked away and shifted in her seat. "This business with the Marked," she began. "It makes no sense."

Parno took a swallow from his cup. "You read too much

poetry. This is all about power. The Jaldeans assert themselves at the expense of the Marked. When the Marked are gone, the Jaldeans fill the void."

"Fill it with what? Promises and platitudes?"

"Fear and righteousness."

"And meanwhile people die for want of Healers, starve for want of Finders, and go mad for want of Menders."

"Not everyone; there's few enough Marked that many don't depend on them."

"Not *so* many." Dhulyn chewed on her upper lip. "Parno, my heart, remember that time you told the tavern dancer that I could See his future for him?"

"I remember what you called me," Parno said, trying for a smile, "and what you told *him* about *me*. And I remember how sore I was in practice for the next few days."

"I don't think you'd better make that offer to anyone else."

"I'd already thought of that." Parno waited a minute before asking. "Did you See anything else?"

"Gotterang." Her lips twisted as they named the capital of Imrion.

"No."

Heads turned and a waiter hesitated on his way across the room. Parno lowered his voice again, shaking his head. "It's back to the *Catseye* for us. Imrion is no longer the land of my childhood, nor even the land we left after Arcosa. Caids know, it's not safe for you there."

Dhulyn nodded, but so slowly Parno knew she was really saying no. "Ship's gone," she said. "Tide turned while we were with the Finders." She looked up and gave him her wolf's smile. "If any of the Marked are safe, it would be me. No one thinks to meet a genuine Seer; most people don't even believe in them anymore. Besides, since when do we look for safety, my heart? We're Mercenary Brothers."

"I won't lose you to the Jaldeans." That was as plain as he could say it.

"And if I lose you?" Dhulyn set her cup down with a thump and looked her Partner in the eye, holding his gaze when he would have looked away. This was neither the time nor the place she would have chosen to speak on this subject, but surely she'd been silent long enough. Partnership was a life bond in the Mercenary Brotherhood. Or was meant to be.

"What do you mean?"

"A demon haunts you," she said. "A demon from your childhood." She waited two heartbeats, three, but Parno made no move to deny her words. "Shall I tell you how many times in the last year I've turned to you on the trail—or worse, on watch—and found you, wits abstracted, staring into the middle distance? Or how many times woken up in the middle of the night and found you awake, staring at the stars?"

"You never said anything." Parno's eyes held hers for a moment longer before falling to where his fingers were clamped around his own steaming cup.

"I waited for you to speak, and the word spoken was Imrion."

"I never meant . . ." Parno heaved a deep breath. "It's only that I began to wonder what became of my Household and I . . ."

"Spoke to me of Imrion." Dhulyn leaned back in her chair, nodding. Of course, she thought. Time had softened whatever had made him leave his House and become a Mercenary Brother. But to tell her so, to ask her openly to return with him to learn what had become of his past—she smiled, a twisting of her lips. How could he ask this of her, who had no past to return to?

"This business of the Marked changes all of that." Parno took a deep breath and released it slowly, pushing his cup to one side. "Very well, I admit that I've wondered about my House, my father . . . but going there endangers *you*. If the *Catseye* is gone, then we'll take another ship."

"Do you hear yourself?" Dhulyn leaned forward, though her voice was already too low to be heard beyond their table. "You actually counsel the safe and the secure to a Mercenary Brother—to *me*? What next? I should open a book shop and die in my bed? We're *Mercenary Brothers*. One day we'll make a mistake, and someone or something will kill us. This is our truth."

"It's everyone's truth," Parno began.

"But we know it, and we don't run away." Dhulyn licked her lips. "We don't run away."

"In Battle," Parno said.

"Or in Death," she answered.

Parno leaned against the serving bar, the common room of the inn slowly filling with customers as the afternoon lengthened and laborers came in for a midday meal or a quick mug of ale on their way home. Those who were already drinking something stronger had neither homes nor meals to go to. The serving girl had just swept up the last of the broken crockery from around the table where he and Dhulyn had been sitting when Linkon Grey the innkeeper, a little stouter and a little grayer than when Parno had last seen him, came out of the serving door behind the bar.

"Hot stones will be ready in a minute," Linkon said.

Parno turned. "Sorry about the mess," he said, jerking his head at the girl moving toward them with her broom and dustpan full of what had been two plates and a pottery mug.

"Not your fault, Lionsmane," Linkon said. "Though I'll have to replace them, and with no Menders the blasted potters are charging an arm and a leg. But not to worry, I took the price out of the man your Partner threw out the door. He should have taken no for an answer. If you didn't want to work for him, you didn't want to work for him. And I don't blame you, if he was lying about the job."

"Wolfshead's good at spotting liars," Parno said, "though your house cat would have known the fool was lying, come to that. Normally she's more forgiving. His bad luck he pushed it a little too far at the wrong time, if you catch my meaning."

"Oh, I catch it all right. My wife's the same, though not much capable of throwing me out the door, for which I thank the Caids." The man grinned.

Parno grinned back and didn't bother to correct the man. Dhulyn wasn't his wife, but there were few people outside of the Brotherhood—and even some within—who understood what it meant to be Partnered.

"Though I can't say I'm surprised the man persisted," Linkon continued, as he laid out mugs on the bar ready for spiced cider when it came hot from the kitchen. "There's not so many Mercenaries in Navra at the moment, and for that reason, a word in your ear."

Parno obliged the man by leaning both elbows on the bar, bringing his face within inches of the landlord's. He'd once spent almost a whole winter at the inn, and had developed a friendship with Linkon Grey that even the passage of years did not change.

"Two of the Watch were in here last night, looking for a couple of Mercenary Brothers who'd helped some Finders yesterday."

A chill traveled up Parno's spine. Not Linkon, too. "People had set fire to a house with children inside it."

Two red spots appeared on Linkon's pale cheeks. "Don't misunderstand me, Lionsmane, you did the right thing, though I wouldn't say that to any and everyone."

"Will this bring you trouble?"

"I was able to tell them, truthfully, that I'd not seen you—it was only your baggage was here all night. But they'll be back. It may take a few days; most of the Watch is none too eager to jump to the Jaldeans' orders, but like it or not, they'll have to come around again, sooner rather than later. And then . . ." Linkon Grey pursed his lips and raised his brows.

"Oh, come, Link! We're Mercenary Brothers, what can they do to us?"

Linkon shrugged, turned away to accept a cider jug from the kitchen boy, and turned back to pour out mugs for himself and Parno. He waited until the boy used a second jug to fill a tray of mugs and carry them off to distribute among the tables before leaning forward again.

"I don't know, and I don't want to know. It wasn't so long ago the Marked were saying the same thing." He frowned, brows pulled down, before meeting Parno's eyes once more. "I like the Brotherhood. It's always good to have some of you in the place. It brings custom and it keeps order, all at the same time. But it's my family as well as my business I've got to consider."

"I'll get Dhulyn—"

"Nah, man, you've a day at least—more like two. As I said, the Watch will be in no hurry, so long as you draw no more attention to yourselves. But you'd be doing me a favor if you accept the next offer that'll take you out of the city."

Parno looked around, saw that there was no one close to them. "When did this business with the Marked start? The Wolfshead and I came almost without stopping from Destila," he added, naming the city at the far end of the Midland Sea. "Only changing ships at the Isle of Cabrea. The last time we were on the Peninsula, the Jaldeans were no more than harmless old priests."

Linkon looked into the depths of his cup. "You've been away to the west, you say, Lionsmane, but you're from Imrion yourself, eh?"

"You know better than that, Linkon. We're Mercenary Brothers, the Wolfshead and I, and *that's* where we're from."

The innkeeper nodded, tongue flicking out to the corners of his mouth. "Still. If it were anyone else . . ." He shrugged.

"The trouble wasn't started by the old priests you remember, asking for alms at the shrines of the Sleeping God. It's the New Believers who are preaching against the Marked."

"Any oppose them?"

"They say the Tarkin himself," Linkon answered, "but there's a limit to what he can do."

"What's he like, this new Tarkin? When Wolfshead and I fought with Imrion when they took the field against the Dureans at Arcosa, the old man was still alive."

"They say the son's not the warrior his father was, but he's no fool either. The High Noble Houses acclaimed him when old Nyl-aLyn died, and that says something." Linkon gave a sharp nod. "Still, in this new matter only a few of the Noble Houses have declared themselves one way or the other. It's all the Tarkin can do to prevent an open breach between those as support the New Believers and those who would just as soon let be. The New Believers're saying the Tarkin doesn't see the danger—"

Linkon broke off as his younger daughter came out of the kitchen doorway with a tray of pies.

"*Danger?* From the *Marked?*" Parno cut in as soon as

the girl was out of earshot. "How dangerous can they be? There's not three in two hundred who are Marked."

"How many does there need to be to awaken the Sleeping God?" Linkon had lowered his voice still further. "I'll tell you straight, since it's you I speak to, Lionsmane, no good can come of any persecution of the Marked. It's madness, pure and simple. But the whole of the West country was flooded last spring, an earthquake leveled Petchera in the summer—and there's rumors the Cloud People are looking to break their treaty. Imrion's luck has turned bad, you mark my words."

Parno laughed to cover the chill that had come over him, raising the hairs on his arms. "Why, Linkon, we're Mercenary Brothers looking for work. Imrion sounds like just the place for us."

"Well, you know your own business best, but mark my words—"

A noise from the kitchen doorway made him turn again. "Ah, here's the warmed stones for your Partner now."

Parno accepted the stones, heat palpable through their heavy coverings, smiling his thanks to the kitchen boy. He gave Linkon a we'll-talk-later nod and made his way between the tables to the staircase.

Dhulyn Wolfshead suddenly gasped, curling around her belly, her eyes squeezed shut. Parno froze, one hand holding up the thin woolen blanket, the other stopped in the act of pushing one of the heated stones closer to the small of her back. Which would be safest, hold still until she quieted or finish what he was doing?

"Gotterang," Dhulyn said, spitting out the word between gasps. "Gotterang." Her left hand lashed out, and closed on the air where Parno's wrist had just been.

"I know, Dhulyn, I know," he said, using his voice to soothe where his hands could not. He shoved in the warm stone, lowered the blanket, tucked the edges under the pallet and sat back on his heels. He covered his Partner with the other blankets and both their heavy winter cloaks before raising himself to his feet, movements cautious and slow, and stepping back from the edge of the bed. He went only as far as the doorframe, where he leaned, listening.

Eventually Dhulyn's breaths came slower, took longer, as the valerian mixture he'd put into her cider took effect.

This would make twice she'd Seen Imrion's capital. While that didn't *necessarily* make her Vision more likely to come about—still it made him think.

"We go to Imrion," he said to her, voice still pitched to quiet and soothe. "And Gotterang the capital, no less. You are Senior, and you have spoken." It relieved him of the responsibility, he thought, but not of the knowledge that his had been the hand that placed out the tiles in this particular game. A demon, she'd said. And she was right. The demon of his life before the Brotherhood. Was his father still alive? His sisters?

When he'd found the shadow of his past would not let him rest, he'd persuaded Dhulyn, without telling her why, to come back with him to Imrion. More than ten years had passed, adding some height and more than a little muscle to the boy he had been. Time enough, and change enough, he was sure, to make him unrecognizable to any who might remember him.

Dhulyn pushed an arm out from under the blankets and began to hum. Parno cocked his head to listen more carefully. It was the tune the children had been singing on the pier. He found himself smiling. When his eye fell on the small arsenal of weapons he'd managed to take off her before she'd tumbled into the bed, his smile broadened.

"You'll be safe enough, my wolf," he said. Isn't that what she'd said? Wasn't that all any of them could say? They were Mercenaries, for Caids' sake, not dancing masters. "The path of the Mercenary is the sword." So went the Common Rule, and it was all any of them hoped or expected. There was a Mercenary House in Gotterang; he could find out what he wanted to know about his family there. And then they could be off, to where Dhulyn's Mark would make no difference, no matter who knew of it. What's the worst that could happen? They could die. Well, that was part of the Common Rule as well.

"I swear to you. Jaldeans or no, New Believers or Old. I swear by the Caids, if they still watch over us. You are my Partner and my life. Together. 'In Battle or in Death.'"

The Brotherhood's oath on his lips, he touched his fingertips to his forehead in salute, and turned to go back down-stairs. He must see if Linkon had anything else to tell him.

A CIRCLE OF RED-HAIRED CHILDREN DANCE, HAND IN HAND, REVOLVING AROUND A BLINDFOLDED GIRL. SHE FEELS THE HANDS OF THE CHILDREN NEXT TO HER IN HER OWN. BUT SHE IS ALSO THE BLINDFOLDED CHILD. THIS MUST BE JUST A DREAM, SHE THINKS, AS SHE HUMS THE TUNE. BUT THEN . . .

A TALL, THIN MAN WITH CLOSE-CROPPED HAIR THE COLOR OF WHEAT STRAW, EYES THE BLUE OF OLD ICE, DEEP ICE, SITS READING A BOUND BOOK LARGER THAN ANY SHE HAS EVER SEEN. HIS CHEEKBONES SEEM CHISELED FROM GRANITE, YET THERE IS HUMOR IN THE SET OF HIS LIPS, AND LAUGHTER IN THE FAINT LINES AROUND HIS EYES. DHULYN FEELS SHE WOULD LIKE THE MAN IF SHE MET HIM, AND THAT SHE HAS SEEN HIM BEFORE, THOUGH THERE IS NO BEFORE, NO AFTER, IN THE PLACE SHE IS NOW.

THE MAN TRACES A LINE ON THE PAGE WITH HIS FINGER, HIS LIPS MOVING AS HE CONFIRMS THE WORDS. HE NODS, AND, STANDING, TAKES UP A HIGHLY POLISHED TWO-HANDED SWORD. DHULYN OWNS ONE LIKE IT, THOUGH SHE DOES NOT USE IT OFTEN. IT IS NOT THE SWORD OF A HORSEMAN. SHE CAN SEE NOW THAT HIS CLOTHES ARE BRIGHTLY COLORED AND FIT HIM CLOSELY, EXCEPT FOR THE SLEEVES WHICH FALL FROM HIS SHOULDERS LIKE INVERTED LILIES.

HE TURNS AWAY FROM THE STRANGELY TIDY WORKTABLE AND TOWARD A CIRCULAR MIRROR, AS TALL AS HE IS HIMSELF. THE MIRROR DOES NOT REFLECT THE ROOM, HOWEVER, BUT SHOWS A NIGHT SKY FULL OF STARS. HIS LIPS MOVE, AND DHULYN KNOWS HE IS SAYING THE WORDS FROM THE BOOK. HE MAKES A MOVE LIKE ONE OF THE CRANE *SHORA*, AND SLASHES DOWNWARD THROUGH THE MIRROR, AS IF SPLITTING IT IN HALF. BUT NOW SHE SEES IT IS NOT A MIRROR, BUT A WINDOW, AND IT IS THE SKY ITSELF AND NOT A REFLECTION THAT THE MAN SPLITS WITH HIS CHARMED SWORD AND THROUGH THE OPENING COMES SPILLING LIKE FOG A GREEN-TINTED SHADOW, SHIVERING AND JERKY, AS THOUGH IT IS AFRAID. THE MAN STEPS BACK, HOLDING THE SWORD UP BEFORE HIM BUT IT IS NO DEFENSE, AND THE FOG SUCKS INTO HIS EYES, HIS NOSTRILS, HIS MOUTH, HIS EARS . . .

***

A YOUNG MAN WITH DARK BLOND HAIR AND A SCAR ON HIS LEFT CHEEK
SITS AT A SCARRED TABLETOP AND WRITES ON LOOSE SHEETS OF PARCHMENT
BY THE LIGHT OF A CANDLE. HIS EYES ARE GRAY, AND HE IS SMILING . . .

❧❧❧

Dhulyn woke to the sound of steel on stone and forced her eyes open. A cot had been brought up and squeezed into the only empty corner of their small whitewashed room. A shaft of late afternoon sunlight slanted across it, and in that spear of light Parno sat cross-legged, the sun picking up the golden hair on his forearms and the backs of his hands. He held his sword in his right hand, his left rhythmically stroking the blade with a honing stone. *Her* honing stone. Dhulyn grimaced. Only the certainty that Parno would have sharpened her sword first prevented her from objecting to his taking things from her pack. He would never learn. To a person who had owned nothing—not even her own person—even the smallest possessions had value.

She cleared her throat. "How long have I slept?"

"You missed the midday meal," he said, without pausing or looking up. "Though they've kept a plate for you by the kitchen fire. Are the stones still warm?"

She wiggled her hand down until she could touch the padded stone against her belly, and the one at the small of her back. The weight of her coverings—both their winter cloaks if she was any judge—made her nest warm enough that she had to rest her hand directly on the cloth-wrapped stones for a moment before she could detect a faint warmth. "Well, they're not cold."

"Not so bad then. You talked a bit at first, but you dropped off as soon as the stones began to warm you." He stopped honing, but still avoided her eyes, testing the edge of the blade against the back of his thumbnail. "What do you remember of this morning?"

She shrugged. A most unsatisfactory movement when lying down. She shut her eyes again.

"Do you recall the man who said he was from the House of Sogenso?" Parno prompted. "The man you threw out the door?"

Dhulyn shut her eyes, wrinkling her nose. "Was it open?"

"As luck would have it." The rhythmic sound stopped. "He said he was setting up a pilgrimage to the Mesticha Stone."

"To steal it," she murmured.

"So you told him."

Dhulyn could hear his smile. "What else did I tell him?"

"You told him we were Mercenaries, not thieves." Parno paused. Dhulyn waited. "He thought you were trying to raise the price, so he went on talking. You broke his wine cup. Over his head."

She winced again, squeezing open one eye. "One of the clay cups?" She seemed to remember a glass goblet on the table, and almost made the luck sign with the fingers of her left hand.

Parno shook his head, grinning. "Don't worry, Linkon took the damages from the Sogenso boy."

She opened her eyes. Parno sat relaxed, ankle over one knee, sword across his lap, his face in shadow. He had put the honing stone down on the floor next to his feet. She would have to make sure he did not leave it there.

"Did I . . . tell him anything else?"

"I was afraid you might, seeing how it was with you. There's something to tell, then."

"He shouldn't have touched me," she said, halfway to an apology. "He'll go to the Stone anyway, and he'll die there. It will be quick," she added. "And relatively painless."

Parno swung his head slowly from side to side, lips pressed to a thin line. "Even if you'd said so, people would have taken it for a threat, not a Vision. As I might have done, once." He released a deep breath and slid his blade into its sheath. "I got you upstairs, and Linkon had the kitchen heat stones for your pains, when they came."

"And gave me valerian—don't deny it, I can taste it in the back of my throat. You know it always makes me sick to my stomach." Dhulyn rolled over on her back, pulled her knees up tight against her chest then released them, resting her feet flat against the mattress. "When did all this happen?"

"An hour or so after breakfast." He rose and stretched, coming full into the shaft of sunlight. A golden man, tall, with warm eyes the color of amber. He had let his beard

grow the last few weeks, and it had come in a shade darker
than his sunbleached hair. His summer tan had faded over
the long moons it had taken them to come from the Great
King's court, but he was still much browner than she would
ever be.

Dhulyn rubbed at her temples and her eyes with the
heels of her hands. Parno had taken off her shoes, her sword
belts and sashes, but left her otherwise clothed. Long
familiarity—they Partnered shortly after meeting on the
battlefield of Arcosa—had taught him to touch her as little
as possible during her time. In the beginning, coming as he
did from the decadent north, he had seen nothing wrong
with lovemaking during her woman's time. A single experience had taught him that her people did not refrain merely
from Outlander fastidiousness. It was then she had Seen
the manner of his dying.

"Who else knows?" Parno said, tapping the side of his
face next to his eyes when she looked at him with raised
brows.

"You're the only one I've told." Dhulyn answered the
question he'd really asked. She'd only told Parno himself
when they talked of Partnering—not fair to him otherwise.
And she'd only been able to tell him because she *had* Seen
the manner of his death. Knowing the one thing that she
must never tell him had left her free to tell him everything
else.

At first he'd been delighted, thinking they'd soon be the
richest Mercenaries in the Brotherhood. They'd know
which jobs would be successful, and which would end in
disaster, who would pay up promptly and honestly, and
who try to cheat. He'd soon learned that she couldn't use
her Mark to answer specific questions, and when it did
work, it wasn't reliable and steady like the Finders or
Menders he'd known, but so chancy and sporadic as to be
more liability than asset.

"'Course it wasn't dangerous then, for others to know."

"No," she said. "Just no one's business. I tell you I'm safe
enough." She thought for a moment. "Dorian knows, I believe. Though he's said nothing."

"You'll be safe with any of the Brotherhood, I should
think, let alone the man who Schooled you."

Dhulyn nodded. For Mercenaries, the Brotherhood *was* their religion.

Parno leaned back on his cot and stretched out his legs in front of him, as far as the limited floor space would allow. "Linkon says the last rumors out of Gotterang before the Snow Moon closed the passes fit what the Finders told us. The New Believers are pressing the Tarkin for measures against the Marked, and he'll either have to give in, or refuse outright and take the consequences." Parno looked up from beneath his golden brows. "And, apparently, there will be consequences."

Dhulyn turned over on her side again, this time propping herself on one elbow. The slanted ceiling—their room was under the eaves of the inn—prevented her from sitting up. "I've read of such things in the past, but if I hadn't seen and heard it for myself, I'd find it hard to believe that people could be turned against the Marked."

Parno nodded. "People can be persuaded to hate and fear what they don't understand—even something useful and homey like a Mender or a Finder." He shrugged. "Healers, though, *that* would take *some* persuasion."

"There's not so many Healers, however, even the books mention that. Though more than Seers, that's certain."

"I can remember talk of such things when I was a child," Parno said. "The Market Dance at the Harvest Fair, they'd get someone to stand in the center to be the Seer, usually whichever young maid had been chosen Lady Harvest."

"One of your sisters?" Dhulyn asked with a smile.

"When they could bully enough people into it," Parno admitted, laughing. "Certainly no one ever expected a real Seer to show up."

Dhulyn rolled over onto her back again. There had been a fair amount written over the years about the Marked, but what she had never yet found in any book or scroll was mention of her tribe. Her height and coloring marked her for an Outlander, but she'd met only one man who had seen her and instantly known which Outlander tribe she came from. How Dorian the Black Traveler knew of the Espadryn, Dhulyn never learned. All she knew was that he had taken her from the hold of the slave ship, put salve on her cut face, spoken to her in her own tongue, saying "come with me, and learn to kill whoever hurts you." And she had gone with him, and learned. And somehow she had never asked whether Dorian also knew about the women of her people.

"If you'll be all right," Parno said, getting to his feet. "I have an . . . appointment." Dhulyn saw for the first time that he was wearing his finest clothes, which at this moment meant his cleanest.

"And what are you using for money?" She looked up, and their eyes met.

"I need none," he said. Now she could see his smile as well as hear it in his voice. "This one loves me." He gave her a courtly bow.

"Your wenching will kill you one day," she muttered.

Parno's face drained of color and he clamped his jaw tight.

"Just an expression," she said quickly, hauling herself up on her elbow again. Still pale, he continued to look at her, eyes narrowed, likely calculating whether she might be annoyed enough about the valerian to tell him the one thing she had promised never to tell. She held out her hand to him.

"Never, my soul," she said.

He touched the tips of her fingers with his own, brushed the back of her scarred knuckles lightly with his lips. "In Battle," he said. He gave her a more pronounced bow, and was gone before she could answer.

"Or in Death," she said to the empty room.

Ah well, she thought, settling back into the warmth of the bed. He'd believed her; all to the good since she'd told him the truth. If only she could keep her temper. Her thoughts began to float with her return to sleep.

Never wanted to have the blooded Visions, she thought sleepily, *and less so now.* Unless perhaps something was going to show her why Parno so badly wanted to return to the land of his birth.

❈❈❈

"Are you the one they call Dhulyn the Scholar?" A plump, compact, no-nonsense woman of middle years stood at their table, prosperously but not fashionably dressed in a

good wool overtunic with expensively dyed yellow trim.
This matron was accompanied by a young girl, dressed not
quite so well. Even this early in the evening both women
managed to look out of place in the public taproom of an
inn. Though it was likely the men of their household would
not.

"I am." Dhulyn looked up from the loose pages in her
hands and smiled her wolf's smile, the scar, normally too
small to be seen in itself, pulling her lip up into a snarl.
Parno did not trouble to hide his own grin as he watched
the woman, already starting to seat herself on the stool
across the table, unconsciously check her movement for a
long minute before slowly setting herself down. She then
looked Dhulyn Wolfshead sharply up and down, to show
she had not been frightened.

Parno knew what the townswoman saw—knew what he
had seen when he first noticed Dhulyn across a field of ar-
mored forms fighting and limp bodies fallen. A woman
much taller than the average, hawk-faced, pale skin lightly
damaged by the northern sun, beaded thongs tying back
long hair the dark color of old blood. The hair had been
permanently removed over each ear and the skin tattooed
blue and green in her Mercenary badge. Tonight she was
not in battle leathers, but dressed in loose wool trousers
dyed a dark blue and gathered at the ankle above leather
slippers. A tight vest made from scraps of silks and wool,
and bits of leather, quilted together with ribbon and laces,
left her arms bare as if she did not feel the cold. Armed, but
not obviously, and not for war.

The woman would see an Outlander Mercenary. Nothing more.

"Hmph," the townswoman nodded. "The landlord here
has put out that you're looking for work." She looked
pointedly around the tavern room. The place was almost
empty. Linkon Grey was preparing for his late night by taking a nap, leaving his daughter Nikola in charge. It was
early yet for drinking, though the supper hour was not so
far off. The place smelled faintly of spilled ale, and not so
faintly of the fish oil they used in the lamps. The townswoman's eye rested longest on a table of young persons

near the staircase, too friendly to be anything but professionals waiting for trade.

"Strange place to find a scholar," she finally said.

"I'm a Mercenary, townswoman. Not a shopgirl."

"And that's well." The woman placed her hands flat on the scarred tabletop. "For it's a Brother I need. My name is Guillor Weaver." That explained the quality of her clothes, thought Parno. "This is my fosterling, Mar." A gesture took in the girl who stood close at her elbow. "I need a bodyguard and guide to take Mar north, to Gotterang."

"Gotterang?" Dhulyn drew down her brows and shook her head minutely from side to side. "It would mean crossing through the country of the Cloud People, and according to the treaty, caravan season doesn't begin for almost another moon. Why not wait and send her then?"

Weaver shook her head. "We cannot wait, and we haven't the coin ourselves, so early in the season, to send her round by boat. We'd take her overland ourselves, but we've no one to spare."

"We're not a caravan; the Clouds would likely let us pass unhindered. Still," Dhulyn lifted her shoulders ever so slightly and wrinkled her nose. "Gotterang?"

Parno leaned back on his stool, pressing his shoulders against the wall behind him. He kept his face impassive, content to watch as his Partner did the haggling. Most people found debate with the Wolfshead's cold southern eyes disconcerting enough that they were anxious to come to terms. That he and Dhulyn were looking for an opportunity that would take them southeast to the capital would, of course, go unsaid. Parno rubbed the left side of his nose with his right thumb, and Dhulyn blinked twice.

"What will you pay?" she was saying in a uninterested tone, fingers toying with the edges of her papers.

"I have enough for the expenses of the journey, but not enough to pay you, if you see what I mean. The people you take her to will give you your fee."

Dhulyn lifted her brows and bared her teeth again.

"Slavers?" she said.

Without being aware that she was doing so, Weaver leaned away from the table. Parno touched Dhulyn lightly on the wrist with a finger. He knew that she had been a slave herself, though she rarely spoke of it. Knew, too, what kind of people buy children and youngsters, and to what use they put them.

Knowing nothing of this, the townswoman puffed indignantly, like all those who've had no personal contact with the trade.

"She's no slave! Mar's of our own fostering, orphaned of a House. We send her to her blood kin. It's they who want her, having just learned of her, though don't ask me how. And it's they who'll pay you for her delivery, safe and sound."

Dhulyn looked at Parno, blood-red brows arched. Parno nodded. Very possible for a House of Imrion to have a minor Holding or even a Household in Navra. Distant kin, but kin nonetheless.

"And the girl wishes to go?"

Weaver glanced at the girl standing so sedately at her side. The young girl met her foster mother's eyes steadily until the woman lowered hers and looked back across the table. "We would have kept her and happily, for she's a fine worker—reads, writes, and is learning to clerk. But she has little of her own, and we have no wedding gift for her, not with three of our own to pay for. This is her own kin." The Weaver seemed to be repeating a well-rehearsed speech. Perhaps there was someone at home—a son, maybe—who had needed to be convinced. House or no, the woman was content that the girl was going. "There may be property, there may be money for her. Caids know there should be," the woman muttered, looking sideways at the girl.

Not by smile or change of expression did Dhulyn acknowledge how much the Weaver had unintentionally revealed. "I only wished to know if we must take her bound." She tossed off the mug in front of her—hot sweet cider, no alcohol after the valerian—and handed it to Parno. He sighed and got to his feet, signaling to Nikola where she stood behind the bar.

"Thirty weights," Dhulyn said. "In gold." The Weaver gasped in outrage, and Parno stopped paying attention. He threaded his way between the empty tables, to where the girl was pouring out for him. Two men had come in while the Weaver had been talking and were leaning against the bar.

"I don't care how well the Sleeping God sleeps," the shorter man said in the careful diction of one who's been drinking all afternoon. Nikola exchanged a look with Parno. "Turchara's a good enough god for any sailing man. What I want to know is, why should they set their own prices? These are essential," the man had some trouble with the word and had to repeat it, "essential services. We shouldn't have to pay for them, and they shouldn't be allowed to withhold them." The man looked over and saw Parno for the first time — sure sign, were any needed, of just how drunk he was. "Not like they had to be Schooled, eh, Mercenary? No years hard training for them. They're born with the Mark. It's cost them nothing to get it, and look what they charge!"

"I'd lower my voice if I were you," Nikola said, taking the cups from in front of the two men. "There's a Jaldean at the door."

The drunk who'd been speaking turned slowly in a great show of control, but Parno had to put out a hand to stop the man's elbow from slipping off the bar. The doorway, as he'd known all along, was empty.

"Might have been gone to report you," Nikola said as she wiped off the bar. "Best be off home before he gets back with a Watchman."

Parno watched as the man's friend helped him out the door, before giving Nikola a wink and carrying the cider back to where Dhulyn sat with the Weaver woman. He put the Wolfshead's cup down in front of her and turned his attention to the girl he had no doubt would be their fare to Gotterang.

Even had he not been told, her heart-shaped face made it obvious Mar was no blood of the Weaver's, and it was likely enough that she was indeed orphan of a House. She was already taller than the admittedly short towns-woman, though manifestly young; she looked a marriageable age for a town girl if he was any judge — and he was. Unlikely that she would grow any taller, but she had inherited a good length of bone, regular features, good teeth, and abundant hair, though it did not shine much in the taproom's lamplight. All testimony to good blood and good health. And what was more, sufficient luck to be fostered in a family which fed her well enough to let her keep these advantages.

"So we're agreed?" Weaver was saying as she pulled a pouch from the wallet at her belt.

Dhulyn was still considering. Finally, she lifted her chin from her fist and held out her hand, palm up. "Give me your hand, girl," she said. Parno tensed. What could Dhulyn be thinking? Better she didn't touch anyone than to actually invite a Vision. Weaver looked at the young woman and nodded, but Mar was already holding out her square, ink-stained hand, palm down, for Dhulyn to take in her long scarred fingers.

"Are you afraid?"

"I am," the girl said in a voice little more than a whisper. "But I will go."

Dhulyn nodded, retaining her grip on the girl's hand. Her pale gray eyes became fixed so markedly upon something over the girl's shoulder that Mar turned around to see what it was. Dhulyn stared at nothing. Mar tried to pull her hand away. Dhulyn did not even seem to notice. Parno touched her foot with his under the table.

"She will need a pony," Dhulyn said, finally releasing the girl's hand without comment. "Forty silver weights and we are agreed."

Weaver opened the small pouch, shook its contents into her hand and, coin by coin, counted out the forty weights. Most of the coins were the old minting, ship on one side, the old Tarkin's head on the other, and dull with tarnish, but there were six gold pieces. Parno lifted his right eyebrow.

"It is enough," Dhulyn said. Weaver drew shut the strings of the pouch and slipped it back into her wallet.

"When will you leave?"

Dhulyn looked at Parno. He knew that her bargaining had taken into account several things besides the price of a pony, the purchase of heavy clothing, and provisions for traveling. There was the lodging they already owed Linkon Grey—besides the packhorse they'd bought from him and the extra cot for their room. Linkon might be an old acquaintance, but Nikola had four brothers and sisters who had to be provided for. Parno lifted his left eyebrow.

Dhulyn turned back to Weaver. "Tomorrow."

"I'll leave her now, then," Weaver stood up. "The letter from her kin tells where to go. You can read it yourself better than I," the woman added with a nod to the pages neatly piled on the table. Dhulyn looked up quickly, astonishment replacing the amusement on her face. The expression on the girl's face hadn't changed.

"Stay, stay, my good woman. If we're to have charge of her now, then it's *not* enough." Dhulyn tapped the coins on the table with a long index finger. "You'll have to pay for her lodging tonight, if you expect us to keep her here."

Weaver chewed on her bottom lip. Mar looked away indifferently. A great sigh, and Weaver took another two copper coins out of the wallet at her waist and placed them with the rest on the table. Parno swept them all into his own pouch.

"Behave yourself, child," the Weaver's voice was gruff as she rose to her feet. "Let your House know how much we've done for you." She did not offer to embrace the girl; her arms hung awkwardly at her sides. Parno caught Dhulyn's eye and widened his own.

"I will, Guillor. I will." The girl was soft-voiced, her tone neutral, or was there a hint of steel? Weaver nodded, but Parno suspected the older woman did not leave entirely content.

The young one sat down on the stool as soon as Weaver was gone, eyeing her present guardians like a new puppy caught between two veterans of the dog pack. Catching sight of Linkon behind the bar with his daughter, Parno roused himself with a sigh and went to explain matters.

Dhulyn's gaze drifted idly sideways, until it was caught and held by a line on the pages before her.

"Why Dhulyn the Scholar?" the girl ventured finally in her soft voice.

Dhulyn glanced up. The girl was relaxed enough, seeming to have put the parting from her family behind her. Of course, they were not her own family. Sun and Moon knew that could make a difference.

"Few soldiers can read." Dhulyn smiled gently enough

that the small scar did not pull back her lip. "And it's pronounced 'Dillin.' I am called other things as well."

"Dhulyn—" the girl broke off as the Mercenary held up her hand.

"You must not call me that," she said gently. "Only my Brothers may use my name, and I theirs. You may call me Wolfshead, or Scholar, if you prefer. And Parno you must call Lionsmane, or Chanter. It is our way."

The girl nodded slowly. "My family—my House, *will* pay well for my safe delivery," she said. "That, at least, is the truth."

"I believe it," Dhulyn said, taking mental note of the qualification. So something else wasn't the truth. Time enough to find out what, she supposed, when they were on the road. Her eyes strayed back to the tabletop. If they were leaving tomorrow, she must finish this book.

Parno dropped into his seat. Dhulyn blew out another sigh and looked up again. "Linkon says he has nothing else free," he said. "And he's already given us an extra cot for the room."

Dhulyn shrugged. "I'll take the cot, then." The girl across the table started and then was still. Her tongue darted out to wet dry lips. Dhulyn stifled her laugh. "No need to look like that, girl. There's no help for it, I cannot share a bed for two days at least. It's a vow," she added in answer to the girl's unspoken question. "You'll be as safe in Parno's bed as you would be in your own. Safer. He won't touch you himself, and he'll kill anyone else who tries." Out of habit her eyes strayed back to her page, but she knew it for a lost cause.

"You're too young for my tastes, child," Parno agreed soberly. "I'll put a sword between us if you doubt me."

"What's to do?" Dhulyn asked, surprised when the girl's anxious expression did not change. "Are you virgin? And mean to stay that way? Has it importance, other than to you I mean?"

"It might. There's . . . there's to be a marriage," Mar said, lowering her eyes.

"Oh, come now," said Parno. "It's only the High Noble Houses worry over such things, and, even so, it's just until the birth of the heirs."

Dhulyn drew in her brows and shushed him. "A marriage? Your foster mother didn't mention that." She was annoyed with herself for not getting all the information. Well, she knew now, and this could up the fee at the other end.

"She didn't know." Mar's voice hardened, and she sat up straighter. She drew forth a letter from the bosom of her tunic and displayed the seal in the folds of parchment, lifted but not broken. "She can't read, and she didn't tell you everything, even of the things she does know. My name is Mar-eMar," she said, putting the accent properly on the second syllable. "And my House is Tenebro."

Dhulyn looked at Parno. His lips were pursed in a soundless whistle that changed into a toothy grin. Someone who didn't know him well would think he was delighted.

Dhulyn sat folded into the window seat, reading Mar's letter by the light of the room's single oil lamp. She had made them wait and be quiet while she finished her book in the taproom. By that time it was getting crowded, and Parno had suggested they make an early night of it. Now Mar helped Parno shift their gear while Dhulyn examined the letter from Tenebro House. With three people, the white-washed room under the eaves of the inn's west wing was sadly crowded. Stowing the packs carefully left the beds free, but there was little floor space.

Dhulyn was familiar with this kind of letter: a great deal of style and very little substance. Almost one third of the page was taken up by the titles and lineage of the woman who wrote (or who had it written for her, more likely) and of Mar-eMar herself, as the person addressed. The letter itself was quite short, stating that the family had just learned of Mar's whereabouts and wished her to come urgently to the capital to occupy her place in the House. That was probably the marriage the girl had mentioned. Almost apologetically, a tone no doubt inserted by the clerk, mused Dhulyn, Mar was asked to bring with her any family possessions that might serve as proofs of her identity. What might such things be, Dhulyn wondered? She looked up to see Mar eyeing the bed dubiously.

"I saw a play once about a man and a woman who lay

together with a sword placed between them," the girl was saying. "And it was taken as proof that they were chaste." She looked up at the Lionsmane, towering over her. "But I do not understand how it . . . how it prevents . . ."

"*Lying* between them? Well, no, perhaps that wouldn't be proof of much," said Parno, almost clucking in his imitation of an elderly uncle. Dhulyn smiled, her lip curling back over her teeth. "But then playwrights are not so very accurate. What do you think, Dhulyn? Shall you lay your sword between us?"

For answer Dhulyn unfolded herself from the window seat, reaching out for her sword where it lay still sheathed on the cot. She straightened, drawing the patterned blade out smoothly and in one motion thrust it, point down, into the straw and ticking of the mattress. Two feet of newly sharpened blade stuck out, quivering slightly, a fence post in the center of the bed.

"Do not brush up against it in the dark, my souls," she said, laughing at the shock on the little Dove's face. "It will cut you."

Three

"BUT YOU TOLD GUILLOR you would buy a pony." The girl eyed their packhorse dubiously. It was a small animal, little more than a pony in size, but Mar was also small, and by careful repacking of their weapons into their own saddlebags, the spare horse could carry both the girl and the balance of the provisions they would stop to buy.

"I told her you would *need* a pony." The corners of Dhulyn's lips twitched. "Not that we would have to buy one."

The girl stood still, blinking. "Guillor Weaver's considered a shrewd woman, a hard dealer," she said finally, halfway between admiration and annoyance.

"Nay, don't be offended," Parno said, chuckling at the look on the girl's face. "Your foster mother's reputation stands firm. But Mercenaries deal and bargain with all sorts, not just people buying cloth."

"And we deal for our lives, little Dove," added Dhulyn. "That makes us sharper." When she was satisfied that the girl wouldn't fall off immediately, Dhulyn nodded to Parno and they mounted their own horses. Both Warhammer and Bloodbone knew what packs meant, and were fidgeting, impatient to be off. How they'd feel after a day's long riding in this cold weather was something else again.

Their first stop was the market, where, after buying a good supply of roadbread and dried fish, Parno and Mar waited with the horses while Dhulyn went to the book merchant's stall. There she traded the three books she had finished—carefully rolled and tied into tubes—for a single new one, a copy of Theonyn's poems bound into a traveler's volume made of the lighter, imported paper instead of parchment, cut into pages and sewn into a binding of stiff leather. She could only afford the one book, and the poems would take longer to read than anything else of equal size.

"What is it, little one?" Dhulyn looked up from stowing her book. Mar's fidgeting was enough to make the pack-horse itself restive.

"Nothing, that is . . ." the girl hesitated.

"A heavy silence for nothing," Dhulyn said.

"It's just . . . I was wondering if I might be able to say good-bye to my friend Sarita at the weapons stall."

"Who would stop you? We take you where you wish to go, do we not?" Dhulyn spoke lightly. No point in terrorizing the girl. "Never mind, my Dove. Slip down and go. The Lionsmane and I will wait for you over by that barrel." Dhulyn pointed out an empty barrel holding up one end of a baker's stall. There it would be possible for them to stand at least partly out of the way.

Mar glanced over at the weapons stall and nodded. "I won't be long," she promised as she hurried off.

"You don't think she'll run," Parno said, watching the girl weave her way between early morning buyers and sellers.

"She hasn't the look of it, no," Dhulyn said, drawing down her blood-colored brows. "But then, we have a clear sight of the weapons stall from here, she won't get far on foot, and we've our travel money to Gotterang in any case." She smiled her wolfsmile, and Parno threw back his head and laughed.

It was not possible for them to stand completely out of everyone's way even so early in the day, but marketers tended to part around the two Brothers with little or no complaint. Mercenary badges often encouraged even the most unruly to mind their manners. They stood facing each other, their eyes drifting apparently aimlessly as they spoke, taking in all of their surroundings, never looking in the same direction at once.

"How is it," Dhulyn remarked in the nightwatch murmur that would be unintelligible to any passerby, "that I have lived thus long without ever hearing the name Tenebro, since it makes even strong men pale?"

Parno bit back a curse. He should have known she would notice something. She would never have asked, but this was something he should have told her before. Caids knew, the middle of the market square in Navra was not the best place for his life story.

"What if I told you it was just a trick of the light?" he said, forcing a smile to his lips.

"You'd be lying."

Best place or no, he had to say something; this might be the last chance they had to speak privately for the next half moon.

"I knew them." He watched as her eyes widened and her mouth formed a soundless "oh" of comprehension.

"Will they know you?" She was asking more than if they would recognize him. She was asking whether there was danger in it if they should. There were many reasons a man might leave his Household for the Brotherhood. Blood duel was only one of them.

"*Caids,* not likely," he said, making it sound as certain as he could. The difference between seventeen and thirty-one, he thought. A lifetime of change.

"You *would* tell me," she said, turning to nod and smile as the kitchen boy from the inn passed close to them—marketing on his free day from the look of his good clothes.

"Of course," he said, eyes flicking to her face. How could she doubt that he would fail to warn her of possible danger? They were Partnered, a sword with two edges.

"Any odds it's not the same House?"

"I keep telling you, less poetry and more politics." Parno snorted, relieved that she questioned him no further.

"Then why would I need you, my soul?" She reached out and punched him lightly, barely a touch, above his heart. "All the same family then?"

Parno twisted his lips to one side, resisting the temptation to squeeze his eyes shut. "The same House," he said, indicating Mar with his eyes, "though not necessarily the same family. The Tenebros are one of the five High Noble Houses, the ones most likely to provide a Tarkin should one be needed. They've Households and Holdings of all sizes throughout the Letanian Peninsula. For the sake of influence, and courtesy, we're . . . *they're* all considered kin, though the blood runs thinner the farther away from the main branch. Just the same, every Household and Holding owes their allegiance there, and all are counted as House Tenebro. Both Householders *and* Holdings use the noble form of their names, as Mar-eMar was quick to remind us. But not the *high* noble form—"

"Which is?"

"The mirror reverse. If our little Mar was herself the House, or heir to that dignity, her name would be pronounced Mar-EE-Ram, not Mar-EE-Mar."

"Ah, I've seen that in books, I should have asked you before what it meant." Dhulyn gave herself a nod of satisfaction.

Parno shook his head. "It's an odd time to send for the girl, having let her Holding lapse these ten years. There's more to this than reuniting lost kin. The Tenebros are First Blood to the Tarkin himself. More important than *that* it's difficult to be, though they were so once, and perhaps with these new troubles, they are trying to be so again."

"I *have* read history, which you call politics," Dhulyn said, frowning. "If I recall correctly, was there not a Tenebro Tarkin before Nyl-aLyn, father of the present Colebro Tarkin?"

Parno shrugged. "I think two reigns before his. It seems their luck turned bad. It began within the House itself, a generation or two back. Unexplained, or insufficiently explained illnesses, a disappearance or two. Then it followed as these things follow." Parno shrugged again. "A battle lost here, an ill-advised marriage there, an assassination or so. The High Houses intervened, the Tarkinate was put to the Ballot, and House Tenebro proved to have insufficient support to retain the Carnelian Throne."

"They were not wiped out?" Dhulyn's eyes narrowed and Parno followed her glance over his shoulder to where he could see Mar talking to her friend. A small flat object, which he recognized as parchment even at this distance, was passed between them. Was that a bit of green seal? The girl had more than the one letter then.

"Oh, no," he said in answer to Dhulyn's question. "Too numerous and too powerful for that, for all they'd lost the Throne. Some of the smaller branches, the Holdings, withered, it is true . . ." Parno's voice dried in his throat, and Dhulyn looked sharply back at him, waiting with brows lowered for him to say something more. He shifted his eyes away, pretending to scour their surroundings for enemies. He wanted to tell her, he *should* tell her. But he hadn't thought the pain was still so close to the surface that it could shut his throat.

"And Mar-eMar is a twig from such a branch, or so her letter seems to say," she said finally, ignoring his silence. Bloodbone snorted and stepped back as someone nudged her from the far side. Dhulyn cocked her eye and smiled at a man in a painter's stained work clothes who ducked his head and smiled in return before he dropped his own gaze. She ran her hand along Bloodbone's neck until the mare quieted. "Which means that marriage is not just a wishful thought on the little one's part. Here I thought she had listened to too many bard's songs."

"Not at all. The songs usually have some root in fact, swords on the bed notwithstanding. At these rarefied heights, allegiances can be tricky things, and it's difficult to find someone of sufficiently noble blood who is not politically suspect, or who is not already too closely related for progeny. A country branch of your own family is ideal. In the old days it was not unheard of to begin such branches for that very purpose."

Again their eyes locked. This time it was Dhulyn who looked away.

"Keeps the property together too, I shouldn't wonder," she said. "Now we know why Mistress Weaver was so sure we would be paid, and so anxious for the family to know of her good care." Dhulyn's eyes found Mar again as she moved through the stalls of the market making her way back to them. "Though why would the Weavers not escort the girl themselves, if it comes to that?"

Parno nodded. "True, merchants aren't known for giving away profit. They're towns folk, though, let's not forget," he continued. "They would have had to hire guards anyway, and then . . ." He cocked his head. "Doing favors for the powerful is a chancy thing. Less reward for them this way, perhaps, but less risk, too."

"More risk for us, you mean."

They fell silent as they watched Mar wait for a boy driving a donkey with water jugs in its panniers to cross in front of her. Parno lowered his voice still further. "Dhulyn? When you touched her, what did you See?"

"I Saw our little Dove wearing a cloth-of-silver gown. Hand in hand with a line of dancers."

"Her wedding, do you think? The wedding she expects?"

Dhulyn shrugged. "Rich and alive," she answered. "It seemed like a good omen for us who are to be her guards. And I'll tell you something else, my Brother," she said. "If they were so very anxious to have her back in the bosom of the family, why did the Tenebros not send some trusted servants of their own?" She smiled her wolf's smile. "Perhaps there's more than bandits and Cloud People for us to be wary of."

Parno shook his head. Whatever she might have guessed from his evasions, she was willing to let it drop, at least for now.

"Caids take you," he said, "as if we didn't have enough problems!"

Laughing, Dhulyn thumped him on the shoulder before swinging herself up on Bloodbone, leaving Parno to help Mar regain her seat on the packhorse. When they were both ready, Dhulyn led them north through the market and into the wide avenue that would become the Gotterang Road once it passed through the north gates of Navra. The streets were unusually crowded this morning, and when they were within sight of the town's wall and the gates themselves, she saw why. Only one leaf of the heavy timbered gate was open, and the people, horses, and carts ahead of them had been formed into a line and were being stopped by the Watch before they were allowed to pass through. While Dhulyn was looking the situation over, one short man with a tinker's pack on his back was escorted away to the guardroom while the others in line stood waiting.

Dhulyn checked Bloodbone, keeping the horse to a much slower pace than the animal wanted. Too late to get

out of line and try a different gate—or a different way out
of the city entirely. They were behind two farm carts and a
small company of strolling players, and there wasn't much
room to maneuver. Dhulyn shrugged, making sure the
sword lying along her spine was loose in its sheath. There
were only five guards, and if worse came to worst . . .

Dhulyn spotted the helmet crest of the officer of the
Watch, and even from this distance she had no trouble
making out how his lips were thinned by a look of frozen
displeasure. The very look, Dhulyn considered, of a man
following orders he didn't agree with. Give too many of
those, and you could have a revolt on your hands.

And she'd bet her second-best sword that the Jaldean
standing behind the gatemen had something to do with it.
Looked as if they'd got the Finders out just in time—and
perhaps they should have gone with them.

Casually, as if she were just checking the numbers in line
behind them, she turned to look back at Parno. Mar and the
packhorse were between them, but Dhulyn had no trouble
catching his eye over the girl's head. He scratched his left
ear with his right thumb. So he agreed. Too late to change
their minds. They'd have to see if they couldn't bluff their
way through.

Whatever it was that had the officer clenching his teeth,
his men looked content enough, though there was none of
the relaxed informality Dhulyn would have expected from
gate guards in a country at peace. And now that she was
looking for it, there was a tall fair guard having trouble
hiding his smirk, grinning openly whenever he was sure
that his officer wasn't looking. Dhulyn smiled. That kind of
discord spelled real trouble, and where there was trouble
in the ranks, there was room for a good Mercenary to maneuver.

The two farmers and the traveling players passed
through without incident, and Dhulyn pulled up as Bloodbone came abreast of the officer's crest. The nearer guards
gave ground, and the three farther away came closer, until
there was a cleared circle with Dhulyn, Parno, and the girl
in the center. Dhulyn glanced up. There were crossbow
men at the top of the gate. Still, if Parno took care of the
bowmen, she could manage the five guards down here

before any others arrived. And from the wide-eyed look on the face of the nearest one, he knew exactly what she was thinking and believed it as well. If she hadn't already taken money to make sure the girl was safe . . . She smiled her wolf's smile at the officer.

"Step to the side, Mercenaries, please," he said, staring steadily at a point just over her left shoulder. "Over there if you will."

And if I won't? Dhulyn didn't say the words aloud. "But you know us, Officer." She tapped her Mercenary badge with the fingers of an obviously empty hand. "Mercenaries of the Brotherhood. This young one's Mar, fosterling of the Weavers in Threadneedle Alley. We've been given the charge of taking her to her family in Gotterang." Dhulyn was careful to keep her tone light, as if she were just gossiping, and the guard officer was just a friend.

The Jaldean pushed his way forward and laid his hand on the thin wool covering Dhulyn's knee. "You go to Gotterang, Mercenary?"

Dhulyn bit down to keep from gasping as

❧

THE MAN IN FRONT OF HER CROSSES THE STREET, HIS EYES GLOWING GREEN

❧

flashed through her mind almost too quickly to see. It took all of her training and concentration not to flinch away from the Jaldean's hand.

"We do," she answered, pleased at how steady her voice was. "Would you mind stepping back, friend? You're making my horse nervous." Dhulyn took hold of Bloodbone's mane in a special twist, and the mare tossed her head and brought her right forehoof down on the Jaldean's foot.

The officer suddenly looked away and Dhulyn was quick to draw in her brows and "tsk," as Bloodbone continued dancing and rolling her eyes like a horse about to bolt. Nursing his foot, the Jaldean flicked his hand toward them and the officer, eyes now bright in his stiff face, acknowledged Dhulyn with the slightest of bows, and waved them through the gate.

As soon as they were through Mar's packhorse fell into

place at Dhulyn's right hand of its own accord, even though Dhulyn was still having trouble with Bloodbone. When Parno took up position to Mar's right, the girl looked from one Brother to the other.

"I don't understand," Mar said. "Were they going to stop us?"

"Seems like they meant to," Parno said. "At least until they knew where we were going."

"Almost makes you wonder why, doesn't it?" Dhulyn said. Bloodbone was now perfectly calm, except for the head tossing that looked remarkably as though the animal were laughing.

"I've got a bad feeling about this," Parno said, turning back to stare at Navra's wall.

Five days later they were in the foothills of the Antedichas Mountains, heading for the pass, and Cloud Country. Dhulyn and Parno rode with bows strung and arrows ready. Even if the packhorse could carry food for three almost a whole moon—which it could not and carry Mar as well— they'd be heartily sick of roadbread and dried fish if they did not hunt.

Dark still came early at this time of year; the search for a place to spend the night began after the midday meal, which was roadbread and dried fruit eaten on horseback. It was obvious the town girl did not have the trick of eating the roadbread, and finally Dhulyn took pity on her.

"You'll break your teeth, my Dove," she said. "The stuff's dense as bricks. Break off a small piece in your hands, or with your knife if your fingers aren't strong enough," she advised. "Then hold it in your mouth until it softens enough to chew." Dhulyn watched to make sure Mar could manage before turning her attention back to the road ahead.

She'd learned on their first campaign together not to let Parno choose their camps. He *always* stopped too early, and so the journey took half again as long as was needed. Twice, Dhulyn turned down likely looking places without comment before settling on a hollowed clearing nestled in a small copse of half-grown pine trees.

"Toss you for it?" Parno dismounted and shook a cramp out of his left leg.

"No," Dhulyn said, "you go ahead and set up the perimeter, I'll help the Dove." As with the roadbread, Dhulyn watched Mar before offering any advice. It didn't take long to see that the town-bred girl knew nothing about travel. She was clumsy with her bedding, shy about her personal needs and, Dhulyn sighed, no doubt useless as a cook. And how could she not be? Weavers were not known as great travelers. And those like Guillor Weaver traveled less than most, since her business was in a port town, and trade would come to her.

Not for the first time Dhulyn wondered what it would have been like to grow up with walls that did not move. Not a tent or a ship or the back of a horse. Where the same people were there every day.

"That is not the way," Dhulyn said when she'd finished laying out her own bedding with Parno's and turned to where Mar fumbled with hers. "First, if you put your bed there, you will lose the benefit of the fire."

"But I'm closer to the fire than you are."

"And I'm closer to this tall brush that will reflect the fire's heat down on me," Dhulyn responded. "Put your bedding here, next to ours. No, a good layer of these old needles first. You'll find the ground quite hard enough the first few days, I'll wager."

The girl eyed Dhulyn's own bed. "Don't you have to sleep alone?" she asked shyly. "I mean, your vow?"

"My vow's over, but I will be sleeping alone," Dhulyn said, grinning. "I'll sleep when Parno's on watch. Then he'll sleep while I watch. When it gets colder, the two not on watch will sleep together for added warmth."

"Colder?" squeaked Mar.

"Colder as we move into the mountains, closer to the pass."

Both women turned as Parno followed his voice out of the darkness, a skinned rabbit hanging from his hand. "Then warmer again once we're through. That's why we want to get through as quickly as possible." Parno took in the campsite with a quick glance and nodded. "Who is cooking tonight?"

Dhulyn skewered the cleaned rabbit on a short iron rod and propped it between carefully set rocks close to the fire.

"There are traveling tools, then, for every thing," said Mar watching closely. "Just like at home? Things to cook with and clean with?"

"Not so much cleaning on the road, as you'll find out," Dhulyn said, sitting down cross-legged within easy reach of the spit.

"Not that you'll notice after a while, since we'll all be equally dirty," agreed Parno. "I once traveled without the benefit of cooking rods, pots, or skillets, however."

"What did you do?" said Mar.

"Roasted rabbits, just like today," he said. "But I used my sword for a spit."

"Doubtless all it was good for," Dhulyn remarked solemnly.

Mar shook her head, but Dhulyn saw the ghost of a smile on the girl's lips and relaxed.

"How did you learn to do all of this? Find your directions by looking at the sun? Learn where to set up your camp? How to cook?"

"We have close to twenty years of Brotherhood between us," Parno said. "Much of that time spent on campaign. Not surprising that we should know how to set up camp."

"Are you so old, then? Old enough to have been Mercenaries all that time?"

"I have seen the Hawk Moon twenty-six times," Dhulyn said, unsure what prompted her to answer in the Outlander's roundabout way. "Parno, to be sure, is an old grandfather next to me."

"Alas, too true," Parno said, shaking his golden head. "And yet there's no respect for my ancient bones and hard-learned wisdom."

"You don't look like town people," Mar said. "I couldn't guess your ages. I've seen the . . . the Hunt Moon eighteen times," she added, smiling at the Wolfshead.

"Still not old enough for me," said Parno lying back on the bedroll. "So you may rest easy. Wake me when the food's ready, would you, young ones?"

When Mar awoke that first morning in camp, there was something very hard bruising her left hip, her back felt sore, and her nose was cold. And there was an odd, rhythmic chuffing sound, familiar, and yet too quick to be the sound of the loom. She sat up, suddenly remembering that her mornings might never start with the sound of the loom again.

Lionsmane was blowing on the embers of the fire, but that wasn't what Mar had heard.

Movement caught her eye, and Mar saw sunlight flash on the edge of the blade before she saw the woman who wielded it. Suddenly she realized that the rhythmic sound was Dhulyn Wolfhead's breathing. Little puffs of fog left her lips as she danced around the clearing where they camped. Mar had seen the City Watch doing this once, also early in the morning when she had been unable to sleep and had volunteered to fetch the early milk. *Shora,* it was called. A kind of mock combat that could be practiced alone or with others. But the City Watch's practice was clumsy beside what Mar saw now. The Wolfhead's every movement was precise, fluid and effortless, like the running and leaping of a deer, and with something of the deer's grace and heart-stopping beauty. The swords moved faster and faster, the blades disappearing as the air around the Wolfshead blurred, until they abruptly took on form once more as she regained perfect stillness.

And the Wolfhead's breathing never changed.

Mar released the breath she was holding, truly frightened for the first time since she had received the letters from Gotterang. Looking at the Mercenary woman's cold face, it seemed that what Mar had agreed to do might be considerably more dangerous than she'd thought.

"Practice, practice, practice," Lionsmane said in a comfortable voice. "And yet it was I who saved Dhulyn Wolfshead from death at Arcosa, the day we met."

Mar turned her eyes away from the motionless Wolfshead, relaxing into the warm rumble of Parno's voice. She looked again at the expression on his face as he watched Dhulyn. That's *why I'm safe with him,* she thought with a sense of awakening even further. That's *why he says I'm too young. Because he can look at her like that.* Mar took her bottom lip between her teeth. If Ysdrell had ever shown her such a look, she thought, she might have ignored her

Tenebro letters, and none of them would be here—or would Wolfshead and Lionsmane be on their way to Imrion just the same? As if he could feel her eyes on him, the Lionsmane shook himself and looked back at her.

"You've never seen the *Shora* practiced?"

"I've seen the City Watch." She glanced back. The Wolfshead had lowered her blades and was automatically wiping them clean, though there was no blood on them. "But it wasn't like that, exactly."

"The difference you cannot explain is the difference between Mercenaries and ordinary soldiers. I know," he added as she turned to him, "because in my time I have been both. The word *Shora* means patterns in the old tongue, the tongue of the Caids, as our friend there would be the first to tell you, and there are eighty-one of them. Each with at least three, but some with up to one hundred and eight separate moves. *Shora* for the sword—single-or double-handed—*Shora* for the knife, the dagger, the razor, the club, the stick, and the stone. *Shora* for the hands, feet, and head. For anything held in the hand, as well as for the hands alone. *Shora* for breathing, for smell and sight and hearing. I know the basic twenty-seven that all Mercenaries must know to be considered Schooled." Parno Lionsmane shrugged. "Maybe a few others. The Wolfshead knows over fifty. If she lives, she will know them all, and she will School others."

If she lives. Mar shivered, watching Dhulyn sheathe her weapons. The morning was colder than she'd thought.

Four

I N THE AFTERNOON of the twelfth day, with the pass
two days behind them, Parno stopped on a small rise
and let the two women ride past him. Dhulyn pulled up
her horse and halted Mar with a gesture when he did not
follow them.

"What?" she called.

"Look at those clouds," he said. Dhulyn turned in her
saddle to follow the direction of his gaze. The sky was dark
and heavy. "If that's not snow, and soon, I'm a blind man."

Dhulyn nodded, sighted back along the trail and bit her
lower lip. Earlier that morning they had seen what might
have been a herder's hut off to the south of the trail, but
Dhulyn had decided it was far too early to stop. They might
pay dearly for that decision now. It wasn't often she laid out
the tiles and lost the game.

She looked around at the uneven landscape, rocky and
full of pines, pockets of old snow drifted into spots the sun
did not reach. "This part of the hills, we should be able to
find some reasonably sheltered place," she said, sighing.
They were Mercenaries; they didn't expect either rain or
snow to kill them. If the weather were better, the long-lost
Tenebro cousin would be traveling in the company of a
merchant's caravan, and she and Parno would be lucky to
get guard's wages for the same journey they were making
now.

"As well we're not twenty or thirty people," was all
Parno said.

The sky was turning ominously black when the tiles

came up swords after all. What looked like a shoulder of hillside jutting out from among a small grouping of firs proved to be two enormous boulders, one partially leaning on the other to form a shallow cave where they touched.

"Plenty of shelter in those trees for the horses," Parno said.

"And we can cut branches, layer them across the top, extend the shelter right out to here." She indicated the point where the rocks were farthest apart. "With a fire close to the opening, we'll stay snug and dry."

"What odd shapes." Mar edged the packhorse closer. "I've never seen rocks like this."

"They are not rocks, little Dove."

"What then?" Mar dismounted and, holding the pack-horse's lead, stepped closer.

Dhulyn brushed off a piece of dried lichen, revealing a remarkably smooth section of whitish stone. "Remnants of a wall, I'd say. Relics of the Caids."

"The *Caids.*" Mar stepped back, putting her horse between her and the wall. "I thought they were spirits."

Dhulyn looked sideways at the girl. "They may be, now. People do swear by them, it's true. But the Scholars say that they're an ancient people, long gone. Ancestors to us all, they say. It's sure that everywhere *I've* journeyed I've seen their traces—bits of statues, places too flat for nature that must have been roads, odd formations of rock like these. There are even bits of books left from those times, though all I've ever seen were translated copies." Dhulyn smiled, pushed Mar a little with her fingertips. "Don't worry, my Dove, the place isn't haunted."

Mar nodded, but not as though she was reassured.

"Get the packs stowed," Dhulyn told her, "then go and collect firewood while Parno and I cut branches."

Snow began to fall as the two Mercenaries placed the last of the branches across the opening and Mar carefully laid and lit the fire as Dhulyn had shown her. With large flakes and fluffy, the snow fell quiet and soft, and at first melted as it hit the ground. But long before they were ready for their suppers, it began to accumulate, thick and light as down.

"No point in setting watch," Parno said. He crawled past

Dhulyn deeper into the cave. "We'd neither see nor hear anyone coming."

"Any sign of wind?"

"No, thank the Caids." Parno grinned, touched his forehead with the tips of his fingers in the Mercenary salute. "That would be all we'd need."

Dhulyn tucked Mar into the warmest corner, from where the girl watched with wide eyes as, after they had eaten their supper rations, the two Mercenaries took it in turns to unpack, testing and examining each item of their clothing, and each piece of metal, checking for signs of dampness or rust. Their bedding was already toasting in the warmth from the fire, and now cloaks and damp hoods were spread out as well.

Parno unwrapped and was assembling the pipes that gave him his nickname "Chanter" as Dhulyn checked over her book and the few writing materials she carried. There'd been precious little playing—or reading for that matter—since they'd left that last inn, and Dhulyn had noticed that Mar had taken to calling them Wolfshead and Lions mane, dropping their other nicknames entirely. She supposed it was hard for a town-bred girl to watch them at their daily *Shora* and think of them as anything but Mercenaries.

As Dhulyn stowed away the last of her belongings she gestured to Mar. "Come, my Dove, your turn. The damp will spoil your things if you don't take care."

Mar unpacked slowly, and it seemed to Dhulyn that the girl was shamed to display how little she owned, even to two of a Brotherhood known for traveling light. Her few pieces of clothing were well made of good, if plain, cloth, befitting the foster child of weavers. There was also a very fine pair of bright yellow trousers that Dhulyn eyed covetously, knowing they would never fit her. And a single glass bead on a strand of copper wire, more a child's plaything than a piece of jewelry.

The girl's writing supplies were the goods of a professional, not a hobbyist like Dhulyn. Four good pens, their nibs fresh and ready for trimming, and two bottles of differently colored inks, stoppered and sealed with wax. Instead of Dhulyn's few scraps, Mar had several large sheets of parchment, not new, but carefully scraped clean. Shuffled in among these Dhulyn saw the green-sealed letters Mar had picked up from her friend in the market at Navra. Information from her House, it seemed, that Mar didn't want to share.

Dhulyn flicked a glance at Parno, and he nodded with the barest inclination of his head.

"How much neater you keep your things than I do mine," Dhulyn said, reaching out to touch the parchments Mar was shuffling back together. "Are you sure none of these have taken any damp?"

"Oh, yes," the girl said, thrusting all the pages into the bottom of her pack before picking up the pens and inks with more care.

"I'm glad to see you take such care of the tools of your trade," Parno said, solemn and sincere. "They're proof to any who need to know it that you have the means to earn your own living. You have relative wealth and independence even without your noble House, don't forget it."

"What's this last thing?"

Once again, Dhulyn reached out, and this time Mar did nothing to stop her from unwrapping an old cloak, worn, but still showing something of a vivid rose dye in its folds. When there were only a few layers of cloth left, Dhulyn pulled back her hands and let Mar, almost ceremoniously, finish unrolling what was clearly her greatest possession. A bowl, shallow, perhaps as wide as two narrow hands, its exterior intricately patterned and glazed, colors glowing like jewels in the fire's light. Dhulyn met Mar's gaze and smiled, her own delight mirrored in the younger woman's eyes.

"It is beautiful," Dhulyn said simply. "May I?" Mar passed it carefully into the older woman's hands. Dhulyn turned it over a few times in her long fingers, measuring and weighing it unconsciously as she examined the patterns. Along the narrow base there were geometric shapes—lines, triangles, circles and squares—but on the upper edge . . . "I know these designs," she said softly, "Look! Am I wrong? What's this along the edge?" She held out the bowl at an angle, so the light fell clearly along its green-bordered rim.

"It's forest creeper," Parno said.

"No it isn't." Mar's voice was quiet, matching her smile. "It's a chain of people dancing. Isn't it?" she added, looking across at Dhulyn.

The older woman nodded. "I believe so," she said. "And in that case . . ." she turned the bowl upside down, the better to study its patterns. Squinting in the changeable light of the fire, she could see how the chain of dancers along the rim crossed over itself, as if in a country dance, and turned down, forming garlands around the body of the bowl and framing spaces which had been filled with small scenes. "Yes," she said. "See here, there's a woman, noble from her gown, laying out the vera tiles for a solitary game." Dhulyn glanced up at Parno. "You've seen that posture a thousand times, my soul. And look at this old fisherman," she turned the bowl slightly, "hanging up his nets, checking for tears and snags. Look how his muscles stand out as he lifts them. And here's a young boy walking back and forth along the rows in a vineyard, no doubt keeping the foxes out!"

"This one's a man," Mar said, tapping an image on the side of the bowl closest to her. "It must be a father," she added, "he's tossing up a small child and catching him again." She looked up, a catch in her voice. "There's a woman watching them, smiling."

"What's the last one," Parno said. "I can't make it out."

"It's a young woman again—no, a young man, and he seems to be holding a harp." No amount of squinting brought out further detail. "Do you know, Mar?"

Mar shook her head. "I've always thought it was a mirror." She took the bowl completely into her own hands and tilted it to catch the dying light of the fire on the final scene. "It's been a long time since I really looked at this. I didn't like to bring it out at the Weavers."

"It's a beautiful thing," Dhulyn said. "Worth another look and then another. Do you know what you have here, my Dove?"

"I thought I did," faltered Mar. "Now I begin to doubt." Dhulyn's heart warmed. It was easy for her to find a look tinged with fear on someone's face. Only when people saw the Scholar and not the Wolf did she ever see this kind of warmth.

"It comes from my mother," Mar said, "and her mother before that. The property of the eldest daughter of my Household. It's my proof, if I need it, that I am Mar-eMar Tenebro."

"Making it valuable enough," Dhulyn said. "But it has other significance. A bowl like this is described in Tarlyn's *First Book of the Mark*."

"It would bring a good price," Parno said putting his hand on Dhulyn's wrist. "I marvel the good Weaver left it to you."

"You mean she might have taken it?" The girl's genuine astonishment caused the two elders to glance at each other and quickly away.

"Nay, child, she's been proven an honest woman, even without this." Parno put a comforting hand on the young girl's shoulder. He ventured a glance sideways at Dhulyn. "You don't think it could be . . . ?"

"What? Tarlyn's bowl? Oh, Sun and Moon, no! The *Book of the Mark*, like these designs, goes back to the time of the Caids." Dhulyn returned to her scrutiny of the bowl. The silence made her look up into Mar's stricken face. "Oh, it is real, little Dove. A Scholar's artifact. But," she shrugged. "It could not be Tarlyn's bowl, is all. The designs are the true ancient ones, but the colors, see how sharp the blues and greens?" She traced her finger along the line of dancers. "These have been no more than five generations in use."

"And that's not ancient?" Mar's eyes were wide with surprise. "My grandmother's grandmother's mother?"

"Ancient for people, assuredly," Dhulyn said. "But a mere five generations is nothing as artifacts are judged. The roads and other objects the Caids have left," she gestured around her at the walls that sheltered them, "are much older even than our oldest writings. Still," Dhulyn caught Parno's eye again. "Valuable as it is to anyone, it has a meaning for you and your House that it cannot have for any other."

Mar took the bowl from the Mercenary's outstretched hands and lowered it back into its wrappings. She did not see the Brothers share another glance over her head.

"Are you happy to leave them, then, the Weavers?"

Dhulyn watched the girl's face closely. This would make twice the girl had lost the only family she had ever known. Once upon the death of her own parents, and now again at this parting from her foster family. That she went to her own House, her own people, would be no great comfort, considering she had never seen any of them before.

"I think I would have had to leave anyway," Mar said.

"How's that," Parno asked from where he sprawled. "There seemed to be enough business to need you."

"Oh, yes," Mar said. "They'll have to hire another now, and someone not as well trained in their ways. But I think it would have come to that anyway." She looked between their interested faces. "You see, the younger son asked for me."

"Not in itself unheard of," Dhulyn said dryly.

"No," Mar agreed. "His father was not against it. He was willing to apply to House Tenebro for permission and dowry, but Guillor Weaver felt it might offend them." The girl shrugged. "If he marries elsewhere, Ysdrell can bring money to the business and the family with his marriage. Until my letters came I was no one, with nothing. After that I was too much a someone."

Dhulyn carefully ignored Mar's slip. It remained to be seen what importance the number of letters had. It crossed her mind, however, to wonder whether the male Weaver had, in secret from his wife, contacted the girl's House, and if this "urgent" summons to Gotterang was the result. "At least you do not sound brokenhearted, my Dove."

"Oh, no. You see, for me, that was the real problem. I did not want Ysdrell." She added another stick to the fire and looked up again. "That's why I would have had to leave."

"A good enough reason," Dhulyn said, feeling a knot of tension release. "So this is as good a way as any, and better than most." And it explained why the girl was so ready to go to Gotterang.

"How do you get your names?" Mar asked as she knotted the ties on her pack.

Dhulyn laughed. It appeared it was a night to ask questions, and not for Parno to play while she and Mar sang. "Oh, different reasons at different times. Parno, for example—"

"I have the strength, the lordliness, and the beauty of a lion," he cut in.

"And the smell," said Dhulyn, and smiled as Mar laughed.

"What about you? You explained Scholar, but why Wolfshead? Is it because of . . . because of . . ."

"Because of the scar? Because of this?" Dhulyn smiled her wolf's smile, lips curling back off her teeth in a snarl, but she made sure the eyes above it were smiling, too, and Mar grinned back at her, not in the least afraid. "Quite right, exactly because of that."

Mar frowned, her head on one side, as if she was trying to picture Dhulyn without the scar.

"Do you mind it?" she asked finally.

To her own surprise, Dhulyn Wolfshead began to laugh. There was something about the young woman that made it easy to tell her. "Mind it? Why, it was my salvation. If I'd thought of it, I would have done it myself."

"You're just confusing the girl, Dhulyn, my heart," Parno said. "Tell her what you mean."

"Ah, well, it was long ago, and the story means nothing to anyone but me," Dhulyn said, drawing down her brows. "It's the tip of a whip, not sword or dagger, that gave me this mark. The metal-coated tip of a whip clumsily applied that flicked 'round me and caught me on the face. That was enough to ruin me in my master's eyes, so to the auction block I went. And from there to the slave trader's ship, and from the slave ship to Dorian the Black Traveler. And from his hands, to this moment. And from this moment . . . to a new subject," she said, seeing Mar's stricken face. "Tell me, little Dove, do you know a child's game called Weeping Lad, or Weeping Maid?"

"I know one called Sweeping Man," Mar said.

"Do you know other variations?" Dhulyn said. "We sang one when I was very young and I've been trying to remember the words."

Late in the night, while Mar slept, Parno and Dhulyn lay wrapped in their bedrolls. They spoke so softly, lips to ear, that had Mar been awake, she would have been ready to swear they made no sound.

"It is a scrying bowl," Dhulyn breathed into Parno's ear.

"To See?" Parno asked.

"More likely to Find," she said. "Did you not see how, though the outside is patterned with people and scenes, the inside of the bowl is a plain pure white? Like the bowl Grenwen Finder used in Navra? Only this one is much more costly."

"Does the little one know?" Thus Parno avoided even the chance that Mar's sleeping ears might hear and register her own name.

"There have been Marked in the family, Finders most likely, and someone knew it, for it to have passed so carefully, mother to daughter."

"The Dove herself?"

"Not likely. She lost her parents early, but she would have noticed the signs when she grew old enough, as I did myself."

Parno drew in a cautious breath. "Do we tell her or no? With things the way they are, it may be dangerous for her to have it. You won't be the only one who can recognize it."

"She'll need it to show her family, if what she says of proof is true."

Dhulyn felt Parno's muscles tighten and then relax once more. "We might do her a great favor if we broke it for her," he said finally.

Dhulyn pressed her forehead against his shoulder.

"But it's so beautiful," she finally said.

THESE ARE HER OWN HANDS. THERE'S THE PUCKER OF SCAR ON THE BACK OF THE RIGHT HAND, WHERE A SMOOTH TARGET ARROW WENT THROUGH DURING TRAINING. SHE IS NOT STANDING OFF TO ONE SIDE, A WATCHER. SHE SEES HER HANDS AS IF SHE WERE SITTING AT A TABLE LOOKING DOWN AT THEM, LAYING OUT A GAME OF VERA, THE TILES SMOOTH AND COLD IN HER FINGERS. THIS IS NOT THE USUAL SOLITARY HAND SHE LIKES, COMPLICATED AND DIFFICULT TO WIN. THIS ARRANGEMENT IS QUITE SIMPLE, A CROSS, WITH A COLUMN DOWN ONE SIDE. "WHAT DO YOU SEE?" A VOICE SAYS AND WHEN SHE LOOKS UP, SHE SEES A MAN WITH A LONG FACE, DARK HAIR, AND ONE EYE. NO, TWO EYES. NO, ONLY ONE. "WHAT DO YOU SEE?" HE SAYS AGAIN, AND SHE LOOKS BACK AT THE TILES.

"I SEE A FIRE," SHE TELLS HIM. "SEAS AND MOUNTAINS ARE BURNING, SHORES AND RIVERS. . . ."

***

A BOY CHILD RUNS ACROSS THE COBBLES OF A COURTYARD IN THE AFTER-
NOON SUN, A PRACTICE SWORD IN HIS HANDS. SHE KNOWS THE SHAPE OF HIS
SMILE, AND HIS EYES. HE'S GOLD BLOND ALL OVER, EVEN HIS EYES ARE AM-
BER, WARM. HE TURNS AND PACES OUT A REASONABLE VERSION OF THE
STRIKING CAT *SHORA*, GIVEN HIS YOUTH AND SIZE. HE LOOKS UP, SEEMINGLY
INTO HER EYES, AND SMILES AGAIN. . . .

❧

Dhulyn blinked awake, lying on her left side, her right arm
around Mar, Parno's right arm around her. The banked fire
was hardly a glow in the darkness. What had she Seen? A
golden child with Parno's familiar smile and eyes. Was this
Parno's child? Is that where traveling to Imrion would
lead? Was this Parno's future?

Dhulyn squeezed her eyes shut, tried to slow her breathing before it woke the others. Where was the courtyard?
And who the child's mother?

The next day's warmth brought on a fog so thick that
Dhulyn decided they should stay where they were until it
cleared, using the time to rest and pamper themselves a
little more. The horses could be left to luxuriate in the absence of riders and packs. The fog was a good sign, she
judged; the weather would be getting warmer from now on.

That morning she and Parno practiced the lengthy Bear
Cub *Shora* while Mar watched wide-eyed from the entrance of their shelter. By midmorning the fog lifted enough
that their campsite seemed to be in the midst of a clearing
in the clouds. The midday meal, eaten outside of the shelter,
where an outcropping—no doubt another piece of wall—
provided dry seats, was accompanied by debate on whether
it was worth continuing their journey, trusting to find another good shelter before nightfall, or to wait until the following day.

"It's only been seven days since we left the inn at the
crossroads," Dhulyn was saying. "We won't lose any time by
waiting until tomorrow."

"I didn't say we should go on," Parno said, sitting up to
better make his point. "I only said that it's been *eight—*"

Dhulyn held up her hand, the gesture sharply cutting through the Lionsmane's lazy iteration of his point of view. He put his hand on the sword resting by his right side, and without the slightest sound drew it from its scabbard.

Mar opened her mouth, but before she could speak, Dhulyn efficiently gagged her with the hand that did not have a sword in it.

"Can't shoot at us if they can't see us or hear us," Parno mouthed in a voice that barely carried to Mar's ears. "Stay between." Both Mercenaries stood now, facing away into the fog, crouched slightly forward, knees flexed. Mar slowly stood and looked between them, clearly not knowing what to do.

"Dhulyn?" Parno bared his teeth though his murmur could not support a snarl. "What say you, my heart?"

Dhulyn glanced over her shoulder at him. "Cloud People," she said. "Victory or death, I'll wager. And the choice won't be ours." She reached behind her, pulled a knife out of the back of her vest, and held it out to Mar; watched the Dove take it gingerly in her hand, and then grip it with more determination. Dhulyn gave the girl an encouraging nod.

"We'll earn our pay. Don't you worry, Dove."

Parno had his own long dagger in his right hand, sword in his left. Dhulyn pulled her short sword from where her harness sat draped over a rock and, straightening, held it ready. Back to back with Mar between them they began to circle, Dhulyn twirling her two blades at random intervals. The silence was thick and so complete that she began to wonder whether her ears still worked, or indeed, whether there was anything out there that could make a sound.

And then movement—a shadow in the surrounding fog, became an arrow knocked aside by Parno's sword, startling Mar into dropping her dagger.

A woman's voice rang out. "Hold. Put up your swords. You wear the Mercenary badge. Tell your history."

Dhulyn stopped circling, though her swords stayed poised. "I am Dhulyn Wolfshead. Called the Scholar. I was Schooled by Dorian the Black Traveler. I have fought with my Brothers at sea in the battle of Sadron, at Arcosa in Imrion, and at Bhexyllia in the far west with the Great King."

Parno called out, "I am Parno Lionsmane. Called the

Chanter. Schooled by Nerysa of Tourin the Warhammer. I, too, have fought at Arcosa, and at Bhexyllia, and I fight with my Brother, Dhulyn Wolfshead." Parno's history would tell their questioner that he was junior to Dhulyn, Arcosa being his first battle as a Brother, and that since he fought with her specifically, they were Partnered. Would the Cloudwoman understand?

The voice called out again. "I have heard of you, Dhulyn Wolfshead, daughter of the Red Horsemen. I am Yaro of Trevel, once called Hawkwing. I, too, have fought with my Brothers. Now I fight with my Clan." Parno glanced at Dhulyn and she gave him the smallest of nods. Both Mercenaries lowered their weapons.

Dhulyn remained alert as a handful of people, most carrying spears or bows, but with a few swordsmen to season them, stepped into the clearing. It was hard to tell exactly how many there were, and many seemed to have no heads, no faces, until Dhulyn realized they were wearing scarves or strips of cloth wrapped around their heads. Thick leather vests, worn with the fur or wool side next to the skin, left either arms bare to the foggy chill, or long-sleeved tunics of undyed homespun. Dhulyn grinned. She had learned the art of camouflage from an expert, but this impressed her.

One of the anonymous forms laid its spear on the ground and stepped forward, unwrapping its head covering as it neared them. From the quality of the voice which had spoken to them out of the fog Dhulyn expected an older woman, and she was right. Yaro was short and thickset, her dark brown hair liberally salted with gray. The gold-and-green colors of the Mercenary's tattooed badge had faded, but were still clear enough to be recognized in the misted light.

These were not Yaro's only tattoos, Dhulyn saw, her eyebrows raising in surprise. On the left side of the Cloudwoman's face was a tattoo of two feathers, the second partially overlapping the first, like the feathers of the Racha bird it symbolized. These were so old and faded that only a sharp eye would see them. Much clearer, and obviously much more recent, was the complete set of seven feathers on the right side of her face.

Dhulyn's lips formed a soundless whistle as, glancing

around for the Racha bird itself, she touched her fingertips to her forehead to echo Yaro of Trevel's Mercenary salute. What could possibly be the meaning of the Cloudwoman's Racha tattoos?

She glanced at Parno, but her Partner's face showed no expression. Rare as it was for a Mercenary Brother to live long enough to retire, Yaro of Trevel, once Yaro Hawkwing, had clearly not simply retired. She had left the Brotherhood and returned to her own Clan. Dhulyn would not have thought such a thing possible, and her teeth clenched as she forced herself to pay attention, and to show no sign of the chill that squeezed her heart.

"Brothers, I greet you," the tattooed woman was saying. "We are Clan Trevel. And the land where you stand, and for many days' travel around us, is also Clan Trevel." Dhulyn nodded. Like Imrion's Noble Houses, the Cloud People used the same words to identify both the relationship of blood and the relationship of land. The group of people surrounding her made gestures of assent, and a few murmured. Yaro glanced quickly to each side and the murmurs died down. Several of the group followed their leader's example and, downing their weapons, began to unwrap their own coverings. They were mostly young people, Dhulyn saw, with only two others nearing Yaro's age.

"We are on the Life Passage of our young people, or I would welcome you to the shelter of our homes. However, for the sake of our Brotherhood, if not the Tarkin's treaty," here her words called out a few grins, "we give you safe passage."

"No tribute?" one young man blurted out. His astonishment was clear in the squeak of his voice.

Yaro turned to the youngster, staring at him long enough that his wide shoulders squirmed under her scrutiny. "Tribute?" she said. "These are still my Brothers. You'll be asking *me* for tribute next, Clarys." Several of the others smiled, their teeth flashing white. The young man shifted his gaze, silenced but not satisfied.

"What about her?" he said, pointing at Mar with his chin. "She's no Brother of yours." This time all the people of Clan Trevel turned to look at Mar.

"She is in our care, Brother." Dhulyn spoke only to Yaro. "We ask that you extend your courtesy over her as well."

"I am content." Yaro nodded.

"Well, I am not. And I see no reason to be. They trespass. You say we must let your Brothers pass—well and good. But this person who hires them can pay us for her passage."

"And if she has nothing of value?" Parno said.

"Let us see this for ourselves," suggested a more reasonable voice.

Dhulyn stood still, eyes locked on the young man who had started the trouble. She knew the type. Not so much younger than Mar herself the way time was counted, ready to be a man among his people, as his presence on this Life Passage demonstrated—but still a child in many important ways. Tall, broad-shouldered, and with the long arms so helpful to a fighter. But a little sullenness around his pretty mouth. A little poutiness to the bottom lip, and a top lip too ready to curl. A boy who thought well of himself and thought others should do the same. Trouble, in other words.

Parno touched Mar on the shoulder and then stood back, sweeping a mocking bow in the direction of her pack. Mar tried to nod at him curtly, but trembling spoiled the girl's performance. Once more Dhulyn watched as the little Dove untied her pack. Again the scanty belongings were exposed, looking even more meager and ordinary without the magical glow of firelight to give them life. Even the bowl, when her hands, slowed by reluctance, were able to uncover it, showed its colors dully in the foggy light.

"Why should we not take that bowl," Clarys said immediately.

He ignored Mar's cry of protest, but Dhulyn did not.

"It is the only thing of her family that she has," Dhulyn said. "Would you take from her the symbol of her Clan?" She tried to sound as reasonable as she could. As much as it soured her mouth to let people under her protection be robbed, she disliked unnecessary killing—a sentiment many of her Brothers found ironic. "This comes from the mother of her mother's mother, and is not hers to give away. It can bring no good to any who takes it from her by force." The two older people in the group exchanged nods and murmurs of agreement.

But the boy Clarys also had his fellow, a stocky boy with a dark widow's peak, to murmur in his ear.

"No good?" said Clarys mockingly, as Widow's Peak nodded. "Why it would feed a family for a season, that bowl of no value." More murmurs of agreement, but this time only from a handful of youngsters Dhulyn marked as the rest of Clarys' admirers. If it came to a fight, would these others stand back? Dhulyn marked in her mind the position of the archer, and the three who still had spears in their hands.

And whose side would Yaro of Trevel be on?

Dhulyn turned to Mar. The girl stared fixedly at her prized possession. "Mar?" Dhulyn said, and waited until the girl looked at her. "How say you? Will you trade the bowl for your passage?"

"Is there some other way? Some of my other things? If I come to my House without it," the girl said, tears filling both eyes and voice, "they may deny my claim."

Dhulyn looked at Clarys, but the boy set his mouth firmly and folded his arms. "Idiots," she said, under her breath. Time to put an end to this. She looked at Parno. The Lionsmane tilted his head to the right, as she'd know he would. The Wolfshead nodded.

"You are refused," she said, looking directly at Clarys. "Thus far, this has cost you nothing but a wasted hour. I advise you to renounce your claim before it becomes more costly."

"If she will not pay, then she is herself forfeit. We will take *her*." Both Parno and Dhulyn moved to stand between Mar and the Clouds. Clarys stopped with his hands already reaching out for the girl.

A short, sharp silence as all waited. Dhulyn nodded again. "You'll take nothing but my fist in your teeth," she said evenly. "She is in our charge. *Renounce your claim.*"

Widow's Peak nudged him and the young man cocked his head, his eyebrows raised. "Will you fight?" he challenged.

"I will."

Several of the younger element in the group exchanged looks of triumph. The older ones looked on grim-faced, shaking their heads.

"Wait," Yaro said, the authority of a Racha woman giving weight to her words. "Clarys, think what you do. This is a Mercenary Brother, not one of your cub pack. She has skills beyond what you can imagine."

"No one can best me with sword or spear. You have said this yourself," he said. "This is my Life Passage, my Hunt. This is the proof I choose."

With her eyes shut, Yaro blew out a disgusted sigh. Not even a Racha woman could step between a young Cloud and his chosen Hunt.

Dhulyn shrugged. "First blood, then?" she said.

"No—" Clarys was silenced by Yaro's upright hand.

"First blood is sufficient for a Passage Duel," the older woman said.

"She insults me by suggesting it."

"Don't be stupid, boy," Parno cut in. "In the Brotherhood we don't maim. For us, it's cut or kill."

Clarys' lips curled back from his teeth. "Then kill it will be, *flatlander*."

Dhulyn was careful to address only Yaro—and to keep her voice businesslike. "He renounced his claim on the bowl when he offered to take Mar instead. It's now his life for hers, are we agreed?"

Yaro cast a look around the group assembled in a shallow arc behind her. There were nods, a couple of shrugs, but none shook their heads. One or two even looked speculatively between Clarys and Dhulyn. Either the young man wasn't as well liked as he thought, or these people didn't know much about Mercenaries, Yaro's presence notwithstanding.

"Agreed," Yaro said finally. "You kill Clarys, you and the girl go free."

"And if I kill the Brother, the girl is mine." Clarys said.

Yaro didn't bother to answer, cuffing a couple of the youngsters who had crowded close into clearing away packs and people to leave a space for the duel.

Dhulyn was already stripping off her outer clothing. Parno stepped in closer. "Give him every chance."

"I've given him two chances already. Should I let him kill me?"

"Would you prefer that I fight him?"

"I'm Senior." Dhulyn looked at him sidewise as she kicked off her boots. On this uneven ground, bare feet were best. "And I thank you, my Brother, for your confidence in me."

Parno rolled his eyes upward, calling upon the Caids to witness his frustration. "That is not what I meant, and you know it, my most stubborn heart. You'll mind killing him, and I won't. Rudeness and stupidity should be properly rewarded."

Dhulyn shook her head and turned from Parno, indicating Clarys with the tip of her sword. "Ready," she said.

Clarys stood already stripped and grinning, his friend Widow's Peak still whispering in his ear. Dhulyn nodded and lifted her sword. The boy fell into his stance, and her heart sank. His weight was too evenly balanced for this rough terrain, she saw, and his right elbow stuck out too far from his body. If no one in his clan could best him, it was because the boy had been making do with strength and length of reach, not skill.

Now that she saw him stripped for fighting, Dhulyn could more easily gauge the width of his shoulders and the size of his wrists. He carried the longest possible sword, and that alone could have told her both of his strength and of his vanity. She saw his eyes flick toward her own blade, and the way his full lips spread in a smile. She, too, carried a very long sword, though not so long as his, and he probably thought it too long for her. And so it would have been, had not years of practice made her wrists very nearly as steellike as the blade itself. The length and the weight would not tire her. Many had already died from making that mistake.

As she lifted the point of her own blade in salute, Dhulyn fell automatically into the familiar calm of the Crab *Shora* for the right-handed sword and uneven ground. Her heartbeat slowed, her breathing changed to match it.

Clarys began to circle her, and Dhulyn turned to follow him, her sword swaying lazily, almost as an afterthought. She looked not at his blade, or his eyes, but the center of his chest. A movement of his shoulders signaled Clarys' lunge at her unprotected side; Dhulyn knocked his blade up with a negligent tap and stepped half a pace to the left. She sighed and parried two more cuts with casual flicks of her sword. As she thought, the boy was going for showy high strikes only, counting on his strength and reach, and forgetting the lower half of the body completely. As they continued to circle, Dhulyn kept track of Parno, Yaro, Mar, and especially Widow's Peak in her peripheral vision. She saw several of the Cloud People shaking their heads and felt like shaking her own. What were they about, letting her kill this boy?

"Cry mercy, boy," Parno coolly advised, in an echo of Dhulyn's thought. "The Wolfshead will kill you like her namesake kills a lamb."

"She could not kill a—" Thinking to surprise her, Clarys broke off his circling and attacked without finishing his sentence, coming at her from the side. But Dhulyn was not where he expected her to be. She had stepped inside the reach of his sword and, mindful of Parno's request, did not gut the boy immediately, but cut him neatly on the left cheek with the tip of her blade. Too bad. Using the minor distraction of the conversation might have worked too, Dhulyn thought as she cut him again on the right cheek—on someone who was not a Mercenary.

Dhulyn parried two more blows—both to her head—before Clarys began to breath more heavily. He was used to the fight being over by now. A few murmurs from among his followers indicated that they thought so, too. Yaro had already turned away and was looking up into the clearing fog. Her Racha bird was coming.

"I have cut you twice," Dhulyn said, fixing the boy's eyes with her own. "I am satisfied. I ask you for the last time to renounce your claim." *Pray Sun and Moon,* she thought, *he'll notice he's tiring and hasn't killed me yet. Many men will learn caution if you give them a chance.*

But not this one. She grimaced as Clarys swung at her again, stopping the blow easily with her upraised sword. Time to end this. "I salute your courage, Clarys of Trevel, if not your wisdom." A twist of the wrist and Dhulyn Wolfshead sent the tip of her spinning sword through the front of Clarys' throat. He cried out then, the sound flying outward with a spray of blood, though his mouth did not move.

Dhulyn heard the meaty sound of his body as it fell to the ground. Watched as his heart pumped its blood onto the stones.

The entire clearing was as silent as the fog.

"Are you content?" Dhulyn said, her breathing even, her sword still raised. She spun around as Parno's dagger flew past her, and pinned the sword hand of Widow's Peak to his left side.

The boy went white, and looked down at his hand, mouth trembling, as Parno approached him and took hold of the dagger's hilt.

"We cut, or we kill," Parno said, slowly drawing the blade free. There was, as Dhulyn expected, very little blood. "You've been cut. Shall I go on?"

Widow's Peak shook his head, squinting at the thin wound where the dagger's blade had sliced between the bones of his palm. He touched his side with the fingers of his left hand and drew them back lightly stained with blood. The point of the dagger had barely nicked him. The boy looked from his hand to Parno, to the body of his friend. To Dhulyn.

"We fight every day," he said. "Clarys trained his whole life."

"On the day your lives began," Dhulyn said. "I had already killed."

Yaro gestured, and two of her men stepped forward to pull the body away from Dhulyn's feet. "Clarys of Trevel," the Racha woman called out in a voice of proclamation, "has died during the trial of his Life Passage. His soul will rest content until the Sleeping God awakens and has need of him."

"Not if the New Believers have any say in the matter," Parno said, almost under his breath.

Yaro made a face and spit, carefully avoiding the blood on the grass. She turned to Dhulyn, a look of sheepish sympathy on her face. "He beat me once in practice," the older woman said. She shrugged at Dhulyn's raised eyebrows. "He wasn't so much the rooster as he became." She turned to watch Clarys' body as it was carried off into the mist. The Cloud People would bear it away and bury it that night. "Still, he never seemed to notice that he never beat me again. Some won't learn that there's a difference between practice and killing."

Dhulyn turned to look at her young noblewoman and smiled, her lip curling back, knowing her face was marked by Clarys' fountaining blood. Mar turned away and was abruptly sick in the grass.

Five

"MANY OF THE OLD BELIEVERS have come to us, those from the cities, especially." Yaro led the way down a steep and rocky path to a stream running along the bottom of a narrow vale. They were only over the ridge from the Caid ruins, but with the snow falling the previous afternoon, the stream had been easy to miss. Dhulyn followed closely, carrying the empty water bags and taking care not to crowd Koba, the Racha bird balancing on the Cloudwoman's shoulder.

Koba cocked his head, and shook it slightly from side to side. "True," Yaro said, in answer to some remark only she could hear. "Those who were content to stay in their shrines and hold their tongues were left there; especially the unimportant shrines, which held no relic of the god. But since the priest Beslyn-Tor has become head of the Jaldean sect—" Yaro stopped and turned to face Dhulyn. "You know there are others besides us Clouds who follow exclusively the Sleeping God?"

Dhulyn nodded. More than half the soldiers she'd fought with were followers of the warrior god, praying before each battle that if they should fall, they might sleep with him until they were needed again.

"Things have changed with the Jaldeans since Beslyn-Tor became their head, up there in Gotterang. They're saying he's been touched by the god, knows things he cannot know, and sees more than a man can see. And there are others who have been visited in the same way." Yaro reached the water, and her Racha bird dropped off her shoulder to perch on a nearby rock. Yaro crouched at the edge of a small pool, dipping up the cold water into her hand and tasting it, smacking her lips with pleasure. "And there are many new priests now."

Dhulyn set the water bags down next to Yaro, and passed the Cloudwoman the first one. "And what do they do, these new priests?"

"Preach against the Marked, as far as any of us can make out," Yaro said as she maneuvered the opening of the first water bag under the surface of the pond. "This new heresy you say you've heard from the Finder in Navra—he reached us, by the way, we heard by Racha from Langeron—the Sleeping God must be kept asleep, our safety lies in his unbroken dreaming, and the Marked are the incarnation of evil in the world, trying to awaken the god and destroy us all. That nonsense."

"But the armies would rebel—"

"And are being told they're *already* the soldiers of the god, *already* fighting to keep the world safe."

Dhulyn frowned, rubbing her temples with her fingertips. "We are more sensible in the southern ice," she said. "The Sun and the Moon are always with you, the Weather gods, and the gods of the Hunt and the Herd."

"We're not so changeable here in the Clouds either." Yaro exchanged her full bag for the next empty one. "We'll keep to the old ways."

Dhulyn waited until the third bag was filled, and then the fourth, before sitting down next to the Racha bird; Koba blinked at her companionably. Yaro pushed the stopper into the final water bag, dried her hands by running them through her hair, settled herself on a patch of last year's grasses, and leaned back on her elbows, legs stretched out before her.

Dhulyn leaned forward. "You spoke of the old ways, Brother," she said. "I must ask you . . ." She tapped her own face, indicating where the tattoos marked Yaro's. The Cloudwoman lowered her eyes, nodding. After a moment she looked up again, but not at Dhulyn, at her Racha bird. Koba turned his head, returning her look first with one eye, then the other, before nodding in turn.

Yaro sat up, crossing her legs and resting her hands on her knees.

"I lost my first Racha," she said. Her eyes unfocused, as if she no longer saw the world around her—the stream, the pool, and Dhulyn Wolfshead—but the past. Koba left his perch next to Dhulyn and half flew, half hopped until he was beside Yaro, crooning deep in his throat, a keening sound. "I was very young, and I found him, you see, fallen from the nest."

Dhulyn made a querying note in her own throat and Yaro glanced at her. "It does happen," she said. "Rarely, but it happens. Perhaps too many chicks hatch, perhaps there is a shortage of food that season, and one chick or more is pushed or falls from the nest."

"But the trial," Dhulyn said. "I thought for the bond to form, there had to be a trial?" That was why bonding with a Racha was usually part of the Life Passage.

"I saved him from a wolf," Yaro said. She breathed deeply in through her nose and, blinking, turned to the living bird beside her and smiled. Koba rubbed his hooked beak against her right cheek.

"That was considered enough of a trial, you see, and we were bonded." Yaro cleared her throat. "We were two months together," she tapped the faded tattoo of feathers on her left cheek, "when I fell ill of a brain fever. I was near death for days."

Yaro looked up, and Dhulyn saw the young girl, and the young girl's sorrow and loss in Yaro's face. Her living bird pressed his head against her, and both closed their eyes for a moment.

"My Racha, my—" Yaro pressed her lips tight, as if she could not say the bird's name. But, gaining strength from contact with her living bird, she opened her eyes and continued. "My *first* Racha died during my fever. I fell into what all who saw me thought would be the final sleep, but Sortera the Healer came." Dhulyn looked up and Yaro nodded. "Two weeks before she was expected, she came and Healed me. But when I finally woke, I was alone, my bond broken, and that she could *not* Heal."

Dhulyn cleared her throat but remained silent when Yaro again touched the faded tattoo on her left cheek.

"I believe it was the Healing that kept me from following my soul into death," she said. "But I believe I should have died before ever Sortera came. My Racha gave me *his* life, and that is how I lived long enough to be Healed.

"I could not throw away his gift, but neither could I remain in the Clouds and see around me every day the space where my soul was not. So I went to serve the Sleeping God another way." This time Yaro touched the green-and-gold tattoo above her ears. "I have no talent for scholarship, and I feared the meditative life, so I became a Mercenary Brother."

Dhulyn nodded her understanding. Though she did not know where the belief originated, she knew the Clouds considered the Scholars, the Jaldeans, and the Mercenary Brotherhood to be three orders of the ancient priesthood of the Sleeping God, and therefore three disciplines open to any Cloud who chose to leave the mountains.

"In the Brotherhood I found another kind of bond; you will understand me, you are Partnered. But while I was Healed, still I was not whole."

Dhulyn touched her own tattoo, her Mercenary badge, traced her finger along the black line that threaded through the colors. The line that showed she was Partnered. *Did* she understand? She had always believed in the bond of Partnership. But now, after Parno's insistence that they return to Imrion, and especially after her Vision of his child—was it possible that he might leave her, leave the Brotherhood as Yaro of Trevel had done, and return to his House? Marry? Father children? Did this mean their souls were *not* one? She pushed the thoughts away. *Today's worry today,* so said the Common Rule.

"One day," Yaro was saying, "I found myself thinking again of my home, the color of the sky above the mountains, the smell of the pines. Alkoryn Pantherclaw, who is Senior Brother to us all here on the Peninsula, advised me to make a visit home." Yaro looked at Dhulyn from under her lashes. "My coming was seen as the direct intervention of the god. My cousin Evela, who had been a toddling child when I left my clan, had become a young woman, a Racha woman. Two days before I arrived she had fallen ill. Of a brain fever." Yaro leaned forward, elbows on knees. "My bond had been broken, and I lived. It was hoped I could help my cousin do the same. But it did not fall out that way."

"Was the Healer . . . ?"

"Arrived too late. This time it was my cousin who died, having given her soul to her Racha, who lived."

Koba keened again, this time a throat-rasping cough that had almost the sound of a sob in it. Yaro rubbed Koba's face with her hands, smoothing the feathers, somehow not cutting herself on the razor-sharp beak.

Dhulyn looked from woman to Racha and back again. "But that's not possible . . ." She let her voice die away.

"So it was thought." Yaro looked Dhulyn directly in the eyes. "The Healer came too late to save my cousin, but when she came, she had a Mender with her. They, Healer and Mender, saw that there were two of us, each with our broken bond—and so together they Mended us, and we were Healed."

It *had* to be true. The bond was there, obvious. Real.

"You were Mended *and* Healed?"

Koba hopped up to Yaro's shoulder as the Cloudwoman raised herself to her feet. "Together they did what neither could do alone. Koba and I were broken, sick at heart. Now we are whole."

As she followed Yaro of Trevel and Koba the Racha back to camp, Dhulyn was conscious that she should feel honored by the woman's confidence—and awed at the achievement of the Marked, Mender and Healer. But she went with her eyes cast down, paying special attention to her footing, struggling to keep her face from showing the churning of her thoughts. She found that, after all, she could not rid her mind of the other part of Yaro's story. That part in which a Mercenary Brother left the Brotherhood, to return to clan and family.

The next day found them with a Cloud escort, following the caravan road west to avoid the Dead Spot, where legend had it that some magic of the Caids had gone badly wrong.

When the trail they followed came close enough, Mar looked out over the silent and empty expanse of twisted rock and sand.

"It looks like a glassmaker's pot," she said. As she let the reins fall slack, the packhorse came to a stop. "But only the dirty bits they don't use."

"There are three such places in the Letanian Peninsula," Dhulyn Wolfshead said. "But whether that means that the Caids had their principal places here," the Mercenary woman shrugged, urging Bloodbone along with her knees. "The Scholars are still arguing over it."

"But what happened here?" The packhorse followed Bloodbone, and Mar looked back at the Dead Spot over her shoulder. "What went wrong?"

"Only the Caids know," the Lionsmane said from where he rode behind her.

"The knowledge was lost," Wolfshead added, "like so much of what the Caids knew."

"And perhaps for the best, if their knowledge could do this." Lionsmane gestured with a wide sweep of his arm. Wolfshead shook her head, but Mar couldn't tell if she disagreed.

Their Cloud escort left them when the road turned northeast once more, though Yaro's Racha bird Koba soared high above them a while longer, looking out and communicating with his bond mate in their private fashion. The whole morning Mar had kept to herself, unable to fully trust the Clouds, and finding herself looking even at her bodyguards from the corners of her eyes.

"That would be the first time you saw someone killed," Lionsmane said.

Mar's neck felt stiff as she nodded in reply. "I've seen dead people, but never . . ." Her voice trailed off as her gaze moved ahead to where the Wolfshead rode several horse lengths ahead of them. *All because of me,* she thought. Because of some letters from Tenebro House, a young man, younger than she was herself, a boy really, was dead.

When the letters had come, her world had suddenly opened to so broad and wide a thing that she could barely sleep for excitement. She hadn't been unhappy with the Weavers, exactly, but she'd been just old enough when the sickness had taken her family to remember what it was like to have a Holding, to know that you were a part, however small, of a Noble House, part of a greater whole. The letters brought the chance of going to the capital and taking up her rightful place as a cousin of that House, and even the possibility of the restoration of her Holding, if she could show how well she understood her allegiance. She had letters she hadn't shown Dhulyn Wolfshead, letters which had given her a job to do, for which she could be rewarded. Her task had been to hire two particular Mercenaries to guide and protect her instead of waiting for the spring salt caravans. A woman of the Red Horsemen and her Partner, the letters had said. Mar'd had all her friends on the lookout for them, and as soon as Rilla Fisher had seen them come off the *Catseye,* Mar had practically dragged Guillor Weaver to the Hoofbeat Inn to hire them. Dhulyn Wolfshead and Parno Lionsmane. She'd liked them, and even being on the trail with them had seemed like an adventure, once she'd got over the discomfort and the strangeness.

But the adventure had ended with the sight of Clarys' blood spilling on the ground.

Mar risked a glance at the Wolfshead's straight back. Lionsmane gave a great sigh, and she froze.

"Seeing someone killed does make a difference, doesn't it?" he said, as if he were commenting on the sunshine.

Mar shivered, making the packhorse toss his head. "I must seem such a child," she said, hardening her voice to make it stop shaking. "It's not as though I didn't know what soldiers and Mercenaries do." She looked up at the golden-brown man beside her. "You'll have seen many like Clarys?"

"I have," he said quietly. "The first when I was much younger than you."

"And killed them, too," the girl said, her eyes returning to the back of the tall woman with blood-red hair.

"Yes," he said more quietly still. "But that was later." Mar glanced at him again, lowering her eyes quickly when he held her gaze.

"That's not all that's frightened you, is it?"

"I didn't know if you were paid enough." Mar cleared her throat. "I thought you might let them take me."

"Fine bodyguards we would be," Lionsmane said softly, "to let that happen. You needn't worry about that." He indicated his Partner with a tilt of his head. "Dhulyn might kill you herself, but she wouldn't allow you to be taken and sold."

"She might kill *me*?" Mar rounded on him, twisting in the saddle. *Was he joking?*

He shrugged. "No need to look like that. *Anyone* might kill you. Dhulyn's been in slavers' hands herself. Death is easier, she says. Not necessarily preferable, just easier. She was lucky enough to be taken from a slave ship by pirates when she was eleven, maybe twelve."

"Lucky? Taken by pirates is lucky?"

"Of course lucky. She was first captured at eight, and no one takes an eight-year-old child to be a household slave."

"What, then?"

Lionsmane looked sideways out of narrowed eyes. "A nice respectable family, the Weavers, eh? Did a good business but didn't travel much?" He shrugged. "Ah well, it's easier for the rich to indulge such vices. In certain circles, small children are sold as bedslaves."

Mar felt her face grow stiff. Lionsmane nodded at her.

"The pirate who took Dhulyn was the Schooler Dorian the Black. He recognized her as one of the Red Horsemen from the south and put a sword in her hand." Lionsmane looked ahead once more to where Dhulyn Wolfshead rode, and Mar, released from the focus of his eyes, relaxed. "We are members of the Mercenary Brotherhood. Soldiers and killers by trade. But certain kinds of people we—she and I—will kill for nothing."

Mar looked down, concentrating on her clenched hands. "Now what?" he said.

"I'm happy to be free . . . and safe. But that boy died because of me. Wolfshead killed him so that he would not take my bowl." She stopped, unable to complete the thought aloud.

But Parno Lionsmane was nodding. "There's guilt in being the one who walks away, don't I know it. You're wondering whether you should have given him the bowl, and taken your chances with your House. You're wondering whether your comfort is worth a man's life," he said finally. And you're wondering," he continued when Mar still did not speak, "what kind of person kills for a piece of pottery, and what kind of person asks someone to do that for her?"

He shook his head, his mouth twisting to one side as if he would spit.

"Listen, little Dove, never think for a moment that Dhulyn did not save your life. He was ready to take *you,* that hothead boy—to sell or to slave for him, whichever took his fancy. We were past bargaining for the bowl by the time the swords were out."

"I tell myself that," Mar said. "But at the time I thought . . . I didn't think . . ."

"You didn't think she would actually have to kill him," Lionsmane said. "You thought 'this is real life, it'll all end before the bloodshed.'" He sighed. "Mar-eMar Tenebro," he said, "you did not kill Clarys of Trevel. His own people lifted no hand to stop him. He was given every chance to avoid his end, and he took none. The Cloud People are hard fighters, none better, but it would take three, maybe four of them to kill Dhulyn Wolfshead, and at that they'd have to trick her. It was Clarys' own arrogance killed him, more than anything you did, or said. More, even, than anything Dhulyn did or said. No one else blames you," he added when she did not reply. "And one day you'll stop blaming yourself."

Mar looked down at her clenched hands. Her head told her he was right—but her head had been telling her that for hours, and her heart felt no better for it. She wasn't sure she'd done the right thing about the bowl—and she wasn't sure she'd done the right thing about the letters. How much *was* she willing to trade to regain her noble life?

From where she rode ahead of Parno and Mar, Dhulyn had no trouble making out their words. She wrinkled her nose. That was the trouble with towns people. The little Dove had known that Dhulyn was a killer, back in the taproom in Navra. But she'd known it without *thinking* about it. During their journey, Mar had forgotten this thing she never thought about, and Dhulyn had become a kind of knowledgeable older sister, a guide and teacher of the secrets of the trail. More than once, Mar had even called her "Scholar." That had ended with Clarys' life. Now, Dhulyn knew, she would always be "Wolfshead."

Nothing to be done, she thought, pulling her shoulders

straight. *Such is the way of things.* Dhulyn did not have Parno's natural warmth, his skill with people. Even when they saw him kill someone, he never entirely stopped being "Chanter." Parno's childhood had been spent in a Household—why, he and the Dove were probably related in some distant and complicated way, Dhulyn realized, her heart skipping a beat. Small wonder they were comfortable together. Bloodbone tossed her head and snorted. "Easy," Dhulyn said, knowing it was her own uneasiness the mare was feeling. Mar was not the only one on her way back to her own family, her own people. Only Dhulyn had no family to return to, and perhaps no people. And if she had? she thought, frowning. If she had?

They entered Gotterang six days later. Dirty, tired, and bored with each other. The gates stood open, and while the guards were stopping everyone—Dhulyn saw some travelers being turned away—she saw no watching presence dressed in red and brown. She squinted. There was something else she couldn't see.

"Parno," she said, drawing in Bloodbone until she was riding knee-to-knee with her Partner. "What are the odds that in a capital city like Gotterang there should be no Mercenaries among the guards at the gates?"

"High, but not impossible," her Partner replied. His eyes took on the faraway look that meant he was calculating. Dhulyn had first seen that look at Arcosa, where Parno had figured the enemy numbers by counting their cook fires. "I'd put us at about one in forty, in terms of Imrion's soldiers. So, yes, there should be a few Brothers among the City Guard."

"That's what I thought," Dhulyn said. "Yet I see no Brothers ahead of us."

"They could be on another watch, or at another gate."

"They could." But somehow Dhulyn had a feeling they weren't.

When they got close enough, Dhulyn examined the arched gates themselves with professional interest. They were two thirds the height of the walls, three man heights at least, and the rounded opening was wide enough for four horsemen to ride through abreast. She would give half a moon's pay at campaign rates to get a look at the machinery that would shut the gates quickly across so large an opening. Had there been any Brothers among the guards, she might have asked for a viewing, but likely, as this was Gotterang, the Seat of the Tarkin, she would have been refused.

"Your business here, Mercenaries?" The guardswoman spoke with barely a glance at them.

"We escort this young lady to Tenebro House," Parno said.

"Tenebro House, eh? I don't suppose you'll want to tell me what that's all about?" the woman said, stepping forward.

"You suppose correctly, my friend," Parno smiled.

"Coming from?"

"Navra."

"Navra? Is the Pass open?"

"For military information, you'll have to consult our House."

"No need to get huffy, man. I was only asking out of curiosity."

"It's open enough for three people on horseback," Parno said with a shrug. "If that's of any use to you."

"See any Cloud People?"

"Plenty of clouds, no people."

"Some people have all the luck," the guardswoman shook her head. A tall man in a crested helmet approached, and the woman questioning them drew herself stiffly to attention. "Two Mercenary Brothers, and their charge, to House Tenebro, Captain."

"Very well," the officer said. "Carry on." He turned to speak to Parno as the guardswoman began to deal with the people behind them. "Dismount, please." He waited, but none of them moved. Even Dhulyn would have been just as glad to be on her feet; the last two nights her bed had seemed to sway, and she'd been riding in her dreams. But Mercenaries didn't get down off their horses for no reason.

"Except for those on City Guard business, and the Noble Houses, riding is not permitted in the city." The Guard

Captain had the air of someone who was repeating himself for the thousandth time. "You'll go directly to your House," the man stated flatly, biting off his words. "They'll tell you what parts of the city you are free of, and what parts you'll need business to enter."

"My friend, we're of the Brotherhood," Parno said. "Since when are we to be treated like thieves and rogues?"

"I'm not blind, man. And I'm not your friend. If you wish to enter the city, these are the conditions. If not, move away from the gate."

"The young lady stays mounted, then," Dhulyn said as she climbed down from Bloodbone more slowly than necessary. "She is of the Tenebro," she said to the man's lifted eyebrow. "Nobles, you said, may ride."

The officer nodded brusquely and stepped back. "Your pardon, Lady. Would you like a guard escort? These two must go directly to their House to report themselves. It would save you time."

"No, thank you." Mar spoke quietly, but with some composure. "I am in no hurry." That almost made Dhulyn smile again. From the look on the little Dove's face, any delay would be welcomed.

"Very well, Lady." The officer turned back to Parno and rattled off the directions to Mercenary House as the Lionsmane listened, gravely nodding as though every Mercenary did not know where every one of their Houses could be found. He gave Mar another sharp nod, almost deep enough to be a bow, and turned his attention back to his guards.

Parno followed Dhulyn's example and dismounted, exaggerating his stiffness as much as possible.

"It used to be they waited for you to make trouble before they decided you were a troublemaker," he said casually as they strolled through the gate, but loudly enough for the retreating officer to hear. Dhulyn laughed. It would have been out of character not to grumble, however false it may have sounded to their own ears. Dhulyn shifted her shoulders, feeling the knife resting in its harness under her vest. She had the oddest sensation that she was being watched. She turned around, but no one at the gate was following their progress, nor did they seem the focus of anyone's attention. She stroked Bloodbone's nose. The horses seemed quite content.

Still. "Parno," she said, keeping her voice level and quiet. "Does anything seem odd to you?"

"Besides these blooded rules, you mean?"

"I mean something like what seemed odd to you that afternoon in Navra." At this Parno gave her a sharp, comprehending look, and then frowned, concentrating within, rather than without.

"Nothing," he said finally. "You? Any green-eyed priests?"

She shrugged. "No green eyes at all. Not now at any rate."

"Careful it is, then," he said.

❧

Wolfshead and Lionsmane had been in the city before, but nothing they had told her prepared Mar for the sounds, colors, faces, and—above all—smells that assaulted her senses as soon as they exited the cold stone tunnel that passed through the thick walls into the cleared space on the inner side of the city gates. At first she was glad to be left on her old friend the packhorse, relieved to be out of the crowd that jostled even the walking Mercenaries and their led horses. Relieved until she noticed how many glances were directed at her. Most of the looks showed simple curiosity, but some she had seen before on the faces of other town girls when they saw how well dressed the Weaver's children were.

"Can't I walk, too," she finally whispered to the Wolfshead, who was nearest.

"Best not," the Mercenary answered in the whisper Mar had heard her use so often on the trail. "Dismounting would draw even more notice. Rest easy, we're not so far from our House."

Mar was more relieved than she could say when they finally rode up a crooked street, past a large archway through which she could see a vast square filled with stalls and kiosks, and finally, through a much smaller arched entrance into the courtyard of Mercenary House. A young woman whose dark brown hair was pulled back off her face with a leather thong, but not yet removed for her Mercenary badge, ran out to take charge of the horses. Lionsmane himself reached up to help Mar down.

"Make yourself comfortable here," he said. "This youngster will see you get something to eat and drink."

"There's fresh cider," the girl offered with a smile, "nice and hot, and almond cakes baked this morning."

"There you are, little Dove," Wolfshead said, rubbing Bloodbone's nose before handing the bridle to the waiting girl. "Tell the House that Dhulyn Wolfshead and Parno Lionsmane are here."

"Can't I come with you?" Mar clung for a moment to Lionsmane's sleeve.

"Sorry, little Dove. None but Brothers may enter further."

Another smile, a touch on her shoulder, and Mar found herself alone. She took a deep breath and looked around her, oddly uneasy with the by-now-unfamiliar sensation of being alone.

The courtyard was as quiet and solitary as she'd always imagined Scholar Houses would be. No clattering groups of armed Brothers, no one practicing *Shora,* no horses, dogs, or chickens. Not even any raised voices from within, as there would have been at the Weavers' home. Scattered through the courtyard were grapevines growing out of old ceramic urns, chipped and discolored with time. Spring was far advanced in Gotterang, and Mar could see the new growth of leaves along the tough old wood stems. Someone had strung cords across the courtyard high enough that they would be well above the head of even someone on horseback. When the heat of full summer struck here, the courtyard would be roofed in with cool greenery.

It was hard to imagine that this small garden oasis existed in the middle of Gotterang's stone. It was harder still to imagine that any harm could come to those who lived here and used this garden.

"Are you the one come with the Brothers?"

Startled, Mar almost slipped on the cobblestones under her feet as she spun around to face the voice.

"Watch yourself, Lady, best you sit down. Days on horseback don't make for steady footing, not on these stones." A small boy, his shock of red hair escaping from a leather thong identical to that of the young woman who'd taken the horses away, stood near her with a tray containing a large cup full of what smelled like the best spiced cider Mar had ever smelled, and a small blue plate of almond cakes covered with a square of linen.

The boy smiled at her and, blushing, set down the tray on the end of the bench next to the studded door that had swallowed her friends.

Mar sat down and nudged the plate toward the boy. "I'm Mar," she said.

The boy took her gesture for the invitation it was and sat also, helping himself to one of the cakes. "Nikko," he said. "I've been here a month, and they're sending me to be Schooled as soon as Dorian the Black puts into port, or there's a Brother heading toward Nerysa Warhammer in the southern mountains, that is. They wouldn't send me alone. Are you coming to be Schooled?"

"No," Mar answered gravely, taking a sip of cider to clear her throat of almond cake. "I'm being taken to my House here in the city."

"So it *was* you that came in with Parno Lionsmane and Dhulyn Wolfshead?"

"You know them?"

"*Everybody* knows *them*! Dhulyn," Nikko blushed again as he called his future Brother by her name. "Dhulyn's a Red Horseman, they say the last of her Clan, the others are all dead, but nothing can kill her, she killed a whole boat-load of slavers when she was just a kid like me, and Parno, he freed the kidnapped heir of Bhexyllia and got decorated by the Galan himself and rewarded with a golden sword, which, of course, he gave to our House, because a real Brother doesn't use such things."

Nikko stopped to take a breath and another bite from his almond cake, and Mar fought to keep herself from smiling.

"So you want to be just like them when you grow up?"

"Oh, I'm not waiting until then. Alkoryn, our Senior Brother here, he says you can be a good Mercenary before ever you have a weapon in your hands. Alkoryn says a good Mercenary—" Nikko broke off and sprang to his feet, his previous blush seeming like pallor next to the dark color that now suffused his cheeks.

"We're not supposed to talk to strangers," he said, and ran off before Mar could reassure him that she wasn't, exactly, a stranger.

Mar leaned back, smiling, against the warm stone of the courtyard's inner wall. This was a sunny corner, and she could feel the tension seeping slowly out of her body. It was clear that Nikko had a case of hero worship, but it was also clear that his Brothers Parno and Dhulyn were forces to be reckoned with. Whatever House Tenebro wanted with these two particular Mercenaries, Mar felt sure that two such legends among their kind would prosper. Even if only half of what Nikko believed was true. Even if she didn't tell them about the letters. Mar closed her eyes. Her head fell back against the warm stone and she slept.

The office of the Senior Brother of Mercenaries in Gotterang was a small but comfortable room tucked into a corner of the House's stone outer wall. When the old building had been a noble family's palace, back before larger houses were built on the more fashionable eastern side of town, this room had been the anteroom to a sleeping chamber. As indeed it still was, Dhulyn reflected, as Alkoryn actually slept in the inner chamber. The office's interior walls, and its floor, were hard oak, stained dark with time. Its two windows, just wide enough, she noted with a frown, to let a slim man pass through, had been paned with real glass lights, shut now against the cool of the spring morning. The window wells were as deep as the thickness of the wall itself, and obviously built for archers. A large worktable with a single armed chair drawn up to it took up most of the floor space. Matching side chairs with thin cushions on their seats were pushed back against the wall between the arrow-slit windows. An enormous parchment showing the map of the Letanian Peninsula with Imrion in pink was fastened to the table with metal clamps. Stains on the map showed where glasses and plates had been put down on it. Racks, shelves, and pigeonholes around the walls held books, smaller maps, and dozens of scrolls.

Dhulyn eyed the man in the room with the kind of interest she would normally have given only to his books. She had never met Alkoryn Pantherclaw, but she had heard him described by Dorian the Black. Alkoryn had seen his birth moon some fifty times, she estimated, and had been a Mercenary longer than she herself had been alive. It had never been Alkoryn's ambition to Command a House, but that was before he had taken the blow to the throat that had robbed him of his voice. A man whose orders cannot be heard loses his value as a field officer. Thwarted in his first ambition, Alkoryn had turned his attention to developing quieter skills. Though he was still considered a formidable warrior and tactician, even among a Brotherhood of warriors, Alkoryn Pantherclaw was now more often called the Charter, and, among other things, he was the chief mapmaker for the Brotherhood.

Alkoryn waited to speak until Dhulyn and Parno had drawn up chairs, and they had all been served with sweet cakes and hot cider mixed with a little ganje.

"Your arrival is timely, very timely." The old man's voice was rough and barely louder than a whisper. "How was Navra when you left it? What of the Pass?"

As Senior Brother of Imrion, Alkoryn Pantherclaw was, in effect, the Senior Mercenary for the whole Peninsula — should his authority ever be required by one of his Brothers. As such, he had a responsibility to collect any information that might touch upon his charge. He listened patiently while his junior Brothers told him of the dredging being planned in Navra's harbor, the new salt mine, and the expansion of the evaporation ponds. He heard with some amusement their story of what had happened to them in Clan Trevel.

"So Yaro Hawkwing prospers," the old man croaked. "I rejoice to hear it. Do we now have allies among Clan Trevel?"

"We might," Dhulyn said. She glanced at Parno in time to see him nodding. "Perhaps if we sent them some acknowledgment. . . ."

"I'll think what form it could take. I have my contacts with Clan Pompano, but we may have need of all the Clouds if what I think is coming comes," Alkoryn said dryly.

He took up the ceramic jug of cooling cider and refilled the cups. Dhulyn saw that two knuckles of his left hand were swollen, but whether from old breaking or from arthritis she could not tell. "You came as bodyguards?" he continued as he set down the jug.

Parno exchanged glances with Dhulyn. She gave him a slight nod. "Not merely bodyguards, Alkoryn my Brother," he began. He paused and took a sip from his cup. Dhulyn suppressed a smile. The way he was drawing out the moment, Parno should have been an actor, she thought, as her Partner blotted his lips carefully with the square of linen provided. "We have come to Gotterang as the guides and bodyguards of a Lady orphan of House Tenebro, no less. Any reason for such an exalted House to be gathering up their lesser kin?"

Alkoryn's lips formed a silent whistle and his eyes narrowed. "She's not the first, and that's a fact," he said. "My bones tell me this may be part of what I see coming," he said. "Though I don't know how." He sat back, leaning his right elbow on the arm of his chair. "The Tenebroso is an old woman and gossip says she's failing. The Kir, Lok-iKol, is a forward-looking man, and may very well be thinking to reestablish the Tenebro claim on lost lands. But that in itself is no reason to bring the girl here."

"Mar-eMar feels there's a wedding in the wind, and it's true she has letters she hasn't shown us," Dhulyn said.

"She's not advantageous enough a match for the Kir himself," Alkoryn said, taking a sip of his cider and returning the glass to the table. "Though there's a cousin in the House, Dal-eDal, from an Imrion Household, not a Holding as is this Mar-eMar. A marriage there would be a way to increase the young man's property without losing anything of value to the main branch. House Tenebro has had bad luck enough in the last twenty years or so; Lok-iKol has no cousins of his own generation left, they say, though there are some few of their children about, like this Mar of yours, and Dal-eDal himself, for that matter." He glanced at his younger Brothers. "With things the way they are at present, it's no bad idea for those in the Houses to put their hands on all their kin."

"The way things are at present?" said Parno. "Like these new regulations governing who may ride? This has some connection with the doings of House Tenebro?" Something in his voice made Dhulyn glance at him. Was he a little paler than before? What had there been in Alkoryn's remarks to give Parno that stricken look?

"Perhaps only in the mind of an old Brother, but I've seen too much to be easy with the changes of the last few years—still less with those of the last few months." Alkoryn took a deep breath and let it out slowly. "The riding law is just the latest, and unpopular as it is, it helps more than it hinders. There's always trouble in a city," he said. "The bigger the city, the more trouble. You'd think that people weren't meant to live together in such quantities, but there, that's a subject for another time."

Dhulyn exchanged a look with Parno as the older man pushed his white hair back from his face with both hands.

"It would be hard to pinpoint exactly when things began to go badly, or why it began, for that matter, but the normal incidents one expects in city life have grown more frequent, and more disturbing. More knifings and fewer fistfights, if you follow me. Associations and clubs are becoming gangs, and it's not unusual now for a quarrel between two merchants to turn into a full-blown riot in a matter of minutes, or for groups to be set upon in the streets."

Parno searched the tabletop for a moment before finding a relatively empty spot to set his glass down.

"You could see something was off-center," he said, "Even walking here." He glanced at Dhulyn. "It's been a few years since either of us were in Gotterang—before we Partnered—but there's a bad feeling in the streets. I can't put my finger on it—"

"Not enough children," Dhulyn said, and lifted her blood-red brows as both men looked at her. "None playing games in the streets, anyway, and the people who *were* out, looking at each other sideways."

Alkoryn nodded again. "You can *see* the tension now, those of us who know what to look for. The City Guards are always on the alert, and they've taken to traveling in groups of five, instead of the usual pairs. The order restricting riding gives the Watch greater mobility, and lessens the chances of troublemakers getting away, but honest people feel it's too severe."

"Can't make the nobles walk, I suppose," Parno said.

"That would make them more trouble, not less," Dhulyn said, her eyes round and innocent in her scarred face. Both men smiled.

"There was a riot in the Calzos district two months ago, and the City Guards were overwhelmed. The Tarkin sent the Guard from the Carnelian Dome and the crowd dispersed. There were delegations to the Tarkin after that and things looked to be getting better, but every time the violence dies down for a few days, something happens that starts it up again. Things are now at the point that only the presence of the Carnelian Guard will convince people to disperse."

"Let me guess," Parno said. "Something to do with the Marked or with these New Believers we've heard about."

"What haven't you told me?"

Parno looked at Dhulyn, and she nodded. "There was a fire in Navra," she said. Alkoryn Pantherclaw's face grew grimmer and grimmer as she told the story, and he was silent a long while when she finished.

"I did not realize it had spread so far. There have been fires here as well and, I think, worse things. Nor is there doubt in anyone's mind that the new sect of the Jaldeans are behind it," Alkoryn said. "But proving it's a different matter. Even those who don't follow the Sleeping God are being turned against the Marked, being told that they profit from the misfortunes of others."

"Well, so do we if it comes to that," Parno pointed out.

"Yes," Dhulyn said. "But we risk our lives doing it; that may keep us safe a while longer."

"Oh, in public and during the day the New Believers preach tolerance and understanding, pleading with the Marked to come to their shrines for guidance and cleansing." The old man shook his head. "I see from your faces you've been told what this cleansing means."

"All this turmoil, at least, should mean we'll find plenty of work, once we've delivered our charge."

"Don't count your money yet," Alkoryn said. "There's been no new hiring of Mercenary Brothers for weeks, and some long in guard service have been let go."

"All these problems, the City Guard confounded, and no work for Mercenaries?"

"Nothing overt has been either said or done," Alkoryn said. "But again, this is nothing new in our history. There are changes coming, with these New Believers, and it won't be the first time that as a Brotherhood we ride them out, rather than fight them out."

"And the Marked?"

"We've a little something in hand for them, never fear. When you've finished with the Tenebro girl, I will have an assignment for you myself. But tell me, you heard nothing of this in the West?"

"Not in the court of the Great King," Dhulyn said. "There are Marked there, of course, but very few, and well-respected."

"As bad as it is here in Imrion, this whole eastern end of the world is like kindling awaiting the match. Kondria has warned the Tarkin that if there are any further attacks on the Marked, it will withdraw its embassy."

"That means war."

Dhulyn shot a glance at Parno. Was there worry in his voice?

"And if Kondria is drawn into a religious war with Imrion, their allies will follow," Alkoryn said. The look he gave them was grave. "The Tarkin, and his hold on Imrion, is all that keeps the east from bursting into flame."

"If the east is burning, it may attract the attention of the Great King," Dhulyn said. "And bring the rest of the world into the conflict." She frowned down at the table, tracing her finger along a shoreline drawn in deep sea green. She froze.

FIRES

She'd Seen fires consuming shores, mountains, and rivers.

"With things so uncertain, perhaps you should consider moving your maps," she said. Parno looked at her, eyebrows raised in inquiry, but she moved her head minutely, side to side.

"What Dorian has said of you is true," Alkoryn said after a short silence. "Your intuition is superb. It is, indeed, part of my plan to move these records to a safer spot."

"I would start moving them now," Dhulyn said, gesturing around her. "I think you are so used to them, my Brother, that you don't realize how much packing all this will take."

"You may be right."

"In the meantime, since Imrion is not yet at war, we'll take the little Dove to Tenebro House . . ." Dhulyn let the words fade away as Alkoryn held up his hand.

"The day's well advanced. Wait until morning and take no chances. And in the meantime, I have something here that may be of use, though it cannot leave this room." He twisted in his seat and reached over the low back of his chair. Dhulyn automatically noted that the old man was still limber enough to perform such an action. After a moment's hesitation he selected a bundle of thin parchments rolled together and tied with a wide blue ribbon. This he untied and spread the curling papers, turning brown around the outer edges, flat on the map that covered the table. Parno passed over several stone weights from his side of the table.

Floor plans, Dhulyn realized. Layer after intricate layer of floor plans.

"Incredible," Parno murmured, pulling one sheet closer to his side of the table. The house was a maze. Halls that went nowhere, others that simply turned back on themselves, forcing the uninitiated to travel in circles, fake walls, secret passages, more stairwells than normally appear in a handful of buildings.

"Built in the time of Jorelau Tarkin," Alkoryn said. "And reflecting the paranoia of that day."

Dhulyn tapped the corner of one sheet, where the mark of House Tenebro was clearly drawn.

"How is this possible?" she said, smiling her wolf's smile.

Alkoryn shrugged. "Over the years many Brothers have served as guards and instructors in Tenebro House. We have three there now, as it happens. For that reason, I will ask you to exercise the greatest care while you are on their premises."

Dhulyn nodded, her eyes still on the plans. Mercenary Brothers might find themselves on opposite sides on a battlefield, but anywhere else they took care of one another.

She looked up from the drawings. "Is the old Bootmaker's Inn still in business?"

Alkoryn nodded. "You might as well leave your horses here, however. You won't be riding them, and it will save you their board."

"Let's hope that's all we have to worry about," Parno said, still studying the floor plans of Tenebro House.

Six

"**D**O I *HAVE* TO RIDE?" Mar asked from her seat on the windowsill. The Bootmaker's Inn had been almost full, and they had ended up all sleeping in the same room, though not, this time, in the same bed.

Wolfshead looked up from lacing the cuff of her leggings. "Of course not, if you don't wish it," was all she said.

"Then I don't wish it," Mar said.

Wolfshead nodded, straightened to her feet, plucked her sheathed sword off the bed, and hung it on her belt harness. "Not that comfortable riding yesterday?" she asked.

Mar shrugged. "Maybe if I'd been dressed differently. I kept thinking people were looking at me and wondering what a girl dressed in a shop clerk's worn-out clothing was doing on a horse." She looked up to find the Wolfshead watching her, head tilted to one side.

"You're not the Weaver's girl anymore, that's certain. But remember that nobility can insulate as well as expose."

Mar looked down, nodding. She knew what the Wolfshead said was true. But, like so many things lately, it didn't make her feel any better.

"Come," Wolfshead said, her voice soft and kind. "There's no harm in being a weaver's girl for a little while longer."

Lionsmane turned from gossiping with the innkeeper just as Mar entered the yard with Wolfshead.

"All ready, then?" he said, turning toward them with a smile.

The innkeeper shook his head, grinning. "If I'd known you had a cousin of the Tenebros with you, I'd have charged you more for your room."

"Why do you think we didn't tell you?"

The man was still chuckling when Mar followed Lionsmane through the inn's gated entrance out into a wide city street. The Wolfshead, for once, was bringing up the rear, with Mar safely tucked between them.

"It's a long walk, as walking goes, from this quarter to Tenebro House. You're sure you don't want us to get you a horse?" Lionsmane looked back at her over his left shoulder.

Mar shook her head. "I'd rather walk," she said. "I'd like to see something of the city." They wouldn't push her, she knew. They would realize that she was making delays out of nervousness. The Lionsmane was humming and whistling as if there was something about cities that brought out a spirit of fun in him.

As they walked, the narrow street crossed others and widened into squares every now and then, some with public fountains and others with neighborhood ovens. The business of the day had already started for many of the people, and setting aside the difference that sheer numbers meant, Mar saw much that was familiar to her. Shops, homes, and taverns being swept out, stalls being set up in the squares, and merchants laying out their wares. These were not like the large farmers' market she'd known in Navra, but neighborhood places, where people came to do their marketing every day.

"Oh, look," Mar said, as she turned aside to watch two women pulling strands of ever thinner dough from hand to hand, doubling and twisting the strands until they were almost as fine as hairs before hanging them to dry on racks made of thin wooden dowels.

"Noodle makers," Lionsmane said, stopping beside her. "Much more popular than rice or potatoes here. They say you eventually get tired of eating noodles, but it's never happened to me."

After a while the streets got wider, the market squares larger and noisier, and Mar began to wish for a horse after all. Lionsmane and Wolfshead moved through the crowd as if they were alone on the trail. Light glinted off the little beads and bits of metal woven into Wolfs head's narrow blood-red braids. Mar glanced ahead at Lionsmane. They both seemed so relaxed, striding along bareheaded and empty-handed. Both had put away their traveling leathers and were dressed once more as Mar had seen them when they had first met. Both in loose-fitting trousers tucked into half boots, the Lionsmane in a light brown tunic embroidered with gold threads that caught and reflected the gold in his hair, the Wolfshead in her quilted vest, bright with beading and ribbons, her arms bare, her skin white in the chill morning air. For the most part the two Brothers smiled as they spoke to each other and to Mar, pointing out here a spotted horse like Wolfshead's Bloodbone, there a seller of spiced rolls that Lionsmane insisted on buying, and pausing at one point to watch a group of children play a skipping game. But Mar noticed that the Wolfshead in particular scanned the people around them, as though she were looking for something or someone in particular, not just checking for possible danger. Mar followed one especially narrow glance at a redheaded man before she realized what it was the Wolfshead looked for.

Red Horsemen, Mar thought. *She's looking for other Red Horsemen.*

The streets became more crowded as businesses opened and serious marketing began. Still, Mar noticed that people seemed to clear a path for the Mercenaries without being aware of it.

At one point she saw three people dressed in the dark green of the Marked. There were a few stony looks, but most of the passersby ignored them. With the crowds, entertainers appeared, and after so many days on horseback Mar was grateful for the rest stops, once to watch a particularly good juggler, and once a person who seemed to be swallowing swords. Mar turned for one last look as they continued on their way.

"How does she do that?"

"Sword's dull," Wolfshead said, as if that explained everything.

"Oh, and another thing . . ." Lionsmane was imparting a steady commentary on manners and protocol over his shoulder as they walked. Mar swallowed, her head was starting to spin.

"Parno, for Sun and Moon's sake, leave the Dove alone. You told her all this on the trail, and she's asked you all the questions she can think of. If she hasn't memorized the eating tools by now, she's not going to the next few spans."

Mar flashed the older woman a grateful smile, hoping it didn't look as stiff as it felt. Now that she was on the point of putting Lionsmane's instructions to use, Mar was finding it vastly less entertaining than it had seemed on the road. And perhaps less to be wished for than it had seemed in Navra.

"Have we much farther to go?" Her feet hurt, and her legs weren't used to walking. Part of her wanted to get there, to get it over with. Part of her hoped that this walk would never end.

Dhulyn was enjoying herself as much as she could in a city—fine places to visit, she'd always thought, but you wouldn't want to live in one. They crossed a broad avenue and turned uphill, entering a sizable square where three streets met, and the corner of a warehouse butted up against a half-ruined garden wall. Here, such a crowd had gathered that it almost blocked the passage through the area entirely. A man in red-and-brown robes was standing on what was left of the wall, raised above the crowd to about the height of a person sitting on a horse. Dhulyn wondered if this particular bit of wall had been chosen for just that reason. Get the people to see you as an authority, either noble or military.

And the man *was* a Jaldean priest, no doubt about it, though certainly the youngest one Dhulyn had ever seen. Hair and beard close-cropped. High forehead and a spot showing where he would be bald in a few years. A much older man in robes of the same colors stood on the ground near the speaker's feet. Dhulyn slowed to let some of the people coming the other way pass by on her left side. She'd thought she'd seen a flash of green as the older man's head had turned away, but she couldn't be sure unless he turned back again. The crowd closest to the priests certainly looked slack-jawed and blank-faced, but they did not display any of the destructive behavior she and Parno had seen in the mob in Navra.

Mar's hand tugged slightly on the front of Dhulyn's vest

as the press of people moved them farther apart, recalling Dhulyn to her charge.

"Just keep moving," Dhulyn told her. "Keep your hand on Parno, don't worry about me." She smiled when Mar took hold of Parno's sword belt before letting go of Dhulyn's vest. Smart girl. It was hard to navigate in this big a crowd if you didn't know how. Easy to lose your nerve.

"Now there's no doubt," the young Jaldean was saying, "that the Caids knew how to awaken the Sleeping God. And there's no one who has seen the Dead Spots, where the land is blackened and sterile, melted and fused like glass, who doesn't know what happens when the Sleeping God awakes."

Dhulyn raised her eyebrows, but kept her grimace from moving so far as her lips. She remembered, years before, walking through a market square with Dorian the Black, and stopping to listen to an old man, a Jaldean priest. All *that* old man had talked about was how the Sleeping God kept watch always in his dreams, ready to awaken and protect everyone from harm. She'd still been a child then—at least in some ways—with a child's way of looking at things, and she'd wondered just how blooded bad things had to get for the blooded god to wake up and help people.

Today's priest seemed to have come a long way from that.

"And we think—we *hope*—that knowledge has died with the Caids, but has it? I ask you, my friends, has it?" Several voices called out "no," but the man continued as if he hadn't been answered. "We can't know for certain, and that's the fact. But we *can* take precautions, we *can* take care.

"We don't *know* that there are snakes in the grass, but we *can* thump the ground with our walking sticks as we go, to be safe. We don't *know* that the Cloud People are going to rob the caravan, they say they won't . . ." Here the man smiled and shook his head as if he could say a thing or two about that, and smiles and winks passed through the listening crowd as if they, too, knew something about the real behavior of Cloud People. "But we *can* hire guards to keep ourselves safe.

"Now, the Marked say they're not trying to awaken the

Sleeping God, that they don't even know how. And many of you have Marked among your neighbors, kind, helpful people and they tell you they don't know how to awaken the Sleeping God, and you think it must be true. You don't see how they can be so dangerous and so wicked." The Jaldean pursed his lips and nodded, as if conceding the point. "But we *know*," his voice fell like a hammer, "that the Marked are the descendants of the Caids. Where else would their special talents come from, remember, talents that can't be taught to all or any—talents that draw on the Sleeping God's power, draining it, bringing him ever closer to wakefulness. No my friends, however kind and helpful they might be as individuals, as your neighbors, as your friends, the Marked are a danger to you, and a danger to themselves. They *must* stop. We *must* learn to do without their aid, their *deceptive* aid, in order to preserve the world. We must take steps to save ourselves. And to save them too! All they have to do is come to the shrine to be blessed. All they have to do is come to the shrine to be cleansed, to be purified. Let us help them to keep us all safe . . ."

The Jaldean's comfortable tone, the throaty murmurs of the crowd, died away as Parno led them slowly out of the square.

"Sometimes," Mar murmured to Dhulyn, "they seem to make sense."

"Yes," Dhulyn's tone was carefully neutral. "Yes, they do." In public they were all tolerance and forgiveness, Alkoryn Pantherclaw had said, and Dhulyn saw what he meant. *That's what makes them so dangerous,* she thought. Much of what was said seemed so logical, people tended not to question the rest. Dorian had always said to be careful of logic. While one was using logic on you, another was stealing your purse. Or slitting your throat. She met the eye of a man behind her, also trying to leave the square, who murmured something under his breath and shook his head, holding Dhulyn's eye. She kept her face impassive, but did not turn away.

The streets became wider still, and better paved, with fewer people on them and no one, now, in the dark green of the Marked. Walls of undressed stone lined with the doorways of shops and workplaces gradually turned into unbroken whitewashed stucco. At one point bells started ringing the midmorning watch.

"Do you recognize that tune, my heart?" Dhulyn called out.

"I've heard it, certainly," Parno said. "But I don't place it. Dhulyn began to sing.

"Weeping lass, weeping lass,
Where have you been?
Weeping lass, weeping lass,
Walk right in."

Mar joined in, her rounded notes a counterpoint to Dhulyn's throaty purr,

"Step to corner, step to fire . . ."

Dhulyn laughed. "You haven't sung that one before, Dove. I'd forgotten that. We used to sing a verse like that when I was a very young child, though not those words. At least, I don't think so. Try that again, Mar, and perhaps my childhood words will come back to me."

Halfway through a second verse, their voices faltered as a burly man running to fat went past on a roan horse being led by a servant. He turned his head to watch them as he passed. The servant and the horse didn't look. Dhulyn laughed and began to whistle the tune.

When they were still a street away from Tenebro House, Dhulyn called to Parno and drew her companions to one side.

"Well, little Dove," Dhulyn said, the corner of her mouth lifting. "This is your last chance. Do we go on?"

The girl looked from one to the other. Parno raised his eyebrows but said nothing. Dhulyn hadn't consulted him, knowing he would be with her on this. Better the girl should freely choose.

Mar nodded absently, her eyes focused somewhere between the two Mercenaries. She parted her lips, thought better of what she was about to say, and shut her mouth again. "What about your pay?" she asked finally.

"We'd want to be paid, rightly enough," Dhulyn told her. "But in this case we're not particular by whom. Plenty of work to be found in this city now that we're here. For you *and* us." Dhulyn smiled, no need for the Dove to know what Alkoryn had told them. "We could wait to be paid if you decide so. Or simply," she said, her voice more gentle, "we can wait if you need time to be certain."

Mar nodded again. She looked up, meeting Dhulyn's eyes directly. "Suppose I go to my House, I might still change my mind," Mar said. "And you would have been paid, but not by me." She grinned in response to Dhulyn's wolf's smile. "In the meantime, they sent for me, and I have come. There is no way for me to be more certain."

Mar turned her head away. If it were possible, Dhulyn would have said that the girl's pallor had increased. She looked almost green in the morning light. Dhulyn caught Parno's eye, but he only shrugged, and set off toward Mar's House.

Tenebro House was a walled enclave, high up in the streets near the Carnelian Dome, almost but not quite a part of the Tarkin's grounds. The huge doors of the gateway, large enough to admit carriages, were heavy wood reinforced with iron bars. But there was a pass door in the right-hand leaf, with a pull chain beside it. Mar took a deep breath and pulled the chain, jumping back at the sudden loud rattle. The two Mercenaries stood, hands resting on hilts, looking over Mar's shoulders as she waited. After a long interval, the pass door opened, revealing an unarmed man with another stone wall perhaps a half span behind him.

Not any movement of face or body revealed Dhulyn's alert interest. She had read that many of the older Noble Houses were doubled-gated, and the plans had shown her that Tenebro House was one, but she had never seen such a thing with her own eyes. There would be two walls, she knew, with a gate in each, offset so that forcing one gate could not force the other. Rather, attackers could be trapped between the inner and the outer wall, easy prey for anyone standing on the inner battlements.

Dhulyn looked with even more interest at the man who

stood so calmly within the pass door. This would be the Steward of Walls, a House's equivalent of the Captain of the Guard, a responsibility so weighty that once it had been accepted, he could never leave the House's walls again. It was part of his undertaking to inspect any who entered the House for the first time. It was he who decided whether to open the pass door or gate. And at times he staked his life on his judgment, since the inner gate was opened only when he allowed it. Intruders might kill him, but killing him would not open the inner gate.

This Steward was a tall, lean man all arms and legs, dressed like a minor nobleman in soft woolen leggings tucked into short boots, linen shirt with wide sleeves and a blue silk tunic. A teal-and-black crest was sewn into the left shoulder of his tunic, the colors of House Tenebro. His dark hair showed some gray, and the skin had begun to turn to paper around his eyes. But those eyes were still a sharp crystal blue. He stood calm, his wide mouth faintly smiling, a man still hard. Had he been a Brother, he would have many years of good service still to give. The man took time to appraise Parno and Dhulyn, their Mercenary badges, their swords ready to draw, their proximity to their plainly dressed charge. His gaze lingered on Dhulyn. She could feel herself starting to smile. He did not seem surprised by what he saw, but then, he did not seem like a man who could be easily surprised.

"In what way can I assist you?" he said, inclining his head to Mar.

"I am Mar-eMar, a daughter of this House."

Nothing changed on the man's face. He would have seen that her clothes, while well made, were nothing more than serviceable by the standards of a Noble House, that those clothes had seen plenty of recent service, and that she and her guards had collected a portion of dust walking in the streets. His face showed nothing of this. "You'll forgive me, Lady," was all he said. "I do not know you."

Mar drew up her shoulders. "I am the daughter of the Lady Tam-uTam, who was the daughter of the Lady Wat-aWat, who was the daughter of the Lord Dow-oDow. I am summoned by the Tenebroso Lady Kor-iRok, who is my House." Mar reached into the front of her tunic and pulled out the letter that Dhulyn had seen and read in Navra. Mar held out the parchment so that the seal could be seen.

The man had started to nod long before Mar had finished her account. "You are expected and welcome, Mar-eMar Tenebro. I am Karlyn-Tan, your Steward of Walls. Pray, enter." He bowed his head more deeply and stepped aside to let them into the space between the doors. The pass door closed behind them, and bars were thrown before the inner gates—a good five paces to the left—opened to reveal the interior courtyard.

As soon as the inner gates had closed behind them, what little street noise existed here so close to the Carnelian Dome faded completely. The courtyard was much larger than had seemed possible from the street, holding a fountain—dry at this time of year—as well as several small trees. To the left and right, doors and windows indicated quarters built into the walls for the guards and outer servants who did not live in the House. Across the yard and up three broad flagstone steps were the double doors of the House itself, elaborate carvings and metal inlays presenting the emblems of the Tenebro. No hinges were showing. That confirmed the detail shown on Alkoryn's plans. A banner hung from a standard, indicating that the Tenebroso, the head of the House, was in residence.

The courtyard was large enough to seem uncrowded, though there were at least twenty people passing through it as the two Brothers entered with their charge. A few of these were guards, but most were obviously servants of the House, lingering to see who was coming in, looking for excuses to pause in their work. Even the children playing with wooden balls in the far corner left off and came to see what the visitors were about. Unlike Karlyn-Tan, all of these wore a kind of livery with the house colors of teal and black showing on collars and cuffs.

The Steward of Walls led them across the yard.

"You may wait here if you wish," he said, turning to address Dhulyn and Parno. "You have Brothers within these walls, and they can be summoned to attend you."

"We are not yet discharged," Parno said.

"Of course." A slight bow. "In that case, I must ask that

you leave your weapons here." He motioned, and one of the watching guards approached. Dhulyn smiled her wolf's smile, drew her sword, and presented it with a flourish. A broad smile passed over the Steward's lips as he accepted her weapon with a bow. She could like this fellow, Dhulyn thought. Only a special kind of man retained his sense of humor in this position. Parno handed his sword without ceremony to the waiting guard.

The Steward waited a moment more, but neither Mercenary moved. "I'm afraid I must ask for *all* of your weapons," he said.

Dhulyn's own smile became more pronounced. "You could strip us naked, and still not have *all* of our weapons," she said, lifting her left eyebrow.

"Lady, I would wager that was so." Karlyn-Tan held her gaze with his very clear blue eyes as the people in the courtyard gave up any pretense of passing through and began to gather more closely around them.

Parno coughed. Dhulyn gave him a sidelong look, but he was only gazing at her blandly. She shrugged and nodded. They'd done this before, and they knew how to make a show of it—and that *making* a show of it would enhance their reputation without frightening anyone. She and Parno began to shed weapons like a wet dog sheds water. Between them they disposed of three knives, one almost long enough to qualify as a short sword, four thrust daggers, and two wrist knives and five throwing stars. They paused. The crowd of House people began to whisper among themselves.

The children crept closer still and poked at each other. Parno winked at the nearest, stroked his now well-established beard, reached into the back of his tunic, and pulled out a silvered throwing quoit. Dhulyn rolled her eyes to the heavens, as though calling on the Outlander gods of Sky and Rain to witness Parno's foolishness. Parno shrugged and smiled sheepishly, making the children giggle. The Steward grinned and said nothing. People in the small crowd surrounding them muttered and Dhulyn heard the chink of coin. She reached over her shoulder with her left hand, pushing it down the back of her vest as if to reach a bad itch, and drew out a tiny hatchet. Parno looked thoughtful, drew four black metal tubes from the top of his boot and added them to the pile.

The Partners looked at each other. Parno frowned. Dhulyn shrugged, unbuckled the wallet at her waist and simply added it, belt and all, to the pile. Parno nodded. They turned their attention back to the Steward of Walls, eyes wide and innocent, hands clasped behind their backs, looking almost exactly as they had looked before. There were grins and murmurs of admiration among the watching gatemen, and a small child whistled and started to clap.

"What, no maces, pikes, or longbows?" the Steward's voice was dry, but his eye sparkled. Someone laughed aloud.

"Awkward to carry through the street, don't you think?" Dhulyn said, her eyebrows innocently raised. "It would be better if these were not touched," she added more seriously, indicating the collection of cutting edges and sharpened points piled on the ground beside them. "Some have more edges than are apparent to the untrained eye."

Still smiling, shaking his head, Karlyn-Tan handed Dhulyn's sword to the young woman who had stepped forward to assist him. "I doubt you would find many willing to try," he said. "I'll see that they're kept safe." He gestured, and the young woman bowed.

When they turned once more to the House door, it was to find a plainly but richly dressed woman standing on the bottom step, her House crest sewn into the left shoulder of her overtunic. Karlyn-Tan turned and stepped closer to Mar. "Lady Mar-eMar," he said. "May I introduce your Steward of Keys?" This was a small woman whose slimness made her appear taller. The skin of her face was smooth and unlined, her hair completely covered by the embroidered headdress that marked her position and status. Dhulyn looked closely at her. Tradition had it, Parno had explained, that the Steward of Keys could never leave the House itself. This lowest doorstep was as close as the woman would ever come to the world outside.

"Welcome, Mar-eMar," the woman said. She bowed from the waist. "I am Semlin-Nor, your Steward of Keys." Her voice was sharply rough, like metal that had been through a fire. "If you will follow me, I will take you to the Tenebroso."

❧

Noises in the courtyard had drawn Gundaron the Scholar out of the narrow room he used as his private study to the window built into the wall outside his door. At first he couldn't follow what was happening three stories below him. A small crowd of idlers were gathering around two, or perhaps three, people in the courtyard. Gundaron recognized Karlyn-Tan standing to one side, but . . . was it jugglers or actors? It seemed there was some kind of performance. Conjurers? Gundaron leaned out as far as he dared through the window, taking a firm grip on the sill. He'd always loved conjurers, ever since one had come to the farm when he was a child and made all the kittens in the house appear and disappear.

These two—no, three, that young girl in dusty clothing was definitely with them—were performing that old favorite, pulling improbable things out of their clothing. The slighter of the two conjurers, a red-haired woman—

Gundaron sucked in his breath, his hand going to cover his mouth. These weren't conjurers at all, they were Mercenary Brothers; he'd seen the woman's badge clearly when she twisted to pull something out from between her shoulder blades. A pair of Mercenaries being admitted into the House. One of them a tall, redheaded woman.

The Red Horseman. It had to be. Dhulyn Wolfshead herself, and much earlier than he would have expected. She and her Partner must be everything their Brother here at Tenebro House had said they were. And she *was* a Red Horseman; no one could be in any doubt about that. He could see her natural southern pallor from here, and no dye would get hair quite that blood-red color, even if a Mercenary Brother would trouble to dye it. He let his hands fall from his face and dragged in a lungful of air. *Finally,* a chance to prove his theories. There'd been nothing new added to scholarship on the Marked since Holderon's day. Nothing until now.

Gundaron rapidly reviewed the list of questions he would ask her. He was fairly certain the books he needed

to refer to were still in the large workroom where he'd first
assembled them when he'd learned of Dhulyn Wolfshead's
existence. His methods might be considered a bit unortho-
dox by the Libraries if they ever came to light, but the benefit to the body of knowledge was incalculable.

He blinked back to the present moment when he realized that the activity in the courtyard had changed. Karlyn-
Tan had taken the hand of the young girl with the Brothers
and was presenting her to Semlin-Nor. The girl was standing awkwardly, her hand looking stiff in Karlyn's grasp, but
she was acknowledging Semlin's bow very bravely, very
properly, like a frightened but well-brought-up child.

A chill threaded its way up Gundaron's spine. *This* was
the Lady Mar-eMar? *She's just a girl,* he thought. *Younger
than me.* He rubbed his mouth with shaking fingers. For
some reason, when he'd told Lok-iKol about her, he'd
imagined Mar to be an older woman. Unconsciously, he'd
thought of her as a stout matron, rather like the cook's first
assistant, the woman who made those delicious pastries. A
woman well able to look out for herself. Not this, this *child*.

Gundaron the Scholar found himself for the first time in
his life hoping he was wrong, that the girl wasn't a Finder
after all. That no Jaldean would become interested in that
bright, heart-shaped face and those eyes that showed dark
blue even from this distance. His eyes moved to the Mercenary Brothers, and what was clearly a pile of weapons beside them on the flag stones of the courtyard. His plans
would remove their protection from the girl. If he called
out now—but it was already too late, wasn't it? The gates
were closed, the Brothers disarmed.

The wheels Gundaron had set in motion those long
months ago couldn't be stopped now.

❧

When the Steward of Keys turned and pushed open the
right-hand House door, it opened inward, just as the plans
had indicated. Parno gave Dhulyn a wink and nodded at
the space now visible. Behind the doors was a landing only
deep enough to allow the doors to swing open, and which
gave access to a staircase on either side. If both doors were
opened at once, the stairs would be blocked, and those en-

tering would find themselves in a shallow room open to the outside. Only a handful of people—say, three if they were carrying both shields and swords—could enter at a time, and whether or not their business was legitimate, they could go no farther unless they had opened only one door.

An invading force which could only enter three at a time would be cut to pieces on the stairs.

Dhulyn glanced back at Parno and nodded, smiling. Like him, she had Alkoryn's floor plans in her head, and was even more likely to notice a certain paranoid pattern.

They followed the Steward of Keys up the left staircase. Dhulyn walked immediately behind the woman, with Mar behind her, and Parno serving as rear guard. The hall at the top of the stair was narrow, and they continued to walk along in single file. Parno grinned after they had been led past the third window high up on a wall. From the outside, it would be impossible to tell which of these windows opened onto rooms and which into empty space. When he was a young boy in his Household, he had had a large wooden puzzle that could be put together into four different mazes. Tenebro House was like that puzzle, Parno realized, if you took all the mazes and stacked them, one on top of the other.

Finally, the halls they walked through widened, and the walls began to be covered by tapestries and paneling. They were shown through several carefully furnished public rooms, one blue with dozens of mirrors, one gold with groupings of armchairs, one dark enough that Parno couldn't guess its predominant color, until finally the Steward of Keys led them up another narrow stone staircase and into a large chamber made small with furnishings. Its unseen floor was completely covered with rugs and carpets, piled to several thicknesses, and its walls were hung with more rugs and the same kind of embroidered cloths that had appeared in the halls. Parno thought the effect not unlike one of Dhulyn's vests, only duller. The other parts of the House had been cool, the stone still retaining the cold of winter, as it would until summer truly began, but this room was noticeably hot.

Even without having seen the maps and floor plans, the Mercenaries would have known that they were now at no great distance from their starting point at the House doors. It was much too easy to get turned around in the heat of battle for any of the Brotherhood to have a poor sense of direction. No very careful observation was actually needed to tell them that they had been escorted around the long way. Each had taken care to look about them as they went, had done their best to imitate Mar's wide-eyed awe. Their country-cousin act was wasted on Semlin-Nor, who did not even turn her head as she walked ahead of them, but Lionsmane and Wolfshead knew that there would be spyholes in the walls. The age of paranoia is never really over.

At first, all they could see in the room was a lean, dark-haired man standing with his hand on the back of a large chair. His age was probably half again as much as Parno's. He was richly dressed in dark blue, his fashionably short surcoat teal and black with an edge of deep red at least two fingers wide. When he turned his head to look at them as they entered, the light showed a well-healed scar on the left side of his face where someone had struck him with a mailed fist and taken out his eye. When that cold blue gaze turned in his direction, Parno shifted his own eyes away.

The man might have been considered good-looking before his disfigurement. But maybe not.

Parno at first thought him the sole occupant of the room, totally out of place amid the dainty padded chairs, the small stands, and the scattered tables with their carved legs. But gradually he realized that the chair over which the one-eyed man hovered protectively had an occupant. An elderly woman with a scroll in her hands sat in it, close to the brazier table whose quilted cover had been thrown back to expose the glowing coals within. The lady was small, thin, and elegantly dressed in stiff brocaded velvet. There was no gray in her golden hair, but her amber-colored eyes were clouded with age. Neither the one-eyed man nor the old woman seemed at all surprised to see them, though the Steward of Keys said nothing before ushering them in. Of course, their roundabout route had allowed someone else to reach this room ahead of them and prepare the way. Parno watched carefully, but he couldn't see that either of the Tenebros showed any special interest in the Mercenary Brothers.

"You are Mar-eMar," the old woman said in a voice low and still vibrant, though faded. "I am Kor-iRok."

As if there were any doubt, the mirror reversal of the woman's name declared her the Tenebroso, the House.

Without speaking, Mar bowed low to kiss the older woman's hand, but remained standing. Parno raised an eyebrow in approval. At least the child remembered some of what he had taught her.

"This is my first child, Lok-iKol."

The Kir. Bet you he's tired of waiting for his mother to die, Parno thought, as the man reached up to touch his eye patch in what was obviously an unconscious tic.

The one-eyed man bowed, but made no move to take Mar's hand, though as Kir, heir to the House, he might have had her kiss his hand as well. "I greet you, Cousin," he said. His voice was low, musical. Mar inclined her head, trying to imitate the motion the older woman had made.

Parno's eyes narrowed, and his mouth twitched. Dhulyn kept her face impassive and her eyes moving between the people and the covered walls. She'd be looking for the secret entrance the plans showed in this room.

"Mar-eMar will have the green room in the south tower, Keys," the Tenebroso said. "You may have her luggage and her maids sent there."

"The Lady Mar-eMar arrived without maids, Tenebroso." Semlin-Nor did not comment on the sparsity of Mar's luggage. "The two I have assigned her await in her rooms."

"You have come without servants? What possessed you?" The words lacked any emotion, but it was evident her indifference was a symptom of her true physical weakness, not her lack of interest. Her face was capable of expressing the patronizing dismay that her voice was not strong enough to convey.

"As you see, my Mother, I have nevertheless arrived safely." Mar addressed the old woman formally, as a member by blood of the House. The corners of Dhulyn's mouth moved.

"And these persons?"

"Of the Brotherhood, my Mother. My guides and guards. To be paid upon my safe delivery."

"Of course, of course." The Tenebroso searched the table at her side, sifting through numerous small ornaments, two books, several curling sheets of parchment, setting to one side two heavy bracelets, before finding a small pouch of embroidered suede. Dhulyn and Parno both recognized this dumb show, meant to underscore the Tenebroso's distance from such crass matters. Of course the woman knew exactly where the purse was. It would have been brought to her while they were being led around the long way. The Steward of Keys moved forward to take it from the Tenebroso's hand, before presenting it to Parno. He kept his eyes down, and his face lowered as he stepped forward a pace to take it.

Dhulyn's eyes flicked from Parno to the old lady seated at the table, and back again. There was something in the old woman's face—something in the way the old eyes narrowed as she looked up at Parno, and in the way she so carefully did not look again. For an instant, it actually had seemed that the Tenebroso was going to forget herself enough to speak directly to a Mercenary Brother. But no, perhaps she was wrong, Dhulyn frowned, perhaps it was only Mar, after all, who drew the old lady's attention.

Money in hand, Parno stepped back, but when they made no further move to depart, the Kir raised the eyebrow over the missing eye. Probably meant to strike terror into their hearts, Dhulyn thought, amused. Finally, she looked at Mar.

"Are we discharged, Lady?" she asked.

"What? Yes, yes, of course," Mar cleared her throat, pink cheeked. "I thank you for your service," she said, as Parno had taught her, "Mercenaries, you are discharged."

❧

Semlin-Nor, Steward of Keys, waited for the Kir to leave before returning to the Tenebroso. She found the old woman exactly where she'd left her—no surprise, since the Tenebroso was no longer able to walk. Her vanity was such, however, that she made everyone else leave the room before she had her women in to carry her.

"What did you think of the Mercenary Brothers?" Kor-iRok asked. Semlin was surprised enough to leave tidying the table, to turn and look at her House. Questions about the country cousin she might have expected, but about Mercenaries?

"The red-haired woman is very striking," she said.

"Yes, that's so. But it's the golden-haired man I'm asking about. He has a mole near his right ear, the Mercenary badge does not quite cover it. Did you see it?"

"No, my House, I have to say I didn't."

"Nor did anyone else, my Keys. Nor did anyone else." The old woman smiled, mouth closed, lips pressed tight. "But I saw." The House turned to look directly at Semlin, her head shaking ever so slightly. "I knew a young man with a mole in that precise place, Semlin. A man of my House. Of my blood. A promising young man. A wronged young man. I have plans to redress those wrongs."

Semlin knelt, laid her hand with the greatest gentleness on the old woman's arm. "But, my Lady, he is a Mercenary now. He is no longer of this House."

"He is Tenebro." Kor-iRok's colorless voice left no room for disagreement. "He is my blood. I will bring him back to us." The old woman looked at her with the remains of what had once been a dazzling smile. "And you will help me."

"Of course, my House."

"Send for him tomorrow, when the Kir has gone to the Dome. Send for the Mercenary Brother Parno Lionsmane."

They had only gone a short way down a new corridor when sounds from behind made them stop. A young man approached them with a broad smile on his face. He was more plainly dressed than either the Tenebroso or her heir, but his face, and his fair brown coloring, marked him clearly as one of the family.

"I greet you. I am Dal-eDal. My cousin, the Lady Mar-eMar, begs you to stay and take the midday meal with her, while she adjusts to her new House," he said, his smile never changing and never touching his eyes.

Dhulyn glanced at Parno. "Tell the Lady we thank her," she said. "But we cannot stay weaponless."

The man inclined his head. "Of course. Now that you are guests, you can, of course, retain your swords. If you will follow me? Thank you," he said to the page escorting them, "I will take charge of our guests for now."

This was the cousin who lived in the House, Dhulyn thought, eyeing the golden-haired man with interest as he led them away. The form of his name—repeated Dal-e*Dal* and not the reversal, Dal-e*Lad*—marked him as having Household status, and not in line to inherit, as was Lok-iKol.

As they followed Dal-eDal down the passage, Parno locked eyes with Dhulyn. The corners of his mouth moved. Dhulyn shrugged. Of course the man was taking them by yet a different route. Anyone providing security would make maximum use of the tools at hand—and the mazelike design of this building, however archaic, was a first-class tool at hand. Karlyn-Tan had not impressed her as the kind of Steward of Walls who would overlook any aids to his security arrangements.

The passageway narrowed until they were walking in single file, Parno's shoulders brushing the wall coverings to each side. When the passage widened again, Dal-eDal lengthened his stride slightly, his hand reaching out to the handle of a door at the end of the passage. He was three paces ahead of Dhulyn when she heard a soft *snick* and lunged forward, heartbeats too late. A thick, weighted net fell from the ceiling and clung to her, muffling her arms and dragging down her head. Dhulyn was aware that somewhere the scholarly part of her mind was registering shock—surprise that anyone, even in the middle of their own House, would attack Mercenaries unprovoked. But even as that thought arose, she was taking a steadying breath and bending even further, slipping the fingers of her left hand into the space between her right calf and her boot. Without hurry, without panic, she took out her moon razor, a small rounded coin of metal, flattened and sharpened along one curve, and slashed at the net in front of her. The strands parted immediately and she stepped through the cut opening and moved to one side, her left arm arched above her head, her right poised with the moon razor. She felt Parno's back against hers in the narrow passageway and knew that his arms were raised like hers, and his hands full of blades.

Another net fell and Parno cut through it. A third net

fell before they could step from the cords of the second. A fourth while they were cutting the third. Dhulyn heard footsteps and braced herself, but the blow came not at her head or shoulders, but at her legs. She felt a hard arm around her thighs and, already off-balance, she went down in a tangle of cords and weights. She twisted and slashed. A high-pitched scream and the warm gush of blood across her hand and arm. She heard a wet crunch and Parno's voice softly cursing.

She was raising herself to her feet, pressing upward on the weight of net that tried to crush her to the floor, when the ceiling fell on them.

Seven

GUNDARON THE SCHOLAR chewed the side of his thumb, hovering just down from where his room's corridor met the wider passage leading to the great hall. He checked for the third time that he'd wiped all the powdered sugar off the scroll of the first act of Bartyn's *Maid of the Forest*. When he'd finally found it, it had been behind his copy of the eighteenth book of the *Hahrgis*, under a plate of jellied sweets. He cleared his throat, as a little finger of guilt scratched at the back of his mind. Good thing his old tutor hadn't seen that. Gundaron had never been tidy by nature, and in the two years since he'd left Valdomar, some of the Library's meticulous discipline had faded. He was still careful with his books—mostly, he thought as he brushed at the scroll again—kept his ink pots and pens clean, even if the cats did play with them. But a plate of jellied sweets on the worktable, *that* would never have been allowed in Valdomar.

Voices. Gundaron straightened his tunic with a tug, tucked the scroll under his left arm, and walked casually toward the main passage. *Caids,* he cursed under his breath. There were three women coming toward him, not one. The two in front, bodices laced fashionably tight, sleeves uselessly long, were the Tenebroso's youngest great-nieces, NoreNor and her sister Kyn-oKyn. Even here in the House they followed the latest fashion of carrying dainty handkerchiefs in the Tenebro colors, rather than showing those colors in their clothing. He'd known someone would be coming with

Lady Mar, but he'd assumed it would be one of the lady pages, not these two giggling fools.

He inclined his head, as courtesy required, his lips parted, ready to return their greeting—then felt his ears blaze hot as they passed him with identical curled lips and heads turned away. Until yesterday they had at least acknowledged him, so that snub was not so much for his benefit as it was for the newest member of the House walking slowly behind her distant cousins—but not so far behind that she'd missed the little scene, worst luck. Mar-eMar wore a good gown made of fine wool, but even Gundaron could see that the sleeves were last year's length. Instead of a laced bodice, Mar-eMar wore a tunic like an elderly woman would. A teal-and-black tunic with a thin red stripe on its half-sleeves, no dainty handkerchief for her. He wondered if she realized the clothing the gigglers had picked out for her was hopelessly out of date.

From the whiteness of her face, and the sharpness of the two dots of color on her cheeks, Gundaron suspected that she knew. He swallowed, all doubts suddenly gone.

"Uh, hello, Lady Mar," he said, stepping forward. As he'd hoped, she stopped, hesitant, her eyes flicking forward to the backs of the two sisters who were leaving her behind. When she turned to look at him, however, Mar-eMar's gaze was steady. Her hair was the exact shade of the rich brown velvety moss that grew in the Tenebroso's rock garden, and her eyes were so deep a blue as to be almost black.

"Yes?"

Gundaron blinked. He cleared his throat again. "I am, ah, I'm Gundaron the Scholar. Gundaron of Valdomar."

"Mar-eMar Tenebro," she said inclining her head in a short nod. Gundaron thought she might have relaxed just a little.

"I was wondering—I thought—that is, can you read?"

Instantly, the red spots on her cheeks stood out like paint, and a muscle jerked in the side of her jaw as she clenched her teeth.

"Yes," she hissed, barely moving her lips.

"Oh," he said, in sudden understanding. "No. That's not what I meant at all. I only meant to ask if you'd *like*

something to read." He held out the scroll he'd had under
his left arm. "It's a play, Bartyn's *Maid of the Forest*." When
she didn't move he said. "I have others, if you don't like
Bartyn."

"A play? To read?" Suddenly her eyes seemed even
darker, and she lowered them, looking away from him.

Gundaron swallowed, his throat suddenly thick, and
held out the scroll. She took it without looking up again.
"Thank you." If he hadn't been watching her lips so closely,
he would never have known she'd spoken.

"You're welcome," he said. He held out his hand, indicating the direction of the great hall. "Shall we . . . ?"

He'd get up early tomorrow and clean up his room, he
thought, as she fell into step next to him. He would. Or if
not tomorrow, the next day, for certain.

Mar began to think that the meal was never going to end.
She'd been seated between her two girl cousins, undoubtedly by someone who thought she'd welcome companions
of her own age—and who didn't know Nor and Kyn very
well. They'd come to her room, speaking to her with every
evidence of courtesy which, thanks to Parno Lionsmane's
tutoring, she was able to return in kind. As soon as they'd
dismissed the lady page who'd been waiting when Mar arrived in her room, however, and seen how few and how
poor Mar's possessions were, their remarks had taken on a
different, sharper tone, and Mar began to realize that they
were laughing at her. Mar wasn't going to give them the satisfaction of either crying or losing her temper, however. She
thought about how little Jarla, the youngest of the Weavers'
daughters in Navra, would have acted if she were in this
room, and pasted a smile on her face, made her eyes as wide
as possible and cooed over everything the sisters said.

Strangely, watching them snub the Scholar Gundaron
had made them less intimidating, not more. There was obviously nothing personal in their attitude toward her; they
were snobs pure and simple, and working in the household
of the best Weaver in Navra had taught Mar how to deal
with those.

Under the guise of moving her goblet of watered wine,

Mar managed to look down the table to where the Scholar sat, holding his fork very gracefully in his strong fingers. He was very fair, even his eyebrows showing almost white on his square face, and his eyes were a warm light brown. And obviously he hadn't let the sisters' treatment turn him into a snob and bully in his turn. Mar touched the scroll in the wide pocket of her gown. Perhaps, once she had read it, the Scholar would like to hear about her experiences with Dhulyn Wolfshead, who was also a Scholar, in her way.

There were others in the House besides Gundaron of Valdomar who were not of the same mind as Nor and Kyn. When she'd first come into the hall, Mar had looked around the table and found other intelligent and friendly faces. A young man whose golden hair reminded her of Parno Lionsmane had come to her before he sat down and introduced himself as Dal-eDal. But both he and the lady seated next to him, an older woman named Lan-eLan, were too far away for conversation. Gundaron was seated closer, and seemed to be looking at her every time she glanced his way, but he only smiled, blushed, and lowered his eyes. Eventually, he was taken up with the Kir, Lok-iKol, and didn't glance her way anymore.

Mar forced herself to eat, taking small bites as the Lionsmane had instructed her, not that she could actually taste anything. The last time she'd felt this out of place she'd been six years old, her first meal at the Weavers after her Holding had disintegrated following the fire and the sickness, after the three months she'd spent at the Jaldean Shrine while they found her a foster family.

Where were you people then? Mar thought with a shock that made her put down her fork. Surely the Jaldean priests would have sent word to her House? They'd known who she was; it was one of the reasons it had been easy to foster her. But why hadn't her House sent for her then?

"Sweetest, you don't use a fork for this dessert." Kyn-oKyn's tinkly voice broke into Mar's thoughts. "You use this special spoon."

"Pardon me?" Mar turned to her left, making sure the edge of her napkin caught the plate of custard and cream that had just been put down in front of her, and tipped it neatly into Kyn's lap.

"Oh, dear, I'm so sorry," Mar said, as Kyn squealed and pages ran up with cloths. "How clumsy of me."

✤✤✤

Gundaron looked up with dismay when the commotion at Mar-eMar's end of the table drew the attention of everyone seated, even the Tenebroso herself. Worse, from Gun's point of view, Lok-iKol was now looking at the Lady Mar as well. Gun had been hoping that the Kir had forgotten all about this little cousin, now that they had the far more important Mercenary woman in their hands.

"She has the bowl," Lok-iKol said, when the servants had finished serving the dessert, his eye still fixed on Mar-eMar. "So the pages tell me."

"Oh, the bowl in itself proves nothing," Gun said as casually as he could. He and the Kir had had many conversations like this one—Caids, *how* many? he thought with a sudden and unexpected twist of nausea in his guts as he pushed the thought away—and he hoped he sounded just as objective and disinterested this time. Most of the Marked that he'd located for Lok-iKol over the past eighteen moons or so had been older, some much older than the Lady Mar. *But they probably had families, too.* Gundaron let his eyes fall again to his plate, pretending interest in the dessert as his stomach churned. That thought felt familiar, as if he'd had it often, but . . . he couldn't remember thinking it before.

"There's no doubt she's the right girl," Lok-iKol was saying, stroking his eye patch with his fingertips. Gundaron came to with a start, realizing with some shock that Lok-iKol was standing. He rose with as little fuss as he could manage. Fortunately, he was on the man's blind side, and with any luck his lapse of attention would go unnoticed.

"She's the very image of her grandmother," Lok-iKol continued. "I remember the wedding very well. The Tenebroso had us all attend, even though she was only marrying . . ."

Gundaron waited a moment for the man to finish before he finally gathered his nerve and looked Lok-iKol in the face. What he saw almost made him look away again, but his scholarly habit of investigation was stronger than his fear. The Kir's lower lip had fallen slack, and all the muscles of his face drooped. Only the scarred skin around his left eye was still stiff.

"Lord Kir?" Gundaron put up a hesitant hand; Lok-iKol much preferred not to be touched uninvited. Gun let his hand fall back to his side; he could see that, for all the slackness of the face and mouth, the Kir's eye was sharp and clear.

And focused on Mar.

What does he see? Gundaron thought, that makes him look like this?

As if Lok-iKol could hear his thoughts, the man turned, oh so slowly, to focus his attention on Gundaron himself. In the slackness of his face Lok-iKol's right eye was unnaturally bright, almost as though the man had a fever, and Gundaron could swear that instead of a clear blue, the eye glowed a brilliant jade green. Gundaron parted dry lips, about to call for a page, certain the Kir was having a brain storm. Then the green tint passed, the muscles in Lok-iKol's face returned to normal, and his eye restored to its natural icy blue.

"You were saying?"

Gundaron cleared his throat, throwing a glance around the room. No one else seemed to have noticed anything; everyone's attention was still at the other end of the table, where Nor-eNor had suddenly burst into tears. "I think it unlikely the Lady Mar will give us any interesting information," he said, using the euphemism that allowed them to discuss their work in public. "Situated as she was, she would have had great difficulties in hiding it."

"Nor, in Navra, would she have had reason to, I agree," Lok-iKol said. "In any case, we need be in no hurry where Mar-eMar is concerned. We can examine her at our leisure."

Gundaron nodded slowly, unable to explain, even to himself, his reluctance to let Mar-eMar be questioned by Lok-iKol and the Jaldean Beslyn-Tor the way other suspected Marked had been questioned. He looked down the table again and saw her bow to her cousins and walk up the other side of the long table to pay her respects to the

Tenebroso before leaving the room. He'd have to think of something. Gun stepped back to allow the Lord Dal-eDal to pass between him and the table.

Of course the interrogation of the Mercenary woman would take some time, Gun considered, as he and Lok-iKol followed Lord Dal from the room. And the longer it took, the more time Gun would have to come up with a plan to help Mar-eMar.

❧❧❧

When she awoke, Dhulyn Wolfshead found herself sitting in a heavy carved chair, its knobby, uneven surface tight against her spine. There was a strap around her forehead—though it didn't seem attached to anything—and someone had tied her arms down at elbows *and* wrists, her legs at knees *and* ankles. Not entirely amateurs, then.

Ignoring the throbbing in the back of her head, she tensed first the muscles of her forearms and wrists, then her calves and ankles, without receiving any encouragement. Her bonds were loose enough to let her blood flow, but tight enough to restrict her movements. For certain, not amateurs.

She could tell from the sounds of breathing that there was only one person in the room with her, and that it was not Parno Lionsmane. She let her eyes open the merest fraction.

Standing with his hand on a table a span in front of her was a fair-haired young man in a mixture of Scholar's and nobleman's dress, a short dark blue tunic over black hose instead of brown leggings, heeled shoes instead of leather half boots, and a bright enameled brooch where his Library crest should be. Dhulyn let her eyes open another fraction. The hand she could see looked soft and dirty, his tunic was too tight over his middle, and there was an incipient puffiness to his face. There were *Shora* for Scholars, too, Dhulyn knew, slow motion versions of the Mercenary *Shora,* designed for use by Scholars as exercise. From the look of him, the young man in front of her hadn't practiced any for some time.

The sound of the door latch was followed by booted footsteps moving from wood to carpet, but Dhulyn couldn't see who had entered the room without turning her head.

"My lord Kir, I found her like this."

"As well you did not release her, the order was mine." It was indeed the silky voice she remembered from the Tenebroso's room. She should have known; only the Kir of the House could order two Mercenaries detained.

"I don't understand . . ."

"Did you think that a Mercenary Brother would simply answer our questions because we asked them? Ah, your face tells me that you did. Very well. If you find that, after all, this worries you too greatly, you may leave." Even her limited view showed Dhulyn the boy's negative response. "I thought not. Shall we begin?"

The Scholar moved directly in front of her, leaning forward and peering into her face. Dhulyn opened her eyes. Behind him, the Kir Lok-iKol was sitting with one hip braced on the wooden table; from the look of its heavily carved legs it must be the match of her own chair. She smiled her wolf's smile and the boy edged away from her. He licked his lips and lowered his eyelids.

"The One-eye's name I know," she said to him, "but not yours."

The young man's mouth twisted. He shot a glance at the Kir, but the older man had picked up a goblet from the dark wooden table and was drinking from it. His single eye regarded them over the silver rim of the cup. The Scholar looked back at Dhulyn. His mouth opened and the tip of his tongue sneaked out to poke at his upper lip.

"I am Gundaron," he almost whispered. "From the Scholars' Library of Valdomar."

"I greet you, Scholar Gundaron," she whispered back. "You are very soft and very puffy and the whites of your eyes are dull," Dhulyn said with the greatest innocence and truth. "Are you sure you are of the House of Scholars?"

She grinned when the boy straightened quickly to attention and tightened his lips. He opened his mouth and shut it again. His tongue licked again at his parted lips.

"Best you let me go," she said in her steadiest voice. "Are you certain what you want from me is worth the risk you take?"

The young Scholar shot a quick glance at the Kir. "Are you one of the Espadryn?" he asked her. "Can you see the future?"

Dhulyn drew back her head and knitted her brows, giving him her best confused look to cover the cold sinking of her stomach. It wasn't all that difficult.

"My name is Dhulyn Wolfshead," she said. "I'm called the Scholar. I was schooled by Dorian of the River, the Black Traveler. I have fought with my Brothers at the battles of Sadron, of Arcosa, and Bhexyllia. Parno Lionsmane is my Partner—and where is he by the way?"

Again, the boy glanced over his shoulder at the Kir.

"For the moment safe," the One-eye said, "though if you do not answer our questions, I may be forced to injure him. Or worse."

Dhulyn didn't bother to stifle her snort of laughter.

"We're Mercenaries, you blooded fool. We already know we're going to die. Kill us, don't kill us." She shrugged as well as she could with her arms bound to the chair. "Save your threats for someone you can frighten. Here's a threat for you." She paused to give the word weight. "Pasillon."

One-eye didn't react, but the young Scholar paled even more, and his lips trembled. "Get book boy here to explain it to you."

The Scholar turned to face the one-eyed man.

"My lord Kir," he said. But One-eye didn't even blink. In fact, Dhulyn thought he might have smiled, just for an instant.

"Pasillon is an empty threat, Scholar. The world has changed and no one will come for her, any more than they came for the others."

Others? Dhulyn pressed her lips tight. He had done this to other Brothers? Or just other captives? One-eye directed his words to the young Scholar, but his gaze never left Dhulyn's face. "This one and her companion were seen leaving Gotterang by the north gate. Their Brothers will think that, having been paid for the delivery of the Lady Mar-eMar, they have gone vagabonding."

Dhulyn kept her face impassive. One man, at least, would know exactly where they were, would not be fooled by any stories of the North gate, no matter how well witnessed. But was Alkoryn Pantherclaw likely to knock at the House Door and ask the Steward of Walls for his missing Brothers in time to do them any good? And if they were asking about her Mark, it wasn't just their lives at stake here, and these people might, in fact, be able to do much worse than merely kill her.

"If she will not answer the easy way, then we must try the hard." Lok-iKol stood and revealed a tray of small bottles with waxed stoppers and an apparatus in the shape of a glass funnel with a long, curving spout.

The Scholar's eyes widened. "My lord, you can't—"

"I have said you may leave, Scholar. Though I understood that this time, at least, you had questions of your own."

The boy licked his lips again, looked at the door, looked at Dhulyn's face. There was an armless chair next to the table. As if against his will, he sat down.

The One-eye picked up the funnel and edged around her chair. Dhulyn heard a sharp metallic click, and felt a pressure on the strap around her forehead, increasing as her head was pulled back and down until her throat was exposed, her mouth sagging open, and she could see behind her to where he stood at the mechanism, part crank, part ratchet, to which the strap around her head was attached.

"I advise you to relax," the silken voice said. "I am going to use this tube to deliver some liquid into your stomach. If you struggle, I may miss and get your lungs instead. I advise you to be still."

Briefly, Dhulyn considered struggling anyway, but with her head in this position, she couldn't even keep her teeth clenched tight. It wouldn't be poison—there were faster and easier ways to kill her, if that's all they wanted. While she still lived, she could get out of this—or Parno could get her out. She closed her eyes, made all her muscles relax, and tried to concentrate on what she'd told Mar about the sword swallower.

❊❊❊

Parno always woke up instantly alert. Which was a very lucky thing for the hazel-eyed woman inspecting the binding on his right arm. The heel of Parno's left hand stopped just inches away from the bridge of her nose. The hazel-eyed woman, her hands still on Parno's arm, never moved.

"My Brother, I greet you," she said formally. "I am Fan-ryn Bloodhand. Called the Knife. Schooled by Bettrian Skyborn, the Seeker. I have fought with my Brothers in the north, at Khudren and at Rendia. I fight with my Brother, Thionan Hawkmoon. The smaller arm bone is cracked, my Brother. Careful how you move it."

"I am Parno Lionsmane," Parno said. His voice came out in a stiff croak and he cleared his throat. "Called Chanter. Schooled by Nerysa of Tourin, the Warhammer. I have fought with my Brother Dhulyn Wolfshead at Arcosa and Bhexyllia. Is she with us?" He knew she couldn't be. If she were in this cell, Dhulyn would be in his line of sight. But he had to ask.

"I'm afraid not, Brother," Fanryn said. "With us is my Partner, Thionan Hawkmoon. Also Hernyn Greystone. But the one called Dhulyn the Scholar was not brought here."

Parno nodded. "We'll take it that she lives, then." Mercenary lore always said one Partner would know if the other died, but Parno wasn't sure he believed it. "How long?" he asked.

"A day and most of the second," Fanryn said. "I thought you might wake up when I first bound your arm, but I had no such luck."

Parno began the slow process of sitting up. Bruises and abused muscles had stiffened as he slept. When she saw that he was determined, Fanryn slipped an arm behind him and helped him settle his aching arm in a sling she had ready, evidently torn from her own tunic. He looked around him. Fanryn sat back on her heels, her Partner Thionan hovering over her shoulder. At a guess they were close to his own age. Both women were tall, though not so tall as Dhulyn, both with the catlike grace that comes of good training and better muscles. They might have been sisters, except for their coloring. Fanryn was as golden blond as Parno himself, while Thionan had green eyes and hair close to black. Even so, Parno had known of parents who had produced such disparate offspring.

The third Brother, Hernyn Greystone, was by far the youngest. A lanky boy with mousy brown hair, and a black eye that discolored most of the left side of his face. There was another pallet against the far wall of their prison, but the young Brother sat on the floor with his back to the wall, his arms wrapped around his knees.

The room itself was cool, the walls dry, made of large blocks of undressed stone. What debris there was was surprisingly clean, scraps of straw and chips of wood, as from packing cases roughly opened. Whatever this room had been originally—and the heavy door with the small barred opening suggested a cell—its most recent use appeared to have been as a storage room.

"Well, I've been in worse places," Parno said, grateful for the steadying arm of Fanryn the Knife.

"All this is due to me." Young Hernyn Greystone lifted his head off his knees.Thionan Hawkmoon shut her eyes and made an impatient sound with her tongue.

"You are here through my fault, my Brother," the young man continued in the slightly righteous tone of someone determined to speak the truth, come what may. "You and the Wolfshead. They asked if I knew of a Brother, a tall woman with blood-colored hair. I knew of her, schooled by Dorian of the River as I was myself. So I gave them her name."

Parno winced as he leaned forward. "Who are 'they'? Who asked you these things?"

"Some of the guards here," Hernyn said. "I thought them just curious. I meant no harm."

Thionan made her impatient sound again. "There is always harm in flapping the tongue. I'm surprised you didn't learn *that* with Dorian." Her voice was unexpectedly deep and rough.

"Have done, Thio," Fanryn said. Parno could tell they had tossed this bone back and forth many times already. "Anyone could go to our House and get the same answer. What harm could there be in repeating common knowledge?"

"I should have thought the answer self-evident." Thionan spread her hands out to take in the walls around them. She shook her head and stalked all of three strides across their cell to seat herself on the other cot.

"Wait, wait," Parno said. He tried to pat the air in front

of him in a "calm down" motion, hissed in his breath, and bit down on a grunt. Hernyn buried his face again. Thionan stood up once more but was waved off by her Partner.

"Sit still, my Brother," Fanryn said. "I'll have to bind that more tightly. Ask all the questions you wish, but for the Caids' sake, sit still." Fanryn folded Parno's arm delicately across his stomach and began to tie it in place with strips of the same heavy cloth she'd used as the sling. The immobility of his arm made him more uncomfortable than the pain, but he did not protest. Mercenaries made the best surgeons, for obvious reasons, and he was not fool enough to argue.

"Perhaps you might start at the beginning," he said. "I know, more or less, *how* I got here, if not *why*. What are your stories?"

"Simple enough," Thionan said. "Straightforward guard detail. The Tenebros lost a few guards on caravan last fall. I think the Cloud People, wasn't it?" She waited for her Partner's nod before continuing. "Anyway, it's hard to get good men in the city. If you're in the country now, that's different. You just promote some of your yeoman's children, your farm boys who don't care too much for farming, and there's your new recruit. But here in the city—well, there aren't so many extra pairs of hands here. The children of House servants rarely make good guards, even if they're willing, and as for hiring outsiders—the questions come up, don't they? 'Why did you leave your last place of employment?' People looking for a change aren't the kind you want guarding your walls. And it's too blooded dangerous to take some one else's castoffs."

"So they hire Mercenaries," Parno said. There was nothing new for him in what Thionan was saying. *Let her talk,* he told himself. *Let's get comfortable with one another.* He knew from the battles they'd fought in that he was the Senior Brother present—though that would change when they found Dhulyn—let Thionan give him her report. They would all feel better for a little ordinary discipline.

"So they hire Mercenaries," Thionan agreed. "Specifically myself, my Partner and, not many moons ago, our Brother Hernyn here."

"When did they ask about Dhulyn Wolfshead?"

Fanryn tied off the last strip of cloth and eased Parno back against the cold stone wall.

"They never asked me," Thionan said.

"Or me," Fanryn echoed. "Though, I daresay, we might either of us have answered. In our Brotherhood, your names are well known."

"Aye, you're probably right," Thionan conceded with a shrug. "After all," she added with a neutral look at Hernyn, "what harm?"

Hernyn shrugged and bit his lip. Parno sighed. They didn't have time for the boy's self-pity.

"Come on, man," Parno said. "We're all of us alive and, if we keep our heads, alive's how we'll stay. So snap out it, you sniveling brat!" Parno's sudden roar popped the boy's head up so fast he cracked it against the wall behind him. "We're a council of war here. Stop wringing your hands and come be of some use."

The boy looked at the faces looking at him. Thionan patted the cot beside her. Slowly, with a shy bewilderment, Hernyn rose to his feet and sat down with his Brothers. He gave a sharp nod and squared his shoulders.

"We were on watch one night," he began. "Myself and two others of the guard."

"Which ones?" Fanryn asked.

"The tall dark one with the broken nose, Rofrin, and Neslyn the Fair. Anyway, they were asking about how we live, the Brotherhood. Whether we marry and have children. Neslyn had just spoken for the son of the Steward of Keys, so there was much talk of such things. Everyone thought it would make a fine match—"

"When was this?" Parno said. Best to keep the boy to the point.

"Just over a moon ago," Fanryn said.

"So they were asking about Mercenary customs," the boy continued. "And I tried to explain about Partners." Here he looked at the two women. "How it really isn't a marriage, the way outsiders think, but that it's a kind of . . . of . . ."

"Never mind, Hernyn," Fanryn said, smiling. "We all know what it is." Small wonder outsiders had difficulty understanding Partnering, her glance at Parno and Thionan seemed to say, if even Brothers got tongue-tied and embarrassed trying to explain it.

"And so they asked about famous Brothers, and did I know any and I told them who I'd been Schooled by, Dorian of the River, the Black Traveler, because everyone's heard of him. And I told them about some of the Brothers Dorian's Schooled, Samlind the Nightbird and Pakina Swifthorse, that I thought they might've heard of. And they asked me if I knew a Mercenary *they* had heard about, and Rofrin described Dhulyn Wolfshead."

"They didn't know her name?"

"No, but they described her pretty well, even the scar on her lip. But it was the coloring and the build that they knew best. Tall as a man, they said, very lean, fair skin, gray eyes, blood-colored hair. Good with horses, used maybe a sword, maybe an ax. And I knew her, how could I not, with both of us Schooled in the same place, by the same hand? I told them her name." Parno could hear in Hernyn's voice how flattered the boy had been by their interest, how proud to know someone, even in so indirect a way, who was known to them. Borrowing a little glory from his better-known Brothers.

"So they were looking for her, for Dhulyn Wolfshead? Her, particularly?" Thionan asked, breaking the silence before it could grow awkward.

Parno shook his head slowly. "Barring the scar, they might have been looking for anyone like her, anyone of her Clan—though from what she tells me, the Espadryn are no more. Just our bad luck that she was the one they found."

"But what is it they want her for?" Fanryn asked.

Parno looked his Brothers in the face. "I do not know," he said, lying with the strictest truth.

Thionan slapped her knee and stood up. "I've gone and forgotten," she said. "Here, we've saved some stew for you, against the time you woke up." She reached under the cot and pulled out a flat clay bowl, with another bowl turned over on top of it. "Hernyn ate a portion first to be sure it wasn't drugged."

"Optimistic of you," Parno said, his stomach rumbling.

Good stew it was, too. Plenty of meat, if rather over seasoned for his taste. He'd paid for and eaten much worse any number of times.

"If this is the kind of food they give prisoners," he said aloud, "this must be a very prosperous House."

"Long as we don't take it as a sign they mean to let us live," growled Thionan. Hernyn curled back into the corner of the cot.

"Relax," Fanryn said when she noticed him. "It's not what they've got planned will decide our fates, but what we let happen." She turned back to Parno. "What will Dhulyn Wolfshead do, my Brother? It's my guess they've kept her alone—otherwise why not keep us all together—and if I'm right, she'll have no one to share the food."

"She won't eat," he said.

"But she'll have to drink," Fanryn pointed out. "She can go a long time without food, most of us can. But she'll die quickly without water."

"So they'll drug the water," Parno said.

"And then?"

Parno shook his head slowly, mouth twisted to one side. "That depends." He wished he felt more confident about what he was going to say. *His* Schooling had not included any drug *Shora*. "Dhulyn knows the *Shora* for the fressian drugs," he said. Both the older Brothers looked up at this. Most Brothers chose not to learn those particular *Shora*. As well as being one more way to die in Schooling, it diminished any future enjoyment a person might obtain from drugs. "And the iocain, too; plus one other, I think," Parno told them. "If they give her one of the drugs using those bases, Dhulyn will manage."

"But how can they do this?" Hernyn burst out. "With Pasillon . . ." His voice trailed off under the steady looks of his Brothers.

"Pasillon was long ago," Parno said. "There are no longer thousands of Brothers who would come to avenge us."

"A better question is *why* do this," Fanryn said.

Parno nodded, more in response to the tone than the words.

He'd have liked an answer to that same question, himself, if only to be sure that it wasn't the thing he feared. But what else could it be? Since it wasn't *him* isolated, it had to be Dhulyn they were after. He didn't see how Lok-iKol could have found out, but he could easily see why such a man, a man with political ambition, would want a Seer, if he knew where to put his hands on one.

What else would be worth so much trouble and risk?

"Have you been out of the cell yet?" he asked, more in an attempt to change the path of his own thoughts than because it would be useful to know. When his companions did not answer right away, but exchanged looks out of the corners of their eyes, he feared he did not have to look far for more to worry him.

"Well . . ." Fanryn scratched her elbow. "We were taken unprepared."

"Unprepared? How did that happen?" Parno kept his voice carefully neutral, though from the silence of the other three, he hadn't quite managed to keep the censure from his tone.

Fanryn shrugged. "Have you never taken service in a House, Parno? Things can look a bit different, you know."

"Different, indeed," Parno agreed, "if it means you can end up in a cell without the means of freeing yourselves." He shook his head. No point in being delicate about their feelings. If it came to that, he'd been caught himself. For years, he'd chafed under what he'd always thought to be Dhulyn's unnecessarily strict discipline. After all, he'd been Schooled the same way she had; all Mercenaries were. The three Schools might have different philosophies, as befitted their Schoolers—the nomadic Dorian the Black, the mountain-bred Nerysa Warhammer, Bettrian Skyborn of the western plains—but the *Shora* were the same, as was the Common Rule. If this kind of slackness actually did exist—and three Brothers in a cell without lockpicks seemed to say it did—maybe Dhulyn Wolfshead was less fanatical than he'd thought.

"Hold, Brother," Thionan said, her hands raised, palms out. "We know. 'A lazy Mercenary is a dead Mercenary.' Believe me, we know. That's not a lesson any of us will have to learn again. But telling us what we should have done doesn't get us out of this cell right now."

Parno nodded. The woman was quite right. Recriminations didn't solve problems. "How *did* you get taken, if you don't mind the question?" They all three exchanged another look. "It might be useful for me to know," he added.

"They put something in our food," Hernyn said, glancing at the stew bowl Parno had scraped clean. "It was just after you and Dhulyn Wolfshead came in with the young woman, that same day. Wasn't it?" He turned to the two women.

"It was," Thionan said. "A day, no, two days ago now. It was at the midday meal. They managed it the only way they could have, they put the stuff in the common dish. For the Caids' sake, Parno." Something of what he felt must have appeared on his face. "We've been here fourteen moons. We work for these people. We thought we'd be safe enough if we ate from the same dish as all the rest."

"They must have knocked out seven other people just to get us," Fanryn pointed out.

"And to confuse things," Parno spoke his thought aloud. "No one could tell where you had gone or why."

"True," said Thionan. "But according to the keeper who was talking to us before he was told to hold his tongue, one of the people at table with us didn't get up. I don't know what they used on us—Fan says something called cyantrine—but apparently they risked poisoning their own people, just to make sure they had us."

"What else could they do?" Parno said. "You would have known we never came out." All four Brothers looked at each other. The word Pasillon went unspoken, unneeded.

"*You'll* get us out, though. Right, Parno?" Hernyn asked. Parno saw the boy had color in his face and had lost his hangdog expression. Though there was still something doglike and devoted in his eyes. At least he seemed to have taken Parno's advice to heart, and was putting his indiscretions behind him.

"Don't see why not," Parno said. "But let's not rush ourselves. Getting out of the cell is one thing—out of the House another. I can't leave without my Partner, so my first concern is to find her. Are we agreed?"

Fanryn nodded. "You're Senior, Parno, so even if we didn't agree—"

"Which we do—" Thionan cut in.

"Wonderful," Parno smiled back. "Help me get my boots off."

Eight

"SO, THIS IS WHAT you did when you were living in Navra?"

Mar raised her head from the poem she was copying. She couldn't tell which of her two new cousins had spoken. Their voices were very much alike, and now they both wore the identical wide-eyed look of innocent interest. The three of them were sitting on stone benches set around a stone table topped with small colored tiles that formed a picture of a flowering tree. The morning sun was bright, the garden protected, and here against the south wall it was warm enough for cloaks to be laid aside. A hard embroidered cushion protected her from the cold stone she sat on.

The question sounded polite enough, but in the last two days Mar had answered many questions that had hidden stings in their tails. Still, it was easier to answer with the truth.

"No," she said, dipping the end of her pen—a beautiful thing, carved from a single piece of inglera bone, with a real gold point fitted on the end—into the marble inkwell. "The Weavers didn't own any books for reading. I kept the accounts for their business. You know," she added, determined not to let them make her feel ashamed, "lists of inventory, of customers, and orders, estimates for work, records of bills. That kind of thing."

"But why didn't the clerk do this work?"

There it was, the sidewise glance from one set of blue

eyes to the other as Nor-eNor and Kyn-oKyn exchanged a not-so-private look.

"I *was* the clerk." Mar looked back at her work just in time to prevent a large drop of ink from falling to the tiled tabletop. She bit the inside of her bottom lip. At the Weavers' house, it would have been a serious and costly offense to waste ink and spoil table, paper, or parchment. Here, it would probably go unnoticed. But Mar wasn't used to being here, copying poems instead of doing accounts.

"Ohhh." Nor's tone of enlightenment rang archly false. "So these weavers weren't working for *you, you* were working for *them*!"

"I've explained it several times," Mar said as innocently as the growing lump of unhappiness in her throat would let her. "Was I speaking too quickly?" She moved her eyes back to her work and kept them there until the two girls had gone off, their noses in the air.

The knots of tension in Mar's shoulders loosened a little. Her moments of solitude had been few and far between since she'd been whisked out of the presence of the Tenebroso—and away, incidentally, from her friends the Mercenary Brothers—and rushed away to bathe and dress properly in time for the midday meal. Her own clothes had been taken away to be "laundered," and she'd since had to be very insistent to convince the lady page assigned to help her that she wanted the clothes back. She wasn't sure herself why she wanted the clothing, worn and out of place here as it was; she'd only known that she'd wanted something familiar around her. As for her new clothes, Mar was still not used to the sheer *amount* of them. The hose, the chemise, the long gown with close-fitting sleeves covered by the loose tunic in the House colors that was so clearly unfashionable when compared to the tighter bodices of Nor and Kyn.

Mar wrote three careful words on the parchment in front of her. She wished she didn't mind looking poor and frowsy next to the glittering sisters . . . but she did. Would it scandalize the lady page even more if she were to ask for needles and thread with which to stitch her clothes into a more up-to-date look? Or was that a task some other servant was supposed to do for her? Mar sighed. This was an area which Parno Lionsmane hadn't touched on.

"Those two couldn't be more ignorant and foolish if they took lessons, and I hope you don't let them bother you more than you can help."

Mar jumped, startled into looking directly at the older woman sitting on the far end of the bench, where the sunlight shone on the embroidery she held in her lap. Mar had forgotten that Lan-eLan was even there. A widowed cousin-by-marriage Mar had been told, Lan was older than herself, but still young, small, and pretty, with smooth olive skin and thick dark hair.

"The Weavers were all I had," Mar said. "I'm not ashamed of them."

"If you were, you'd be even more foolish and more ignorant than those two." Lan snipped off a hanging thread with a tiny pair of gold-handled scissors. "Do you think the Tenebroso can't read and write? Can't add up figures? Can you imagine how those two are going to be cheated by their servants, if we're ever lucky enough to find Households for the conceited little half-wits?" Lan-eLan turned her embroidery over and frowned at it. "They wouldn't know accounts from a country dance."

Mar could feel her mouth hanging open with shock. Lan-eLan looked up and smiled, and suddenly Mar burst out laughing.

"Is there anything else worrying you, my dear?" Lan asked when the laughter had finally died away. "Anything important, I mean?"

Mar smiled at her older cousin. Somehow Lan's sweet-voiced "my dear" was better than her formal name, but not as warm and comfortable as the Wolfshead's gruff "my Dove." Which reminded Mar of one of her worries.

"I didn't get a real chance to say good-bye to the Mercenary Brothers who brought me here, and to thank them," Mar said. "I was with them almost a moon, and they were dismissed so quickly . . ." Mar hesitated to ask anything directly. So far, at least, no further mention had been made of her part in bringing Dhulyn Wolfshead and Parno Lionsmane to Gotterang. Was it possible they were still in the House?

Lan's dark brows drew together as she thought, head on one side. "Oh, yes, I remember seeing them. Most impressive,

I must say, particularly the Outlander woman. I think they had a short interview with the Kir, but then they left." Lan smiled, turning her attention back to the embroidery in her lap. "Perhaps you could send a message to their House. It might catch them before they take their next assignment."

Mar nodded, conscious of an unexpected disappointment; she hadn't realized how much she was counting on their still being in the House. But either the Mercenaries hadn't been wanted after all, or they'd turned down whatever work the Kir had offered them. *No point in us all being stuck here.* Mar blinked, half surprised and half frightened by a feeling she hadn't admitted before.

"You still look a touch worried, Mar. Are you sure there isn't anything else?"

"There is something." Mar took a deep breath and looked directly at Lan. "I know the Tenebroso is . . . is very busy," Mar substituted for the more honest but less tactful "very old" she'd been about to say. "But when would it be right to ask about the restoration of my Holding? And who should I ask? I don't even know if the land still belongs to the Family, or . . ." Mar let her question trail away.

The older woman had recovered her poise very quickly, but not before Mar had seen the look that crossed Lan's face.

"Well, it would be the Kir you should ask, though Dal-eDal handles a great deal of the House business for him just lately," Lan said with her warm smile. "But you know what my advice is? Let it be for now, give yourself a chance to settle in. After all, it's a great honor to be received in the House, and you don't want to look unappreciative. I know you don't feel so at the moment, but given the chance you might come to like it here, and you might prefer, as I did, to remain a part of this House."

"Of course," Mar cleared her throat and forced her lips into a smile to match Lan's. "That's very sensible. I thank you for your counsel."

And all was as it should be. Except that Mar had seen how Lan's face had changed, how surprised she'd been by Mar's question. Obviously, Lan-eLan had absolutely no idea what Mar was talking about.

When a servant came to call them in to luncheon, Mar

was able to smile pleasantly, rise, and follow her cousin-by-marriage into the House. Not at all as if her whole world had just been turned upside down.

THE TALL THIN MAN STANDS BEFORE HIS MIRROR THAT IS NOT A MIRROR. THIS TIME IT SHOWS HIS REFLECTION. HIS HAIR IS LONG AND UNKEMPT. IT APPEARS HE HAS NOT SHAVED IN MANY DAYS, NOR EATEN. HIS EYES ARE NO LONGER THE COLOR OF OLD ICE, BUT THE COOL GREEN OF JADESTONE. HE HAS THE SAME LONG SWORD IN HIS HANDS AND HE CUTS DOWNWARD, SLASHING AT HIS IMAGE IN THE MIRROR FRAME. IT IS AS IF HE LOOKS AT HIS REFLECTION IN A POOL OF WATER. THE SWORD PASSES THROUGH IT AND LEAVES IT RIPPLING AND DANCING UNTIL IT SETTLES AGAIN.

THE MAN SLASHES AT HIS IMAGE AGAIN AND AGAIN. . . .

A CROWDED STREET, A HOUSE WITH A SQUARE TOWER. PEOPLE WEARING CRESTS OF TEAL AND BLACK ARE KILLING GUARDS DRESSED IN DARK RED. THE BLOOD LOOKS BLACK IN THE MOONLIGHT. . . .

A GOLDEN-HAIRED CHILD IS RUNNING WITH A SHORT SWORD IN HIS HAND. HE TRIPS OVER HIS DOG AND CUTS HIS CHIN. . . .

Fresnoyn was the thought that chased the Vision through her head and followed her mind to consciousness.

From the taste in the back of her throat, and the way the inside of her head felt like a very large space, the drug One-eye had given her was fresnoyn. But from the way her hands and feet seemed so remote, the basis of the mixture was poppy, so perhaps there was not so very much fresnoyn in the mix. She began taking long slow breaths. Breathing alone would not clear the drug from her body as quickly as sleep or heavy exercise, but it would help somewhat.

Fresnoyn *was* a truth drug, and Dhulyn wondered how the Kir had managed to obtain a supply. Made from the mold which grew on the bark of a particular tree in the rain forests of the lands across the eastern sea, fresnoyn was ruinously expensive. She herself had trained with it twice while studying the poison *Shora*. She only hoped she could remember what she had been taught. Even though Dorian the Black had been given his particular supply of fresnoyn, he could not afford to waste any in extra training.

Dhulyn continued to breath deeply and slowly, and in her mind began a chant which, if she remembered it correctly, was intended to help channel her thoughts. She would have to answer with the truth, otherwise her skin would flush a deep red as the drug reacted to the lie, but clarity of thought would enable her to answer with the truth she chose.

"Dhulyn Wolfshead." The silky voice had already said her name twice.

Dhulyn opened her eyes. There he was, right in front of her, the one-eyed son of a diseased inglera.

She smiled her wolf's smile. One-eye pulled his head back. Dhulyn laughed. That was fun. She resumed her measured breathing. She could not really afford such tricks.

"Wolfshead," he said. "Will any of your Brothers come for you?"

She considered the question for the space of a slow breath.

"Parno Lionsmane will come," she said. That was easy, no more than the real truth.

"Parno Lionsmane is captive and cannot rescue you," the Scholar said. "Will someone else come for you?"

"Yes," she said, responding to the question and not the statement. "Parno will come," she repeated. "He will always come." That should do them, she thought, watching them exchange looks. What's the best lie? A truth that won't be believed.

One-eye nodded at the Scholar. "You see? So much for your fears of Pasillon." The boy sat on the edge of the armless chair. His hands were at his mouth. Clearly, he was regretting his decision to stay, but even as she watched, his hands fell to his knees, and he straightened in his chair. His face relaxed, the frown of concentration melting away as his features grew slack, and his eyes glowed a soft jade green.

There, she thought, the hairs on her arms and the back of her neck rising, sure she was seeing what Parno had seen. Green eyes again. *What makes your eyes so green, little Scholar?*

One-eye had already turned back without, Dhulyn was certain, seeing what she had seen. She settled her face to show no reaction.

"Who are you?" he said.

Dhulyn smiled as softly as she could. There was only one answer to this. Clearly, they must have tried this only on the unSchooled, otherwise they would have learned to ask better questions. "I am Dhulyn Wolfshead the Scholar—" She stopped at the man's abrupt gesture.

"And before?" One-eye leaned forward again in his eagerness.

Dhulyn drew her eyebrows together and pretended to have difficulty focusing on the Kir. Again, this one was easy. For Mercenaries there was nothing "before"—or shouldn't be; she dragged her thoughts away from Parno. They had no history before they joined the Brotherhood, no country, no House, no family. When they received their badges, their real lives began. This was their truth.

"There is no 'before,'" she said.

"What was your tribe?"

Now she did smile. "I am Dhulyn Wolfshead," she repeated. "Called the Scholar—"

She saw his arm tense and braced herself for the blow, but One-eye did not actually raise his hand.

"The Scholar tells me you are Espadryni. What the common folk call the Red Horsemen."

It was not a question, so Dhulyn did not have to answer.

"What do you remember of that tribe?"

Wrong question, Dhulyn thought as she shook her head and then pretended she couldn't stop shaking it. All too easily done. Maybe the drugs were more effective than she'd thought.

"Nothing," she said. Again the strict truth—if not all of it. She remembered sitting astride behind her father on the back of his horse. *A woman wearing leathers and furs, with her face completely wrapped in cloths, only her ice-gray eyes showing, leaning over to me from her own mount, adjusting the scarf around my face. That woman is my mother, that I know, but I never remember her face, only her eyes, peeping out between the wrappings of scarves. And never anything more of my father than his wide back in front of me. Of the tribe, nothing. Just my mother's eyes, the color of ice. But warm, very warm.* She shook herself. But of her band nothing, of her tribe, nothing. And Lok-iKol, Kir of House Tenebro, had asked no questions about her family.

"I think you people must be insane," she heard herself say in a bright friendly voice. One-eye glanced at the boy behind him but without noticing anything.

"The eighth book of the *Rhonis* tells of a city named Shpadrajh, so old that the book claims it dates to the time of the Caids."

Dhulyn made a rude noise with her lips. "No one's read the *Rhonis*," she said. "Are you telling me *you've* read the *Rhonis*? There's only—what, two copies of the *Rhonis* in the whole world." What were they trying to prove?

"One of those copies is at Valdomar."

"Really?" Dhulyn's thoughts skittered down a path all their own. "Would I be able to come there and read it?"

Lok-iKol smiled. "Of course. If you answer our questions thoroughly, I'm sure I'd be able to arrange that."

"What questions," Dhulyn said, twisting her head and squinting her eyes at the green-eyed Scholar. "Blood, old One-eye's ugly, isn't he? I mean, uglier than a one-eyed person generally is, don't you think? Listen, I've seen some ugly one-eyed people in my time, but really . . . What? Did I speak aloud?" Dhulyn grinned. "Sorry, my lord Kir. But really, you must own a mirror. I'm not telling you anything you don't already know, am I? And you're the Kir of a High Noble House, for blood's sake—it's not like you're going to have any trouble getting lovers, is it? Oh, all right." Seeing that she'd made the impression she wished to make, she stopped talking. This would teach them to give her drugs. Give her a headache, would they? "Sorry, what was the question?"

"Spadrajh was a city of Seers. Tall, red-haired people. Lords of Clans and Households, Great Houses, even Tarkins, even the High Kings when they still ruled in the north came to Shpadrajh or sent their First Children to speak for them, all asking for a glimpse of the future."

"No," Dhulyn said, throwing as much skepticism into her voice as she could. "Where are they, then?"

"The Seers began to tell of a coming plague and finally

an ambassador of Kadrath came to find the city deserted, the Halls of Sight empty. Shpadrajh was no more. All felt that the plague they had spoken of had finally come upon them. But our Scholar here does not think so." The One-eye gestured behind him without turning. "There is no plague that doesn't leave bodies, bones, behind. He thinks they Saw something else and fled before it could destroy them. The first mention of your tribe, the Espadryni, comes after this time. The Shpadrajha had been nomads in their time, and it is his theory that when the thing they called the plague neared, the Shpadrajha abandoned their urban lives and returned to a wandering, reclusive existence. And so they survived until the present day, as the Espadryni."

The space in Dhulyn's head was suddenly larger, more echoey and very, very cold. And her hands and feet were cold, too, and she hoped her mouth would freeze solid before they asked her again the question she saw coming.

THE SCHOLAR GUNDARON IS STANDING OFF TO HER LEFT, WATCHING, BROWN EYES DARK WITH FEAR AND LINES OF HORROR ON HIS FACE. THE SCHOLAR GUNDARON IS AT THE DOOR, PULLING AT THE LATCH, BUT HIS HANDS PASS THROUGH THE MECHANISM WITHOUT TOUCHING ANYTHING AND THE DOOR REMAINS CLOSED. THE SCHOLAR GUNDARON IS SITTING IN HIS CHAIR, LEANING FORWARD WITH HIS JADE-GREEN EYES FOCUSED ON HER, HUNGER IN HIS FACE. THE GUNDARON AT THE DOOR LOOKS OVER HIS SHOULDER, SEES THE ONE IN THE CHAIR, AND REDOUBLES HIS EFFORTS TO OPEN THE DOOR. . . .

THE SCHOLAR GUNDARON, THIN AND DRAWN, STANDS WITH THE LITTLE DOVE, SHOULDER TO SHOULDER. THEY ARE LOOKING DOWN AT THE TOP OF A TABLE, BUT DHULYN CAN'T SEE WHAT THEY LOOK AT. A MAP? A BOOK? MAR MAY BE CRYING.

Dhulyn blinked and took in a ragged breath of air. Where was Mar? Hadn't she seen the little Dove just now? But the Scholar was looking heavier again, and Mar was nowhere in the room. What had just happened?

One-eye leaned toward her again, his knuckly hands with their long fingers grasping the back of her chair to either side of her head. Leaned forward until his face was only a few fingerwidths from hers. Dhulyn could see the hairs of his beard growing in crookedly where his face was scarred. Smell wine on his breath.

"I think you can see the future, what do you think?"

Dhulyn wanted to laugh, but was afraid it would not sound real. "I think you're foolish and stupid, too, as well as ugly. Get your Scholar to read less and think more." She had shaken her head. "If I could see the future, how could you have captured me? Why did I walk into this trap?"

She looked up to see One-eye still looking at her, the muscles in his face, still moving to focus two eyes, gave him a most peculiar squint. *Here it comes,* she thought.

"Can you see the future, little wolf? Can you?"

He was close enough to her. And she had an answer to give him. A true answer. "I can See your death," she said finally, smiling her wolf's smile. "But what does that prove?"

He reached out his left hand and stroked her cheek with the back of his fingers. Dhulyn opened her mouth to scream as images blasted their way into her mind.

❦❦❦

SHE SEES AN OLD DOG, PUSHING WITH HIS NOSE AT HIS MASTER'S SLACK HAND. THE DOG IS WHINING. HIS MASTER, A BEAUTIFUL MAN WITH LARGE BLUE EYES IS SPRAWLED ACROSS THE TABLE, ONE ARM FLUNG STRAIGHT OUT, HIS CHEEK RESTING ON THE ARM. HIS BEAUTY IS MARRED BY DARK DISCOLORATIONS IN HIS FACE, POINTS OF RED IN THE WHITES OF HIS EYES. THOSE EYES ARE WIDE OPEN, STARING, THE PUPILS TINY POINTS OF BLACK. THERE'S FOAM DRYING ON HIS LIPS, AND A LINE OF BRIGHT YELLOW DROOL HANGS FROM THE EDGE OF HIS MOUTH AND TOUCHES THE TABLE. THE DOG WHINES AND PUSHES AT HIS HAND AGAIN.

A PLATE OF KIDNEYS CONGEALING IN SAUCE SITS ON THE TABLE, JUST TO THE MAN'S RIGHT. THERE IS A FORK LYING WHERE IT FELL FROM THE MAN'S FINGERS, AND A PIECE OF BREAD BROKEN OFF FROM A SMALL LOAF HAS FALLEN TO THE FLOOR. AFTER NUDGING THE MAN'S HAND ONCE MORE, THE DOG EATS THE BREAD.

THE DEAD MAN WEARS THE DARK RED SURCOTTE AND THE THIN GOLD CIRCLET AROUND HIS BROWS THAT MARKS HIM FOR THE TARKIN OF IMRION. . . .

***

SEVEN WOMEN WITH BLOOD-RED HAIR STAND IN A CIRCLE SINGING. DHULYN BELIEVES SHE WOULD RECOGNIZE THE TUNE, BUT SHE CANNOT HEAR ANY SOUND. THEY HOLD EACH OTHER'S HANDS AND DANCE, FIRST ONE WAY, THEN THE OTHER, CALLING OUT THE STEPS, ENDING WITH A CLAP AND STILLNESS ONCE AGAIN. THE TALLEST WOMAN LOOKS UP, RIGHT INTO DHULYN'S EYES, AND SAYS HER NAME. . . .

THE CARNELIAN THRONE. A ONE-EYED MAN SITS ON IT, HIS DARK RED SURCOAT OVER HIS TEAL-AND-BLACK CLOTHES. HE TURNS THE THIN GOLD CIRCLET AROUND IN HIS FINGERS, THEN REACHES UP TO TOUCH HIS EYE PATCH. BEHIND HIM STANDS A MUCH OLDER MAN IN RED WITH A DARK BROWN CLOAK, CASTING A GREEN SHADOW. THE MAN ON THE THRONE CASTS A GREEN SHADOW HIMSELF. HE LOOKS UP FROM THE CIRCLET IN HIS FINGERS AND LOOKS RIGHT AT HER, HIS EYE GLOWING A SOFT JADE GREEN. HIS EYES GLOWING GREEN. SHE TURNS TO RUN FROM THE ROOM, BUT THERE IS NO HERE, NO THERE TO RUN TO. . . .

A CLOUDMAN WITH A TATTOOED FACE LEANS AGAINST A STONE PARAPET AND LOOKS INTO THE SKY. . . .

SHE BEARS TWO SWORDS, THE LONGER IN HER RIGHT HAND. SHE PARRIES A BLOW WITH THE LEFT, CIRCLING AND PULLING HER OPPONENT'S SWORD FROM HIS GRASP AS SHE STEPS FORWARD, THRUSTING HER LONGER SWORD THROUGH HIS BODY WITH THE WEIGHT OF HER OWN BEHIND IT. THE GREEN FADES FROM HIS ONE EYE AS HE FALLS TO HIS KNEES.

Nine

MAR HAD LEARNED long ago that if you walked with a purpose, and nodded at the people you passed, everyone who saw you assumed you had business, and let you go without comment. She found that this was as true in Tenebro House as it had been in the streets of Navra. So far, none of the people in the passages, most wearing the livery of servants or guards, had done more than return her nods, and many not even that much. If anyone asked her, she planned to say she was looking for the Scholar to return his play, and she had it in her gown pocket for proof. But also in that pocket was a piece of drawing chalk she had pilfered from a box in Lan-eLan's rooms after luncheon.

Every now and then she would make sure no one was looking, and chalk a mark low on the wall, pattern marks like weavers used to record how a pattern had been woven. Meaningless to anyone else, they would tell Mar which passages led toward exits, and which deeper into the House.

She didn't have a plan, exactly, but Dhulyn Wolfshead had once said that you should always be sure of the way out.

She had just backtracked out of a passage that led only to bedrooms and was trying another turning when she saw there was someone sitting in the seat fitted into the window embrasure halfway up the passage on the right. She fixed a modest smile on her lips and prepared to stride purposefully by when recognition made her slow her steps.

"Gundaron," she said, her heart beating faster. He was leaning forward, his elbows on his knees, staring at his clasped hands. He didn't look up.

"Scholar." Mar raised a tentative hand to touch him on the shoulder. He shuddered and straightened, showing her a pale face with dark circles under the eyes.

Gundaron blinked, for a moment not recognizing the silhouette, backlit by the branched candlesticks farther down the passage. *Scholar,* he thought, shaking his head and blinking again to clear the fog from his brain. This was Mar-eMar. He straightened. Had she asked him a question?

Mar motioned with her hand and Gundaron shifted over. The window seat was more than wide enough for them to share.

"I said, are you all right? You look very pale."

"I don't know," he glanced around. "I must have dozed off. I . . . I don't remember."

"Did you hit your head? What's the last thing you *do* remember?"

"Pasillon." The word popped out of his mouth before he could stop it. "Oh, *Caids,*" he said, as the scene in the Kir's workroom came spilling into his mind. What was he doing sitting here? How did he get here? The light spun, and he clutched at the hand Mar had placed on his arm to steady himself.

"Who is Pasillon?"

Could he tell her? Certainly he had to give her some reason for the fear he saw mirrored in her face.

"Not a who, a what. When I was a boy, in the Library at Valdomar, I used to sneak downstairs, late at night when I was supposed to be asleep, to read the books we weren't old enough to read yet." He swallowed, and a smile's ghost rested a moment on his lips. "There was one in particular, the *Book of Gabrian,* that told of Pasillon."

Mar-eMar settled herself, half-turned toward him, her face steady and unsmiling.

"It's a plain," he said. "Far to the west of here and south, in the country that's now Lebmuin. The plain has another name now, but when it was Pasillon, there was a great battle there, between two city-states, Tragon and Conchabar. It was Tragon that won."

"I've never heard of them."

"Practically no one has, but that's not why people

remember Pasillon." Gundaron twisted to face her. "There were Mercenary Brothers on both sides—"

"*Both* sides?"

"They're like Scholars, the Brotherhood, free of all countries, citizens of the world. And during battle—" All at once Gundaron was back in his midnight Library, shivering in the cold. Mar took his hands in hers and began chafing them. "During battle they'll kill each other, if they come upon other Mercenaries on the opposing side. They think it's the best way to die, at the hands of one of their own."

Mar drew down her brows, nodding. "Yes, that's what they would think."

Gundaron took a deep breath and released it slowly. He could feel sweat on his upper lip. He freed his hands from hers and rubbed them on the smooth cloth of his hose.

"That day, the day of the battle at Pasillon, the lord of Tragon had been killed, or maybe it was his son—I only read *Gabrian* that one time, so I'm not sure. But, with this special grievance, the Tragoni fought harder and won." Gundaron looked closely into Mar's face, searching for the glimmer that showed she understood. "But their loss made it a sour victory. And the taste of it left them angry, so they chose to take no prisoners. The Tragoni killed the Conchabari as they fled, allowing no one to surrender."

"Oh, no." Mar raised her shoulders and drew her sleeves down over her hands.

"But the Brotherhood, the Mercenaries, they had no reason to flee. Their Common Rule says that those who fight on the losing side submit to the victors and are ransomed by their own Brothers. But not that day. Not at Pasillon. Blinded by victory, enraged by its cost, the Tragoni pursued their fleeing enemy and fell upon any who stood in their way. They did not see why a Mercenary badge should buy someone's life.

"They'd forgotten they had Mercenaries on their own side. And those men and women were quick to come to the aid of their Brothers. And then the real battle of Pasillon began." Gundaron leaned back against the cold stone embrasure, eyes closed, looking back at the boy he had been, reading an exciting and forbidden book by candlelight when he should have been in bed.

"Exhausted, outnumbered," he went on, "some injured, forty or fifty Mercenaries stood against more than five hundred. *Gabrian* describes how they stood back-to-back on a rise of ground and cut down wave after wave of enraged Tragoni until finally, long hours later, when the sun had set, three injured Brothers crept off in the darkness, leaving the rest to cover their escape. And finally, finally, the last Mercenary fell. The victors—the few Tragoni who were left, looked about them and shook their heads, thanking their gods that it was over."

Gundaron blinked, and focused on Mar once more. Her eyes were wide, whites showing all around, and the corners of her mouth were turned down.

"Except it wasn't over." His voice dropped to a whisper. "The army of Tragon continued to die after that day. Not everyone, just the men who were there that day. Just the men who had killed Mercenaries. And the officers who did not stop them. And the lords who gave orders to the officers.

"People spoke of bad luck and the Curse of Pasillon, and many went to Healers and Finders and Menders, even Jaldean shrines, since they were soldiers, to see if the Sleeping God would cleanse them. The Healers saw no illness, the Finders found no poisons, the Menders nothing broken, and the Sleeping God slept on. But many shrines housed Scholars, and the Scholars saw that this was the work of the Brotherhood."

"I don't understand."

"Don't you see? It was the Mercenaries, the Brothers who escaped. They carried the story back to their Houses, and their Schools, and the Brotherhood acted, to teach everyone in the world that mistreated and betrayed Mercenaries would be avenged." He looked away. "Will be. Still will be."

"No, I understood that part. I don't understand what made you think of all this now? Why you're so frightened."

He looked at her, licked his dry lips. Realizing that he could not tell her. Could not tell her of the look on Dhulyn Wolfshead's face and the word Pasillon on her lips— Gundaron pressed his clasped hands between his knees to steady them.

"It was seeing the Mercenaries," he said finally. "Not the tame ones who live here and guard the walls, but the strange ones, *your* Mercenaries. They made me think of it and I had a nightmare . . ."

The girl pressed her lips together, frowning. "*Something else has happened.*"

Gundaron looked down at his hands, suddenly clenched into fists without his even realizing it. What else happened? He'd been in the Kir's workroom and Dhulyn Wolfshead had said "Pasillon," and then . . . and then. Nothing.

He looked at Mar-eMar. His hands were shaking.

"Nothing," he said. "There's nothing there." He pitched forward as the yawning blackness swallowed him again.

❧

Dal-eDal shook the box of vera tiles, listening with half an ear to the rattle, spilled them onto the tabletop, and began laying them out in the Tarkin's Cross, one of the old patterns, the Seer's patterns. As a child he'd wished for the Sight, sometimes even pretended he had it, and he'd brought his box of tiles with him when he was summoned to Tenebro House on the death of his parents. If he'd been the Seer he'd pretended to be, would he be sitting now in his own Household, he wondered, his mother and father still alive? His sisters nearby instead of married away, and himself at home instead of a Steward he knew only through the man's reports. But perhaps then he'd have been summoned to Gotterang after all, like little Cousin Mar, who might yet find herself in one of Lok-iKol's windowless rooms, on the receiving end of uncomfortable questions, with the chance of an unwanted introduction to a highly-placed Jaldean staring her in the face.

While her cousin Dal-eDal sat in his room and played vera with himself.

Dal didn't even bother to sweep the tiles back into their box when a knock sounded at the door.

"Come," he said, looking up from the pattern on the table and smiling his inquiry at the man-at-arms who came in.

"I don't know how you knew it, my lord, but you're right. The upper armory's been unlocked and restocked, though nothing's missing from the lower armory, and nothing's been delivered from outside so far as I can find out."

Dal tapped the tabletop with the tile in his hand, keeping his face impassive. "And the other matter?"

"I did as you told me, my lord, and asked in the kitchens. The Scholar and the Kir *are* using the big workroom, leastways food and drink have been taken there, and up to the small room in the north tower as well. But there's something else, my lord. Lights and braziers have been taken down to the western subcellar, the wine rooms."

Dal lifted his eyebrows, but slowly, careful to keep his excitement off his face. Lights to the wine rooms were one thing, but lights and *heat*? He sat back in his chair. Wine rooms indeed. Cells didn't stop being cells because you called them wine rooms. Light and heat down there, that meant new prisoners in the old cells. And new, unaccounted-for weapons in the armory? That gave him an idea of who the prisoners were.

If he was right, if the Mercenaries were still in the House—what, if anything, was he going to do about it?

He knew what his father would have done, if Lok-iKol had left Dal's father alive to do anything. Mil-eMil would have gone straight to the nearest Mercenary House with his tale of kidnapping and forced imprisonment. And not because he wanted to remove an obstacle to his own ambition—he'd had none, though Lok-iKol had never believed it—but to protect the House. And maybe, said the voice of the little boy who still lived inside Dal, maybe just because it was the right thing to do.

What would my father do? he thought. Something more than stand back collecting information, that was certain. And what had happened to make him think of his father just now?

"Thank you, Juslyn, you've done well. Ask the Steward of Walls to be good enough to join me in the upper armory at his earliest convenience. I require his advice for a new sword."

"Very good, my lord. Thank you, my lord." The man-at-arms bowed his way out of the room, his crooked teeth showing in his wide grin.

Dal turned over the tile he'd set down and looked at it.

The picture on its face was tiny, but unmistakable. A Mercenary of Swords. He sat up straight, concentrating on the tile. There *had* been something. Something that had made him think for a split second of his father. When he'd led the two Mercenaries through the halls to the trap point, something—a shiver of familiarity—about the man Lionsmane had triggered a thought, a memory. What had it been? He frowned, placed the Mercenary of Swords back into the olive-wood box and began sliding the others into his palm. No time to chase down stray thoughts now.

He closed the lid of the olive-wood box with a snap.

And if his one-eyed cousin *was* keeping four Mercenary Brothers in a cell and one in a nice room—when she wasn't tied to a chair—what, precisely, could Dal do about it now?

A brisk knock, and Lan-eLan entered with a click of high heels. She shut the door behind her, leaning against the knob.

"Why knock if you don't wait for me to say 'enter'?" Dal said, good training bringing him to his feet. As usual, she ignored him. They'd long ago come to an understanding; a free exchange of information between them helped them both.

"Mar-eMar was told she'd get her lands back."

Dal sat slowly, holding the edge of the table like an old man.

Lan nodded, a stiff smile on her lips. "She wondered, as innocent as you please, should she ask about it now or wait. I told her she should wait, of course, or speak to you."

"Sound advice, in any case. Though she'd wait a long time. Do we even own the lands still?" Dal shook his head. It felt strange to know that once upon a time he'd been this naive himself. "Did she say what she'd done to expect this gift?"

"I gave her every chance to tell me," Lan said, spreading her hands wide. "But the moment passed. She must have been asked for *something* . . ."

Dal thought he knew what Mar-eMar had been asked for—and what she'd brought. But *why*?

"I'll find a chance to speak to her myself," he said. "See what I can get from her." Lan nodded and left as abruptly as she'd entered.

What was so important about these Mercenaries? Dal pushed his chair back from the table, stood, and picked up his box of tiles. He'd asked the Steward of Walls to meet him, and he'd better go. He could give the good Walls a nudge in the right direction. With luck, this affair might become his chance to finally do what his father had asked of him. Avenge his death. Stay alive himself.

Maybe the Mercenary Brothers would solve his problems for him.

❧❧❧

"You sent for me, my lord?" Karlyn-Tan waited in the doorway of the old armory, letting his eyes adjust to the light of the oil lamps within the room, so much darker than the sunlight streaming into the passageway from slits high in the stone walls.

Dal-eDal looked up from the dagger he was examining. "We're alone, Karlyn, or will be if you shut the door."

Karlyn took a step forward and let the oaken door, reinforced with strips of iron, swing shut behind him. Sturdy wooden shelves lined the walls, and low tables divided the floor space into long sections with clear pathways leading toward the far end of the room. A fine layer of dust covered innumerable pieces of weaponry laid out in orderly rows, everything from a gilded mace to a dagger small enough to fit in a glove. Many pieces were ceremonial, or so jeweled as to be almost useless.

"What's this Juslyn tells me about a new sword? Are you sure you don't want one new-forged?"

"I'm afraid I misled Juslyn slightly." Dal was looking him directly in the face, but Karlyn thought there was something stiff and unnatural about the man's smile. "It's not so much a new sword I'm looking for, as a particular one. My father's, to be precise. I seem to remember it was among the effects I brought from my Household."

Karlyn started off to the left, heading for the far corner. "If it was, this is the place to look, right enough. Private blades—family blades that is, or anything jeweled should be along here."

"Do you remember my father?"

Karlyn nodded, without turning around. "I met him once, just before I became Walls. A big man, golden-haired like a lion." Karlyn turned to look more carefully at the other man.

"Like you. You must look quite like him, though I won't lie to you, I don't remember his face. That would be, let me think . . . I've been Steward of Walls in Tenebro House for fifteen years, and served almost as many before that, since *my* father brought me here. So close to twenty years ago."

"The Tenebroso never objected to your father bringing you?"

"Because he was her husband, you mean?" Karlyn shook his head. This was a question he'd answered many times over the years. "His children by other women did not affect the succession. And she liked me," he added, seeing that it was Dal he spoke to. "Trusted me enough to make me Walls when old Norwed-Gor died, though my father was gone himself by then."

"A man's made Walls of a House as much for his judgment as for his skills," Dal said. "I think we may have need of your judgment now."

Karlyn heard Dal's last words, but at first they did not register. He had reached the section of the tables where the swords were laid out in wooden racks, hilts first. He had stopped at a particular sword about one third of the way down the rack on the left. A sword lacking the patina of dust worn by those around it. A sword he knew.

Dal's father might very well have had a sword like this one; forged by a master, perfectly balanced, sharp along the full bottom and back perhaps two thirds of the top edge. But this was not Dal's father's sword. Karlyn knew this sword. Knew the horsehead pommel, knew the very slight nick in the guard. He'd had this sword in his hands within the last three days. And if her sword was here, then the red-haired, gray-eyed Mercenary and her companion had *not*, after all, left Tenebro House two days ago—Karlyn-Tan struck his thigh with his fist and turned on Dal-eDal.

"What do you know about this?"

"Little more than you."

"You helped him, don't deny it."

Karlyn saw Dal consider reprimanding him for his tone, saw the noble's face relax as he changed his mind.

"My cousin the Kir doesn't always leave me in a position to refuse when he commands—as you very well know."

Yes, Karlyn knew. Dal had come to the House a frightened boy, hostage for the good behavior of his mother and the safety of his sisters. The women were gone now, dead or married off, but the habits of years were not so easily shaken away.

"I heard the same story as you. The Mercenaries gone from the guard after the incident of the bad food, as their Common Rule requires. Mar-eMar's escort seen leaving Gotterang by the North Gate. I was relieved when I learned that they were gone."

"Looks like your relief is short-lived," Karlyn said. *And mine,* he added to himself.

Dal was nodding, as he brushed the dust off the sword next to Dhulyn Wolfshead's with a fingertip. "Lok's not impressed by the Curse of Pasillon, you know. He says the power of the Brotherhood has passed, and there are too few of them left in the world to pose such a threat."

"He's a great one for logic, is the Kir," Karlyn said, his anger rising hot enough to burn his throat. "But logic's a two-edged blade, and can cut both ways." He hefted the Mercenary's blade for emphasis. "Even in these times, people have a way of dying when Mercenaries go missing or abused. How's this for logic? If their numbers are fewer in these years, would they not be all the more careful of each other?"

"What is so important that Lok would put the whole House into danger this way?"

Karlyn spat to one side. "It's that snake spawn Beslyn-Tor behind this." Dal's head jerked up, and his eyes narrowed as he studied Karlyn's face. "Did you think I didn't know? I'm Walls, for the Caids' sake. That poison's been coming to the House for months now." Karlyn laid the sword back down in the rack. He'd never regretted having to let anyone into the House as much as he regretted having to let in the leader of the New Believers. Not that he much liked the Jaldean's underlings either. Hard to make out which was worse, bona fide poisonous snakes, or their tail-kissing followers.

"What will you do?"

This time Karlyn did not trouble to hide his disgust. "I am Steward of Walls of Tenebro House," he said. "My oath, and my responsibility are not to you, Lord Dal, nor to

Lok-iKol, nor even to the Tenebroso herself. My Oath is to the House. And it is the House I will protect."

Karlyn-Tan swept by him so brusquely that Dal had to take a step back to keep from being shoved off his feet. The hand that he put out to steady himself knocked against the rack of swords, setting the blades of some ringing like bells. The nearest blade was knocked from the rack entirely, its dusty tip rapping the tabletop sharply. This sword was marginally shorter than the Mercenary's weapon, slightly curved and sharp on only the bottom edge. However, it, too, had an animal's head for a pommel, this time, a mountain cat. One of the cat's ears had been hammered flat, when the pommel itself had been used to strike a blow. Dal sucked in a breath, wrapped his hand around the cat's head.

This was his father's sword.

※

IT IS COLD. THE WOMEN HAVE ROSY CHEEKS IN PALE FACES; A FEW HAVE COVERED THEIR BLOOD-RED HAIR WITH SCARVES OR HOODS. THEY STAND IN A CIRCLE, HOLDING HANDS, EYES CLOSED. ALL CHANTING THE SAME WORDS, OVER AND OVER. ONE OF THEM APPEARS TO BE HERSELF, OLDER, BUT WHERE IS HER MERCENARY BADGE? SHE TREMBLES. . . .

AND SEES THE FIRE. THE MOB MILLING ABOUT IN FRONT, THE FLAMES LICKING AT THE WINDOWS. THERE ARE CHILDREN INSIDE, AND UNLESS SOMEONE ARRIVES IN TIME TO SAVE THEM—

※

Blood. And. Demons. Dhulyn turned on her side, hugging herself in the feathery warmth of the bed. That was the Finder's fire in Navra, certain sure, so why should she be Seeing that now? And as for the circle of women . . . Espadryni women. Herself older she'd Seen, many times, but never without her tattoo. Dhulyn blinked. Not herself without her Mercenary badge, but her *mother.*

Not the future, but the *past.*

Could this be the work of the fresnoyn? Or had she been having Visions of the past all along, and never known it? Dhulyn laughed aloud. No *wonder* the Sight had been of so little practical use to her—she'd have to look at each one more carefully than before. She squeezed her eyes shut. Perhaps the fair-haired boy she'd seen was not Parno's child, but Parno himself?

Dhulyn shook her head and took another, deeper breath. She had no time to fully consider these questions now. First things first. They had looked for her, old One-eye and his leashed Scholar. Looked for her specifically because she was who she was . . . *what* she was.

Dhulyn's eyes flicked open. Because the women of her Clan—no, of the *Tribe* were Seers. She frowned, digesting this information. So the Mark had not fallen on her from the clear blue sky, as she'd always thought. Her mother had been Marked as well, and the other women of her tribe. Seers all.

And I have seen your face, Mother.

Gone. All gone. Not just her mother, her father, aunts, uncles, cousins. Her Clan, and likely her whole *Tribe.* Everyone who might have helped her when her Mark came. Everyone who might have had some answers. Why hadn't the Sight helped them?

Why hadn't the Sight helped *her*? Kept her out of Lok-iKol's hands? Dhulyn rubbed at the still-numb skin of her face. Had they asked her anything else? For a moment the smoky darkness, the face of a man turning purple as he choked to death threatened to rise again, but she gritted her teeth against it.

The Tarkin, she thought, remembering the color of his tunic and the golden circlet around his brows. The Tarkin of Imrion was going to be poisoned, by the Sun and Moon, and she knew who would gain by it. Though not for long. This was information she should take to Alkoryn Panther-claw—if she could think of a way to explain how she came by it.

Dhulyn blinked. The important thing right now was escape. She pulled her hands out from under the warm covering and ran her fingers over her head. Contrary to how it felt from the inside, it was in one piece, though her scalp, like her face, felt numb. That was the fresnoyn and the poppy still in her blood. Her hair was untouched, neither unbound, nor cut nor shaved. She started to sit up and stopped abruptly, hissing at the throbbing of her head. This was not good.

She gritted her teeth. Pain or no, she had to get up, get out, find Parno. And all without finding herself again in that chamber, with the fresnoyn fresh inside her, when they'd thought of better questions to ask her.

The shape of the present room told her nothing. Alkoryn's floor plans had shown dozens of squarish rooms. Heavy hangings covered the walls entirely, the only furniture her bed, and, just within reach on the floor, a glazed pitcher with a matching cup. She scrubbed her hands over her face and again ran her fingers over her hair, this time feeling carefully at the beads and baubles, ribbons and thongs, all intact, tied and woven through it. She touched the wire she was looking for and released a breath she hadn't realized she was holding.

All right. She must put aside her fear, her anger, and be patient. Her Clan might be gone, even her Tribe, but she was not alone. As Dorian the Black Traveler had once promised her, she had a House, Brothers, a place to stand in the world. She would hold fast to that and she would not fail them. Nor would she fail herself.

As soon as this cursed drug wore off, she would find Parno. She would free him. They'd kill the One-eye. And maybe his Scholar boy as well. Then she and her Partner would return to their own House.

Lok-iKol, Kir of House Tenebro, signed his name to the bottom of a letter, adding the glyph that indicated he had indeed signed it himself, and not given it to one of his clerks.

"Just these three more, my lord," Semlin-Nor, Steward of Keys murmured, selecting another sheet of paper from the sheaf she held in her hands to place on the table in front of him. Lok glanced over the list on the paper before him, mentally comparing figures and amounts to what his Keys had already reported to him. He did not trouble to look up when the door opened.

"My lord Kir, the priest Beslyn-Tor—"

Lok raised his eyebrow as the Jaldean did not wait to be further announced, but entered the room before the page had finished speaking. Lok pressed his lips together, but stifled the major part of the annoyance he felt. His need for the services the Jaldean and his fanatic followers had been providing, and were still to provide, brought him to his feet, and turned what could have been a gesture of dismissal into a signal for Keys to bring another chair that his guest might join him at his worktable.

"It has been some days since I have heard from you, my lord Kir," Beslyn-Tor said, standing in front of the chair brought for him.

Lok repressed another grimace at the sound of the Jaldean's honeyed voice, the kind of honey that caught unsuspecting listeners in a golden trap. Surely the priest must know by now that Lok was anything but unsuspecting. He took up his pen and, leaning back in his chair, began to turn it over in the fingers of his right hand, making it dance down toward his smallest finger, and back again.

"I have not sent for you, Beslyn, no," Lok said, deliberately using the diminutive of the man's name. "But now that you are here, will you not sit?" Lok allowed himself a small smile. The chair that Semlin had brought forward for the priest was the very chair that Dhulyn Wolfshead had been sitting in. Two of the silk scarves which had been used to bind her wrists were still draped over the left arm. Lok lowered his eyes to the papers in front of him and without turning to her said, "Semlin, would you be so kind as to bring our guest some wine?"

The Jaldean's raised hand stopped her when she had only half turned toward the door.

"I have very little time this evening," the honeyed voice said. "I was the more surprised not to hear from you, Lord Kir, given the arrival of your recent guests."

At moments like these, Lok welcomed the advantages of his injury. It was almost impossible to register any emotion at all—even when he wished to—and equally impossible to give anything away. So he could be certain that the shock that struck him like a blow to the heart at the priest's words never showed on his face. Who among his household was selling information to the Jaldean?

"If our guest needs nothing, Semlin, perhaps you might return to your other duties?" The woman's well-trained face remained expressionless as she made her courtesies and left the room.

"We have an agreement, Lord Kir."

Lok turned to the Jaldean, setting his quill pen down to the right of the documents on his table. Beslyn-Tor was sitting on the forward edge of the chair, statue-still, as he always did. The man didn't fidget, didn't scratch, didn't chew his nails or rub at his hands. It seemed at times as though he didn't sweat.

"I have met my part," Lok reminded the motionless man. And he had. Eleven Marked had been found by the Scholar Gundaron—though only nine had been turned over to the Jaldean. Until a moment ago, Lok would have sworn that Beslyn did not know about the Healer and the Mender secreted in the Tenebro summerhouse. But he also would have sworn the man didn't know about Dhulyn Wolfshead.

"As I will meet mine. You will not sit on the Carnelian Throne without my help."

Lok inclined his head in a shallow bow. *But once I'm there,* he thought, *that will be help I no longer need.* Especially if he was the only person in the country—perhaps the peninsula—with Marked in his service. Especially if one of those was a Seer. The Jaldean was a fanatic and, like all fanatics, out of his depth when dealing with an equally ruthless but rational man.

"We have had some arrivals, as you say, but it is merely our cousin Mar-eMar, with her bodyguard."

"And that bodyguard? I had heard one was an Espadryni woman." A warmth lit up the jade-green eyes until they seemed almost to glow. "I have been given the benefit of your Scholar's theories."

Lok sat back and waved his hand in the air. "She answered the physical description," he said, using his most reasonable tone. "But it is not *so* unusual. We were able to fully account for her background. She is not Espadryni."

"You are certain?"

"As certain as we can be. We used fresnoyn in her food."

The Jaldean nodded. "The chance of a Seer," he said, so softly he might have been speaking to himself. "There are so few." He raised his head and once more Lok had the benefit of his level jade-green stare. "It was necessary to be sure."

"I believe the woman and her companion have already left Gotterang," Lok continued, once more picking up his pen.

"What of the Mesticha Stone?"

"According to my last report, the ship had left Navra on its way to the shrine on the Isle of Etsanksa to retrieve it. We cannot expect to hear again for some weeks."

"He is a good tool, your little Scholar."

"He is," Lok agreed. "I could not part with him." *Certainly not,* Lok thought, *until I find out what you want with all these relics he's located for you, and why the Mesticha Stone is so important.*

"Are you sure you will not have some wine? Can I offer you other refreshment?"

Ten

IN THE MIDDLE of the first watch of the night, while most of the Household were seeking their bedrooms, Karlyn-Tan checked that he had his set of master keys hanging from his belt and set off down the corridors and passageways of Tenebro House. As he inspected the watch—something he did often, if irregularly—he could take the most roundabout and quiet route to the room that held the Wolfshead.

His first checkpoint was a young guardsman standing with a drawn sword in her hand, her back to a tapestry that depicted, in fading colors, a boar hunt. Word had it that the Tenebroso herself had worked the tapestry as a young woman, before the deaths of her two older siblings had made her Kir, and turned her attention to other matters. The tapestry hung at the apex of a long curving corridor, where the guard who stood before it could see down both sides.

"All quiet, Steward of Walls." The young woman standing watch at the tapestry saluted with her sword as he passed her, giving her nothing more than a nod of acknowledgment. He knew her well, as he knew all of his own people. He even knew what special feat in practice had won her the honor of standing guard inside the walls and not out. The honor was always a coveted one, but especially on very hot nights when the stone walls gave some cooling to the House. Or on nights like this one, when spring's cool drizzle misted the battlements.

The thought that Lok-iKol would endanger this young woman, and all her fellow guards as well as everyone else in the House—Karlyn's hand had touched his sword hilt before he brought it back, relaxed, to his side.

Karlyn nodded to four more guards before he finally reached the room that held the Wolfshead. He waited for several minutes, listening and taking deep breaths, before he unlocked the door and stood on the threshold.

The first thing he saw was the bed placed against the middle of the far wall, and Dhulyn Wolfshead sitting cross-legged upon it, composed, and smiling merrily.

"It is Karlyn-Tan, Steward of Walls," he said in a voice that would reach her ears without traveling down the hallway.

"I remember you," she said. She still sat softly smiling, her blood-red eyebrows slightly raised. Suddenly, her smile broadened. "Have you come to release me, Steward of Walls?" she asked.

Karlyn took three paces into the room until he was no more than the length of a sword from the woman on the bed. He cleared his throat. "Yes."

The look of blank astonishment on her face, though quickly masked, made the Mercenary woman look younger. "You surprise me, Steward of Walls. Did you not think that my Partner and I left the city through the north gate?"

Karlyn shrugged. "Wolfshead, that is the tale told in the House. But I have seen your swords and weapons hanging in the north tower armory."

She raised her eyebrows a fraction and inclined her head once.

"I must ask something of you."

Her lips twisted to one side. "You and everyone else in the blooded House."

"Will you tell me what the Kir wants of you?"

The stony immobility of her face gave him his answer. Did not know, or would not say.

"Can you tell me at least whether it brings danger to the House—other than the danger you represent yourself?"

This time Dhulyn Wolfshead drew down her blood-red brows and pursed her lips. "That would be hard to say. He takes a great risk, I would judge, but whether it endangers the House . . ." Her frown deepened. "When you invade another's territory, do you endanger your own?"

Lok was planning an assault on another House? Karlyn found himself nodding. Yes, that would fit. Perhaps even explain the Jaldean.

"I will free you, Dhulyn Wolfshead. And in return, may I ask you to spare my guards? They are innocent in this."

Dhulyn sat up straight, hands on her knees. She had rarely seen a man look as troubled as the Steward of Walls looked at that moment. The little muscles around his eyes and mouth were sharp with tension. As if he'd spent much time in thought before coming to her. But his request was sincere. That, Dhulyn was sure of. She had been right to approve of him when they had met at the gate. That he did not ask for himself, only for his men, showed his heart moved him in the right way. Dhulyn found she was glad of this. And that gladness surprised her, a little.

"Why should I do this thing, Steward of Walls?"

"I will set you free with my own hand, and give my word that my guards know nothing of your captivity," he said.

"Someone must know."

This closed his eyes, as a look of pain shot across his face. "None of *my* people, Wolfshead. I cannot speak for the Kir's *personal* guard."

"You have named the Kir," she said, leaning forward.

"My oaths are not to the Kir," he replied. "But to House Tenebroso. That House is more than the Kir or even the Tenebroso herself. Like me, my people do not belong to the Kir, but to House Tenebro. They are innocent in this," he repeated.

Again, he did not ask for himself. "Blade oath, Steward of Walls?"

"Blade oath, Dhulyn Wolfshead."

A long moment passed. "I believe you," she said finally. He bowed to her, but made no move to leave.

"I will leave the door open," he said. "May I ask you to wait until the middle of the third watch?"

"What of this?" Dhulyn Wolfshead uncrossed her legs; as she lowered her bare feet to the floor, a heavy chain rang against the metal of the bed frame. Karlyn felt his stomach clench. He did not have the keys to that manacle.

"A hacksaw—" he began, already turning to the door.

"Wait." He turned back. "You are an honorable man,

and I will take your word in this as in the other. Go, lock the door behind you lest another come. Best you be able to say you do know not how I escaped."

Karlyn-Tan gave the Mercenary a deep bow, and turned to the door.

❧❧❧

"One thing is certain," Parno said. They had waited until the middle of the second watch to make their attempt on the door. He gritted his teeth and coaxed the bent-and-folded wire he had inserted into the lock a little to the right. Stupid lock was blooded stiff. And using his left hand was not making a hard job easier. Trial had shown, however, that left-handed or no, he was still better at lockpicking than the other three. He closed his eyes the better to feel the mechanism. "What I'd like to know," he said through his teeth, "is how much the little Dove knew when we were looking after her on the road and making sure she wasn't eaten by Cloud People."

"Your coming was not just coincidence, you think?" Thionan said.

"Perhaps," Parno jerked his head and young Hernyn eased in beside him. "Hold this just where I have it, my Brother." Parno waited until the young man had slipped his hand into position and grasped the wire before moving his own hand away. The cracked bone made his right arm throb. "But it's certain they were ready for us. Perhaps the little Dove's an innocent bystander. And the letter we never saw a love note. It's just that I'd like to know before I cut her throat." Parno thought of Mar white-faced and vomiting after Dhulyn had cut young Clarys' throat. It had taken days for that big-eyed look of apprehension to fade from the girl's face. She had looked at Dhulyn the way one looks when one realizes that the house dog one cuddled in the evening was really trained to kill strangers who came uninvited. Had that pallor and those sidelong glances been no more than a performance? Or was it just that the girl had found it was one thing to act as lure, and another to travel with killers?

"The Lady Mar-eMar's really a member of the House," Fanryn said. She crouched on the floor near Parno, her back braced against the wall. "That much you may believe. They've been sending for cousins and second cousins and even more distant relatives since last planting season. Some stay, some go forth again." She handed Parno the wire she'd finished bending for him. She'd been the one who'd helped him off with his boots. The pattern of beading around the boot tops still looked intact, but some of the beads were gone, worked into the dirt floor, and the wires which had held them on were picking the lock of the cell door.

A dull click, and the Brothers smiled at one another in satisfaction. Parno and Hernyn eased the door open a fingerwidth, and they all fell silent, listening. They quieted their breathing, waited with trained patience for one thousand heartbeats, before Parno slowly twisted the picks out of the lock. "There we are, my lords and ladies," Parno looked around at the three faces grinning back at him. "Off you go, Hernyn, and mind you don't get caught. In Battle, my Brother."

"Or in Death." Hernyn gave Parno a grin of his own and snaked himself out of the door on his belly. Parno relocked the door. Always easier to relock than to unlock. A twist to the old proverb Dhulyn was always quoting, "easier in than out." Too bad she hadn't remembered it before they'd come into this place.

"He'll be all right." Parno hoped his words did not sound like a question. It was not something he could have said while the youngster was still in the room. Fanryn, Hernyn, and Thionan had matched fingers for the job and the boy had won.

"Oh, blood, yes," Thionan snickered. "He's new in the Brotherhood, but that makes him old for outsiders. You or I might see him, Parno; Fanryn here knows his smell and could track him by that alone. But none of these people will see him." She tossed her head at the corridor on the other side of the door. "We used to go roaming at night—blood, during the day sometimes, and none of us were ever seen."

Parno nodded. He would rather have gone himself, of course, but there was no way to convince the others in view of his injury. No way to explain the map in his head, if it came to that. And these three had more than maps in their heads. In their time in the House, they had been over the whole edifice several times, they'd told him. And it was from Brothers like these, Parno knew, that the maps he and Dhulyn were shown had come. They knew where every member of the household slept, and with whom, and what many of them looked like in their sleep. They knew where the chamber pots were kept and how often they were emptied; where the Tenebroso kept her jeweled gloves, and what kind of sweetmeats the tame Scholar kept under his bed.

Most important, they knew of the places that a prisoner like Dhulyn Wolfshead—someone who had to be kept secret from the rest of the household—might be hidden. According to Thionan, there were three small rooms that, going by their placement within the maze of Tenebro House, were without windows and had only one door. Thionan knew of at least one other visitor who had been kept in the room she considered most likely.

"Look there first," she'd said to Hernyn. "You know the place I mean. Around to the left and down the short flight of stairs beyond the Kir's suite. Across from the hallway that goes nowhere."

"That's not the place to start," Fanryn had said, shaking her head. "You want to check that chamber next to the Kir's suite first, the one he and the Scholar use for a workroom." When the other three waited for her to go on she shrugged. "That's where they question people. He should make sure she's not there before looking for her cell."

Hernyn had looked at Parno and waited for the older man's nod. No one thought it odd that the man who knew the least about the House should be the one to decide. Even if he had not been Senior, Parno was Dhulyn's Partner, the only one who could speak for her.

Parno sat propped on one of the cots while Thionan quickly put together what spare clothing and blankets they had between them to look like Hernyn was asleep on the other cot. They'd need all their luck and the bad lighting to fool anyone for long, Parno thought.

"How's this look?" Thionan flopped herself on the cot along with the make-believe Brother and drew a length of twisted tunic around her own waist. Parno squinted, then began to laugh. By the Caids it did look like Thionan was sharing the cot with someone else. She rolled back up to a seated position and bowed her acknowledgment of Parno's tribute.

"What shall we do to pass the time?" Parno said. "I'm no Scholar, but I know a good many tales, or I can sing."

"A song by all means," Fanryn said, leaning back and shutting her eyes with a smile.

❧

Dhulyn stood ignoring the passage of precious minutes, waiting with a cat's patience for the sound of footsteps in the hall to move away. When she'd heard them approaching, she'd ducked into the nearest open door and found herself unmistakably in the anteroom of the Tenebroso's chambers. Two sleeping women, wearing the silken sleeping shifts and loose hairnets of senior lady pages, with heavier but no less finely woven robes across the foot of each bed, explained the absence of any other guards. Handmaidens or dressers would be sleeping elsewhere—these women would be nurses and companions, as well as bodyguards. Though the one to the left was too rolled up in her bedding to come to anyone's quick assistance, Dhulyn thought, her lip curling slightly.

Still, here in the heart of the House, surrounded by her people, the Tenebroso was evidently thought sufficiently well-guarded. And so she would have been, from any intruder other than a Mercenary Brother.

Not that Dhulyn wished to intrude upon her. She stood not quite in front of the closed door, the well-oiled hinges at her back. She tried not to think about time passing slowly and inexorably by. She tried only to listen to the breathing of the two women with her in the softly lit room, until she was sure they breathed at the same moment, as people who sleep together over long periods of time often do. If she needed to—and then the footsteps of the guards outside stopped in front of the door at her back.

Like a cat, Dhulyn walked quickly, softly across the room's thick carpets to the interior door, keeping her footsteps timed to the breathing she felt more than heard, and slipped behind the heavy quilted curtain that marked the archway into the main bedchamber. She moved immediately to the right of the doorway and slowed her breathing, hoping her heart would follow suit and stop its hammering.

The Tenebroso's room was so large that the small oil lamps placed one to each side of the doorway did very little more than create deeper shadows. It had been a long time, evidently, since anyone other than Kor-iRok and her women had needed to navigate this room in the dark. Dhulyn heard sounds and murmuring voices from the anteroom and froze. After an eternity her heart resumed beating. Would they come into the Tenebroso's room, or would they take it for granted that no one had been able to pass the lady pages?

More importantly, was this a routine check, or were the guards looking for her? Had someone found her cell empty?

Like her sitting room twenty paces farther down the hall, Kor-iRok's bedroom was crowded with furniture. Little tables, stools, cabinets as tall as Dhulyn herself, some with open shelves and some with closed doors. Dhulyn edged over farther and squatted, adding herself to the shadow of a round table with thick carved legs. From here, she had a clear view of the large bed at the far end of the room. A small bedside table held a bowl of fruit and a light horn cup with a hinged silver lid to keep insects out of the drink. The Tenebroso Kor-iRok did not stir. The woman was warmly dressed and covered. At her age she would feel the cold more than would her ladies asleep in the outer room. Without cosmetics to give it color, the skin of her face was papery and pale. On a stand near the bed rested the elaborate golden-haired wig the old woman had been wearing when Dhulyn had first seen her, a gold, Dhulyn realized with a jolt, the exact shade of Parno's hair.

More light entered the room as the curtain was noiselessly pushed aside. The rings must have been bound with cord to prevent them rattling against the curtain rod. *Wish I'd known that before,* Dhulyn thought. One of the lady pages from the anteroom took a step into the bedroom.

"What is it, Jhes-iJhes?" came a whisper from the bed. Only years of discipline, and her teeth in her lower lip, prevented Dhulyn from making any sound.

"One of the guards in the west wing thought he saw something, my House," the woman said.

Not me, then, Dhulyn thought.

"Well, there is nothing in here," the papery whisper sounded once more from the bed. "Pray shut the door until the alert is over."

"Yes, my House, sleep well." The woman stepped out of the room, drawing the curtain closed as she went. Dhulyn heard the "snick" of the latch as the door she hadn't noticed in the anteroom was closed. She squeezed her eyes shut. This was all going to take much longer than she'd thought. She'd hoped to find Parno and go tonight, not take the chance of another day in One-eye's interrogation room.

"Come sit by me, Mercenary," came the whisper again. "They will take a few minutes to sleep again, and you will be more comfortable here."

Dhulyn squeezed her eyes shut. Why didn't her Sight ever show her something like this? Suppressing a sigh, she straightened out of the shadow of the round table.

"When did you know?" she asked, as she sat down on the edge of the bed.

"When you moved the curtain," the old woman said. "The air changed."

Dhulyn eyed the distance to the door, and turned to watch the old woman's thin chest rise and fall. If she took a breath deep enough to call out, Dhulyn could stop her before any sound got farther than the edge of the bed. Though it was bad luck to kill someone so old.

"I did not want to be Tenebroso, you know," Kor-iRok said as though she was continuing a conversation. "But my brother died, and then my sister. I had a daughter who died also, an elder daughter. Two months before her presentation day, dead of a fever. Young. I believed it to be natural; eventually, I learned differently. Now my time comes, though I am the only one who knows it." She looked directly at Dhulyn, the force of her stare belying her words. "You may help me. Your coming is most advantageous. I fear I have less time than I had hoped."

Dhulyn pressed her lips together. There was no doubt, not even any real sense of request in the Tenebroso's voice. She was used to being obeyed, and she expected to be obeyed now. What help would the old woman need? And what would she do if Dhulyn did not provide it?

"I do not see how I may be of aid," she said. "We do not kill people in their beds."

"The only killing needed here will be done by me." The old woman indicated the bedside table with a glance from her still bright amber eyes. Following that glance Dhulyn saw what she'd missed before in all the shadows of the place, a glass vial no longer than her smallest finger, and stopped with a waxed plug. Dhulyn pursed her lips in a soundless whistle.

"Grandmother," Dhulyn said, finding herself instinctively reverting to the courtesy of her Clan. "I do not understand."

"I will ask three—no—four things of you. First, unstopper the vial and hand it to me." She waited. "I *am* ready, my child," the papery voice whispered when Dhulyn hesitated. "More than ready."

Dhulyn looked at the vial, at the old woman, saw the determination and certainty in the Tenebroso's face. She picked up the vial. She wondered what kind of poison the old woman had decided on. She ran her thumbnail around the edge of wax and worked out the cork before placing it into the Tenebroso's waiting hand. The old woman smiled, and tipped the contents of the little glass tube into her mouth. A small grimace of distaste, as when one takes a mouthful of sour wine, and then she held out the vial once more.

"I wish you to take this with you when you go." The Tenebroso suddenly gasped and shut her eyes tight before blinking them open again. "I will not give him the satisfaction . . . I would not have him think I have killed myself because of him."

No need for Dhulyn to ask who the man in question might be.

"That is only two things, Grandmother."

"I would have you listen to my curse," the old woman said. "Another's ears will give it weight and power. And I wish it to fall upon him as heavily as might be."

"You would curse your own Kir?" *Townsfolk. Who could understand them?*

The old woman's eyes must have been very accustomed to the darkness in her room for her to catch Dhulyn shaking her head.

"It is not what you think, Mercenary. I would curse him for killing my daughter, all those years ago. For killing his sister."

"But your House . . ." She'd condemn her House to the chaos and turmoil that would follow the cursing of its Kir? Not that Dhulyn would stand in the old woman's way. As far as she was concerned, a curse was just what the One-eye needed.

"The House will continue. I was afraid," the old woman said in the voice of one confiding in a friend. "I thought I might have waited too long. Dal is not what I had hoped. He watches, but he does not lead. He hates Lok, but he cannot make up his mind to kill him."

Dhulyn smiled at this insight.

"But now Par-iPar has come, as I arranged, and you will bear my message to him. He is strong. A true Heir. Now I may die content, cursing my son who robbed me of my daughter, and my House of its true Kir."

Par-iPar? Dhulyn stared again at the golden wig, this time really seeing how exactly it matched Parno's hair. Lok-iKol thought he was bringing her here for her Mark, and all along his mother was bringing the One-eye's replacement. Parno. *Parno* was the heir. Not just a younger son of some Household of the extended House Tenebro, noble but unimportant. *When this woman dies, my Partner will be* heir.

"I am glad he has you, my dear. What a consort you shall be. What a House you will make between you. Carry my words to him, and my blessing for him and our House."

Dhulyn let her mouth close, her words of refusal fading on her lips. It was too late for the old woman, let her die in peace at least. She managed a nod as she took the Tenebroso's hands in hers and squarely met her bright amber eyes.

The woman's pupils suddenly shrank.

"Your death is here, Grandmother. Begin your curse."

Eleven

THE ROOM WHERE the Kir of House Tenebro questioned his prisoners was, as Hernyn Greystone had expected, unlocked and empty. Though, perhaps, prisoners was too strong a word. After all, some of the people questioned had gone in smiling, had been given wine and dainty edibles before they came out, still smiling, restored to their normal routine. Others, Hernyn knew, had gone in and never came out again—at least not under their own power. What exactly distinguished guests from prisoners—and what made some remain guests while others became dead—had been beyond the concern of Mercenaries employed in the guard.

Lucky thing he was so good at the Stalking *Shora*. He'd had to dodge three people on his way out of the cellars alone, and there seemed to be an unusual number of the Kir's guards patrolling the hallways.

Hernyn had been pleased and excited to find two Brothers already in the guard at Tenebro House when he signed up. Fanryn and Thionan were both older, but they'd treated him right, and he'd been careful to follow their examples, especially when it came to being discreet. "Nothing you see or hear ever leaves your eyes or ears." That was Common Rule no matter who you worked for. The only people you ever told about anything you saw or heard while on an assignment was the Mercenary House itself.

"Do nothing to lose trust and respect, or you'll lose it for all your Brothers." That was Common Rule, too.

And, Hernyn thought, a blush rising over him even now,

he'd seen some very interesting personal behavior in the months that he had been in Tenebro House. Had even been invited to join in—and by some most unexpected people. The Mercenary's code prevented him from gossiping about what his old grandmother had called "that kind of thing," even as it stopped him from discussing the routine security measures of the House. And the kind of people who went into the room he was going to now. Their names. Which ones walked out on their own limbs, and which ones did not.

He hadn't needed the presence of his Brothers to remind him of the Common Rule. He just hadn't expected it all to be so complicated. Because he'd gone and made a mistake after all. That he couldn't have known it would be a mistake, didn't make him feel any better. He should have known better. Because he'd been bragging. And he'd thought he'd been cured of that, long ago. The hard way. He rubbed the scar on his right forearm.

He crossed quickly to a window, let himself out into the cool night air. *Frost before morning,* he thought, using the finger- and toeholds provided by old and crumbling mortar to move up to a similar window on the floor above. No one bothered to latch these windows; they were too high up, and gave only on an inner courtyard.

When Rofrin and Neslyn the Fair had asked him about a Brother who was obviously Dhulyn Wolfshead, he'd told them *far* too much about her—everything he knew, in fact, and he'd known quite a lot. And he hadn't told them to be helpful, or even to enhance the reputation of the Brotherhood; he'd told them to show off. And just as he'd been warned, showing off had brought trouble—had put another Mercenary Brother in danger.

The long corridor of the south wing took him past the first of Dhulyn Wolfshead's possible prison rooms. The door stood open, a good sign the room was empty. Hernyn hoped that Dhulyn wouldn't kill him when she learned what a fool he'd been, even though Parno had said that she wouldn't.

A noise?

Hernyn held his breath and concentrated, exerting all the skill born in him from generations of desert hunters and honed to perfection by the Stalking *Shora* of the Mercenary School. Yes. Noises. Still a ways away, but possibly coming closer.

Hernyn eyed the next slot of shadow, marginally darker than the hall around it, created by a bit of uneven wall and a hanging that was just a handbreadth too wide. He took two silent steps and eased himself into its protective embrace.

An arm clamped around his chest, trapping his left arm at the same instant that a hand covered his mouth. He whipped up his right hand, aiming for where his captor's eyes should be, and cracked his fingers against the stones of the wall.

"Quietly, my Brother," the soft murmur in his left ear froze him. "Did no one ever teach you to make sure the dark is empty before you hide yourself in it?" The arms around him loosened but did not drop.

"Dhulyn," he breathed. He had not realized he was holding his breath. He felt her nod, and relaxed against her. Suddenly he was acutely aware of her breasts and stomach pressed against his back and buttocks. He released his mind from the Stalking *Shora*. This was not the moment for heightened senses. If he moved away from her, he knew, he would be out of the shadow that hid them both. He was embarrassed to react to her physically, but more embarrassed at being so easily caught. It was like being back at School. He should have known better, he thought. Good enough to avoid ordinary people just was not good enough to fool another Mercenary. Nor was he particularly surprised that Dhulyn Wolfshead had stood in the shadow unseen by him. Outlanders were notoriously good at keeping hidden, and an Outlander with Mercenary Schooling, well, you'd need a Finder even to notice them.

Hernyn's lungs refilled with air. "My name is Hernyn Greystone," he said. "I was schooled by Dorian the Black. Parno Lionsmane, Fanryn Bloodhand, and Thionan Hawkmoon await in the cell of our confinement. I will lead you there."

"I thank you for finding me, Hernyn. Is the Lionsmane well?" Dhulyn rested her forehead against the back of Hernyn's shoulder. He could smell a faint odor of sweat, dust, and a sharp but not unpleasant herbal scent rising from her skin. He found himself thinking of a time that he'd had a bad fever while he was being Schooled. He'd been given a drink that had smelled the way Dhulyn smelled now.

"He is," he replied. "His right arm bone was cracked, but Fanryn Bloodhand has seen to it. Come, I will take you to them."

He felt the slow release of her breath. Some of the tension left her body.

"Weapons first," she said. "Brothers second. Do you know where the north armory is?"

⊗⊗⊗

Gundaron stood in the carpeted passageway outside Mar-eMar's rooms and rubbed his upper lip with a hand that trembled. It was early, still dark, in fact. Mar-eMar had helped him to his rooms after he recovered from his faint, but he hadn't slept. Since discovering the gap in his memory— He shook himself. He'd already spent most of the night chasing the same thoughts around and around. He'd tried everything he could think of, every technique of focus or relaxation, but nothing had worked. His memory simply hadn't been there to . . . he swallowed. To *Find*.

There. He could admit his Mark to himself, if to no one else. None of his usual methods, untrained and almost unconscious as they were, had helped him at all. He was here to try the only other thing he could think of. He gritted his teeth, squared his shoulders, and knocked.

"Just a minute," came her voice from within, much more quickly than Gun had expected. It looked as though he was not the only one who'd spent a sleepless night.

The door cracked open, and a deep blue eye looked out.

"Lady Mar, I'm sorry to disturb you so early, but I have need of your bowl."

"My *bowl?*" The door swung open, and Mar-eMar stepped back in invitation, one hand still on the edge of the door, the other holding the throat of her dressing gown closed. There were oil lamps burning in this outer room, and neat piles of folded clothing on the low chairs and the single brazier table, but he barely took them in as he scanned the surfaces for the patterned bowl. Could she be keeping it in the bedroom? He glanced from the girl, still standing with her hand on the open door, to the inner door leading to the bedroom.

"I'd only need it for a few minutes, I won't harm it."

"But why *my* bowl? There must be bowls in the kitchens you can use."

"It's—" Now that he was faced with it, Gun realized he had no idea what to say next. He hadn't seen beyond the point at which he had the scrying bowl in his hands. It simply hadn't occurred to him that he would have to explain what he wanted it for. He glanced over his shoulder at the open doorway, but there was no help there. When he turned back, Mar-eMar was watching him with her liquid eyes.

She had relaxed her hold on her dressing gown. The neck had fallen open and he saw that, under it, she was wearing not a night dress but a shirt and tunic. There was no fear in her face, just a calm query as she waited for him to answer her—and the certainty that he would. *She's very brave,* he thought, taking a deep breath. She had to have been, to come all this way not knowing what waited for her. *Braver than I am.*

"It's a scryer's bowl, Lady Mar," he said. "A Finder would use it to focus the Mark."

Mar-eMar glanced into the passageway and shut the door.

"Are you sure?" She came toward him. "Dhulyn Wolfshead only said it was very old."

"I'm sure. Please, my lady. I've lost something, and I—" Gun swallowed the sob that threatened to break out. She was from Navra, the Marked were still safe in Navra. She must not think him a coward, she *must* not. "I have to Find it."

"*You . . . ?*" Mar gestured without completing the sentence. "Please."

She stared at him a moment longer and then turned to the pack that lay open on the round brazier table to the left of the inner door. She removed two rolled gowns, a pair of light brown sueded half boots, and finally the old thick cloth he'd seen when she'd shown the bowl on her arrival. As Mar-eMar turned back the faded folds of material, she looked once more at the door. Gun followed her glance and went himself to secure the latch. When he turned back, she had tossed the old cloth over a chair and set the bowl on the round table.

"Do you have water?" he asked. Without another word, Mar went into the bedroom and returned with a pitcher of water. Gun took it from her and, after moving the bowl nearer the edge of the round tabletop, filled it two-thirds full. He looked around and found Mar taking three folded tunics from a chair. He positioned the now empty chair in front of the bowl and sat down.

His Finding had always been most successful when he was researching. He placed his fingertips lightly on the edge of the table and leaned forward, keeping his back straight, his shoulders down. He was researching again, that's all; all he had to do was relax.

Gun licked his lips. Research so often started with the printed page. A scroll, or book. The flame of the lamp cast little highlights on the surface of the water, standing out against the pure white of the bowl. A little like letters meticulously copied onto a page of parchment or paper. This was how he'd *Found* things. Hypnotizing himself with the ink and page. The water—

✖✖✖

It's not water, it's a bright page of paper. Suddenly he's in a Library. Familiar. Not one he's been in, but Libraries are Libraries. He should be able to Find the text he's looking for. There's a beautiful jade-green line on the floor before him, fuzzy at first, but stronger and more precise as he follows it. He walks swiftly now, down the main aisle, shelves and scroll holders branching off to left and right. The place is enormous.

He walks faster, following the thin jade line as it rounds a corner into a narrower aisle. The aisle ends, opening into Lok-iKol's workroom. Of course, this is where his memory must be. There. The Kir is bent over Dhulyn Wolfshead in her chair, her face frozen in that snarling smile. And there he is himself—Caids, how fat he's become!—sitting in the other chair. Something has frightened him because he has his hands up to his mouth and his eyes are very wide open.

They are motionless as a painting, as if the jade-green mist that fills the room, the exact shade of the line he's been following, is a kind of ice freezing them into stillness. But his memory is in there, it must be. He focuses, straining to move forward again, and the mist is sucked away, so suddenly that he takes an unintended step forward into the room just as sound and movement returns to the people in it.

Dhulyn Wolfshead stiffens and looks at where Gun sits in his chair, but she also looks at him now, right now, where he's standing watching them all, and with a shock he realizes that she can *See*. That she Saw him when they were all in this room together. *She* is *a Seer*. Part of him feels triumphant. Her eyes shift and he follows the angle of her glance and sees himself at the door of Lok-iKol's workroom, trying to work the latch. But he's transparent, and his hands pass through the mechanism without affecting it. *I don't remember that.* Gun looks back to where he was sitting and sees his body is still there, filled with a jade-green light, that makes his eyes glow green in his slack face.

Gun takes a step back toward the Library he has come from. He remembers seeing that green glow, that slack face, in Lok-iKol. With that thought images, memories, cascade through his mind and he remembers—for the first time—seeing the glow, but with no slackness whatsoever, in the eyes of Beslyn-Tor as the Jaldean has passed him in the doorway of this very room. And he remembers that the Jaldean has passed him many times, over and over. All those memories lost—taken, he realizes—until this very moment. And now that he has those memories again, standing there in his mind's Library, Gun realizes there is a difference between the green glow when it is in Beslyn-Tor and in Lok-iKol, and that same difference—please, blessed Caids—is in himself as well.

There is something living inside Beslyn-Tor, he thinks, his Scholar's mind weighing and assessing. He and Lok-iKol were tools only, something to look through, as a jeweler looks through a lens. Somehow the Jaldean priest, or the thing living inside him, has pushed Gun out of his own head, out of his own body, and that's why he has no memory of this. He couldn't remember what he wasn't in his body to experience.

And Gun realizes something else.

This is what happened every time I left the room. All those people I've Found for them. This interrogation, this torture, this is what happened to them.

At that moment the head on the body he's not wearing begins to turn to him, and Dhulyn Wolfshead starts to scream, the sound a horrid tearing of the throat. Fear chokes him as he backs away, faster and faster, finally turning and beginning to run as shelves and tables of books and scrolls move to block the aisles between him and the image of the room, shutting it away.

Not that he will be able to forget it now.

❈

"Gundaron?" Mar put out a tentative hand and touched the Scholar's shoulder with her fingertips. His muscles were so rigid, it was like touching wood.

At first he'd been relaxed, watching the water as though he were reading, eyes flicking back and forth. As the minutes passed, however, he'd become gradually more rigid, and now his grip on the table's edge showed white knuckles. Mar leaned forward. He seemed to have stopped blinking. She took a firmer hold on his shoulder and shook him. It was only slightly better than pushing at a wall. She reached out and gently touched his face. The skin soft, the muscles under it rigid.

Mar shot a quick glance around. She'd have to hide all her packing before she went to fetch help. Whoever came would be sure to notice it and guess exactly what it meant. Her eyes returned to the Scholar. There was one more thing she could try. She picked up the bowl and dashed the water into Gundaron's face. He sputtered, blinked, and shook his head.

"I didn't know," he said, clutching at her arm as he came fully awake. "I swear I didn't know."

"Of course not," she said. The pressure of his fingers on her forearm made her wince. She gently pulled free and set the bowl back on the tabletop. "I take it you Found what you were looking for?"

He started to nod, turned a pale green, and retched, gagging. Nothing came from his mouth but a thin line of saliva.

Mar ran into the bedroom, snatched up a towel from the washstand and brought it out to him. He disappeared into the towel, and for a moment Mar thought he wasn't going to come out. When he did, he had rubbed some color into his face, and looked less as though he were about to faint again.

"Don't tell anyone. Please."

"What can I tell? I don't even know what it was."

Gundaron looked up, eyes wide. "No," he said finally. "I meant don't tell anyone I'm a Finder."

"I won't."

"Promise?" His voice was thick, giving weight to the childlike request.

Mar hesitated, but there was something in his face that touched her—something more than fear. She held out her hand, waited until he'd taken it.

"Yes, I promise, but—do you mean no one knows?"

Gundaron rubbed his eyes with his fingertips, lowered his hands, and looked around the room.

"I wanted to be a Scholar. I wanted it so badly. I moved the sun and the stars to be allowed to go to Valdomar. And I'm *good* at it; I knew I would be. The best Scholar in my class. If they'd known I could Find . . ."

"You'd have gone to the Guildhall."

He looked at her. "And now . . ."

Mar took the towel from him, shook out the creases and began to fold it. It wasn't the Guildhall he'd go to now if the wrong people learned he was a Finder, but the Jaldean Shrine. "I'll keep my promise," she said. "I won't tell." She sat down in the other chair, still holding the towel. "What was it you Found?"

A muscle jumped in his cheek as he clenched his teeth. "I Found what they're doing here. Lok-iKol and . . ." his eyes shifted away, "and the others."

Mar waited some minutes before deciding that Gundaron wasn't going to say anything more. But as she rose to her feet, thinking to take the towel back into her bedroom, the Scholar spoke again.

"This was my first assignment." He stroked the edge of the bowl with the first two fingers of his right hand. "The Tenebros asked for our best Scholar to write a history of the House, and the Seniors at Valdomar chose me, even though I was their youngest graduate. I've never been anywhere but home and Valdomar; I'd certainly never seen such a place as this. I was all alone here—"

Mar thought of the twin sisters Nor and Kyn and knew just how alone he had been. Suddenly she wanted to put her arms around him, stroke his hair, but she knew that if she did, he would stop speaking. And whatever it was he was about to say, he needed to say it.

"Then to have the Kir of such a Noble House take me into his confidence, treat me with respect . . ."

Mar lowered herself into her seat once more. His words and tone had the flavor of explanation, almost apology, and she waited for him to continue.

"There's so much data in a Noble House's archives," he said. "The kind of private things that never get into the history books. Things that could help me with my personal researches—and I was promised all the information I needed—" He got up and moved the short distance between the table and the window, his steps small and abrupt. "I was so excited, I got so interested in what I was learning that I—I forgot to keep my distance."

"Is that what you Found? Your distance?"

Gundaron licked his lips and Mar got up once more, this time to bring him a cup of water.

He took a deep swallow and gripped the cup tightly in both hands. "Yes. I think I can say that." He took a deep breath. "I've stepped back and taken a good look at what I've been doing, and I don't like what I've seen."

Mar put her hand on his arm. Gundaron was the only person here who had been kind to her, really kind to *her*, as herself. The only person who had never made her feel apart. "I'm sure whatever you've done couldn't be all that bad," she said.

The look of despair that passed over his face at her words almost frightened her.

"I've been Finding Marked for them," he said, so quietly that Mar actually leaned toward him to be sure she'd heard him correctly.

"For whom?" The words came out in a hoarse whisper.

"Lok-iKol, for one." What Mar thought must have shown

on her face because he threw himself down at her feet and clutched at the skirt of her dressing gown. "I didn't know, I swear I didn't know. I thought it was just research. Families, bloodlines, how talents pass through kinships. I didn't know about the Jaldeans." He looked at the bowl. "I didn't know until now. It's memories I've Found."

"But Gundaron, *you're* Marked."

"They don't know!" He waved her words away. "I'm a Scholar."

Mar shook her head. Surely it wasn't possible. Surely it wasn't possible that you could be so focused on your craft, on your *research,* that you could overlook what was being done with it. Surely you couldn't feel so separate and apart from people just like yourself.

Families. Bloodlines. She looked from his face to the bowl on the table. Her bowl. Passed through five generations. A scryer's bowl. A *Finder's* bowl. A cold hand closed around her heart.

"That's why *I'm* here," she said. "That's why they sent for me. And you—"

"I told him you weren't," Gundaron said. "I wouldn't have let them—please, believe me."

So he *had* known. Even if some of his memories were missing, to lie to Lok-iKol about her, Gundaron must have been aware that *something* wicked was happening, even if that awareness had been buried deep. Mar reached to push him away from the skirts of her dressing gown, but something held her back. What had he done, really? Found innocent people and, in return for certain promises and favors, arranged to have them brought to Tenebro House. Hadn't she done much the same thing herself? In return for comfort, riches, her Holding restored, hadn't she brought them Dhulyn Wolfshead and Parno Lionsmane? Hadn't the Wolfshead killed a Cloudboy in the Mountains for her? Were her hands any cleaner than Gundaron's?

She put her hands on his head, patted his rough hair.

"The Mercenary Brothers," she said. "That's why you're afraid of Pasillon, because you—we—brought them here for Lok-iKol as well."

He was motionless, but Mar saw in his face that it was so. She looked around the room at her folded clothing, her half-filled travel pack. Her instincts had been better than she knew.

"What can we do?"

"Go to the Tenebroso." Gundaron got to his feet. "She's the only person in the House more powerful than the Kir."

"Will she stop him?"

"I'm sure she will." But Mar saw the uncertainty cloud his eyes as he turned his head away. What odds the old woman didn't already know?

A knock at the door startled them both.

Guilt, Mar thought. *That's what's wrong with us.*

Gundaron looked at her and she swallowed, straightened her dressing gown and, closing it once more with her hand to her throat, went to the door.

"Who is it?" she called. *And how long have you been standing there listening?*

"Okiron, Lady Mar."

Gundaron motioned to Mar and she backed away, letting him open the door. Standing on the threshold was the boy page who served this corridor. He looked pale, and there were the marks of tears on his cheeks.

"What is it?"

"The House is fallen," the young boy said, shock apparent in the reediness of his voice, "The Tenebroso Kor-iRok is dead."

Mar felt her hands and feet go icy cold. *Too late,* she thought. *We've left it too late. Is this Pasillon?*

❧❧❧

Dal-eDal stood at the doorway to the Tenebroso's—no, Kor-iRok was no longer Tenebroso, and these were no longer the Tenebroso's rooms. The woman whose rooms these had been was now the Fallen House, and he and everyone else in the family, Households and Holdings, would have to teach themselves to think of her in that way. He'd been young when he came here, but there were others here, many much older than himself, grandparents some of them, for whom there had never been any other Tenebroso but Kor-iRok. For them, this was worse than the death of a parent. For them, the whole world had changed overnight; nothing now could be safe or secure, ever again.

Dal-eDal looked at his cousin, the new Tenebroso Lok-iKol, and knew exactly how that felt.

The man who stood in Kor-iRok's bedchamber with him, and watched with him while the Steward of Walls and the Steward of Keys examined the room and the tiny figure on the bed—when had the old woman become so small?— was Tenebroso now. Lok-iKol stood halfway between Dal-eDal's post at the door and the bed on which the body of the Fallen House still lay, observing without apparent emotion as his servants performed their duties.

He is the Tenebroso, Dal thought, watching his cousin, *and that means I am the heir.* Though he was sure Lok was in no hurry to hold the ceremony that would acknowledge Dal, and change the format of his name. Even if there was no one closer to the succession until Lok married and produced his own First Born, his Kir. Dal tapped his thigh with his closed fist. That wasn't strictly true, now that he thought about it. There *was* someone closer than himself to the succession. It must be fifteen years or more since *that* particular cousin—Dal glanced up at the ruin of Lok's left cheek, his missing eye—had been Cast Out.

"A seizure of the heart," Karlyn-Tan was saying. Dal-eDal turned his attention back to the bedside of the Fallen House. Karlyn-Tan rose from the bed, finished with his examination of the body. Semlin-Nor was bent over the Fallen House, making the body straight and covering it with the bedclothes until the lady pages would be allowed back in to tend to it. Both Stewards were in full formal livery, as was every servant and guard in the House by now. Karlyn even wore his sword.

"Are you certain, my Walls?" Lok-iKol's beautiful voice was softer than usual. Was it possible that he actually had some feeling for the woman who had been his mother? At that moment Dal-eDal realized that he was taking it for granted that Lok-iKol had had his mother killed.

"I am certain, my House," Karlyn-Tan said. "You may note the color of the skin, and the slight amount of froth on the lips. There are no other marks or wounds." The man looked up. "It would have happened during the second watch of the night, my House."

Dal-eDal noted the emphasis on the formal titles absently. Everyone would be very sure to observe strict protocol for the next moon or so, until they had all had a chance to accustom themselves to the new regime. After that, the level of formality would depend on the wishes of the new Tenebroso.

Lok-iKol nodded. "Do you concur, my Keys?"

"I do, my House." Semlin-Nor gave the heavy quilted bedcover a final tug and stepped back from the bed and its burden. "As the Steward of Walls has said, there is no mark or wound, no sign of struggle."

"Poison?"

"None we can detect, my House," the woman continued. "There is no change of skin color, the eyes appear normal. I would also say a seizure of the heart, my House."

"Very good," Lok-iKol said, though what exactly he intended by that was not clear, thought Dal. Dal watched his cousin slowly nodding, the man's gaze fixed on the still figure of the woman who had been his mother, the head of his House, and perhaps, in these later years at least, thought Dal-eDal, the thwarter of his ambitions.

"That will be all, I think, for now," Lok-iKol said. "Have her people prepare her. Dal, Cousin, may I ask you to send the proper messages?"

"Of course, my House," Dal replied, inclining his head in a slight bow.

"I thank you all for your service." It was so obviously a dismissal that Dal bowed again and gestured to the others to precede him out of the room. *Perhaps Lok would like to check for himself, make sure the old woman's really dead,* Dal thought.

❧

Lok-iKol, the new embodiment of House Tenebro, looked down at the corpse of his mother. Death had aged her, robbing her face of its stern animation and adding to its lines.

"Thank you, Mother," he said, sitting down in the slipper chair next to the bed and taking an apple from the bowl on the bedside table. "The timing of your death could not have been more perfect." In fact, if she hadn't died in her sleep, he would have had to take measures himself. All his work, all his planning, had not been done to place his mother on the Carnelian Throne.

His mother gone, a Finder, a Healer, and now a Seer in his hands. A Mender located. Lok turned the apple over in his fingers, automatically noting the perfection of its skin. A Seer was the rarest, and the most useful of the Marked. Not to be wasted by giving her to the Jaldeans, watching her disappear or be ruined as others had been.

Let Dhulyn Wolfshead choose to stay, Lok-iKol thought. There must be some way to persuade her. There always was. She seemed to like the Scholar; perhaps something useful could come of that. Lok needed to know what was to come, if he was to perfect his plans.

In any event he had to act quickly. Beslyn-Tor's unexpected visit had shown him that. Should he wait until the Jaldeans became too strong, he would never free himself of their hold. For it was in no way a part of his plan to become a puppet of the priests. Let them help him to the throne, and then they might find that the pursuers often became themselves the pursued. He knew how to use the Tarkin's power, better than that soft-handed weakling who had it now.

"Will you excuse me, Semlin?" Karlyn-Tan and the Steward of Keys waited in the outer room of the Fallen House's suite. "I need a moment."

"Up to your battlements, are you? I wish I had such a place to help me think. I'm afraid times like this will find me in the kitchen eating the sweetest thing I can find." Semlyn-Nor's tone was light, but her face never brightened.

"There are no times like this," he said, getting to his feet.

"When I think that, but for an accident of birth, it might be you in there . . ." Semlyn shook her head.

"Rather an accident of marriage, wouldn't you say?"

"Don't look at me like that, Kar. There's plenty in the House will be having these same thoughts just now."

"Perhaps," Karlyn acknowledged. "But you should not say them aloud, all the same." It was a reflection of just how badly she was shaken that she said such a thing at all, he thought. Semlin had been very close to the Fallen House, and this would come harder on her than it would on him.

He patted his fellow Steward on the shoulder and left, directing his steps through the maze of hallways and stairs that would end with the room where Dhulyn Wolfshead undoubtedly lay wondering what had delayed her breakfast. This would be the perfect time to use the hacksaw blade that rested in his scabbard, alongside his formal sword.

This time Karlyn made no attempt to be quiet as he unlocked the door. He was not hiding anything from anyone. He pushed the door open slowly, and as it cleared the bed, his heart stopped.

The cell was empty, the chains with their manacles neatly coiled on the bed.

When his breathing had returned to normal Karlyn left the room, relocking the door behind him and headed to Dal-eDal's rooms in the east wing. Dhulyn Wolfshead was gone, safe, and therefore his people were safe also—though Karlyn wouldn't take odds on how long Lok-iKol might live. The man might as well be cursed.

And it was very unlikely he himself would ever see Dhulyn Wolfs head again.

He told himself that what he felt was relief.

He had to breathe carefully, hold this body, this *shape* together, when everything in him, every instinct, every thought, wanted to dissolve, to undo, to make NOT. But not yet, there were still too many of them, the Marked. They might yet rally and remember him. But it would be soon now. The old House dead. Lok-iKol would move quickly. At any moment would come the summons he expected. Then there would be a new Tarkin in Imrion, and the Marked would be his. *All* the Marked. Even those the new Tarkin thought were hidden away.

Twelve

"YOU HAVE NEWS that will not wait?" Alkoryn Pantherclaw's voice was as thin as paper. He lifted his blue eyes from their scrutiny of the map fixed to the top of his table, looked from Dhulyn to Parno and back again. "Tell me."

Dhulyn stifled the impatient movement of her right hand before it became anything more than a tremor in her nerves. The captive Mercenaries had split up upon making their escape from Tenebro House, she and Parno taking one route while their Brothers took another. Besides being good strategy, it had given her a chance to tell Parno privately of Lok-iKol and her Visions. And given them the chance to prepare a report for their Senior Brother that did not mention her Mark.

She took a deep breath to steady herself as she began to speak.

And stopped.

She had never lied to a Senior Brother, never once since Dorian the Black took her hand in the hold of the slave ship. Neglected to tell things, perhaps, but *lie*? She looked over to Parno, leaning against the table to her right, saw concern mingling with fatigue in his face, clouding his amber eyes. Untold secrets hovered in the air between them, as well.

This was not what she wanted. This was not what the Brotherhood meant to her. *I cannot have this*. She sat up straight, hands firm on the tabletop, and hoped her judgment was not as clouded as Parno's eyes.

She cleared her throat. "My Brother," she said. "I bear a Mark." From the corner of her eye, she saw Parno's head jerk up an inch before he regained control.

Alkoryn's fingers froze in their idle tracing of the lines of river and road. He lifted his hands from the map, sat up straight against the back of his chair, and let his hands fall to his thighs. When he had stared at her without speaking for some time, she continued.

"I am a Seer."

Alkoryn struck his thigh with his fist. "A Seer. By the Caids, a *Seer*." He looked at her sharply. "Does Dorian know?"

"I believe he does. But, Alkoryn, hear me." She did not know the Pantherclaw well, but she had to hope so Senior a Brother would listen, would not let his obvious excitement rule *his* judgment. "My Mark is unschooled, untrained. No Guild trains Seers, at least none that I have ever found, and so my Sight is clouded, erratic, and . . ."

"Not to be relied upon?" Alkoryn's whisper was dry, a little of the animation dying from his face.

"It shows me true Visions," she said. "But not with regularity, nor in any way that allows me to plan."

When Alkoryn looked at Parno, her Partner nodded. "It's as she says. I could give you dozens of examples of true Visions, and perhaps twice when it's been useful."

"And that is why you've told no one." Alkoryn placed his hands palm down on the tabletop. "Everyone thinks as I did, of how to use you, and doubts it when you tell them it cannot be done." Had his glance been a blade, she would have been cut to the bone. "And Lok-iKol? This is what lies behind his actions? Does he know?"

"No more now than before. His Scholar told him that the women of my tribe *might* be Seers. It was enough for him to lure us—" she glanced at Parno, "—to lure *me* in." Dhulyn leaned forward, resting her forearm on the tabletop. "My Brother, hear me. My news is of such weight—"

"Of course, of course." The Pantherclaw picked up his cup of cider and drained it. "You have kept your silence too long to break it for trivialities. Pray, tell me what you Saw." The hand that lowered the cup from his lips trembled.

"I have Seen the Tarkin Tek-aKet dead by poison," she

said in what she considered a remarkably steady voice. At least the shock and immediacy of the Vision had faded, though the images remained clear. "Men in Tenebro colors killing the guards of the Carnelian Dome. I have Seen the One-eyed Tenebro with the coronet in his hands, sitting on the Carnelian Throne. And I have Seen the Jaldean who stands behind him."

"Allied with the Jaldeans," Alkoryn said. "That in itself makes a degree of sense." He looked up to meet her eyes. "Is it Lok-iKol behind this persecution of the Marked?"

Dhulyn shook her head. "That is more than my Vision can tell me."

Parno cleared his throat. "He'll have promised them something for their support."

❈❈❈

RIOTS. FIRES. GUARDS IN DARK RED PULLED FROM THEIR HORSES AND KILLED.

❈❈❈

"I said, 'are you all right, my Brother?'" Alkoryn's voice was rough and whispery. Parno's hand on her arm. Dhulyn licked suddenly dry lips and swallowed.

"Yes, I am more tired than I had thought. Your pardon."

"What did you See?" Parno said. Alkoryn looked from Parno's face to Dhulyn's.

"Carnelian Guards being pulled from their horses in the streets."

Alkoryn shook his head, but not as though he did not believe her. "When the old Tarkin died," he said, "and Tek-aKet his son was confirmed to follow him as Tarkin, Lok-iKol did not put his name forward in nomination, nor did he request a Ballot."

"It would have been his mother, then, would it not?" Parno said.

"So it would, so it would," Alkoryn nodded, rubbing the scar on his throat. "This is no time for me to be growing old." The Pantherclaw sighed and drew himself up until he sat tall and straight in his chair.

"You may not have heard," he said. "This morning brought news of the Fall of Tenebro House. The old woman no longer stands between Lok-iKol and the Carnelian Throne."

"Then he'll make his move." Something in Parno's voice made Dhulyn look up. The light coming through the window made his hair glow golden and warm. She saw the old woman's false hair shine in the light of the oil lamps, and the Fallen House's words echoed in her ears. *Par-iPar has come. A true heir.* She squeezed her eyes shut. *I will have to speak,* she thought. *She charged me with the message.*

Their Senior Brother was nodding gently, once again appearing to give his whole attention to the study of the map in front of him, his fingers softly stroking the parchment. Watching him, Dhulyn forced her lungs to release her breath, slowly, softly. Had everything now changed? Did she still have a Brotherhood? Or would her Mark, which set her apart from all others, set her apart from her Brothers as well? Dhulyn started to rise, froze as Alkoryn looked up.

"Three days ago you advised me to move my maps."

"I Saw them burning."

"They shall be moved. Beginning today. As for what you tell me now . . . I wonder if I could ask a boon of you, my Brother," Alkoryn said.

Surprised, Dhulyn lowered herself back into her chair. "Ask," she said.

"Will you come with me to the Tarkin," was Alkoryn's reply, "and tell him what you have told me?"

Dhulyn's dry lips parted, but she could no more speak than she could fly. With a thump, Parno returned the cup he still held to the table. Alkoryn spoke before either of them had gathered their wits.

"Not all of what you've told me, clearly," the older man said. "But the portion which concerns him."

"Is the Brotherhood in the Tarkin's employ, that we would run to him with this news? We are not spies—" She held up her hand, hearing her own words, and worse, the tone she'd used. "Your pardon, my Brother, this is not mine to question. If you feel the good of the Brotherhood in Imrion demands the Tarkin be told what I have learned, then tell him."

Alkoryn's glance had drifted back to his beloved maps.

"When I accuse Lok-iKol, I accuse Tek-aKet's own cousin, even if not a very well-loved one. I think he would be the readier to believe this tale if he heard it from your own lips, my Brother. He may have questions only you can answer." Alkoryn looked up at Dhulyn, fixing her with his cat's eyes. "There is too much here we do not know. Lok-iKol wants the Throne—very well, there's nothing new in political ambition, and war is what we deal in. But with the Jaldeans in the mix . . . if the New Believers gain much more power . . ." Alkoryn tapped the tabletop with his index finger. "What they do is genocide, not war; but it will lead to war, and worse, if they have the full backing of the Carnelian Throne."

"Alkoryn," Parno leaned forward before Dhulyn could speak. "May we think about this, my Partner and I? It is an unusual request, and touches her closely. We must think of a way to tell him without revealing her Mark," he added when the older man hesitated. Dhulyn kept her face still, her features impassive. What was Parno up to?

"Certain you may," Alkoryn said. He glanced over at the shaft of sunlight that angled into his office from the high window. "But if we are to speak to Tek-aKet, it should be as quickly as possible. Tonight, by preference. Will you give me an answer soon enough?"

"Certain we will," Dhulyn heard her voice come out as little better than a croak. Whatever Parno wanted to say to her, he could say quickly. There should be nothing to stop them giving Alkoryn Pantherclaw his quick answer.

"And Parno?" They turned back at the door. "There is a Healer in the caves below the House—yes, we have been hiding the Marked and smuggling them out of the city; this was the assignment I had planned for you, my Brothers. Go to him and have your arm seen to."

In less than an hour they were back in their assigned room, Parno flexing his right arm in pleasure after his visit to the Healer. Dhulyn threw herself on the bed and wriggled around to face him.

"What are you doing?" she asked him.

"You were about to say 'no,'" he said, "and I wanted a chance to talk you."

"You suggest I *should* tell my tale to the Tarkin?" Dhulyn punched at the stuffed straw mattress to find a comfortable position on the bed. "What is Tek-aKet to me, or I to him?" She punched the mattress again, aware that her exasperation had little to do with the Tarkin.

"You told Alkoryn," Parno pointed out reasonably, sitting down on the stool close to the bed.

Dhulyn rolled her eyes up to the heavens, though from this angle she was really rolling them at the heavy wooden bed frame. "That would be a little thing called the Common Rule, no? You remember the Common Rule, I suppose, my Brother?"

Parno stood and strode away from her to the window. He leaned his hands on the sill, looking out, before turning back to her. "Is it not also the Common Rule for us to be guided by the advice and suggestions of Senior Brothers?" Parno's tight voice showed an increase of sarcasm and decrease of patience.

"And *I* am the Senior Brother in this room!" Dhulyn shot back. She sat up, thumping her booted feet to the floor and leaning forward, hands on her knees. "I repeat, what is the Tarkin to *me*? You call on the Common Rule, you question my obedience to it. Are you so sure it's not *your* old loyalties which command here? *You* wanted to come to Imrion. *You* . . ." She stopped, suddenly aware that words which could not be called back were dangerously close to the tip of her tongue. But she was between the sword and the wall. If she spoke, she risked losing her Partnership; if she was silent, if she could not speak, she had already lost it. There was only one action to take.

"Are you certain you're not willing to risk me in order to save your Tarkin?" Dhulyn stopped, suddenly breathless.

"How is he *my* Tarkin?" Parno stood facing her with his arms folded across his chest, the sunlight coming in the window making a golden aurora around him.

"You are more to the Tenebros than you let me suppose." Dhulyn's hands and feet felt cold, as if her pounding heart did not push her blood. "You're not some third son of a minor Household. With the House Fallen, you are now the next heir. If Lok-iKol Tenebro is cousin to the Tarkin, what are you?"

He took two steps toward her, arms swinging to his side. "It's not so simple as that. I was Cast Out!"

"You could not tell me of your nobility? I told you of my Mark, first off, *before* we Partnered."

"The Mark is not something that you could leave behind—it's not just a part of your life before. House Tenebro is. When I became a Mercenary Brother, I left it behind me. That's the Common Rule, too."

Dhulyn swallowed around a tight throat. Could it really be that simple?

"You were not hiding this from me?"

"I had put it behind me. True, I did want to see Imrion again, but everything else . . . *I was Cast Out.* That life is gone."

Not hidden from her because too important to tell, but left aside because not important enough to mention. Dhulyn dragged in a deep lungful of air.

"We are beating each other with the Common Rule," she said. "We are Partnered. I never thought we would quarrel in this way—never thought we *could*."

"Never Saw it coming?"

Dhulyn looked up, Parno's mouth was twisted to one side in the grin that woke her heart. "Tell me now," she said, patting the bed beside her. "I will listen."

Parno sat down next to her, slipping his right arm around her. "I am the son of Wen-eWen Tenebro—" She shifted to look at him but he held her fast. "No, let me speak. It will be easier. My father was the military commander for House Tenebro, and the much younger half brother of the woman who is now the Fallen House."

"*Was?* This was the demon haunting you? Why you wanted to return to Imrion? To see if your father still lived?"

"I got my temper from him, though mine's Schooled now. Lately, as I near the age he was then, I wondered if he managed to stay alive and well. If I am, as you say, the heir, then I have my answer."

"Sun and Moon shine on him. Wind blow warm." Dhulyn touched her fingertips to her forehead.

"And you *are* the One-eye's cousin?" she asked, after a moment had passed.

"And the reason that he has one eye."

Dhulyn twisted around to better see his face. He inclined his head. "You are my very favorite Brother," she said, smiling.

"Save your flattery. It was an accident of temper, though afterward I wished I had done it on purpose. I had seen the Harvest Moon seventeen times, and we all met at another Household for a wedding. He was rude to my sister, and when I asked him to apologize, he baited me, not realizing, perhaps, how much better a fighter I was. I lost my temper and struck him, forgetting that I came from hawking, and wore metal gloves." Parno shrugged. "He lost his eye. He claimed that I had attacked him unprovoked. My father was left with no choice but to cast me out. If he had not done so, he would have lost everything, he and my mother, my sister. I came to the Brotherhood, to Nerysa Warhammer. And to you."

"She meant for you to come, the Fallen House, she wanted you here." In as few words as possible, Dhulyn told him about the old woman's death. "The One-eye wanted me; but the old woman had her own plans all along. I was to tell you to be ready, that Lok-iKol had been cursed."

Parno blew out a deep breath. "That is what has been bothering you? Not the fall of the Tarkin, but this? You thought I might turn back into a son of House Tenebro?" To her surprise, Parno grinned his old, loose grin and pulled her closer, resting his forehead for a moment against her hair.

"Forgive me. This is not the first time such a thought has crossed your mind since I began to speak of Imrion, and I said nothing. You came young to the Brotherhood, with nothing but pain and loss behind you, and it has been—as you have reminded me often enough—your whole world, your whole life. I came to the Brotherhood a man grown, with a world and a life behind me. So that though I am longer in the world than you, my heart, you are the Senior in Brotherhood. I know what you've thought. You've wondered if I value the Brotherhood less, because once I was of a House, because I once had family, servants, people to command, a place in an ordered life. You've thought, once or twice, that I would not have come to the Brotherhood had my life not undergone such a change by force." He took hold of her shoulders, looking her in the eyes, his own clear under his golden brows. "Could I not say the same of you? Would you not even now be away in the cold south with the Red Horsemen, if they still rode? Tell me, what have you lost that I have not also lost?"

Dhulyn shut her eyes tight, only opening them again when Parno smoothed her brows with his thumbs.

"I am not a Tenebro. I am Parno Lionsmane, the Chanter. I was Schooled by Nerysa of Tourin, the Warhammer. Since we first met at the battle of Arcosa, here in Imrion as it happens, since you skewered that westerner who was trying to skewer me, I have been *your* Brother. And you mine." The grip on her shoulders tightened painfully. "*And you mine.* You'll have to kill me to be rid of me. And though I have no Sight," he said, "I tell you that is not how it happens. Neither the Tenebros, nor even the Tarkin himself is the reason that I counsel you to speak."

Her anger, and the fear that caused it, had drained away, leaving her limp, muscles trembling with fatigue. She leaned her forehead against his shoulder, breathed in his scent of leather and sweat. "Why should I speak, then? If not because *you* love him, then why?"

"Not because of the Tarkin, but because of the Jaldeans. You're right. The Tarkin is just one person or another, and we're Mercenaries. And if there's war? What's it to do with us who sits on the Carnelian Throne, besides more work and better pay?" He kissed her knuckles and placed her hand gently on the woven bedcover. He pulled his legs up beneath him and sat cross-legged, facing her from the end of the bed.

"I don't say we should fight for the Tarkin, I'm saying we should fight *against* the Jaldeans." From habit, Parno lowered his voice to a murmur that went no further than the bed they sat on. "You have never made any great show of your Mark—"

"Even if I wanted to, you know I cannot—"

"Hush for once and listen to me, woman." The bare injustice of this silenced her. She was not the talker of the two of them, and Parno knew it. "The Mark is an old problem for us, one we might easily have lived with forever. The

Jaldeans have changed that. Your Mark is now an active danger, not merely a nuisance. Where will we go, my heart, if the Jaldeans come into such power, here in Imrion?"

"Imrion is not the world—"

"Imrion is the seat of the old civilization, and there are many places which still look to it for guidance. And there are Jaldean Shrines everywhere besides Imrion, in the desert, even in the Blasonar Plains. How long until this New Belief reaches there?"

"Small shrines, a monk or two . . ." Even she could hear the lack of conviction in her voice.

"They were small shrines here in Imrion, if it comes to that," he pointed out. "Look how they have grown."

Dhulyn frowned. Parno was right. If what she had Seen came to pass . . . try as they would, they could not hide her Mark forever. And she would endanger Parno as well, not just herself. Perhaps even the rest of her Brothers.

"But my counsel to you would be the same, even if you were not a Seer. This killing of the Marked is wrong of itself. What tells us the Jaldeans will stop with the Marked?"

That brought Dhulyn's head up again.

"The New Believers gather power and importance to themselves by turning the world against useful, talented people who provide a service for a fee. Can you think of any other groups of whom these things might be said?"

Dhulyn sat up straighter, put her hand on the hard muscle on Parno's thigh. "The Scholars," she said. "That's obvious. But we also. The Mercenary Brotherhood is also such a group." She pulled her lip back from her teeth. "In the Marked, the New Believers remove a source of competition, an alternate center of power. They make the people a sword, and once the sword is sharpened, they can use it to cut anyone."

"True words, Dhulyn, my soul." Parno nodded.

"We're not so few as the Marked," Dhulyn said. "And better armed than the Scholars." She dragged her lower lip between her teeth. "But we're spread thin, so thin. It would take some time to kill us all . . ."

Parno nodded. "But kill us all is how it would end."

"No." Dhulyn shifted away so she could look Parno directly in the face. She tapped the air between them. "You are right. It ends here."

"So we will warn the Tarkin."

"If we're to die with swords in our hands, why delay it?" Dhulyn smiled. "You are wrong about one thing, however."

"I am never wrong."

"This time you are. It occurs to me, Parno, my soul, that it does matter to us which man is on the Carnelian Throne."

"It does?"

"Yes," Dhulyn let her lip curl back from her teeth. "It may be anyone except that one-eyed piece of snake's dung. Anyone except Lok-iKol Tenebro." She opened her eyes and looked at Parno's grinning face. "I witnessed his mother's curse, that twisted turd, I cursed him with Pasillon myself, and it's Pasillon he shall have."

❦

"They have *what*?" The menace and anger in Lok-iKol's voice was enough to stop in their tracks the two servants who were busy ferrying out the Fallen House's rugs and tables, now unwanted since the new Tenebroso had taken possession of the office that the old woman had used as her sitting room for so many years.

Dal-eDal had spoken to his House in a practiced murmur that would not carry beyond the worktable at which Lok-iKol sat, but now he pointedly looked at the servants and waited until Lok-iKol had waved them out of the room before he spoke again.

"They have gone, my House," he repeated. "Escaped."

"Impossible. Who freed them?" His hands were fists, and the scarring stood out bone-white from the rest of his face.

Dal had never seen Lok-iKol so angry. Fear could take a man that way, but somehow Dal doubted what he saw in Lok's face was fear.

"Your pardon, my House," he said, keeping his voice neutral. "No one needs to free Mercenaries; they free themselves. The cell was found locked, but empty."

"The cell?—Etkyn! Etkyn, here!" One of Lok-iKol's personal guard charged in from the anteroom, sword drawn. "Go to the east room immediately and check it."

"But, my House—"

"Don't argue, GO!" The man ran from the room.

Dal remained standing at the side of the worktable, watching Lok rap his knuckles against the tabletop. As Heir he was entitled to a chair, but he knew the answer Etkyn would bring, and he thought it best to remain on his feet.

Running feet in the outer room announced Etkyn's return. His face announced his news. Lok's scarred countenance darkened even further. "Search the House," he whispered. "They may not have gone far."

"My House, hear me." Lok looked at him as if he had forgotten Dal was still in the room. With a raised hand he signaled to Etkyn to wait.

"Let them go, my House," Dal said. "They have left without killing anyone. If we let it end here, they may take no action against us." *And we should count ourselves as lucky,* he thought better of saying.

The new Tenebroso nodded slowly. "Perhaps you are right, Cousin. Perhaps so." He sat back in his chair. "Very well." He picked up the parchment he had been studying when Dal had broken the news. Etkyn glanced at him, and, Dal giving him the slightest of nods, left to return to his post outside the door. Dal prepared to follow.

"Cousin," Lok said before Dal had managed more than a couple of steps. "I had intended to meet with our little cousin, the Lady Mar-eMar, this morning. Would you see her for me and ask her something? Ask her—" Lok broke off, staring unseeing at the ceiling of the room. "Ask her at which inn the Brothers who brought her to Gotterang stayed when they arrived."

"Certainly, my House." Dal waited, but Lok returned once again to his parchments.

So much for letting them go, Dal thought, as he, too, bowed and left the chamber. Dal didn't know what was so important about these Mercenary Brothers that Lok would endanger the House in the first place, and go looking for them in the second. Karlyn-Tan did not know either—though the Steward of Walls had now made it his business to find out. The problem was the number of men-at-arms who reported directly to Lok-iKol, and who were not part of Karlyn's guard. The Scholar, Gundaron, he would know. And little Cousin Mar might know something as well. Dal began to walk faster.

Lan-eLan had called the younger relatives and senior staff to meet in the south sitting room, with the Stewards of Walls and Keys in attendance. Like Mar, most of those gathered had heard the news already, but this was the official announcement. The two sisters looked pale, Nor-eNor as though she was about to cry genuine tears, Mar thought. *Ah, well, they knew the Fallen House. Only right they should really mourn her.* This death changed their whole world.

And mine as well, Mar thought, as she watched the older girl wipe her eyes.

As soon as she could, Mar left the assembly and headed back to her room, threading the corridors carefully to avoid getting lost. She was mounting the second staircase when Gundaron caught up with her.

"You're leaving the House," he said, so quietly Mar had to tilt her head toward him to be sure she'd heard him correctly. "Your things this morning," he went on. "You were packing."

Mar risked a glance at his face. He was frowning, but not the kind of frown that seemed about to raise the alarm.

"That's nonsense," she ventured. Her hand slid forward on the banister as she continued up the stairs.

"I'm not going to stop you. In fact," he swallowed. "I'm coming with you."

"You are not." Mar stiffened, her right foot raised for the next step. She couldn't believe how easily he'd tricked her into giving herself away.

He patted the air between them. "Not so loud; do you want to be stopped after all?" He looked down the staircase behind him, and up to where it curved to the right. "Get your things, come to my room and I'll explain."

❦

Mar wasn't sure exactly how she managed it, but it seemed no time at all until Gundaron was showing her into his room, where she sat gingerly on the edge of the round stool at his worktable, watching him empty books out of stiff canvas bags and arrange them in tidy rows on the shelves.

"Here," he said, handing her an empty book bag. "Put your things into this."

"Why?"

"Because neither of us would ever be carrying around bags of clothing in this House, let alone out the gates. But we might be carrying books. I'd be returning them to the Library of Scholars, and you might be interested in coming with me, since you can read. We've no duties to perform for the Fallen House, either of us," he added. "If no one sees us for a while, they'll just be glad we're not underfoot."

Mar swallowed, the words she had to ask trembling on her lips. "Not that 'why.' I meant why would you come with me?"

He lowered his eyes, but not before she saw the fear.

"I can't stay, knowing what I know. I can't do it again. I could have gone to the Fallen House and resigned. She would have accepted my Scholar's oath to keep the House's business to myself. But Lok-iKol . . ." He turned away, began picking up his own clothing. "If we leave together, it's like the book bags. Misdirection. We've no reason to run away together, so no one will think we are." Gundaron took a deep breath and stopped, a clean and neatly folded undershirt in his hand. "I don't want to stay here, and from the look of things, neither do you. We might be able to do together what we'd fail to do alone."

Mar was aware of a small hollow in the center of her body, where she hadn't been aware anything existed. He was coming with her because he had to leave the House, and doing so together made logical and tactical sense. *Well, of course,* she thought, gritting her teeth. *What other reason could he possibly have?* And yet there was that little hollow inside her.

Gundaron didn't know how much he was depending on Mar's agreement until she stood up from the chair and began transferring her clothes and possessions into the book bag he'd given her—and his heart started beating again. Most of what she was shoving into the book bag was clothes and similar bundles, but he recognized the oiled canvas package that held her pens, inks, and spare parchments. *We have a lot in common,* he thought. *It makes sense for us to be together.* He turned back to his own packing, struggling to keep the smile from his face.

He had been afraid to approach Dhulyn Wolfshead, but after learning of the Fall of the House, he'd left Mar and gone down to the cell in the western subcellar where the other Mercenaries were, hoping to explain and apologize. He'd found it locked, but empty. The Mercenaries had left without killing him. And maybe, just maybe, if he kept his head down, they wouldn't come after him—they'd be satisfied with Lok-iKol. He and Lady Mar could get away. Together. He was starting to feel good about this.

"Will these really get us through the Gates?"

"I go to the Library often, and there's no reason for them to stop you, is there?"

The girl shook her head. "They've reason to think I wouldn't dream of running away."

When she didn't continue, Gundaron shrugged. Looked like the Lady Mar-eMar had some secrets of her own.

"Where are we going once we get out of here?" she said.

Once again he hesitated, tongue flicking out to lick his lips. "One thing at a time," he said. "First we get out."

❦

Karlyn looked up from his desk. If it did nothing else, the Fall of the House created another swamp of paperwork, much of it the kind that could not be delegated to his clerks. He smiled with encouragement at the young woman who was his Deputy.

"You asked for anything unusual, Steward of Walls," Jeldor-San said.

"I did."

"The Scholar Gundaron and the Lady Mar-eMar left the House; they claim they go to the Library, and they were carrying book packs."

"Did you send someone to follow them?"

She grinned. "I sent Ollivan, the new man. They're neither of them likely to recognize him, but he knows the city well."

He smiled back at her, pleased with her initiative. This one would make a fine Steward of Walls one day. "Have him report directly to me, when he returns."

"As you wish, Steward of Walls." When his Deputy did not move, he looked up at her with raised brows. "The Lord Dal-eDal was looking for the Lady Mar earlier and not finding her."

"Was he? Never mind, Deputy of Walls, I will speak to him myself."

⧈

Leaving the House had been just as straightforward as Gundaron had thought. Anyone who might normally have exercised their curiosity had other things to think about to-day. Even the offer to get the Lady Mar-eMar a horse had been perfunctory and easily turned down.

Gun led her away to the left, trying to stride along confidently and keep his relief from showing too obviously in his face.

"Slow down," Mar-eMar said. "Why are we going this way?"

"We told them we're going to the Library," he said, slowing his pace to match hers. "So we're headed that way." She was right, though, they should look as though they were out for a stroll, their destination not particularly important. He found himself wishing, as he smelled the sharp bitterness of ganje beans roasting, that they really were just on their way to the Library. They would turn into one of the little shops along the road and sit down, order some ganje or some chocolate, and while away the morning. It wasn't unheard of that a Scholar and the child of a minor Holding could— Gun felt his face grow hot as he cut off the thought before it could complete itself. No point in daydreaming. They'd go their separate ways; Mar had no reason to stay with him, though Gun found himself wishing he could think of one.

"You'll tell me which street I need for the Mercenary House? I don't think I'll recognize it going this way . . . what is it?"

"You c–can't," Gun stammered, stopping dead in his tracks. She couldn't have said what he thought she'd just said.

"Oh, I think they'll still be there," Mar-eMar said. "It's only been a few days, and they were going to look for work here in Gotterang, so even if they've found it—"

"No, I mean—" A large man carrying an iron bedstead

cursed them, and Gun got out of his way, drawing Mar-eMar into the closed doorway of a nearby shop. He hadn't planned to tell her, he didn't *want* to tell her, but how could he live with himself if he let her go to them, knowing what he knew.

"They've not been gone for a few days," he said. "They only escaped last night."

She pulled her sleeve out of his grasp, her face pale. "What do you mean 'escaped'?"

He looked away from her suddenly fierce eyes, but there was nothing to help him in the comings and goings of the late afternoon foot traffic.

"Dhulyn Wolfshead—" No, that wasn't the way. "There was something Lok-iKol wanted from them, something they weren't likely to simply give him or sell him, so he held them until he could persuade them."

"Something he wanted from them?" Mar's brows drew down until they almost met over her eyes. "*This* is why Pasillon made you so afraid. It isn't just a story from your childhood."

Gun clenched his teeth and said nothing.

"It wasn't just the Marked you were Finding, you Found Dhulyn and Parno as well." She looked away from him, the corners of her mouth turned down.

"Mar, I—" Her upheld hand silence him.

"They escaped, you said."

"Yes, but . . . the House Fell."

For a moment Mar just looked at him, eyes wide, mouth fallen open. Then she shook her head, lips thinned to a stubborn line. "They wouldn't have killed her. Lok-iKol, perhaps, but not the House. They'd have known who was to blame."

Almost against his will, Gun found himself agreeing with her.

"No," she went on. "It's Lok-iKol who needs to worry about Pasillon."

"But, Mar," Gun said, not noticing until now that he'd twice used the familiar form of her name. "As you say, they'll know who to blame." When she still looked at him, a puzzled frown twisting her brows, he went on. "I Found them, and you brought them here."

"You don't understand," Mar said, the words clear despite her clenched teeth. "One person's already dead because of me, and I don't want there to be any more."

"But—" Gun was beside himself. "I only told you about this to *prevent* you from going, don't you see? They have every reason to kill you, and you're going to walk right up to their House."

"You're the one who doesn't see. I've got to explain, I can't have them thinking that I *knew*—" Her voice cracked, and she took a breath that shuddered all the way in. "That I knew about this. You'll see. They won't kill me."

Gun wasn't sure if he could explain how thoroughly he *wouldn't* be seeing this. "How certain are you?"

Mar swallowed, her lips trembling. Clearly, she wasn't as sure as she pretended. Her eyes dropped to focus on a pebble at her feet. "They won't kill me," she repeated.

"And if you're wrong?"

Her chin lifted. "According to what you say, it doesn't matter what I do. This is our Pasillon. 'Harm one, harm all.' That's one of their sayings, isn't it? If they want to kill me, they'll find me and do it." She licked her lips. "Well, I don't want to live my life that way, hunted, on the run."

As Mar's words sank in, Gun swallowed against the acid in his stomach. *Hunted. On the run.* He was a Scholar, for the Caids' sake, not a soldier, or a Cloud. Where would *he* suddenly develop the skills to hide from the Mercenary Brotherhood? Was he ready to spend the rest of *his* life looking over his shoulder? He squeezed his eyes shut.

"Thank you for being so worried about me," Mar said. "But I'm sure I'm right."

Here he'd thought there was no way he could feel worse. "I'm in it just as deeply as you are," he heard his voice say. "Deeper."

He felt the gentle pressure of fingers on his shoulder. He couldn't look at her.

"I'm not as brave as you," he said, finally lifting his head to meet her dark blue eyes.

Mar looked back at him, her eyes, so warm and expressive moments ago, shuttered now and cold. After what felt like a long time, she spoke.

"Maybe you're right," she said, letting her hand fall to

her side. "Maybe you'll never have to face it. Good luck." Without another word she set off toward the main street that would take her to Mercenary House. Gun watched her walk away, head up, pack shouldered. Once she turned the corner, he'd never see Mar-eMar again.

Maybe he'd never have to face it. Maybe he'd never have to face anything. What, after all, had he ever faced in his life? He couldn't face being a Finder, he'd wanted Scholarship instead. He hadn't wanted to face what was going on in Tenebro House—hadn't wanted to face losing his research. No wonder Beslyn-Tor had found it so easy to make him forget.

She was almost at the corner. She'd begun the turn, he could almost see her profile.

"Wait!"

Thirteen

DHULYN LOOKED WITH INTEREST around the small reception room. It was sparsely but very expensively furnished, and while the chair opposite the entry doors was too small to be a throne, it was decorated with the distinctive red carnelians that were set aside for the exclusive use of the Tarkins of Imrion. The floor, a soft creamy marble, still had its carpets laid down against the winter chill, and likely would for a few weeks yet. The light oak panels on the walls, even the double doors on the left side of the room, were inlaid with silver hooded snakes, the symbol of the ancient House of Culebro, founders of the Tarkinate of Imrion. Two men and a woman stood close to the Tarkin's chair, and it was the younger man who turned, saluting Alkoryn with a smile and a lifted hand, before taking the seat.

Like the room, Tek-aKet, Tarkin of Imrion, Consage of the Lost Isles, Darklin of Pendamar, and, as it happened, Culebroso, was plainly but richly dressed in the dark red of the Tarkinate. On his left sleeve were two thin stripes of color, yellow and brown, to show his Culebro heritage. As tall as Parno, but as slim as herself, the man was well-muscled, with his northern father's dark hair and his southern mother's fair skin setting off eyes so pale a blue as to be almost colorless. The woman, olive-skinned, her eyes a glowing black, her hair and most of her dark red gown covered by a long veil of purple silk shot with gold, took her place to the Tarkin's right, and Dhulyn realized that it was the Tarkina herself who was taking part in the audience.

Dhulyn hooked her thumbs in her worn leather sword belt, unsure whether the Tarkina's presence would make things easier . . . or harder.

The older man, skinny, and wearing more jewelry than either Tarkin or Tarkina, Dhulyn noted with a grimace, also wore the Carnelian badge on his left shoulder, marking him for some upper-level aide of the Tarkin.

"I greet you, Alkoryn Pantherclaw." The Tarkin's voice was surprisingly gruff coming from so smooth-looking a man. And there was a smile in it, Dhulyn realized, which explained how Alkoryn had been able to see the Tarkin so quickly. Some connection, whether friendship could be the word or no, existed somehow between the two very different men. "My aide Gan-eGan you know," the Tarkin said, gesturing at the older man, "and my Tarkina you have met. You say there is a threat against my life?"

"I greet you, Lords, Lady," Alkoryn said, bowing his head and touching the empty loop on his belt where his sword normally hung. "May I present my Brothers, Dhulyn Wolfshead the Scholar, and Parno Lionsmane the Chanter. It is the Wolfshead who brought this news to me, and I bring her now that you may hear her own words."

The Tarkin turned his pale blue eyes to her, the strange etiquette of the Carnelian court allowing him to notice her for the first time.

"Lord Tarkin," Dhulyn said, lowering her gaze for a moment and touching her sword belt in imitation of Alkoryn's example. Her Senior had heard and approved the version of the story she and Parno had planned, and she began it now. "I have recently been in House Tenebro, and while there I overheard the present Tenebroso speaking with a Jaldean priest. They were discussing your assassination, my lord, and making plans to put the Tenebroso Lok-iKol—the Kir as he then was—on the Carnelian Throne."

The Tarkina lifted her hand, as if to put her fingertips on her husband's shoulder. There was no other movement in the room.

Finally, the Tarkin leaned back in his chair, rested his chin in his right hand. The red stone in his seal ring caught the light, twinkling.

"The newly risen House and a Jaldean priest?"

"Yes, Lord Tarkin."

The Tarkin looked at his aide. "Have your people heard anything of this?"

Gan-eGan shook his head. "No, my lord, and I do not see how this could be so. The Jaldeans have made no changes in their usual demands."

Out of the corner of her eye, Dhulyn saw Parno rub his upper lip with his left index finger. She, too, imagined she knew what the "usual demands" were. Judging from what they'd heard preached on the street, the Jaldeans wanted arrests and detainments, not just green headdresses, curfews and pressure to come to their shrines voluntarily.

Alkoryn cleared his throat. "Nor would there be, if they had something like this in view. You are too moderate for them, Lord Tarkin . . ."

"It may be, as some suggest, that I would prefer the Jaldeans had never found their new teachings," the Tarkin said. "But they are here, many listen and believe, and that is a reality of my reign. I am sorry for the Marked. I have instructed my soldiers, and the guards along my borders not to hinder or stop them if they wish to go, though the Jaldeans would prefer I did otherwise. I am not myself a New Believer, but I will have order, and until I find some other way, the Marked are the price I must pay."

"It is as I have said," the aide said. "The Jaldeans have no need to support the claims of another for the Throne."

"Perhaps the need is Lok-iKol's," Dhulyn said.

"You should be more careful, Mercenary. This is a High Noble House you speak of."

Dhulyn smiled her wolf's smile, and Gan-eGan edged farther away from her. The Tarkin looked quickly aside, lifting his hand to rub at his upper lip. *I could like him, were he not so wrong,* Dhulyn thought, stifling a genuine smile of her own.

"May I ask, Dhulyn Wolfshead, how it is you came to overhear this conversation?" the Tarkin said.

Dhulyn swallowed. This was the tricky part.

"They thought I was unconscious, and so spoke freely before me."

The Tarkin sat up straight. "They thought you were unconscious? How?" He transferred his look to Alkoryn. "Drunk?"

"Drugged, my lord."

The aide sniffed. "Is that not much the same thing?"

"Drugged by *them*."

"To what possible purpose?"

The Tarkin was content, Dhulyn saw, to let his weasel of an aide pursue his questions for him. She drew in air through her nose.

"I did not catch your name, sir," Parno cut in. Dhulyn ground her teeth but stayed silent. This was Parno's world, as she herself had said. She'd do best to let him handle it.

"I am Gan-eGan," the aide said through stiff lips. "I am the head of the Tarkin's private council."

"I am surprised, Gan-eGan, to find you so hostile to persons who have come here with a warning."

"The Brotherhood's neutrality is well known, so you may therefore understand my caution when one of you, claiming to have been drugged, comes with an accusation against a High Noble House," Gan-eGan said.

It was all Dhulyn could do not to throw her hands in the air. This would get them nowhere. "My partner and I delivered a cousin of theirs whom we'd guarded from Navra, and when the job was done, we were set upon and held. We don't know why—perhaps you could ask the Tenebros? They gave me fresnoyn, and while they were waiting to question me—again, I don't know why—I overheard the conversation I've described. The interrogation was interrupted, and we escaped before it could be continued. We thought about remaining in captivity•and asking a few questions of our own, but rational thought prevailed."

"Do not take offense." The Tarkin's eyes danced in an otherwise straight face. "The Carnelian Throne is not an easy seat. Even the accusations of friends must be examined, when they come without proof. Is there proof you can offer me?"

Dhulyn closed her eyes and gritted her teeth. "I thought it was a mistake to come here," she muttered. "Believe us, don't believe us—it's all the same to me."

It was as if Dhulyn had thrown a cat into a dovecote. The weasel of an aide yammering his indignation, Alkoryn's rough whisper failing to catch the Tarkin's ear, and Parno also trying to be heard. Dhulyn ground her teeth together.

This would all be for nothing if she could not get them to believe her. She caught Parno's eye and raised her eyebrows. He grimaced and shrugged, leaving it up to her. She looked from Alkoryn to the Tarkin and back. She was here. Her decision, she realized, had already been made.

She grasped Gan-eGan by the shoulders and moved him to one side as though he had been a child, stepping into the space he had occupied, stepping to within striking distance of the now silent Tarkin. If details were what they wanted . . .

"They will poison you in a dish of kidneys."

Every tongue stilled. Every eye in the room turned to her, and the Tarkin's were not the only ones which had narrowed. Dhulyn took a deep breath, now she was for it. At least the weasely clerk had stopped his yammering.

"You'll be in a little room, much smaller than this one, in an old part of the palace where the walls are very thick. There's a tall, thin window with an archer's grille, and a shutter on the inner wall, with glass panes in it." The Tarkin's chair was elevated enough that Dhulyn looked straight into Tek-aKet's blue eyes. "The lower left-hand pane has some words scratched on the glass; I don't know what they say, it's a language I don't know. I could write it for you, though. There's a worktable, with an armchair on each side of it, both cushioned. A fireplace on the side of the room farthest from the window, with a small fire laid but not yet burning. A dark patterned carpet on the floor, old with worn spots, but you can still see the outline of snakes. A cloth covering the table with weights sewn into the corners—"

"Enough," the Tarkin said, his voice harsh and abrupt. "I know the room."

"Well, they'll bring you a dish of kidneys there, Lord, and you'll die from it."

"How can you know—"

"She's Marked." Only the Tarkina would interrupt the Tarkin, and she'd been silent so long they had all forgotten her. She sounded as though she smiled with delight under her veil, and her voice had the liquid lilt of her northern homeland. "She's a Seer."

"*That's* why you include the Jaldean priest in your accusation." Gan-eGan stabbed the air with his beringed index finger. "Now your motives come clear. The Marked have ample reason to wish the Jaldeans accused of the assassination of the Tarkin." The man's eyes narrowed with calculation as he turned to the Tarkina, "My lady, this is not proof."

"You could always let the Tarkin be poisoned, then you'd know for sure." Parno said in his most reasonable tone.

"I Saw what happens to the Tarkin, and I Saw Lok-iKol on the Carnelian Throne," Dhulyn continued, leaning forward against the grip Parno had on her arm. "I don't need the Sight to know what will happen to you. It's all the same to you who sits on the Carnelian Throne, providing you keep your office—" She poked the aide's shoulder with her index finger.

※

GAN-EGAN STANDS IN THE COUNCIL CHAMBER AND TALKS TO A TALL MAN IN A DARK RED GUARD'S UNIFORM. HE IS CALM AND SMILES A SMALL, VEE-SHAPED SMILE; HIS EYES ARE A WARM JADE GREEN. ANOTHER GAN-EGAN, TRANSPARENT LIKE THE IMAGE OF THE SCHOLAR SHE HAS SEEN BEFORE, STANDS BEHIND HIM, WEEPING, AND WRINGING HIS HANDS. WHEN HE IS FINALLY ALONE, IN HIS OWN ROOM, AND HIS EYES ARE GRAY ONCE MORE, HE FITS A ROPE AROUND HIS NECK AND STEPS ON TO A CHAIR.

※

Dhulyn sucked in air and clung to Parno's arm. The green again. The green fog. In the priest's eyes, in the one-eyed Lok-iKol, and now in this old man. What was it, and how did it move? And why did it seek out the Marked? She swallowed. Gan-eGan's eyes were gray now. If she saved the Tarkin, would she save this counselor as well?

"You will feel differently, sir," she told him. "You will. If this man falls—" she jerked her head toward the Tarkin, "so will you."

Dhulyn stepped back into Parno's circling arm and hung her head, swallowing. They were fools, all of them. Listen to them now, Alkoryn's urgent whisper going unheard, drowned out by the clerk bleating his outrage. Only Parno's murmur in her ear made any sense. She wished she hadn't come.

The doors to the anteroom opened, and the slim, golden-haired young woman who'd been their escort through the winding corridors of the Carnelian Dome came in with a unit of six guards in the Dome colors at her back.

"My lord Tarkin," she said, "a report has come from House Tenebro. It seems the old House did not Fall of age and infirmity as was thought at first. There is now evidence that the Fallen House was poisoned, and two members of the House have run away, suggesting their guilt."

"I grieve to hear it, Amandar," the Tarkin said. "But why must I hear it now?"

"One of the runaways is a distant cousin, Mar-eMar, recently come to the House, and brought by these Mercenary Brothers."

"Who else ran from the House?" Parno said.

The young woman shot a quick glance at Parno out of the corner of her eye before focusing again on the Tarkin.

"The Scholar Gundaron of Valdomar," she said when the Tarkin had nodded his permission for her to answer.

Dhulyn looked at Parno and raised her eyebrows.

"And do we know where these people are now?" the Tarkin asked.

"They were followed almost to the doors of Mercenary House, and then lost, my lord."

"Alkoryn Pantherclaw," the Tarkin said. "You will understand that I must detain your Brothers—" He raised his hand to halt Alkoryn's whispered protests. "This is the Fall of a High Noble House, and not any House, mind, but one closely related to my own . . . and it places into a different light the tale that these Brothers have brought you. Some will say," here he looked aside at Gan-eGan, "that they wished to make the first move in a game of accusations—but enough! Questions must be asked, and these Brothers will remain here, well-treated, until the answers are found. You, I hold blameless; you may go. But see that you send the Tenebro cousin and the Scholar Gundaron to me, should you have occasion to find them."

"My lord, we are neutrals, we cannot merely—"

"You may go." The Tarkin stood and looked to his wife, who shook her head and remained standing beside the chair. He nodded to Alkoryn, and left the room by the double doors to the right of his chair, accompanied by Gan-eGan. Once her husband had cleared the door, the Tarkina turned back to the young woman and the guards.

"Amandar, you will give me a moment with these Brothers. You guards may wait outside. Alkoryn Pantherclaw, I know you have matters to attend to at your own House."

"I do, my lady, but I expect to return for my Brothers." He turned to them and touched his forehead.

Dhulyn caught herself before the smile reached the surface of her lips. It was not the Tarkina, but she and Parno who were being reminded. Dhulyn remembered Alkoryn's workroom, and the charts and floor plans that lined his shelves, and thought she knew how Alkoryn intended to return for them.

"Dhulyn, Parno," Alkoryn touched his forehead with his fingertips. "In Battle."

"Or in Death," they replied in unison, saluting him in return.

The young woman, Amandar, hesitated but finally made a short bow and gestured the guards out of the room. The Tarkina waited until they were alone before sitting down in the Tarkin's chair and throwing off her veil with a sigh. The face revealed was striking, her olive skin darker than the norm for Imrion, and her profile too pronounced, too hawklike, for conventional beauty. But her eyes, the darkest Dhulyn had ever seen, were large and lustrous, her lips full, warm and ready to smile.

Dhulyn pressed her own lips together. She'd wondered what the presence of the Tarkina might mean; perhaps she was about to find out.

"Do you know when this will come to pass?"

For a moment, Dhulyn wasn't sure what the woman was asking about. Then she remembered it was the Tarkina who had guessed she was Marked.

"You believe me," she said.

The dark woman in the Carnelian chair nodded slowly, the jewels in her hair twinkling in the light of the oil lamps. "Most people think there are no Seers left in the world, but I know differently. There was one, an old man from the far west, at my grandfather's court when my father was a child. Long before my time, truly, but unlike Gan-eGan, I do not need to experience something personally to know that it exists."

"And you do not mistrust the Wolfshead's words, simply because she *is* Marked?" Parno said, his head tilted to one side as he considered the woman in the chair.

"No," the Tarkina said, leaning back in such a way that it was obvious she'd often sat in her husband's chair. "By what I was taught, the New Believers are heretics, and in Berdana the Queen, my sister, provides asylum to the Marked, and refuses the demands they are starting to make. Here in Imrion they are my husband's subjects, and therefore safe from my bad opinion."

"You're not afraid of what you don't understand?"

The dark woman shrugged. "I don't understand higher mathematics, but I am not afraid of the Tarkin's accountants nor yet his astronomers. And I'm not afraid of the Marked, that's certain. Whether I understand it . . ." She shrugged again. "When we were young, my sister and I, in our father's palace in Berdana we had many companions from among the children of the noble classes, and my favorite, the one who I think would have loved me even if I were not the daughter of the King, she was Marked. Not a Seer, no, but a Finder. Because of my love for my friend, our tutors told us stories of the Marked, and made their histories part of our studies."

The Tarkina brought her gaze back from the shadows of her childhood to focus once more on Dhulyn. "If I can persuade my husband, will you help him? And if I cannot, can I hire you myself, to act as eyes and ears about the Dome?"

"Lady, I believe we are being detained under suspicion of abetting in the Fall of a House."

"Yes, that is a small problem."

"I'm glad you think so."

"You misunderstand me. I'm not concerned with the Fall of Tenebro House. I'm concerned with the Tarkin—personally," she said, giving Dhulyn a direct look from her raven-dark eyes, "not just for the sake of my position, and the position of my children. I believe it would be a tragedy for Imrion to loose Tek-aKet as their Tarkin, but it would be more than a tragedy for me to lose my husband. At the moment, Tek and the moderates among the Houses who support him are keeping the Jaldeans in check in this country. If the New Belief wins here, there will be war. War here will mean war for Berdana; my sister cannot remain neutral."

The Tarkina leaned forward and rested her chin on her right fist. "Gan-eGan is a fine man, whatever you might think, but he lacks imagination. Unlike him, I believe the Jaldeans will not stop their persecutions with the Marked, and if the Carnelian Throne will not give them what they want, I believe they will take the Throne. For Imrion, which is now my home, for Berdana my homeland, for my sister as well as my husband and children, I would push the Jaldeans back into their temples, and out of the council halls. For the sake of my old friend, I would have the Marked free again. Will you help me?"

Dhulyn glanced at Parno and found him looking at her, the same thought, she knew, in both their minds. This is what they had talked about, back in the Mercenary House, when she hadn't been sure about warning the Tarkin. The Tarkina saw the same things in the Jaldeans that they had seen themselves. The balance would be upset, no matter what the Tarkin thought, and she and Parno needed to know on which side of the scales they were weighed.

"If we are free and alive," Dhulyn told the dark woman in the Tarkin's chair, "we will help you."

⊗⊗⊗

The woman they brought him had a strong golden fire, small but perfect. He shuddered, knowing that he was broken and in pieces, who should never have had form to begin with. The shape of Beslyn-Tor was whole, and wearing it was less exhausting than trying to form and hold a shape of his own; it was easy to gather his powers—to gather *himself*—and push into her eyes, probing into the flame, smelling it, tasting it, feeling its strengths. Holding it in his hands.

A Mender.

In an instant he was in the mirror room, standing over the Mender woman holding her head between his hands; holding it high and tight so that her neck stretched uncomfortably and her eyes flared with alarm. This is where it had begun. Where he'd been *Seen* and *Found* and *Healed* and

Mended. No matter that he had not been lost, and was neither sick nor broken.

"Do you know this room? Have you seen me before?" She had a different form, but that did not mean this was not the Mender who had first given him shape. Even now, even after all this eternal passage of time in this world of forms and solids, he did not understand all that it was possible for shape to do. "Are you the one? Can you open the door?"

Her eyes flicked from side to side, seeing the great round mirror that held the doorway, the worktable with its scrolls and books. The sword.

"No, my lord. No." She would have shaken her head, if he had not been holding it so tightly.

At once they were in the priest's room in the Jaldean Shrine in Gotterang, he still holding her head between his hands. He reached into her with his own essence, sought out and found once more the golden flame. It burned hot and chaotic, almost shapeless. But he knew what true shapelessness was, and this was a mockery. He touched the golden flame and released it, dissolved its form. Made it NOT.

The woman fainted. When they took her away, her face was empty and she cried.

He was resting when the Tenebro Lord Dal-eDal came. His was a red flame. No danger there. The man held himself stiffly, as if he would rather be elsewhere.

"I am sent by the Tenebroso Lok-iKol," Dal-eDal said, coughing to disguise the roughness in his voice.

"It is true, then. The House has Fallen."

"It has."

"He gives me a time?"

"Tonight, if it is possible."

He nodded. "Tonight it shall be." He closed his eyes, and the Tenebro Lord went away.

"Go out, my eyes and ears," he whispered when he was alone again. "Go out, all my tongues, and whisper. It is time."

"Are you sure we're not lost?" Mar pulled the hood of her cloak closer around her face as the rain that had started threatening soon after they'd left Tenebro House began to fall in small, sharp drops. The balcony under which they stood was too narrow to give them any real cover, but at least the rain was keeping most of the townspeople off the streets.

"Of course I'm sure."

Mar pressed her lips together. Why was it that fear so often made people angry? She'd been so pleased when he'd called after her, she'd known that Gun was braver than he'd thought. She only wished he was brave enough not to be annoyed now that he *was* doing the right thing. Though, with luck, he wasn't irritated enough to be mistaken about the way . . . she'd followed his lead, trusting that he knew where he was going, but once they'd left the wider avenues for the warren of alleys, laneways, and courtyards that lay to the north of the Great Square, she was well and truly adrift.

Gundaron tapped the wall they stood by. "This is the east wall of the Bootmaker's Inn, the one you told me about." His fair brows drew down in a vee. Mar opened her mouth . . . and closed it without asking again if he was sure. Gun looked over at her.

"I'm thinking," he said, "that we might not want to just walk up to the Brothers' front door. Maybe we should be a bit more circumspect."

"If this is some way to get out of going there," Mar began, but was silenced by his tight-lipped headshake.

"We're not having that argument again," he said, voice gruff. "But we might not be the only ones looking for Dhulyn Wolfshead." His lips trembled as though there were words he held back before continuing. "I'd like a chance to see if there's anyone there we wouldn't want to run into."

Mar nodded. That made sense. She shifted her pack higher on her left shoulder.

"If you follow along until the end of this wall and turn right, a little ways up you'll come to one of the big archways, one of the entrances to the Great Square; then, just a bit farther along, Mercenary House is on the right-hand side, the same side as the entrance," Gun said. "There's another laneway on the left, just before you get there."

"And so?"

"So you can walk down and then turn into the other

lane. You'll look like you're going down toward the Old Market, but you can see if there's anyone suspicious around Mercenary House."

Mar took her lower lip in her teeth. "Why me?" She thought it extremely unlikely she'd know what "anyone suspicious" looked like.

"Because no one from Tenebro House is likely to recognize you in clothes they saw you in for five minutes four days ago. Me, they've been living with for two years."

At first Mar was inclined to argue further—after all, no one could be looking for them yet, and when the search began, *if* it began, surely no one would think to look for them here. Still, she felt Gundaron's logic, and second thoughts persuaded her that this was exactly what Dhulyn Wolfshead and Parno Lionsmane would have done.

"Mar-eMar," Gundaron said, when she still hadn't spoken. "If you're not sure—you don't have to do this."

Mar looked up sharply, but his eyes were firmly on hers, his gaze direct and open. This was no ploy to get her to change her mind; Gundaron was really worried about her, was really offering her a chance to think about it. It had all seemed so clear when she was explaining it to him around the corner from the Scholars' Library. She couldn't believe she was in any danger, but now she couldn't help remembering what the Lionsmane had told her on the way to Gotterang. *Anyone might kill you.*

She dragged in enough air to fill her lungs. They'd saved her life. Dhulyn Wolfshead had killed someone for her. The Caids only knew what had been done to them in return. She owed them an explanation and an apology. Nothing changed that.

"Keep my pack for me," she said, slipping the book bag off her shoulder and stepping out around the corner.

Gun watched her walk away, head high, step sure. Everything he'd said to her was true. It *was* better, and safer for both of them for Mar to go. But he felt like a coward just the same. Was there anything he could do to help her? Could he Find danger? He closed his eyes.

The Library. Something trying to reach him . . . he recoils. The green fog. The shelves and tables laden with scrolls and books form walls around it, keeping it away, keeping him safe. Gundaron looks at the book nearest him and sees a name. *Mar-eMar.* He puts his hand on it. Stay here. Stay with me. It's safe here.

The rain was a bit heavier away from the shelter of the wall, and Mar hunched her shoulders against it, holding her cloak closed in front of her. *Makes it less likely anyone's around to see me,* she told herself, hoping that it was true. She followed the wall down to its end and turned right. The street jogged to the left—something Gundaron hadn't mentioned—and Mar's heart thumped loudly as at first she saw neither the Mercenary House, nor the laneway that she was supposed to dodge into before she got there. But as she followed the street along, she recognized the arched entrance to the Great Plaza and breathed more easily. A man came sauntering out of the archway, and her heart skipped a beat until she saw that, though he wore a sword under his cape, he was far too well-dressed to be on any guard's payroll. He was bareheaded, his hair cropped short, and his face was clean-shaven, revealing a tattoo of thin black lines over the left side. He acknowledged her with a shallow bow before he turned and walked toward the Mercenary House.

Cloudman, she thought, *Racha man, too.* Mar remembered seeing the same tattoo on Yaro of Trevel. She continued down the road until she'd passed the archway and crossed as she drew abreast of the lane leading away on the left, just where Gun had said it was.

And there was the small gated archway of Mercenary House, and the Racha man just going in the postern door. Mar had taken a half step toward the House, forgetting Gundaron's plan, when a guardsman wearing a black cloak with a familiar crest on the left shoulder and a broad teal stripe along the bottom approached the Mercenary's gate from the far side, and called out to the still open door. Mar ducked into the lane before the man could turn to look in her direction. Only after several minutes had passed did her heart slow down and her breathing return to something like normal.

Mar could hear voices as the guard in Tenebro colors exchanged words with the Brother answering the gate at Mercenary House, but their voices were low, and the rain was noisy enough that she couldn't overhear what was said. *Now is the time to move,* Mar thought. *While the attention of the guard from Tenebro House was taken up by the Brother.* Mar took three slow, deep breaths and stepped out of the lane, turning immediately back in the direction she'd come from. Remembering something Dhulyn Wolfshead had told her in the mountains, Mar dragged her left foot a little with each step, changing entirely the way she walked, and forced herself to go slowly, as if she hadn't a care in the world besides getting home for her supper.

By the time she got back to the semi-dry corner where Gundaron waited, the pain in her left foot was real, and her stomach was tight as a fist. She pushed back her hood, welcoming the cool touch of the rain, as she told Gundaron what she'd seen.

He licked his lips, looking from her to the corner of the wall and back again.

"Most likely it's the Mercenary Brothers they're looking for, but I'd be very surprised if that guard hasn't orders to watch the place, at least for tonight."

"Where does that leave us?"

"It's late, and later still for us to find a room somewhere even if we could afford it." He frowned. "If we can make our way into the Old Market, we should be able to find somewhere to lay up until morning. Give us a chance to figure out what to do next."

Mar swallowed, picked up her pack. If he was anything like as exhausted as she was, he'd be glad of any place out of the rain where they could sit down.

"I'm not promising much," he said, and he started to re-trace their steps.

"I was almost a moon on the road with Mercenaries," she said. "I don't expect much."

❈❈❈

Hernyn Greystone was making himself small and unno-ticed behind a pillar in the Carnelian Dome's outer court-yard when his Senior Brother came out of the building alone. With his damaged voice, Alkoryn Pantherclaw rarely went about the city unattended, and Hernyn had begged for the privilege of accompanying him on his errand. The chance to be of service to Dhulyn Wolfshead and Parno Lionsmane was only part of it, he assured himself. Only people with necessary business were let inside the Dome, however, which left him cooling his heels out here. With a sinking feeling in his stomach, Hernyn made his way across the cobblestones and around a carriage being pulled out of a nearby stable entrance to Alkoryn's side.

"Tenebro's Deputy Steward of Walls came in half an hour ago," he reported to the older man.

"With news I'll tell you as we go," Alkoryn said, walking briskly to the Dome's open gates. "Did the Deputy see you?"

"No." Hernyn hesitated, but as Alkoryn Pantherclaw was already on his way across the courtyard, he could do nothing but follow.

"Our Brothers?" he managed to murmur once they were out in Tarkin's Square, a broad expanse of normally sun-drenched pavement fronting the massive pile of buildings that was the Carnelian Dome, seat of the Tarkins of Imrion.

"Detained."

Hernyn listened in growing disbelief as Alkoryn told him of what had passed within.

"But—did you know this of Dhulyn Wolfshead?"

Alkoryn shrugged. "It's rare for the Marked to become Mercenaries, and Seers are the rarest of the Marked. . . ." His whisper died away. "There's nothing in the Common Rule about such a thing. Nothing to tell us what to do or, or what to think."

"Is she still . . . ?" It was so unthinkable Hernyn couldn't bring himself to say it, but fortunately Alkoryn knew exactly what he wanted to ask. And he knew the answer, too.

"Of course she is," he said. "Brotherhood ends only with death."

But for all that, there was something troubling the older man, Hernyn could tell that much.

The streets near the Dome were much more crowded than Hernyn would have expected, given that it was late and just beginning to rain. As they turned into the avenue that would eventually lead them to the Great Square and their House, they ran into a group of men blocking almost the whole of the way. Hernyn stepped forward.

"If we may pass?" he said.

Several young men, and one not so young, stepped back out of the way with nods. *What I wouldn't give for a horse,* Hernyn thought as Alkoryn returned the nod of a bearded shopkeeper he obviously knew by sight. *And what's a silk merchant doing here?* Hernyn wondered, making his own assessment of the man's clothing. They passed out of the quarter of Noble Houses that crowded as closely as they were allowed to the Carnelian Dome and through the neighborhood of jewelers and metalsmiths. Here there were still shops, but these were the lesser trades: food sellers, weavers, cobblers, bakers, and the like. Though rain was falling more heavily, and the shops were closed and closing, there were still a surprising number of people, both men and women, on the streets at a time when most should be at home preparing for their suppers. Nor did they appear to be on their way home. Small groups formed and re-formed, and some, though talking in friendly enough fashion, kept looking over their shoulders. One tall fellow with a smith's heavy shoulders and a familiar amulet around his throat, stared hard at Hernyn's green cloak as they walked by.

Hernyn tossed back his hair to draw attention to his Mercenary badge, bared his teeth in a strained smile, and placed his hand casually on his sword hilt. And knew without looking that Alkoryn had done the same.

"If I were you, my Brother," Alkoryn said, tugging at Hernyn's dark green cloak once they'd left the smith behind, "I'd think about getting something in a different color."

"It was a good price," Hernyn said.

"And now you know why."

As streets wide enough for two coaches became narrower and shorter, they passed shops which were now closed for the night, and the small knots of whispering folk grew fewer, and farther between. They were able to make better time here, and Hernyn had picked up the pace when Alkoryn spotted a woman in dark green creeping from doorway to doorway, taking advantage of every shadow the rainy evening offered her. As they drew near, she pressed herself into a doorway, turning her face away from them and waiting to let them pass. Hernyn was just thinking that she'd better hurry—curfew for the Marked was the setting sun, and with the rain it was hard to prove that the sun had not already set—when Alkoryn signaled to him with a quick finger snap and stopped in front of the woman, effectively shielding her from any others who might pass by.

"Korwina Mender," he said, his soft whisper making it perfectly safe to say her name. "I thought you were gone from Gotterang."

Seeing who it was, the woman looked up, but didn't leave the deep shadow of the doorway. "Your advice was good, Charter, but we left it too late. We were turned back from the gate."

Hernyn winced at a sudden bad taste in his mouth.

"I'm sorry, Korwina, that can't be good," Alkoryn said.

"So we thought, and it's followed by worse. I'm to present myself and my family at the Jaldean High Shrine tomorrow morning."

Alkoryn shook his head. "Do they know your family? How many. . . . ?"

"If they don't, there's plenty of my neighbors will tell them." The woman's tone had no resentment, no bitterness, Hernyn noticed. They'd got used to this kind of thing in Gotterang. She shrugged. "They'll have to, to save themselves. Still, I've been going round now, to my best customers, to see if there's any will hide my children. If they're not there tomorrow, the Jaldeans can't take them, no matter what tales the neighbors tell. But no one dares." Again, she sounded as if she didn't blame them. "They don't know, you see, what the Jaldeans may do to us once we've gone to them. They can't risk that I might tell . . ." the Mender drew in a shaky breath. "That I might tell where my babies are hidden."

"Send them to us," Alkoryn said.

Hernyn looked up in surprise.

"Come to Mercenary House." Alkoryn's voice sounded harsher than usual. When the older man turned to him, Hernyn had had time to school his face.

"You go with her, my Brother, make sure she and the children are safe and none see you. Your Brothers in the House will know what to do with them. Tell your Brothers further what has occurred at the Dome; tell them to bar all doors and gates, and to make the lower chambers ready. Then join me yourself at the Dome." Alkoryn looked off into the middle distance, as if he were listening to some music only he could hear. "Tell them that if we are not back by sunrise, Fanryn Bloodhand is Senior."

"But, Alkoryn—"

"I'm a fool, Hernyn, I've been too long with my maps. The time for counsel and waiting is passed. Go now, do it quickly."

His mouth suddenly dry as sand, Hernyn nodded, and stepped round to take the Marked woman gently by the elbow.

"Waste no time," Alkoryn said. "In Battle."

Hernyn touched his forehead. "Or in Death."

"The Caids bless you," the Mender said in the ancient way, "the Sleeping God hold you in his dreams."

"Someone'll have to," Hernyn muttered, as he followed the Mender woman down a narrow corridor between two buildings. *She did that well,* he thought, almost like a Mercenary. It was surprising what people could learn when they had to.

❧❧❧

Tek-aKet, Tarkin of Imrion, stood a long time at the window of his private room, watching his reflection dance on the rain dripping down the panes of glass, and running his fingers from time to time against the five words scratched there by some unknown ancestor's jewel. Like Dhulyn Wolfshead, he did not know the language, though he also thought he could draw the letters from memory.

The sound of the door latch drew him around, and made the old dog sleeping in front of the fire raise its eyelids.

Larissa-Lan, junior page for this old tower, and therefore the one who usually brought whatever was required to the Tarkin's private workroom, entered balancing a tray with practiced ease on her left hand. On the tray, along with cutlery, linen, and a breadbasket, was a heavy ceramic dish whose close-fitting lid barely contained the familiar odors of a wine sauce.

"Here we go, sir," said the young woman, smiling. "Still hot, and unsampled, though I had to threaten Kysh with a beating."

"What is it?" Tek asked, though he thought he knew.

The page looked up in surprise. "Why, your favorite, Lord. Kidneys in jeresh sauce." She advanced on the work-table, set down the tray, and laid out a heavy place mat for the hot dish. Beside it on the right she placed a crisp napkin folded in the shape of a crane, along with one of the new silver forks, and arranged the small breadbasket to the left.

Tek did his best to nod naturally even while his throat closed and his stomach dropped abruptly. This was coincidence with a vengeance—and altogether too pat for comfort.

"And who ordered this treat for me?"

"The Tarkina, my lord. At least, that's what the cook told me. I was to say, with the compliments of the Tarkina."

"Excellent, Larissa, thank you."

"A pleasure, sir. Enjoy." With the confidence of familiarity the young woman left the room.

Enjoy. Well that was going to be difficult. Tek almost wished young Kysh *had* taken a taste of it. Then at least he'd know. . . .

He shook his head and sat down at the table. He already knew. Of course he did. There was nothing wrong with these kidneys and he didn't need a taster. Tek broke off a piece of bread and picked up his fork in his right hand, speared a particularly juicy looking bit of kidney, and, using the piece of bread to stop the sauce from dripping on his clothes, lifted the tasty morsel to his mouth.

The Tarkin of Imrion let the fork clatter down on the plate. The old dog raised its head.

Larissa said the Tarkina had ordered the dish. Any other day Tek would have believed it—but not today. Just this morning, long before the request for an audience had come from Alkoryn Pantherclaw the Charter, Zelianora had talked to him about how tight his clothes were getting, and how little exercise he'd managed to get over the winter. A nice dish of steamed carrots, flavored with cumin. Apples spiced with cinnamon—even a hot soup. Those he would have expected Zella to send him. But kidneys in jeresh sauce? Not likely.

That didn't mean the dish was poisoned. And it didn't mean that it wasn't.

Old Berlan got up with difficulty from his spot by the fire and walked his old dog's walk to nudge his master's hand. Tek absently stroked the bony old head, pulling the long silky ears through his fingers. The dog laid his head on Tek's thigh and snuffled. Tek looked at the dish of kidneys, at his dog, and back to the dish. Berlan was too old to hunt, too old even to go outside, almost too old to eat. His pain was not yet great, but that day, too, would come.

Tek took in a deep breath and let it out slowly. He thrust one finger into the center of the ceramic dish to test for heat before placing the dish on the floor. He watched as Berlan, tail wagging, began to eat. No great harm, perhaps even a kindness, if the dish *was* poisoned.

And if the dish wasn't poisoned? No great harm there either.

Tek-aKet, Tarkin of Imrion, Consage of the Lost Isles, Darklin of Pendamar, and Culebroso, sat back in his chair to watch his dog eat.

Fourteen

"MY INSTRUCTIONS WERE very clear, Mistress. I'm to escort you *and* the children to Mercenary House." Hernyn hovered in the doorway to the Mender's inner room, frustration and impatience making his skin crawl. The family were living in the two back rooms of what had been a decent tradesman's dwelling—before the furniture had been sold and the family tapestries and ornaments taken from the walls, leaving pale marks behind to show where they had been. There were two tick mattresses on the uncarpeted stone floor that had obviously seen their bedsteads sold out from under them, and the outer room held only three mismatched chairs, an unpainted wooden table, and a carefully arranged stack of pottery plates and mugs.

Three children, a boy of about eleven, and two younger girls, perhaps seven and four, sat close-mouthed and wide-eyed on the edge of the larger mattress.

"I must wait for my man." Korwina Mender fastened the ties on a small leather pack and handed it to the older boy. "He's been out same as I have, looking for a place to hide the children. I can't let him come back to an empty house. Please," she turned to Hernyn, showing him a face that wouldn't accept a "no." "I'll wait and bring him with me. But please, Hernyn Greystone, take the children now."

Korwina Mender looked at him, mouth set, the words she wouldn't say in front of her children shining from her eyes. That her man would come back too late, if he came back at all. That, having seen her children safe, she would wait to share whatever ending fate brought her husband.

Hernyn looked from the children to the door and back again. Time was wasting. "Say your good-byes," he told Korwina.

The older boy stood and went to his mother, the pack clutched in his hands, his face solemn. He was almost as tall as she, with the same soft brown hair and hazel eyes. Korwina brushed the hair back off his forehead with a steady hand.

"I'll not be long," she said. "But you are the head of the family until your father and I come. Watch out for your sisters." She turned to the two younger children. "Mind your brother, and the good Mercenaries, until . . ." her voice faltered and she looked back at her son.

"Don't wait too long, Mama," the boy said.

"I won't, my heart." But the look they exchanged showed that both knew the truth. There was not luck enough left in the air tonight to bring the husband and father home in time, and this was good-bye. The boy swallowed and blinked rapidly, as if he knew that tears would frighten the younger children. But his lips were trembling too much for him to say anything more.

Korwina Mender took her son's face once more between her hands and shut her own eyes. After a moment she opened them again, and her son's face was calm, peaceful. He pressed his lips together and nodded, touching his mother's face lightly. Hernyn looked from one to the other, knowing that something had happened, but unsure what it could be. The boy looked more solid somehow, more *whole*. *She's Mended him,* Hernyn thought, licking suddenly dry lips. *By the Caids, she's* Mended *him.*

"Hernyn Greystone," the woman said, lifting her hands slightly as the boy led his sisters from the room. "I should tell you, my boy shows signs of Mending, like me. We've told no one else."

"I don't care if he shows signs of being a vulture plant," Hernyn said. "Good luck to you, Korwina."

"And to you, Greystone."

As soon as they were out on the street, Hernyn picked up the older girl and set off as quickly as the boy, carrying his younger sister, could manage.

"What's your name, boy?"

"Jerrick."

"Come along, then, Jerrick."

Close to an hour later, Mender's children safely stowed in Mercenary House and managing to eat the food Fanryn had set before them with a surprising appetite, Hernyn Greystone was on his way to the Carnelian Dome through back alleys washed clean by the rain. As he sprinted toward the main avenue, he became aware of the sounds of a crowd ahead of him. He slowed, drew the longer of his two swords, and shifted over to the right-hand side of the alley as three men, two carrying long butcher knives, the third with a rusty short sword, ran past him on the left. The last man looked over with a hard eye, but Hernyn's Mercenary badge showed well in the moonlight that had followed the rain, and he had to stifle the laughter that bubbled up in his throat when he saw how quickly the man's belligerent look became polite. Instead of saying whatever he had intended to say, the man ducked his head and hurried after his friends.

As he neared Tarkin's Square in front of the Carnelian Dome, the rumbling he'd heard in the distance grew louder, becoming murmuring, with individual voices raised in shouts Hernyn couldn't quite make out. It seemed like every corner he passed had grown a knot of three or four men. This was no ordinary crowd, Hernyn thought, his stomach muscles tightening, but a mob in the making.

He slowed his pace still further and sheathed his sword, but kept his hand resting lightly on the grip. Trying to appear nothing more than curious, he sauntered up to the nearest group of men. "Hey, friend," he said. "What's caused all this buzz? Are we invaded?"

"Have you not heard?" the man said, his smile wide, plainly pleased to be giving news to a Mercenary Brother. "There'll be work for you boys, that's certain. Imrion's Fallen."

Hernyn hoped his raised eyebrows disguised the shock he felt.

"The Tarkin's been poisoned," the man continued. "They say it's those cursed Marked."

Hernyn walked away, his eyes fixed on the towers of the Carnelian Dome, still some blocks away. The distant shouting had become screaming, and he could hear the sounds of metal clashing on metal.

Hernyn began to run.

⊱⊰

Dhulyn was getting tired of these very nice rooms. This one had a deep pile rug on the flagstone floor, a highly polished table with two comfortable chairs, a pitcher of wine with matching glazed cups, and a plate of one-bite meat pies. Everything, in fact, to entertain waiting guests except music, windows, and an unlocked door.

She looked up from the vera tiles she was laying out on the table as Parno asked the same question for the third time.

"Alkoryn says he'll return for us," she said, giving the same answer she'd given twice already. "Compose yourself in patience, my soul."

"Caids take it, of course he'll come," Parno said. He turned back to the door and stroked the lock with the fingertips of his right hand. "You're certain we shouldn't help him a bit ourselves? Meet him halfway, as it were?"

Dhulyn shot him the look she usually reserved for people cheating at tiles and put down the tile she was holding with an audible click. "You're the expert on politics and Noble Houses," she said. "You tell me. Tell me you think it's a good idea for us to wander about the Carnelian Dome hoping to meet our Brother in hallways crawling with servants, pages, and nobility both high and low, to say nothing of the Tarkin's Personal Guard. Tell me this, and that lock's as good as picked." Dhulyn went back to studying the hand she was laying out before Parno had even finished rolling his eyes. She moved a page of swords from its place in a sequence of sword tiles so that it stood next to the seven of staffs. The two tiles, though of different suits, had the same color pattern. Green. There was a hand. A winning hand called Tarkin's Jade. She looked at the tiles, frowning. She could have sworn that for a moment she'd seen something else, not a pattern exactly, but some total lack of . . .

"Parno—" she began.

"Shhh. Someone comes." From habit, Parno moved

away from the door to stand where he wouldn't be immediately visible when it was opened. He needn't have bothered. The Tarkin's Guard weren't Mercenary Brothers, but they weren't common idiots either; the one who opened the door checked both walls before he allowed the tall young man behind him to enter.

"I greet you," the young man said. "I am Far-eFar, Senior Page of the Old Tower. The Tarkin Tek-aKet thanks you for waiting so patiently and sends me to ask that you join him at your earliest convenience."

Even Dhulyn could tell that this was mere politeness for "now and be quick about it."

"We're at his lordship's disposal," Parno said, with a bow that Dhulyn was sure gave credit to his childhood tutors. He gave his arm to Dhulyn, and she put her fingertips on it, exactly as she'd seen noble ladies do. The Senior Page smiled and, nodding to the guards who remained at their stations, led the Mercenaries out of the room.

"You have no guards with you?" Parno said, as if he were remarking on the weather.

"No need," Far-eFar said. "I assure you I know the way."

Dhulyn exchanged a look with Parno behind Far-eFar's back. This did not have the smell of a trick. So the Tarkin no longer felt the need to guard them? Was this the work of the Tarkina, or had something else happened? They knew there was no point in questioning Far-eFar; no one could be in the Tarkin's household for long and not have learned when to speak and when to hold his tongue.

Though this did not mean that the young man stayed silent, Dhulyn observed with a grin. He was a well brought up lad, Far-eFar, and he made a polite inquiry about archery that soon had Parno chatting with him as if they were on their way to the supper table at the young man's home. Dhulyn listened, half-entertained and half-annoyed. That nobles, whether of Houses, Households, or Holdings, couldn't go ten breaths without speaking was something she already knew. Nor was Parno acting, aping the manners of the noble class; this was the voice, the manner, even the way of walking that he'd practiced for years before he had come to the Brotherhood. Before she had met him on the field at Arcosa, before they had become Partnered.

Dhulyn pressed her lips together. No point in lying to herself; being so close to the lures of Parno's old life still worried her. Even if her Vision had been of his past and not his future—something she could not be sure of—that did not mean that all would be well for them now. Parno was so sure there was nothing here to entice him, he did not even have his guard up. She looked at him out of the corner of her eye. The sooner they were out of *these* noble lives and back to their own, the better.

The hallways through which they walked became narrower, dating from more austere times when ladies' skirts were not so wide as fashion had them now. The walls were dressed stone instead of paneling, the ceilings squared instead of arched, and made of inlaid woods instead of painted plaster. Dhulyn gave a silent whistle. Was it possible she'd recognize the room they were heading for?

Far-eFar stopped in front of a heavy oak door reinforced with bands of metal. There was an old lock, the kind that had a key as big as a man's hand, but one of the smaller, more difficult to pick modern locks had been added above it. Far-eFar rested his long-fingered hand on the heavy iron handle that lay between the two locks.

"I wait here," he said, as he opened the door for them.

Dhulyn took a step forward and looked around her with interest. There was the table with its cloth, weights sewn into the corners so that breezes wouldn't disturb it. The fireplace, ready to be lit. The window with its etched pane.

The Tarkin on the floor with a dog's head in his lap.

"He wasn't in a lot of pain, not yet," the Tarkin of Imrion said without looking up. "But he was old, and soon the pain would have become much worse." He looked up at Dhulyn. "They brought me a dish of kidneys in jeresh sauce," he said. "I gave them to Berlan. He took my death."

Dhulyn crouched down next to the Tarkin. She stroked the still-warm muzzle with the backs of her fingers.

"Do you think he would have preferred it otherwise?"

The Tarkin looked at her, frowning, before his countenance cleared. He almost smiled. "No," he said, his voice sounding much lighter. "Not at all. Thank you." He gently placed the old dog's head on the curly wool of the hearth rug and stood, shrugging the stiffness out of his shoulders as he returned to the chair behind his worktable. He stood for a moment, his eyes on his old dog, before waving at the chairs on the opposite side with an open hand.

Parno had long ago given up any expectation of ever again finding himself sitting down in the same room as his distant kin, the Tarkin of Imrion. In the back of his mind a much younger version of himself was making a very childish gesture at his father. Parno grinned, leaned back in his chair, and propped his right ankle on his left knee.

"And so I take it from this that neither you nor the Lady Mar-eMar, nor even the Scholar of Valdomar had anything to do with the Fall of Tenebro House? As the poet says, 'True in one thing, true in all things?'"

"Take whatever you like," Dhulyn said, shrugging. "Proving it's a different breed of horse altogether."

Parno was never sure why Dhulyn, who'd read far more than he and could speak in as cultured a manner as any Library Scholar, often took great care to sound as barbarous as possible. He'd have thought her nervous with the noble classes — if he'd ever seen her nervous. He'd opened his mouth to speak, thinking in any case to take the pressure of conversation with the Tarkin from her, when an urgent tap sounded on the door. From the look of astonishment on the Tarkin's face, it was a sound he'd never heard in this place.

"My lord." Far-eFar, pale as a piece of bleached parchment, entered without waiting for a summons. "I beg your pardon, my lord. Alkoryn Pantherclaw the Charter is here saying there are rioters in the streets, proclaiming your death by poison. The Guard Captain's sent men out to find out what he can."

"So quickly." The Tarkin blinked slowly. "My cousin has nerve, I'll give him that. I'd have waited until I saw the body."

"It's possible they won't let him wait."

"Ah, yes, the Jaldeans." The Tarkin turned to the page. "Does the Charter tell us anything about them?"

Far-eFar glanced behind him and bit his lip.

The Tarkin sighed, and stood. "Don't keep him standing there, Far. Let's have them in, by all means."

Parno and Dhulyn came to their feet as the Tarkin stood,

moving silently off to one side as the page pushed the door full open, allowing Alkoryn to enter. Parno, catching a glimpse of Hernyn's Mercenary badge among the soldiers waiting in the hallway, signaled the boy with a flick of his fingers to come in and indicated the corpse of the dog with a tilt of his head. Hernyn nodded, bending over at once to pick up the body and carry it out into the hall. No use having people step on the poor beast, and it was one less thing to distract the Tarkin.

Hernyn slipped back into the room on the heels of the arriving Guard Captain. The man was flushed, out of breath, and accompanied by only three more soldiers in the dark red surcoat of the Tarkin's Personal Guard. One of these had an arm dangling limply at her side. *Numbed by a blow,* Parno thought. *No blood.*

"How bad does it look out there?" he asked Hernyn.

The young Brother shrugged, trying his best to imitate Parno's relaxed tone. "Bad, but the looting hasn't started."

Dhulyn dragged her eyes away from them and addressed her Senior Brother. "What news?"

The older man shook his head. "Worse than I would have expected, given the time," he said. As quiet as his voice was, everyone in the room stopped to listen. "There were people inside before we could get the gates shut, and the Dome is full of House soldiers." Alkoryn caught Dhulyn's eye. "Not just Tenebro either. It seems Lok-iKol has allies in the other Houses. I saw the colors of both Jarifo and Esmolo. The Carnelian Guard is scattered; half of them think the Tarkin is dead." His disgust at poorly managed security was evident. "As for the Tarkin's Personal Guard," he shrugged.

"How could this happen?" Parno said. "Where is the rest of the Dome's Guard?"

Dhulyn found it more than interesting that such was Parno's natural tone of command the Guard Captain answered without questioning Parno's authority to ask.

"The Carnelian Guard is out in the city, helping to quell the rioting in the merchant quarter."

"Making obvious the purpose of the rioting," Dhulyn observed under her breath.

"The discontented have always dispersed in a very orderly way upon the arrival of the Carnelian Guard."

"Of course they have, Din-eDin." The Tarkin's even voice silenced everyone. "Making us all the readier to send the Guard out tonight." The Tarkin drew back his gaze from the distance.

"How many do we have?"

"No more than fifty at the most, my lord," he said, looking up from the strip of cloth he was using on his wounded guard, strapping the woman's arm immobile. "But they are scattered through the Dome and some do not know you still live. With us now, a dozen of your Personal Guard, no more."

He caught the look that passed between the Mercenary Brothers.

"Our security was not lax!" he said, straightening to his feet. "We're a Personal Guard, not an army. As recently as this morning, all was at peace."

"The Sleeping God?" Dhulyn murmured.

"Think you're funny?" Parno said under his breath.

"What do you know, Dhulyn Wolfshead?" Alkoryn said.

Dhulyn gave a pointed glance at the number of people in the room, and waited to speak until she saw her Senior Brother's face change in acknowledgment of her point that this was neither the time nor place to speak of her secret. "This isn't a simple coup on the part of an ambitious House, and we all know it," she said. "This fire has the Jaldeans for fuel. And whatever it is that stands behind them, pushing them forward." She turned to the Guard Captain. "Your security was not lax," she told him. "You did not know you were at war. Neither your men, nor your preparations, took the followers of the New Believers into account."

"My Brother's right, Tek-aKet. Even had you believed her immediately, our warning may have come too late to do more than save your life. The Carnelian Throne we cannot save, not tonight at any rate. Once you're upon it again, that will be the time for us to talk about what the duties of the Tarkin's guards *should* be."

Dhulyn did not trouble to hide her grin. The look on the Guard Captain's face as he looked openmouthed from

Alkoryn to the Tarkin and back again was almost worth the trouble that brought them together. She'd wager her second-best sword—or she would if she knew where it was—that the man had never heard anyone speak to the Tarkin that way before. Let alone use the man's name without his title attached.

"How steadfast are your men, Din-eDin?" Alkoryn asked.

The Tarkin's raised hand stopped Din-eDin from answering.

"Perhaps that, too, is a question to be answered later, since there is only one way to test it." Was it possible that the man was smiling? "I am open to suggestions for present action."

"A strategic retreat, my lord," Alkoryn said. "Get the Tarkina and yourself to a safe place, and regroup."

At that moment a disturbance came at the door as the guards let in another man wearing their dark red uniform. He was panting, his hair stuck to his forehead with sweat, but the blood on his clothes was evidently not his own.

"My lords," the man spat out as soon as he had gathered breath. "They draw nearer. We will be cut off if we do not move."

"Nonsense," Din-eDin said. "We can hold these rooms indefinitely until relief comes."

"And from where is this relief to come?" Dhulyn's voice rang out, in stark contrast to Alkoryn's thin whisper.

In the silence that followed, Dhulyn leaned back against a table and crossed her arms, watching indecision fight its way across the Tarkin's face. It hurt his pride, she could tell, to abandon his palace, his throne. His jaw firmed, and Dhulyn raised her eyebrows. He would make the grand gesture then, make his stand and die, here and now. She was wondering where their weapons had been taken when the Tarkin's face softened.

"We will run," he said, "and see what the future brings us." He looked around him. "But how can we leave the Dome without bringing our enemies with us?"

Dhulyn shrugged and relaxed into immobility once more, exchanging glances with her Brothers. She saw the same thing on their faces as she knew to be on hers. They would die here or somewhere else; today or on a day to come. They were Mercenaries.

Not that they were in any hurry, she grinned as Parno winked at her. She'd just as soon escape as die trying.

"Captain Din-eDin." Alkoryn was now very careful to observe the formalities. "Are there enemies between us and the old keep where the summer kitchens once were?"

The Guard Captain was shaking his head, his mouth twisted in thought. "There may be a few, but most are coming in from the front and western gates. They're in the Throne room, and the Tarkin's suite of rooms behind it. They'll seek to isolate us here, but they'd have no reason to go into the old keep. There's nothing but offices and workrooms there now."

"Then there is a way to leave the Dome unseen. But we must spend some of your men to keep your enemies from following."

The Tarkin grimaced, his handsome face a twisted mask. "How many?"

"You may spend as many as you like," Din-eDin said. "That is what we are for."

"You know your men," Alkoryn said to the Guard Captain. "You tell me how many we'll need. There are three points that should be held. Let men stand at the two staircases, the Coral and the Ruby, that lead down to the old summer kitchens. Let them hold as long as they may, and then fall back to the intersection where the old serving corridor meets the Onyx Walk. That is the final point. If that is held long enough, we'll be able to get away. But," he looked Din-eDin in the eye, "if we are hard-pressed, the men who hold that point will not escape with us. They must stand."

The Guard Captain stopped nodding. "There's no escape through the old kitchens."

"And as long as everyone believes that, we'll be safe." Alkoryn said.

"What do you know, old man?" The Tarkin had some hope on his face.

"Enough to get us out of here safely."

Din-eDin shook his head, "They will know where we went."

Alkoryn bared his teeth. "They will know *where,* perhaps, but unless we have no luck at all, they will not know *how*."

"Jay." Din-eDin turned to a young dark-haired man. "Take two men and hold the Ruby Staircase. Taryn, it's the Coral Stairs for you and two others. Send anyone of ours you see, any you know to be with us, to the old kitchens. You know your orders."

It was not a question, but the dark-haired guard answered. "Hold our positions as long as we can. Do we fall back, Captain, or would you prefer us to die at our stations?"

He was grinning, but Dhulyn could tell from the set of his jaw that his question was meant seriously.

"Why don't you improvise, man?" Din-eDin said with a grin of his own that was answered by all the guards. "The rest of you are with us. Stay with the Tarkin, no matter what passes. After we reach the Onyx Walk, you'll take your orders from Alkoryn the Charter until you're free of the Dome, and then from the Tarkin himself."

"Dhulyn Wolfshead will be my voice," came the harsh whisper of the old Mercenary. "Listen for her."

The guards nodded, some of them studying the Mercenary woman covertly. A few looked as though they would have felt better if Alkoryn had said Parno was to be his second, not, she knew, because she was a woman, but because she was so obviously an Outlander.

The Tarkin had not moved. He was still leaning against his worktable, arms folded across his chest, frowning down at the spot where his dog should have been lying.

"My lord," Din-eDin said.

The Tarkin blinked and stood up straight. "Zelianora and the children."

Dhulyn glanced at Alkoryn and waited to speak until he'd nodded.

"Tell us the way, and if you've arms for us, Parno, Hernyn, and I will go for the Tarkina," she said, "and meet you by the Ruby Stairs." Or even if you don't have arms, she refrained from saying out loud. Guard Captain Din-eDin no doubt felt inadequate enough.

❈❈❈

Fanryn Bloodhand stepped off the last of the twisted narrow flight of treads cut into the rock deep under Mercenary House and felt her eyebrows rise and her mouth form an "oh" as her lantern illuminated what Alkoryn had called the lower chamber. A grunt reminded her she wasn't alone and she moved forward out of Thionan Hawkmoon's way.

"Well," Thionan said after a minute of staring about her. "Big enough, isn't it?"

Fanryn nodded. The chamber was a good four spans long, partly natural, and partly cut out of the rock, with beds for at least twenty and space for twenty more.

Holding her lantern higher, Thionan moved deeper into the room. "There's bedding," she said, "and the air's fresh enough. Cold, though."

"We'll send one of the youngsters down to start a fire," Fanryn said, indicating the iron stove along the right-hand wall and the pile of neatly cut logs stacked next to it. "Make sure everything is warm and dry."

"What is it?" her Partner said, as Fanryn stood still near the bottom of the stairway.

Fanryn shrugged. "I didn't like sending Hernyn off again like that. One of us should have gone."

"And spoil the fun of his first real danger? Go on, he wouldn't have thanked us. And besides," Thionan said, putting her arm around Fanryn's waist. "Our orders were to hold the House."

Fanryn nodded, doing her best to smile. "And with luck, Hernyn'll come back with whoever it is Alkoryn wants this room made ready for."

"There you go," Thionan said, giving her Partner a squeeze. "Let's get out of here, it's too blooded cold."

⁂

Dhulyn followed Parno and Hernyn, their feet silent on the winter matting of the corridor, hefting a blade unusually well-balanced, considering the amount of gold and jewels decorating it. She supposed it followed that the nearest weapons to the Tarkin's private study should come from the Tarkin's personal armory. Even the dagger she had in her boot was worth more than all her other possessions, books included. Good thing, too, as so far in this campaign they'd made no money at all.

"Parno, my soul," she said in the voice one used on nightwatch, the voice that didn't carry. "What happened to that purse of money the old Tenebroso gave us?"

"Gone when I woke up in the cell with our Brothers."

"Another thing that one-eyed piece of inglera dung owes us," she muttered under her breath.

They had advanced as far as the end of the final dressed-stone corridor that led away from the Old Tower, and had turned into a wider, wood-paneled hallway when they heard the soft tramp of careful feet, offset by the muted jingle of soldiers' harness. The Mercenaries slowed, if possible becoming even more silent than they had been before.

Parno raised his brows at her. "For or against?" he asked in the nightwatch murmur.

"Against," she answered.

"How do you know?" Hernyn said.

Parno shut his eyes and shook his head slightly, but Dhulyn answered. "Their footsteps are hesitant. If they were on our side, they'd know where they were going. Since not for us, against us."

"They're closer," Parno said.

Dhulyn looked around quickly. The hallway was a long one, and they had come too far down it to be sure of getting back to the cross corridor without being seen. And, unlike Tenebro House, there were no hiding places in the hallway itself—the original designer had seen to that, and the later inhabitants had been careful not to disturb it.

"Dhulyn." She'd known Parno long enough to hear the impatience in his voice.

"Fine. We kill them."

"I don't understand," Hernyn said, stepping into the lead at Dhulyn's gesture. Dhulyn merely shook her head.

"She doesn't like to kill people," Parno said. Hernyn looked at Dhulyn and back at Parno. "It's an Outlander thing," Parno added, shrugging.

"Advance," Dhulyn said, pulling the dagger from her boot. "Or we lose the element of surprise."

Not that they needed it, she thought moments later. They reached the end of the wide hallway just as their quarry rounded the corner. That they did so without either looking first or sending a man ahead was testament to their carelessness. Hernyn spitted the first one on his sword as quick as breathing, and had the sword out and killed the next man while the first body was still slumping to the floor. Parno kicked the feet out from under a tall, thin man who obviously thought he had the reach on everyone, gutting him with his left-hand short sword as the man went down, while blocking another blow with the short sword in his right hand. The fifth man turned to run, and with a call to warn her Brothers, Dhulyn threw the jeweled dagger and caught the runaway squarely under the left shoulder blade as Parno pulled his sword from the fourth man.

Dhulyn stepped around the bodies and blood on the floor, grasped the jeweled hilt, and pulled the dagger free.

"Throws well, too," she said, wiping the blade clean on the dead man's shirt.

"Look what I have." The dead soldiers had all been wearing badges in the Tenebro colors of black, teal, and dark red pinned to their chests. Hernyn had removed them. "We can wear them as a disguise."

Dhulyn leaned forward and picked one out of his hand. "This one has blood on it."

They had not progressed much farther when noises came from behind them. Parno twisted around to listen more carefully, holding up his hand for Dhulyn and Hernyn to be still.

"We're between them and the Tarkina's rooms," he said. "But they sound like they're coming this way." He lowered his hand. "Dhulyn? You're Senior."

"You wait here for them. Join us if you can. If not, we'll be back for you."

"My Brother, I could stay."

Parno caught Dhulyn's eye but should have known better; of course she'd seen what he'd seen. The nervous half smile that appeared on Hernyn's face whenever he stopped controlling his features. Those two Tenebro soldiers could very well be the first people he'd killed since his Schooling had finished. The boy had done well, and he knew it, but was trying to be as offhand about it as his Senior Brothers. Since he was paying more attention to his attitude than his job, this was not the time to put Hernyn in charge of their rear guard.

"My Brother," Dhulyn said with command in her tone. "This is not your time." Parno caught her eye and winked.

"In Battle," he said.

"Or in Death," they responded as they trotted down the hall toward the Tarkina's rooms. Parno adjusted the badge pinned to the front of his tunic and stood, feet shoulder width apart, knees slightly bent, shoulders relaxed, swords held out from his body. He released all the breath from his lungs and breathed in, consciously beginning the rhythms of the Eagle *Shora*. His heartbeat slowed, sounds became clearer, the light brightened.

The first man into the hallway was Dal-eDal Tenebro.

Parno felt his lips peel back from his teeth. The blond man motioned his fellows to wait, stepped forward himself to striking distance and stopped, but Parno wasn't stupid enough to move. He was already in the best spot to stop them from advancing, close enough to the corner to crowd them as they came around, far enough from the other end to give him room to fall back.

Dal's eyes flicked to the badge on Parno's chest.

"We've engaged no Mercenary Brothers to fight for us," Dal said.

"Do *all* your allies know? Because once I've killed you, you won't be telling anyone else."

"I would tell you something, Mercenary," Dal-eDal said, with a noticeable pause before the last word.

"And what might that be? If I recall correctly, the last thing you told me was a lie."

"This is not. You might wish to know that your Household fell almost two years ago. The Lady Pen-uPen is Householder now."

Parno managed to stop himself from lowering his sword, but his heart rate did speed up. His father was gone, then. But his sister had been allowed to inherit. He shook his head. "Who do you think you're speaking to?"

"My cousin, Par-iPar Tenebro. I didn't remember you at first, but the only time I was here in Gotterang with my father, you were here as well, and you helped me with my pony. My father liked you."

"The man you speak of was Cast Out," Parno said, gratified that his voice was steady. "I am Parno Lionsmane the Chanter, I fight with my Brother, Dhulyn Wolfshead."

"Don't be ridiculous, man. You're closer to the main line than I. If Lok-iKol dies, you would be Tenebroso."

"And Tarkin, too, I suppose?"

Dal shook his head. "With Lok gone, no need for Tek-aKet to die. And the man has children to inherit, besides." Dal sheathed his own sword and took a half step forward. For a moment Parno saw, not the tormented, torn man Dal had become, but the laughing child he'd once put on a pony. "Think about all you give up!"

This time Parno did lower his sword. Dal wasn't going to hurt him. Not here anyway, maybe not ever, if he thought there was a chance that Parno would step back into the life he'd left. *The life I was Cast Out of.* He shrugged one shoulder. When he'd talked of this to Dhulyn—was it only hours ago?—he had no way of knowing such a temptation would come his way. His sister would keep the Household; he'd be taking nothing from her. He thought of his mother, still alive. He could place House Tenebro and all its power behind Tek-aKet and defeat the Jaldeans. His thoughts faltered as he remembered the green shadow that looked from men's eyes. What power would they need to defeat that?

He thought then of his Schooling, of the feeling in his stomach on the morning of a battle; of the smell of spring as he rode his horse down from the mountains; of the way the air of a foreign country filled his lungs. Of the look on Dhulyn's face when she turned over the right vera tile. Of her husky voice singing while he played the pipes. Of the smile she smiled only for him. He thought of the years on the road together since Arcosa. *In Battle or in Death.*

"You have no idea what I'd be giving up," he said finally.

❈❈❈

Hernyn rattled the door latch to the Tarkina's suite with no results.

"Locked and barred," he said. Dhulyn rolled her eyes. "And there is no light that I can see."

"I doubt she'd bar the doors if the rooms were empty."

Dhulyn took her Brother firmly by the sleeve and pulled him to one side. She gave the door three sharp blows with the side of her fist and called out. "Tarkina! It's Dhulyn Wolfshead. Let us in."

There was a thump, and a small bang on the far side of the door as the bar was removed and laid to one side. The door cracked open and a woman's hand beckoned them in. Dhulyn wasted no time entering, and she and Hernyn made short work of rebarring the door. It was good stout work, she saw with satisfaction, the insets for the bar not merely attached to, but part of the structure of the walls. They were as safe as could be—short of treachery or starvation.

Dhulyn almost didn't recognize the woman who'd let them in. Gone were the Tarkina's veils, and her palace gown with its fluttering sleeves. In its place Zelianora wore the loose trousers, long-sleeved blouse, tight vest, and short boots of her own desert people. An older woman, similarly dressed, stood at the doorway across the drawing room with a curved knife in her hand. Her surprise must have shown on her face, because Zelianora Tarkina took one look at her and smiled.

"Denobea saw strange soldiers in the courtyard," she said, "and what with the noises . . ."

"Strange soldiers?" Dhulyn said to the older woman.

The nurse Denobea cleared her throat and gestured to the arrow niche that served this drawing room for a window. "They wear Tenebro color." Her accent was the same as the Tarkina's, but her words more hesitant.

"For them to be in that courtyard, someone had to let them in," the Tarkina said, sinking into a nearby chair. "One of my husband's people."

"Not necessarily." Hernyn spoke from the doorway to the suite of rooms. "The Tenebros were Tarkins not so long ago. They might know a way in that doesn't rely on treachery."

Dhulyn snorted, then rolled her eyes as everyone turned to her. *Youngsters.* "Say what you like, my Brother, but treachery's the simpler answer and you know it."

"I was trying to spare the Tarkina suspicions of her own household," Hernyn said shyly.

"Please don't." The Tarkina stood up. "I may not be a

Mercenary, young man, but I prefer not to be told that the wolf at the door is only a pet dog. We must go at once to my husband."

"It's under his orders that we're here, Tarkina." Dhulyn eyed the other woman's clothing. "You're Berdanan, aren't you, Lady? As you've been Tarkina of Imrion for several years, I must ask, do you still keep your travel packs ready?"

"I was Berdanan long before I became Tarkina of Imrion, Dhulyn Wolfshead; our packs are in the bedroom."

"Get them, then, and we will go."

The Tarkina spoke softly to the nurse in her own tongue and Denobea ran into the other room, coming out so quickly with two well-balanced travel packs that Dhulyn assumed they must have been taken out of their storage place already. Following her, eyes big in faces too serious for their ages, were a slim girl of perhaps nine, leading a toddler still chubby with baby fat.

"I will carry my son," Zelianora Tarkina said, picking up a wide shawl of heavy linen and wrapping it around her upper body with practiced ease, tying it to form a sling across her chest. She held out her arms and the small boy let go of his sister's hand and ran to her. "With the pack on my back, my weight will be even."

For an instant Dhulyn flashed to the memory of warm wrappings supporting her own legs and back, and the smell of leather and spicy sweat that was her father. She blinked and breathed deeply.

"The little one looks to be asleep, already," Dhulyn said, a question clearly in her voice.

"I gave Zak valerian, a safe dose," the Tarkina said. "It seemed the best way to keep him quiet."

"And what about this lady?" Dhulyn looked down at the nine-year-old girl who looked back at her with the Tarkin's firm jaw and blue eyes, but her mother's steadfast gaze.

"This is our daughter, Bet-oTeb," the Tarkina answered.

"The Tarkin-to-be." Dhulyn bowed to the child.

"Exactly," the child said in a soft, clear voice that only wavered the slightest bit.

"Are you armed, Lady?" Dhulyn said, doing her best not to smile.

For answer, the child drew a knife long enough to be sword-sized for her out of a stiff sheath at her waist.

"And do you know how to use it, Tarkin-to-be?"

"I've trained with the Personal Guard since I was six," the child said.

"Then, if it please you, Lady, you shall walk by your mother, and help to keep your sibling alive."

The child nodded. "It pleases me."

Dhulyn bowed again.

Hernyn coughed from his post by the barred door. "Someone comes."

"I'm getting tired of this." Dhulyn drew her sword and motioned the Tarkina back toward the inner rooms.

"Dhulyn, my heart." The voice was unmistakable, even through the door.

"Parno," Hernyn said, sheathing his sword and helping Dhulyn with the bar on the door. *Parno for certain,* she thought, but something had happened. His voice sounded thick, as if he were about to start a cold.

"Someone could be forcing him," the Tarkina said.

Dhulyn looked back over her shoulder. "No," she said. "Someone couldn't."

Parno came into the room out of breath, and startled Dhulyn by taking her immediately in his arms.

"My soul," she said, with the little breath he left her. "The enemy."

He let her go, whirled to face the door, and drew his right-hand sword all in one movement.

"Not just now," Dhulyn said, "but at any moment." She turned back into the room. "Lady Bet-oTeb, Nurse Denobea, my Partner, Parno Lionsmane the Chanter."

"Ladies." Parno gave his best bow and accepted the young Tarkin-to-be's acknowledgment. "Do you know the fastest way to the Onyx Walk?"

❈❈❈

Din-eDin left the three volunteers at the top of the Ruby Stair and led Dhulyn and her charges down the Onyx Walk to the corridor that serviced the old summer kitchens.

"The Tarkin has gone ahead with Alkoryn Pantherclaw," he told them, as they reached the opening of the service corridor. "You are to join him immediately, Lady Tarkina. He will send back the volunteers for this spot."

"No need for them, I'll stand with you." Every head in the corridor, even that of little Bet-oTeb, turned to look at Hernyn.

"Demons and perverts, Hernyn. There's no need." Parno grasped the younger man's arm. "Dhulyn, tell him there's no need."

Dhulyn looked at Hernyn but waited, knowing the young man had to speak. For the first time since they'd made it to safety after their escape from Tenebro House, he met her eyes squarely, and held them. His glance didn't fall away in embarrassment after a few blinks. She saw strength there now, courage and resolve. It seemed what was left of the School boy had faded away, and Dhulyn saw the man, her true Brother.

"It's for me to do," Hernyn said. "Not for your sake, my Brother, for my own."

Dhulyn clasped Hernyn's hands in a firm grip. "Captain Din-eDin, if my Brother, Hernyn Greystone, called the Shield, will stay," she said, still holding Hernyn's eyes with her own, "you will need no others."

Hernyn nodded, once down, once up, taking her words as they were meant, as a blessing.

"I welcome the Shield's assistance," Din-eDin said. He turned to the Tarkina. "You will be safe with these Brothers, my lady, and the Lord Tarkin."

"Din-eDin, I thank you."

"There is no need, my lady, but you are welcome."

The Tarkina stepped forward from her spot between Parno and the nurse Denobea and kissed both Din-eDin and Hernyn Greystone the Shield on the cheek. The child, Bet-oTeb stepped out also, though not before the nurse made a move to stop her. She gave one hand to each of the two men.

"Thank you," she said, her child's voice ringing softly against the cold stone. "Thank you for my life."

Oh, yes, Dhulyn thought as the two warriors—Mercenary and Guard—blushed and ducked their heads to the child before them. *She'll be Tarkin one day, and people will fall over themselves to follow her.* Only then did the child turn, and let her mother and her nurse lead her up the corridor toward the kitchen.

Dhulyn embraced the younger Mercenary and said. "We will tell your tale, Brother."

Din-eDin waited until the nobles were out of earshot. "My Tarkin is in your hands, Mercenaries. See that you hold him."

"Mercenary House will know where to find us, if you should live through this day."

"Can you close the passage behind you?"

Dhulyn looked to Parno, who shrugged.

"If you can, close it," Din-eDin said. Dhulyn nodded, gave Hernyn's shoulder one last squeeze, and ran down the corridor toward the old kitchen.

Fifteen

A WOMAN USING the public fountain at the east end of the Old Market had taken pity on him and given Gun a clay pitcher with a cracked lip to take water away in. Though he'd known better than to try paying her—he hadn't completely forgotten being Gundy the horse boy—he had still tried to give her something in return.

"Keep your scarf, youngster," she'd said to him, though Gun was fairly certain the woman wasn't *that* much older than he was. Poor nutrition during childbearing would account for more of her lost teeth than age—obviously she didn't come from the part of society who normally had access to Healers. Not that anyone did now.

"You'll need all you have an' more, I should think," the woman added, eyeing him up and down and appeared to make up her mind about him, for she went on in a quieter voice.

"Don't take this amiss, boy, but have you any other clothes? Rumor on the street says they're looking for a Scholar, something to do with the Fall of Tenebro House what happened last night. There's a reward offered an' all. I'm not saying you're the one they're looking for, but you stick out, boy, that's a fact, and if you don't want to be answering questions, you'll try to look less like what you are."

"But I—" Shock stopped Gun's voice. Looking for him *because* of the Fall of the House? Water began to dribble from the pitcher as his hand relaxed.

"Watch it, boy, watch it. No need to waste water." The

woman propped up his elbow with her strong fingers. "I'm not asking any questions myself, mind, just passing along a bit of advice. If you've no other clothes, go down to old Semplon-Nast, south corner, the rag and bone man. Tell him Nessa sent you, and he'll give you good trade for what you're wearing."

"And why won't *he* turn me in?" Gun said, abandoning all pretense that he was not the Scholar being looked for.

"Three reasons. One, I sent you; two, he's got no love for the Noble Houses and won't care if one's Fallen; an' three, he's blind. He can't see a Scholar, but he can feel the quality of the cloth you're wearing."

Gun unwound his scarf and held it out to her. "Not for the water," he said. "For the warning, and the advice." This time she nodded once and took it.

Still, he waited until she had gone on her way before taking a firm grip on the clay jug of water and starting back to where he'd left Mar. He was careful to take a different route from the one he'd come by.

⬩⬥⬩⬥⬩

Bracing herself on the arch of the opening, Dhulyn leaned into the old kitchen fireplace, large enough, she was sure, to roast a mature inglera whole. She was just starting to feel the burn in muscles overtaxed by hauling wine casks out of the way, and firmly ignoring the familiar feel of cramping in her lower back. Even in the lantern light, you could still see the marks fire had made on the brick walls, particularly at the back, where Alkoryn now tapped upon the stones. Parno stood by him, a war hammer ready in his hand, the closest thing to a mallet they'd been able to find in the Tarkin's armory, and just as extravagantly decorated as every other weapon there.

This was the middle one of three fireplaces in the old summer kitchen, and though Alkoryn Pantherclaw had known perfectly well which of the three was wanted, he'd insisted that all of them be emptied of their contents.

"We hope to mislead those who'll come after," Alkoryn had whispered to the Tarkin. "If they do not know which of these holds the passage, they will have to break into all three. They may even think we escaped elsewhere."

One of the guards had dropped a cask during the moving, shattering it on the worn stone floor, and now the heady smell of aged liquor mixed with the dry dust smell of the old kitchen itself made Dhulyn's stomach lurch. She swallowed, looking for something to distract her. The Tarkin, Tek-aKet, was only a few paces away, half-sitting on an upright cask, his right arm around the Tarkina, his left hand resting on his daughter's shoulder.

"Look, Zella," he was saying, pointing with his chin to several barrels that had been rolled to one side. "That sweet wine was laid down by my father when I was born." He looked up at her again. "We should have been able to drink it next year."

"We still shall," she said, in a voice so firm that even her little daughter nodded.

Dhulyn straightened as Alkoryn stepped back from the fireplace wall and motioned Parno forward. The Senior Brother indicated five particular stones, waited for Parno to nod, and then touched them again in a different order. Parno nodded again, rubbed his upper lip with the first two fingers of his right hand, and touched the stones himself.

"Tap there, my Brother, but gently. Say that you wanted to knock out a sentry, rather than kill him."

Parno nodded, and hefted the war hammer.

"Want me to do it?" Dhulyn said.

Parno just showed his teeth as he swung the weapon forward and lightly but firmly tapped the stones in the order he'd been shown.

With a grinding Dhulyn felt in her bones, a section of wall moved backward. Two of the guardsmen helped Parno push it aside to reveal a long tunnel. Alkoryn caught Dhulyn's eye and nodded.

"Lord Tarkin," she called over her shoulder. "We're ready. Alkoryn Pantherclaw will go first, seeing he knows the way." Dhulyn tapped the shoulder of a tall guard with thick black hair. "Kole, isn't it? Go with him. Then you three," she said, nodding at the remaining guards. "Lord Tarkin, you and your family next, and Parno Lionsmane and I will come last."

The Tarkin was nodding, but his mouth was twisted as if he'd eaten something unpleasant. "I don't want to seem ungrateful," he said. "But I cannot honestly say I'm pleased that the Mercenary Brotherhood knows of secret passageways in my Dome."

Dhulyn shrugged. "It was someone else's Dome before you, Lord, and the Brotherhood is older even than the Dome, older than the reign of Tarkins. Older than Imrion, if it comes to that. There's many things we know."

❧❧❧

Hernyn wiped his mouth with the back of his hand, and resisted the desire to spit. Then he thought about where he was, and how long he was likely to be there, and spit freely on the inlaid tesserae of the Onyx Walk. He heard an unmistakable clatter in the distance, and looked to Din-eDin, who nodded his acknowledgment that he, too, had heard the approaching noise.

"Won't be long now," the older man said.

It was Hernyn's turn to nod. When they'd first taken up their station an arm's length down from where the narrow service corridor met the Onyx Walk, they'd heard the sounds of voices and what seemed like moving furniture echoing up the long hallway from the old kitchen, but now, while they could still hear voices, the louder noises had stopped.

A shadow moved into their field of vision. Hernyn glanced at the extra weapons he'd lined up behind him on the floor of the passage and picked up a handheld crossbow he'd found among the Tarkin's things. A toy, really, and he'd blushed when he saw that Dhulyn Wolfshead had seen him pick it up. But she hadn't said anything, she hadn't even smiled. It was a beautiful little piece, finely constructed out of ash wood and inlaid with mother-of-pearl, and probably intended for ceremonial use. *And deadly just the same,* he thought. Not very good for distances, of course, but he was willing to let the man approaching get close enough.

"Hold." Din-eDin put up his hand; he'd squatted down to take a quick look about waist height around the corner of the wall, and was now straightening. "He's one of mine."

The Guard Captain was stepping forward to meet his man when Hernyn put out his arm, blocking his advance.

"Don't step into the Walk," he said. "Not for any reason. That's how we get flanked. Make them come to us." A part of Hernyn felt like a School boy reciting his lesson, as if Din-eDin had been only testing him; a part was embarrassed to have to correct an older, more experienced man; a part—and this by far the largest, was rolling his eyes at the carelessness of those who were not Mercenary Brothers.

He leaned against the cold stone of the left-hand wall and angled his head until he could see the approaching man clearly. He was in the uniform of the Tarkin's Personal Guard, right enough. But why wasn't he running? The only reason for the men at the other points to come down here was to fall back to this position when their own was overwhelmed—and if they were quick enough, to get out through the tunnels Alkoryn had said were there. And this man didn't move like someone who'd been overwhelmed. He moved like someone taking a walk—or no, amended Hernyn as the man stumbled and put out a hand to the plastered wall of the Onyx Walk. He walked like a man who was drunk and determined not to show it.

Drunk . . . or wounded?

"Are you hurt, man?" Hernyn called out.

The approaching guard shook his head, but kept advancing at that strange, overly-careful pace. As if he pushed against a stiff wind, though no air stirred in the halls.

"Ask him where the others are," Din-eDin said. Hernyn flicked his eyes to the older man. There was sense in that, at least.

"Do your comrades still stand?"

"Let me pass," the guard said.

Hernyn resisted the urge to rub the back of his neck, where it felt like all the tiny hairs were standing up. There was no urgency in the man's tone, no fear, no excitement. Nothing, in fact. And surely his shadow should be angled the other way?

"That's Ennick," Din-eDin said.

"No," Hernyn said. "I don't think it is."

The guard Ennick was now close enough that they could see his face clearly in the light from the wall sconce near the intersection in which they stood. Hernyn could see the man had the most beautiful jade-green eyes.

"Let me pass," he said again. He had been looking beyond them, down to the far end of the Onyx Walk, but now he brought his gaze to bear upon them. "Let me pass."

"He's in shock." Din-eDin pushed Hernyn's restraining arm out of the way and stepped into the Onyx Walk.

Ennick brought up his sword and slashed at his captain, catching him on the arm as Din-eDin lifted it to block the blow to his head.

Hernyn raised the crossbow and let the bolt fly, feeling a hot burst of satisfaction when the bolt buried itself in the guard's neck. The man put his hand up to the bolt and stood swaying for a moment before he dropped to his knees.

"Captain?" he said.

Hernyn broke his own rule and stepped into the corridor to help Din-eDin pull the other guard back into the relative safety of the narrow kitchen passage. They shifted him until he was sitting with his back to the wall. The bolt was plugging the hole in his neck, but turning his head to look at them started the blood flowing in earnest.

But he *was* looking at them now, and the strange, staring green of his eyes was gone. His eyes were very dark brown.

"Ennick?" Din-eDin said.

"Captain," he said again. "Don't—" He coughed, and a bubble of blood broke on his lips. "Don't."

"No fear, my boy," the captain said. "We won't."

Ennick nodded, and his eyes closed.

"What was that?" Din-eDin frowned down at the body of his guard.

"Whatever it was," Hernyn said, "it means we can't trust anyone else who comes down this corridor."

Din-eDin shut his eyes. "Makes things easier for us."

"It does at that." Hernyn glanced up at the older man. His jaw was set, and his eyes sharp, but the wound on his arm was bleeding. Hernyn quickly tore two strips of cloth from the dead man's tunic. One he folded, and used the other to tie it securely in place over the gash on Din-eDin's arm.

"Can you handle a sword left-handed?"

"As it happens."

"Better to be lucky than good, isn't that what they say?" Hernyn bent to strip Ennick's body of weapons before rolling it back out into the wider corridor. "Let him be useful in tripping up the rest of his companions." Hernyn glanced behind him. Amplified by the stone corridor, the voices of those in the kitchen echoed in the air around him. He was sure he'd heard Dhulyn Wolfshead's ringing tone.

"This changes things," Din-eDin said. "We can't let anyone past us now."

"That's not all," Hernyn said. "We've more to worry about as well."

The man glanced from the corner of his eye. "Explain."

Hernyn nodded at Ennick's body. "It looks like there's worse than death might come to us. Did you see how his eyes were glowing green? That wasn't just Ennick, not at first anyway."

The other man tapped the dagger he had at his waist. "We'll have to be sure, then, won't we?" His eyes narrowed. "Can we warn the others?"

But then they finally heard the sounds they'd been waiting for, rushing feet, jingling harness. Men who weren't taking the trouble to be quiet. Din-eDin stepped in front of Hernyn. Hernyn was about to say something when he realized the man was right for once. Older, injured, and not a Mercenary. Three reasons to put him in front.

"Here they come," Hernyn called back over his shoulder, hoping the amplification of sound in the service corridor worked both ways. Before picking up his second sword, he checked that he had a dagger in each boot, and that the one strapped to his left arm wouldn't stick in the sheath. He stood squarely in the passage with the Guard Captain in front of him, facing the opening to the Onyx Walk, and lightly·tapped the walls with his swords, fixing the space well in his mind.

He would rather have died with his Brothers, but if he could die _for_ them, well, that would be enough.

❦

The Tarkin and his family had followed the last three guards into the tunnel. Dhulyn hesitated at the opening.

She was sure she could hear the sounds of conflict coming from the far end of the hallway.

"Should we wait?" Parno asked.

One of the many cords that bound her hair must have broken, for a fine blood-red braid fell over Dhulyn's forehead with the minute shaking of her head. She pushed it back.

"We told Din-eDin we would close the passage," she said.

❈❈❈

Someone was yelling. Her hip was pressing against something hard. She must have fallen asleep waiting for Dhulyn to come back with wood for the fire. She could smell damp wool and smoke. Mar blinked, took a deep breath, and shifted. That had been the mountains, and long behind her. This was Gotterang, and Gundaron, and the ruins of the Old Market.

Maybe if she ignored it, the yelling would stop and she could go back to sleep. They'd spent more than half of the night hiding in a crawl space Gundaron had found, under a surprisingly intact floor of thick oak planks, but they hadn't had much sleep. Trying to get comfortable on ground made uneven by loose foundation rocks and ancient garbage, with nerves stretched to the snapping point by the drizzly rain and the knowledge that they were being accused of having a hand in the Fall of Tenebro House, would have been difficult enough. As it was, the night had been marred by the noises of screams and running. A fire had broken out in the Old Market itself, and it had been close to dawn by the time she and Gundaron had been able to fall into sleep.

"Mar!" A hand shook her shoulder.

She cracked open one eye. From the look of the light that slanted down through the breaks in the old floorboards above them, the sun was well up.

"Did you hear what he said?" Gundaron shook her shoulder again. "Mar, did you hear?"

Without waiting for her answer, Gun crawled out of their hideyhole. Still blinking sleep from her eyes, Mar followed, afraid to lose sight of him. Lionsmane and Wolfshead had been teaching her to navigate out on the trail, but in Gotterang she felt it would be all too easy to get completely lost.

Mar had a moment of panic when she didn't see Gun right away, but then she remembered he no longer wore his Scholar's tunic and, looking for the gray-brown of homespun rather than the bright blue of the Libraries, she spotted him. Gun stood on the fringes of a group gathered around a thickset man in breeches, boots, and a full-sleeved shirt who must have been standing on a broken bit of wall, as he was head and shoulders above the crowd. She blinked at him, holding up her hand to shield her eyes. Ran the taproom down by the fountain, she thought. That's where she knew him from. She'd bought food from there last night.

"Imrion's Fallen, I'm telling you that's certain, they're crying it in the Great Square. Lok-iKol Tenebro is Tarkin by acclamation."

The taproom keeper had plenty more to say, but Mar had stopped listening. She tugged Gun by the sleeve.

"Gundaron," she whispered, tugging again until he turned to look at her.

For a moment the sight of her face stopped Gundaron's breath. A wisp of hair had fallen out of her head scarf and swayed over her right cheek. In the vivid depths of her blue eyes, her pupils shrank to pinpoints as she blinked in the morning sun.

"Is *this* what I helped him do," she said. "Bringing him Wolfshead and Lionsmane? He wanted to be Tarkin? That's what this is all about?"

His thoughts spinning, Gun followed Mar back into their hiding place. She was right, wasn't she? Lok-iKol was Tarkin. The things that he had done, the people he had harmed, all that *research,* not for scholarship—Gun's stomach turned at the thought of his own naïveté—but to put Lok-iKol on the Carnelian Throne.

Mar was still waiting for an answer. He swallowed, mouth suddenly dry. "There must be more to it than that." He blinked, eyes narrowing as he followed the pattern of his thoughts to its logical conclusion. "The Carnelian Throne's what Lok-iKol wanted—but not what the *Jaldeans* want."

"But if the New Believers want the Tarkin's full backing . . ."

Gun realized he was shaking his head. "But what they're saying about the Marked and the Sleeping God—that the god should stay asleep and the Marked are trying to wake him—none of that is true."

"I never thought it was, but—"

"No, no. I mean they don't believe it themselves, at least, not the ones in charge, not Beslyn-Tor. There's something else going on." Gun hoped Mar wouldn't ask how he knew—in fact, he was afraid to examine the knowledge too closely, afraid that it might be yet another thing the Green Shadow had helped him forget.

"If the Jaldeans have some other trouble in mind," Mar was saying, "we have to tell someone."

Gun nodded. "Who?"

"Come on," Mar said, swinging her pack up on to her shoulder.

"Where?" Gun drew himself straight and formed his hands into fists when they wouldn't stop trembling.

"Mercenary House."

❧

Parno rolled his shoulders, trying to work out the cramp that threatened to spread down into his lower back. The tallest in their group, most of the tunnels and passageways—some of them apparently natural, made by the passage aeons before of water long gone, some bearing the unmistakable signs of picks, chisels, and rock hammers—were just low enough to make him walk with his head ducked and his shoulders raised. Just as he thought he'd have to ask everyone to wait while he sat down and straightened his back, Parno saw what could only be the flicker of moving light reflected off the rocks as the tunnel they followed bent to the right.

"Something up ahead," he said to Dhulyn's back. *She* was just enough shorter, he'd noticed with disgust, to walk upright through most of the passages.

"Lamplight, not torches," she whispered back to him. "Alkoryn's not stopping."

Which meant the old man expected to find lights ahead

of him, which meant there was nothing for the two of them to worry about. Except whether he'd ever be able to stand upright again, Parno thought.

Exhausted as they all were from close to two hours of walking from one sealed entrance to another, everyone managed a short burst of speed once it became clear there was something besides more tunnel ahead of them. When Parno finally followed them all into the lamplit room, however, he saw that they were still underground, although in a chamber large enough—with a ceiling high enough, he found, straightening gratefully—to accommodate all of them easily.

The Tarkin led his wife and children immediately to the nearest beds, making sure they were seated comfortably before leaving them in the hands of the nurse Denobea and joining Dhulyn, who had stepped around them and the guards to stand beside Alkoryn. Head lowered and tilted to one side, she listened to his whispered orders, nodding, though at one point her face went completely blank.

Something she doesn't like there, Parno thought, maintaining his position as rear guard just inside the entrance to the chamber. With his eyes still on his Partner, he arched his back and raised his hands over his head, willing his abused muscles to stretch out.

"Lord Tarkin," Dhulyn said, her voice pitched to carry to everyone in the chamber. "My Brother Alkoryn Pantherclaw suggests that you rest here in comfort while he and I continue to the surface. There is fuel, food, and drink. We will return or send for you as soon as we are able."

"Why must we wait?" The Tarkin, Parno was impressed to see, was not arguing, but simply asking the question.

"It's very likely Lok-iKol will want Mercenary House searched," Dhulyn said. "This chamber can be closed off and hidden, so you'll be perfectly safe here. If it comes to the worst," Dhulyn added, "my presence in the House is natural. Yours, Lord Tarkin, could not be explained. My Brother Parno Lionsmane will remain here with you."

Parno met Dhulyn's eyes over the heads of the Tarkina and her children. *That's what made her face change,* he thought. *Is it the thought of separation she doesn't like, or the idea of leaving me here with my cousin, the Tarkin?*

She smiled at him, lifting her shoulder in the slightest of shrugs.

In Battle. Only her lips formed the words.

In Death, he answered.

⚜

He was close now. Only a matter of hours until the decrees went out. He wiped sweat from the forehead of the body he wore and shuddered. And then only a matter of days until he had all of them, even the Seer, and the danger would be over, and he could throw off this disgusting *shape*, and undo, and unmake. Turn the whole shape-filled place into NOT. Perhaps find the doorway once again.

⚜

"No one in without a badge, my little quails." A dark-haired Mercenary leaned out of the sentry's window next to the gate at Mercenary House, tapped her own tattooed badge, her green eyes flashing.

"But we've important information," Mar said, craning her neck to see the woman.

"Oh, I've no doubt *he's* got information enough—but I'm not inclined to let him in, no matter how important it might be."

"Then let Mar in," Gun said, placing a hand on the gate in his eagerness. He swallowed, realizing that he'd just called Mar by her personal name. Out loud. "The Lady Mar-eMar I mean. You've nothing against her, let her in." He looked at Mar, looked back up to the sentry window. "You're Thionan Hawkmoon, aren't you?" he said. "That's how you know me." He waved his hand impatiently. "It doesn't matter about me, but you can let Mar-eMar in, she needs to speak to Dhulyn Wolfshead, or—"

"Ah, so you're the little trickster from Navra, are you? I hadn't seen you before now."

Any hope Gun might have had that they'd do as he asked died at the tone in the Mercenary woman's voice.

"Listen, children, we've our orders, and if I was likely to break them—which I'm not—it certainly wouldn't be for you two. And besides—"

Thionan Hawkmoon froze in mid-syllable, her attention caught by something within the walls.

"And besides," she took up where she'd left off. "There's an order out for both of you. Seems you ran away after the Fallen House Kor-iRok was found dead." She looked down at them with a wink. "Don't make me send for the City Guards, now."

•

Sixteen

FANRYN BLOODHAND AND Thionan Hawkmoon were both waiting when Dhulyn swung the counterweighted chunk of flooring to one side and climbed out, reaching back in to give Alkoryn Pantherclaw a hand up.

"We've left the others in the lower chamber," Dhulyn said, telling her Brothers in a few words just who those "others" were. "Hernyn?" Thionan said.

Dhulyn's lips parted, but her throat closed on the words.

"Hernyn Greystone the Shield remained behind," Alkoryn said for her. "That we might escape."

"In Battle or in Death," Fanryn said after a long pause. The eyes of the four Brothers met, and for another moment they were silent, in honor of the one who had fallen. And in unspoken prayer that they should fall the same way, on their feet, swords in hand.

"Since his body will be found," Alkoryn said, breaking their silence at last. "We can expect inquiries, perhaps even a request to search our premises before the day is out. What is it, Thionan?"

Even Dhulyn could see and recognize the slightly furtive look that had crossed Thionan's eyes.

"About an hour ago," she said. "I turned away the Tenebro's tame Scholar and that Navra girl you and Parno brought, Dhulyn, telling them I'd call the City Guard on them. I was joking, but . . ."

"You spoke truth without knowing it," Alkoryn said. "Well, at least they have been warned. What else can you tell me?"

Dhulyn only half heard Fanryn's first words. So Mar and Gundaron of Valdomar *had* come here. Looking for what?

"Lok-iKol holds the Dome and the city," Fanryn was saying, leading the way out of the room that, to anyone who didn't know better, held nothing but the old cistern of Mercenary House. "Of the High Nobles, Jarifo and Esmolo Houses are with him—"

"We saw their men in the Dome," Dhulyn said as she followed the other women up a short flight of stone steps and through another counterweighted chunk of wall.

"The other Houses are holding off, waiting to see how true Lok-iKol's arrow will fly, though there's talk that the Tenebroso will be acclaimed by midday," Fanryn continued, her face showing her displeasure. "The only one demanding to be shown Tek-aKet Tarkin, living or dead, is the Penradoso."

"I know that House," Dhulyn said, thinking back over the years to the last time she'd fought in Imrion. When she and Parno had met.

"You should," Alkoryn said, pausing with his hand on the wall to take a deeper breath. Dhulyn didn't like the look of the man; his color was worse than a sleepless night walking underground should make it. "Fen-oNef Penrado was an old ally of Tek-aKet Tarkin's father, and he fought on the old Tarkin's side at Arcosa. You'd have seen him there. The odds are very short that he'll come to Lok-iKol's side without proof positive that Tek-aKet's dead."

"Lok-iKol's gone ahead and scheduled his anointing for next new moon," Thionan added. "Twelve days from now. And the Jaldeans have agreed. So old Penrado hasn't much time to decide."

They'd reached Alkoryn's map room by this time, and the old man looked better for being able to sit down in his own chair. Dhulyn leaned against the wall between the two windows, angled into a corner of the map shelves where she couldn't be seen from outside, and stifled a yawn. If she sat down, she thought, she'd fall right to sleep.

"Is there anything more?" Alkoryn said.

Fanryn considered, her head to one side. "There's seventeen Brothers in the House," she said. "Eleven of those from the Carnelian Guard who were out in the streets overnight. They felt their oaths were to Tek-aKet Tarkin, rather than the Carnelian Throne, so when he Fell, they came Home."

"Did any die in street fighting?" Dhulyn asked.

"None. In fact, they saved some of the other Carnelian Guardsmen, and we've got them hidden around the quarter, some in the Old Market. None in the House, of course." Fanryn looked over at Thionan when her Partner cleared her throat. "Besides the children you sent us, we do have a guest, however, who was visiting in the House when your orders came to shut the gates." Fanryn waited to be sure she had both Dhulyn and Alkoryn's attention. "Cullen of Langeron is here," she said, "an intimate of Yaro of Trevel, and a Racha man, no less. Seeing that Yaro was once of our Brotherhood, we gave them sanctuary."

"That may turn out to be very lucky." Alkoryn leaned back in his chair, folding his hands over his stomach. "How many Marked have we in the tunnels?"

"Including the Mender's children Hernyn brought us, seven."

"Delay no longer. See that they go now, before the day is out. Send also our own youngsters, any waiting for Schooling and any not ready for their badges. Let them go with the Marked as far as the Tourin Road, then to Nerysa Warhammer. The Marked to Pompano, unless Cullen would like to take this opportunity to return to his home, in which case he may want them to accompany him to Langeron. Who is scheduled for the task?"

"The sisters, Jenn IceSea and Jess Riverhorse."

"Let them choose two others to help them and go with the group to Nerysa. If Cullen of Langeron decides to go, ask him to have word with me before he departs." He nodded twice and looked up at Fanryn. "If there is nothing else pressing, I'd like a few minutes with Dhulyn if you would, my Brothers."

Both Fanryn and Thionan straightened to their feet. "I'll have some food and drink sent up," Thionan said.

"Considering we may need a place to hide the Tarkin Tek-aKet and his family, it's a very lucky thing indeed that the Racha man is here." Alkoryn spoke half to himself. "No one would think to look for them in the Clouds."

Dhulyn stayed at her perch by the window, consciously relaxing each muscle group as she waited for Alkoryn to turn his full attention to her. She could think of only one reason Alkoryn would have sent both Fanryn and Thionan away. *He's going to ask me to* See, she thought. *That's the reason I'm not in the caves with the Tarkin.*

"I must say, Dhulyn, my Brother, if the reaction of the Tarkin and his counselor is any indication, I am not at all surprised that you tell no one of your Mark." Alkoryn sat up straight and laid his hands palm down on the map of Gotterang that still covered his table. "But I would fail in my duties as Senior Brother and Commander of this House if I did not ask you, despite what you and Parno have told me of your experience, is there no way you can look for a Vision that may be of help to us?"

Dhulyn looked at him for a long moment. He was asking her in the same way he would ask a swordsmith how many weapons were ready for use. No judgment, just a request for the kind of information that would help him plan his strategy. A tightness she had not been aware of loosened in her chest. Whatever she said now, he would take her at her word. She was still among Brothers. In Battle or in Death.

"It's worse than Parno told you," she said. "Worse than I knew myself. Only very recently I have learned that some of what I See is not the future at all, but the past. If I cannot even tell which is which, the Visions I *do* See are useless to us."

The knock at the door was soft, almost as if the person outside wanted the room to be empty. Karlyn-Tan's "Enter" was so automatic he did not even look up from his lists of work orders. A moment passed before he realized that someone had indeed come in, and that she was waiting for him to speak. He glanced at Semlin-Nor's face and he sat back, lowering his pen to the tabletop. Born in the House, Semlin was the most unflappable of the House Stewards, and not even the fall of the Old House had given her that gray skin, that tremor in her clasped hands. Seeing her face, Karlyn had the feeling he was going to be sorry to have answered the knock. Maybe even that he'd got up at all today.

"Word has come from the Dome," Semlin said, and cleared her throat. "The Tenebroso is on his way."

"Sit down, Sem." Karlyn shoved his paperwork to one side. There would be time to do it once Lok-iKol had come and gone. Both he and Semlin-Nor had received messages from the Dome in the twenty-four hours since Lok-iKol had taken the Carnelian Throne, asking for one thing or another that the new Tarkin had decided he wanted from his own House. A levy of men from Karlyn-Tan, a favorite chair from Semlin-Nor. There were only two things the Tenebroso could not send for, Karlyn thought, and they were both in this room.

Semlin had shaken her head and remained standing, her hands on the high back of the chair across from him. "Which of us do you suppose he wants?" Semlin's voice was steady and true, but Karlyn-Tan had an idea from the whiteness of her knuckles on the chairback how much that steadiness cost her.

"I can think of no area in which you've failed the House," he said. "And I shall say so, should I have the chance."

"As will I for you," Semlin said, nodding.

Karlyn looked at her carefully, but there was no insincerity in her face. "No." Karlyn leaned back in his chair, tapping his lips with the fingers of his right hand. "I have reason to believe it will be me. Don't try to shield me, you can't know the cost."

The woman across from him took her lower lip into her teeth, shot him a glance from under her brows before focusing once again on the papers which layered the top of his desk. Karlyn raised his eyebrows as awareness dawned.

"How long did you know?" he said, sitting forward again.

"The House knew, and told me." The words tumbled from her mouth. "She'd been looking for the golden-haired one, the Lionsmane, for some time. As for the rest," she spread her hands, "I keep the Keys, man, how could I not know when food was prepared, when rooms were cleaned and light taken to them? Heat? Bedding? As for the rest . . ." Semlin lowered her eyes, the corners of her mouth turning down. "I gave the Fallen House my solemn oath to make no mention of it, nor of her plans. The next I knew, she was Fallen, and the Mercenary Brothers were gone."

"That going will be on my head. As well as the going of the Scholar, and the Lady Mar-eMar. As Keys is your function, so mine is Walls."

The tightness in Semlin-Nor's shoulders relaxed, but her face did not regain its usual color.

"You'll see I'm right," he said, getting to his feet, and taking his sword of office down from its bracket on the wall near the door. *Might as well be formal,* he thought, *it may remind Lok-iKol of his obligations to me, as well as mine to him.*

When he looked up from the silvered clasp of his sword belt, Semlin was already at the door. Her smile was a mere baring of teeth and her nod set her earrings swinging. There was little that his reassurances could do. She knew as much as he did about what had gone on in Lok's rooms when he was just Kir. Maybe more.

They walked without speaking from Karlyn's tower rooms to the main doors, silent even in those portions of the corridors where they knew they could not be overheard. Semlin-Nor came as far as she could with him, stopping in the outer courtyard, at the lowest steps of the House.

"The Caids bless you," she whispered through barely moving lips as he stepped off onto the stones of the yard. "The Sleeping God keep you in his dreams."

"And you."

He could feel her eyes on his back as he crossed the outer courtyard to the gates to greet his House, the new Tarkin.

"Tell me again of the escape of the Mercenaries."

It was as he'd suspected. It was only Karlyn-Tan that the Tenebroso had asked to accompany him to his workroom. Lok-iKol sat behind his worktable, staring at the sharp nib of a pen as he rolled it between thumb and fingers. For the first time in many years, he had not invited Karlyn-Tan to sit.

"With respect, my lord," Karlyn said, "I remind you that they were not in my keeping, and that I know nothing of their leaving." It was safe for him to say so, as he knew that the keys for Dhulyn Wolfshead's shackles never left Lok-iKol's own hands. "Mercenaries do not require assistance in these matters. It is known they cannot be held, if it is their own wish to be gone."

"And the Scholar, and the Lady Mar-eMar? Were they assisted?"

"Once more, I remind you, my House, that neither I nor any of my men had orders to prevent any members of this House from proceeding about their affairs. We knew of no reason to prevent them from leaving."

"You remind me." Lok-iKol pursed his lips and straightening in his chair, dipped the pen into the open bottle of ink lined up perfectly with the piece of parchment waiting to be written on.

"My mother, the Fallen House, often said that as a young man there was no hunter as skilled as you. You will find my Scholar. You will find the girl, and you will find me the Mercenary woman, the Wolfshead."

"My hunting days are past, my House. I am Walls now."

"I know you cannot leave the House," Lok-iKol said. "But you will direct the hunt."

"Let me speak more plainly, my lord. No, I will not."

Lok-iKol looked up, lifting the pen from the paper. Karlyn-Tan watched the ink gather into a large drop at the tip of the nib, grow large enough to shiver for a moment in the morning sunlight streaming through the window and fall onto the page beneath. Still he said nothing, waiting for his House to speak.

"I am your House," Lok-iKol said finally. "And now I am your Tarkin as well. You are my Walls, and you will do as I ask."

"I *am* the Walls of House Tenebro, my lord." Karlyn-Tan nodded, looking directly at the man seated at the worktable. "I am neither yours, nor mine, but Tenebro's. As I have said to you before, I serve only the House, with my own obligations, and my own judgment. It is my judgment that pursuing these Mercenaries will bring danger to the House. As Tenebroso, you may discharge me, but you cannot overrule my judgment."

"Then you are discharged." Lok-iKol looked down at the page before him, twisting his lips when he saw the stain of ink. "Be gone by sunset. Take nothing that belongs to me."

Karlyn fought to keep his knees locked, to keep his hand from reaching for the support of the chairback next to him. It was as though he suddenly found himself on the edge of a chasm, and only firm control would keep him from plunging down. The chasm had always been there, but he had grown so used to it, he had forgotten it could harm him. As he managed to forget, most of the time, that this man was his half brother. A voice inside him, the voice of the boy who had never known any other home but this one, cried out that he should submit, that he should agree to anything, and his lips parted, but the words that came out. . . .

"I'll give you a piece of advice," he said. "There'll be no need to hunt for the Mercenaries, Lok-iKol. They will come hunting for you."

⌘

Afterward, Karlyn was unable to recall whether he passed anyone on his way back to his rooms. He remembered thinking that he should have been surprised to find Semlin-Nor waiting for him when he got there, but he was not. She was, after all, the closest thing to a friend he had. She did not speak, but he answered the question on her face.

"I am Cast Out."

She put out a hand for the edge of the table, lowered herself into a chair.

"Do nothing. Say nothing. You are not safe here. Go, we never spoke." He could not endanger her. He, at least, had seen the outside world, even if not for fifteen years. She had been born in this House, and had never left it. If she were Cast Out, guilty by her association with him, it would destroy her.

Still, he could not help feeling hurt when Semlin ran from the room without further word. The touch on the hand she gave him as she pushed past was not much consolation. He sat down in the chair behind his worktable and let his face fall into his hands. He had until sunset. Until sunset to decide what, if anything, he was allowed to take with him. He had a little money of his own, saved up over the years. A ring and a dagger the Fallen House had given him. They could be considered his. Surely not even Lok-iKol would put him into the street naked, but was there anything in his rooms that was not of Tenebro colors, or which didn't bear the Tenebro crest?

Karlyn took a deep breath and looked up. From the angle of the sunlight on the desk, he'd been sitting here the better part of an hour already. And he had not given any thought to where he would go, once he'd found clothing. Was the Blue Dove Tavern still in business, he wondered, thinking of the last place he had stayed before coming to Tenebro House, and did it still rent rooms cheaply?

Leave the House. The fiery heat of his anger had finally died away, leaving a tightness in his throat and chest. He forced himself to take a deep breath, and then another. A sound made him get to his feet just as the door to the hallway opened. It was not, as he'd expected, Semlin-Nor, or even his assistant Jeldor-San, having just learned of her unexpected promotion, but the Lord Dal-eDal.

His hands full, Dal-eDal kicked the door shut behind him. In his right hand he carried a bulging saddle pack, and in his left, held by the scabbard, a sword. Both of these he put on the table in front of Karlyn.

"I did not knock, since I have learned that these are no longer your rooms."

Karlyn-Tan inclined his head.

"I have further learned that you have been told to leave with nothing that the Lord Lok-iKol has given you. Therefore, I have brought you clothing and a sword."

By the tone of his voice, and the expression on his face, Dal-eDal might have been passing Karlyn the bread at a communal table and not the tools that might save his life.

"I may need to report that they come from your hand."

Dal-eDal shrugged. "Consider it reported. My cousin has returned to the Carnelian Dome, and I am the heir."

Karlyn nodded his understanding, feeling a tightness in his shoulders relax. It was to find Dal-eDal that Semlin-Nor had left in such a hurry. "In that case, I accept."

It was Dal-eDal's turn to nod. He straightened his cuffs as if searching for something more to say.

"Did he want you to find the Tarkin?"

"You mean Tek-aKet Culebroso? The *former* Tarkin?" Dal smiled. "Yes, that is what I meant."

Karlyn took a deep breath, found further tension releasing. "No," he said. "The Scholar, the Lady Mar-eMar, and the Mercenary Dhulyn Wolfshead."

Dal leaned against the doorframe, folding his arms across his chest. "What is it about this woman? He tricks Mar-eMar into bringing her to Gotterang, and now, with all that must be occupying him in the less than two days he's been on the Carnelian Throne, he finds time to leave the Dome to ask you to find her?"

"The Scholar would know."

"And if we had the Scholar," Dal said, "we would know."

We? Karlyn thought. Dal presumed much on the basis of clothing and a sword. Karlyn believed he could put his hands on both the youngsters pretty easily, thanks to Jeldor-San's fast thinking in having them followed and to his own tracking skills, but he saw no need to tell Dal-eDal as much.

The two men exchanged a long look.

"If you would," Dal said finally, "once you know where you are, send me word."

"Why not?"

Dal-eDal's parting smile was more than half grimace.

"Just as soon as I figure out who you'll tell," Karlyn-Tan said once the door had closed again.

❧

Parno was using the sharpening stone he'd found in the underground chamber's weapons kit to put a better edge on one of the knives he'd been given from the Tarkin's armory. As soon as he could get upstairs, he'd be able to recover those of his own weapons—including his best sword—that had, along with the rest of his pack, been left with their horses at Mercenary House. He scowled at the knife, moving it this way and that as the light caught the edge. Was it really only a week ago?

Parno looked over the edge of the blade to find Bet-oTeb looking at him. The Tarkin-to-be looked very solemn, her eyes huge in the chamber's uncertain light. "My father wants you," she said. "If you would be so good as to come with me."

Parno bowed to her, put the knife back into the sheath he wore at his belt, and followed Bet-oTeb to the far end of the room, where the Tarkin sat with his wife. Tek-aKet smiled his thanks to his daughter and indicated that Parno should seat himself on the next bed.

The Tarkin looked tired, as well he might, having slept only a few hours after being up most of the night. Parno doubted he would have recognized the man had he merely encountered him on the street, any more than his second cousin appeared to recognize him. There was a world of difference between the seventeen-year-old he had been and the bearded, tattooed, and heavily-muscled Mercenary Brother he had become. The last time Parno had seen Tek-aKet, back when he himself had still been Par-iPar Tenebro, Tek had been thirteen, gangly and round-shouldered from study. Fourteen years later, Parno could see the old Tarkin in the shape of Tek's eyes, the breadth of his shoulders, and the firm set of his jaw.

Tek-aKet now leaned forward until their heads were almost touching.

"Zelianora and I have been taking thought," the Tarkin of Imrion said. "Am I correct in my understanding that you can speak for your Partner?"

Parno nodded. "We are the same person," he said.

"Can you tell me, then, whether she will use her Mark to help me?"

"More than she has already done," the Tarkina said, acknowledgment and gratitude in her voice. Her husband flashed her a smile and nodded.

Parno looked down at his hands, clasped between his knees. The man thought he had a great tool, and who could blame him . . . Parno had once thought so himself. Experience had taught Parno differently, but how was he to convince Tek-aKet? Did Dhulyn escape from Lok-iKol only to fall into his cousin's hands? Parno looked at Zelianora Tarkina, who was watching her husband's face with steady dark eyes. Composed, almost serene. He looked back at the Tarkin. This man was not like Lok-iKol, he thought. Nothing like.

"One time," he said quietly, "Dhulyn woke up crying. She'd Seen a farmer drowning a basket of kittens. Is that the kind of thing you want her to tell you?"

Tek-aKet sat up straight, letting his hands fall to his knees. "You're saying she can't control it."

"I'm saying she can't control it." Parno rubbed his chin. He'd kill for the time to shave and a nice sharp razor, though he feared he'd have to wait until he left Imrion to do it. "At first, I thought it was just some kind of Outlander stubbornness. She hated the thought that I might be watching her in the morning, trying to see in her face some sign that she'd Seen something in the night. That I was waiting for her to tell me what to do next, instead of using my own brain. 'I'm not a crutch,' she used to say to me. But then I realized that she wasn't trying to teach me a moral lesson, but telling me the real truth. Her Mark wasn't something that we were going to able to use, to lean on."

"How does it work, then?" the Tarkina asked in her musical voice.

Parno shrugged. "It comes when it comes, waxes and wanes like the moon. Strongest with her woman's time, as if the blood brings it, and if she's touching someone, she's likely to See something pertaining to them. But not always. And sometimes she'll get Visions in between, not so clear, but sometimes." He looked up to find them both watching him.

"And you have to understand, there's never any context to them. The farmer with the kittens? She didn't know what country he was in, or when it would happen. If we'd wanted to stop it, we wouldn't have known where to go. She'll help you," he said. "We both will. But don't count on her Mark to win for you."

❊❊❊

"And since the foreign ambassadors should be met with as quickly as possible, my lord, I've arranged for an informal supper in the east reception room. That way you can speak to them all at once. The Berdanan ambassador is particularly insistent concerning the whereabouts of the Tarkina and her children, as they are the heirs of her sister, Queen Alliandra." The voice of the Tarkin's Chief Counselor, Gane-Gan, was flat and colorless. But then, Lok-iKol thought, that more or less described the voice of everyone in the Carnelian Dome.

"It would not be more diplomatic to see him at least individually?" Lok-iKol frowned, resisting the desire to rub at his eye. He'd managed only a few hours' sleep in the last two days, and right now he felt they hadn't done him much good. The day had started well, the Dome and city were his, and the Assembly of Houses had met and accepted him as Tarkin—though not quite by acclamation. House Penrado had pleaded illness and absented himself, as Lok had expected, but he had not actually protested. Lok would do something about that later.

But the day had not continued well. Lok closed his right hand into a fist. He had not expected Karlyn-Tan to defy him, and now he would have to find someone else to hunt for the Seer.

"A meeting at this time, my lord Tarkin, is a mere formality. They acknowledge you, and you remind them that existing relations will continue. Your reassurances to the Berdanan ambassador will carry more weight when spoken in front of such witnesses. When I said 'informal,' I meant in dress and preparation, not in topic of discussion."

"Very well."

As Lok spoke, a page entered the spacious room that had been Tek-aKet's public study. Lok-iKol let out his breath with such force that Gan-eGan looked up from the mark he was making on his parchment list.

"The Priest Beslyn-Tor is here, my lord," the page said. Gan-eGan dropped pen and parchments, and the page courteously stooped to help him retrieve them.

"My apologies, but I have no leisure for him today."

"My lord Tarkin."

Lok realized that Beslyn-Tor had followed on the page's heels and was already in the room. He suppressed the irritation that immediately rose to twist his lips. Gan-eGan looked around, brows raised and head twitching as he backed away from the priest. Lok's eye narrowed. It seemed there was something between Gan-eGan and the old priest. Something unpleasant.

Lok smiled. He'd expected Beslyn-Tor to turn up, though not quite so quickly.

"More wine and a glass for my friend," Lok said to the page, ignoring the Jaldean's shaken head and gesture of refusal. He'd never seen the man take either food or drink, and Beslyn-Tor was noticeably thinner than he had been when Lok had first met him, though he showed no other signs of ritual fasting. His color was good, his grip firm, his jade-green eyes particularly clear and his movements, as he took the chair next to the worktable without waiting to be invited, graceful.

Once more Lok-iKol suppressed a frown. "As you heard me say," he began, "I have no great store of leisure today. If you would tell me in what way I can assist you?"

"I have given you what you desired, yet you withhold my payment."

Again a darting glance from Gan-eGan, and another from the page, as he came in with a tray bearing a fresh flask of wine and a second goblet.

Lok looked at the tray as the page set it down on the table. "Leave us," he said.

Unexpectedly, Gan-eGan did not protest. Hugging his parchment lists to his chest like a shield, he scuttled from the room. The page looked from the old counselor to Lok-iKol and back again, as if he might speak.

Lok raised his remaining eyebrow.

The page inclined his head, though his lips thinned as he turned to go. No one in Tenebro House would ever have looked at Lok like that. *What has Tek-aKet been teaching his servants?*

Only when they were alone did Lok sit down in the Tarkin's chair.

"I must have time to solidify my position before I can give you what we agreed upon. A moon, perhaps two." As the priest narrowed his eyes, Lok smiled and spread his hands. "Come," he said. "Have we not prospered?" He leaned forward and poured himself a glass of the wine. It was a dark, full red that Lok knew from experience would taste of the oak it had been aged in. "When I am anointed, I will prepare the proclamations that shall give you what you've asked for." He sipped at his cup of wine, savoring it in his mouth a moment before swallowing. *And, once I'm anointed, I won't need you.* "The support and countenance of the Tarkin for yourself and your followers. Dominion over the Marked."

"Why do you wait? Every delay allows the Sleeping God more time to awaken."

Lok ground his teeth. The man's beliefs were becoming

more than a nuisance. Lok set his wineglass back on the table, fixing his guest with his eye. The Jaldean was not even looking at him. "I have declared Tek-aKet Fallen, but in the absence of a body, there are rumors," he said, with more force than he had intended. "Rumors which force me to move much more slowly than I had originally planned."

Beslyn-Tor brought his gaze back from the distance and fixed it on Lok-iKol, the jade-green eyes as bright as though they'd absorbed the light of the setting sun that streamed through the windows. The new Tarkin of Imrion suddenly wished he was not sitting down. He would feel stronger on his feet. It seemed the whole room had darkened.

"You think to put me off. I warn you, do nothing you will regret."

Lok brought his fingertips together and tapped his lips. "Do you threaten me? You stirred the people against the Marked; that is a great power you have. But Tek-aKet was taken by surprise, I will not be. That trick cannot be played again."

The Jaldean priest waved the statement away with the closest thing to a smile Lok had ever seen him make.

"I seek to give you what you want most."

"And that is?"

"You have named it. Power."

Lok-iKol felt the cord of his eye patch move as he drew in his brows. "I am Tarkin."

"Is that the extent of your ambition? What if there was more power to be had?"

Lok sat back, gripping the chair arms with his hands. This was too much.

"What? Will the Sleeping God bless me and hold me in his dreams? Do you think me as gullible as the rabble you rouse to frenzy? You are a useful tool, Beslyn-Tor, and I will reward you as promised, but do not presume too much on my gratitude."

As a sign that the audience was over, Lok-iKol stood. Beslyn-Tor sighed and heaved himself to his feet, his age suddenly showing in the noise of his effort.

"My lord Tarkin, " he said, lowering himself to one knee. "Forgive an impatient man. Allow me to be the first to give you my allegiance." He bowed his head and reached up his right hand.

Lok-iKol hesitated, but there was no irony, no smug sarcasm, nor even any calculation on the old man's face. He took the offered hand between his own. The priest's skin was warm and dry, his grip firmer than Lok would have expected in so old a man. Lok licked suddenly dry lips.

"I receive . . ." he began, and shook his head in irritation. For a moment he couldn't remember the words. He blinked and focused again on Beslyn-Tor's face, the man's jade-green eyes. The room around them grew darker.

❈

He threw back his head, lungs breathing deeply. He had touched this shape before, used its eyes, so it took only moments of weakness, seconds of disorientation before he wore it easily. Younger. Stronger. For a moment the lost eye distracted him, but a second's concentration removed that difficulty. For another moment the original inhabitant's shrieking drew away his attention, but that was swiftly dealt with. The same concentration allowed him to review what this one knew.

The Seer was lost.

For a moment the body's heart stopped beating.

She must be found, this Mercenary, this Wolfshead. Who could do so?

The Scholar. He had Found once already. But the Scholar himself was missing. Karlyn-Tan Cast Out. Dal-eDal. That one always knew more than he told.

He looked down at the old man on the floor.

"Jelran," he called and was pleased by how swiftly the page entered.

"Have the junior priest who accompanied Beslyn-Tor enter. His master appears to have suffered a stroke."

The young page glanced at the figure on the floor and licked his lips. "Of course, my lord."

He watched, feeling the inside of this shape, testing the strengths, tasting the skills, as they helped the stricken man dodder out of the room.

"Jelran? Tell Gan-eGan to cancel the ambassadors' supper and send for my cousin Dal-eDal to come to me."

"At once, my lord."

❈

I have got nothing to worry about, Dal-eDal told himself, nodding to the pale-faced Dome Guard as he dismounted at the Ironwood Gate. If Lok was ready to have him killed, he needn't bring Dal to the Carnelian Dome to do it. Far more likely to suffer some "accident" at home, like so many others of the Tenebro family. No, the difference today was that the summons came not only from his House, but from his Tarkin.

Or someone's Tarkin, anyway.

Dal smiled and tossed his reins to the waiting stable girl, thanked his escort and began the long walk across the fitted flagstones of the wide interior yard to the Carnelian Dome's Steward of Keys, waiting on the steps of the grand entrance known as the Tarkin's Door. Like the stable girl, and a couple of the Carnelian Dome Guards for that matter, the Steward's face showed a pallor and a stiffness that spoke of underlying uncertainty. Not unlike, Dal thought, the look on the faces of the people in Tenebro House on the morning the House fell.

"Not *your* first time here, at any rate, Lord Dal," the Steward said with the ghost of his usual smile on his lips.

Dal tilted his head with a smile of his own. He felt and recognized the need for normal conversation in these most abnormal times. "I barely remember that event," he said. The Steward gestured, and Dal preceded the man through the gateway. "I was four when my father became head of his Household, and I came with him to give his oaths to the Tenebroso, and to the old Tarkin."

The Steward made a half-aborted motion with his right hand, and Dal coughed. So it was better not to mention even Tek-aKet's father, was it?

"I wasn't Steward then," the man said. "I don't believe I remember your father."

"He was only in Gotterang once more. In fact, he died on his way home from that last visit to the Tenebroso. Fell from his horse."

"You became Household then? Or was there an older sibling?"

"No, I was Kir for my Household, but at eight years old, my House thought it better to put a Steward in place and brought me to her in Gotterang." No need to tell the Carnelian Dome's Steward of Keys that such young children were used as hostages; the man well knew that for himself.

"And, of course, you've been here ever since. Once in the capital, who would want to leave?"

Dal smiled, his lips pressed tightly together. Ever since. Ever since his father, who must have guessed *something* about that summons from which he never returned, had kissed him good-bye whispering, "Stay alive, Son. See you survive to avenge me."

Still alive, Papa, he thought. *Accomplishing that much at least.*

"It must have been strange for you," the Steward said, as he opened the third set of double doors for Dal to walk through. "I remember being very homesick when I first came here as a child." Dal stood to one side as two pages, heads down and mumbling their excuses, came stumbling through the opened door.

"Not exactly homesick. Though there were no children my age in Tenebro House," he said, after the young pages were out of earshot. "And I'm afraid I found my cousin Lok-iKol very . . . impressive."

The Steward of Keys, with a glance at Dal's face, nodded his quick understanding.

At first, Dal had been too shocked by grief and the change in his circumstances to remember his father's last words to him. Afterward, he'd needed to be sure that it *wasn't* just homesickness and an aversion to Lok's company that made him want to kill his one-eyed cousin. The longer he waited, the harder it became to do anything. If he killed Lok openly, he would be killed himself. Failing in his father's first command to him. If he killed Lok by stealth, he'd become the heir, something he'd never wanted—still didn't want. So he'd spent years studying the situation, gathering information, in part to protect himself, in part to find a safe way of enacting his father's vengeance. All in all, he'd been gathering information for a long time.

When he'd realized just *why* Parno Lionsmane had seemed so familiar, only the iron discipline of years had stopped him from running singing through the House. He'd thought all his problems were solved. As kidnapped Mercenary Brothers they would kill Lok, and as a first cousin,

Par- iPar Tenebro would set aside his Mercenary Brother-hood, become heir, and Dal could finally go home.

But the Brothers were gone, and Lok was now Tarkin.

"My lord." The Steward of Keys motioned Dal to one side. Approaching them down the corridor were three indi-viduals dressed completely in dark green, escorted by two guards in Tenebro colors and two Jaldean priests. From the corner of his eye, Dal looked at the Steward's impassive face. For it was clear from their air of stumbling confusion that something had been done to these Marked. One of them, a short stout woman, was supporting a man almost twice her height, holding him around the waist. She merely looked red-eyed and blotchy, tears still rolling down stiff cheeks, but the man was vacant-eyed and drooling. The third, perhaps their son, was white as paper, and breathed shallowly as if in great pain.

"I thought the Marked were being taken to the Jaldean High Shrine," Dal murmured to the Steward of Keys.

"Last night the new Tarkin gave orders for them to be brought here," the Keys said. Something in the man's voice made Dal look at him closely, but the Keys kept his eyes lowered. His lips, Dal saw, were trembling.

Once the Marked had passed, Dal and the Steward of Keys fell silent. They continued down the hall until it wid-ened before the delicately carved doors of the Cedar Room, the small audience chamber. Here, there were com-fortable cushioned chairs set out for waiting dignitaries, grouped around small empty tables that normally carried jellied fruits, salted nuts, and carafes of wine and cider. The place, usually crowded with petitioners and the younger children of the Noble Houses, was deserted.

Suddenly, Dal didn't want to go any farther.

"If you would wait a moment," the Keys of the Dome said. "I will see if the Tarkin is ready for you."

Dal sank into one of the cushioned chairs. Once again he reminded himself that Lok need not bring him to the Dome to kill him. So what *did* Lok want? Dal thought about the message he'd received this morning from Karlyn-Tan, that the former Steward of Walls could be found at the Blue Dove Tavern. And where, Dal wondered would Gundaron the Scholar and the Lady Mar-eMar be found? Dal did not believe for a moment that the two had anything to do with the Fall of the House, but it was evident that Lok wanted them, and that meant Dal might gain something by finding them himself.

Lok had asked Karlyn-Tan to find the Mercenary woman, and the Steward of Walls had refused and been Cast Out. Was Dal now about to be asked? And if *he* refused? What would Lok do then?

The Keys pushed both doors of the small audience room open, gone so pale that his mustache and eyebrows stood out dark against his skin. "You may go in, Lord Dal-eDal." He gestured toward the open doors.

Stomach twisting, wishing he had the courage to simply turn and walk away, Dal went through.

Whatever he'd expected to find, it wasn't Lok in what was clearly the Tarkin's great chair—carved out of white cedar, studded with carnelians, and just smaller than the official throne—talking to Chief Counselor Gan-eGan. Dal hovered, unwilling to approach more closely. The older man was on his knees on Lok's right side, his hands clinging to the arm of the great chair, as a man in the sea clings to the side of a raft. Dal licked his lips and took a hesitant step forward.

With a soft sigh the counselor stood, lifting a trembling hand to his mouth, sketched a shaky bow, and headed for the door. Dal actually had to step out of the man's way, as Gan-eGan—usually so punctilious it was almost laughable—passed him without acknowledgment of any kind.

"Cousin." Lok's voice was curiously flat, as if he was too tired to speak with more animation. Perhaps he'd found being Tarkin to be more work than he'd expected, Dal thought as he crossed the floor to his cousin's side. He performed a more elaborate version of the counselor's bow and straightened, forcing a smile to his lips.

"All is well at the House," Dal said. "Tenryn-For is settling well into his duties as Walls." *As well as he can after less than twenty-four hours, and after Karlyn-Tan's Deputy Jeldor-San had unexpectedly refused the post.*

Lok nodded, but with an air of a man who is listening to something else. He got to his feet and gestured to Dal to fall in beside him as he walked toward the smaller, private door behind the great chair.

"Come with me, Cousin," he said. "I would ask something of you."

If I didn't know better, Dal thought as he followed Lok through the door and nodded at the redheaded page who waited there and fell into step behind them, *I'd think he was drunk.* There was just something a bit too careful, too focused, about the way Lok was speaking—and walking, now that Dal thought about it.

Any other time Dal would have welcomed the chance to walk through the private corridors of the Carnelian Dome, places that the public—even relations like the Tenebros—never saw. As it was, he kept his eyes on his cousin, and only took in the occasional detail, here a portrait of a heavily bewigged Tarkina, there a rug showing the bright dyes that marked it as a product of Semlor in the west.

Lok finally stopped outside a thick oak door, reinforced with embedded iron bars, whose massive frame was carved to look like snakes. *Treasure room or armory,* Dal thought, recognizing the motifs of the Culebro Tarkins. The page, pale, wide-eyed, and tight-lipped, once more took up his position to the right of the door, ready to wait until he was wanted.

Lok unlocked the thick door with a final twist of the key and walked straight into the room. Dal stopped dead on the threshold, until he realized that the reason his mouth felt dry was that it was hanging open. Treasure room he had thought, and treasure room it was, but thought is one thing, and sight another. A long central aisle stretched out between tiered shelving, every shelf covered with dark blue felted cloth, and every finger span of cloth covered. Plates and tableware used on state occasions filled more than half the room, personal jewelry by the basketful—including the cat's-eye rubies the Tarkina had brought with her on her marriage—and, halfway along one side, the Tarkin's gold crown, bracelets, ear clasps, and pectoral of woven snakes, every one with gleaming carnelian eyes.

"The lists say there is a relic of the Sleeping God here,"

Lok said, so quietly that Dal almost did not hear him. "A bracelet with green stones."

Dal took a step forward. "Did you wish me to look for it?" His voice sounded harsh in his own ears, but Lok did not seem to notice.

"No, I wish you to find me the Mercenary Dhulyn Wolfshead." Lok stopped, turned to the shelves on his right and picked up a pendant, a square-cut emerald set in silver wire. He frowned and set it down again.

Dal almost smiled as he watched his cousin pick up yet another piece of jewelry with a green stone and set it down again. Finally, a chance to learn why Lok found this woman so important.

"The Mercenary?" Dal said, careful to show no real interest. "What is it about this woman . . . ?"

Lok had stopped again, this time to pick up a bracelet made of gold links set with square smooth-polished stones. From that, and from the color and thickness of the gold, it was obviously very old. These stones, too, were green, but seemed likely to be jade. As Dal watched, Lok pushed it on over his hand, barely able to move it past the root of his thumb, to where it hung closely about his wrist.

Dal cleared his throat to ask his question again, but he hesitated, as his cousin had closed his eye, tilting his head back as if he were listening to some favorite music. Glancing down, Dal saw the bracelet on Lok's wrist move, as if it were suddenly a living thing, its colors suddenly painfully bright, and then fading, dissolving as it was absorbed into Lok's wrist, until it seemed he had a tattoo there, where his skin had been clear and clean a moment before. Even as Dal took a breath to exclaim, the tattoo faded, and Lok's skin was clean again. Dal looked up, but his cousin's eye was focused on the spot on his wrist where the bracelet had been. And his shadow, cast on the wall behind him was not his own, but larger, darker, than it should have been, and somehow the wrong shape. Dal's own shadow was beside it, pale and small and normal.

"Lok, what . . . ?" His voice was paper thin and Dal cleared his throat. Without moving the rest of his body, Lok twisted his head to look at him and Dal saw that Lok's right eye, clear and beautiful in the unmarred side of his face was *green.* Not crystal blue as it had always been, but a soft jade green. And Lok's eye patch had shifted, perhaps because of how he'd turned his head and Dal lifted his left hand to his own face, as if to indicate to his cousin what had happened, but he froze, unable to move.

Both of Lok's eyes were green. *Both* of them.

Seventeen

KARLYN-TAN HAD TO STEEL himself not to twitch away from people, not to hug the walls as he walked down the street. He recognized his feelings as the horizon sickness, though he'd never suffered from the fear of open spaces before. There *was not* too much space, he told himself, just more than he was used to—and too many strangers. Already this afternoon he'd had to convince two young toughs that he wasn't someone they could prey on. Thank the Caids, Dal-eDal had given him a sword. He now walked with his hand openly resting on the sword's hilt, as a message to any other tough boys in the area.

He kept walking, following the market crowds into the Great Square, resisting the urge to run back to his inn—run away from *outside*. He took a deep breath and looked around him, forcing his shoulders down. Was it his imagination, or was everyone around him walking too quickly, heads ducked, cloaks held more closely than the warm day called for? He frowned. He'd been Walls too long to remember what people on the outside were like.

Karlyn walked directly across the square, heading for the steps in the southeast corner that would lead him out into Swordsmiths Street and Mercenary House.

There were several people on the wide stone steps leading from Great Square to the street below and Karlyn's attention kept being drawn to one of them in particular. Fair-haired, medium height, fair width of shoulders . . . and the right shoulder hitched up a bit, as if he was used to carrying a pack or heavy bag slung over it. Horizon sickness forgotten, Karlyn increased his pace. He knew that walk and that shoulder hitch even without the Scholar's tunic; he'd been watching them around Tenebro House for the last two years. So Gundaron of Valdomar *was* still in Gotterang, and where was he heading now?

❧❧❧

Mar sat in the window hole of the ruin just an alley length away from their hiding spot under the old floorboards of the abandoned granary. She'd been the one to go for water this morning, while Gun went to see if he could get into his Library. They weren't going to be able to stay out on the streets very much longer, not unless they wanted to start selling things—and what did they have to sell but a few articles of clothing and the tools of their trades? If it wasn't for having to hide from every pair of guards, and every sound of horses' hooves, they would have been well able to make a living selling their skills, but as it was, they'd be running out of money and things to barter very quickly.

She was listening carefully for the short three-note whistle that would mean Gundaron had entered the alley. She'd answer with the agreed-upon variation, and then watch from her hiding spot as he walked to the end of their lane past the entrance to their cellar and turned the corner. She'd wait for a count of fifty and, if the lane stayed empty, she'd whistle again. Gundaron would double back and meet her as she let herself down from her window hole. This was just one of the ways they'd figured out between them—her from stories she'd picked up from Dhulyn Wolfshead and Parno Lionsmane, Gundaron from his fund of reading—of watching if anyone was following them, or if anyone had found their hiding place. Still, Mar was getting heartily sick of spending most of her time watching her back.

When the whistle finally came, she answered it, and Gundaron glanced up to where he knew she would be. When their eyes met, a new look passed over his face, a familiar look.

Oh, Caids. I know that look. She'd seen it on Parno Lionsmane's face when he looked at Dhulyn Wolfshead. She'd wanted someone to look at *her* that way. The blood hammered in her ears and her hands shook, even as a small flower of joy bloomed under her heart.

"We can't go on like this much longer," Mar said, keeping her eyes on the ties to her pack, the knowledge of what she'd seen on Gundaron's face too new, too fresh to acknowledge. "Money's not all we can run out of. So far we've been lucky, no one's cared enough about us to steal from us or to turn us in, but how long will that last?" She groped into her pack for the metal cup they shared. "We need help, and we need it soon."

"It's a judgment on us," Gun said.

Mar's hand stilled. "What do you mean?"

"We're surrounded by people we can't trust," he said, looking up from the small lamp he was refilling with the last of their scrounged oil. "Maybe it's because *we* can't be trusted."

"I'm trusting you," she said, touching his forearm lightly with her fingertips. It felt just as hard as the metal cup in her other hand. "And you're trusting me. And . . . we were used by the people we did trust, both of us," she added. "That makes a difference."

Gundaron rubbed his face with both hands, the corners of his mouth turned down. "I don't think the Mercenary Brotherhood are going to feel that way about *me*."

Mar pressed her lips together. She did trust him, just as he trusted her. And yet there was still something Gun wasn't telling her. What could be worse than what she'd done, betraying people who had saved her life? Maybe it was because she hadn't read the stories Gun had, maybe it was because she'd spent so much time with the Mercenaries, but she honestly didn't believe she or Gun were in any danger from the Curse of Pasillon.

"Gun," she said finally, handing him the cup. "Maybe we should try to get out of the city."

He looked at her, their fingers touching on the cold metal of the cup. "But you wanted to tell them, the Wolfshead, I mean, and Lionsmane."

She nodded, lower lip caught between her teeth. "We've been sent away from Mercenary House twice now," she said. "What if we don't get a chance to tell them?"

"Tell them what, Lady Mar?"

❧❧❧

Interesting, Karlyn thought once the cup had been picked up and they'd made room for him in the only corner high enough to let them all sit upright. They'd dropped the only thing that they might possibly have used as a weapon, to cling to each other. He wondered if they'd realized it themselves. Judging from the way they carefully avoided touching in the confined space, Karlyn rather thought they had.

Like anyone who'd commanded troops, he was a good judge of character. The girl looked nervous, he thought, and a little too pale. But her jaw was firm, and her mouth a resolute line. She was tougher than her noble birth and her town fostering might lead some to believe. After all, she'd come over the Antedichas Mountains with two Mercenaries, met the Cloud People, and lived to tell of it—not to mention surviving those particular four days in Tenebro House. Karlyn looked to the Scholar.

Though he was a few years older than Mar-eMar, Gundaron was likely the younger in experience—that being the trouble with book learning. The boy was frankly terrified, in Karlyn's opinion. Where the girl was pale, the boy was white-faced; where she was firm and resolute, he held himself so stiffly he had a slight tremor in his hands. And he blinked too much. But for all that, Karlyn thought, impressed almost against his will, Gundaron was keeping his fear firmly in check. What could have frightened him so badly? This was the first real emotion Karlyn had ever seen in the boy. What had woken him from his Scholar's daydream? Was it the girl? Or something more sinister?

"We didn't harm the House," Lady Mar said, breaking into his thoughts. "I know you have no reason to believe us, but we didn't."

"Perhaps I have no reason," Karlyn said, "but I believe you. What decided you to leave when you did?"

Lady Mar took a deep breath. She was wearing the same clothes she'd had on when she'd arrived with the Mercenary brothers, now much creased and dirty. But she seemed not to notice any discomfort. "I'd been used," she said, a bitter twist to her mouth. "I didn't know how badly just at first. I knew I'd been lied to, though, and I couldn't stay where there was no one I could trust."

Tough, all right. Tougher than some other cousins of the House he could name. Karlyn turned to Gundaron. The Scholar clamped his jaw, not like someone determined not to speak, Karlyn thought, but like someone who expected the words to burn on their way out. The Lady Mar put her dust-grimed hand on the Scholar's arm.

"I know you have no reason to believe me," Karlyn said, deliberately echoing Mar-eMar's words. "But you *can* trust me. I did not choose to leave Tenebro House, I have been Cast Out for refusing to hunt for Dhulyn Wolfshead and Parno Lionsmane. I believe we are allies." The two youngsters glanced at each other before looking back at him. Was there hope in their eyes? "What is this you were saying about Mercenary House," he asked them.

"We've amends to make," Lady Mar said, her eyes flicking toward the Scholar. "And information to give. But we can't get anyone to listen to us."

Karlyn nodded. "I believe *I* can," he said. "Let's get you cleaned up. I believe they might listen to me."

◄►

Parno turned the Tarkin's sword gently out of the way, using the palm of his hand against the flat of the blade, and, letting his own sword drop to the floor, poked Tek-aKet in the sternum with the forefinger of his right hand. Both men, the Tarkin red-faced but smiling, stepped back from one another.

"You're not afraid of the blade, which is good," Dhulyn said, stepping forward as Parno retrieved his sword. "But you kept your own too low, and too far off the central line. Watch." She took the Tarkin's place and came at Parno slowly, her movements exaggerated in such a way that Tek-aKet Tarkin would have no trouble following. She held her sword so that the sharpened tip sagged below her waist. As she advanced on Parno, he once again turned the blade aside with the palm of his hand.

"Do you see?" Dhulyn said. "Your blade was off-center, and at an angle that made it easy for him to turn it aside, even without another weapon of his own. Now watch where I have mine." Dhulyn executed almost the identical move, except this time Parno was able to turn her blade aside only by sacrificing his own forward momentum, and losing any chance to turn the move to his advantage. She and Parno lifted their points and stepped back.

"Did you see, Lord Tarkin?"

Tek-aKet nodded, brow furrowed. "I thought I'd had good teachers, but you've shown me things—" He lifted his shoulders and let them drop. "I didn't think to watch his bare hand."

Dhulyn sheathed her sword and extended both her hands to show the fine scars on the palms. "When it's life and death, and not for show, *everything* is a weapon. Kill or be killed, all battles come down to this."

"Kill or be killed," Tek-aKet repeated, his dark brows drawn down into a vee over his clear blue eyes. "I think you have shown me more than a *Shora* of offense and defense, Dhulyn Wolfshead, I think you have answered a question for me." He looked up at them, the sheen of sweat drying on his upper lip. "I think I must take back the Carnelian Throne."

"There was some doubt of this?" Parno's eyebrows could not raise any higher.

Tek-aKet nodded, his eyes hooded. "I never wanted to be Tarkin," he said, a half smile playing about his lips. "My brother died of a fever, and I had to take his place. It did actually occur to me that this was my chance to take Zella and the children and go to her sister in Berdana."

"And what decides you against that?" Dhulyn said.

"Zella and the children," he said. "My family will never be safe with Lok-iKol Tenebroso on the throne. No matter where we go, what we do, he will see us as a threat until he hunts us down and kills us all. He's been doing exactly that to his own House for years." He lowered his eyes again, and his face turned to stone. "But there is also this. Lok-iKol is not Tarkin of Imrion. Neither by inheritance nor by Ballot. I find it is, after all, that simple. I will not walk away from my throne, my people, my responsibilities, and leave them to that jackal. I must find some place, some fortress or other, that I can use to rally my army. If I move quickly, then many who are now confused will come to us."

"Well," Parno said lightly. "We're looking for work, Lord Tarkin. We'd give you a good rate."

❧

The sound of hoofbeats on the cobbles of the lane outside the tavern drew every eye to the window and three of the regulars to the door. Karlyn-Tan stayed in his seat by the inner window that let out on the stable yard, polishing the buckle of his sword belt in the sunshine that found its way through the open shutters. The two youngsters were in his room upstairs, smuggled in the back way and even now taking advantage of warmed water and soap. It wasn't until it was obvious the horse was stopping that Karlyn put aside the buckle and polishing cloth and turned toward the door. He knew the sound of a horse that was being ridden, and there was only one noble he could think of who might have reason to come to this particular inn.

Dal-eDal entered and stepped immediately to one side so as not to present a silhouette in the entrance—and also to let his two guards enter with him. As soon as his eyes adjusted to the relative dimness of the taproom, his chin lifted as he caught sight of Karlyn-Tan. He crossed the half-empty room with a nod at the innkeeper behind the bar and joined Karlyn at his corner table. Karlyn smiled when the nobleman sat down with his back to rest of room—evidently Dal was sure that Karlyn would warn him if there should be any trouble. Or perhaps he was counting on the loyalty of the two guards, now being served at the bar? The young nobleman looked paler than usual, with lines around his eyes Karlyn had not seen before. When his cup of wine arrived, the fingers that turned it around on the tabletop without lifting it to his lips trembled slightly.

"You might have been better to come afoot," Karlyn-Tan said. "You'd attract less attention." He threw a pointed glance around at the patrons of the barroom, only some of whom were minding their own business. Others seemed to think that a well-dressed and mounted nobleman, even with two guards, *was* their business.

"I will not be in Gotterang long enough for attention to harm me," Dal-eDal said, turning to sit sideways in his seat.

That was enough to make Karlyn look up once more from his polishing, as Dal-eDal must have known it would.

"My House and lord, Lok-iKol," Dal said quietly, his eyes now idly drifting over the room, "has an errand for me outside the city."

"Lok-iKol wishes you to *leave Gotterang*?"

Dal-eDal inclined his head once.

Karlyn-Tan relaxed, allowing his shoulders to rest against the wall behind his bench. No one in the House had thought it strange that this younger cousin had been kept on a short leash. Younger cousins who were part of the succession, even if they had no apparent ambition, were always a danger to heirs, and best kept where they could be carefully watched. This was no less true now that Lok-iKol was calling himself Tarkin. And yet Lok-iKol was now sending Dal away?

Karlyn let his eyes drift over to the two men watching from the bar. "Is he so sure of himself, now that he is Tarkin?"

Dal shook his head impatiently. "It's more than that. He . . ." Dal looked across the table from under his brows. "I've been long a coward, Karlyn-Tan, or so I thought. But yesterday I saw something that makes me understand what fear is. I need help."

Karlyn raised his eyebrows, his lips parting of their own accord. He quickly lowered his own eyes back to the bits of buckle, the polishing paste and rags on the tabletop. Dal *had* to be afraid, to say such a thing aloud.

"I appreciate the help you have given me," he said slowly. "But I remind you that I am no longer a Steward of Tenebro."

Dal stopped turning his wine cup on the table and took a long draw from it, setting it back on the table with a sour twist to his mouth. *Serves him right,* Karlyn thought. *This isn't the kind of place you should order wine.*

"This is a greater concern than who is Tenebro and who

is not. We speak now of the fate of Imrion." Dal wiped his lips with the back of his hand. "You haven't asked about my errand."

Karlyn-Tan waited.

"He sends me to find the Mercenary Brother, Dhulyn Wolfshead. I feel it is imperative that we find her, if only to learn why Lok-iKol wants her. If only to use her ourselves."

Karlyn-Tan felt himself go perfectly still. And kept perfectly silent.

"How?"

"How else? Against Lok-iKol."

Ah. Karlyn drummed the tabletop with his fingers. The fate of Imrion, indeed.

"Can we rid ourselves of the two men with you? I have someone I think you should meet."

Dhulyn looked out through the spy hole and nodded slowly, almost unable to believe what her eyes told her.

"He does not lie," she said to Tyler Nightsky, the Brother who had called her to the gate. "That is Karlyn-Tan, last seen as Steward of Walls at Tenebro House." She turned to Tyler. "I will speak with Alkoryn. In the meantime, allow him to enter the outer courtyard."

Karlyn-Tan had been told to stand at the end of the courtyard nearest the gate. Dhulyn let herself into the yard from the kitchen end and waited, without moving. Except for the missing Tenebro crest, he looked very much the same as the last time she had seen him, eyes narrow, lips unsmiling.

"Dhulyn Wolfshead," he said, taking half a step toward her before remembering his instructions and standing still.

"I did not think it possible that my ears and eyes both should deceive me," she said. "And yet here you are."

"You are not deceived, Wolfshead," he said. "I am here."

"And your Walls?"

"Are mine no longer. I am Cast Out."

For a moment Dhulyn could think of nothing to say that was adequate to what he'd told her. Finally, she nodded. "For whom do you speak?"

"To you, I speak for myself," Karlyn glanced away before returning his eyes to hers. "I rejoice to see you well, and alive. And I bring you warning that Lok-iKol Tenebroso seeks everywhere for you." She bowed toward him. That was certainly no news to her, whatever he thought, but his goodwill in warning her had to be acknowledged.

Karlyn took a deeper breath. "To Tek-aKet, Tarkin of Imrion, I speak for Dal-eDal Tenebro, who comes with news, and brings himself and eight others as a token of the force of allies he can add to the Tarkin's strength."

"You bring messages *here* for Tek-aKet Tarkin?"

"I do. Mercenary Brothers helped him escape, and he is either with you, or his whereabouts are known to you."

Dhulyn kept her face still as stone, giving nothing away. Of course Dal-eDal knew they had been in the Carnelian Dome, helping the Tarkin. Did anyone else know? Were the tunnels secure enough for the Tarkin and his family? Alkoryn certainly believed so, but better careful than cursing, Dhulyn thought.

"Does Dal-eDal hope to become Tenebroso? And will you then be restored to your Walls?"

"We have no such hope or expectation," Karlyn-Tan said. "There is too much future for us to see what will come."

Dhulyn narrowed her eyes, but it was clear his words were innocent of any hidden meanings as he continued with his message.

"Our purpose is to remove the usurper Lok-iKol Tenebro from the Carnelian Throne, and restore the Culebro Tarkin, Tek-aKet." He cleared his throat, giving her a chance to respond, but she only smiled her wolf's smile. "If we live, there will be time to see what will follow."

Dhulyn crossed her arms and, with her head to one side, studied the former Steward of Walls. If their House was being watched, no one, not even Karlyn-Tan, could simply enter and not be seen to come out again. Fortunately, Alkoryn had thought of even this contingency when she'd gone to consult with him.

"When the moon has set, bring Dal-eDal to the Fountain of the Rivers. You will be met and taken to the Tarkin."

"There are two others I believe you will want as well, for

the information they may have, Mar-eMar Tenebro, and the Scholar of Valdomar, Gundaron."

She raised her eyebrows. They were alive, then, and likely to stay that way if Karlyn-Tan had taken them under his wing. Still, she told herself, she had no wish to see either the Scholar or Mar-eMar Tenebro again.

"The Scholar, at least, was intimate with Lok-iKol, and has information that may be of use."

Dhulyn sighed. Of course he did. And she was a blooded fool not to think of that herself. "Very well, you may bring them."

Dhulyn found Parno and Alkoryn already seated with Tek-aKet at the table farthest from the low entrance, with Fanryn and Thionan half-sitting on the edge of another table against the left wall. This was another one of the many caves that honeycombed the earth under Mercenary House and even the Great Square itself. Dhulyn had no idea what its intended use had been, perhaps a storeroom for contraband; the uneven ceiling was low enough in places that she had to duck her head, and those taller than she, including Parno and Tek-aKet Tarkin, had found themselves seats as quickly as they could to remove the strain of standing hunched over. The Tarkin had chosen the two shortest of his guard to stand against the rock wall behind him. Dhulyn hoped the sweat on the face of the blond on the left came from too much clothing, and not the enclosure sickness.

Instead of a large council table, such as could be found in the public meeting room in the House above them, here were half a score of small round tables, scattered over a floor leveled with sand and inlaid cobbles, each with chairs or stools to allow three or four to sit, making the place resemble nothing more than the taproom of a small tavern. All it lacked were windows and a serving bar. Ganje, water, bread, and dried fruit had already been laid out on the tables.

Dhulyn was alerted by noises in the passages behind her to the arrival of Cullen of Langeron, a lean, wiry man with steel-gray hair and the feather tattoo covering the left side of his face. The ceilings did not allow for Cullen's Racha bird, Disha, to ride in her accustomed place on his shoul-

der, and Dhulyn was intrigued to see that the bird nevertheless accompanied her Partner, walking on the ground
almost under his feet in the manner of a playful cat. The
Cloud went immediately to Tek-aKet and saluted him with
the formal bow of an ambassador.

"Don't stand on ceremony, Cullen of Langeron," Tek-
aKet said. "At the moment I'm Tarkin of nothing but this
room."

"On the contrary, Tek-aKet Tarkin," the Cloudman said
sharply. "It is precisely *because* you are Tarkin of more than
this room, that ceremony will be observed." The two men
locked gazes, and after a moment Dhulyn saw a loosening
of the tension of Tek-aKet's shoulders, a lessening of the
darkness in his eyes. *Guard yourself better,* she thought,
make your thoughts harder to see. The Tarkin of Imrion
nodded, just once, as if in answer to her thoughts, and gestured to seats at the nearest tables.

"I have just been telling our host that most of the army is
away on the borders to the south and west, keeping the Kon-
drians honest. I don't know how many might come to us."

"I believe we may have time to put that to the test,"
Alkoryn said. He signaled to Fanryn Bloodhand.

"The latest news," Fanryn began, "is that the Anointing
and Dedication scheduled for the new moon has been postponed. Lok-iKol has sent for the Mesticha Stone, and tells
people he'll wait for its arrival. What this means, no one
knows, but it's only the last and strangest of the changes the
latest days have brought us. As we know," Fanryn said, tossing her hair back out of her face and accepting the cup of
ganje Thionan had brought her, "the first few days found
the Houses of Jarifo and Esmolo coming and going in the
precincts of the Dome, giving themselves airs about the
court and the city itself."

"It seems there was to be a wedding," Thionan added,
"between Lok-iKol and Riv-oRiv Esmolo."

"She's young," Tek-aKet said. "Too young to marry in
any case."

"Too young to marry, but not too young to be promised
in marriage." Parno drew their attention as he leaned forward, elbows on the table. "It's a good move," he added.
"Buys the support of an important House without really

committing himself to anything." He shrugged. "A great deal can happen between now and the time the girl can actually marry."

"Well, the wedding's no longer spoken of," Fanryn said. "Now both those Houses have taken down their flags and flowerets, pulled their men off the streets, closed up their enclaves. Like those other Houses who were neither for you nor against you, Lord Tarkin, they now bide their time, waiting to weigh Lok-iKol's power, waiting to see who they should salute. What's changed them, though, *that* we can't find out."

Disha the Racha bird suddenly hopped from the floor to the back of an unoccupied chair. As if it were cause and effect, Cullen spoke, his soft voice cool and dry.

"So the Houses are playing their tiles carefully. There's nothing new in that," he said.

"But if the Houses have withdrawn their support, it may be we have a chance to regain the Throne if we act quickly. I've sent out word through the old network," Alkoryn added, "letting people know that you're alive, Lord Tarkin, and that you will return. Soldiers and guards alike are presenting themselves at safe contact points. One who's come to us quietly with no fanfare and on foot so as to draw no attention is Fen-oNef Penradoso. He says to tell you that he doesn't forget his promise to your father, nor yet the one he made to you. If you want Lok-iKol dead, say the word."

Tek-aKet exchanged looks with those around the table, returning Parno's broad smile with one of his own. Tek-aKet's skin looked less bleached, Dhulyn thought, and the muscles of his face had regained their youthful firmness. This was what he needed to hear; that there were those who had believed in him, who were willing to support him still.

"He's a tough old man, Fen-oNef," he said, still smiling. "And I've no doubt that he would try. But it's too dangerous."

"Exactly what I told him. And it's too dangerous for him to house the would-be soldiers who keep turning up. One of the things we must think of is a place to gather troops."

"What of the Jaldeans," Dhulyn said, leaning forward. "And the Marked?"

Fanryn's eyes flicked at the Cloudman, her question as clear as if she'd spoken it aloud. *How much did they know?* Dhulyn shrugged. It no longer mattered, she thought. As the Clouds revered the Marked, she was probably safer with them than with anyone besides her own Brothers.

"There's a mystery there somewhere." Fanryn shook her head. "At first, there was great rejoicing from the Jaldean Shrines, and people were talking about the dream of the Sleeping God as if they were about to join it.

"But now petitioners are being turned from the shrines, told to come back, and when they do, they're turned away again with excuses and soft words. There are no services or meditations, and the priests aren't seen in the streets. Beslyn-Tor has not been seen in over two days—not even by his own people—and some others who were believed touched by the god are also conspicuous by their absence. People are wondering what has happened to the promises the Jaldeans were making before the fall of Tek-aKet Tarkin. The very people who were so quick to support them, are now murmuring against them."

"Helped by the rumors we and the Scholars are spreading, of course," Thionan said with a grin.

"And the Marked?" Tek-aKet asked.

Thionan's voice came low and rough. "Two days ago they started being taken to the Carnelian Dome, and not to the Jaldean Shrines. None have been seen, city or country, since."

The silence in the room was as thick as inglera fleece.

"We will hope there are some in hiding," Cullen of Langeron said, as his bird Disha nodded.

Thionan cleared her throat. "There's something else, though it's hard to know how significant it is," she said. "I'm sorry to say, Lord Tarkin, that your counselor, Gan-eGan, was yesterday found hanged in his private chambers. Hanged by his own hand, it appears. It seems a small tragedy in the face of everything else, and in the face of what the Marked have had to endure, but we thought perhaps you would want to know."

Dhulyn shut her eyes, seeing again the two images of the skinny, overjeweled old man, one with green eyes, the other standing behind, weeping. She blinked. Green eyes again. Like the Mage in her Visions. And the Scholar. Who was on his way even now with information. Perhaps more information than he knew.

Dhulyn glanced at Tek-aKet. He was pale again, his face fixed and resolute. But before she could ask any questions a young woman appeared in the cave's entrance. Dhulyn recognized her as the same one, Rehnata by name, who had greeted them when they first arrived in Gotterang. Since then, the dark brown hair above her temples and ears had been removed in preparation for the tattooing of her Mercenary badge.

"They are here, my Brothers," she said to Alkoryn, acknowledging Dhulyn as well with a bob of her head. "Shall we bring them?"

"By all means," Alkoryn said.

⧟⧟⧟

"Watch your head."

From the sound, the warning had come just a second too late for Karlyn-Tan, Gundaron thought. He himself was too short to worry about bumping his head, but being led blindfolded through passages and tunnels meant bashed elbows and stepped-on toes, no matter how careful your guides. As things were, however, Gun was grateful to have sore elbows and bruised toes to distract him from what was coming. He knew Mar and Karlyn-Tan were right—this was what he had to do. But just at the moment, he was more than half convinced he'd been persuaded against his will.

Finally the blindfolds came off. They'd had them on so long that even the soft light of the lanterns carried by their guides was enough to have all four of them blinking and squinting. Gundaron tried not to hang back as they approached the open doorway of the underground meeting room. Not that he could do much more than drag his feet a bit since there were Mercenary Brothers both in front of and behind him. From what Karlyn-Tan had said, he'd expected Dhulyn Wolfs head herself to lead them to Tek-aKet, but it had been two black-haired Mercenary Brothers with Semlorian accents. The smiles they'd given him when they'd met them at the fountain made the skin on the back of his neck crawl.

Dhulyn Wolfshead would be inside the room, he thought, watching Dal-eDal pass through the entrance. Along with the Brother he hadn't met, her Partner Parno Lionsmane.

The first Brothers he saw as he followed Mar into the room weren't the two he was dreading the most, however, but Fanryn Bloodhand and Thionan Hawkmoon, who went so far as to lay her hand on her sword hilt and grin at him. Gun looked away and, seeing Mar's face, followed her line of sight to where Dhulyn Wolfshead stood to the left of Tek-aKet. Mar stepped toward the Outlander woman with her hands lifted, reaching out, but hesitated, coming to a stop as the Wolfshead gave her the half bow that was the very knife edge of courtesy among the Noble Houses. Such would be the greeting—Gun had seen it many times— between two nobles who had some long-standing grudge, but were forced to be civil in some public gathering. Dhulyn Wolfshead straightened and turned her eyes away, and Gun braced himself . . . but her stone-gray eyes moved over and past him as if he was not even there.

He immediately looked down, heart thumping. It seemed he had nothing to fear from Dhulyn Wolfshead. It seemed that as far as she was concerned, he didn't exist. He found himself hugging his arms around his chest, to convince himself he *was* there, he *was*.

When he had enough control of himself to listen, he found that he had missed Dal's first words. The Tarkin was speaking.

"To say that I am surprised to see you does not begin to describe my feelings, Dal-eDal Tenebro." He put up his hand and Dal stilled. "You are heir to your House, and now to the Carnelian Throne, and yet you come with your oaths of loyalty to me."

It was not a question, but Dal-eDal answered it.

"My lord—" he cleared his throat and began again. "I am not an ambitious man. I have never wanted more than my own Household. But my cousin Lok-iKol sees a mirror in every man, and his own image grinning back at him. Fate may lead even a distant cousin to become House of his family, whether he wished it or no, but the Tarkinate . . ." Dal shook his head.

"I was warned to be skeptical of your loyalty," Tek-aKet said, nodding at where Fanryn Bloodhand and Thionan Hawkmoon stood leaning against a small table to Gundaron's left. "Perhaps you do not want the Carnelian Throne, but you would have me believe that you choose this moment to act against your House?"

Dal licked his lips. "I do not believe I go against my House, my lord," he said, in that quietly strained voice that had been all Gun had heard from him for the last day. "I believe my House has Fallen."

At this everyone, Gun included, edged forward. Fanryn Bloodhand straightened to attention and Thionan Hawkmoon put a restraining hand on her Partner's arm. Even the Wolfshead and the Lionsmane exchanged glances.

"Who is it, then, who sits on my throne?" Tek-aKet's voice was hard as the rock overhead.

"I do not know," Dal said. "Outwardly, it seems to be my cousin." Dal glanced suddenly at Parno Lionsmane, but Gun couldn't see that the Brother had moved in any way. "Possibly, in some way, it is. But I do not believe it. Something else occupies . . . something else is there." He straightened, and Gun saw for the first time the dark smudges under the man's eyes. "Indulge me, my lord," Dal said. "I have waited what seems an age to tell the full story only once, and it is choking me."

Tek-aKet glanced at the older Mercenary Brother seated next to him. When the man nodded, the Tarkin gestured at Dhulyn Wolfshead, indicating that she should take the seat next to him. That left an empty seat across the table.

"Sit, Dal-eDal Tenebro. Refresh yourself, tell your story."

Dal nodded, waited until a cup was poured for him, but made no move to pick it up. He took the chair, though, Gun thought, feeling the ache of his own muscles.

"I have spent my whole life waiting, and watching, my lord; so long that perhaps I forgot what it was that I was waiting for." As Dal folded his hands on the table in front of him, Gun saw them trembling. "Lok had my father killed, and I believed I was waiting for the right moment to avenge him. I wonder if I would ever have found it." Dal drew in his brows, frowning at his hands on the table.

Mar shifted, stepping forward as if she would move closer to the table. Gun put his hands on her shoulders, and pulled her back a little, until she was standing against his chest. Her skin felt warm, even through two layers of clothing, and she relaxed under his hands, though she kept her eyes on the faces of the four seated at the table.

Dal glanced up at Tek-aKet and waited until the man nodded before he continued. "Perhaps three days after he took the Dome, my lord, my cousin called me to him, saying that he had an errand for me." Keeping his eyes fixed on Tek-aKet, Dal's voice did not falter. "For years he has kept me under his hand, and I have not left Gotterang unless as his companion. Yet he has now, suddenly, asked me to do so, in order to find the Mercenary Dhulyn Wolfshead."

Mar glanced at Gun over her shoulder, her eyebrows raised; Gun pressed his lips together and nodded. A quick look around the room showed much less puzzlement than he would have expected. *She's told them,* he thought, *by all the Caids, she's told them.*

Dal, too, had noticed the change of atmosphere in the room. "Apparently, you know more of this than I, though I knew that my cousin had shown interest in this Brother before he took the Carnelian Throne.

"He said no more of her at that moment, and I walked with him to the room where your crown, my lord Tarkin, and your treasures, and the jewels that your wife brought with her to her marriage are kept. He said he was looking for a relic of the Sleeping God."

Tek-aKet nodded. "An old bracelet," he said, "with green stones. I know of it. The Jaldean Shrine here in Gotterang has been asking for it for months."

"As you say, my lord. Lok found it, a gold bracelet in the antique manner of the Caids, and he put it on." Dal picked up the cup of ganje that had been poured for him, looked inside it, and put it down again. *He's not looking anyone in the face,* Gun thought. *When did that start?* Dal had always been the most watchful of men.

"What of it," the Tarkin said. "My mother wore it often. I've worn it myself."

Gun wouldn't have thought it possible, but at these words Dal paled even more, the shadows around his mouth stained a faint green.

"Drink something, man; you're no use to us if you faint," Dhulyn Wolfshead said in her rough voice. The Cloudman to the Tarkin's left stood and with his own hand poured out water from the glass jug on the table and handed the mug to Dal-eDal.

"Thank you." His voice was a thread of air. He sipped at the water and set the mug down next to the untouched ganje. He cleared his throat, but his voice when he continued was still rough. "Lok found the bracelet," he said, "and slipped it over his hand. As I watched, the bracelet faded, dissolved, and was absorbed into his skin. I looked up, and Lok was watching the spot where the bracelet had been and smiling. And his shadow, on the wall behind him, was not his own, but larger, darker, than it should have been—" Dal sucked in a short, sharp sip of air, "and was the wrong shape, as if it had wings about to open."

Parno Lionsmane's cup tilted, but he caught it before it fell.

"The lantern—" Tek-aKet started to say.

"No, my lord," Dal interrupted. "My own shadow was there, pale and ordinary, as familiar to me as my own hand. Except that my shadow seemed to shrink from his, as if it knew something I did not." This time, when Dal stopped speaking, no one else moved or spoke, so obvious was it that he had not finished. "There is more, my lord. When I looked again to my cousin, to ask him about what I had seen, his eye was green. Not blue as it has always been, and, his eye patch—" Dal lifted his left hand to his own face, as if to show them where the eye patch should be. "I don't know, perhaps because of the angle at which we were standing, perhaps because he had touched it somehow—" Dal looked across the table at his Tarkin. "My lord, I could see that *both* his eyes were green. *Both* of them."

Mar shifted abruptly and Gun loosened the suddenly tight grip he'd taken on her shoulders. His breathing came uncomfortably quick, and in his mind he saw again the barricade of shelves and books that kept away the Green Shadow. The Cloudman at the table with the Tarkin made the old sign against evil, thumbtip to tip of index finger, the Mercenaries standing around the room developed suddenly neutral expressions, and Wolfshead and Lionsmane looked at each other, recognition in their faces. But Dal spoke matter-of-factly like a man beyond caring what other people thought.

"Clearly, you believe what you saw," the Tarkin said finally. "What do you believe it means?"

"It means you must not wait, my lord," Dal said. Suddenly reaching out his hand to the man across from him, Dal looked the Tarkin directly in the face. "Listen to me. This is no ordinary coup. I have thought that it did not matter to me who sat on the Carnelian Throne, but I tell you, it matters to me *what* sits there, and that green-eyed thing is not my cousin." Once again he spoke, not as a frightened man who expects to be held in contempt, but as a man freely owning a fear in the face of which the opinions of others were meaningless. "It has the Marked brought to the Dome, and they leave broken and mad. The Carnelian Guard—" He broke off, frowning. "Elite troops injure themselves with carelessness or in quarrels, except for those who go off duty and disappear. Gan-eGan has killed himself. Children are weeping in corners. Whatever this is, its poison is spreading. You must waste no time. You must act *now*."

Gun licked his lips. One pair of eyes had left off looking at Dal-eDal and had fixed on him. One pair of stone-gray eyes that had slid over him, unable to see him when he had entered the room, were focused on him now.

"Let's ask the Scholar," Dhulyn Wolfshead said. "I'll wager my second-best sword he knows what this is, or can guess. He knows more than anyone what the formerly one-eyed Lok-iKol has been up to."

Gun's hands formed fists at his sides. It felt like every eye in the room was on him. Even Mar had turned around and was searching his face, her eyebrows drawn down, her lips parted.

"Come, Gundaron of Valdomar." Gun winced at the tone in Dhulyn Wolfshead's husky voice. "From the look of you, Dal-eDal's not the only one here who's seen this green-eyed thing."

Everyone *was* looking at him, Gun saw as he tried to swallow with his suddenly dry mouth. Everyone except Parno Lionsmane. He stood behind the Wolfshead, his hand on her shoulder, his eyes squeezed shut.

"Come forward, boy, and tell us what you know of this."

Gun found himself responding to the tone of command in the Tarkin's voice, stepping around Mar and coming closer to the table before he realized he'd made up his mind to do it. Mar touched him on the arm as he passed, her worried eyes searching his face. He looked away from her. He couldn't tell them *everything*. He couldn't tell them that he, himself—they would never understand. Mar would never understand. He would lose all that was growing between them.

When he was facing the Tarkin, he cleared his throat, and released the breath he was holding. "I have seen it, my lord Tarkin. It is real." Gun glanced around, but except for Mar, there was no friendly face. "I—we've been hiding," he said. "Can you tell me, Lord Dal, have the Marked been going to the Dome only *since* the . . ." Gun bit his lip and then continued. "Since the green has come into Lok-iKol's eyes?"

"I believe the decree changed that morning, just hours before my cousin, or the thing that he has become, sent for me."

"What can you tell us, Scholar of Valdomar?"

Gun drew in a deep breath and settled his shoulders. He found himself folding his hands in front of him, as if about to recite his lesson. If only this was just another lecture, another examination in his Library. That what he was about to say was only interesting history, and not something that might very well change the lives of everyone in this room, including his own.

"I believe it is this Green Shadow that seeks for and destroys the Marked. That the teachings of the New Believers are nothing more than an excuse, invented to give it freedom to act."

Gun saw movement out of the corner of his eye and hesitated. The Cloudman was nodding, a satisfied smile on his face.

"Continue," the Tarkin said.

"I cannot explain how, my lord Tarkin, but I have only recently remembered seeing what Lord Dal describes, the green light, the misshapen shadow, the . . . the feeling of otherness, in Beslyn-Tor, the Jaldean High Priest. It seems I took no notice of it at the time, but afterward, as I say, I *remembered* seeing it many times." Gun waited for the murmurs to die away.

"I think I saw it in Lok-iKol once, but not in the same way," Gun continued when no one else spoke. "At that time, Lok-iKol did not move or speak, but stood slackly, like a rag doll, as if the Green Shadow only looked through his eyes. In any case, it was the priest who wanted Marked brought to him, not Lok-iKol."

"The Green Shadow," Parno Lionsmane said under his breath.

Gun *meant* to continue, to tell about himself, to tell everything, but his throat closed. He looked down at his clasped hands, trembling, knuckles white. When he looked up again, he met Dhulyn Wolfs head's eyes. *She knows,* he thought.

"They say Beslyn-Tor has suffered a stroke, and lies feeble and raving in rooms Lok has given him in the Dome," Dal said, leaning back in his chair with a thoughtful look.

"Always the Jaldeans," Tek-aKet said. "Zella warned me they were the real danger, and I didn't listen."

"They supported Lok-iKol's coup," Dal pointed out.

"But *why?* Was it this Green Shadow?"

Gun nodded. "It wants the Marked."

"The Marked." Tek-aKet let out a forceful breath. "I did not give the New Believers what they wanted."

"And so they gave their support to someone who would." Parno Lionsmane focused his attention on Gun over his Partner's head. "But what did that support entail?"

"The people." It was Dhulyn Wolfshead's raw silk voice that answered. "How did the traitors get into the Dome so easily? Almost all of the Carnelian Guard, soldiers whose duty it is to protect the Dome, and more than half of your Personal Guard, Lord Tarkin, have been in the streets for the last moon, helping the City Guard keep order, quelling little riots and mob violence. All started by the Jaldeans."

The Tarkin was shaking his head. "They wouldn't have done so much on Lok-iKol's bare word that he would enact their laws. Lok-iKol must have been doing something for them already."

Gundaron swallowed. "Lok-iKol was collecting Marked for them, my lord."

"Explain."

"Not everyone came voluntarily to the shrines to be blessed by the Sleeping God. Some even left the city, or moved to new quarters, never obeying the edicts about their dress. Lok was seeking these out and holding them for the Jaldeans when he found them."

"And how was he finding them?"

Something in the Tarkin's tone, in the glint of his eyes, made Gundaron look away, down at the white knuckles of his clasped hands. He licked his lips. "I found them for him, my lord."

"How?"

Gun bit his lip, his throat tight as a fist. He risked a glance at Mar. Her face was still as stone, but she said nothing. "Research." His whisper sounded uncomfortably loud in the silence of the room. Dhulyn Wolfs head looked at him with narrowed eyes; he shifted his own and was startled to find the same searching look in the eyes of the Racha bird.

"What were the Jaldeans doing with the Marked you helped locate?" Tek-aKet's voice was silkily quiet.

"I don't know. That is—" Gun kept his eyes fixed on his folded hands. "I didn't take any part after the people were found. Afterward, when I remembered . . . now I know that Beslyn-Tor came to give them what he called the Sleeping God's blessing. But as for *why* . . . I think he—I think *it*, the Green Shadow, is destroying the Marked; it fears them, as if they can harm it somehow."

"You never tried to find out?" Gun glanced up at Parno Lionsmane, but immediately dropped his gaze. The Mercenary looked like he'd opened a pie only to find snakes writhing inside.

"I didn't *know*." He couldn't tell them everything, they wouldn't believe him.

"It may be that the Green Shadow took the memories from him," Dhulyn Wolfshead said.

"And it was for this that you brought my Partner, my soul, to Gotterang?" The growl in the man's voice showed it wasn't just for his coloring that he was called Lionsmane.

"No!" Gun cried out, holding his hands up, pushing away the worst of it. "Dhulyn Wolfshead wasn't for the Jaldean. Lok-iKol wanted to keep her for himself."

"And who else?" Dhulyn Wolfshead glanced over his shoulder and suddenly Gun knew exactly who was standing just behind him. He could almost smell the distinctive sweetness of the soap they'd used in Karlyn-Tan's room.

"And Mar, too, if she proved to be a Finder as he suspected." He squeezed the words out through the barrier his throat had become.

"As he suspected because *you* had told him so—"

"Enough, Parno." The Wolfshead's voice, though soft, had the force of a cracked whip. All the murmurs in the room died away. "We are all alive, which is more, apparently, than can be said for Lok-iKol," she smiled her wolf's smile, "on whom, as his mother wished, has fallen a terrible curse." She turned to Gun. "What of you, Scholar of Valdomar?"

"I'll kill him if you like," Parno Lionsmane said, and there were a few murmurs in the room that showed others agreed.

"He meant no harm," Dhulyn Wolfshead said, steel showing in her voice. "You forget the Scholarly mind, my soul. It isn't real to them unless it's in a book."

Gundaron looked up at her. There was no horrified disbelief on her face, as there was in Parno's. He felt a crumbling hollow in his mind where there had been a good solid wall. A wall that he'd built by sticking to his books, his notes. By not asking awkward questions and by telling himself that everything was all right. He had a sudden mental image of the little page Okiron once telling him that Lok made him nervous, and of himself telling the boy that everything was all right. He'd told himself over and over, since leaving Tenebro House, that he was doing all he could to make amends and there was no point in dwelling on the past. But he'd still been hiding something behind that wall. Of course he'd been horrified when he'd finally remembered, finally realized, what Lok-iKol and Beslyn-Tor were doing. But that hadn't been why he'd wanted to leave. He'd wanted to leave out of fear for himself, not out of horror at what he'd done to others. Out of fear of the Green Shadow, and what it might still do to him. Out of fear of Pasillon. Not out of resolution and defiance, as Mar had done, but out of fear.

Of course the Outlander woman showed no surprise now; she'd known all along, she'd seen him in Lok-iKol's study, and known what he was.

"We have strayed from our point." Gun roused himself at the sound of the Tarkin's voice. "What of the green-eyed Jaldean spirit? What can be done now?"

Gun cleared his throat. No one had offered him anything to drink, and he was afraid to ask. "Lord Dal is right, this is not Lok-iKol. The Shadow does not want what Lok-iKol wanted. If you wait to gather an army, my lords, there may not be an Imrion to save. From what I have seen, the Shadow doesn't care about the country, only about the Sleeping God and the Marked." Gun coughed again.

The Racha bird startled them all by suddenly opening and closing its wings.

"These people came together, my lord," the Cloudman said. "Shall we accept what they told us without verification? You can withdraw to the mountains. An army can't fight the Clouds," he said, reminding them all of the old saying.

"Never before," Gun agreed, "because the Tarkin always counted the cost of it, in time, in soldiers, and in lost revenues. But what if the cost was immaterial to him? What if it's the Shadow that comes? The Green Shadow cares only to destroy the Marked."

"What is this Shadow?" Fanryn said. "Is it the Sleeping God, awakening to destroy us?"

The Cloudman's bark of laughter brought every head up. "Don't be misled by the lies of fools. We have nothing to fear from the Sleeping God, awake or asleep. This is some enemy."

"Enough." The Tarkin's soft baritone cut across and silenced all other noise. "Dal-eDal, if you have nothing further to add, would you withdraw, and allow me to consult with my advisers?"

"I am entirely in your hands, Tek-aKet," the Tenebro man said. "But I urge you again, waste no time."

Eighteen

"SO THE LORD DAL-EDAL is certain." Cullen's Racha bird Disha had hopped up on the table in front of him, and was eating tiny pieces of hard cheese from the palm of his hand. "I don't find his certainty altogether reassuring, do you?" He and his Racha tilted their heads at each other, their movement a perfect mirror image. "It's madness to believe him." Cullen's quiet tone was at odds with his words. "It is a trick. These men have been sent by the Tenebroso Lok-iKol to lure you into acting before you are prepared."

"Mercenaries?" Tek-aKet looked up from the food lying untouched on his plate.

"What of Karlyn-Tan?" Dhulyn said. "The oaths taken by the Stewards of a House are as binding as those taken by Mercenaries . . . or by Racha Clouds," she added, inclining her head toward Cullen and Disha. "Do you suggest that he has not been Cast Out? A Steward of Walls does not leave his post for a trick, not even so weighty a trick as this one."

"But, Dhulyn." Now it was Thionan who spoke up from her perch on the nearby table. "Demons? Possession by green shadows? We can't make plans based on such ravings. Has any of us, any we can trust, seen this thing?"

"I have."

In the silence you could hear the rustling of Disha's feathers as she turned her head to look.

"You, Lionsmane?" Alkoryn's harsh whisper held the surprise that was mirrored on every other face in the room.

Dhulyn almost smiled. Parno was supposed to be the ordinary soul, *she* was the strange one.

"In the eyes of a Jaldean priest in Navra. A priest who was standing at the back of a mob while that mob burned down a Finder's house, with his children still inside."

"I also have seen it," Dhulyn added.

"In Navra?"

"In a Vision."

Cullen and Disha leaned forward, their heads at an identical tilt. Disha half opened her wings and took two rocking steps toward Dhulyn on her taloned feet. Dhulyn hesitated, aware that everyone in the room waited for her next words. Should she reveal what she'd seen of the Scholar, or should she keep it to herself until she'd had a chance to investigate it further? Did Gundaron of Valdomar know that the Green Shadow had also looked through *his* eyes? It might be an idea to find out before exposing him.

"I have Seen a green-eyed Lok-iKol on the Carnelian Throne, his shadow misshapen on the wall behind him."

Cullen and Disha nodded, satisfied, but the Tarkin's two guardsmen showed by their thinned lips and narrowed eyes that belief was mixing with something closer to fear in their thoughts. Dhulyn sighed, and pressed her lips together. It was exactly to avoid that look that she'd always kept her Mark to herself.

The Tarkin had seen it also. "Let me remind you," he said to his men. "If Dhulyn Wolfshead was not Marked, I would be dead. And you, who gave oaths to defend me to the death, would be either dead as well, or alive and forsworn. She has done us all a great service." Both men had the grace to look shamefaced at their feet. Tek-aKet nodded, satisfied.

"May I have your counsel for action?"

Slowly Dhulyn realized that everyone in the room, Cloudman, Racha bird, Mercenary Brothers—Tarkin and his guardsmen—all were looking at her. She glanced first at Parno, then at Alkoryn. Both men nodded to her.

"The Green Shadow exists," she said. "Whatever its ultimate goal, it begins by destroying the Marked." She glanced around at the faces intent on her words. "That is where it *begins*. We cannot know how it will continue."

"It begins where it fears the most, you think?" Parno had obviously been giving this some thought.

"Very likely," Dhulyn agreed. "If it fears the Marked, it means the Marked can harm it somehow. We need to find out how."

"No." They turned to the Tarkin. "We must remove it from the Throne."

Tek-aKet Tarkin raised his hands, palms toward her, and Dhulyn fell silent. "With respect, Dhulyn Wolfshead, hear me out. Perhaps we can destroy it, but perhaps we cannot. Our first act *must* be to remove it from the throne, to regain control of Imrion. At the moment, its power does not extend past Gotterang, and if we act quickly, it will not. Once we have the city, now that we know what we must fight, we will have a position of power from which to do it." He placed his hands palm down on the table. "We must act and act now."

Alkoryn was nodding, his fingers tracing lines on an imaginary map. "A frontal assault will not work. We have not the numbers needed, and unlike Lok-iKol, we've no trick to empty the Dome of its Carnelian Guards." He looked up from his tracing to indicate the rock walls around them. "Fortunately, we know a way into the Carnelian Dome that has nothing to do with front gates, or the number of guards. Dhulyn, my Brother, if you would."

Dhulyn bowed and turned to the door. "Rehnata," she called, and waited for the girl to appear in the entrance before turning back to Alkoryn.

"Fetch my maps of Gotterang," Alkoryn said now that the girl was within reach of his voice. "The blue series, not the green, and the plans of the Dome. When you have done that, bring back our guests."

❧

Two tables were pushed together, and Cullen of Langeron looked on with interest as the maps and drawings were spread over them. He'd seen such things of course—though the Clouds did not use them, relying on their own memories and training to find their routes and ways through the Antedichas—but never so detailed, and so beautifully drawn. Disha walked about on the table, looking over them carefully, with first one golden eye and then the other. For an instant Cullen saw the image of the drawing's lines superimposed on his own image of his Racha and the room.

"If you would stand here, Lady Disha," Alkoryn the Senior Brother said in his scarred voice. Thus courteously addressed, Disha was happy to move. There weren't many who knew the Racha would understand them—as, of course, she could, so long as Cullen himself was in the room. If it were possible, his already healthy respect for the Mercenary Brotherhood increased.

"There are three layers of guards," Tek-aKet Tarkin was saying. "Those here, in the outer perimeter, allow access to the public rooms and galleries where any petitioner may enter; here the second, letting pass only those who have business with the Throne. And finally, here, the innermost circle," he looked up. "These posts are usually taken by my own Personal Guard, and they watch the family and private rooms."

"So far as I can tell," the Tenebro Lord Dal-eDal said, frowning down on the drawings, "the guard postings have not changed—though the guards themselves are different." His brows drew down even further. "No, there *is* one change. There are now guards here, in the Onyx Walk."

Cullen's eyes narrowed as Disha cocked her head to look closely at the Tenebro man. He'd no trust of this one either, cousin to the usurper, a man who stood to gain no matter who died. Cullen shifted his gaze across the room to where Dhulyn Wolfshead stood, relaxed, her eyes on Dal-eDal, her wolf's smile on her lips. Except for that, and their intent stares, the Partnered Brothers could have been asleep on their feet, there was so little tension in their bodies. Disha transferred her golden eye to the Wolfshead in response to Cullen's thought.

+SEER+ was the thought that Cullen caught. +YES+ he answered. The balance of power in the room had changed utterly for him when he understood the direction of what had been said. Menders, Finders, even Healers were to be found among the Clouds—and if Lok-iKol was hunting the

Marked, that was reason enough for him to help kill the man. But a *Seer*. His mother had spoken of one that had been known in *her* mother's day. Cullen had no more hoped to be in the same room as a Seer than he would have hoped to fly without Disha.

We are here for you, Seer, he thought, knowing that Disha heard him and agreed. *My soul and I. Yours is the lead we follow.* He and his soul turned their attention back to the man speaking.

"That need not preclude our using that entrance, though we would lose the element of surprise," Alkoryn Pantherclaw was saying, tapping his gnarled index finger on the plans in front of him. "And there are other secret ways by which we can enter into the Dome, but," and here the old one paused, looked at the Tarkin and at the Tenebro lord. "But I will not take Dal-eDal through these ways."

The Tenebro lord hissed air in through his teeth, plainly displeased, and Cullen smiled, Disha shifting from foot to foot.

"Surely—" The Tarkin broke off in the face of Alkoryn Pantherclaw's slowly shaking head.

"You objected, Tek-aKet, that the Mercenary Brotherhood knew of ways into your Dome, and now you ask that we tell others? I should not even have taken *you* that way, but what's done is done. As Senior Brother, I must consider the future and not merely the needs of the moment. In any case, we could not take many through the tunnels and passages. I advise sending only those who have already been. What say you, Brothers?"

Dhulyn Wolfshead grimaced, considering. "It seems to me these passages were never intended to be used by soldiers—to the contrary. In many places they are so narrow, that we could pass only one at a time, considering that we will be carrying weapons. That would likely also be true of whichever secret door we used." She turned to Parno Lionsmane and added, "Remember the engagement at Lashar? Where we used the caves beneath the escarpment? One company of men was caught and slaughtered because of just such a bottleneck in the passages. Besides Tek-aKet, I would recommend no more than six Brothers."

"*We* can't walk in the front door," Tek-aKet said, rubbing his chin with the fingers of his right hand. "But Dal-eDal can, and he can bring others with him."

"That I can't do. I was sent for Dhulyn Wolfshead, and I can't return without her."

"Then Dhulyn Wolfshead you shall have," she said.

Cullen clenched his teeth and remained silent. The Wolfshead waited patiently until the storm of protest died away before continuing as if she had not been interrupted. "We'll be able to operate from two fronts, allowing us to flank if need be." She looked up, not at her Senior, but at Lionsmane, her Partner. "I'll be perfectly safe," she said in her honey-rough voice, "until I get to the Green Shadow, and by then you'll be there."

"We are for you, Dhulyn Wolfshead," Cullen said. "Disha and I. We also should not be shown the secret ways," he added.

"I can't bring back more than the eight I brought away with me," the Tenebro lord said. "In fact, it would be more convincing if I returned with fewer."

"You would have needed a tracker to find a Mercenary Brother," Cullen said. "I am that man, come with you in the hope of greater rewards."

The Tenebro lord spread his hand. "A good enough notion, but surely there is another way to get our own people into the Dome. Could some of the Mercenary Brotherhood not take work there, to act as spies, if nothing else?"

Disha moved closer to the Tenebro man. +BITE+ was her thought. +NO+ he responded, though he stifled a smile.

"What have I said?" the Tenebro lord said when the silence grew lengthy.

"The Mercenary Brotherhood does not take someone's pay in order to spy upon them," Alkoryn Panterclaw said. "Not even when it appears to suit our purposes to do so. We are true to our employ, always. This is one of the reasons the Brotherhood is as old as it is."

"And one of the reasons there are so few of us," Dhulyn Wolfshead added.

"Your pardon, Alkoryn Charter." There was a hint of sarcasm in the Tenebro lord's tone, as if he had himself taken offense. "Ordinarily I wouldn't argue with a policy that has stood so well the test of time. But as I've said, this is no ordinary foe. Now, if ever, is the time to suspend such rules, before you find yourself and your Brotherhood destroyed."

Maybe he should have let Disha bite him. +YES+ she thought.

"What difference?" Dhulyn the Seer broke in. "If we suspend our rules, there is no Brotherhood, we would have destroyed ourselves."

Tek-aKet held up his hands. "Dal, please. I know you are anxious—"

Cullen remembered that these two were also, in some way, cousins.

"With respect, Tek, you didn't see—"

"No, I didn't see. But these others have, and yet they are not ready to plunge headlong in. Things are as they are. We work with what we have." He turned to Alkoryn Pantherclaw. "What of loyal guard within the Dome?"

Dhulyn the Seer and Parno Lionsmane both shook their heads. Dhulyn shrugged and signaled to Parno to speak. "In view of what the Scholar Gundaron has told us, I don't think we can count on any who are still within the Dome," he said. "They may prove to be free of the taint of the Green-eyed Shadow," here Parno paused and looked pointedly at Dal-eDal, "but we can't be sure enough to trust them with our plans and our secrets."

❦

"Of course, we can't trust any of them," Parno punched the plaster wall of their bedroom, several flights above the underground meeting room, with the side of his fist. "But I tell you in particular I don't trust *him*."

"Either the Scholar or the Lord Dal might have been touched by the Green Shadow without knowing it." Dhulyn pulled a chair away from the wall, turned it around, and sat down astride it, twisting her spine from side to side; the last thing she needed at this moment was cramping muscles. "The Scholar, I believe, has been."

Parno sat down on the edge of the room's only bed. "What do you mean?"

By this time in their Partnership, Dhulyn had had a fair amount of practice describing her Visions to Parno, and this one went quickly. "It looked to me," she said finally, "as if there were three Scholars, one the body being used, one a spirit trying to escape, and one a spirit watching."

"If he watched, then he knows." A muscle in the side of Parno's jaw popped out. "And he made no mention of this."

"Some *part* of him does know, I'm certain, but can you be surprised that he would keep this to himself?"

Parno looked at her with narrowed eyes. "He is a danger."

"We must warn Alkoryn to keep the boy watched, I agree, and to limit most strictly where he goes, and what he sees."

"If the Green Shadow is looking for you . . ."

Dhulyn folded her arms on the chairback and rested her chin on her hands. "I understand the Tarkin's wish to regain his throne, but it is the Green Shadow that is the real danger to us all, I think."

"With luck," Parno said, "we will destroy it when we kill the body it wears."

"And Lok-iKol does die by my hand, I have Seen it."

"Then we proceed, and we're back to my concerns." Parno leaned forward, his elbows on his knees.

Dhulyn shook her head, her eyes shut. "Dal-eDal would be a problem if we *did* trust him. We've already agreed we don't, so he's no more dangerous now than he was before."

"You'll be bound—"

"I won't really be bound, you dolt," she said. "I'll even be on my own horse, as if Bloodbone and I between us can't confound Dal-eDal and his plans. *If* he has any. Now tell me what the real problem is."

"Then I'll come with you." Parno spoke through his clenched teeth. "No disrespect intended to your *horse*."

Dhulyn laid her forehead down on her crossed arms. "This has been decided. You're to go with the Tarkin. I'm to go with Dal, and Karlyn-Tan and two others. And Cullen, don't forget, which gives us the Racha as well. What can go wrong?"

"You're the Seer, you tell me. Do you hear yourself? 'What can go wrong?'" He threw out his hands and widened his eyes in a parody of innocence. "If I started listing things now, I'd still be talking when it was time to leave."

Dhulyn slammed her hands down on the chairback.

"That's right," she said. "*You'd* still be talking. The rest of us would be at work." She rubbed her face with her hands. "'Let's go to Imrion,' you said. 'We haven't been there in years,' you said. 'I miss the smell of my own hills.' If we'd followed my advice we'd be in Voyagin even now, helping to plan the summer campaign." She sucked in a deep breath, grimaced, and let it out as slowly as she could. "And the Green Shadow would be destroying the Marked. I'm sorry, my soul. These politicians waste my patience. Come, it's not the first time a campaign has separated us, and it won't be the last."

"I'm not so sure about that," he muttered. "I'd rather have Dal with me."

She shook her head slowly. "And *I'm* supposed to be the inarticulate Outlander. Even if you did doubt my own abilities—which I know you don't, bound and gagged I could still kill him easily—I won't be alone. The way they feel about the Marked, do you think Cullen and the Racha bird will stand idly by if Dal-eDal threatens me?"

"They won't be watching him carefully enough."

"Carefully enough for *what*? Why should it prove so much more dangerous for Dal to be with me than with you?"

He stared at her for a long moment before speaking, his breath coming short and fierce through his nostrils. "Because Dal has no reason to want *me* dead. He may think he has such a reason for you."

She looked up at him, eyes widened in surprise. "Nice to know I make enemies so easily."

"I told you we met and spoke in the Dome. I didn't tell you that, like the Fallen House, Dal wants Lok dead, and me to become Tenebroso. I told him I would not leave the Brotherhood. I would not leave you. What if he thinks my answer would be different if you were dead?"

"The old woman," Dhulyn said. "The House-that-was. She thought I would make a fine consort."

"And so you would, if we were not Partnered, and Mercenary Brothers. That life is gone."

She nodded, rubbing the small of her back with both hands. "Parno, my soul. Would you fetch me warm blankets, please?"

***

Parno put down the pipes on which he'd been rhythmically playing the same seven notes over and over and smiled his thanks at the young Brother standing in the doorway with a pile of heated blankets in her arms. Glancing at Dhulyn's face, he saw she was well and truly asleep; neither the interruption in the playing nor the arrival of the blankets had disturbed her. He laid his pipes aside and rose to take the blankets from the youngster. The mountain wool had been folded twice, as he'd asked, and he laid them, warm and heavy, across Dhulyn's lower body and legs.

Parno glanced at the open doorway, sensing the youngster still hovering, obviously torn between courtesy and curiosity.

"You're Rehnata, aren't you?" he asked, straightening from the bed and walking cat-footed closer so she wouldn't have to raise her voice. "Go ahead, ask."

The girl licked her lips, and pulled herself up straighter. "Two things, Parno."

Parno needn't have worried about moving closer, she'd been well-trained in the nightwatch whisper.

"First, if this were the morning of a battle, what would the Wolfshead do for her pains?"

"First," Parno said quietly. "When there is training, pain can be ignored, as I'm sure you already know. But in order to ignore pain, there must be a distraction. When there is no fighting, distraction of a kind can be found in drugs. Your herbalist can tell you which are best. The Wolfshead does not like drugs. She says that the pain exhausts, but the drugs make you stupid. Better tired than stupid, she says." Parno smiled. Dhulyn had never been any great fan of the stupid. "As for the day of battle, the necessity to kill others is often in itself a powerful distraction." He turned and looked again at Dhulyn. She slept, but under the weight of blankets she still moved and shifted as if, even in her sleep, she sought relief in movement for overtaxed muscles.

"And the second?" he said, turning back to Rehnata.

"Is she," here the girl looked away, not wanting Parno to see what was in her eyes, "is she *Seeing?*"

Parno frowned. This would be the first of many such

questions, now that Dhulyn was no longer hiding her Mark. "I think so. She has not said it, but it seems when there is more pain, there is more Sight."

A TALL THIN MAN WITH CLOSE-CROPPED HAIR THE COLOR OF WHEAT STRAW, EYES THE BLUE OF OLD ICE, DEEP ICE, SITS READING A BOUND BOOK LARGER THAN ANY SHE HAS EVER SEEN, TRACING A LINE ON THE PAGE WITH HIS FINGER, HIS LIPS MOVING. STANDING, HE TAKES UP A HIGHLY POLISHED TWO-HANDED SWORD, AND HIS LONG LILY-SHAPED SLEEVES FALL BACK FROM HIS WRISTS.

HE TURNS TOWARD A CIRCULAR MIRROR, AS TALL AS HE IS HIMSELF, REFLECTING A NIGHT SKY FULL OF STARS. HIS LIPS MOVE AND DHULYN SEES THE WORDS FROM THE BOOK. ******* HE SAYS, AND **********. HE MAKES A MOVE FROM THE THIRD PASSAGE OF THE CRANE *SHORA*, AND SLASHES DOWNWARD THROUGH THE MIRROR, THROUGH THE SKY, SPLITTING IT, AND THE GREEN-TINTED SHADOW COMES SPILLING IN LIKE FOG THROUGH A CASEMENT. . . .

CHILDREN TURNING A LONG ROPE; ONE RUNS IN, TIMING IT JUST RIGHT TO BE ABLE TO JUMP OVER THE ROPE AS IT SWINGS UNDER HIS FEET, OVER HIS HEAD, UNDER HIS FEET. HE SINGS A CHANT, AND ANOTHER CHILD, A CHILD WITH HIS OWN DARK COLORING, RUNS IN AND JUMPS WITH HIM. THEY BOTH SING, AND ANOTHER GIRL JOINS THEM. . . .

MAR SITS DOWN, FROWNING, HER DELICATE BROWS DRAWN AS FAR DOWN AS THEY WILL GO, HER MOUTH TWISTED TO ONE SIDE AS IF SHE IS CONCENTRATING WITH ALL THE STRENGTH OF HER MIND. SHE WEARS A LIGHT LINEN SLEEPING SHIRT THAT HAS BEEN TORN ON THE LEFT SHOULDER AND CAREFULLY MENDED BY A HAND SKILLED WITH THE NEEDLE. SHE BREATHES HEAVILY THROUGH HER NOSE AND STANDS UP, STILL LOOKING DOWN AT WHAT NOW APPEARS TO BE THE TOP OF A TABLE. THERE IS SOMETHING ROUND AND WHITE ON THE TABLETOP, BUT IT ISN'T UNTIL MAR RESTS HER HANDS ON IT THAT DHULYN CAN SEE IT IS MAR'S BOWL. AT THIS TOUCH THE WATER IN THE BOWL SHIVERS AND MAKES THE REFLECTED IMAGE OF CANDLE FLAME DANCE. SO IT IS NIGHT. AS DHULYN HAS THIS THOUGHT, MAR LOOKS UP AND TO HER OWN RIGHT, AND DHULYN SEES THAT THE SCHOLAR GUNDARON STANDS NEXT TO HER, AND HE ALSO IS

LOOKING INTO THE BOWL. AND SHAKING HIS HEAD. HIS HAND GRIPS MAR'S SHOULDER MORE TIGHTLY, AND THEY BOTH TURN TO LOOK OFF TO THEIR LEFT PAST WHERE DHULYN IS STANDING WATCHING THEM. THEY DO NOT SEE HER. WHEN DHULYN TURNS TO SEE WHAT THEY ARE LOOKING AT, SHE SEES. . . .

A GREAT THRONE IN A ROOM VAST WITH DARKNESS. NOISE AND MOVEMENT AROUND HER, BUT MADE OF SHADOWS ONLY, NOT OF THIS TIME. THE ONE-EYED MAN SITS ON THE THRONE OF TIME-DARKENED WOOD AND DULL RED GEMS, LOOKING AT HER WITH TWO GREEN EYES. DHULYN PLUNGES HER SWORD INTO HIS HEART. THE FINE TELISCAN BLADE PASSES CLEANLY THROUGH HIS BODY AND PINS HIM TO THE THRONE AND HE CANNOT MOVE. THE BLOOD SOAKS INTO THE WOOD, AND WILL NEVER COME OUT. HIS EYES ARE GREEN. HIS EYE IS BLUE. SUDDENLY IT IS NOT LOK-IKOL SITTING ON THE CARNELIAN THRONE, BUT TEK-AKET, AND YET SHE IS STILL THERE, SWORD IN HAND. ARE HIS HANDS BOUND? THE TARKIN LOOKS AWAY OVER HER SHOULDER, HIS EYES FOCUSED FOR THE LONG DISTANCE, AND WHEN SHE TURNS TO LOOK, SHE SEES. . . .

A GRAY DAY, A COLD GRANITE CLIFF, CRAGGY AND HIGH ENOUGH TO HAVE SNOW THOUGH THERE IS NONE TO BE SEEN. A MAN WITH A FACE TATTOOED BLUE WITH FEATHERS FALLS, PLUMMETING STRAIGHT AND TRUE AS A STONE FALLS, AND SO SHE KNOWS HE IS ALREADY DEAD. A BIRD FALLS WITH HIM, BLUE-TIPPED WINGS HELD TIGHT AGAINST ITS BODY, AND DHULYN KNOWS THAT THE BIRD HAS TIME—MORE THAN ENOUGH—TO SPREAD ITS WINGS AND SAVE ITSELF, BUT SHE KNOWS THAT IT WILL NOT, THAT THOUGH ITS HEART BEATS AND ITS EYES ARE CLEAR, IT, TOO, IS ALREADY DEAD.

⸎

Dhulyn sighed and tried to turn over, opened her eyes when she found the weight of bedcovers impeding her. Mountain wool blankets, from the weight, and the sharp smell. She snaked one hand free and felt it caught by Parno's, larger, rougher, but as familiar to her as her own.

"Have I been asleep long?"

"A few hours. Is the pain better, or worse?"

"Better, I think."

Parno turned her hand over and kissed the palm. She pushed herself up on one elbow, and, using her grip on Parno's hand for leverage, managed to roll onto her side so she was still lying under the covers, but able to see her Partner without twisting her neck.

"Anything?"

"More discussion, but they're agreed. Dal will meet you at Yerloa's Spring at the hour the moon sets tomorrow night. That will bring you to the north gates of the city just as they open, and we'll meet inside the Dome just as the morning watch is settling in and getting complacent."

"What of the Tarkina?"

"She'll stay here where it's safer. Mar and that Scholar boy as well." He took the hand he still held, and bumped it softly against his lips before adding, "Well-watched, as you advise, but I still say you should let me kill the twisted little book reader."

Dhulyn sighed. "It is the purpose of Scholars to learn, and this one has learned something of the world that his Library neglected to show him. Let him live with that knowledge, and with the knowledge of the evil he is capable of. And let us not forget, we may yet learn something from him ourselves."

Parno shrugged, though his own smile did not touch his eyes. "It's your decision, I suppose. Let me know if you change your mind, though. I'd be happy to kill the little dung eater later."

Dhulyn tugged his hand. "I've Seen Gun helping Mar. They were both looking into that bowl of hers."

Parno sat back, releasing her hand and placing his own on his thighs. "They've been wondering, the Tarkin especially, whether you've Seen anything. I don't think they're going to care much about Mar and her bowl."

"Daresay you're right." Dhulyn began pushing back the blankets that covered her. "I saw Lok-iKol again, and I killed him again. Sometimes he had two eyes, sometimes one."

"But you still See his death, so that's to the good. Nothing we've done so far changes that?"

"Evidently."

"What aren't you telling me?"

"I Saw Tek-aKet on the Carnelian Throne."

"So why don't you look happy about it?"

She shrugged as best she could lying propped up on one elbow. "I was standing next to him with my sword out."

Parno nodded his understanding. "Armed in the presence of the Tarkin is one thing, but weapons out in the throne room? That's not likely."

"Exactly what I thought. The throne room might have been just an overlap from the image of Lok-iKol, but . . ."

"You don't know for certain."

"I don't know for certain."

When she looked into Parno's eyes, she saw there the same knowledge he would see on her face. She couldn't know for certain. She never had, and this is what the loss of her tribe really meant—not just her mother and father, but the loss of all and any who might have taught her to School her Visions, to read them properly, even to guide them. That had always been the drawback, the flaw, to using her Sight. But with so much, and so many, relying on her now, what else could she do?

"I need to know more about how the Sight works," she said. "I can't go on hiding from it." She looked up at him. "That's the lesson the Scholar has taught *me*."

"When this is over, we'll go looking for some answers."

"It seems the Scholar might have answers."

"You just don't want me to kill him." Parno's swift grin faded just as swiftly. "There's something else, isn't there?"

She nodded, lower lip caught between her teeth. "The Green Shadow fears the Marked, for reasons unknown to us. It follows that the Shadow has knowledge of the Marked, also unknown to us. In killing it, might I be destroying the source of the very information I seek?"

"Do we have a choice?"

She kept her eyes down.

"You Saw Tek on the throne, so that has to be good," Parno said, in the firm tones of a man telling the surgeon to go ahead and cut.

"I Saw him on the throne," she agreed.

"Watch Dal, my soul," he said after a moment's silence. "I've made it clear he's not to think of me, but . . . watch him."

"I do not like these Houses of yours," Dhulyn said, taking his offered hand and letting him pull her out of the bed.

"They're none of mine," he said.

But Dhulyn had noticed that he'd called Lok-iKol—and even the Tarkin himself—by their diminutives, Lok and Tek. As if he felt somehow free to speak of his old kin as he must have done when they had all been young together.

❦

When Mar saw Parno Lionsmane run down the steps and into the entrance on the far side of the inner courtyard, she immediately abandoned the stone bench where she'd been told to wait for the Tarkina, and flew up the stairs the Lionsmane had used. Earlier, he'd been carrying blankets, and the only person Lionsmane would be carrying blankets for would be the Wolfshead. And that meant she was up these stairs. Mar went directly to the only closed door on the floor above and opened it without knocking.

"Dhulyn Wolfshead."

The Wolfshead had her heel hooked on the sill of the window casement, and was leaning over, stretching out the long muscles in the back of her leg. The older woman looked over her shoulder, lowered her heel to the floor, and straightened to her full height.

Heart still pounding from her run up the stairs, breath still coming short, Mar took one look at the Wolfshead's face and flung herself into the Mercenary's arms.

"Dhulyn, I'm so sorry," Mar said, sobbing out the words. "This is all my fault."

Mar felt the Wolfshead relax, ever so slightly. The muscled arms came up, and the long-fingered hands took Mar by the shoulders and held her away.

"Sun and Moon, Lady Mar." The words were kind, but the tone, and the face when Mar had courage to look up at it, were cool and closed. "Don't make yourself so important, child," the Wolfshead continued. "You didn't make the Jaldeans insane, and you didn't make Lok-iKol rebel against his Tarkin."

"But you and the Lionsmane—"

"We're still whole and hearty, no harm done; in fact the contrary, if our help to the Tarkin has come in time."

"But I betrayed you." Mar wiped her face with her sleeve. "Please, let me explain. You must forgive me."

"Tchah. There's nothing to forgive. How could you betray us? It's not as though we're Brothers."

Mar swallowed with difficulty, the Wolfshead's face blurring as she blinked away tears. Finally, she nodded, and, keeping her eyes lowered, left the room.

❧❧❧

"I give you notice, Scholar, that my Partner keeps giving me reasons I shouldn't kill you. The day will come she'll run out." Parno had found Gundaron of Valdomar exactly where he'd looked for him, coming out of the underground council room after a short audience with the Tarkin. The boy had what seemed like a bundle of cut paper in his arms.

"I would like to live, Lionsmane. What can I do?"

"Don't wait." At the boy's raised eyebrows, Parno added, "*You* give me a reason not to kill you."

Nineteen

MAR AND GUN HAD been given beds in the same large underground chamber that housed the Tarkin and his family, though screens had been brought in to give some semblance of privacy. Mar opened her pack and took out her writing supplies, laying pens, inks, and parchments carefully on the small table that sat under the largest of the chamber's lamps. Her hands trembled, and she took a deep breath as she steadied the carefully stoppered glass bottle of black ink. Mindful of her reception at Tenebro House, only Mar's determination to confront Dhulyn Wolfshead had distracted her from her dread of meeting with Zelianora of Berdana.

As it was, she'd almost knocked the Tarkina down as she rushed, blind with tears, across the inner courtyard of Mercenary House. The Tarkina had given Mar a fierce hug, kissed her forehead, and dried Mar's tears with her own neck scarf, making Mar blow her nose as if she was no older than little Zak-eZak who even now was pushing a small wooden horse across the chamber's uneven floor. Mar had been so astonished at the Tarkina's behavior, that any uneasiness she might have felt had disappeared entirely, and she realized that she felt more at ease with the Tarkina of Imrion than she ever had with her own family in Tenebro House, or even with the Weavers in Navra.

It wasn't the same kind of comfort as sleeping snug and safe between Dhulyn Wolfshead and Parno Lionsmane, but comfort it was.

"I hear you are lettered and have worked as a clerk,"

Zelianora Tarkina had said, once Mar's eyes were dry. "Will you help me with the children? This is so hard for Bet-oTeb, her tutors and friends gone. If I could re-establish in some small way her regular routine . . ."

"Perhaps you'd prefer—Gundaron is a Scholar . . ."

Zelianora Tarkina had waved this away, linking her arm through Mar's and leading her inside. "With respect to the Libraries and their teachings, we had Scholars in Berdana as well, and undoubtedly the time will come for economics and the philosophy of history. At the moment, however, I'd be happy if Bet could add and subtract."

So while the Tarkina had sent the guard to find her daughter, Mar had gone down into the chamber to set up her classroom. Mar picked up the better of her two wooden pens, tested the seat of the steel nib, and set it aside for Bet-oTeb's use. For herself she applied her penknife to an uncut quill. She thought about the two giggling sisters in Tenebro House and suppressed a smile. The idea that she was about to begin teaching the future Tarkin of Imrion the basics of accounting was giving Mar an unexpected sense of satisfaction.

She could almost forget the cold lump of wretchedness that sat under her heart. She'd thought she'd been alone and miserable in Tenebro House, but that was nothing compared to what she felt now. Was it possible to be *more* miserable because you *weren't* alone? What was she going to do about Gun? Was she even sure of what she felt?

Suddenly Mar remembered Lan-eLan, and that woman's kindness to her. Where was Lan now? Mar hadn't even thought to ask Dal if the older Tenebro woman was safe and well. Mar blinked rapidly, willing the tears not to flow. She was always leaving her friends behind. Sarita in Navra, Lan-eLan in Tenebro House. Even Dhulyn Wolfshead.

"I'm scum," she whispered.

"Nonsense." The Tarkina's gentle voice startled her, the slight Berdanan accent giving a musical lift to the word. "I've known women like the Wolfshead, she'll forgive you."

Mar felt the heat rise to her face.

"Maybe," Mar said, lining up the edges of her parchment squares. "If she thought she had something to forgive."

Zelianora took the parchments and set them to one side,

sat down beside Mar in the chair that Mar had drawn up
for Bet-oTeb. The Tarkina just sat, quietly waiting, and
somehow this loosened the knot in Mar's throat, allowing
her to draw in a deep, ragged breath.

"The Wolfshead said that I hadn't betrayed her, that I
couldn't because, well, because I wasn't her Brother."

"And that doesn't help, because you feel that you did."

"Yes."

Zelianora reached across the small space that separated
their two chairs and laid her fingers, the signet of the
Tarkina twinkling in the light of the lamp, on top of Mar's
clenched hands. "She is right. You can only be betrayed by
someone you trust. In that pure sense, a Mercenary can
only be betrayed by another of their Brothers, because she
would never give her trust to anyone else."

"That's what I thought she meant." Mar hung her head so
as not to meet the Tarkina's eye. Zelianora hadn't seemed
like one of those lecturing grown-ups who pointed out the
obvious as though it was wisdom's best pearl. She twisted
her mouth to one side. Must come from being a parent.

"We have a saying in my homeland: 'there is more than
sand in the desert.' Dhulyn Wolfshead may tell you she is
not angry with you, and it could be so. It could be herself
she is angry with, and in her strict honor, she refuses to be
angry with you." Zelianora lifted her hand and sat back in
her chair. "But I don't believe it. I was one of those watching, and I saw her face when she told us you were with Dal-
eDal. The Wolfshead was happier to know you were safe
with him than she should have been, seeing you are no
Brother of hers. Somehow during that journey through the
mountains I have heard of, she grew to trust you. It's hard
to sleep with someone you don't trust."

"We only lay together for warmth."

"Lie down together, yes. Even with your arms about one
another, with certainty. Even guards traveling with prisoners have been known to do this, when it was their duty to
return alive. But sleep? With the prisoner unbound? No,
my dear." Zelianora shook her head, and Mar glanced at
her out of the corner of her eye. "Mercenary Brothers
would never have fallen asleep in the arms of someone
they did not trust."

"So I did betray her, and she knows it." Mar took another deep breath. "Why do I feel better?"

"Well, it seems you *are* important to her, after all. And since she *is* angry with you, whether she believes it or not, it will be possible for her to forgive you." The Tarkina stood. "If we all live long enough."

Mar stood up, too, smiling for what felt like the first time in days. "Then we'll just have to live long enough."

Gundaron selected another waxed strand of cotton and held it up into the shaft of sunlight that hung, warm and bright, from an opening high in the wall across from his bench. He threaded it through the finest curved bone needle in the sewing kit Alkoryn Pantherclaw had given him. These weren't the best bookbinding tools he'd ever seen, but he'd been taught at his Valdomar Library to make use of materials at hand when a book needed to be mended. He'd no idea where this quantity of paper, cut and folded to table-volume size, had come from, but no one here in Mercenary House had the knowledge or skill to turn the paper into a proper book. And Alkoryn wanted one to make a portable set of maps. This was good useful work, Gun knew, tapping together the first bundle of sheets . . . only not needed, or important, or even wanted particularly urgently. Except as a way to keep him out from underfoot, while the real work was done. Now that he'd told them what he knew, given them his warning, there wouldn't be anywhere he was really needed, or wanted. Not after what he'd done.

He sighed, letting his hands fall into his lap, the pages slipping from slack fingers. Neither he nor Mar was considered physically dangerous to anyone here, that was obvious enough from the way they were treated, but he didn't miss the point that they'd been put into the one chamber that was, for the sake of the Tarkina, constantly guarded. So he and Mar could be watched at the same time, with no wasted effort.

Zelianora Tarkina had been pleasant to Mar, asking for her help with tutoring the Tarkin-to-be, but with him the Berdanan princess was distantly polite, like an upper Scholar whose classes you were not yet a part of.

Gun told himself he was happy that Mar was being accepted more easily. After all, she'd only been tricked and lured into a mistake in judgment—a mistake, what's more, she'd set out immediately to correct as soon as she had learned of it. It was obvious to everyone, even to himself, finally, that what he'd done was far worse. He hadn't set out to betray or destroy anyone, but he'd ended up betraying and destroying everyone.

Even himself. There was no doubt in his own mind who was to blame. How many times had he been told while still in his Library not to become too focused, too narrow in his methods and his theories? Too sure of himself and his abilities? To do his best to keep the greater whole always in view? In his zeal to track down the ancient Shpadrajha, and connect them with the modern Espadryni, he'd done a good job of forgetting that particular lesson, and making himself an easy tool for—he shivered. For Beslyn-Tor. For the Green Shadow.

He picked up the pages and rescued the needle from where it had fallen into the crack between two flagstones and found himself staring at the bone implement's sharp point, wondering how large a hole it would make in a vein. There were other needles in the kit. How large a hole would he need?

He gripped the needle fiercely, eyes shut. He might as well stop playacting. He was too big a coward to solve his problems that way.

"Didn't anyone ever teach you how to hold a needle?" Mar's head popped up over the ladder from the lower level of caves.

"What are you looking so cheerful about?" Gun pushed the needle carefully through the scrap of soft cloth that held its brothers.

"The Tarkina says that Dhulyn Wolfshead will probably forgive me."

"May the Caids continue to smile on you." Gun was sorry as soon as the words left his lips, even before her face fell. He knew he should be happy for her, but . . .

"I'm sorry," he said, shifting over on the bench and indicating the space next to him. "I mean it, I really am happy for you. It's just hard to tell you so when I'm feeling so sorry for myself."

"Well, if you *know* you're feeling sorry for yourself, you're already well on the path to recovery."

"If you'd like to stop talking like someone's nurse, maybe you could actually be of some use."

"Or I could go and find better company if you can't be civil."

Gun took a deeper breath, let it out slowly. "I'm sorry, really, I am."

"Yes, you've said that," Mar said dryly, but Gun looked up in time to catch the sparkle in her eyes before she turned her head. "You know it isn't *me* you need to apologize to— well, yes, it is, and I forgive you, just don't do it again—but there *are* others who need your apology. For . . . what happened, I mean."

"You mean for helping a madman hunt down and destroy innocent people?" Gun waved away her protest. "I knew what you meant." He squinted up at the lowering sun. No one seemed interested in accepting his apologies anyway. "I *am* sorry," he finally said. "But who am I going to tell?" Certainly not the Marked he'd help find and turn over to the Green Shadow.

To his surprise, Mar was actually considering his question seriously, resting her elbows on her knees and her chin in her hands. He was even more surprised when her brow cleared and she smiled.

"Tell the Tarkina."

"What?"

"I'm serious. She's the representative here of the Tarkin, or I suppose Bet-oTeb is, really, but she's still so young. Tell them both. Tell them . . . tell them everything." Gun looked away; he knew she meant his Mark. "Ask them what you can do to make amends. You *can* help them, you know."

"They won't care. They don't trust me."

"Give them a reason to."

Gun sighed. Isn't that what Parno had said? He looked up to find Mar watching him, her eyes warm, but the corners of her mouth turned down. He found himself sitting up very straight. He thought he had faced what he was capable of when he admitted to himself what he'd done in helping Lok-iKol. But like the Wolfshead, he'd been hiding a part of himself that could be useful. A part that could help.

"Mar, you're wonderful."

"Did I help?" She was smiling, her dark blue eyes shining.

Gun took her by the shoulders, spilling the papers to the ground, and kissed her on the mouth.

❦

The call of the Racha bird told Dhulyn that Cullen had been able to leave Gotterang unmolested and reach Yerloa's Spring. The Cloudman himself was nowhere visible, however, only Dal-eDal, Karlyn-Tan and two guards, palefaced strangers alike enough to be brothers. All four wore dusty clothing in the Tenebro colors of black and teal. The breeze penetrating into the small copse of trees promised a warm day, bringing smells of damp earth, and, from somewhere nearby, the scent of apple blossoms.

Karlyn-Tan was evidently looking out for her, and as Dhulyn had made no attempt to hide her approach, stood as soon as she came into view. He held his place, however, making no move toward her. She smiled in the darkness. *No one's fool,* she thought. The less movement, the less noise.

"Your Cloudman has not come, Dhulyn Wolfshead." Dal-eDal's was the hunter's soft murmur. "Will you take one of our horses, or ride double with one of us?"

Dhulyn smiled her wolf's smile and there was evidently enough light to see by, for the Tenebro lord backed off a pace.

"Cullen," Dhulyn called softly. Dal-eDal snapped his head around and one of the two brothers swore as Cullen stepped out from cover so thin even Dhulyn had trouble believing he'd hidden there.

"Your horse is on the far side of the spring, Dhulyn Wolfshead," Cullen said. "Disha tells me no one is near."

Dhulyn measured the light in the east with a practiced eye. They were little more than an hour from Gotterang's main gate, enough time, once she'd fetched Bloodbone, to finish her preparations.

She was leaning over from her saddle, practically upside down, tying her bent left leg to the saddle leathers in such a way that she looked safely trussed up, when Karlyn-Tan came to her, soft cloth bag in his hand.

"Well, Karlyn-Tan," she said, before he had a chance to speak. "Once again, we meet under strange circumstances."

"Once again, Dhulyn Wolfshead, you seem to be bound." He answered her smile with a careful one of his own. His faded more quickly. "I'm afraid this time you'll be blindfolded as well. I regret the necessity, Wolfshead," he said, as he handed her up the cloth hood. "But best to put this on well before we get to the gates."

Dhulyn shrugged. "I thank you for your concern, Karlyn-Tan, but a blindfold won't unnerve me at all. We've had occasion, Parno Lionsmane and I, to learn how to fight blindfolded."

"I'd like to hear that story."

"If we live, I'll be sure to tell you." She looked over her shoulder. "Pull on that thong, would you? It needs to be tighter."

"It seems far too tight already," he said, though he reached to comply. "You are not meant to be truly bound."

For answer Dhulyn thrust downward with her left leg, heel out as if she were kicking someone in the throat, and all the bindings that held her leg fast to her saddle fell away as if by magic.

"Any more observations, Karlyn, and we shall miss our appointment."

❈❈❈

Fanryn looked around from staring out the window at Swordsmiths Street and stepped over to help Alkoryn Pantherclaw strap the last packing case shut.

"That will be the lot of them," he whispered, the light from the windows picking out every line and wrinkle on a face suddenly old.

Fanryn straightened up and looked over her Senior with her surgeon's eye. Like his namesake the panther, Alkoryn had been pacing the room since Dhulyn had left before midnight, and the grayness around his mouth and eyes testified to that. She picked up a glazed jug of ganje from its place on the strangely naked worktable, poured out a cup, and placed it in front of Alkoryn's customary seat.

"I was surprised when the Racha man offered to go with Dhulyn," she said. "From the look on his face when he learned Dhulyn's a Seer, I don't think he'll be parted from her until all this is over."

"The Clouds have claimed since the times of the Caids that the Marked are under their personal protection. The fact that until recently the Marked needed no special protection has never changed their attitude."

Fanryn picked up her own mug of ganje and tossed it off in one swallow. She made a face.

"Cold," she said.

Before Alkoryn could do more than smile, Thionan came striding in, Oswin Battlehammer, one of the two Semlorian Brothers in Gotterang, in tow. "I hope this is the last," she said, tapping the travel case with the side of her foot. "We're starting to run out of room."

"It is. As soon as you have it safely stowed, Parno will want us in the common room."

Thionan glanced at the window, checking the amount of light showing above the rooftops. "They'll still be in the copse. We've got the better part of an hour before they come through the gate, and at least two until they arrive at the Carnelian Dome."

"When you reach my age," Alkoryn said, "you'll realize that you can never have too much time."

Fanryn glanced at her Partner over their Senior Brother's head. She knew Thionan's grin was a mirror for her own. And she knew why. Neither of them expected to reach Alkoryn's age.

⊰⊱

Almost an hour later Parno stood beside Tek-aKet in the Mercenary House's small whitewashed common room and counted over in his mind the group assembled there. Half a dozen Brothers only, including Fanryn and the two Semlorians, but not Thionan who'd gone off to watch for Dhulyn's party to come through the north gate.

"You've all seen the maps," he said. "There's only one tricky part, so watch the walls for our marks." Parno indicated the man leaning against the trestle table to his left. "The Tarkin and I will be first, with Jessen and Tonal of his Personal Guard. Oswin Battlehammer and Tyler Nightsky will follow next, and then the rest of you behind us by twos." He tapped a small sand clock he'd borrowed from the kitchen. "Use this to time yourselves, we can't afford to get bottled up. We'll be going through the northwest passage, exiting in the Steward's room behind the main dining hall."

"Remind me to brick that up when all this is over," Tek-aKet said with a smile twisted sideways. Parno waited for the laugh to finish before he went on. It wasn't much of a joke—in fact he was sure that Tek meant every word of it—but anything helped to relieve the tension.

"Fanryn, you and Thionan—"

"If she ever gets back," Fanryn said, rolling her eyes and shaking her head.

Parno grinned. "*When* she gets back," he said. "You'll stay with Barlen Jadestar and Noshun Icehawk. Try to make it look like there's still twenty of us here, and keep the Tarkina safe until . . ."

"Until you send for us," Fanryn said. "Or until you don't."

"If it should be that we don't," the Tarkin said in a quiet voice that nevertheless reached every ear, "will you see that she reaches her sister in Berdana."

"We'll do it ourselves, Lord Tarkin, my Partner and I," Fanryn said.

Instructions given, Brothers and Guards started to leave the common room, some laughing or whistling, some studying the floor with narrowed eyes as they went. *Everyone reacts differently,* Parno thought. It was something he'd seen before, every experienced soldier had. He saw the look on Tek-aKet's face and smiled. Every *experienced* soldier. Tek looked like he didn't know whether to be scandalized at their levity, or to laugh himself.

All thoughts of laughter vanished as Barlen Jadestar burst into the room.

"Fanryn," Barlen said. "Come quickly, it's Thionan."

Parno wasn't very far behind Fanryn as she ran down the short corridor that led to the entrance courtyard. There would be only one reason, he thought, his heart heavy, that Fanryn should come quickly. A small, selfish part of his soul sagged with relief that Barlen had not come calling for him. Still, he cursed himself when he reached the outer courtyard and found Fanryn taking Thionan into her arms, easing her Partner down onto the bench under the plum tree, and pushing Thionan's hands away from the bloody rag she held to her chest with both hands.

Parno sucked in his breath when he saw the blood-darkened arrow shaft sticking out between Thionan's hands. She'd been surprised coming back from the gate, and not too far away, judging by how far she could walk with that shaft in her chest. And the Healer who'd fixed his arm long gone.

"Traitor's soldiers surround the House," she said, blood bubbling through her lips as she breathed.

"That dung eater Dal-eDal has sold us to the Shadow," Parno said.

"No." Thionan coughed and tried again. "Not here for Tarkin. Looking for Dhulyn."

"They don't know she's at the gates with Dal?"

"Save your strength, just nod," Fanryn said, her own teeth clenched.

Thionan nodded. Her lips formed the words "passed" and "gate."

Parno looked at the angle of the sun. This changed all their plans—and yet it couldn't. They couldn't leave Dhulyn and Dal-eDal to enter the Dome alone. He looked up as a shadow touched him to see Alkoryn studying his face.

"Pasillon, after all," the Senior Brother said with a sour smile.

Parno nodded, grim-faced. "They'll wish it was only the Sleeping God they had to worry about, when we are through," he said. He turned back to Fanryn and Thionan. "Can you cut it out? Or can we move her?"

Fanryn shook her head. "It's in the lung." She turned her face toward him, though her eyes never left Thionan. "And it's barbed."

A war arrow, then, not the kind the City Guard would normally use on citizens. This was war, the kind of death they all expected—for many, the death they hoped for. Parno could imagine many worse ways to spend his final moments than in Dhulyn's arms, her cheek against his forehead.

So long as it was not the other way around, he thought. Please all the Caids, demons and fates, not the other way around.

❦

After passing through the gate in the city wall it took Dhulyn a few minutes to place her companions once again. Linn, the guard who'd eaten onions yesterday, had moved from his position behind her and slightly to the left, and was now directly behind her. His brother, Joss, whose saddle gave off a rhythmic squeak, was still directly ahead. Dal-eDal's horse had a distinctive wheeze in its breath—nothing serious, but the horse probably shouldn't be used for racing—and the sound placed the noble in the lead, where he should be.

Cullen, who somehow managed still to smell of mountain thyme, moved suddenly to her right.

"Disha tells me the banner does not fly from Mercenary House."

With an effort Dhulyn kept relaxed and still. She could not risk loosening her false bonds. "Let her tell us when it does."

"And if it should not?"

"There's no turning back now," Dhulyn said.

"But, Wolfshead—"

"My Brothers will reach us," she said.

"And if they do not?"

"Then we will kill the Green Shadow ourselves."

"Or die in the attempt."

"Or die in the attempt," she agreed, with a careful shrug. "It is all that is required of us."

❦

The sound of breaking glass took Parno on the run past Alkoryn's deserted map room. He'd already been on his way up to shut and bar the only second-story windows that gave on the outside world, but as it was, he'd almost been too late. Sword ready in his hand, he cut with one downward motion through the hand that groped on the windowsill, wincing as the blade clanged on the stone. There went a carefully honed edge. He used the fist that was holding the hilt to push the man—screaming at the loss of his fingers—off the ladder he was standing on and took only another second to shove the ladder away from the wall as Sharan Owlclaw ran into the room behind him.

"Get those shutters," he called, jerking his head toward the other window as he closed the ones in front of him and threw up the first of the three solid iron bars that fit horizontally across, locking the iron-reinforced shutters tight. He glanced over, saw that Sharan had her shutters closed, and felt along the baseboard for the vertical rods he knew would be there, sliding them through the bars and locking them with sharp turns before going to help Sharan.

"They've backed off downstairs," she said. "Shall I watch here?"

Parno nodded, his breath a harsh rasp in his throat, and headed back down the stairs. Now that this first assault had been repulsed, he was free to think about Dhulyn, knowing she would continue to the Dome, signal or no signal. He'd known her going off on her own was a cyantrine sniffer's dream. He hoped he would be able to tell her so.

The first person he saw when he reached the outer courtyard was Tek-aKet. The Tarkin had a streak of dirt on his face and blood on the point of his sword.

There was silence from the street outside, when Parno would have expected the shouts of the troops and the sounds of running feet. It reminded him of that day in early spring, when he and Dhulyn had found the crowd watching the Finder's home burn down with the children inside.

"It's so quiet," Tek-aKet said, coming up to Parno as he entered the courtyard. "Everyone is so quiet."

Parno knew who "everyone" was to the Tarkin. "We're killers, Tek," is what he answered. "We're trained to be quiet." Though that didn't account for the silence outside the gate.

"Parno," the Tarkin said. "If we delay much longer, they'll be in the Dome without us."

"I know, Tek, I know. Just a few minutes more."

Parno's searching eyes froze on the spot where the plum tree in its pot had shed some late blossoms over Fanryn, still sitting with Thionan in her arms. Alkoryn, his sword in one hand, stood over them.

"Lionsmane." Tek's voice brought Parno around with a jerk.

"Sorry," he said. He sheathed his own blade and went to Alkoryn. "Time for everyone to get into the tunnels."

"Not everyone," Alkoryn croaked. "I will not leave my House." At Tek-aKet's protesting noise, Alkoryn raised his hand and glanced behind him at the Brothers under the plum tree. "They will not move, and how could I leave them? Besides," the old man shrugged. "If Lok-iKol's men find the place empty, they will look for the tunnels. Barlen and Noshun will stay, Sharan has asked to remain also, that the rest of you may escape."

"This is the second time people will die in order for me to escape." Tek's voice was calm, level. "I don't like it."

"Your time will come another day," Alkoryn said, turning away.

"In Battle or in Death," Parno said, knowing from the Senior Brother's tone that it would be useless to argue. This was the end the old man sought. He hugged his Brother to him with one arm, kissed an oblivious Fanryn on the forehead, and touched Thionan's hot cheek.

"We're to the tunnels, then. Any who do not stay, send them after us." He clapped for the attention of the Brothers in the courtyard and signaled to those who'd been assigned to go with him. The rest he would leave in Alkoryn's hands.

Twenty

❧❧❧

H E GOES SWIFTLY to the corner of the Library where the books and shelves make a great wall and begins to pull at the volumes, his hands going unerringly to one special section and pulling enough books and scrolls out of the way to make a tunnel in the wall, a tunnel he can enter only on his hands and knees. He encounters no shelves as he goes, just book after book, scroll after scroll, as tightly packed as unripe seeds in a flower head that lift away and disappear as he moves them out of his way. He tunnels for what seems like days, and he begins to fear that he cannot Find his way out again, even though the books and scrolls he removes go on disappearing as he pulls them free of the wall in front of him as the tunnel he crawls through gets smaller and smaller until he is reaching almost at his arm's length to move the final small scroll aside so that he can see the Carnelian Throne and the man sitting on it with his eye patch not quite covering the steady green luminescence of the left eye.

The wall begins snapping back into place.

❧❧❧

Gundaron pushed away Mar's bowl forcefully enough for the water it held to slop out onto the tabletop, and released the breath he hadn't known he was holding. He'd Found what he was looking for, no doubt there. Give Parno Lionsmane a reason not to kill him. Give them all a reason to trust him, to want him. Gun could almost hear his mother's voice "For the Caids' sake, Gundy, make yourself useful."

It had taken him the better part of the night to think what to do, but he hoped that this would be useful enough.

"Gun?"

More water slopped on the table as Gun jerked upright and spun around. Mar stood with her hand on the back of his chair, dark brown brows drawn down into a vee over her eyes. He blinked. How could he have forgotten she was there?

"What did you Find?"

Gun stopped short of answering her as a fair-haired Mercenary Brother he didn't know appeared in the doorway behind her.

"The Tarkina wants you," the Brother said. "Quickly."

Gun tossed the water on the floor and handed the bowl to Mar, ushering her out of the room in the Brother's wake.

They found Zelianora Tarkina placing packets of dried food into her travel bags, the nurse Denobea tying young Zak-eZak into his sling, and Bet-oTeb dressed and ready, her long dagger in its sheath at her side. The two Personal Guards the Tarkin had left behind were waiting, arms crossed, just inside the entrance to the sleeping chamber.

The Tarkina glanced up but kept packing. "The House is under attack," she said. "We're to follow Parno Lionsmane into the tunnels."

"We're not safe enough here?" Even as she asked, Mar went to her own bags and began to restow her bowl and pick up her writing tools.

Zelianora tied the last loose thong on her pack and hefted it, nodding, before answering. "If Tek and Lionsmane succeed," she said, "we can return to the Dome." Her hands stilled. "And if they fail, we will need to leave here in any case. I prefer to be prepared."

Gun took his lower lip between his teeth. "Mar, can you pack for us both? I've got to speak to Parno Lionsmane."

The fair-haired Mercenary Brother shook his head. "He'll have started—"

Gun didn't wait to hear more. He ducked under the arm of the man at the doorway and dashed off in the direction of the deeper tunnels. There were only four of these tunnels in this section of the caves, and only one that led in the direction of the Dome. Logically—

Gun ran headlong into the chest of a large, hard Mercenary. Prevented from ducking around him, Gun strained to look over the Brother's shoulder. Was that a glimmer of light he could see?

"Lionsmane," he called. "Listen! You need the throne room. He's . . . *it's* in the throne room."

The light stopped moving.

"Let him come."

The Mercenary holding him let go and Gun dashed down the tunnel toward the light.

❧❧❧

Telian-Han hesitated at the door, raised his hand to knock, and lowered it again. Though many of the doors in this wing had bolts on the inside (and some even locks that would work from the outside), to Telian's knowledge the man he still privately thought of as *the* Tarkin, Tek-aKet Culebro, had never used them—at least not here in the private wing of the Carnelian Dome. A well-run Household doesn't need locks, Tek-aKet used to say. A closed door is as good as a bolt to an honorable person. Since Lok-iKol had come, however, the bolts at least were almost always used. And some said the locks, too, though Telian pushed that thought away almost as soon as he had it.

What all this meant for him was that if you knocked, the person on the inside had to stop what he was doing, and come to let you in. Or not.

Telian's hands formed fists at his sides. There had been lots of changes since the night Lok-iKol had come, but it was the more recent ones that were especially worrying. At first, when they'd heard the noise of feet pounding and steel clashing, Tel and some of the other pages in his dormitory had wanted to rush into the passages and find out what was going on. But the Steward of Keys had sent senior pages to keep all the younger ones in their rooms and dormitories. The next morning Keys had called them all into the big kitchen where the chief cook and his assistants, the kitchen help, the household staff—cleaners for the most part—and the pages had been asked to gather. Tel had missed the Keys' first few words—something about a transfer of power that hadn't sounded too scary—he'd been too interested in the kitchen to pay attention. He'd been here before, but always on an errand, and the noble staff weren't encouraged to loiter down here.

"Each will remain in his or her own post," Keys had said, nothing in his voice showing that he'd drunk three bottles of the Tarkin's best jeresh the night before and must have had a splitting headache because of it. "You'll find men with Tenebro badges,"here he'd tapped his chest on the left side, "in the public rooms and at cross corridors in the Dome. Be ready to explain who you are and what your errand—and as I said," here Keys had looked 'round at all the staff, junior and senior, "this is nothing to worry us; it's just while they get to know us."

One of the Tarkina's lady pages, tall, dark-haired Rab-iRab Culebro was bold enough to interrupt and ask about her mistress, but Keys had told her to stay in the Tarkina's suite with her fellows and await orders.

"Your families may send for some of you," Keys had said, though everyone knew *that* wasn't likely to happen, at least not until they all saw how things were going to fall. No one wanted to risk offending the new Tarkin by appearing to remove their support along with their family members. Tel, for one, had been hoping no one came for him. Minor son of a Holding, a position in the Carnelian Dome was the best thing that could have happened to him.

He'd been so excited, he saw now, looking back on a morning that was only a week ago, though it felt like a month. All he knew was he was a lot more than a week older. He hadn't admitted to himself, possibly hadn't realized, how much he'd been hoping that some miracle would happen, and Tek-aKet Tarkin would come back. After the last few days, a return to minding his father's almond groves and vineyards under his older sister's supervision didn't seem like such a bad thing. Locked doors were not the only changes for the worse in the Dome.

He took a deep breath and knocked, waited, standing with his back straight, elbows in as he'd been taught, straining to hear any command, any footsteps nearing the door, and finally hearing only the bolts being pushed back. He took two more slow breaths before pushing the door lightly aside with his fingers and entering the room.

Lok-iKol was sitting as usual in the armchair by the open window, the papers and documents on the worktable against the far wall untouched and gathering dust. He allowed no attendance, not even from his own people.

"My lord Tarkin," Tel said, and waited to be acknowledged.

"Speak," the man by the window said in his heavy voice.

"The Lord Dal-eDal has returned, and brings with him a prisoner."

Tel gasped with pain as Lok-iKol was suddenly beside him, holding his upper arm in a grip that stopped Tel's breath.

"Where?" The man's breath was like rotting fish and Tel did his very best not to turn away.

"City gates, my lord." Tel spoke through clenched teeth, unable to keep himself from squirming in an instinctive attempt to pull free. The man holding him took no notice whatsoever.

"The throne room," the man said, dropping Tel's arm and turning away. "When they come, tell them the throne room."

"Yes, Lord." Tel blinked back tears and sucked in air as circulation restored itself to his lower arm and hand. Lok-iKol turned away, no longer paying him the least attention, so Tel just turned and ran from the room.

Maybe he would send a message to his father, after all, and beg to come home.

⋙⋘

The part of him that was Lok-iKol squirmed and would have turned aside, preferring not to enter the throne room. But he ignored it. He needed to know for certain whether this woman was a Seer. He needed to know whether she had already Seen the Lens. Then he could deal with her as he'd dealt with all the others.

And then he would only have to wait for the last piece to arrive and he would be whole again, in the first shape he'd known, in the shape that, perhaps, might be the key to freeing him from any shape. Whole, he would be safe, for without the Seer, there could be no Lens. And without the Lens, the Sleeping God would never awaken.

He saw the men who waited in the throne room, but he didn't speak. They talked too much, these shapers. He sat on the throne.

※※※

As they rode along the narrow streets immediately inside the city wall, heading for the wider avenues that surrounded the precincts of the Dome itself, Dhulyn had to stop herself from taking off the hood. It was not the lack of sight that disturbed her, but the way her skin crawled and the hairs stood up on her arms. There was something wrong. She'd expected what Parno called city noise to disorient her, to mask the little telltales of scent and sound she'd been using to keep track of her group, and stay aware of her surroundings.

So where was it, then, the city noise?

These were, more or less, the same streets she'd been through not that long ago, and she wasn't hearing what she should, nor smelling what she should either.

It was much too quiet for early morning. In this part of Gotterang there should have been—there *had* been when she'd come through with Parno and Mar—people hawking their wares, the squeaking ungreased wheels of hand- and donkey carts, children running and playing, chanting their games, and the buzz of conversations, the tiptap of hundreds of footsteps, the hum of hundreds of pairs of lungs pushing air in and out. But the noises were few enough that Dhulyn could detect and identify them almost as easily as she did the people who were with her. A woman wearing stale perfume scurried by on the right with what smelled like a basket of radishes, fresh from the ground with the earth still on them. Dhulyn's stomach growled, and she realized that there was no smell of foods cooking, but only the smell of burning, faint but noticeable. Not so faint was the smell of filth—clearly the night soil had not been picked up in days.

"Turning left in a few paces," murmured Karlyn, with a light touch on her left leg.

As they turned, the breeze brought the unmistakable

odor of a decomposing body. Her companions were singu-
larly silent, though Dhulyn knew they must have noticed
the stench. *Better not ask,* she told herself.

Closer to the Dome, the streets smelled marginally
cleaner. but there were even fewer sounds of people. At
one point Dhulyn heard rapid hoofbeats in the distance,
but they came no nearer.

Bloodbone's muscles bunched and relaxed in a new
way, and Dhulyn sensed that they had started up the in-
cline that was the road to the Carnelian Dome. The Dome
itself had originally been a fortress on the edge of the escarpment that overlooked the Talgus River, but as Imrion
had grown, and the Tarkins had settled on Gotterang as its
capital, they had all added to the original structure. Rather
than building outward, however, when each subsequent
Tarkin had needed more space, they had built up so that
the Carnelian Dome was, in fact, layer upon layer of buildings, from the lowest ancient kitchens, to the highest lookout towers. The outer wall was almost as thick as the city
walls, and built in the time of Jorelau Tarkin, that most paranoid of leaders.

Their hoofbeats made an entirely different kind of echo
when they reached the open plaza of the Tarkin's Square.
Another touch on her thigh told her they were stopping—
but at a point she judged well back from the gates themselves.

"The gates are open," Dal said. He kept his voice pitched
low and soft, so that it would not carry over, but his shock
was evident. Dhulyn understood. The outer gates of the
Carnelian Dome stood open only when the Carnelian
Guard was parading in the square, and her ears told her
that other than themselves, the square was empty.

"It's only the pass door," Karlyn said. "Whatever may be
the explanation for this, we cannot turn back now."

"In a tale," Dhulyn said, "those words would be the signal for an attack."

"That is what comes of reading too much."

They stopped again at what Dhulyn estimated was well
within bowshot of the gates, and therefore too close for
comfort if they really expected to be attacked. She heard
the creak of Dal's saddle as he stood up in his stirrups.

"Give answer," he called. "Who attends the gates, give answer."

"I attend," came a man's voice out of the air.

"I am Dal-eDal Tenebro, the cousin of Lok-iKol Tarkin. May I pass?"

Dhulyn grinned. Would anyone else find it significant that Dal-eDal was so careful to say *which* Tarkin he was related to?

"Enter, enter, enter . . ." said the voice in the air, fading as though the speaker was turning and walking away. Around her were the noises of her companions dismounting, but Dhulyn stayed where she was.

"You'll have to duck down," Karlyn said from around her right elbow. "You'll just fit through the door if Bloodbone walks carefully."

"I'll do what I can," Dhulyn said rapidly reviewing the knots she'd used before deciding none of them would either pull loose or become dangerously tight if she bent enough to get through the door. Such doors, she knew, were specifically designed to prevent the entrance of people on horseback, but Bloodbone was not large, and if Dhulyn could lay practically flat along the mare's neck. . . .

She pressed her cheek against Bloodbone's mane, and felt the loop around her right knee tighten painfully. Just as she was about to sit up again, she felt a hand loosening it. "Thank you," she said, knowing it was Karlyn-Tan.

The quality of the echoes thrown off from hooves and footsteps once they'd passed through the gate told Dhulyn the inner gate was already open, and she could picture the look of disgust that must have decorated Karlyn-Tan's face at the carelessness which allowed both gates to be open at once.

Dhulyn closed her eyes and concentrated her senses— there was more wrong here than sloppiness with the gates.

"Are there archers in the recesses?" she asked. There should be, she knew. There had been archers at the slitted openings high in the curve of the tunnel walls when she had passed through here with Parno and Alkoryn.

"I see no one," Karlyn said.

A shifting of air and the feel of sunlight on the skin of

her arms and hands told her they were through the inner gate and into the main courtyard of the Dome.

"You there," Dal called out. "Where are the Stewards? Our horses need attendance, as do we."

Nothing more than muttering, and what sounded like fingers snapping in time to an unheard tune. The muscles in Dhulyn's stomach tightened. The last time she'd felt this way had been in Navra, watching the crowd around the Finder's fire.

"What is happening?" she said, not caring who heard her speak.

Before anyone could answer Dhulyn heard the unmistakable sound of an arrow whistling through the air, and a grunt behind her, a swift click of hooves as a horse shied to one side, a jingle of harness, followed by the unmistakable dull thud of a body hitting the cobbles.

Without conscious thought she squeezed her knees together and Bloodbone obeyed the signal, rearing as Dhulyn thrust out both heels, pulling free of her leg bindings and sliding off Bloodbone's back to land squarely on her feet as the mare took a step forward. Lifting and uncrossing her arms over her head freed them, and Dhulyn yanked off the hood, ducking just in time to avoid another arrow as it fell bouncing on the stones beyond her. The flagstones underfoot were swept relatively clean, but as she straightened, Dhulyn mimed tossing dirt into the faces of the two nearest strangers, who flinched without thinking. She pulled her boot knives free and used them to deflect yet another arrow.

Not that the arrows appeared to be specifically aimed at anyone, Dhulyn realized as she glanced around, squinting against the light, near blinding after so long in the hood. The second flight of arrows seemed let off from loose strings, so haphazard as to be no real danger. Not like the armed guards running from the doorway beside the gate. They were badly dressed and disorderly, but heavily armed and deadly serious. Though if they hadn't been coming from what was obviously a wardroom, Dhulyn would have sworn these were soldiers coming spent and dirty from the battlefield.

One even had dried blood on the blade of her sword. And a moment later, Dhulyn's dagger growing out of her eye.

Dhulyn turned and pulled her own sword from the scabbard lying hidden along Bloodbone's side under her woolly oversized saddle pad. Why would a professional soldier not clean her weapon, Dhulyn thought, as she automatically brought up her blade to block a blow aimed with great fury but little skill at her head. And since when did the guards of the Carnelian Dome have little skill?

"This way," Dal-eDal called from behind her, and Dhulyn automatically stepped back, throwing a quick glance over her shoulder. Dal was heading toward a small arched doorway on the far right of the courtyard, not the elaborately carved main entrance Dhulyn had used when she'd come for her audience with the Tarkin.

Three more guards came trotting into the courtyard, but instead of coming directly to the help of their fellows, they hesitated, looking from friend to foe with frowns. One of them stared about as if he wasn't even sure where he was. Dhulyn moved her sword with more discretion, hitting with the flat of the heavy blade, pushing one youngster away with a boot to the midsection, unwilling to kill people who didn't seem altogether certain that they wished to kill her.

She was one of the last to reach the doorway Dal stood guarding, and she helped him slam the heavy door into place, stepping aside as Karlyn and Cullen thrust down the bar. A quick look around confirmed only minor injuries, barring the unlucky Linn, who'd been hit by the first arrow—the only one which had come with any force. They had left his body outside with the horses.

"This doesn't make any sense," Karlyn said. "Where are the Stewards? Why were the gate guards not better organized?"

"And cleaner. And aware enough to actually do some damage with their swords," said Dhulyn.

"What do you mean, Wolfshead?" Dal-eDal said.

"Did you not see it?" Cullen said. "They moved as if they knew what to do, but had forgotten how." He looked between Karlyn and Dhulyn.

"Or as if they'd forgotten *why*," Dhulyn said. "There was no coordination, as if they'd never fought together before. As if they were each of them alone."

"We were lucky," Karlyn said. "You can be killed just as dead by someone who doesn't know why he's shooting at you."

"This is a kind of madness," Dhulyn said. "We saw this in Navra, Parno and I. Did you see their eyes? It is some effect of the Green Shadow."

"We waste time with questions we cannot answer," Dal said pushing away from the wall. "Come."

Three identical dressed-stone passages led from the entrance hallway, each as wide as her outstretched arms, each carpeted with runners of woven matting to deaden the sound of servants' feet. Dal had chosen the one on the right, and they had advanced as far as the first cross corridor when they heard footsteps running. Dhulyn and Cullen had been walking with their swords at the ready, and now Karlyn and Joss lifted theirs, bracing themselves. Dal held up his hand and after a few moments it became clear that the running feet came no nearer, but were fading into the distance.

"They go to the throne room," Dal said.

"If our people are the target of those running guards, they will need our help."

"Throne room it is."

They lit the cressets when the third lamp they came to was out of oil and covered in dust, as was the smoothed stone floor under their feet. Those who carried no lights held to the belts of those who did. They'd left the natural caves under Mercenary House behind them, and were now in the secret tunnels that generations of Mercenaries had discovered, used, and expanded upon.

And even though they were helping him at the moment, Tek-aKet Tarkin didn't like it. He didn't like the darkness, the closed-in spaces—hadn't liked it the first time through, but then he'd had Zella with him and the children and that had made a difference.

He didn't at all like that the tunnels existed, and he

especially didn't like that the Mercenaries knew so much about them.

The passage they followed now was narrow enough that in places they had to turn sideways, and Tek found himself thinking how lucky he was that he took after his slim mother, and not after the hulking bear of a man his father had been. As it was, there were one or two places where even walking sideways made for a tight fit. Parno Lionsmane, with the maps Tek didn't like to think about firmly in his mind, led the way. After a long, unbroken stretch of bricked tunnel, they came to a crossroads and the Mercenary Brother hesitated.

"Tell me again, Scholar, which way we should go."

Unable to turn completely, Tek looked over his shoulder at where the Scholar stood between Jessen and Tonal.

"He's in the throne room, Lionsmane. I'm sure of it."

Because of the confinement of the walls, Tek was the only one of the group who could see the man's face—and Tek was fairly certain even Parno Lionsmane didn't realize he could be seen. Tek saw distrust flit across the Mercenary's features, strangely bronzed by the light from the cresset he held. The distrust was followed by frustration as Parno Lionsmane shut his eyes tight. And finally the man shrugged.

"Throne room it is," he told the pale-faced Scholar. "If we live through this, you're going to tell me how you know."

Using his dagger, he scratched a pattern on the tunnel wall at eye height and added an arrow.

The tunnel grew gradually wider, and narrow slitted openings began appearing high in the stone walls, letting in some outside light. There was something familiar about the pattern of the light, and it dawned on Tek that this was the outer wall of the Soniana Tower, so called after a long-dead Tarkina, and the present-day location of the Carnelian Throne. He had seen these narrow slits in the walls from the outside, and thought them decorations.

There was light enough for them to see the end of the passage before they walked into it. Parno Lionsmane signaled, holding up his left hand with the first two fingers extended. Tek passed the signal back to his guards. The Lionsmane stuck the cresset into a bracket to the left of the wall in front of him and ran his fingertips over the bricks, feeling for the one glazed smooth. Tek saw him take a deep, quiet breath and let it out slowly, before he ran his hands over the bricks again.

"Should I hold the light?" Tek said.

Lionsmane shook his head. "The maps say the brick won't show, no matter where we hold the light, that only— here it is." Tek put out his hand and the Lionsmane guided it until Tek could feel the smooth glazing for himself. It was one of the smaller tying-in bricks, he thought smiling, placed sideways to the others both to create a pattern and to strengthen the double-layered wall. Unless you knew what to look for, the smooth surface was too small to draw attention to itself.

The Mercenary braced his fingers and pushed the smooth brick with his thumbs. "Lord Tarkin, your hands under mine, please." Even straining as they all were, Tek heard nothing, and it wasn't until they released the catch that Tek felt the wall give, shuddering slightly under their hands. According to the instructions that had been hand-written on the map, this section of wall was cantilevered, and they should be able to swing it open by pushing on the left-hand side.

Lionsmane drew his sword, and motioned Jessen and Tonal forward, showing them with the point of his blade where he wanted their hands. "I'll go through first and to the left; the Tarkin behind me and to the right. Guards, you follow up the middle. Scholar, stay out of the way of the blades." When everyone was in position, the Mercenary nodded and the two guards pushed against the wall to the left of the trigger brick. As promised, the wall opened, so quietly that without the change in light Tek wouldn't have been sure that it had happened.

"Who's been keeping this oiled?" he whispered as he followed the Mercenary through the narrow space into the dressing room and stepped to the right. Lionsmane threw him a glance that made Tek's ears burn. *Of course. The Brotherhood maintains the tunnels.*

When Tek was growing up, this room had been filled with his father's robes of state, the Tarkin's coronet and the spear and sword, symbols of the Tarkin's office. Tek preferred less ceremony, and had always used the room as a private salon, where he could retreat to rest and refresh himself without technically leaving the throne room, or to send petitioners to wait for a more private audience. A thick rug covered the stone floor, with two comfortable chairs placed near a table covered with an embroidered cloth, tall enough to serve for either writing or dining.

As Tek stepped to the right out of the opening, he glanced down at this table. It held the cut-glass inkwell that Zella's sister Alliandra had sent him from Berdana's new glassworks. The ink had dried, and inkwell, pens, and embroidered cloth were all covered with a fine layer of dust. Tek tightened his grip on his sword and felt a chill trickle up his spine. His whole life he'd lived in the Carnelian Dome, and he'd never before seen dust on the furniture.

Lionsmane waited until everyone had come out of the secret passage before he swung the wall shut behind them. The paneling was decorated with an inlaid pattern, and with a tap of his forefinger, he drew their attention to the piece of inlay that marked the door's trigger from this side. When Tek and his two guards had nodded, the Mercenary turned to look at the room.

"Does that door open directly into the throne room," he asked, his voice a quiet growl, "or is there another, connecting room?"

"I'm surprised you don't know," Tek said, smiling to take the sting out of his words. *Well,* he thought, *first you kill the wolf,* then *you worry about the holes in the fences.* He would deal with the extent of the Mercenaries' knowledge when they lived through this. "Not a room, but a connecting passage," he continued. "Go immediately right. The door on the left wall at the other end is the entrance to the throne room proper. The entrance will bring us out to the right of the Throne itself. The door opens toward us and will lay flat against the far wall."

Parno Lionsmane nodded, his eyes still on the door.

"Your best guess as to the number of guards in the room, Lord Tarkin."

"There are always two standing at the throne itself. This is not the normal time for audiences . . ." Tek turned to look at the Scholar, looking all the paler for a streak of dirt on his face, standing close to the hidden opening, as if he would like to go back through.

"He's there," the boy said. "Or the Green Shadow is."

Tek nodded. "Then there may be more guards. We should be able to hear voices through the second door."

"Very well," Parno said. "Keep the same formation, but come out striking."

Twenty-one

ON THE COUNT of three, Parno dove out through the door held open for him, tossing throwing stars to the right and left and making an automatic count of the men in the room as he rolled up onto his feet. Five against each side wall, two flanking the formal entrance. None close to the throne. Twelve. Not so bad, if he didn't have Tek-aKet to worry about. But with luck there should be Brothers only minutes behind him in the tunnels, and Dhulyn only steps away. Between them he and his Partner could handle twelve easily, even while keeping the Tarkin and his guards alive. Tek-aKet had already followed him into the throne room and was engaging one of the guards standing against the right wall, with Tonal and Jessen running up to help.

Three guards in Tenebro colors approached him warily as Parno straightened to his feet and lifted his sword, already deciding which he would gut first. Just as he shifted his weight to make the first move, he was grabbed in a bear hug from behind, clamping his arms to his sides.

Idiot! he thought, cursing both himself and his assailant. He should have been aware of his own back, not watching for Tek's. As for the fellow who'd grabbed him, he must have been unarmed—otherwise why waste time with wrestling moves? Even as he was thinking this, Parno squatted, bracing his legs and bending forward to tip the man off-balance. The guard was not unskilled, however, and he countered Parno's shift of weight by thrusting his own leg forward between Parno's braced legs. The man was barrel-chested, the strength in his arms astonishing, and Parno felt his lungs close down, refusing his next breath. But he had some experience of his own, and this was no simple wrestling match, skill against skill alone, undertaken for money or glory, and over when one man was pinned to the ground. Years of Schooling allowed Parno to ignore the burning in his lungs, the pounding in his blood, and focus on distribution of weight, on leverage, angles, and cutting edges. Still squatting, he turned his dagger a few degrees of arc, stabbed back and upward, felt the hot gush of blood as he severed the artery in the man's thigh, took a deep welcome breath of air and shrugged his way out of the man's suddenly limp grasp.

As he straightened, Parno lifted both his blades, swinging his sword through the arm of the Tenebro guard who was closing in on Tonal. Of the three who had been approaching him, only two were left and Parno leaped to engage them, forcing them back toward the throne itself. Lok was standing, a sword in his hand, looking out at the men fighting like an owl sitting on a perch, turning this way and that, watching for prey.

❊❊❊

The part of him that was Lok-iKol recognized the golden-haired man with the Mercenary badge as soon as he stood up out of his roll. The surge of adrenaline that passed through the body was unpleasant, burning and leaving a metallic taste in the mouth. There was some fear, but also something he had come to recognize as hope. Lok-iKol thought there was something this man could do for him, and there was something . . . the body's heart rate increased. Where this golden-haired man was, he understood, the Seer would not be far away. He stepped forward and around two men fighting, lifting his hand to TOUCH the man, when another body stepped into his way. This dark-haired, bearded man was no stranger to Lok-iKol, though it took a moment to recognize him, bearded and disheveled as he was. Another surge of emotion, this time colder, bitter. Their swords met with a clash and he fell back, making the dark, bearded man follow. The golden man called out, "No, Tek," and began cutting through the wall of men preventing him from coming to the dark one's aid.

The dark man was Tek-aKet. The golden man would fight to save the dark man. Interesting. He could not TOUCH the golden man from here. But he could TOUCH the dark one.

❦

"This way."

Mentally checking and approving the direction against the map she'd seen days before in Alkoryn's workroom, Dhulyn ran down the corridor after Dal-eDal. This was the right direction for the throne room, even though they'd missed the formal public approaches that would have taken them directly there. She quickened her pace until she was just behind the Tenebro lord. If he was leading them into a trap, she was willing to let him spring it. As they came up on a second cross corridor, they slowed. This passage was not as wide as the one they were using, but its carpet was good wool, not the woven matting they were walking on. Here they might run into someone with authority.

"Hold your sword down and just walk straight across at a normal speed," Dhulyn told him. "From a distance we'll pass for Dome Guards. It's the stealth and the running that attracts attention."

They slowed to a walk, but just as they reached the other corridor, a slim, dark-haired young woman turned briskly into their passageway. She yelped, took a quick step back, turned, and ran off. Training made Dhulyn pull out a throwing dagger before she thought again, and resheathed it. Killing the girl would accomplish nothing.

"So much for stealth," Dal said. "Let's hope she doesn't bring the guards."

"You mean *more* guards?" Dhulyn said.

They were no more than ten or twelve paces past the intersection when a small group of six guards burst into the passage behind them. They came, Dhulyn noticed, not from the arm of the corridor down which the dark-haired girl had fled, but from the opposite direction.

"Sun and Moon take them," Dhulyn cursed. They couldn't

hope to outrun soldiers on their own ground, and while six were not too many to deal with, it would cost them time they might not have.

"Let me try something," Dal said. He took a step toward the approaching Guards with his hands up, palms toward them.

"We come to kill Lok-iKol," he called out, "and restore Tek-aKet to the Carnelian Throne. We'd just as soon not kill you, so are you with us or against us?"

Dhulyn grinned, seeing that the man in front, while unshaven, was otherwise tidy in the solid dark red uniform of the Tarkin's Personal Guard, as were three others. The remaining two wore the multicolored sleeves of the Carnelian Guards. Dal-eDal had good eyesight.

The lead guard rubbed his face with his free hand. "You've got Tek-aKet? He's alive?"

"He should be ahead of us," Dhulyn said. "With my Partner."

"You swear it's so?"

"I'm Dhulyn Wolfshead the Scholar, I was Schooled by Dorian the Black. I fight with Parno Lionsmane the Chanter. I swear by my Partner, may we both die in battle." Dhulyn touched her forehead with the back of the hand that held her sword.

The man reversed his own weapon and held it out to Dhulyn, hilt first. "I'm Dernan. We're with you. Lead on."

"You won't mind keeping your weapon, and taking the point position? It's not that I don't trust you," Dhulyn said, with a smile. "It's that I trust no one."

With their reinforcements surrounded, they crossed three more corridors on the way to the throne room, but the only other people they saw were two young pages. Unlike the dark-haired young woman, these two boys did not run away, but stood looking at them as they approached. They clung to each other, though Dhulyn was sure they weren't aware of it.

"Telian-Han," Dernan called out. "Go for Talya. Tell her to come help us kill the Tenebroso usurper."

Both boys broke into wide smiles and ran off down the corridor behind them.

The waiting area outside the wide oak doors of the

throne room was just as dusty and neglected as the corridors had been. But somehow it made Dhulyn's skin tingle to see the tastefully organized chairs with their side tables carrying dead greenery and guttered candles.

"Take care, my lords," Dernan said, as Dhulyn, shoving her sense of unease to one side, ran across to the closed doors. "If you stay too long with the Tenebroso, or too near him, some illness takes you."

"I don't want to stay long in One-eye's company," Dhulyn said. "I want to kill him." She seized the gilded pommels in the center of the ornamental doors and threw them open.

Even as the others spread out, Cullen behind her, Dal to her right, Karlyn-Tan to her left, Dhulyn assessed the room, mentally ticking off friend from foe, looking for the one she wanted most to see. She found Parno just as he shrugged a guard off his back and cut off another's hand with a casual stroke of his sword before turning to engage two others. A guard she recognized as one from Mercenary House, who had been facing two opponents until one suddenly found herself handless, dispatched the man left to him with a broad cut to his head. Dhulyn was more than halfway across the room herself when she heard Parno cry out "Tek, no!" and increased her speed.

Parno's cry had a strange impact on the people in the room. Fighting all over the room faltered as several of the Carnelian Guards raised their weapons and stepped back from their opponents, looking around them as if unsure what to do. One even nudged a fellow guard who was still fighting out of the path of his adversary and called something Dhulyn couldn't hear into the man's ear.

Dhulyn ran past them and skidded to a halt.

Tek-aKet Tarkin and Lok-iKol Tenebroso were circling each other in front of the Carnelian Throne. Lok looked as though he had been wearing the same clothes for some days, and his hair hung stringy and unwashed. He still wore his eye patch, but a green glow shone from behind it, matching the color that shone from his good eye.

Dhulyn caught Parno's attention across the room and flashed him a grin as she circled around to the left, hefting her dagger. Now if only the Tarkin could maneuver the green-eyed dung eater around so that she could plant a blade in him. Her experienced eye was just telling her that Lok was holding his blade a shade too low, when Tek-aKet, remembering what they had taught him, swept the other man's blade aside and planted his own squarely in the center of the taller man's body.

For a moment they stood there frozen, Lok's arm falling limp by his side, his sword dropping to the floor with a clang of metal on stone, his green eye hooded. He coughed and a dribble of blood ran out of the corner of his mouth. Then Lok moved, reaching out for Tek-aKet, pushing himself up the blade until he clutched at Tek's clothing, staring the Tarkin in the face as if he would say something important. Perforce, Tek let go of his sword, grabbing Lok's wrists to prevent being pulled off his feet. Dhulyn saw the green die out of Lok's eyes, saw the lips form the words, "Tek, Cousin" as Lok-iKol's knees sagged, and he slid slowly to the floor, taking the blade with him, hands still clamped to Tek's arm. Lok's mouth still worked, but the lips formed no words. Dhulyn ran forward to catch the Tarkin's arm before he joined his cousin on the floor.

Tek-aKet screamed, yanked his arm loose and fell, cracking his head against the foot of the Carnelian Throne.

⬥⬥⬥

He cried out, letting the new body scream for him. The light. The searing light. She Sees. She was not to touch him, with her all-seeing eye. He withdrew, diving deeper, until the darkness covered him.

She *Sees*.

⬥⬥⬥

"How can you be humming?"

Dhulyn lifted her fingers from the charred window frame. "What?"

"You're humming that children's tune, the one from the game you're so interested in."

"It's going through my head, I can't get it out."

"Come, the floors are unsafe here. We must go."

Dhulyn followed Parno out of the charred ruin that had once been Alkoryn's map room. It had taken them some time to get away from the rejoicing at the Carnelian Dome, but as soon as they could find enough horses, they'd gathered the Mercenaries who had come up through the tunnels and returned to Mercenary House through streets filling with people as news of Tek-aKet's restoration spread through Gotterang. They'd found the gates battered but still closed, no attackers outside, and nothing living inside.

It didn't need any great experience to see what had happened. Unable to breach the gate, the attackers had resorted to fire arrows and scaling ladders. From the body count, seventeen had made it inside the House. They'd been laid to one side in the courtyard, as far as possible from the four bodies of the Brothers who'd been found. Parno had found Thionan's body where he expected, under the plum tree. Fanryn was lying over her, sword bloody.

"Another one this way," Tyler Nightsky stuck his head in the door.

"We'll help," Parno said, turning away from the stairs and following his Brother to the rear of the House. He stopped Tyler with a hand on the arm. "Dhulyn," he said, motioning her forward. "It's Alkoryn."

From the look of the bodies, Alkoryn Pantherclaw had killed one man as he came through the second-story window, and had been backed into a corner by a second man in a Tenebro uniform. This second man was spitted on Alkoryn's sword, the pool of tacky blood beneath him showing the wound to be immediately mortal.

"Does he live?"

Dhulyn pulled the Tenebro man's body away and squatted next to Alkoryn. In death, his hand had fallen away from where the hilt of a dagger stuck out, just below where his navel would be, if she could see it. He'd held it in place, keeping the blood in, until he'd been able to dispatch his opponent.

"In Battle or in Death," Dhulyn saluted him, touching her fingertips to her forehead.

❦❦❦

"Zella."

Zelianora looked up from where she sat in the window seat of her bedroom, the shutters angled to throw the morning sunlight on the book in her hands, and keep it from the bed where Tek was resting. At the sound of her name, she put the book aside and stepped over to the bed.

"How are you feeling?" she said, sitting down on the edge of the thick mattress, and drawing her hand down the side of Tek's face, letting her fingertips linger on his warm skin. She had caused him to be shaved as he slept, and though he was thinner, and there were new lines on his face, he looked more like the man who had met with and disbelieved the Mercenary Dhulyn Wolfshead—was it only a half moon ago? It felt like three moons at least.

Tek had been unconscious for almost a day after the fight to restore him to the throne, and of course there were now no Healers to be found in all of Gotterang. A surgeon had come from the Mercenary House, a "Knife" as they called him, but the Brother had found nothing physically wrong with Tek beyond the lump on his head.

Zella took the hand that lay on the outside of the thick feather bedcover. "Here I thought that, once we were back in the Dome, all our troubles would be over. I would rather have you well, than all the thrones in the world."

Tek squeezed her hand and she thought she saw him smile.

"It is only a headache, Zella," he said. "The Mercenary Knife said, from the knock on my head. It will pass."

Zella nodded, smiling. "Dal-eDal is suggesting that you show yourself to your men, and to some of the other Houses, now that you are awake. They need to know that you are well, and Tarkin again."

"I'm so tired." And indeed, his voice was lower than she had ever heard it, even the time that he'd had the coughing sickness and had lost his voice for three days. There had been no Healer then, either, now that she thought about it.

"I thought perhaps a short audience," she said now. "It would have to be in the throne room itself, I'm afraid, but we could get you seated before inviting your nobles in . . . And we could be careful of the light, so long as they could clearly see you."

"No Mercenaries," he said. "Not Dal-eDal."

Zella licked her lips, hesitating. Dal had been a great help to her while Tek was unconscious, and she well understood that without the help of the Mercenaries, neither she nor Tek—nor their children—would be alive to have this discussion.

He seemed to take in what she left unspoken.

"It's the appearance," he said. "I—we. We mustn't look as though we were relying on paid troops, no matter how respected the Brotherhood is. And even if Dal has not yet been confirmed as Tenebroso, his attendance might send the wrong message."

Zella nodded, relief making her smile come naturally. Tek was talking and thinking like his old self. "I see, that's well thought out," she said.

"Get Gan to arrange it."

Zella felt her face go stiff. "Gan-eGan is dead, my heart. Don't you remember?"

❦❦❦

The man's mind told him how to speak to her, what to say. He wanted to send her away, but that would cause remark. Remark he could not afford now, not while this pain throbbed its way through the head, pulling at his attention. He had considered taking another shape, an uninjured one, but Tek-aKet was Tarkin, his was the most useful shape. No other so powerful, so safe. Once the pain was gone, once the body was well, *then* the Seer. Not now, not yet.

❦❦❦

Dhulyn sucked in her stomach as the point of Parno's blade passed within a hair's breadth of the skin on her belly.

"Trying to tickle me?" she said, aiming a blow at his left shoulder which he parried, making her duck under a cut to her head.

Parno grinned. "And why, exactly, shouldn't I tickle you?"

"Because you know what tickling leads to." She saw her opening, slapped his sword aside with the palm of her hand against the flat of the blade, and stepped into him, taking his wrist in her left hand and throwing her sword arm around his neck. She kissed him, light touches on cheeks, chin, and lips, as he laughed. "And we have company." She made to step back, but his arms had gone around her, so she turned in their circle and smiled her wolf's smile at the two men approaching from under the arches of the arcade along the north side of the courtyard.

Parno whistled softly next to her ear as he let his arms fall away, releasing her. She gave Dal-eDal and Karlyn-Tan a short nod before turning to the stone bench where they'd left their other weapons. She tossed Parno his shirt and slipped her vest on over her breastband.

"I see we're not the only ones left uninvited to Tek-aKet's audience," Parno said, as he wiped the sweat off his face and arms with his shirt.

Dal-eDal shrugged, tilting his head to one side. "I could see how my presence might be awkward, but I was surprised when I heard that you were also excluded."

Parno grinned. "Politically, it's an astute move. Now isn't the time to remind the Houses that the Tarkinate was restored by a handful of Mercenary Brothers."

"You were always more politically aware than I," Dal-eDal said, with a short bow. "And that is why I have come to you. I felt you should be told. The Tarkin has sent word that he will confirm me as Tenebroso four days from now."

"You don't need *my* permission."

Dal shook his head, lips pressed tight. "Nor do I ask for it. But I find that I would like your . . . your approval."

"You have it." Parno's voice was low and cool.

"The reason for your Casting Out has been removed, and I would like to offer you the shelter of the House once more. So that you are Tenebro again."

Dhulyn's heart thundered in her ears as Parno remained silent a long moment. Would he give the same answer here, in front of others, that he had given her?

"Don't take offense at what I'm about to say, Dal," Parno finally said. "But I want you to remember that I didn't leave the House. Do you understand? It was taken from me. I was Cast out." Karlyn-Tan's head came up, and he looked sharply at Parno. "I have another House now, one that I can never lose. And I have a Partner. Not even death will release me from that bond." He looked down at Dhulyn and touched her cheek with his fingertips. "In Battle," he said.

"*And* in Death," she answered, forcing her voice through the barrier in her throat.

"I understand." Dal-eDal swallowed. "But I *will* consider you my cousin. A Tenebro." He looked at Dhulyn. "Both of you. The task of being Tenebroso will be difficult enough without you."

"Want my advice?"

"Always."

"Just ask yourself, what would Lok do? And do the opposite."

Dal-eDal joined the laugh, but Dhulyn thought his eyes were not smiling.

⚜

Dhulyn was quiet as Parno followed her to the baths in the Tarkina's wing. She had neither spoken nor answered any greeting since they'd left the courtyard. The corridor to the baths was deserted, and as she reached for the door latch, Parno put his hand on top of hers.

"All's well, my soul?" Was it possible that the woman was still worrying about Dal-eDal and the lure of House Tenebro? Would this uncertainty haunt her forever?

His heart froze as she looked up the short distance between them, frowning, her blood-red brows drawn down in a sharp vee.

"I don't like Tek-aKet's behavior," she said. "I don't like our being excluded."

Parno let out his breath slowly. After all this time, he still expected her to react like a civilized woman—as his mother or sisters might have done, wanting to talk it over, reassuring themselves again and again. Was he ever going to know her well enough to know what she was thinking? Did he want to?

"Tek's position is logical, politically speaking."

"There is no such thing as logic, *politically* speaking."

"Ah, so young to be so cynical."

She shook her head, lips pursed. "There's something off. Something wrong."

Parno pushed the door open and let Dhulyn precede him into the baths before he answered. "Let me see if I understand. We've killed Lok-iKol, restored the rightful Tarkin to the Carnelian Throne, we're valued guests of the

Tarkinate . . ." He imitated Dhulyn, shaking his head, pursing his lips. "No, I can't say that I see a problem."

Parno doubled over, gasping, as Dhulyn poked him in the solar plexus with stiffened fingers, and stepped around him to shut the door against the cooler air of the corridor. "You've forgotten the Green Shadow."

"Well, I was *trying* to, yes." Parno dragged in a ragged breath, fully aware that he didn't sound as lighthearted as he was pretending to be. "Unlike some overeducated Outlanders of my acquaintance, I don't like to dwell excessively on the negative. As I said before, evil defeated, Tarkin restored, Mercenaries luxuriating in well-appointed baths of Carnelian Dome—no, I see no difficulties here."

Dhulyn sat down on the cedar wood bench just inside the door and pulled up her right foot, but made no other attempt to remove her boot. "I hope you're right," she said. "But, somehow, I'm not so sure about evil's being defeated." After a moment she looked up, her eyes still focused inward. "Zelianora tells me that other than the bump on his head, Tek-aKet has no injuries."

"And so?"

Dhulyn sighed, shutting her eyes. "Why are you being so stubborn? If his arm was not broken, why did the man scream when I touched him?"

"What are you saying?"

"Has anyone noted the color of his eyes?"

❦❦❦

From his vantage point three steps down from the Carnelian Throne, Telian-Han watched the select group of Houses, which included all the High Nobles and quite a few of the Lower, mill about the throne room, noting who spoke to whom, and which House courteously ignored which. His post today, as on many an audience day, was Tarkin's Runner. He was here to fetch anything that the Tarkin might want from elsewhere in the Dome, or to run with any message. It was always his favorite post, to stand almost on a level with the Tarkin himself, with strict orders to listen to any discussion Tek-aKet might have with any of his guests—the Tarkin would sometimes quiz him on the talks he'd overheard, using it as part of Tel's training. Tel once again thanked the Caids that he hadn't, after all, sent to his father asking to come home.

He knew there were some among the staff and Carnelian Guard who hadn't thought that well of Tek-aKet Tarkin, who'd maybe been a bit pleased when he was gone. But there were few—*very* few—who had found they actually preferred Lok-iKol Tenebro. For the last three days the halls and corridors had been filled with smiling faces, Rab-iRab, the Tarkina's lady page, was practically dancing in her work, and altogether everything, Tel thought with satisfaction, was once again as it should be.

Today he was so happy that he wasn't really listening very hard to the conversations behind him. After the first few they were pretty much the same. The first House into the room had been Fen-oNef Penrado, no surprise there. His support for Tek-aKet Tarkin had been unwavering. The second *was* unexpected. It was Jor-iRoj Esmolo's daughter whom rumor had promised to Lok-iKol. Either the rumor had been false, or the Esmoloso was anxious that Tek-aKet believe it so. After that bit of excitement, the conversations had been boringly repetitive. If everyone was so glad to see Tek-aKet in what they all referred to as his "rightful place," how had it been so easy for Lok-iKol Tenebro to sit in it?

Tel stood straighter to attention and pricked up his ears. Old Fen-oNef was approaching the throne again, and since he'd already paid his respects, this meant that he had some other business with the Tarkin, business that might require the Tarkin's Runner.

"My lord Tarkin," the old man was saying. "I see there are no Jaldeans present this afternoon."

A little surprised, Tel glanced around the room. No, there weren't any of the recognizable dark brown robes. How had he missed that?

"They are saying, my lord, that the Jaldean Shrines are shut, and petitioners are being turned away."

"Is this so?" The Tarkin sounded tired. Tel hoped the audience would be over soon.

"My men tell me that one of the shrines has been broken open by discontented believers, and found empty, not a priest or acolyte in sight."

Tel carefully kept his face from showing his surprise. He knew that Lok-iKol had stopped supporting the New Believers as soon as his particular friend the priest Beslyn-Tor had become ill, but he hadn't been aware just how far the fortunes of the Jaldeans had fallen.

"My lord." Old Fen-oNef was still speaking. "If you would take the frank advice of an old ally, let me remind you what your father would have done in these circumstances." Fen-oNef waited for the Tarkin's nod before proceeding. Old family friend he might be, fool he was not. "Once or twice it seemed that the Houses had lost confidence in Nyl-aLyn Tarkin." Here the old man smiled, brushing back his long mustaches with the back of his hand, but Tel managed to keep his face straight. He knew that with his "once or twice" Fen-oNef referred to the near-rebellions that Tek-aKet's fierce father had suppressed. "At those times, you may remember," the old man continued, "your father held a Ceremony of Dedication, where each House reaffirmed its loyalty and support. Why not do the same? If nothing else, it is a marvelous excuse for a banquet."

At this Tel did smile, almost squirming at his post in excitement. He'd been too young to be a page when Tek-aKet became Tarkin, but a Dedication was almost as good as an Anointing.

"An excellent suggestion, Fen," Tek-aKet said, his hand straying up to his left cheek. Tel frowned. He'd seen that gesture once or twice already, and if the Tarkin's head still pained him, this audience should be cut short.

"It will take some organization, I know," Fen-oNef said. "But I'm sure Gan-eGan has left able assistants, and, if I may, I would advise this as soon as possible."

The Tarkin tapped his mouth with the first two fingers of his right hand as he considered this. "I agree," he said finally. "Preparations can begin immediately, but I would suggest the ceremony itself wait for the arrival of the Mesticha Stone. That should serve to quell any fears felt by the Jaldeans and appease their faction."

The Tarkin and the Penradoso went on speaking, but

their words were drowned by the buzzing in Tel's ears. The Mesticha Stone? Tel had almost forgotten about it, even though he himself had helped the Steward of Keys arrange with a representative of the Jaldeans for the Stone's arrival. One of the small rooms behind the throne had been designated as the artifact's resting place, though as yet no changes had been made.

But it had been Lok-iKol who had asked for these arrangements, not Tek-aKet. He risked a glance over his shoulder at the Tarkin. What did Tek-aKet know about this? *How* did he know?

It wasn't until after the evening meal that Telian-Han decided he would, after all, speak to someone about what he'd overheard.

❧❧❧

Mar looked up from her book when Rab-iRab Culebro led a younger, male page into the receiving room of the Tarkina's suite. She and Rab had become friends over the last few days, finding that they had oddly much in common, seeing that their backgrounds were so distinct. Rab was from the Tarkin's own House, and had grown up in a country Household, riding and roughhousing with her three older brothers, living the life that Mar had lost when the sickness had taken her parents. There was no snobbery about her, however, and Rab had been indignant when Mar had told her of the reception she'd had in House Tenebro.

"One of those Tenebro girls came to be a lady page with us last year," Rab had said. "Zelianora Tarkina gave her a three-month trial before sending her home. She won't tolerate any of that type here." Rab had welcomed her Tarkina back with laughter, and not a few tears, and had embraced Mar willingly, all the more so as her fellow senior page had left to be married some few weeks before the night of terror.

Of course, it didn't hurt that Rab had been much impressed by Mar's adventures. "It reminds me of the *Tale of Evanian the Carver*," she'd said. "I hope your life has every bit as good an ending."

It was the same excited but serious look that Rab-iRab was wearing now.

"Mar," she said, barely waiting for the door to close behind them. "Is the Tarkina still asleep?"

Zelianora had come back from the audience in the throne room exhausted, her emotional resources worn to thinness by all that had happened in the last half moon. Now that she was finally enjoying a deep and satisfying sleep, Mar was reluctant to wake her, and said so.

"This is Telian-Han," Rab said, indicating the younger boy. "He's one of the Tarkin's pages."

Mar smiled at the boy and he smiled back, though the frown that drew down the corners of his eyes did not go away. "Can your message wait until the Tarkina awakens?"

"It's not a message, Lady Mar," the boy said, clearing his throat as his voice croaked. "It's something that happened in the throne room this afternoon. Something that worried me."

"It won't seem like much," Rab said. "But it made me think of something you'd told me in your adventures. How the Wolfshead said that a scout's report should include everything, even the details that don't seem important because you can't tell what's important until you have *all* the details."

Mar looked from one young face to another. The boy was definitely frightened, and desperately hiding it. Rab's flushed cheeks showed her excitement, but her eyes were steady and serious. *These two lived here with Lok-iKol,* Mar reminded herself. *And with whatever Lok had become.* They'd been having their own adventures.

"Tell me," she said. "Maybe together we can decide what to do."

Mar could tell from the practiced way he told the story that Tel had given this a great deal of thought. What she couldn't see was why the boy was so frightened.

"The Mesticha Stone is an important artifact," she said. "And it would take time to prepare a Dedication Ceremony in any case, so why not wait for it?"

"It was the way he said it," Tel said. "It . . . I'd heard *him,* the other one, say it just about exactly the same way. The same tone in his voice, the same words. Even the part about 'appeasing the Jaldean faction.' Tek-aKet Tarkin never cared about appeasing Jaldeans," the boy said, his lip curling. "And even less so now, from what we've been told. It was as if I was hearing Lok-iKol speaking with the Tarkin's voice."

"Lok-iKol or something else. Mar fought to keep the sudden surge of fear from her face.

"What color are the Tarkin's eyes," she asked.

"Blue," said both pages in unison.

"And are they still blue? They don't seem green?"

The two pages looked at one another, looked back at Mar and shook their heads, confusion evident on their faces.

Mar was not reassured. "I don't think we'll go to the Tarkina with this," she said finally. "Not quite yet anyway." Gun had gone to the Library, and might not return tonight if he found something useful among the books and scrolls. That left only one person she could take this to. Mar rose to her feet and set down the book she'd been reading. "Let's find Dhulyn Wolfshead."

Dhulyn Wolfshead had turned the corner from the outer courtyard into the passage that led to the rooms she and Parno had been given close to the Tarkina's suite when she heard the unmistakable footsteps of her Partner behind her.

"I thought you were there for the rest of the day, challenging all comers," she said as he caught up with her.

His pipes bleated a mournful note as he tucked them closer under his elbow, freeing his other arm to slip around her waist as they continued down the corridor.

"Pah," he snorted, a feigned disgust wrinkling his lips. "As if there's any contest when the Tarkin's own Chanter gets involved. The woman does nothing all day but play. Small wonder she can best the rest of us."

"There, there, my soul," Dhulyn said, grinning. "There's plenty you can do better than she."

"As I hope to be proving to you in a few minutes," he said, squeezing her closer and brushing his lips against her cheek. Dhulyn hugged him closely in turn, sighing as the muscles in her neck and shoulders relaxed.

"How long do you think we'll stay?" she asked him.

"Well, at least let's get paid," he said. "Or do you find

you simply can't take the luxury of fires, feather beds, and regular baths a moment longer?"

Dhulyn smiled at the undercurrent of laughter in his voice. "It isn't that," she said. "And you know it."

Parno nodded without speaking, and held his tongue until they were at the door of their rooms. "We must stay and keep watch, in case there's reason. So you told me this morning, and I agreed. But there's something we should do," he said, "so as to be ready when the time for leaving comes."

"I believe we did that, too, this afternoon," she said, trying to make him laugh, "and unless I'm mistaken, we're about to do it again."

"Never you fear," he said, smiling and shaking his head. "We'll never go short, not so long as we're both alive, and I, at least, have breath enough for my pipes. But there is a place here where a Brother of ours fell. Let us visit it while we have the chance."

Dhulyn pressed her lips tightly together. "You are right, my heart. Bring your pipes, and I will fetch my sword."

Parno patted the bed with his free hand. "I didn't mean we should go right now."

This time Dhulyn laughed out loud. "Oh, yes, you did."

Dhulyn set the oil lamp down and crouched to touch the dark stain on the flagstones deep beneath the oldest tower of the Carnelian Dome. To her left was the Onyx Walk, to the right the long corridor stretching down to the old summer kitchen. She frowned and straightened once more, touching a similar dark stain on the wall. Her brow cleared. "This one," she said.

"Died on his feet," Parno said. "Good lad."

"So may we all," Dhulyn said, leaning her shoulder against the wall to one side of the bloodstain. "Tell me," she said, beginning the ritual, "how did you first know our Brother Hernyn Greystone the Shield?"

Parno made himself comfortable against the wall on the other side of the stain. "I knew him when he was only Hernyn Greystone," Parno began. "And he was a sorry sight when I first laid eyes on him, let me tell you . . ."

The exchange of story and anecdote that made up the

Mercenary's Last Farewell did not take very long, even though Dhulyn and Parno tried to remember everything they had seen Hernyn say or do.

"We stand now where our Brother stood at the last," Dhulyn said finally. "And we say farewell to Hernyn Greystone the Shield, who gave his life for ours. Farewell, Hernyn, we stood together in Battle, and we will stand together again in Death."

"In Battle and in Death," Parno said, lifting his pipes into position, and fitting the chanter to his lips. The melody that he played then was not traditional, but one of his own making, and Dhulyn thought that if he had played it in the guardroom, he might have beaten even the Tarkin's piper, in spite of all her practice.

When the final notes died away, they stood a moment or two longer in respect for the music, and their fallen Brother, before Dhulyn gave the bloodstained wall a final salute, touching her fingertips to the bloodstain, and then to her own forehead. Holding hands like children, they retraced their steps to the upper floors.

They had not yet reached the first staircase when Dhulyn hesitated between one step and the next, holding Parno back with a tug on his hand. He caught her eye, and nodded; he'd heard it, too.

"That was not the last dying away of the pipes' music," he whispered. "There's no echo so long as that."

"Speak again," Dhulyn called, her voice pitched carefully so as not to echo too much in the deserted stone passages. "Speak that we may find you. Do you need our help?"

Again there came the low moaning that had first caught at Dhulyn's ears. There was, indeed, something of the mournful notes of the pipes in the sound.

"This way," Parno said, as he turned to go back the way they came. They were not far on the other side of the narrower passage that led to the old kitchens when they found a series of rooms, roughly the size appropriate for storage, the bolts on the outside of the doors showing evidence of what had been stored there. The man making the sound was in the third room.

He cowered away from them, pushing himself with his

feet into the corner of the cell and covering his eyes against the brightness of the lamplight. It took a few minutes, along with some gentle words, for his eyes to adjust enough to allow Dhulyn to coax his hands away from his face.

"He hasn't been here long," Parno said, joining her after a quick look into a pail in the far corner of the cell. "But I'd say no one's been near him in a few days."

Dhulyn nodded, pulling her small emergency flask of water out of her belt pouch and holding it to the man's lips.

"Can you speak, Grandfather," she said as gently as she could.

The prisoner worked his lips, licking at them and swallowing. "Mercenary," was the word that finally found its way out of his mouth.

"That's right, sir," Parno said, squatting down next to the old man. "Can you tell us who you are?"

Suddenly the old man grabbed Dhulyn by the front of her vest, his gnarled fingers tangling in the bits of lace and ribbons. "Did you see him? Has he found you?"

"Who would that be, sir?" Parno said.

"The Sleeping God," the old man said, subsiding once more into his corner, one hand still clutching Dhulyn's vest.

They became aware that the torn and stained robes the old man was wearing had once been the dark brown of a Jaldean priest. Their eyes met over the prisoner's head.

"You've seen the Sleeping God?" Dhulyn asked, just as Parno said, "Does he have green eyes?"

"I thought he was, do you see? I thought he was. I thought I was helping him. Helping him to awaken because his time had come." The old man subsided. "I thought he *was* the God. At first. I thought I was touched by the God."

"Who are you?"

"Beslyn-Tor." He looked around, his eyes clearing. "Have I been sick? This is not my hermitage."

"Is he here now? The Sleeping God?"

"No, no, why don't you listen? I tried to tell everyone, but no one listened. I *thought* he was the God. I *thought* he was. I'd been collecting relics, you see. I found five, do you see, that's one more than Arcosa Shrine and the people will come to us, to *our* shrine, to Monachil. He spoke, and I thought it was the God." The old man repeated the phrase several times before putting his dirty index finger, with its cracked nail, to his lips, tapping them in the "shhh" sign, all the while his head trembling as if he had the palsy. "But no," he said finally, the words a mere whisper. "But no." He caught at Dhulyn again. "I welcomed him. I rejoiced!" He shook his head again, but this time like a man who just can't believe he could have been that stupid. "But he *isn't* the God. He fears the God. He *fears* the God, do you see?" He collapsed backward. "And then he left me."

"Where did he go?"

"To Lok-iKol. To Lok-iKol. Like this." And here the old man took Dhulyn's face tenderly in his hands, and focused his eyes on hers. "Like this. That's how it's done."

It took all of Dhulyn's force of will to take the old man's hands off her face gently, without breaking his wrists.

"That's how he does it, is it?" she asked.

The old man nodded again. "That's how. But he always came back. Before. He always came back. It's hard to be alone. Hard now." His eyes came abruptly into focus. "You be careful, young woman. He looks for a Mercenary. You be very careful." His voice dropped to a whisper. "Don't let him touch you, my daughter. He looks for a Mercenary. Be careful."

The focus faded once again from his eyes and the hand that clutched at Dhulyn's vest relaxed. She felt for and found a pulse under his jaw, but it was fitful. She glanced up at Parno, found him grim-faced.

"Can you carry him?" she said. "I don't think he'll last long anyway, but we can't leave him here."

"Take my pipes," Parno said. "Dhulyn," he added as she straightened to her feet and held out her hands for the instrument. "Do we understand him to mean . . . ?"

"I think we must," Dhulyn said, tucking the pipes under her left arm and picking up the lantern. "From what he's said, I think it means the Tarkin."

"Who should we tell?"

"That's a good question." Alkoryn was dead, she thought. And as little as she liked it, that might very well make her Senior Brother in Gotterang.

They left Beslyn-Tor to be made as comfortable as possible in the guards' infirmary room before looking for the

Tarkina. They were just entering the corridor that led to Zelianora's room when they heard three people behind them.

"Dhulyn Wolfshead? Lionsmane?" came a tentative but familiar voice. As she turned, Dhulyn did not trouble to suppress a sigh that was so short as to be almost a snort of annoyance. Mar was part of the Tarkina's household now; what could she possibly want from Dhulyn?

She raised her eyebrows as she turned and recognized the youngsters with Mar. One she knew as Rab-iRab, senior lady page to Zelianora Tarkina. Younger than Mar, but tall for her age, and with an air of having very recently learned how serious the world can be. The other was a page of the Tarkin's whom Dhulyn had now seen several times without learning his name. Dhulyn felt a heavy weight settle into her stomach. What would bring pages from the Tarkin's household looking for Mercenaries? She was very afraid that she knew.

"Wolfshead and Lionsmane,". Mar said. Dhulyn knew that look—half fear, half resolution—she'd seen it in Mar's face in the mountains. "May we speak with you in private?"

"We've business of our own to attend to, Lady Mar," Parno said. "Can this wait?"

Mar exchanged looks with the two pages. The young boy spoke up. "It's about the Tarkin," he said, eyes glittering.

"You're his page, aren't you?" Dhulyn asked him. "You know our names, what is yours?"

"I am Telian-Han, son of Debrion-Han of Culebro Holding." The boy had to clear his throat halfway through, as his voice threatened to crack.

"You knew the usurper, Lok-iKol Tenebro? You were here?"

The boy nodded. "We both were."

"And you have something to tell us?"

Again the nod.

Parno raised his hand to his face, placing the tips of his index and middle fingers on his lips. Dhulyn saw and silently agreed. She wasn't the only one with a sense of disaster.

"Come with us," she said to the youngsters.

Twenty-two

PARNO LEANED FORWARD in his chair, elbows on his knees, hands lightly clasped. *Demons and perverts.* He looked from one white-faced page to the other, and fixed a look of confident encouragement on his face. Behind him, Dhulyn leaned against the window frame, arms folded across her chest, ankles crossed, eyes almost closed. They'd taken the youngsters straight to their own quarters where the first thing he'd done was shut the windows—though it was very unlikely that anyone could overhear them, here on the fifth floor. Their three rooms here in Zelianora Tarkina's tower made up a small suite, with this outer, double-windowed room furnished as a sitting room with a long upholstered settee, a round table covered with a weighted cloth, thick patterned carpets on the dark oak floor, and heavy armchairs made soft with bright cushions.

Rab-iRab and Telian-Han, though they would ordinarily bear no resemblance to each other, now wore identical pale, wide-eyed looks. Parno and Dhulyn had listened to Telian's story without commenting, yet somehow, in the repetition of it, both young pages had become aware of the gravity of their suspicions.

"Lady Mar," Dhulyn said, her eyes still resting on the face of the young Telian-Han. "Would you be so kind as to find Zelianora Tarkina and bring her here?"

"Dhulyn," Parno began.

"We are still, technically, in her employ." Dhulyn turned to Mar. "Come straight back to us here, Lady, if you would be so good. I need hardly tell you, speak to no one of this, not even the Tarkina herself, until you are both safely in this room. Until we are sure, any and all of us may be in danger."

Or may be the danger, Parno thought.

"The children?" Rab-iRab said. Parno's jaw tightened as he exchanged a look with Dhulyn. Just when they were thinking things could not be any worse.

"They should both be asleep," Mar said, getting to her feet. She spoke more than half to herself. "Denobea will be with them." She looked up at Parno, glanced at Dhulyn. "They've seen very little of their father these last few days."

"Perhaps you could make sure of their whereabouts somehow, my Dove, without alarming the Tarkina."

It was a shock to see what a change two small words could bring to a young woman's face. Suddenly there was a brightness in Mar's eyes, and she left the room with a light step and more heart for her errand than she had when she'd entered it. Parno shook his head, smiling. Leave it to Dhulyn to know the right thing to say, and the right moment to say it. What a Schooler she would make, if they lived so long.

As the door closed behind Mar, Parno turned to the two pages, sitting close together on the settee, holding hands.

"Would you youngsters be so kind as to wait in the inner room while my Partner and I consult?" The two pages exchanged identical worried glances. "You'll be safest there," Parno continued, "and no one will be able to ask you any questions you'd rather not answer."

This reassured them, and they both stood. "Come, Tel," Rab-iRab said as they walked toward the door Dhulyn held open for them. "You look as though you could lie down." Dhulyn gently closed the door behind them.

"What are we going to tell the Tarkina?" Parno said.

"I think we'll rather ask her if she's seen anything unusual, anything that has given her pause." Dhulyn rubbed her eyes. "Are we crackbrained? Do we make too much from the maunderings of a half-crazed old man and the nerves of a young page who has seen perhaps too much in the last half moon?"

"A half-crazed old man who knew the Shadow well, and a young page who knew his Tarkin. Add to that the fact that we've not spent time in the Tarkin's presence since the restoration, when he would hardly be parted from us before." Parno shrugged. "Evidence enough at the least for us to investigate further."

Dhulyn tapped the table lightly with the side of her right fist. "Think what we risk if we don't learn the truth. I'd rather beg pardon if I'm wrong, and take what punishment might be awarded me, than be sorry I never tried to be sure." Her eyebrows drew down in a frown. "Where's Gundaron, where's the Scholar? It's not like Mar not to go to him first."

"Set your mind at ease," Parno said. "He went off this morning to the Library and hasn't returned; likely intends to spend the night there. He's been poring over all the old books he can find, looking for any mention of the Green-eyed Shadow."

"Send Corin Wintermoon to fetch him," Dhulyn said. "All things considered, whatever he's found so far, I'd like to have him here while we discuss this."

"And sending Corin has the added advantage that it will stop her flirting with the guards before she hurts one of them."

❧

Zella turned over on her couch and blinked herself awake. What was that sound? Sitting up at night with Tek had left her exhausted, and she must have dozed off without realizing it.

There it was again, a low thumping, as if—Zella shot to her feet, almost falling as she tripped on the shawl Denobea must have tucked around her legs. The sound was coming from her own bedroom, where Tek was yet again lying down. Pushing open the door, she ran into the room and found her husband by the side of the bed on his hands and knees, crawling toward the door. He shrank back as she entered, blinking at her in the dim light that followed her through the doorway.

"Zella?"

"Tek, what's happened?" She ran forward to help him to his feet. He hunched his shoulders, cowering from her and narrowing his eyes to a squint.

"Zella?" His voice stronger now, but there was a note of

query in it that made her pause, her hands still outstretched, ready to raise him to his feet. Before she could help him, he clutched at her forearm with such force that her sleeve tore.

"Tek—" she gasped. "You're hurting me."

"Zella," he shook her. "Where's Dhulyn Wolfshead? Bring her, get her now." The fierce focus died out of his face, the painful grip on her arm relaxed as he collapsed onto the floor.

❈❈❈

Gundaron pushed his chair back from the table and rubbed his eyes with the heels of his hands. *Here since daybreak,* he thought, *and all I have to show for it is headache and eye-strain.* He'd found the first scroll he was looking for—an early history of the Marked in the last days of the Caids—but not the equally important commentary written by the Scholar Holderon. Without it, all he could do was try his best to duplicate the other man's work. And somehow he felt he didn't have that much time.

The Index of Materials told him this Library did indeed have a copy of Holderon's *Commentaries,* but no one could find it on the shelves. Yet Gun was certain he'd seen the scroll himself.

The history covered a period about which there were more legends known than facts, the early rise of the Marked, before they had formed into Guilds, and, interesting but not so significant for his present purpose, it had a section on the Sleeping God as well. But it was Holderon's interpretation of this piece of ancient learning—if Gun remembered what he'd read correctly—that the Mercenary Brotherhood, the Jaldean Priesthood, the Marked, and even the Scholars themselves all appeared at the same time—just after the fall of the civilization that was now called the Caids. If Holderon was right, Gun thought, if there was a connection of some kind between the disparate groups, surely that could be a starting point, a guide for them to—

The sound of footsteps made him look up, and the sight of Karlyn-Tan heading toward him brought him to his feet. He found his mouth dry and tried to swallow, brushing down his tunic with trembling hands, conscious of being once more in Scholar's dress. Logic told him he had no reason to fear the former Steward of Walls, but he found he still wasn't really comfortable with anyone but Mar.

"Karlyn-Tan," he said. "I didn't think to see you still outside Tenebro House."

The older man smiled and shrugged one shoulder into the air as he propped his hip on the edge of the next carrel. "Nothing's made permanent, Gundaron. The Lord Dal-eDal is giving me time to think. I'm not altogether sure that I want my old post back. I was Walls for fifteen years, never thinking to come out."

"But now that you *are* out . . ."

Karlyn nodded. "Exactly. Now that I am out—I may be more useful outside the Walls, and, well, it's rare a Steward has a chance to rethink such a choice, and I'm using the opportunity."

His own heart being well awake now, the significance of certain looks and gestures suddenly dawned on Gun. "It wouldn't be Dhulyn Wolfshead who's making you rethink your choices?" Gun asked, made bold by Karlyn-Tan's friendly tone.

Karlyn-Tan laughed. "It might, though perhaps not in the way you're thinking."

Gun sat down again. "What brings you here?"

"Dal needed a message sent, and I felt like a walk. When they told me you were in here, it seemed like a gift from the Caids. There's a deal of scrolls and books left in your room at Tenebro House, Gundaron of Valdomar, and—what have I said?"

Gun stopped striking his forehead with the palm of his hand. "I was looking for a scroll and wondering why I couldn't find it and all the time it's probably sitting in my study at Tenebro."

Karlyn-Tan looked at Gun with such sympathy that Gun lowered his eyes. "You'd rather not think about Tenebro House, wouldn't you?" the man said. "Put it all behind you, as it were?"

It was Gun's turn to shrug.

"Your pardon, Scholar Gundaron." It was one of the youngster Scholars that Gun didn't know. "There's a Mercenary Brother at the gate. You're to come to the Dome."

Gun glanced at Karlyn-Tan.

The older man nodded. "I'll come with you."

⊱⊰

Running footsteps in the outer room warned them as the door was flung open, and Zelianora Tarkina, a white-faced Mar behind her, swept into the room. The sleeve of the Tarkina's dress was pulled loose from the shoulder seam, and her dark hair was escaping from her court veil.

"The Tarkina was on her way here," Mar said.

"Mar has told you, then?" Parno said, rising to his feet as Mar entered behind the older woman and shut the door. The young woman was shaking her head even as Zelianora spoke.

"Told me? Told me what? No." She looked wildly around the room before focusing her eyes on Dhulyn. "Dhulyn Wolfshead," Zelianora said, reaching out her hands, "Please come, Tek asks for you."

Dhulyn stood slowly. "What are you not saying?" Four days ago this request would not have brought the Tarkina herself. Four days ago Zelianora would have sent a servant.

The Tarkina hesitated, lips parted, before turning to glance at Mar. As she turned back, she faltered, as if her knees were failing her. Parno stepped forward and took the Tarkina's arm to steady her and led her to a chair, but let it go immediately as Zella gasped in pain. Dhulyn sprang up with a snort of disgust and pulled back the woman's sleeve, to reveal bruises darkening on her forearm.

"Zelianora," Dhulyn said, her voice sharp enough to shock the Tarkina to attention. "The Tarkin did this."

"No! Yes, but hear me out." The Tarkina waved Dhulyn away with impatient hands. "This is not important."

"We are listening, Zelianora Tarkina," Parno said.

"I don't know that I can make you understand." She raised her hands to her head as if she would cover her ears. "He is terrified. I have never seen anyone so afraid." She looked directly at Dhulyn. "And yet . . ."

Dhulyn took Zelianora's hands and led her to a seat. "And yet?"

"He is himself in a way he has not been these past few days. Since the blow to his head, he's been like a man suffering from an illness. Now it is as though a fever has broken and—he is himself again. He is Tek. Do you understand?"

"Before this," Dhulyn said, indicating the bruised arm. "Did he stare into your eyes? Touch you in any way that made you feel dizzy? Ill? Are there gaps in your memories?"

"No, indeed," Zelianora said. "Nothing like that. Since his illness Tek . . . he has *not* touched me," she said, as if realizing it for the first time. "But he's been ill, I thought nothing of it."

"If I might interrupt," Parno's voice was vibrant with urgency. "I rejoice that Zelianora Tarkina is well, but she tells us that the Tarkin is more like himself than he's seemed in days. In the light of what we were discussing, perhaps we should go and see for ourselves."

❈

"Don't let him touch you," Parno said, as he helped Dhulyn lift her sword belts over her head.

"If you'd rather do it yourself . . ." Dhulyn pulled her multicolored vest back into place. She needed no help to remove harness or weapons—she could have done it by herself, in the dark, and one-handed—but Parno had needed the reassurance that helping her disarm, that touching her, would bring. *And he's not the only one.*

"We've been through that," he reminded her. "Do you want me to say it again?"

Dhulyn smiled, patting him on the shoulder. Once they had explained their fears to a white-faced but resolute Tarkina, Parno had made everyone see that they had to send someone in to speak to Tek-aKet. And once they'd persuaded Zelianora Tarkina that it should not be her, he'd insisted that Dhulyn was the only logical choice. "There's no one faster," he'd said. Out loud, too, where everyone could hear it, even if he didn't want to repeat it now for her ears only. "If it becomes necessary to disable the Tarkin without permanent harm," he'd said. "Dhulyn is the only one who can do it."

Dhulyn handed Parno the long dagger from her left boot. She still had her holdouts hidden, but there were no more weapons that someone else could reach easily. They both knew that this was precaution only. So far as they knew, Tek-aKet Tarkin—if this *was* Tek-aKet Tarkin—had no reason to harm her. But they both knew of many people killed by those with no known reason to harm them.

Parno, her dagger still in his left hand, brushed something off her shoulder with his right. "Do you know what you're going to do?"

"Come out alive, and in my right mind," she said, giving him the smile she saved only for him. The smile that had no wolf in it.

He laughed without making a sound and stepped back from her.

"In Battle," he said, touching his fingers to his lips.

"Or in Death."

Dhulyn slid through the barely opened door and waited, listening, while Parno pulled it shut and latched it behind her. She could see at once that things were not as Zelianora Tarkina had left them. Dhulyn had expected the room to be dark, the windows shuttered. The Tarkina had left her husband tucked up in the bed, shivering and semiconscious. This man was standing at the window, shades thrown open to the early evening.

"You sent for me, Lord Tarkin?"

"I sent for you." The tone was ambiguous enough that Dhulyn could not be sure whether it was question or statement. The man turned to face her.

She took a step toward him, and then another. With the light behind him, his face was shadowed and she couldn't be sure . . . She took another step. And stopped, repressing a shiver as the hair on her arms and the back of her neck stood up. There was no doubt. The man's eyes were green. Whatever Zelianora thought she had seen, it was gone.

"What is it, then?" she asked.

"You take a very informal tone with your Tarkin."

"But you're not the Tarkin, are you? Mine or anyone else's." she said, strolling casually closer, fingers reaching automatically to tap the place on her hip where her sword hilt should rest. Could she keep him from hearing the noises in the anteroom?

"What am I, then?"

Dhulyn frowned. She would almost swear the question was asked in earnest. "You best know that yourself." She moved still farther into the room, beginning to circle around to the right, keeping his attention on her, and away from the door.

"Will you tell me something? I am curious." He turned to follow her, stepping away from the window and into the room.

"You are capable of curiosity, then?"

"I am capable of worlds."

Dhulyn wanted to snort in disbelief, but found she couldn't. "Ask."

"How was it known, so quickly, that Tek-aKet was not here? With the others, with Beslyn-Tor, with Lok-iKol, no one knew."

A sensible question. How did you catch me? A very sensible question. Would the Green Shadow understand the answer?

"They had no one close enough," she told him. "No one who knew them well enough to see a change."

"No one who could see *me*?"

"No one who could see you," she agreed. It didn't know about Dal, then, or Gun; nor was she about to tell him. She stepped around a long padded bench, still moving toward him. They were only a few spans apart, almost close enough, and she was eyeing the precise spot on his neck where her blow should land.

"What do you want?" she asked. Keep him talking, keep his attention from what she planned.

"Nothing."

"Your actions say otherwise. Have we no common ground? Can we not negotiate?"

The thing that possessed Tek-aKet closed its eyes. "Common ground." Its voice, Tek's and yet not Tek's, trembled with some unnameable emotion. "Too much shape." The eyes opened, bright as gemstones. "All things here have shape. Everything. Shapes. Edges. Start, stop. Here, even *I* have shape. Even I. Can you send me back, Seer? Can you or any of your kind do more than force me to a different shape? You ask me what I want. Give me nothing." The right hand rose up and, fingers curled, tapped it on the chest. "Make this nothing. *I want NOTHING.*"

She blinked, and shifted her gaze. The far end of the bench, the end closest to the Shadow . . . *shimmered* like the air above a fire. It was not there, then it was. She blinked again and shook her head. A fog grew out of nowhere and swallowed the bench, and the Tarkina's room, and the world, leaving a curious emptiness. A *NOT.*

Dhulyn stopped walking. A corridor formed around her and dissolved as she stepped forward onto a beach . . . the Tarkina's bedroom again with the Green Shadow who inhabited the Tarkin looking at her . . . the hold of a ship . . . a window, a mirror—no, a window, the night sky cut and a green fog spilling down. The corridor again with the fog, a cloud like hot dust eating the air, consuming all that lay before it, making *NOT.*

Advancing toward her.

This was death coming. Now. Death was *now.* No battlefield. No sword in her hand. No hot rush of blood, heart pounding in her ears. A slow dissolve, the world like crystals of ice slowly melting and becoming not water, but nothing, nothing at all.

NOT. . . .

Why had she never Seen this? Never *this* Vision?

The world changed again. Not a Sight. A memory. A dark-skinned man, his teeth white in the darkness of the hold as he smiled at her where she stood over the corpse of the careless slaver, that same slaver's sword in her hand. "Come with me," the smiling dark-skinned man had said, "and I'll teach you to use that thing." Suddenly that sword was once again in her hand, the memory sword, her first sword, that Dorian the Black had let her keep, and taught her how to use. Sharp, clear, its edges well-defined and solid. She brought the sword up in a salute, and then brought it down and up again, in the sweep she would use to clear space before her when she was being crowded. The blade passed through the stones of the corridor before the dissolve could reach her, cutting them cleanly and leaving a sharp, distinct edge. A gap like a firebreak.

The fog was on the other side, and, now that she was

focused, now that she was armed, she could see the two spots of green that were the eyes. She smiled, lifted her left hand and made a beckoning motion.

She was back in the Tarkina's bedroom. Back with the Green-eyed Shadow before her. But this time she knew what to do. Her breathing steadied, and she fell into the first position of the Wading Crane *Shora*.

Focus. Like light through a lens. Sharper. Cast out all noise, all smells. See only the strike. When you strike, with blade or with hand, with stave or with elbow, you strike *through*, not at. The blow does not stop at the target, but goes through. See nothing but the target. See only the strike.

SEE the Strike.
SEE the Fall.

⊱⊰

Parno spit out the piece of nail he'd chewed off his thumb. Strain his hearing as he might, no sound came from inside the room. He'd thought he could hear some conversation at first, if he hadn't imagined it. After all, this was the Tarkina's bedroom, the walls and door were practically sound-proof—

Was that a thump? He shook his head. He didn't care what he'd agreed to, he was going in. He drew his sword, unlatched the door, grabbed up Dhulyn's sword in his free hand, and kicked the door open.

Dhulyn was dragging Tek-aKet's unconscious body toward the bed. One of the clothes presses was open and a number of silk scarves had been pulled out, their colors spilling over the thick rugs.

Parno frowned, blinking. For an instant the far end of the padded bench that stood between him and Dhulyn had looked somehow melted and blackened. Then it had appeared whole again. He stepped forward to examine it more closely and found that his initial assessment had, after all, been correct. The end of the bench was melted and fused like glass, as was a large section of carpet and floor under it.

"Since you're here, you can help me tie him up."

Parno looked around. "It was the Shadow?"

Dhulyn gave him a look that would turn wine into vinegar, and Parno felt his muscles unknot, felt the grin spread across his face. Only the real Dhulyn could look at him like that. He sheathed his sword, tossed hers on the undamaged end of the bench and grasped the Tarkin's wrists.

"On the bed, I thought," Dhulyn said. "We'll have to keep him comfortable, and he'll have less leverage lying down."

"Facedown?"

"And feed him how?"

Parno shrugged again. The fact was that Dhulyn had far more experience with keeping prisoners—or being kept prisoner, than he had himself.

"What if Tek, the Tarkin I mean, comes back to his senses?"

Dhulyn pulled a final silk scarf around the unconscious man's head and secured it as a blindfold over the eyes.

"Always supposing that's possible, that Zelianora actually did speak to her husband, and not the Shadow." Now it was Dhulyn's turn to shrug. "We'll explain to him why he's tied up." She walked back over to the damaged section of the floor. "Does this look at all familiar to you?"

Parno squatted beside her. "How do you mean?

"Does it not remind you, in a small way, of the Dead Lands?"

Parno pursed his lips in a silent whistle.

After checking the ties one last time—better careful than cursing, is what Dhulyn always said—they came out into the anteroom to find Gun and Karlyn-Tan waiting for them. The former Steward was wearing a politician's face, telling nothing, but the young Scholar had his lower lip between his teeth.

"What now?" Dhulyn asked. Parno smiled. Someone was going to regret creating that edge of exasperated impatience in her voice.

"It's Beslyn-Tor," Gun said, shooting a glance at Karlyn and waiting for his nod to continue. "He's left. Just got up and walked out."

"What do you mean 'walked out?'" Parno asked. When he'd seen the old Jaldean priest that morning, it was all the man could do to find a chair with his backside. "Who'd he go with?"

"No one," Karlyn said. "It seems he simply walked away. The guard at the gate included it in his usual report at the transfer of shift, but had no orders to stop him or to report it earlier."

"Of course he didn't." Parno could have kicked himself. "The man could barely walk to the door unaided. Who thought he could walk out the gate?" He turned to Dhulyn. "Was he shamming all along?"

She was shaking her head, slowly, her eyes looking at but not seeing the tables and chairs of the Tarkina's anteroom.

"When did this happen?"

"Just before we arrived. Perhaps ten minutes ago, a little more."

"What color were his eyes?" she asked. Parno looked to Karlyn, but the man was shaking his head. That was a detail no one would have thought to check.

The silence lifted Dhulyn's eyes to meet Parno's.

"We're going to have to leave him tied up," she said, indicating the inner room with her chin. "No matter who he is."

Twenty-three

DHULYN LEANED AGAINST the wall behind Zelianora Tarkina, watching the familiar faces around the table. She and Parno could have had seats at the table as well—and maybe Parno would have liked that, she thought, looking sideways at him out of the corner of her eye—but she felt more comfortable on her feet, where she could watch everyone and move quickly, should it prove to be necessary.

They were in the private council chamber in the north tower of the Carnelian Dome. Zelianora Tarkina sat at one end of the oval table, to the right of Bet-oTeb, present as the official representative of her absent father. The Tarkina was pale, and there were lines around her lips that had not been there last night. In no other way did she show the fear and worry that she must have been feeling. The Tarkinto-be was a copy of her mother, down to the rigidly straight back and the frown line between the eyebrows. On BetoTeb's left was Dal-eDal, Tenebroso in all but name, with Karlyn-Tan leaning against the wall behind him, which put the former Steward directly across from Dhulyn herself. To Dal's left was Cullen of Langeron, and the Racha bird Disha paced back and forth upon the table itself, pausing every now and then, turning her head to watch the person speaking.

And to round out the circle of those who knew about the Green Shadow, Gundaron and Mar-eMar sat together at the end of the table farthest from the Tarkina and BetoTeb. Dhulyn narrowed her eyes. They were never far from one another, those two, and Dhulyn wasn't at all sure how she felt about that. She told herself it was none of her business. Mar had made herself very useful to Zelianora and her pages, and whatever had brought her to Gotterang in the first place, she now seemed well placed in the Tarkin's court. Gundaron had pledged himself to the Tarkina also, Dhulyn had heard. All she knew for certain was that the boy was looking thinner than was good for him. He also looked older, more thoughtful, as well he might. But he still had trouble meeting people's eyes.

"The Shadow has left the Tarkin, then?" Dal was saying. "Can he tell us anything?"

Zelianora Tarkina had been murmuring something to her daughter, but at this question she raised her head and looked around the table, taking in each face in turn. Now Dhulyn could see the exhaustion in the woman's eyes, held at bay by the firmness of her mouth. The Tarkina shook her head.

"He is Tek-aKet, of that I'm certain, and Dhulyn Wolfshead agrees," she said. "But his mind still wanders."

Dhulyn cleared her throat. "It was the same with Beslyn-Tor. He could not focus for more than a few moments at a time." The Tarkin had been moved to his own chamber, where Corin Wintermoon stood guard beside the bed. She'd been warned not to untie the Tarkin, no matter what was said, or who requested it—and to be especially suspicious if the man became lucid. Now that they knew the Shadow could revisit former hosts, they could not afford to leave Tek-aKet unbound. Though, Dhulyn admitted to herself, it was all too likely the creature could destroy any restraints holding it, if it didn't mind the cost to the body housing it.

"The Tarkin will know things about the Shadow," she continued, turning to Zelianora and Bet-oTeb. "Just like the Jaldean did. Things that could help us. We must question him, even if his mind is wandering." She could understand that their first concern would be for the father, the husband, the leader of Imrion. But they hadn't seen the Green Shadow, or spoken to it. Hadn't see the *NOT* that it would make of their lives and their world, if they did not find it and destroy it.

Bet-oTeb spoke up, her clear child's voice startling. "Can't we—could we not find a Healer? Somewhere? I have heard that there are Marked among the Cloud People. Would they be willing to help us?"

Dhulyn was pleased that the child who was to be the next Tarkin spoke of willingness to help, rather than of forcing. That boded well for everyone's future, if they all came out of this alive, and in their right minds.

"There is a Healer in the Trevel settlement," Cullen said. Disha shrugged her wings and walked up the table toward him in her peculiar rocking gait. "Disha says that if she leaves now, she can be back before nightfall, but the Healer, even if she's found quickly and is willing to come," he spread his hands. "It would take more than half a moon for someone to get here from the mountains."

"I would be very grateful if you would go," Bet-oTeb said, addressing the bird directly. Disha opened and closed her wings with a snap, hopped to Cullen's shoulder where she butted his cheek with her head as if she were a cat, and from there launched herself out the open window next to Dhulyn.

"I don't think we have half a moon," Dal said. "The Houses are already beginning to ask questions. If Tek is not able to take part in the Dedication Ceremony, they may very well ask for the Carnelian Throne to be set to the Ballot, and if that occurs, we must ask ourselves how likely it is that Bet will be chosen as Tarkin."

"And where will that leave us?" Bet-oTeb asked.

Dal shrugged. "At the moment we are holding secure. As Dhulyn Wolfshead suggested, we've let rumors be spread that Beslyn-Tor is stricken with an illness that spreads on the touch. People are asked to report if they've seen him, without trying to capture him themselves. I think a good many people will be happy to do just that, especially since the rumor carries word of a reward."

"There are still those among the New Believers who may hide him," Karlyn-Tan said.

"That's so," agreed Dal. "But most of the Houses are with us—either really with us, or holding off to see what happens next, depending on their spirit. The conservative faction of the Jaldeans, the Old Believers, are also making overtures toward the Tarkin, now that it's obvious the New Believers have lost so much of their former power. But if Tek-aKet does not regain his health, and a Ballot is demanded . . ." Dal lifted his shoulders and spread his hands. He turned his eyes toward Parno, leaning against the wall within touching distance of Dhulyn.

"We would lose our leverage, our ability to act freely against the Shadow," Parno said. "We stand in a position of strength only so long as we can be seen as acting on the Tarkin's orders. Without him, we have no authority."

Dhulyn looked between the two men. If it was left to Dal, she realized, there would always be a connection between them, no matter what Parno thought.

"He must be made well again," Zelianora said. "There must be a way."

"Gundaron of Valdomar," Dhulyn said, turning to look down the length of the table. "Have your researches told you anything that could help us?"

The boy glanced quickly at Mar before he spoke. "I'm afraid I know of nothing that might help the Tarkin," he said. His voice, though quiet, was trained for the lecture hall, clear and carrying. "At least—there are several indications that this is not the first time we've been visited by this Shadow. The very oldest texts, those which date to the times of the Caids—we always thought they were legends really, myths, but many of them speak of a time of great peril, a time when the world itself was in grave danger. Texts speak of floods and earthquakes, but there's one of the Eshcaidath scrolls—" Here the boy sat up straighter, gaining poise and confidence from the familiarity of reporting on his researches, and looked at Dhulyn, waiting for her nod of recognition before he continued. "It speaks of an 'undoing', a kind of dissolving, of large areas of land where there seemed to be no land, and where beasts and men died blue, as if their breathing had stopped."

Yes, Dhulyn thought, her heart pounding. That's what the Shadow had meant, when it spoke of making nothing. What it had done so casually to the small bench in the Tarkina's room, it wished to do to the whole world.

Cullen leaned forward, drawing in his attention from the

distance where Dhulyn was sure he followed his Racha's flight.

"The Dead Lands," he said. Dhulyn found she was nodding along with the Scholar.

"But the peril was overcome?" Zelianora said.

"It was. The people called upon the Sleeping God, and the God awoke. When the peril was banished, the God slept again, or departed, or, well—again the texts differ."

"But have the same essential meaning." Dhulyn shifted her weight to her left leg. "Beslyn-Tor told us. The Green Shadow fears the God."

"The New Believers said," Bet-oTeb said, her girl's light voice trembling, "that we are the dream of the God, and if he awakens, the world will be destroyed."

Gundaron shook his head, his lips pressed together. "There's just no basis for that idea in any text, book, or scroll. And the Old Believers among the Jaldeans have always denied it. The ancient stories say that the God awakened to destroy this great evil, this peril. So the God *was* awake, do you understand? It destroyed the peril and then . . ."

"Fell asleep again?" Parno's voice was a soft rumble.

Gundaron shrugged, and nodded.

"Are we in any doubt that this is the same peril?" Karlyn-Tan asked.

"Given the use it has made of the New Believers, and its insistence that the Sleeping God *not* be awakened, I think not," Dhulyn said.

"How do *we* awaken the God?" Strangely, it was Bet-oTeb who voiced the question in everyone's mind, as if, childlike, she was not afraid to ask.

Gundaron licked his lips, glanced again at Mar, and seemed to draw strength from her.

"The stories don't say how," he said. "Just that the call went out into the world, and the Sleeping God awoke and came."

"How can they not say?" Zelianora massaged her temples with her fingertips.

"It's not unusual," Dhulyn said. "It's the reason there are so many commentaries on the old books. The writers take a certain knowledge for granted, they assume a shared understanding. They say 'the enemy,' without naming or describing the foe—for them, there can be only one enemy, and description is unnecessary."

"But how could this be?" Dal slapped the tabletop with his hand.

Parno shrugged. "When you tell someone how to catch fish, do you tell them what a fish is? What it looks like? Of course not, everyone knows what a fish is. But when we were in the deserts of Mondothir, we had to draw pictures of fish in the sands, for some of the tribes there had never seen one. These texts, they would be like that."

"So Scholars try to understand fishing, without ever having seen a fish?"

"Something like that, yes."

"We must remember," Gun said. "What we have in our Libraries of the times of the Caids are mere scraps of their writings and knowledge. In his *Commentaries,* Holderon speculates that by the time the Shadow was finally defeated, so much of the land had been laid waste, blighted by its presence, that the rule of law collapsed. There followed a long period—no one knows how long, really, but it must have been generations, not years—before the books were gathered again, and learning reestablished. It was then that the first Jaldean Shrines, the Scholars' Libraries and the Mercenary Schools were founded, then that the Marked were first gathered into Guilds."

"And if the method of calling the Sleeping God is in one of these lost texts?" A silence followed Zelianora's words.

"Excuse me," Mar said, blushing as everyone in the room turned their eyes to her. "But surely calling the Sleeping God must have something to do with the Marked?" Her voice faltered as she took in the faces of those staring at her. "Mustn't it? The Shadow has been gathering and destroying the Marked for months, maybe years. And Tek-aKet, when Dhulyn Wolfshead—I mean, the Shadow tried to destroy her as well."

"Wonderful," Parno growled. "And the only trained Marks more than half a moon away."

"Cullen?"

The Cloudman was already on his feet and heading for

the door. "Let me go to a rooftop. Sometimes I can reach over greater distances if I have greater height."

"Dhulyn Wolfshead." Zelianora Tarkina spoke into the silence that followed Cullen's departure. "Before I return to Tek, I must ask. I have told myself time and again that I will not, but you have saved him twice now. Have you Seen anything?" The Tarkina rubbed her forehead with a hand that trembled. "I'm sorry. I know you would have said."

"I have Seen nothing new for days," Dhulyn said. "And what I have Seen—" she shook her head, frustration rising yet again. By force of will she kept herself from glancing down the table at Mar and Gundaron. "Without a context, the things I *have* Seen mean nothing. I do not even always recognize the people I See. Are my Sights important to our dilemma? How can I know?"

Zelianora bit her lip, then nodded her head. She patted her daughter's arm and stood.

"Send for me if there is any change," Dhulyn said to her. "And, Tarkina, don't release him, no matter what he says or does."

The face that turned toward her at these words was not the face of the loving wife, but the face of a Queen's sister, and a future Tarkin's mother. "No fear," that regal face said. "I will not."

Dhulyn leaned back against the wall as the discussion went on among Dal-eDal, Gundaron, and Parno. Her Partner pulled out Zelianora's chair and sat down. She had nothing more to contribute, they were only rechewing the same mouthful of overcooked stew. She hadn't told the strict truth, but only Parno knew it. She *hadn't* Seen anything useful. She'd had several Visions more than once, but nothing that could help them. Mar-eMar in her silver gown. The unknown man—a mage? a king?—with his magic window. Was that a way to make the Shadow disperse? Would someone else call it into a different land? Gundaron sitting at a table, looking down on something. She repressed the urge to spit, mindful of Zelianora's clean parquet floor. *Now* there *was useful Sight.* A Scholar, seated, looking down at a tabletop. If the Marks were a creation of the Caids, as some of the stories Gundaron had been talking about alleged, she wished she had a few of those old-timers with her now. She would give them the benefit of her thoughts on the subject of the Sight.

A movement at the far end of the table caught her eye, Gundaron fidgeting with his pen case. If *her* Mark could not help them, and there was no Healer near enough to reach them quickly—would a different Mark be of more use?

It was past time this meeting was ended.

Gundaron hung back with Mar, letting the others leave the conference table before them. Karlyn-Tan hovered by the door, exchanging a soft murmur with Dhulyn Wolfshead and giving her a Mercenary's salute, touching his lips instead of his forehead, before following Dal-eDal out of the room. Gun was pushing himself to his feet, hands braced on the edge of the table, when Dhulyn shut the door behind Karlyn-Tan and turned back into the room. Mar licked her lips and looked from one Mercenary Brother to the other and back again. Gun merely sat down and lowered his face into his hands.

Dhulyn Wolfshead sighed heavily, turned a chair around, and sat astride it, resting her cheek on her hands.

"Gundaron—Sun and Moon are my witness, if I were going to kill you, I should have done it long before. Will you look at me, and listen? Mar, can you help us?"

The touch of Mar's hand on his shoulder was like a rope to a drowning man, firm, strong, life-giving. "Gun, *I've* told you Dhulyn Wolfshead wouldn't hurt you, and now *she's* told you. What more do you want than her own word?"

He looked from the Mercenary's face to Mar's and back again. Dhulyn Wolfshead raised one eyebrow and slowly blinked.

"What are you more afraid of," she said. "That I *will* kill you, or that I won't?"

Gundaron's lips parted, but no protest came out.

"Wolfshead!" It was Mar who spoke, a wrinkle forming between her deep blue eyes.

"Would you rather he *wasn't* bothered by what he's done?" the Wolfshead said, her voice calm as still water.

"But he's trying to help. The Tarkina and Bet-oTeb forgave him." Mar spoke her next words to Dhulyn Wolfshead, but she looked at him when she spoke. "I forgive him."

"He hasn't forgiven himself."

Heat burned through Gun's face and he lowered his eyes. Not that Dhulyn Wolfshead wasn't perfectly able to read him without looking into them. How did she do this? How did she know him so well?

"People are dead because of me," he said. "No amount of 'help' can bring them back."

"Many have died at our hands also," Parno Lionsmane's light voice fell softly into the air. "And many are also alive because of us. You still live; you have time to make the second true for yourself as well."

"You're not the first to do what he finds repulsive," the Wolfshead said. "And you won't be the last, blood knows, people being people. But you stopped the first chance you had, hold to that." She shook her head, blood-red braids shivering. "Words won't help you, at least not now. But I assure you, time will, if you let it." She looked at Mar before turning her steel-gray gaze back to him. "In the meantime, since you're sworn to help, I'd like to share a thought with you. I'm thinking that when something is lost, it's a Finder we need, not a Healer."

"You might have thought of this before the Racha bird was sent," Parno Lionsmane said, with just enough sarcasm in his tone to ease the tension in the air. "We've no more a Finder than we have a Healer."

"I think we do," Dhulyn Wolfshead said. "What do you think, Gundaron of Valdomar?"

"How—" Gun's throat closed. He would have said it was impossible, but he was sure he felt the blood drain from his face. He hadn't . . . How *could* she know? Had she Seen? He shot a quick glance at Mar, but she was shaking her head.

"I didn't—" Mar subsided when the Wolfshead raised her hand.

"No one told me," she said. "Except you, yourself, when I thought about what you have done. Found documents left carelessly aside for centuries. Found the secrets of tribes and cities lost for generations. When Marked were wanted, you Found them." Dhulyn Wolfshead paused, tapped her-self on the breastbone, causing tiny bells tied into the laces of her vest to chime. "When a Seer was wanted, you Found her. You told Parno where to find the Green Shadow when it was in Lok-iKol—ah, you thought we'd forgotten that. Even now, you know where to Find the information that we need."

"But that's research . . ." Gun let his protest trail away. He could not use that lie again—not even to himself.

The Mercenary was shaking her head. "You forget, I've been trained as a Scholar myself, though it was not the life for me. I know how research is done, and the kinds of an-swers it produces. And how swiftly. And how many import-ant answers in one person's lifetime. What you do is not research. Your books may have told you *what* to look for, they couldn't have told you *where*. You are Finding." When Gun still hesitated, the Wolfshead went on, her voice rough but warm. "Come now. The time for secrets is past."

"I've never . . ." Gun took a deep breath. He'd never con-vince anyone unless he could speak clearly. "I meant to tell you, after Lok-iKol, it's just . . . I've always kept it secret. I'm a Scholar. It's all I ever wanted. Even before the Jaldeans turned against the Marked, I never wanted to be . . ."

"Do you think I wanted it?" The Wolfshead was quiet but firm. "Untrained and half useless as it is? The world is not what we want, but what we *make*." She paused, as if that word had some special significance for her, before con-tinuing. "I wish your world *was* the Library carrels, the shelves of books, and the under-Scholars fetching ink and pens. Once I wished that for myself . . . I know how precious it is. But you are needed for more than that now. Wish for it or no, you will have to come out of your Library now and join the rest of us out here on the edge of the knife.

"You are a Finder, Scholar Gundaron. I am a Seer. Nei-ther of us wants this. But we are what we are."

Gundaron hung his head, aware as if from a distance that he was shaking it ever so slightly, wanting to deny her words. But Dhulyn Wolfshead was right. He lifted his head and found the Mercenary's cool gray eyes ready to meet his. Next to her, leaning his hip against the table's edge stood her Partner, Parno Lionsmane, the left corner of his mouth lifted. Beside them sat Mar, her blue eyes darker than usual with concern. When his eyes found hers, she smiled, her face lighting as if from within, and for an instant his heart stopped beating as the breath caught in his throat.

He would have to come out into the world. But he wouldn't be alone.

"What do you want me to do?" he said. He'd thought his voice would shake, but it rang out firm and true.

"The Tarkin's mind is lost. I would like you to Find it."

Gun's heart sank like a stone into a lake turning to ice. "The *Tarkin*? But how? I'm not *trained*. To Find something like that . . ."

"How did you Find the Green Shadow?"

Of course she would think of that. Library-trained, Dhulyn Wolfshead the Scholar. Her mind would work like his. Gun looked at them, Mar smiling, the two Mercenaries watching with guarded faces. He had to tell them, he realized. It would change everything, he would lose all the ground he'd gained, but he would have to tell. No more secrets. No more lies.

"I can Find the Green Shadow," he began. "Because it . . . it touched me." He looked up again into the silence. Mar, white-faced, lips trembling; Parno Lionsmane, the killing look back in his face, a knife in his hand. Dhulyn Wolfshead . . . Dhulyn Wolfshead calm and nodding?

"I'd lost some memory," Gun said. "There was time I couldn't account for, so I looked for it, and when I Found it . . ."

"You Found the Green Shadow. I Saw," the Wolfshead said. "When One-eye was questioning me. The Green Shadow was there, looking through your eyes." Parno Lionsmane made as if to move forward, but stilled at the Wolfshead's raised hand.

"But it only looked through my eyes, I swear it! It never lived in me as it did Lok-iKol." Relief at having finally told them warred with fear that they would not believe him.

"And when it comes back?" Lionsmane's voice was a snarl.

"It can't."

"How can you be sure? Convince us." Dhulyn Wolfshead spoke with the voice of command.

How to make them understand? "*It's* not Marked. I've hidden myself. *It* can't Find *me*."

"Dhulyn, we can't be sure," Parno Lionsmane said.

But the Mercenary woman was nodding. "Yes, we can. He is probably the one person we *can* be sure of. Who better to hide, than the one who Finds?" She looked up at her Partner and took hold of his sleeve. "The boy's right. It was not the same. I Saw it in him, and I Saw it in Tek-aKet, and it was not the same." She frowned and then looked at Gun once more. "Still, the Green Shadow has touched both you and Tek-aKet. Can you use that link somehow to Find the Tarkin?"

Could he? Did he dare? He looked at Mar's face, calm now, but wary. If he didn't try, would she ever smile at him again?

"I'll need Mar's bowl."

"Now, Scholar Gundaron," Dhulyn Wolfshead said, stepping back from the scrying bowl and setting the empty water pitcher on the little desk under the window. Gundaron took his seat at the small round table, set his hands flat beside the bowl, and looked down.

"I have Seen this," Dhulyn Wolfshead said, her hand on her Partner's arm.

Gun took a couple of deep breaths and focused on the water. He'd found Tek-aKet before, but that was just . . . the water shimmered, and the image broke. Gun steadied his breathing and tried again.

Parno Lionsmane sighed and Gun jumped in his chair.

"I'm sorry," the Mercenary began, but Gun held up his hand.

"It doesn't matter," he said. "All I'm getting is the Tarkin in his room."

Mar put her hands on his shoulders. "Relax," she said. "Try again."

Gun blinked, his eyes suddenly threatening tears. He dragged in another breath and let it out slowly.

It's not water, it's a bright page of paper. What should he write there? The story of Tek-aKet. Suddenly he's back in the

Library. Of all the lines on the floor before him, he needs to choose one in particular. Dark red it should be, the color of carnelians. He frowns. It's there, but it's stained, as if someone spilled green ink on it and didn't clean it off fast enough. He shudders; the last thing he wants to do is follow anything green. He takes a deep breath, looks around him at the ghosts and shadows of other Scholars and steps out, following the red line. Concentrating on the red. He walks swiftly now, down the main aisle, shelves and scroll holders branching off to left and right. The place is enormous, the silence broken only by the sound of his bootheels on the wooden floor.

He turns a corner and the thread of color is gone. The floor is covered in a thin carpet. The shelving is darker, too thin to carry the weight of the countless tomes on it. He reaches out a tentative finger. It's cold, painted metal. He turns around. The shelves behind him are exactly like these. There is no sign of the Library he came from.

There is a red mark like a small square of paint on the spine of one of the books. Gundaron looks around. There are similar marks on other books as well. Clean red marks with no green stain. He sets off again. This is only a Library. There is nothing to be afraid of.

He walks faster, following the red-marked books as they lead him across a wider lane with a metal cart in it. The cart holds books with green marks on their spines and Gun averts his eyes as he crosses the aisle into the next wall of shelves. There's a man at a desk farther down, his elbows on the tabletop, his head down between his hands. Just a shadowy figure at first, but he comes clearer as Gun advances. Gun knows the man won't look up, that he's afraid to. Gun puts his hand on the man's shoulder, wondering whether he knows the book the man's reading. He can see the writing, but it's a language he doesn't know.

"My lord Tarkin," are the words that come out of his mouth. "Tek-aKet. You must come with me."

Twenty-four

"THERE IS A PRECEDENT for madness."

The next morning, Tek-aKet Tarkin's voice sounded even more gruff than usual, as if someone had been sanding his vocal cords with a metal rasp. Dhulyn frowned. *Or as if someone else has been using them.*

"Madness is not considered grounds for the Ballot. Tau-Nuat Tarkin was always restrained to prevent him from harming himself," Gun said from where he stood, shifting from foot to foot, near the door of the Tarkin's bedroom.

"True," Tek-aKet said. "And he's an ancestor of mine, as it happens, so neither Guard nor Houses will be too shocked if they see me chained to the throne." He lifted his hands the scant inches allowed by the silk ropes to illustrate his point.

It may have been a trick of the light, but Dhulyn could have sworn there was a smile hovering on the man's lips. When Gun had come out of his Finder's trance, they had all rushed immediately to the Tarkina, and they had found her, with tears in her eyes, already in Tek-aKet's room clutching his bound left hand in both of hers. Now, Zelianora still sat on the edge of the bed, across from where Dhulyn had dragged up the chair that had been standing closer to the window.

"Do you remember anything of the Shadow?" she asked.

Zelianora raised her face from where she'd laid it on Tek-aKet's hand. "Give him a chance to rest—" Her words died away as Tek-aKet tried to raise his hand.

"We may not have time, Zella. If it should come back . . ."

The Tarkina swallowed, and nodded her understanding. She reached up and smoothed back a lock of hair that had fallen into his face.

"Your pardon, Dhulyn Wolfshead. Pray proceed."

Dhulyn looked at where Parno leaned with his back against the door of the room. He raised his left eyebrow, and lifted both shoulders the merest fraction. She inclined her head to the same degree.

"Lord Tarkin?"

"The first I remember is the pain in my head. I'd banged it once as a child, falling from my pony, and I thought—" He cleared his throat, "I thought that somehow I was there again, or there still. Thank you." He raised his head to sip at the water cup the Tarkina held to his mouth. "I realized after some time had passed that I did not actually feel the pain." Tek-aKet frowned. "It was as if I stood to one side and *watched* it more than felt it." He turned to his wife. "I've had the same feeling when I've been fevered."

And there were drugs, too, Dhulyn thought, that gave you the same feeling of detachment.

"Suddenly I wasn't off to one side, but *inside*. Inside, looking out through my own eyes as if they belonged to someone else. Pushed to the back like a passenger in a carriage." The Tarkina swallowed, but he shook his head when Zelianora lifted the water cup. His voice dropped to a thread of sound. "More time passed, and—some of that time—I wasn't inside. I was . . . nowhere." He looked up. "It, the thing I was inside, is nowhere."

"NOT" Dhulyn said.

"What do you mean?" Gun took a step into the room.

"When I knocked it out, before I knocked it out. I saw it *changing* the room, and the space around itself, making it nothing." She looked over the boy's shoulder to Parno.

"The damaged part of the floor, in your bedroom, Zelianora," Parno said. "The end of the bench that looked melted."

"Like the Dead Lands." It was no question, but Dhulyn nodded to Gun just the same.

"It is not simple damage," she said. "He makes a nothing. No." She shook her head, the words not making sense even to her. "Not nothing, for that's the opposite of something, and therefore a thing in itself. Unmaking it, as if it never was."

"Yes," the Tarkin said dreamily, his eyes unfocused. "It unmakes, it returns the world to the never was."

"Lord Tarkin." Dhulyn tapped Tek-aKet sharply on the side of the face. "Do not drift away from us."

The Tarkin pressed his lips together and took a deep breath through his nose. "It's so old," he said. "It wants its home. It loathes the body, the . . . the *shape,* and would destroy it."

"Your body?" It was true the man looked older and worn, as though he'd been faded through too many washings.

The Tarkin nodded, but slowly, face contorted with the effort of making himself understood. "Yes, but also . . . the body of the world."

"And the Sleeping God?" Gun asked.

"It fears the Sleeping God. Hates and fears it. It was the Sleeping God who broke it. Into parts. It knew nothing of parts—do you know, I just realized that. That's the reason it hates the world and everything in it." Tek-aKet dropped his voice as if he were sharing a secret. "We're all made up of parts. Shapes within shapes."

Dhulyn looked at Parno, saw her own confusion mirrored in his face. Shape and edges. That's how *she'd* Seen it when she was close to the Green Shadow. What Tek-aKet saw as *parts.* But if what made up the world was strange to the Shadow—how could that be? Unless the Shadow was not of this world.

Then she Saw it. The mirror window that was the night sky. The sword cut that opened the doorway in the stars. The entrance of the mist. The entrance of something not of this world.

A Sight from the *past,* not the future. She'd realized with her Vision of the Finder's fire from Navra, and the circle of Espadryni women that the Sight was showing her the past as well as the future, but, fool that she was, she'd never thought to examine her other Visions. Parno's voice brought her back to the present moment. She would have to consider what the Vision of the doorway could tell her later.

"Does it know how the Sleeping God is called?" Parno was asking.

"It's ironic. It knows irony. Only the Marked can call the Sleeping God. But they've forgotten how. *He's* the only one left who knows. The Shadow."

"But he kills them anyway."

"Surely." The Tarkin nodded, his eyes still focused on his memory. "What if they remember?"

"Now we know," Parno said from the doorway.

The Tarkin licked his lips. Dhulyn leaned forward again with her cup of water. "You frightened it, Dhulyn Wolfshead. It knows what I know. When it rode Lok-iKol, it only suspected, but it knew you were a Seer as soon as it entered m—" He clamped his mouth shut as if against a scream. Dhulyn knew he was drawing upon the rags of his strength to be able to speak to them at all, to tell them what he must. Worse than any rape, the Green Shadow had been *inside* him, inside his mind. He had watched it wear his body, *use* it. Such a thing could do more than make a man mad—it could drive him to his own destruction.

"Enough, Lord Tarkin," she said. "Now you must rest."

"No." It was a command, no matter how faint the voice. "It had to wait to destroy you," Tek-aKet said finally, spittle forming at the corners of his mouth. "It had to wait until the effects of the blow to my head had worn off, and the body—my body, was strong again."

"Lucky it hadn't finished, then," she said.

"You were too fast for it. Then, when the Scholar found me, its attention was turned away; it had gone to look through someone else's eyes for a while."

They all look at each other. "Beslyn-Tor?"

Tek-aKet lifted his right hand as far as the silk bindings would let him and waved it from side to side. "Not then. It was—oh the blessed Caids, it was Far-eFar. Who else?" His hand clutched and Dhulyn grasped it, wincing at the sudden strength of his grip. "Hid-oHid the Steward of Keys and Korvolyn the guard. It can look through their eyes, and," his eyes locked on hers, "it can visit them."

"Parno!"

But her Partner was already on his way out the door.

"Wolfshead, he must rest now. He must." Zelianora rose

to her feet, ready to argue, but Dhulyn also stood. They had heard the meat of it. If the Tarkin regained his strength, there might be more he could tell them, but if they taxed the man too much now—She forced her lips to smile in what she hoped was reassurance. He looked as though he'd been ill of a wasting sickness for months. As she began to release his hand, however, it tightened once more on hers.

"Dhulyn Wolfshead," Tek-aKet said, his voice suddenly strong. "Promise me. If the Shadow returns, kill me. I lived too long in the never was. I can't go back. If it returns, kill me."

Dhulyn knew the right words to reassure him and opened her mouth to say them. Things were never so dark as you thought. He was not alone in the world. He could come back from anything but death. But she remembered her own sight of the *NOT* and the platitudes died unspoken.

"I am Dhulyn Wolfshead, called the Scholar. If the Green Shadow possesses you again, I will kill you."

"Gun's Found it once, why not have him Find it again?" Mar shook her head as Parno offered her a piece of roasted pheasant.

"What if all we'd manage was to chase it into someone else? Even if I find it again . . ." Gun looked at the food on his plate as if he couldn't imagine how it had arrived there. "We need to know how to destroy it." He picked up his knife and fork, but did nothing more.

"We need to awaken the Sleeping God," Dhulyn said. Once Parno had returned from securing the men—all men, she noticed, and wondered if it was significant—and setting Brothers to watch them, they'd brought the youngsters once more to their own rooms.

"We don't know how," Parno said.

"What *do* we know?" Dhulyn said. "Gundaron, an exercise for your scholarship, summarize what we know about the Green Shadow."

"We know it does not have innate shape or substance, and that it views these things as foreign and hateful. Therefore, it must originate in a world other than our own." Gundaron tilted his head to one side, as if examining his own thought, before nodding in satisfaction. He sat up straighter and began cutting his food.

Mar began to protest, but subsided when Dhulyn held up her hand. No time now to describe the links in the chain of theory.

"We know it destroys the Marked to prevent them—to prevent *us*," Gun amended with a nod at Dhulyn, "from calling the Sleeping God. Even though we don't remember how," he added, his voice turning thoughtful. "We know it wants the Mesticha Stone, though again, we don't know why."

"I have a theory," Dhulyn said, "but finish your list."

The corners of Gundaron's mouth turned down. "I think I *am* finished."

"We'd have done better to list the things we *don't* know," Parno said, throwing his own knife down in disgust.

"We may not have *that* much time," Dhulyn said. She looked over her companions. "I've not spent much of my life in Imrion," she said. "What does the Mesticha Stone look like?"

"Well," Mar said when it appeared no one else would speak. "Like all the Jaldean relics, it's believed to be a part of the Sleeping God."

"Like the bracelet with green stones that was in the Tarkin's treasure room?" Dhulyn picked a wing from the platter and tore it in two.

"It's green, all the relics are," Gundaron said. "But the Mesticha Stone is shaped like a hand carved from green stone. There's a treatise—the original's here in the Gotterang Library—that says there was a statue of the Sleeping God that shattered when the God last awoke, or *because* the God awoke, something like that. That's what these relics really are, just bits of the statue."

Dhulyn tossed down a bone. "Bits of a green statue that this Shadow absorbs into itself," she said. "Beslyn-Tor said when he collected five relics of the God together for the first time, the God appeared and spoke to him."

"Except he was mistaken," Parno said. "It wasn't the Sleeping God at all, it was this Green Shadow. And it made him keep on collecting the relics." Parno thought, his head to one side. "Pieces of itself, do you think?"

"But if it has no form," Mar said, "how can there be pieces of it?"

"Pieces of its first shape," Dhulyn said, remembering the Green Shadow's words to her. "Nothing exists in this world without form, so it must have taken a shape—been *forced* into a shape when it entered our world."

"And the Sleeping God broke it," Gundaron said. "'And the awakened God, eyes shut still in sleep, sword aloft, turned his head, listened for the Intruder, and when he heard the cries of the fearful creature, struck again and again, turning the Intruder into dust, breaking it, bone and spirit.'" Gun opened his eyes. "The original's in verse," he said, "but that's the sense of it."

"How can you be so sure?" Mar looked from one to the other.

"Because I've Seen it."

At the fall of silence, Dhulyn looked up from lifting the bones from her fish to see three identical faces frozen in shock. "There's a Vision I keep having," she began, and told them what she'd Seen, the Mage with his book and sword, the mirror that was a window that was a door, the entrance of the green mist. The possessed Mage, green-eyed, unable to open the doorway again.

Parno froze in the act of refilling his wine cup. "It has to be. There are too many details that fit for it to be anything else."

"But how?" Mar said. "I thought Seers saw only the future."

"It's the common assumption," Gundaron said, eyes narrowed in thought. "But when I was researching the origins of the Espadryni," he faltered, licking his lips. "In the city state of Shpadrajh, they answered any question that was put to them, and one old scrap of parchment was a partial list of the questions that had been asked in one year. Many seemed to make no sense, as they obviously concerned events which had already occurred. It was long thought to be a mistranslation, or at the least a misinterpretation, but if it's not . . . the Sight isn't limited in the way everyone assumes."

Parno gave a low whistle. "Tek-aKet said the thing understood irony. Now we see why. It began its present existence in irony. It killed the only person who knew how to send it back."

"Wolfshead." Gun laid his fork down gently. "If you've Seen the Green Shadow coming into the world, you've Seen a time *before* the Sleeping God destroyed it."

"I suppose I have. Blood! The Mage could be one of the Caids."

"That means you could See how the Sleeping God is called."

"I can't make a Vision come when I want it to, and even if we could afford to wait until my woman's time when the Sight is stronger, I can't See what I want to See."

"You must try, my heart. You had clear Visions when we were in Tenebro House, and that was not your woman's time."

"Fresnoyn." Dhulyn and Gundaron spoke at once.

※※※

"I'd much rather have walked," Gun said, squirming to find a more comfortable seat on the saddle.

"I thought you were in a hurry. Stop wiggling, you're only annoying the horse."

Dhulyn Wolfshead sounded as though she might be smiling, but she'd only turned her head enough for him to see the very corner of her mouth. Gun pressed his knees tightly against the saddle and tried to sit up straight as she'd instructed him. It had been years since he'd sat on a horse, and even though it was said that you never forgot how to ride, there seemed to be something lacking in his own recall. Had the beasts always been this far from the ground?

His teeth closed sharply on the inside of his cheek as his horse stopped short. Gingerly, the taste of blood on his tongue, he edged his horse next to Dhulyn's.

"I thought we were in a hurry," he said. He craned his neck to see what had stopped her, but all he could see was a group of children playing Blind Man. Three stood to one side, waiting their turn to play; four were chanting as they danced around the child in the center, blindfolded with what looked like a strip torn from the bottom of his shirt. *Someone'll be in trouble when he gets home tonight,* Gun thought.

***

> *"Blind Man, Blind Man,*
> *Which one will you choose?*
> *Over and through, in and out he goes;*
> *The green tile or the blue, no one really knows*
> *Are you a glad one or are you a sad one?*
> *Are you a good one or are you a bad one?"*

"Three days ago they were afraid to come out to play," Dhulyn Wolfs head said, her eyes fixed on the children and their game.

"They wouldn't be out now, if they knew what we know," Gun said.

The Mercenary smiled her wolf's grin. "We *do* know," she said, "and yet here we are." She clucked to her horse and Gun was jolted upright as his own beast followed.

"If this is a game," Gun said to her back. "I don't want to play anymore."

One of the Tenebro guards must have recognized them as they rode along the street, for the gate of Tenebro House was rolling back as they approached, and a familiar figure appeared in the opening. Except for the change in his clothing and the different braiding of his hair, he looked exactly as he had the first time Dhulyn had seen him.

"Look to the Scholar," she said to him as he came to help her down from Bloodbone. "He's the one's not ridden much."

But another guard was stepping up to help Gundaron, and Karlyn-Tan stayed where he was, smiling up at her. "We thought it would be Parno Lionsmane with you," he said. "Is your errand to the Tenebroso?"

"*Is* there a Tenebroso?"

"The lord Dal-eDal was called to the Tarkin's bedside this morning, and confirmed before witnesses as Dal-eLad Tenebroso."

"And do you address me as his Walls?"

Karlyn-Tan smiled again and shrugged, shaking his head in answer. "But I must do something while I'm here, eating his bread."

"Since you ask as a friend, Karlyn, we come on the Tarkin's orders, to fetch certain needed supplies that the

Scholar knows to be in his former rooms. Whose leave do we ask, if not yours?"

"As you come in the Tarkin's name, I'd say you ask leave of no one."

Dhulyn swung her leg over Bloodbone's head and slid off the mare's back, landing on her feet face-to-face with the former Steward of Walls. He made no step back, just put his hand out for the bridle. "Perhaps, then, the Scholar can find his own way to his old rooms," she said.

"Undoubtedly he can, but Dal-eLad Tenebroso's been told of your approach, and has asked that you speak with him when your errand is done."

Dhulyn looked Karlyn up and down, the beginnings of her wolf's smile on her lips. "It seems to me I've come into this House once before, Karlyn. I'm in no hurry to do so again."

"Ah, but this time you may keep your weapons," the former Walls said, his own grin wide and open. "The new Tenebroso says that all Mercenary Brothers are to be regarded as members of his House. Your Partner and yourself above all others."

Dhulyn absently stroked Bloodbone's neck. "Does he now? That's kind of him." She supposed it was, really, but somehow she couldn't find herself grateful.

"So you may go about your business, Scholar. The Wolfshead will be in the small salon when you are ready."

When Gundaron looked at her, Dhulyn nodded. "Go ahead, Scholar, I've no need to see that room again."

Karlyn waited until Gundaron had run up the left-hand staircase before leading Dhulyn away to the right.

"You won't be familiar with the small salon," he said, holding open a heavy wood door with a small iron grille at eye height for her. "Dal is converting it to his study, and restoring the old Tenebroso's sitting room to its public function."

"I'm surprised to see you still here, if you don't intend to become Walls again," Dhulyn said.

He let her pass through the door, then paused a moment holding it open. Dhulyn stopped and looked back at him. He faced her, but his crystal-blue eyes were focused inward.

"It's not my plan to stay here," he said, finally lifting his eyes to her. "But it's as good a place to live as any until this crisis ends, or until I know where I wish to be."

"You are not too old to make a Mercenary Brother, if you lived through the Schooling," she said.

His smile, for all that it creased his eyes, made him look younger. "I've lived through several things already."

※※※

Gundaron's room wasn't exactly as he'd left it. It was clear that someone had searched it, but it had been someone who had left the room almost as neat as they'd found it. The books and scrolls had clearly been taken from the shelf and then stuffed back in place without regard for either order or bent corners; the bed had been stripped of linens, but the linens themselves had been taken away and the bed restored—almost—to its place against the wall.

He wasn't surprised to find the same partially restored order in his clothespress, though he was surprised that his spare tunics were still there. What wasn't there, however, was the box of drugs that should have been on the top shelf.

Gun chewed on his bottom lip. He'd taken the drugs to the workroom when he'd given them to Dhulyn Wolfshead. He'd brought them back here—hadn't he? He touched the spot on the shelves where the pearwood box should be. Well, if he had brought it back, whoever had searched the room had taken it away again.

That did leave him one other place to look.

He was actually out the door and into the hallway before he remembered there was something else he'd come here to get.

※※※

Karlyn tapped on the right-hand leaf of a set of plain double doors and opened it without waiting. The room within was neither as crowded and carpeted as the old woman's room, nor as cold and heavy-furnitured as Lok-iKol's. The floors were plain golden wood, clean and polished. The furniture, while sturdy, was limited to a few chairs of a light-colored wood, backs, seats, and arms covered with tooled leather, with a few bright-patterned cushions scattered about. The walls held simple ink drawings, there were flowers in low vases, and dried fruit in shallow ceramic bowls. As they entered, the new House, Dal-eLad Tenebroso, was studying the top of a low, round table that sat between two of the leather-covered armchairs. Before he got to his feet, he shifted something on the table with his fingertips with a movement that was very familiar to Dhulyn. She waited until he raised his head and smiled before advancing into the room herself. When she got close enough, she was not surprised to see that the tabletop was covered with what looked to be a very old set of vera tiles. Most were turned facedown, as if a game were about to begin.

"Do you play the tiles, Tenebroso?"

"Please, call me Dal. We *are* related, in an odd way, though it seems we're not to acknowledge it. And no, I get no pleasure from gambling. I don't even play the Solitary hands, really. It's the patterns that interest me most. I lay the tiles out in the old patterns as a way to help me relax."

"The old patterns?"

"The Seer's Patterns, my nurse used to call them. It's why I wanted to see you, as it happens." He gestured for her to sit in the chair opposite him before resuming his own seat.

Dal laid the tips of his fingers lightly on the backs of the tiles nearest him. "My mother brought this set into our Household. I don't know how far back it goes in her family, but it was said the set was made in the time of the Caids."

Dhulyn shrugged, her eyes on the tiles. "It's certainly possible. If parchments and even some paper can last so long, why not tiles? Do you know what they're made of?"

"Some kind of bone or stone, judging by how they change temperature." He picked up a piece and handed it to her.

Dhulyn lifted the tile to her mouth and touched it with the tip of her tongue, tested it with her teeth. "Stone, I would say. I do use the tiles for gambling, as it happens, but I doubt you've asked for me in order to teach you how."

Dal laughed softly. "Quite right. Turn over the tile you've got in your hand."

Suddenly—

❧❧❧

A HEAVY WEIGHT OF TIME; GENERATIONS; HOUSES RISE AND FALL. A
MOUNTAIN PUSHES UP OUT OF THE SEA. AN ISLAND. SHE TOOK A SHARP
BREATH . . .

※※※

"Wolfshead, I said, 'are you all right?'"

"Yes, thank you." Eyebrows raised, Dhulyn turned the
tile over. Rather than being marked with one of the cups,
coins, swords, or spears that she was familiar with, this tile
had a circle with a dot in the middle. She looked back at
Dal-eLad.

He was nodding. "There are tiles in this set not seen in
the sets used for gambling. That's one of that them. There are
four tiles with that dot and circle. And three other sets of
four." He began turning over the tiles in front of him. "A
simple straight line, running lengthwise down the center. A
rectangle, just smaller than the tile itself, and a triangle,
centered along the length of the tile, like a spearhead."

Dhulyn set down the tile she held next to its brothers. "A
line, a circle, a rectangle, a triangle. Four in each pattern.
Sixteen extra tiles?"

Dal shook his head. "Seventeen. This one is unique." He
picked up a tile that lay to his left, and showed, if possible,
more wear than the others. When he turned it over, Dhulyn
could see, faint but clear, a design of three concentric circles.

"Could the other three have been lost?"

Dal shook his head. "My nurse said no, the set had always been like this."

"But surely, if the set is so very old . . ." Dhulyn let her
objection die away as Dal went on shaking his head.

"No other tile is missing, you can tell by the wear and
the patterns that they are all original. What odds would you
give me that three tiles only, and those particular three
would be the only ones lost since the time of the Caids? No.
This tile is unique."

"So." Dhulyn leaned back in her chair, tapping her lips
with her linked fingers. "Seventeen extra tiles we don't use
in the modern sets of vera tiles. And these patterns, what
are they?"

"As I said, my nurse called them the Seer's Patterns. My sisters and I—"

Dhulyn looked up from her study of the tiles. Dal sat with his elbow on the table, chin in his hand, lips pressed tightly together. *His sisters are gone,* she thought, *and it still hurts him.*

"My sisters and I," Dal began again, his voice lower and carefully under control, "would pretend to be Seers, telling each other's fortunes." He cleared his throat and began turning all the tiles faceup. "You know that some of the tiles have names, other than their places in the suits?"

"The Tarkina of Swords is called the Black Maid, the nine of cups is called Wealth, that kind of thing?"

Dal nodded. "Exactly." He held one tile in his hand, leaving the others as they lay. "My nurse said that once upon a time all the tiles had names, and meanings as well. That you would choose the tile that stood for you, and from it your fortune could be told."

Dhulyn leaned forward, placing her elbows on the table. "Show me."

"This is my tile," he said, showing her the Mercenary of Coins. "A young man or woman, golden-haired, brown-eyed. This tile would be placed in the center of a table such as this one. I would ask my question, and this tile," he held up the singleton, "with its concentric circles, would be placed atop my own." He set the unique tile on top of the Mercenary of Coins. "The circled dot above, the triangle below, the rectangle to the right, the line to the left, forming a small cross. We would toss the rest of the tiles, and, drawing one at a time, place one face up above the circled dot, one below the triangle, one to the right of the rectangle, and one to the left of the line, extending the arms of the cross." Pretending to draw tiles from the box, Dal placed them as he indicated. "Lastly, we would choose four more, one at a time, and place them in a vertical here, to the left of the tiles we've already set up. This is the simplest of the Seer's Patterns."

"The simplest?" Dhulyn drew down her brows in a frown, shaking her head. "And what does it tell you?"

Dal spread his hands, palms raised. "That I can't say. No

one in my family ever had the Sight, to my knowledge. But I thought that *you* . . ."

Dhulyn let her lower lip slip from between her teeth. "I've seen these markings before," she said. She tapped one of the rectangle tiles with her fingernail. "Around the base of Mar's bowl. They're—" the blood rushed to her ears. "They're *Marks.*" She looked up, smiling, but Dal was frowning his incomprehension. "*Marks,*" she said again. "This one's a Seer," she tapped the circled dot. "It looks like an eye. This one's a Finder, Gundaron says Finding is like following a straight line."

Now Dal was nodding. "So one of these is a Healer—"

"Probably the square."

"And the other's a Mender."

"But this one," Dhulyn tapped the unique tile with its concentric circles. "I've no idea what this one might be. I've never seen anything like it."

"Because it's a Lens," Gun said from the doorway. Dal jumped in his seat, but Dhulyn didn't even look around. "The missing Mark."

"What do you mean, my Scholar?"

Gundaron held up the scroll in his hand. "It's in the Commentaries, the part I couldn't remember, Holderon writes about an ancient text of the Caids, one that existed in his day but doesn't any longer, though some of the stories it was said to contain have come down to us in the forms of folk songs and plays. Anyway, in the part that I'm referring to, Holderon appears to be answering·the argument of another Scholar, and it's Holderon's position that the other Scholar is mistaken, that the Missing Mark, the so-called Lens, doesn't exist."

"A *fifth* Mark? What was his logic?"

"That while everyone knew of the other Marks, no one had ever encountered a Lens."

"Perhaps it wasn't a person," Dal said. "Perhaps it was an artifact?"

An artifact, Dhulyn thought. *A round artifact.* One, perhaps, that had somewhere along the line been disguised as something more ordinary, and therefore not nearly as old. Something round could easily be disguised as . . . Dhulyn's blood began to pound in her ears. As a bowl, for example.

Dal and Gundaron had gone on talking, and after a moment Dhulyn realized they were suggesting that she try Seeing, using the tiles.

"I'm afraid there is no fresnoyn," Gundaron was saying. "I've tried Finding, but I get nothing."

"Possibly Lok-iKol used it," Dhulyn said, shelving her thoughts about the bowl. It would wait until they were back in the Dome. "Let me see what the tiles can do. Which shall I use?"

"I should think you'd be the Mercenary of Swords," Dal said. "You're not old enough to use the Tarkina's tile."

"I use my own tile?"

"A Sight that involved you might prove to be most useful," Dal suggested.

Dhulyn nodded and took the tile he handed her, setting it down in the center of the table as Dal had shown her. *How do I call the Sleeping God?* she asked herself. As she placed the tiles she thought of as the other Marks, Dal swept the rest off the table, and shook them in their box. As they were placed, Dhulyn tried not to guide her thoughts, but to let them float freely, making whatever associations they might form by themselves. Her Visions usually came to her in her sleep; those very few she'd had in her waking state had always fallen upon her like a blow. Unlike Gundaron, she had never used her Mark deliberately, never sought after a Vision. Perhaps she would See one, though, if their methods were not too broken. And providing the Visions were not so thoroughly linked to her woman's time that this effort was wasted. That tile was the Tarkin of Swords, clearly a man and he was holding a type of sword very much like one she owns, though she doesn't use it much as it's . . .

⊱✦⊰

NOT THE SWORD OF A HORSEMAN. SHE CAN SEE NOW THAT THE MERCENARY'S CLOTHES ARE BRIGHTLY COLORED, AND FIT HIM CLOSELY EXCEPT FOR THE SLEEVES WHICH FALL FROM HIS SHOULDERS LIKE INVERTED LILIES.

HE TURNS AWAY FROM THE STRANGELY TIDY WORKTABLE AND TOWARD A CIRCULAR MIRROR, AS TALL AS HE IS HIMSELF. THE MIRROR DOESN'T REFLECT THE ROOM, HOWEVER, BUT SHOWS A NIGHT SKY FULL OF STARS. HIS LIPS

MOVE AND SHE SEES HIM NOW FROM THAT SIDE, AS IF SHE WERE STANDING IN FRONT OF THE MIRROR AND HIS LIPS FORM WHAT DHULYN KNOWS ARE THE WORDS FROM THE BOOK. *ADELGARREMBIL* HE SAYS, AND THEN *ACUCHEE-YAROB*. A FOREIGN TONGUE?

"Wolfshead. Wolfshead, wake up."

Dhulyn snatched the hand from her shoulder and only just stopped from breaking the wrist when she realized the person shaking her was Mar-eMar. Dhulyn's heart grew cold. The little Dove was out of breath and as pale as lilies. Behind her, in the doorway of Dal-eLad's salon, was the Mercenary Brother Oswin Battlehammer.

"Dhulyn, hurry. Tek-aKet's sitting on the Carnelian Throne and he's—" she shot a glance over her shoulder at the Brother in the doorway. "He's *raving*."

"Where's Parno?" Dhulyn was already into the hallway and heading to the courtyard where Bloodbone waited.

"At the doors to the throne room letting no one in, but you must . . ."

Mar fell behind, but Dhulyn went on running. She knew perfectly well what the girl had been about to say. "You must hurry." Of course she must. Wait too long, and Parno would go in without her.

Twenty-five

"HOW DID THIS HAPPEN?" Dhulyn stood with her right hand pressed tightly against the ornate carving of the doors to the Carnelian Throne Room, as if she could somehow reach through and sense what was happening inside.

"You think I know?" Parno growled. "I was helping the Tarkina with the Semlorian ambassador when the page, Telian-Han, came running for me. He'd gone to the Tarkin's room with the midday meal and found the guard who'd been left there dead on the floor."

"And the Tarkina?"

"Keeping the ambassador calm, I imagine." Parno closed his fingers around her upper arm. "Dhulyn, my heart, don't do it. It doesn't have a head wound now. What if it—it must know you are coming? The best you'll accomplish is to send it to another body."

"You prefer to have the Green Shadow as Tarkin of Imrion?" She looked at him as if she didn't even feel his grip on her arm. Her eyes were as bright as the edge of a knife.

"Besides, I promised him I would kill him. I gave my word."

"We have only you and Gundaron. If it destroys you before you can kill Tek-aKet, we will never prevail against it."

"I gave my word."

"At least let me come in with you." He knew it was no use even before she started shaking her head.

"I can kill *him*," she said. "I don't know that I could kill you if . . .

Parno let his hand drop to his side. He'd known what her answer would be, but he'd had to try. She was what she was. When Dhulyn took his face in her hands, he did not pull away.

"Beslyn-Tor said, 'like this,' did he not?" Dhulyn's steel-gray eyes fixed on his.

Parno closed his hands around her wrists. "He did."

"Eye-to-eye, that's how the Shadow moves, and how, I'll wager, he destroys."

"And so?"

"And so? Blindfold me, you idiot."

Eyes covered with a piece of silk torn from one of the hangings and threaded through the braids of her hair for security, Dhulyn settled her shoulders, breathing deeply, slowly. Beginning the discipline she privately thought of as Blind Parno's *Shora,* from when the horizon sickness had forced her Partner to go blindfolded to cross the Blasonar Plains. She became conscious of the timing of her breathing, the movement of the air, so that each breath took the same length of time going in and going out. In. Out. As her breathing fell into a rhythm, as her body and her thoughts calmed, in the darkness of the blindfold her senses woke. She heard the air move through Parno's lungs, and the soft susurration of his clothes as they adjusted to the movement of his chest. She felt her own skin move against her vest as she breathed, and pushed her senses outward.

Smelled now, not just Parno's familiar smell, but the garlic in the sauce of the partridge they'd eaten for luncheon, the wine he'd had, and the bay leaf in the water he'd used to cleanse his hands. She felt and heard Parno slip the makeshift bar free and eased herself through the opening, moving only enough to allow him to shut the door behind her. She could hear two sets of breathing now--*two*?—and stilled her own to listen better. From the left. Low, steady, almost a snore. Unconscious, then, and neither help nor hindrance. And the second? Above.

Dhulyn stepped to the right in time to feel the displacement of air as the body of her assailant landed to her left, his grunt sounding loud to her sensitive hearing. She ducked under the blow she sensed sweeping toward her head, felt the air push past her face and seized the wrist instead of dancing away as instinct and training demanded. She continued her turn into her opponent until she had it back against the wall, her forearm against its throat, and her knife buried in its chest.

Dhulyn eased the body to the floor, pulled her knife out of the wound and wiped it clean on her breeches before carefully feeling upward with her free hand and covering the dead eyes. Many fights were lost through too early belief that they were won. No point in being careless now. She took a moment to allow her breathing to return to normal, to release herself from the discipline of the *Shora* before laying the knife down behind her and using that hand to dig her fingers into the side of the throat, under the jaw. Nothing, no pulse. The blood had stopped moving from the wound. She made sure the eyelids were closed before she recovered the knife, inserted it with care between her skin and the blindfold, and sliced the strip of cloth free of her face.

"I fulfill my oath, Tarkin of Imrion," she whispered, touching her forehead with her fingertips.

She rose to her feet in one movement and advanced in the direction of the other breathing she'd heard. She stopped when two legs, one folded under the other, came into her view on the far side of the dais. She advanced even more slowly, certain that she recognized those soft-soled boots with their intricate embroidery. Her lips formed a soundless whistle as she knelt, sheathed her knives, and pulled loose one of the braided leather cords that were woven into her vest. Two important questions leaped immediately to mind.

What had Cullen of Langeron been doing in the Throne room? And was this *still* Cullen of Langeron?

Dhulyn had just finished trussing the unconscious Cloudman when the doors of the throne room were flung open behind her. The rapid footsteps stopped only paces into the room, and then advanced once more, slowly. The last knot secure, Dhulyn looked around, knowing already who she would see.

Zelianora Tarkina sank to her knees by the corpse of her husband, laying her fingers lightly on his closed eyelids.

When she looked up, her dark brows were like splashes of ink on her face.

"Did he speak, once the Shadow had departed?"

Shaking her head, Dhulyn rose to her feet and approached the other woman. She stopped when Zelianora held her hand up, palm toward her.

"Leave me, please," she said. "You stood by your word and for that I thank you, but leave me now. Please."

Dhulyn hesitated, looking from the kneeling Tarkina to the trussed Cloudman. Parno left his post by the door to take her by the elbow.

"Come," he said.

"We must bring Cullen," she said.

Parno shrugged and bent over to grasp the front of Cullen's tunic, hauling the unconscious man upright enough to sling him over his shoulder.

"Don't know why you bothered tying him. The Tarkin wouldn't have been attacking you if the Shadow'd left him. Logic tells us Cullen must be clean."

"Logic's killed people before. Better careful than cursing."

At the doorway Dhulyn stopped and looked back into the room. There was something wrong. The throne room showed no signs of the encounter, just the body of Tek-aKet, with his grieving Tarkina kneeling over it. Dhulyn drew in a deep breath through her nose, tasting blood at the back of her throat. But there was something else. Something she couldn't put her finger on.

The new Tenebroso, Dal-eLad, coughed, found himself leaning over the neck of his horse, and straightened, rubbing at the start of a headache over his left eyebrow.

"Dal, are you all right?"

A few blinks assured him he was looking into the blue eyes of Karlyn Tan, riding beside him. He held the focus until he was sure his vision was clear.

"Felt dizzy for a moment." He looked away, rubbing the side of his face.

"You looked as though you were about to faint."

"I'll be fine," Dal said, shrugging away Karlyn's concern.

They had no time for any of this, they had to get to the Dome as quickly as possible. "Let's go."

※※※

"But I don't understand." Mar sat next to Gun on Dhulyn Wolfshead's bed, drawing comfort from the warmth of his body so near hers. She looked between the two Mercenaries. "You did exactly as the Tarkin asked you to do."

Parno Lionsmane closed and tied the silk bag that held his disassembled pipes. "Not everyone will feel that way. The fact remains, little Dove, that my Partner has killed the Tarkin of Imrion, and even though it was at his order . . . well, there's no way to know which way the Houses will jump, if they find out. If we ask for permission to go and are denied," he shrugged, "better to explain, and defend ourselves if necessary, from the mountains."

Gun took her hand. "We'd have to go anyway," he said. "We don't know where the Shadow is now, but we *do* know we need the other Marks. And the only other Marks we know about are in the mountains. Before Wolfshead killed the Tarkin, we *could* have sent Cullen's Racha bird for them—what did I say?"

Dhulyn Wolfshead had frozen in the act of folding her long riding cotte. "Disha," she said. "That's it." She turned to Parno Lionsmane. "When did Disha return?"

"Two nights ago, the same night Gun found Tek-aKet. What of it?"

"Cullen was in the throne room without Disha." The two Mercenary Brothers looked at each other tight-lipped.

"She could be anywhere," Parno Lionsmane said finally. "He could have sent her with a message, or just away, if he suspected something was wrong with Tek. We won't know anything until he comes to himself."

"*If* he comes to himself." The Wolfshead chewed on her lower lip, the half-folded cotte twisting in her hands.

"*That* mistake won't be made again, you can be sure," Parno Lionsmane said. "Cullen's well-guarded and, unlike Tek, has no authority to order himself freed."

"It seems hard to go to the Cloud people without him." Dhulyn Wolfshead frowned at the cotte she still held.

Mar looked down at her hands, clasped in her lap. *Here*

we go again, she thought, surprised to find her hands so steady. Once more on the run. Had she spent longer than three days anywhere since she'd first set eyes on the Mercenaries? She got to her feet, mentally reviewing what she should take with her. No point in packing any of the court gowns Rab-iRab had found for her. However much nicer they were than the clothes she'd had at Tenebro, they wouldn't be much use on horseback. The sound of her own name made her look up.

"Mar can stay here with Zelianora Tarkina," Gun was saying.

A cold shock buzzed in her ears. Did he really mean to go without her? "Not likely," she said, thrusting herself between Gun and Parno. "It's my bowl you need, remember!"

"But, Mar, you're safer here if we—"

"Best if you waste no time arguing."

The voice from the doorway stopped Gun before he could finish giving Mar his excuses. Dal-eLad and Karlyn-Tan had come with them from Tenebro House, but while she and Gun had come straight to the Mercenaries' rooms, the Noble House had gone to the Tarkina. Dal's glance fell to the open packs. "Good. I should have known you would be ahead of me. The Houses are already arriving. Penrado happened to be here when you came riding in and he's called the others."

"And if we're asked for?" Dhulyn Wolfshead did not stop packing to ask.

"Zelianora has told them you've gone after the murderers of the Tarkin," Dal said. "She's said that he told you enough to set you on the trail with his dying words." He entered the room far enough to shut the door behind him. "There is good comes of this, if we are careful. Tek deposed and dead was one thing, the Houses were willing for Lok-iKol to be Tarkin rather than begin a civil war. But Tek assassinated is another. Anyone who steps forward to claim the Carnelian Throne will be suspect. The Penradoso is speaking against a Ballot, and calling for Bet-oTeb to be declared Tarkin, with an appropriate Guardian, of course, and many of the other Houses are listening."

"Enough?"

Dal shrugged. "It will be easier for Zelianora to ask for

the Guardianship herself if . . ." Dal stopped, his unspoken words hanging in the air.

"If she's seen to have acted decisively in sending us after the assassins," Dhulyn Wolfshead finished for him. He nodded to her, clearly relieved that she understood. "These youngsters have yet to pack. Meanwhile we can saddle the horses—"

"You misunderstood me," Dal said. "There were those who wished to question you themselves, and Zelianora has told them you have already gone. You will not ride out of the front gates now without making her a liar, and raising the very questions we wish to avoid." Dal shrugged. "I can have your horses, and even your saddlebags sent after you to the Tenebro summerhome outside of Gotterang." He turned to Parno Lionsmane. "You remember?"

When Lionsmane nodded, Wolfshead turned to Mar and Gun.

"Go, you two, quick as you can and meet back here. Small packs only, Mar, but leave nothing you cannot afford to lose. Be sure to bring the bowl." Dhulyn Wolfshead fastened the last buckle on the straps of her saddlebag.

"And speaking of that." Dal had been carrying a small case made of time-darkened wood with a brass handle set into the lid. "I've brought the vera tiles for you, Dhulyn Wolfshead. They seemed to work at least somewhat. . . ."

"I'll see they come back to you safely."

"Keep them. I can have a new set made." Dal looked at Gun, and then at Mar herself as if he would say something in particular to them, but finally he bowed and left them.

As Mar was pulling the door shut behind them, she heard Dhulyn Wolfshead say, "I wonder. Can the Shadow enter the Racha?"

⊗⊗⊗

"I hope neither of you are afraid of heights." Dhulyn looked with approval at the packs Mar and Gun were carrying. The little Dove's bag was much the same style—if better quality—as the one she'd had on the trail, but without winter clothing, it was less than half the size. Parno was tying their packs to a climbing rope, light but strong, taking care that they would hang true, without twisting or binding.

"Boots off, my Doves, put them into the front of your harness."

"I thought we'd go through the old kitchens," Gundaron said, handing his pack over at Parno's gesture and sitting down to get at his boots.

"We'd have to pass through too much of the Dome to get there," Parno told him. "We're supposed to be gone already, remember."

"We little thought we'd be taking you with us this way, my Doves," Dhulyn said, looking out the window of their bedroom. "But it's not so difficult. If you don't look down."

She looked with longing at her saddlebags. Everything she couldn't do without—including the set of vera tiles—had been transferred to a travel pack, but uncomfortable wouldn't begin to describe their journey if, by ill luck, they lost the bags. And there was her second-best sword, to say nothing of the axes and the longbow. She gave a mental shrug, put her most cheerful smile on her lips. Either Dal-eLad would get them their horses and saddlebags, or he wouldn't. No point in giving the youngsters anything more to worry them. Under her breath, she ticked off a list of weapons. Knives—in boots, wrist sheaths, back sheath under her shirt and the public one at her belt—with short sword, throwing star pouch, and disassembled crossbow, all attached to vest harness, and tied down so as not to snag on anything or tangle the ropes. Parno had, in addition to his own body weapons and sword, the cavalry recurve bow that came apart into three pieces, and the arrows they'd brought back from the Great King's court, steel arrows that unscrewed, patterned after relics of the Caids. Everything else was either too heavy or too long to take by this route. She'd just have to hope that Dal came through for them. She turned her back on the pile of books and scrolls stacked neatly on the room's side table. If she didn't look, she wouldn't think about them. Much.

Her inventory finished, she helped Parno move the roped packs to the window.

"I'll get these up now," he said. "And come back to help with the youngsters." He was out the window and up the wall in a moment, trailing the rope with the packs attached behind him. Dhulyn knew he'd reached the roof when the rope grew taut, and she eased the packs over the window-sill, watching them rise as Parno pulled them up.

She turned back into the room and smiled when she saw Mar and Gun eyeing herself, and the window, in disbelief.

"If you're ready," she said, attaching ropes to the front and rear of Gun's and Mar's harnesses, until they were strung out, herself to Gundaron, Gundaron to Mar. "The ledge is wider than it looks. Follow me out, then Parno will lead us all."

As if hearing his cue, Parno swung himself back into the room and, seeing they were ready, linked himself to Mar with the rope he'd used to haul up the packs. He looked up with a nod as he finished checking the knot.

"Ready?" Instead of just stepping out onto the ledge as she would have done if she were alone, Dhulyn sat on the edge of the window casement, swung her legs out, turned to face into the room, and, gripping the edge of the casement tightly, lowered her legs until her toes felt the ledge.

"You see?" she said. "Just like that. I'll be out here to steady you."

Gundaron followed her out, trying his best to ape her actions exactly. He had a shaky moment when his toe couldn't find the ledge, but once Dhulyn had guided his foot down, he managed well enough.

"Move over here, Gun, and mind the ropes," she said, allowing him to pass between her and the wall. "Let Mar out."

Anyone would have thought that Mar had been climbing out of fifth-story windows all her life—as, indeed she may have been, for all Dhulyn knew to the contrary. The little Dove slid out of the window onto the ledge and over next to Gun without hesitation or sign of nerves. Parno followed her out, drew the casements shut behind him and, using a bit of wire tied onto the end of a string, pulled the latch over as he did so. From the inside, at least, there'd be no sign that they'd left via the windows.

"Eyes on me," Parno said. His tone was even and calm, the same tone, Dhulyn thought, that he'd used to coach Mar in table etiquette when they were on their way to Got-terang. "Watch where I put my hands and feet, and you put yours the same. Don't start up until you see me wave at you. I'll be anchored, so you can't fall, but be careful all the same."

As Dhulyn knew from her own reconnaissance, there were no windows directly above theirs, so Parno could climb straight up until he'd cleared the two stories above them, and reached the battlements at the top of the tower. These were decorative only, intended to match the style of an older tower, with no place for guards or archers to stand behind them, Dhulyn knew, only the shallow-pitched peaked roof of the tower itself. Parno swung himself over the edge of the stone, and after a few moments, they could see his hand waving.

"Up you get, children, fingers and toes now." Dhulyn had tested the route herself only the day before, and knew that there were many finger- and toeholds in the rough stone wall, and more than a few places where the whole foot could be placed to take the weight off the hands.

This time Mar went first, scrambling up the wall like one of the monkeys Dhulyn had seen in the jungles of the northwest. Gun lifted his arms to start up almost as soon as he had room to do so.

"Wait." Dhulyn said, her hand on his shoulder. "Let her reach the top; you would pull her down as well if you fell." *And me with the two of you,* she didn't say aloud. No point in frightening the boy any more than he was already.

Still, his fear didn't stop him from starting up as soon as Mar had cleared the top, and Dhulyn found herself nodding in approval for the first time. He'd learned somewhere not to let his fear stop him. He might make a worthwhile human yet.

Halfway up, he froze, and Dhulyn bit back her thought. "Don't look down," she told him. "I'll be right there." She pulled herself up until she was nearly on top of him, covering his legs with her body, careful not to tangle the ropes. "Take a deep breath and move up. Parno's there, see him? He's got the slack of the rope. You can't fall, just help him bring you up, don't let him do all the work." When he still didn't move, she added, "Look within, Find your courage."

Dhulyn's fingers were just beginning to feel the strain when the boy nodded as though his neck were made of oak, and began to move, first his right hand, then his left, his right foot, his left. Dhulyn held herself back a moment, checking the rope, keeping out of the way of his lower limbs, but not letting Gun get so far ahead that he couldn't feel her presence between him and the long fall.

"Keep breathing," she said. "Let the air move in and out, in and out."

It could not have been more than minutes later that Parno was helping Gun roll over the battlement onto the roof, but Dhulyn was sure that it felt much longer to the boy.

"Not to worry," Parno was saying. "We're only going to walk along this wall to that other tower you see there. No more climbing." Mar had hold of the boy's hand, and his grip on hers was so tight her fingers looked white.

Gun swallowed, but whatever he wanted to say didn't make it out of his lips.

"We'll still have the ropes," Dhulyn said, in her most matter-of-fact tones. "There's still no way for any of us to fall. You keep your eyes on the spot where your rope attaches to Mar, and you'll be fine."

Gun pressed his lips together into a thin line and nodded. When she saw that he intended to stand, Mar helped him to his feet. He looked to Dhulyn, then to Parno, and nodded again. Parno picked up the two heaviest packs, one in each hand to balance himself, and set off. Dhulyn picked up the two remaining packs and watched as Mar and Gun followed her Partner.

They were a little more than halfway across when the boy spoke.

"I thought the Carnelian Dome was impregnable from this side," he said, in a voice that was a tight parody of nonchalance.

"Oh, you can't get *in* this way." Parno answered as if he hadn't heard the tightness.

"But you can get *out*," Dhulyn said.

Parno led them only a few spans farther, until the section of wall that led off from their tower met the ruined corner that was all that remained of a tower that no longer existed. There was room enough—just—for them to stand together.

Parno began unhooking the ropes that tied them together, coiling them neatly at their feet.

"Use these cords to tie your packs to your wrists, my Doves. Mar, check Gun's knots. Use the ones we showed you on the trail."

When her own pack was ready, Dhulyn retied the rope that had attached her to Gun, making it much shorter. When Parno had done the same with the rope between him and Mar, Dhulyn leaned over the edge of the most exposed corner of wall, looked back at them and grinned. "I forgot to ask, can you swim?"

Gun shot a quick look over the edge. "You can't be serious."

"Never more so, my Scholar. The cliff's undercut, and there are no rocks in the river, which is deep enough. I checked. We'll go first," she added, to Parno.

"Got him?" Parno said, as he took Mar's hands in his, moving her away from the edge.

"Got him," Dhulyn said. With her right hand, she gripped Gun's right wrist, and was gripped by him in return. Parno caught her eye above the youngsters' heads.

"In Battle," he mouthed.

Mindful that Gun and Mar could see her face, Dhulyn merely smiled and bowed her head, touching her fingertips to her lips.

"Let's go."

As she and Gun stepped out into space and began to fall, Dhulyn wished she'd really had a chance to check that the river was deep enough. She'd worked it out in her head, but . . .

❦

The shock of the cold as they hit the water was enough to push every fear from Gun's mind, and more than enough to make him gasp. Unfortunately, he was underwater as he did it. His pack dragged heavily at his right wrist and he had time to be thankful that it was not harnessed to his back before he began to cough. Hard fingers caught him by the front of his tunic and heaved him into the air just in time. He struggled to push himself still farther out of the water, stopping only when a bone-crushing grip on his wrists made him realize that the object he was forcing deeper under his weight was Dhulyn Wolfshead. He was lying half across her, facedown, and she had only her face out of the water. The angle she held him at was just such that he was able to cough out the water in his lungs without breathing in any more.

The coughing seemed as though it would last forever, and by the time it had stopped and Gun was able to loosen his grip on the Wolfshead and look about him, the current of the river had taken them away from the Carnelian Dome, and downstream, toward the summer homes of the very rich.

"I can swim," he said.

"Not just yet," she said. "Let the current take us for now. Turn over on your back."

With the Wolfshead to brace against, turning over was easy. Gun had a difficult moment when he thought he'd begin coughing again, but it passed. The Wolfshead slipped her own arm under his and across his chest, holding him against her but with his head well above the water. He forced himself to relax, breathing steadily and slowly, as she used a lazy sidestroke to give them steerage as they floated downstream. The water still felt icily cold, and Gun knew that luck was with them. It was too early in the year for water sports, and the wrong time of day for fishing. It wasn't long before piers and jetties were replaced by boathouses, water pavilions, and long stretches of terraced gardens leading away from the water. Gun's teeth began to chatter and he almost didn't feel it when Dhulyn Wolfshead nudged him on the shoulder.

"Look up," she said, a murmur in his ear.

Gun tried, but could make out nothing beyond the shadowy shapes of clouds partially obscuring the darkening sky.

"What is it," he said, keeping his own voice low.

"A Racha bird," she said. "Time to swim."

❦

If he had to spend three hours in the river, Parno thought, the Tenebro's summer household was the ideal place to come out. Built to provide a comfortable setting for those refreshing themselves in the water, there were numerous pavilions, each with three or four charcoal braziers to help swimmers dry themselves and their clothing quickly after a twilight swim. Parno had indeed remembered the place from his long-ago childhood visits, and it hadn't been hard for him to find his way through the grounds. There had been only one pavilion with lights still burning, and as they'd dragged themselves, wet, cold, and exhausted, from the river's edge, they'd found warmth, servants, food and— perhaps most important of all—their saddlebags.

It didn't surprise him that it was Karlyn-Tan who greeted them, directing the bustle of the servants as they stoked braziers, fetched hot water and food, and led Gun and Mar off for warm baths, hot drinks, and dry clothing. It made sense that Dal would have sent one of the few others who knew exactly what was at stake.

With a nod of thanks Parno accepted a steaming mug from an older man with a Steward's badge in the Tenebro colors.

Dhulyn pulled her wet shirt over her head and handed it to a waiting page, accepting a large towel in exchange. She must have felt Parno's eye on her, for she looked over at him, lifting one blood-red brow.

"I saw a Racha bird," she said.

Karlyn nodded, caught the Steward's attention, and waited as the man gathered up his helpers with a gesture of his hand and left the room. "I've much to tell you, the chief of which is that Cullen is here, with us."

"Why?" Parno said, just as Dhulyn said, "Where?"

Karlyn held up his hands. "He regained his senses, and as the Racha accepted him, and his eyes were normal, we felt he must be clean. Even so, Zelianora Tarkina felt he would be safest with us. If there is any chance the Shadow *is* with him, we are the only people equipped to both recognize and deal with it."

Dhulyn looked up from toweling her hair as dry as it would get while still in braids. "There's merit in that idea, much as I wish she hadn't thought of it," she said. "Now we'll have to spend precious time watching to make sure he isn't trying to escape." She exchanged a look with Parno. In it was the knowledge that so long as they did not know for certain where the Green Shadow was, they would all be at risk, and they could trust no one.

Parno set his cup down. "What else is there to tell us?"

Karlyn had been leaning against the edge of the table near Parno, arms crossed. Now he looked down at the floor, chewing his upper lip.

"Out with it, man," Parno told him. "What could be worse than knowing we might have the Shadow with us?"

"We had not time, before, to wonder how it was the Shadow returned to the Tarkin."

Parno stopped in the act of pulling off his own tunic. "And now?"

Karlyn looked at Parno without raising his head. He shot a glance at Dhulyn, but his eyes did not linger. "The Mesticha Stone came."

Dhulyn finished pulling on the dry breeches she'd taken from her saddlebag, secured the waist, and strode toward Karlyn-Tan. The towel she'd been using was slung over her shoulders like a cloak, not out of modesty, Parno knew, but out of the habit that made her cover the marks of the whip on her back, when they might be seen by strangers.

"The orders to bring it directly to the Tarkin upon its arrival had never been changed," Karlyn said, looking directly at Dhulyn. "And so it was brought to him."

"And Cullen?"

"Saw the Tarkin in the hallway, heading for the gates, he thought, and chased him into the throne room."

"Or so he says," Parno said.

"Or so he says," Karlyn agreed. "Either way, the Mesticha Stone was not found in the bedchamber when it was looked for afterward."

Dhulyn turned aside, tossed her towel across the back of a chair near the brazier, and took a vest made of dozens of strips of supple leather out of her saddlebag, shrugged it on, and began fastening it shut. "The Shadow was in the Tarkin," she said. "It must have been 'visiting' him, as we suspected it might. When the Stone arrived, it seized its opportunity."

"It was the last piece," Parno said. "It's at its full strength now."

Dhulyn looked up from her laces. "And the Racha seems content?"

"As far as any of us can tell," Karlyn said. "Nor does the Cloudman object to riding bound, if we prefer it."

"Well, he wouldn't, would he?"

"What is it you're thinking, my heart?"

Parno looked from Dhulyn to Karlyn and back again. "He'd want to come with us, don't you think?" He held up one finger. "We've got the only Seer he knows of, and," he held up a second finger, "we've got a Finder." A third finger. "We're going to the only place we can be sure there are other Marks. What more does he want? He can let us do his work for him."

Dhulyn had taken breath to answer him when Karlyn spoke.

"So we're safe enough on the journey," he said. "If the Shadow's with us, it won't do any harm until we arrive."

"Us?"

"Under the circumstances, I'd better come with you, don't you think?"

He kept his eyes down and his face animated. Now that he was whole again—he stifled the shape's attempt to retch—he remembered more. He knew better how to hide himself. He had done it in the past. Instead of ignoring the shape's own occupant, pushing its consciousness away once its knowledge had been shifted, he had to wear it as he wore the shape, occupy it as he occupied the shape. With care, he could bide his time. With patience he could deal with the Seer. Patience could lead him to the Lens.

Twenty-six

"**T**HERE IS A SHADOW hanging over us all, a Shadow with green eyes."

Koba the Racha bird eyed Dhulyn from his perch near the fire as Yaro of Trevel gestured her into a seat, hooked the heavy kettle of water on the andiron, and swung it into the fireplace until it rested closer to the flames. As Dhulyn took up her tale, telling what they knew, what they thought, and what they hoped, Yaro watched the kettle, waiting for the water to come to a boil.

When Dhulyn had been silent a moment or two, the woman who was once Yaro Hawkwing the Cloud, Mercenary Brother, tossed a handful of leaves into the now boiling water and, pulling the kettle away from the fire with a heavy cloth, set it on a small iron stand to one side of the hearth. The room began to smell of bee balm.

"I know why you've come to me," Yaro said. She stood a few moments longer, looking into the flames, before turning to face Dhulyn. When their eyes met, the older woman reached up and touched the feathers tattooed on her face. "You would ask of Cullen."

Yaro turned away to take two thick earthenware mugs from a small shelf to the left of the fireplace and set them down on the table between them. She picked up the cloth she'd used to shield her hand from the kettle's handle, but, instead of turning to the fire, stood still, the cloth hanging from her hand, her eyes staring into a distance of time and space.

"If Cullen is not in his body, then Disha would not fly."

And as if the words released her, she was able to turn to the hearth, pick up the kettle, and pour out the strong-smelling brew into the mugs on the table. When she had set the kettle down once again on the hearth, she took the stool across from Dhulyn, wrapped her hands around the mug in front of her, and studied the surface of the tea.

"But if the Shadow is in Cullen's body, would it not be in Disha's as well? Could Disha not fly then?"

Yaro opened her mouth, closed it, and shook her head once more. "I do not know if I can make you see. You told me that Tek-aKet Tarkin was gone from his body until the Scholar Found him?"

"In his own words," Dhulyn said, remembering, "he said that at first he had been pushed out, then allowed to return, but as a passenger. Later, when I struck the Shadow, Tek-aKet was lost. As though the body lived, but he was not in it."

Yaro tapped the tabletop with her index finger. "Without Healer or Mender, in the moment, however short, that the Shadow pushed Cullen from his body, Disha would fall."

"But you—"

"Had a two-month bond, no more, and as it was, only one of us survived. Cullen and Disha have been more than half their lives one being. If they were severed, even for an instant, even for a time so short that the mind cannot conceive of it, they would die." Yaro placed both hands palm down on the table, one to each side of her empty mug. "It is as I say, Dhulyn Wolfshead, my Brother. If Disha still flies, Cullen is free of the Shadow." She breathed deeply in through her nose and, blinking, raised her mug to her lips.

Dhulyn nodded, slowly. There must be such a moment, however short, in which the Shadow *did* move. What Yaro said made sense—but Dhulyn was aware that it was also what she wanted to hear, and therefore suspect. It was clear that Yaro spoke what she thought to be the truth, and Dhulyn believed her. But was that enough? It seemed a small thread from which to hang the fate of the world. Dhulyn rose to her feet, touched her forehead with her fingertips.

"It is good to have seen you, Brother," the older woman said.

"You will see me again," Dhulyn said. Yaro raised her eyes. "In Battle."

"Or in Death," Yaro Hawkwing replied.

⬥⬥⬥

The bird flew overhead, circling, circling, balanced on the currents of air.

What to do, what to do? If he destroyed the Healer now, would they suspect, or would they think it merely her time?

A Mender was coming. If he destroyed any of the Marked now, even the old woman, perhaps the Mender would not come. If he struck, he might lose the chance to destroy the Mender as well. He looked up into the sky and watched the bird float on an updraft, seeming to hang in the air that these folk thought of as nothing, not knowing the true nothing. The *NOT*. If he struck, they would know he was here, now, when they had almost forgotten to suspect, and they would hunt for him. But without the Lens, what could they do?

He could wait. He had overheard the two younger ones talking in the night, when they thought all asleep. They believed they had the Lens, and this belief weakened them. They no longer searched for it, and he could destroy them before they ever realized they should continue to look. He was strong enough, now that he was whole again. He could turn all back to that moment, when he first had form. If he waited, if he managed to find the Lens before them. This time he could succeed. This time he could turn this world into the *NOT*.

Or could there be another way? The bird swept down, and he pushed himself away from the edge of the wall. What if he did not destroy? What if he occupied? Was he strong enough for that? His breath came short, and he tried to steady the pounding of his heart. Was one form any worse than another? He had never looked from the eyes of a Mark—but they would never suspect. Once accomplished, it would be the safest place for him to wait.

⬥⬥⬥

"Oh, I knew Gotterang well. I traveled much in my younger days, as was the rule then, and had been, time out of mind, see you. Scholars traveled then, too, but the only ones who still do are you Mercenaries, and I think that tells us something, don't you?"

Dhulyn glanced up from the washbasin to where the Healer, Sortera, sat in the shaft of sunlight that entered through the doorway of the public washhouse in Trevel. It was the old woman's presence here which had brought them to Trevel, and today she was taking advantage of a warm day and a good breeze to launder her winter garments. After a few minutes of watching the Healer trying to wring out soaking cloth with her crook-fingered hands Dhulyn had asked her to sit down, and had taken over the task of the wash herself, with Mar to help her. Sortera had smiled in such a way, her teeth remarkably good in her wrinkled face, that Dhulyn was certain she'd been outfoxed. But she hid her own smile and kept her thoughts to herself.

Not that laundry was Dhulyn's purpose here this morning. Cullen was as clear-eyed and apparently Shadow free as he had been all the way from Gotterang, but Dhulyn felt only somewhat reassured by what Yaro had told her the night before. After talking it over with Parno, they'd decided that, as far as the Shadow was concerned, very few precautions could be called "unnecessary." She and Mar were watching Sortera; Gundaron they'd left with Parno, going through what scrolls and books the Clouds had in their library. A young Mender boy was coming from Pompano, and until he and his Racha bird escort arrived, no Mark was being left unguarded.

"We Marks didn't live settled into a city in those days, see you," Sortera continued telling them as Dhulyn scooped up another handful of the soft soap in the nearby bucket. "We were all of us on the road, taking our Mark, whatever it might be, to everyone." She leaned forward, resting her hands, with their heavy veins, on the knob of her cane. "Back in those times, people would save only their most important things for a Mender, and they didn't waste a Finder's time on lost scissors or lapdogs, see you. No, it was more like: 'where did Granddad put the harvest money for safety before he fell off his horse and died?' or 'can you Find us the spot for our new well?' That was our work in those times, see you. Marked of the gods, we were. When us

Marked started living in cities," she shook her head, "that was when the trouble started, as far as I'm concerned. Then we were like any tradesman, and people started treating us that way."

Dhulyn carefully squeezed the soapy water out of a thick inglera wool shawl and passed it to Mar for rinsing. Mar pulled the wooden sluice gate from the water channel between the double row of stone sinks and let fresh rainwater flow into her basin from the cistern on the roof. They were the only people in the washhouse this morning, and could use as much water as they liked.

"Eight days on horseback, and all we get are stories of her youth?" Dhulyn said to Mar under her breath.

"I can hear you, young woman," Sortera said, her thin lips pulled back in glee. "I may be old, but I *am* a Healer. My hands may trouble me, but my hearing's just fine."

"Your pardon, Grandmother," Dhulyn said. "How old are you, if you don't mind my asking?"

"Oh, I don't mind, but you won't like the answer, see you. The truth of the matter is I don't know for certain. I remember when there was a Tarkin named Jenshannon—a woman she was—but people tell me that can't be so, that I must be thinking of Jen-aNej Tarkina." The old Healer wrinkled her nose and shook her head in disgust.

Dhulyn rested her forearms on the edge of the basin and thought, mentally ticking off a list of names and dates. It was two hundred years, perhaps more, since noble names began to change to their present mirror-image form. Surely they were right, the people who told Sortera her memory was at fault.

On the other hand, the woman *was* a Healer.

"You may be right, Grandmother," she said. "In any case, don't listen to those who tell you your memory is at fault."

Sortera's laugh was toneless and without heft in the cool mountain air. "I believe you, Granddaughter, I believe you."

"Tell me something else. In all that you have heard of the Mark, do you know of anything called a Lens?"

❈❈❈

"Here it is," Parno came into the room with a belt buckle in his hand. It was cast silver, shaped like a snarling cat's head, and the teeth were sharp enough to cut through rope. "In the outer pocket of Dhulyn's left saddlebag, right where you said it was."

"All right, then." Gun pushed himself back from the table and rubbed his eyes with stiff fingers. "We know it's not me. I've no trouble Finding ordinary things." He looked up. "But I still can't Find the Shadow."

"You're sure you're doing what you did before?"

Gun just looked at him, lips pressed together. Parno raised his hands, palms out. "Forgive me, but you *have* Found it twice before, and somehow I don't think it's just disappeared off the face of the earth."

"I *said,* it's not me." Gun sighed and rolled his left shoulder, grimacing as if at a particularly stiff muscle knot. "I'm not even getting that other Library where I found the Tarkin." The boy looked sideways at him. "I think it's the bowl."

Parno tried not to let his disappointment show. They'd been waiting until they arrived in Trevel to try using the bowl; on the trail there had been no way to hide what they were doing from the others.

"But you have no better luck finding the Shadow without the bowl."

"That's just it, I was getting better results in Gotterang—"

"Caids help us if we have to be in Gotterang for the thing to work." Parno said. He pulled out a chair and sat down, rubbing the edge of the bowl with the tip of his right index finger. "Has the Healer tried it?"

"She has," Gun said. "And reports no results."

"Are we sure . . . she's so very old." Parno hated to say it aloud, but what if the woman was simply too old to Heal?

But Gun was already shaking his head. "I asked. Last week a hunting party came back carrying one of their members with a bad leg break. The bones had pierced the skin. She Healed it.

"And she wants me to go with her this afternoon," he continued. "To help a small girl child who seems to have lost her wits. Together, Sortera says, we'll be able to Find them, and Heal her." Even he could hear the notes of awe and pleasure in his voice as he thought about the old woman's plan.

As Parno Lionsmane blew his breath out with force, making the woven back of the chair creak as he leaned back, Gun forced his attention back to the matter at hand.

"Then this is not the Lens," Lionsmane said. "It works for you because it *is* a scrying bowl. But it would work for everyone, if it were the Lens."

"What about Dhulyn Wolfshead. Can we get her to try?"

The Lionsmane twisted his lips and looked toward the window.

"You've tried already, haven't you?"

The man nodded. "Good news is, the vera tiles seem to work, though that may be because she's closer to her woman's time."

Gun pursed his lips in a silent whistle. "That's it then. We're back where we started. We haven't got the Lens."

"Then you'll Find it."

Dhulyn Wolfshead's quiet voice was filled with assurance, and Gun wished that it could do the same for him. He looked up at her impassive face and told himself there was no mistrust, no suspicion in her stone-gray eyes. He wasn't sure he believed it.

"I don't know what it looks like," he said, sounding, even to himself, like a child trying to escape the blame of eating the family's cakes.

"You didn't know what Tek-aKet's soul looked like either," Parno Lionsmane said. "But you managed to Find that. This is bound to be simpler. It'll be some artifact of the Jaldeans or even of you Scholars that no one thinks is of any importance."

"Try again," Wolfshead said. "Try the way you found Tek-aKet." She sat down on the stool to Gun's right, set her left ankle on her right knee, and folded her hands into her lap. The Lionsmane patted Gun on the shoulder before stepping back from the table himself. Behind him, Sortera sat against the whitewashed wall under the shuttered window, in the room's only padded chair, nodding over the knitting in her lap. Mar had fallen asleep on the pallet next to the old woman, her thick lashes making circled shadows on her cheeks.

Would he ever feel completely forgiven, Gun thought, as Mar so obviously did? Unable to stay awake, sent to bed with a kiss on the forehead like a favored daughter, while he sat here with the scrying bowl in front of him. Gun took a deep breath and set his hands lightly around the edge of the bowl. He was still alive, so he supposed he knew that Wolfshead and Lionsmane both did actually forgive him. He couldn't expect the affection they showed to Mar. Her offense had been against them personally, while his . . . He cleared his throat.

"Move the candle a little closer, please," he said, and out of the corner of his eye saw the Lionsmane's hand reach into the candle's circle of light and move it. The light's reflections on the surface of the water within the bowl flickered and moved, as if someone had taken a page of parchment and shaken it out like a sheet. The water—

❧❧❧

is a bright sheet of paper. And he is to write the story of the Lens. Ah, here is the Library. He wastes no time looking around him, but follows quickly the dark line on the floor that only he can see, the thread that will lead him through the labyrinth of library shelves to . . . Mar?

Mar sits in a carrel, asleep with her head down on her folded arms. Of course. He's thinking about her, sleeping so near him in the room, warm and soft. *Her* affection was in no doubt; bright and shining, he Finds it. He has to stop thinking about her, and think only of the Lens. He sees the line again at his feet and follows it, somehow knowing that this time he is going deeper into the library than he has been before, where he does not see even the shadowy outline of others. The line is fine and dark and leads him to. . . .

Mar again. This time she's snoring.

❧❧❧

There was a quality in Sortera's laugh that made the young Scholar blush. Dhulyn had been willing to swear the old woman had been sound asleep. "Easy to see what the lad's trying to Find," Sortera said. "Whether he knows it or not."

Dhulyn got up and stretched, pushing her hips first to one side, then the other. "She's right, my Scholar. It's late and all you can Find is your bed. We'll try again in the morning."

As Dhulyn watched, Gun took off his boots, shrugged out of his tunic, and in his shirt and breeches squeezed himself onto the pallet beside Mar. He put an arm around her, but Dhulyn couldn't tell if it was from real affection, or from lack of space. She hoped it was the former.

Parno tapped her on the shoulder and motioned with his head to the door, picking up his crossbow and hanging his sword on his belt as he went. The door's closely fitted planks gave immediately onto the steep stone staircase that ran between Sortera's narrow house and the building that was its neighbor.

Parno stepped down until he was standing a stair below her, and cupped her cheek in his callused hand. "My Brother, my soul." He spoke softly, mindful of the Clouds that lay sleeping all around them. "You look tired. Get some rest."

"I know what that means," she said, forcing a smile to her lips. "When a man tells you that you look tired, he's telling you that you look old."

"If this is what you'll look like when you're old, I sincerely hope we both live to see the day."

She felt her muscles loosen as she rested her forehead against his, felt his arms come up around her, drew in a breath full of his scent and nearness. "You'll be late for your watch," she murmured. She felt him nod, felt the touch of his lips on hers.

"I'll go for now," he said. "But I'll be back. I'll always be back."

"In Battle," she said.

"*And* in Death," he answered.

She watched him until he'd gone all the way down the narrow stone steps and turned the corner into the street—just as narrow but not so steep—below.

Dhulyn stood there in her vest and linen trousers until the cold mountain air had time to make her shiver. Then she lifted the wooden latch and stepped back inside Sortera's house.

Gun and Mar were both asleep, nested together like two arrows in a quiver. At first, Dhulyn thought Sortera had fallen asleep in her chair, but something about the length of the old woman's regular breaths, the deliberate movements of her fingers along the needles of her knitting, told Dhulyn Sortera was probably in a Healer's trance.

Wonder if she's Healing herself, Dhulyn thought. One way at least to explain how so old a woman could still be alive.

There was another pallet in the interior room, but Dhulyn's turn at watch along the upper slope would come soon enough to make sleep more of a bother than a help. Instead, she took Dal's small box from the shelf beside the hearth, pulled the chair Gun had been using closer to the table, and sat down in the light thrown by the lamp they'd lit to eat their suppers by. She opened the box and began taking out vera tiles.

❧❧❧

MAR IS DANCING. SHE WEARS A CLOTH-OF-SILVER GOWN WITH A CAREFULLY MENDED TEAR IN THE SHOULDER, A GOWN THIN ENOUGH TO SHOW THE SHADOW OF HER LIMBS AS SHE MOVES. WEDDING CLOTHES? DHULYN THINKS. SHE IS DANCING AT HER WEDDING. DHULYN LOOKS AT THE GUESTS, BUT IN THE WAY OF DREAMS, SHE CANNOT TELL FROM THEIR FACES WHO THEY ARE. AT FIRST THE DANCE IS A CIRCLE, MAR HOLDS THE HANDS OF THE PEOPLE NEXT TO HER, THEN THE CIRCLE BREAKS AND THE DANCERS WEAVE IN AND OUT, TAKING AND RELEASING HANDS AS THEY SKIP AND HOP PAST EACH OTHER, TURNING AND WEAVING A PATTERN IN THEIR DANCE. MAR IS NOT SMILING AND WHEN SHE LOOKS OVER HER SHOULDER AT WHERE DHULYN STANDS, IT IS A DIFFERENT WOMAN, OLDER, AND HER PALE BLOND HAIR IS DRESSED DIFFERENTLY. BUT SHE IS DANCING, STILL. . . .

THE MAGE SITS AT HIS TABLE, HIS BOOK IN FRONT OF HIM, HIS FINGER TRACING THE LINE HE READS, HIS LIPS FORMING THE WORDS.

HIS LIPS FORMING THE WORDS.

DHULYN MOVES CLOSER, UNTIL SHE CAN SEE THE WRITING ON THE PAGE IN FRONT OF HIM, BUT SHE CAN'T READ IT. SHE LOOKS AGAIN AT HIS LIPS.

ADELGARREMBIL, HIS LIPS SAY. *ACUCHEEYAROB. FETENTABIL. DEBEREE-YAROB. ESFUMARRENBIL.*

THE MAGE REPEATS THE WORDS SEVERAL TIMES AND CLOSES THE BOOK.

WHEN HE STANDS, DHULYN SEES HIS SWORD HANGING BY ITS SCABBARD FROM THE BACK OF HIS CHAIR.

"Dhulyn?" Mar's pupils were so wide in the candlelight they looked black.

"Go back to sleep, my Dove."

"I thought I heard you call me."

"You're dreaming, Dove. Go back to sleep."

Mar shut her eyes and Dhulyn began replacing the tiles back into their box.

This would be a good hour. The gold one has gone to stand his turn at watch. Why not slip in now? Their energies would be low; there might be no better time. He looked up, a bird flew overhead, showing its silhouette against the almost full moon. His lips smiled.

"Wolfshead."

Dhulyn had heard the soft sounds of booted feet behind her for some time, and so wasn't startled by Karlyn-Tan's voice when he finally spoke. She stopped at the end of the narrow lane and waited for him to join her before walking beside him across the small square.

"It's late for you to be out."

"I followed Cullen," Karlyn said. "But it seemed he was just giving his bird some hunting, and when I saw him safely back into his quarters, I suddenly felt the need of company."

"A few minutes earlier, and you would have caught Parno still awake."

"I did," he said, looking away from her as if to examine the face of the moon. "I saw him return from his watch and waited for you."

Dhulyn glanced at him, but he was still looking at the night sky. They reached the spot where she was to stand her watch, where a young Cloudwoman yawned, waiting for Dhulyn to relieve her. They exchanged hand signals and the Cloud left them, silently moving through the empty streets to her bed.

The northwestern end of the valley in which the village of Trevel lay was marked with a small orchard of apple trees. There was no wall as such, only a few large boulders placed to give those who took the herds beneath the trees a place to rest their legs. On the far side of the orchard was a stream, and the shallow pass that marked the village's vulnerable point from this direction. It was that pass that accounted for Dhulyn's presence here, as every weapons-wise adult in Trevel—even guests if they were trusted—was expected to take a turn at guard duty.

Telling Karlyn to wait for her by the rocks, Dhulyn scouted through the orchard, ears primed to catch every sound and nose prickling at the sharp, clean scent of trees newly and thickly leaved. She heard the foraging of small animals under the trees halt as she neared and continue as she moved farther away. When she was satisfied that there was nothing in the orchard more dangerous than herself, she rejoined Karlyn at the rocks.

"I have heard," Karlyn said after they had been silent for many minutes. "That Partnered Brothers often have lovers."

It took Dhulyn a moment to realize that her mouth was hanging open, and to shut it. She set her crossbow on the ground, and leaned forward, elbows on knees, chin propped on her hands. She'd had lovers, of course, as had Parno, but she was always surprised by the offer. She let her eyes drop to Karlyn's hands, with their strong fingers, resting on his knees.

"The bond," she said, "is not how you imagine it." They sat so close, she could reach out and touch him with no effort at all. As if he read her thought he lifted his hand and reached toward the side of her face. The moon, shining through the screen of apple leaves, was bright and full enough to give a green cast to the light.

"Look up, my Wolfshead. Let me see your eyes."

Dhulyn straightened until her hands rested on her knees. Without pause, she lifted her head, smiling, and felt the little fold at her upper lip that created her wolf's smile. As her head rose, she took a deep, steadying breath, raised her hands, and—just before their eyes could meet—she struck.

She caught the unconscious man as he pitched forward, easing him to the ground and searching through the laces on her clothing for something long enough to tie him.

"What was taking you so long?" Cullen said, stepping out of the orchard just as Disha landed on his shoulder.

"I had to be certain," Dhulyn said. "Look." She turned one of Karlyn's hands palm up in the moonlight and compared it to her own. Her hand was pale and white in the moonlight, his showed a faint but unmistakable green cast.

Twenty-seven

THE LOCKUP IN Trevel proved to be a disused horse stall in the back of the headman's house. Like every other building in the village, the walls were thick stone covered with whitewashed plaster, but the window opening had an iron grille, Parno noted, not shutters, and the door was barred from the outside.

Gundaron, bent over the trussed Karlyn-Tan, looked up and nodded. "It's here," he said.

Sortera leaned on her staff, shaking her head. "Nothing wrong with him that I can sense," she said. "Barring that he's unconscious, see you."

"We'll want to keep him that way," Dhulyn said. "Can we?"

The old woman's face creased as she smiled. "'Course you can, there's drugs to do it, as you well know. But we'll have to watch him carefully if we don't want to kill him." She thought a moment, frowning heavily. "Let me talk to the village Knife. Between us, we can work out the dosages, see you." She tilted her head, focused her sharp eyes on Dhulyn. "How long do you plan to keep him this way?"

Dhulyn drew her eyes away from Karlyn-Tan. "As long as we have to."

"We'll need to look to our supplies, then," Sortera said. "We can't have innocent people going without because we're using all we have on this one."

"Then we'll have to find a more permanent solution," Parno said. "Wait for us in the other room, Grandmother.

We'll come as soon as Gun's finished." He turned to Dhulyn and lowered his voice still further.

"Are you certain it's trapped?"

Dhulyn shrugged. "I couldn't think of anything else to do. From something Yaro told me, I hoped I could strike at the body fast enough to trap it in Karlyn, especially since it did not know I suspected it."

Parno loosened the muscles in his jaw that kept getting too tight. "I'm surprised he let you get close enough for the Hooded Snake *Shora.*"

Dhulyn shrugged. "Even those who have seen a woman's strength never really believe she'll use it against *them.*"

Parno coughed. "And what about you, Cullen. Why didn't you tell us?"

The Cloudman's teeth gleamed white for an instant as he smiled. He was leaning against the wall next to the door. "What was I going to do, Lionsmane? Swear to you I wasn't possessed?"

Dhulyn and Gun both laughed.

Parno rubbed his face with his hands. It seemed his own bond with Dhulyn helped him to sense the link that they had between them. The Marked. As potent and as real as the bond of Partnership. It was a good thing, he told himself, he was only uneasy because he hadn't experienced it before. Before, it had only been Dhulyn and him, and he could almost forget her Mark.

Surely it was only this uneasiness, this new sensation of exclusion, that gave him the feeling things were getting out of hand?

Dhulyn walked down the long narrow lane that snaked its way through the quarter in which Sortera had her house, having volunteered to fetch water. The tension was beginning to tell on everyone. Even after being up all night, she felt completely unable to sleep. The morning sun was bright, the streets—really more like stone-laid paths slanted to allow the water to run off downhill—still showed the damp marks of dew in the shady corners.

Dhulyn had tried the tiles again after returning to their

quarters in Sortera's house, and even though they'd worked, she Saw no Visions that she hadn't already Seen, although each was clear and precise in a way they had never been before.

She stopped as a door in the wall beside her opened and discharged a Cloudwoman of her own age with a large basket of eggs on her hip. The villager saluted her with a nod and a "good morning" before setting off down the lane at a pace only a native would have found comfortable, given the steepness of the street.

Chickens in an inner courtyard, Dhulyn thought. Enough of them that the excess eggs were going to market to be sold or traded for things that didn't grow in the woman's inner courtyard. The uncomplicated pattern of village life. When had their lives, hers and Parno's, become so complicated? Since Navra. Dhulyn slowed her pace even more. And she'd had more Visions since Navra as well, now that she thought about it. The fresnoyn would account for some of those, she knew, as would the unusual stress and worry of being so near Parno's home. Even the weather might have made its contribution. Blood knew, she'd never been really comfortable in the warmer north.

More Visions; fine, she could account for those. But why clearer ones?

Dhulyn shook off her thoughts and looked around her. Trevel was like no other town or village she had lived in, tucked into its high mountain valley, its location protected by narrow passes and thick forests impenetrable to those who didn't know the ways. Ahead of her now was the tallest structure in town, the stone tower of a Jaldean Shrine—Old Believers, of course—and beyond that, perhaps three days' ride away, the peaks of the Antedichas Mountains to the south. Nothing like what little she could remember of her own birthplace, the cold, windswept southern plains, or even any of the port towns she'd known during her Schooling with Dorian the Black.

Light voices sang out ahead of her as a small group of children ran out from a crossing lane, racing down to the small square between the Jaldeans' tower and the public fountain.

Bursting into the open space, the children did a quick

rhyming count to see who would be the victim—"one two, sky blue, all out but you" was what Dhulyn caught—and one small boy was blindfolded and took his place in the center of four others. As these four joined hands and began to chant, Dhulyn stopped to watch, setting her buckets down on the cobblestones.

> *"Sleeping lad, sleeping lad*
> *Turning, turning, turning*
> *One two three, come to me."*

The children repeated the chant several times, stepping first in one direction, then turning and skipping the other way, sometimes faster, sometimes slower. Finally, they fell silent, stopped, and dropped hands. The blindfolded boy in the middle began immediately to grope for his friends, grabbing the smallest girl as her giggle gave her location away.

They had used almost the same words and a very similar tune as the children on the pier in Navra, Dhulyn thought; children were so much the same everywhere. So much had happened since the evening when they first met Mar and the Weaver woman in the tavern room of their Navra inn. So much—

"Oh, for blood's sake."

A woman passing between her and the children glanced at her with a tentative smile.

The Lens tile in the center with the other Marks placed around it. A child in the center with four others circling around. *Circling.* Herself asleep on the trail with Mar in her arms, Mar with her hands on Gundaron's shoulders.

Not the bowl. *Mar.* Mar herself.

Dhulyn whirled around, almost tripping over the buckets she didn't remember until much later, and ran back up the hill.

❈❈❈

Mar and Gun sat on the stone threshold of Sortera's house, holding hands, squeezed into the doorway, the door open behind them and a beaded curtain let down to keep flies and direct sunlight from inside the house. Not that it was really hot enough yet for either. Mar held his hand, rested her head on his shoulder. A man had passed them a few minutes earlier, giving them the courteous greeting and half bow that all Clouds seemed to give to Marks, with a special smile when he saw their joined hands. Mar knew that, appearances to the contrary, they were holding hands for comfort and companionship, not love.

But the love's here, she thought. *It's here.*

Gun sighed. "I'm so useless," he said.

Mar bit back an exasperated retort. "Come on," she said, as kindly as she could manage given that what she really felt like was slapping him. "We've been through this. You've done the best you could."

"And how good was that? Dhulyn Wolfshead had to find it, and the Shadow was right under my nose the whole time."

Well, no arguing with that, Mar thought. She was trying to come up with an argument, however, when the Wolfshead herself came running up the narrow steps—*smiling.*

"Gun, you were right, the books were right. I should have listened to you from the start. We're just too blooded smart for our own good."

Gun got to his feet. "I was right?"

The beads behind them rattled as Parno Lionsmane joined them in the doorway. Mar felt something tight in her chest loosen as Dhulyn Wolfshead gave her Partner a wide and joyous grin.

"We're making this too hard. The fifth Mark you said, Gun, and the fifth Mark it is. The Lens *isn't* a thing. It's a Mark, like all the others. Not a *thing,* a *person.*"

Shutters popped open in the house across the stairs.

"Inside," Dhulyn Wolfshead said, ushering everyone before her.

"But why hasn't anyone met a Lens?" Parno Liondsmane said. "Not even Sortera, and she isn't sure how long she's been alive."

"Listen!" The Wolfshead sat down on a stool. Her chest rose and fell, but she didn't seem to be out of breath, for all the running uphill she'd just done. She reached out for Gun, and when he was near enough, she took his hands in hers. "You know how all the books and stories say that some Marks are rarer than others. Menders the most common,

Seers the most rare? The Lens must be the rarest of all! There's no general use for a Lens. It only affects another Mark. It's a focuser, a *Lens*."

Gun sat down, and seemed unaware that Parno Lions-mane got a stool under him just in time to prevent his falling to the floor. He was nodding, his eyes focused inward. "It makes sense. It's logical." He looked up at Dhulyn Wolfshead. "That passage in Holderon's *Commentaries* makes sense if what you say is true. That's why I couldn't Find it, I've been looking for a thing. You've *got* to be right."

Mar's cheeks hurt, and she found she was smiling just as hard as the Mercenaries. The weight that had oppressed everyone since the discovery of Karlyn-Tan's possession seemed to be lifting.

Then she saw that Gun wasn't smiling, and she felt her own smile fade.

"But, Wolfshead," Mar said, sure now that she saw the flaw in all this deduction. "We still don't know who . . ."

Dhulyn Wolfshead was holding up one finger. "Oh, yes, we do."

That was when Mar realized that the Wolfshead was pointing at her.

❧

Jerrick Mender was almost twelve years old, thin, with eyes so large and round his name would be Jerrick Owlbeak if he were a Mercenary Brother. When Parno told him that, he seemed quite pleased, and Dhulyn had laughed. Parno had always had a way with children.

"You didn't see my parents in Gotterang? Savern and Korwina Mender?" he said in a voice too old for his child's face. A voice that said he knew the answer, but had to ask.

"No, Jerrick, I'm afraid not."

The boy nodded. "I promised my sisters I would ask. There was another Mercenary Brother who helped us, Hernyn Greystone. Is he with you?"

Parno exchanged a look with Dhulyn, who shrugged. There was no good news to tell this boy.

"Our Brothers are always with us," Parno said gently, crouching down until he was on Jerrick's level. "Hernyn Greystone the Shield is with us in Death."

Jerrick Mender's lower lip disappeared, and he nodded, blinking.

"Will you be able to help us, Jerrick Mender?" Dhulyn asked.

The boy squared his shoulders, taking a deep breath that shook a little on the way in. "I think so," he said. "My Mark's new, but my mother was training me since I was little."

Parno patted the boy on the shoulder.

It had taken what felt like hours to convince everyone that what she'd suggested could be so, and at that, Dhulyn was sure they were willing to try only because no one could think of something else to do.

"Look," she had finally said. "It's Mar that I keep seeing in my Visions—has been right from the start and the same Vision over and over. When Mar is in the room, my Visions are clearer, have more detail, even when I'm using the vera tiles. And it was Mar that Gun kept Finding, not because he was tired and wanted to go to bed, but because he was looking for the Lens."

"There is one thing," Parno said now, making room for Jerrick at the table with the others. "Now that we know what the Lens is, what are we going to do with her?"

Dhulyn looked at Gun and nodded. "There's one of each of us," he said. "It's common for Finders, Menders, and Healers to work together; and Sortera remembers working with a Seer, years ago. With her experience to guide us, we should be able to unite our Marks, and using the Lens . . ." He looked at Mar and seemed to gather strength from her nod. "We're going to call the Sleeping God."

"Oh, good," Parno said. "I was afraid we didn't know what we were doing." Dhulyn rolled her eyes.

"I suggest we use the drying shed," Sortera said. "It's the largest space that's not in use at the moment, and whatever happens, there's not much there to damage."

At this time of year, the drying shed was almost empty, the larger stores of food long since used or moved to more convenient places. The air smelled clean, and slightly spicy from a few bundles of herbs still hanging from rafters high overhead. They stood on a stone floor, so perfect and smooth that Dhulyn knew it for a relic of the Caids. The drying racks, empty now, had been folded and stacked against the walls.

"In my Vision," Dhulyn said when she found everyone looking at her. "Mar was standing, holding the hands of the people next to her." Mar took hold of Gun's left hand with her right, and offered her left hand to Jerrick. Dhulyn shook her head. "But the vera tiles have the Lens in the center and the rest of us around her . . ."

Sortera was nodding. "Take Mar's left hand in your left, Jerrick, now give your right to Dhulyn Wolfshead. And you, Gun, give your left to me. See now, we're all connected."

Mar nodded. "It's like the start of a country dance."

"There was a dance in my youth," said Sortera, "so many years ago now, that began like this—"

"The Market Dance," Parno said. "You remember, Dhulyn, I told you my sisters used to dance it."

"The *Marked* Dance." Both Dhulyn and Gun spoke at once. "But with the Lens in the center," Dhulyn continued, "not the Seer as you thought, Parno, my soul."

"It *is* possible," Gun added.

Parno pulled the chanter of his pipes from his belt. "Do you remember the tune, Sortera? What?" He looked at the faces in the form. "You'll need to focus on something and the music can be just as old as the dance."

Sortera shut her eyes and began to hum a tune. Parno frowned. At first, it seemed the woman's age was against them. Like many elderly people, her voice had lost its ability to modulate itself into notes, but as she hummed, her body began to move in time to the beat, and after a few more tuneless notes, the humming grew stronger, and the notes more distinct. He began to hear hints of the tune and it seemed familiar; much like the one Dhulyn had been humming for months, but also like the one he remembered from his own childhood. Parno lifted his chanter to his lips and began to play. Like all these tunes from round dances, the same short, bouncy melody repeated itself over and over.

"Hey." Jerrick laughed. "I know this song. My father taught us this game when I was little." His feet began to move in short skipping steps, and under his breath, he began to sing,

> *"Sweeping Lad, Sweeping Lad,*
> *Brushing up and down . . .*

Gundaron the Finder frowned. This wasn't going to work. Nobody had taught *him* a game to this tune when *he* was a boy. *Stop it,* he thought. He couldn't be the only one who stood apart, the only one who wasn't doing his best, who wasn't helping. So he didn't know the game, so what? He could *Find* it. He relaxed and let the others lead him, trying to match his pacing to theirs. This was a line, very twisty but just a line, like in the Library in his head. The steps were simple enough. Across and through, let go Mar's hand, turn and catch Dhulyn's, while Sortera was turning and catching Mar's, having let go of Jerrick—he stumbled. *Just let it happen, trust them, don't think about it too much.*

Gun shut his eyes, let the music wash over him. Saw a page with writing. No, not writing, musical notes. He could read them like words, and, under his breath, he began to sing,

> *"Leaping Lad, Leaping Lad,*
> *Where have you been?*
> *Leaping Lad, Leaping Lad,*
> *Step right in . . ."*

Sortera the Healer remembered the dance very well, and laughed aloud with the ease that her feet found in flying through the measure. The circle of the dancers turned, and she threw back her head, remembering. Sunny afternoons, the vault of the sky turning above her as the dance went 'round.

> *"Sleeping God, Sleeping God,*
> *Only you can know, we are where you go*
> *Sleeping God, Sleeping God,*
> *In our hearts we know, all around we grow . . ."*

Dhulyn the Seer thought, *of course, this is why the game and the song, and the dance has survived, and all children know it. In case we should need to call the God.* She thought how much the dance was like the *Shora,* or how much the *Shora* like the dance. The same steps over and over, again and again, until you could do them automatically, blindfolded. Her pulse slowed, her breathing became regular. She could feel herself falling into the familiar trance, the dream state of her Sight. She Saw the dancers and the dance. The calling of the God. Someone was singing, words that matched the steps of the *Shora,* the steps of the dance —

> *"Weeping Lass, Weeping Lass,*
> *Hold with all your might*
> *Win your heart's delight . . ."*

Mar was smiling and humming, her feet moving naturally and freely as if they already knew the steps. *Of course they do.* She remembered the old game well. *She's dancing.*

> *"Sweeping Lad, Sweeping Lad,*
> *In and out he goes*
> *Can we really know . . ."*

Except Mar sang "Weeping Maid, Weeping Maid," and Dhulyn heard "Leaping Lad, Leaping Lad" and Gundaron heard "Sweeping Lass, Sweeping Lass," and they all heard "Sleeping God, Sleeping God."

The right words Found, the steps of the measure Mended, the faulty heartbeats Healed, the Sight cleared, and all

FOCUSED

> *"Sleeping God, Sleeping God*
> *Come into our arms, show us where to go*
> *In our hearts we know, these the parts that grow*
> *One to teach, one to touch, one to reach, one's too much*
> *Bring us an old one, a cold one, a bold one*
> *Give us a sold one, a told one, a gold one."*

The dance goes round and round, every step in time, everything perfect, as if we aren't five people dancing, but one. And we are singing in a tongue we never heard before, but in words we understand. We were scattered pieces until the Finder found us; the Mender put us back together; the Healer gave us the beat of our heart; the Seer looked before and behind, back through the mists to those others, forward into the light of tomorrow's dawns; the Lens focuses all, the power and the light; the parts the form the heart, the light.

No longer parts, but a perfect whole. No longer Sleeping, but Awake.

We are the Sleeping God.

"We can see the whole world. From the roots of mountains to the thinnest reaches of the air. Every heartbeat, every eye blink." There's awe and pleasure in her voice.

"And the Shape and purpose of all these things."

"Look! A wrinkle there in the fabric of the world, just this one spot, where there's a whole."

"You mean a *hole*." We laugh.

"Let's Mend it, it's easy when you know how." The youngest part of us is very happy to be Mending.

Together we're Sight, and we're the Lens turning the Light until in it we See the Shadow. We'll Find, and once Found, we'll Mend and we'll Heal.

"There." The Finding part of us is strong and true now, Mended and Healthy.

"The Green Shadow."

The youngest part is frightened; we all are, but together it is much easier to be brave.

"What is it?"

"It's mad. Forced to 'shape' in our world, its wholeness makes it broken, and drives it insane."

"In its madness it will destroy, unmake, undo."

"To make a home for itself."

"How sad, how frightened it must be."

"We *must* destroy it, or let its madness destroy us. For the safety of all, and for mercy to it as well."

"Please, don't let's hurt it. Can't it be Mended? Isn't it a lost child, singing the same in-and-out song that we know? Couldn't we Find its home?"

"It's too badly hurt, like a dragon, dying, but breathing poison as it dies."

"It's like torn pieces of paper and parchments covered

with writing, glued and sewn together by a child. Form without true content, spilling lies."

"It is a plague victim, innocent but spreading death as it walks."

"We need to see more clearly, focus more. The Shadow is all and none of these things. If we must destroy it, let us give it honor. It will fight us, in its madness and its fear. Let us be a warrior, and give it a clean death."

It is best to be the Wolfshead; skilled, deadly, and unstoppable. I alone of all of us have Seen this room before, and can feel at ease here.

The man looks up from the table, shock showing in his face. "You can't follow me here."

I approach him, looking at him with our head tilted to one side. "Who do you think you speak to?"

"Dhulyn Wolfshead."

The man looks like Karlyn-Tan, but I shake that from our mind. Now he is Lok-iKol, his one eye blazing green, and that is easier. He looks down at his hands, face twisted in surprise.

"How—who *are* you?"

"You *know* who." There is a sword in our hand and I cut, striking off the hand nearest us and a piece of jade-green stone falls to the floor. Its hand and arm remain still whole. I see the comprehension pass over his face like a cloud across the sun. He whirls and snatches the sword from the scabbard that hangs on the back of the chair. He strikes at me, but I jump back.

I look around us. "This is the room where it all began. There's the mirror." I leap on the table and cut at him again, but this time the One-eye parries, and jumps back himself, forcing us to descend once more to the floor. I strike and whirl and strike again, moving our feet in the *Shora,* but he wards off our blows.

"When I am whole—" his mouth twists as if the word itself was poison, "I can come back to this room. Behind that mirror, through that sky, is my home, the real world, not this place of *shape* and *form*." His mouth forms those words, but the thought I can see in his mind is "horror" and "pain."

"I can end your pain." A cut, a thrust, which the one-eyed man does not parry in time. Our sword penetrates his left side to the depth of three fingers. If this were a man, he would be bleeding too freely to continue fighting.

Of course, if this were a man, my earlier cut would have removed his hand, and he would have bled to death already.

"No, you can only break me into pieces. Me, that should never have had form to be made into parts. Do you think that ends the pain?"

"What would end it?"

"Open the door, send me home."

I smile and shake our head. "I would open the door, and others of your kind would come here." But the youngest part of us, the part that is a little boy is crying, he, too, has lost his home. I shake our head again. Our homes are also lost, but I have found another. I have her Brotherhood. I have Parno Lionsmane. He is our home. The little one, he, too, will find a new home. But what about this one's home, the little one asks us?

The man changes again. Now he's the Mage. The sword flicks out, much faster than the One-eye could use it, and I fall back, tasting a sharp flicker of fear in our throat.

"Do you think I would wish this suffering on any other of my kind?" he says. He steps back, lowers his sword, and points to the book on the table.

"I cannot read the book. That is too much form for me, too much shape. It is not just words, but thoughts, the form of form and shape of shape. If I could use the book, I would have gone from here before the madness came."

I keep our sword high, but think. It is true that I have Seen this man trying to open the gate, and failing. And that man wept, not from frustrated ambition, but from despair. I know, because I Saw truly, and I See truly now. I back around the table until I can glance down at the book. It is a language I have never seen before. I can't read it. We can't Find it.

I look up at him. "Would you promise to stay here, in this room, to leave the world alone?"

He shakes his head, rubs at his lips with trembling hand. "I *must* unmake it. It is madness. I must be sane again. I *must*." He snatches up the sword again. He strikes, again, and again, and I fall back, suddenly feeling the young ones' fear weighing down my limbs, the old one's age in my laboring lungs.

The edges of the room begin to waver, the walls to dissolve and I try, my breath short and my eyes watering, to Find my place again as the *NOT* approaches, closer . . .

Focus. I need focus. The Hunting Cat *Shora*. Defense and offense. Stillness and movement. I grasp at the *Shora* and they all grasp with me, all breathe with me; our hearts beat as one. We breathe as one, and together I fall into the Hunting Cat *Shora,* sword up, left hand raised, feet sliding across the floor, keeping our weight balanced.

I glide toward him like the cat the *Shora* is named for and he cuts at our head. I parry, he cuts again, thinking to blind us with his speed, but I move when he blinks, faster than he imagines possible, for I am the God Awake. I cut his arm, slash his ribs, and miss his neck by a hair-breadth. He touches our thigh, but I Heal.

It is like a dance, and I hum a tune under my breath as I strike, and strike. I feel all our thoughts, all I feel, *focus*. The pain of loss. A home gone. The need to have that home restored, and the hateful and the horrible things that need drives us to do. Part of me weeps, and I know I must end this. I am the Sleeping God, but my bodies are human. I cannot dance this measure forever.

But he is so lonely, and all he wants is his home. I stand back, our breath rough and uneven, the sound of weeping in our ears, the taste of tears on our lips.

As if he hears my thoughts, and shares my feeling, the Green Shadow steps away.

"Home," he says. He is trembling, and I see ourselves shining in the light that comes from his eyes. He reverses his sword and plunges it into the floor.

He falls to his knees and bows his head, covering his face with hands that shake. "Break me, Sleeping God," he says. "Let one of us keep their home. Buy your world time. Let us start the long dance again. Until the one is Found who can send me home."

I take the Mage's sword in our left hand, I step toward him, close enough to strike.

"How many times have we danced these steps?" I ask him.

He shakes his head.

I have seen him in this room many times. He cannot read the book, and without it, he cannot cut the mirror, he cannot open the gate. But I also cannot read the book. Even I, the Sleeping God. Healer, Finder, Mender, Seer, held and focused by the Lens. Scholar, warrior, child, maid, crone. I have to strike, to break him once more into pieces, begin the dance of the Sleeping God again. Will another like us See this room? See the Mage reading his book? See his lips forming—

I leap over the kneeling man at our feet and raise the Mage's sword. *Adelgarrembil,* our lips say. *Acucheeyarob. Fetentabil. Debereeyarob. Esfumarrenbil.*

I bring the sword down and cut the mirror, cut the night sky, and the gateway opens. The joy of the Shadow behind us cuts through us like a knife as it blows, flies, ROARS through us and into its own place.

We teeter on the brink of the gate. There is no room behind us, there never was, and there is nothing, no safe-guard, no door to shut, that prevents us, our thoughts, our *selves,* from being sucked through into the formless *NOT.* Nothing, the real nothing, awaits us, our parts unmaking into the *NOT.*

I drop no sword from no hand fall to no knees

Until there is only one small piece of us left.

A thin line of black traces through the blue and the green.

Parno, I think, *my soul.*

Suddenly I Find a sound, a chord of music, playing itself through our mind. Our feet move in the dance. We Mend the cut in the universes. We Heal the holes in our being. We turn to See, and clearly, brightly, with great focus, Dhulyn Wolfshead finds herself in her Partner's arms.

Twenty-eight

PARNO SAT IN the chair by the edge of the bed on which Karlyn-Tan, gray-faced and drawn, lay propped up on feather pillows.

"Sortera the Healer has finished her long journey," Parno said. "She did not wake from the trance of the god."

"We were almost unmade," Dhulyn added from where she leaned on the doorframe. "And she chose to use her strength to Heal us. So you must heal yourself, Karlyn, with rest and good food. We'll wait for you to return to Gotterang with us."

"Don't wait," Karlyn said. "I'm not going back to Gotterang."

Dhulyn approached the bed, stopped with her hand on Parno's shoulder. "Where, then?" she said.

"I'm going to Tourin," Karlyn said. "To Nerysa Warhammer. I'd like a House that won't cast me out."

"You can't do better," Parno said.

"If you live through it," Dhulyn added.

❧

Two days later they were at the edge of the Vale of Trevel, on the unmarked path that led to the Gotterang Pass. Their packs were tied securely to their saddles, and their horses were restive, already looking forward to the road.

"You're sure you won't come with us," Parno was saying to Mar. "Dal would be glad of you, I think. He seems to set great store by his relatives."

"Maybe one day," Mar said, looking over her shoulder

at where Gun was looking down the trail. He must have felt her gaze; he turned and smiled at her, and her face lit up. "We're going to Valdomar. Gun needs to write down all that's happened, and while he does, I'd like to see if the Scholar's life is for me."

"The Scholar is definitely for you, I would say." Dhulyn stroked Mar's hair away from her face, and suddenly found her arms full, as the girl hugged her.

"There, little Dove, we'll meet again, don't fear it."

Mar stepped back, blinking. "We tried again last night," she said. "Not because we don't believe it, but . . ."

"Just to be sure," Dhulyn said, turning to check Blood-bone's girth.

"There no sign of it." Gun drew nearer. "Nowhere in my mind's Library. Even the wall of books is gone."

"Never thought I'd be happy to hear that books had disappeared." She gave Gundaron a friendly shove and was surprised at the flush of pleasure that colored his face.

"And with Mar's help?"

"No difference," the girl said with a wistful look. "I don't think I'm the Lens anymore."

"Broken?" Parno said.

Mar shook her head. "Jerrick says not, he feels nothing broken about me. I don't feel any different, just," she shrugged, "lighter, maybe."

"The Lens has dissolved, perhaps, like the godhood we were; unnecessary now." Dhulyn swung herself into the saddle. "The gods blow fair winds on you, and warm. Farewell, my Doves."

⚒⚒⚒

They had passed over the crest of the first hill, and looking back no longer showed them Gun and Mar standing side by side. Not, Parno thought, that Dhulyn had looked back.

"The God's gone, then?" he asked her.

Dhulyn frowned, her blood-red brows drawn down in a vee over her narrowed eyes. "The Sleeping God is gone. Perhaps forever." She looked up, her brow still clouded. "If its only purpose was to oppose the Green Shadow, then there is no further need of the Sleeping God." She thought for a moment, until her face cleared. "We can't know. As

Mar said, Gun will write it all down, in case the God is ever needed again. Lenses will be tested for, like the other Marks—though, thank the Caids, I don't have to create the test, for I've no notion what it might be."

"But for us, it's over?"

"I won't forget. Shape and form has been at the root of this, and part of me will always remember what it was to be the form of the God."

"Oh, wonderful," Parno threw up his hands. "My Partner is a god. I'll never hear the end of this."

A half moon later they were in Gotterang. They found that Karlyn-Tan could have accompanied them after all, as Dorian the Black had docked his ship in Gotterang's harbor, the better to oversee the rebuilding of Mercenary House.

"The maps are safe, thanks to your warning," he told them, once they had been found seats in a half-restored room and been served with mugs of hot ganje. "Though we've told the Tarkina that they were destroyed in the fire."

"Thus setting any fears of us to rest," Parno said. "So we've only to present ourselves at the Carnelian Dome, collect our wages, with, it's to be hoped, a nice bonus, and be on our way."

Dorian shook his head.

"Bet-oTeb Tarkin, on the advice of her Guardian, Zelianora Tarkina, has sent you your wages here, and begs that you not present yourselves at the Dome. Though it's been proclaimed that you found and killed the assassins of Tek-aKet Tarkin, awkward questions may yet be asked. Bet-oTeb Tarkin suggests that you may wish to find employment elsewhere until interest dies down. Zelianora Tarkina suggests her sister, the Queen of Berdana, may have work for you."

"Essentially, take your wages and leave the country—better yet, the continent?"

"Essentially." Dorian's smile was very white in his dark face. "There's a ship just now in the harbor, leaving tomorrow at dawn. The *Horse's Mane*. A good omen if ever I heard one."

As they walked down the staircase to the sound of carpenters hammering, Parno looked around.

"Well, at least we've been paid this time."

"Do you realize what our expenses have been? Replace at least one horse? Two thirds of our weapons gone and the expensive two thirds at that? A capital city is not the best place for good prices. And now we're to buy passage on a ship at the height of the season?" Dhulyn stopped, her fingers tapping out a now familiar rhythm on the railing. "Did Dorian say the ship leaves at dawn?"

"What of it?"

She gestured at the carpentry work around them. "We can't sleep here, so that means an inn, and where there's an inn there's a taproom . . ."

"And where there's a taproom there's gamblers. Do you think they'll let you use your own tiles?"

THE
SOLDIER KING

Acknowledgments

As always, my first thanks go to Joshua Bilmes and Sheila Gilbert, without whom Dhulyn and Parno would be practicing their *Shora* where no one else could see them. To my friend Barb Wilson-Orange who listened to the story before it reached paper; to Sue Rohland, for her enthusiasm and helpful critiques; to Grant and Jenn Musselman (and Devin) for their unfailing support; to Stephan Furster for looking after my website; to Vaso, Maria, and Jovanna Angelis, for their support, and their help in keeping me decently clothed. To Tanya Huff and Fiona Patton, always for everything. I'd particularly like to thank Brian Henry, for all those useful writing workshops, and all his support since those days, not so long ago.

Megan Primeau, better known as "Megz," purchased at silent auction the right to have a character named after her. I salute you, the Queen's White Blade.

One

PARNO LIONSMANE LOOKED OVER the battlefield that was the valley of Limona with his nose wrinkled. Every soldier became used to the smell of the dead and dying, but not even Mercenary Brothers ever got so that they liked it. From his fidgeting, it seemed to Parno that even his big gray gelding, Warhammer, battle-trained as he was, would just as soon be elsewhere.

"What happened here?" Parno asked.

"Exactly what was supposed to happen. Exactly what I Saw in my Vision." His Partner, Dhulyn Wolfshead, shrugged, making the red cloak she'd won off Cavalry Squad Leader Jedrick swing around her knees. "Against odds, the Tegrians lost and the Nisveans won. Which is why, I remind you, we signed on with the Nisveans."

"So what *happened*? Has the Blue Mage lost his power?"

Still looking out over the field sloping away from them toward the banks of the river Limona, Dhulyn shook her head, her lip curling back in her wolf's smile. "Don't be naïve."

There was movement to be seen between them and the river, the living going through the pockets of the dead.

"Well, I'm not going to rob corpses, no matter what you Saw."

"There's nothing in the Common Rule against it," Dhulyn said. "I once got a very nice thumb knife off a dead man."

"Outlander."

"Town man." She gave him the smile she saved only for him.

As Mercenary Brothers, they were not obliged to pursue those who fled from the field of battle, and Dhulyn—who was, after all, Senior Brother—had decided to look over the fallen instead.

"Do you think it very likely that we will find any of your kin here?" Parno said.

"No more likely than anywhere else," she replied. "But it's easy enough to check."

That was true. Dhulyn's distinctive coloring, pale eyes, pale skin, her hair the color of old blood, would make a person easy to find among the fallen of a battlefield. If, that is, there were in fact any other survivors of the catastrophe which had wiped out the tribes when she was a child.

"But you didn't *See* any Red Horsemen here?" Parno looked sideways at his Partner. Her lips were pressed together, her eyes scanning the far edges of the valley.

"Come now, my heart," he said. "We haven't been looking, *truly* looking that is, for very long, a few moons, no more. Don't lose heart so soon. Your Sight *is* getting better," he told her. "Since you started using the vera tiles, it's not so erratic." He scratched at the stubble on his chin.

Dhulyn's head moved in short arcs from side to side. "My Mark could be more useful if I could control it completely."

Parno drummed his fingers on his thigh. Let her tell him something he didn't already know. "Let's look on the sunny side," he said. "If we meet any more Red Horsemen, and they are anything like you, it might be more than I could tolerate."

Dhulyn looked at him without moving her head. She gestured at the corpse-strewn valley before them. "My people couldn't possibly cause as much trouble as *yours*." She brought her heels in sharply, and her mare, Bloodbone, leaped away.

"In Battle," Parno called out to her back.

"In Death," answered the sign from her lifted hand.

Parno let Warhammer set his own pace as they picked their way slowly out to the eastern edge of the valley. *Not much of a battle,* he thought, looking at the preponderance of Tegriani on the ground. *Slaughter's more the word.* The Tegriani invaders must have been shocked indeed when they began to take heavy wounds, but many were veterans of the days before the Blue Mage began to work his magics on their armies, and they had been holding their own until the Nisvean reserve, which had included Parno and Dhulyn, had fallen on their left flank. Then the Tegriani had broken and run, and far more of them were cut down as they fled than would have been killed had they only stood their ground.

But then, they hadn't expected to be killed. Even now, their dead faces showed surprise.

Parno reined in as Warhammer shied to the left. From the look of the corpse at the horse's feet, this section had been picked over already, though a short cloak had been left behind, evidently too torn and bloody to be worth taking. The body looked to have been a man in his early twenties, his only wound the bleeding shoulder.

Parno leaned out of his saddle, narrowing his eyes. The *bleeding* shoulder? He swung his leg over Warhammer's withers and let himself slide to the ground. Squatting, he gave the body a long hard look, and pulled a corner of the cloak over the wound—and over the corpse's face while he was at it.

"Keep that shoulder covered," he said, his voice a low murmur that wouldn't travel far. "You're still bleeding, and dead men don't bleed. Wait until the moon's set, if you can, and then go south a good few spans before you turn west." He grunted in satisfaction when the man showed no reaction whatsoever and, turning away, climbed back into the saddle.

Doing his best to appear just as relaxed as he had been before, Parno began to angle his horse toward the river's edge, away from the "corpse," toward the bright splotch of red that was Dhulyn. She was leaning so far out of the saddle that anyone other than the Red Horseman she was would have fallen off. When she straightened, and then slid off Bloodbone's back, Parno clucked his tongue, and touched his heels to Warhammer's sides.

***

Dhulyn Wolfshead pursed her lips and blew out her breath in a silent whistle as she scanned the ground. They said all battlefields looked the same, but any real soldier, let alone a Mercenary Brother, could tell you that it depended which side you were on, victors or defeated. That young man right there, for example, with his leather jerkin slipping off his shoulder, holding a bloody cloth to the arrow through his thigh—she'd wager her second-best sword he and she saw the dead and the dying around them entirely differently.

And he'd be watching her approach with an entirely different look on his face if she were an ally.

He looked away when she reined Bloodbone in and, still trying to hold the bloody rag to his leg, twisted around, stretching his hand for the sword that lay just out of reach to his left. Dhulyn dropped to the ground in time to kick the weapon just a little farther away.

"From the angle and distance," she said, as if they were sitting across a tavern table from one another talking about the weather. "You came off this dead horse as it fell, and dropped that Teliscan blade you can't quite reach as you hit the ground yourself." She twisted her lips to one side, propped one fist on her hip, and measured the distances again by eye before nodding and squatting down on her heels.

"Furthermore, that jerkin is too large for you, and no soldier wearing such a thing would be riding this horse, carrying that blade, or—" she poked him in the region of his collarbone where a hard corner clearly showed through the leather. "Or be carrying a book under it." She shook her head. "There's others on this field not so experienced as I, who might actually believe you were just the common soldier you're pretending to be. And they'd cut your throat for you as not worth tending. So right off, my little lordling, I'd remove that leather jerkin you've borrowed and get back into this nice tooled breastplate you've tried to hide under your horse's carcass." Dhulyn straightened and nudged the item in question a handspan closer to him with her toe. "Sorry about your horse, by the way, he looks like a fine animal."

"And *you* won't cut my throat?" Blood and dirt were ground into the creases of his fingers. His hair was black and curly, his eyes dark, and he looked to be naturally olive-skinned under his present dirt and pallor.

Dhulyn raised her left eyebrow, wondering if she should be offended . . . and then smiled. Of course. She pushed back the hood of the cloak she'd forgotten she was wearing. She'd braided some feathers into her hair, and hadn't wanted to get them wet. Now the lordling could see her green-and-blue Mercenary badge tattooed into the skin where the hair had been removed on her temples and above her ears.

"I am Dhulyn Wolfshead, called the Scholar. Schooled by Dorian the Black," she said formally.

The young man relaxed so completely Dhulyn was almost sure a tear or two leaked from his eyes. "I give you my surrender," he said, in a voice that trembled.

"And I accept it. What were you thinking?" She crouched down on her heels and took hold of the bloodied rag, pressing firmly as the young lord stripped off the leather jerkin and struggled back into the inlaid and crested breastplate. She clucked and reached out one-handed to help him with the side ties, pushing the small bound book back into its place against his breastbone. Of course such armor was never meant to be put on by oneself, let alone while lying down in one's own blood.

Not that *much* of this blood was his.

"I didn't want to be held for ransom," he said. "I thought I could get away."

The young man's head was turned away, so Dhulyn smiled her wolf's smile. "This your first campaign, is it? Thought they'd let you walk away, did you? Well let me School *you* a little, young lord. If you're not already dead, there's only three ways to leave a battlefield in this part of the world." She held up her left thumb. "Held for ransom if you're important enough," she held up a finger, "held for the slavers if you're not, and," a final finger, "throat cut if you're not whole enough to ransom or sell."

"There's a fourth way," he said, pulling his lips back in what was meant for a smile. Dhulyn softened her own grin. For all that his hands trembled, the boy had nerve, which was more than she could say for many a noble lord she'd met before.

"What have I forgotten, young lord?"

"Taken by Mercenary Brothers, who don't hold for ransom."

Dhulyn gave a short bark of laughter. "Why, how could we do that? This time next month we might be looking for work from you."

"We're not looking for work *already,* are we?"

It was a good thing she was holding on to the boy's leg; otherwise, the start that he gave at hearing Parno's question would have caused him to do more than hiss as his wound moved.

"Come hold his leg while I pull the arrow out," Dhulyn said to her Partner. "It won't hurt much, young lord," she added, turning back to the boy in time to catch his grimace.

"Just one moment, my soul."

Dhulyn looked up at the hint of warning in Parno's voice. She frowned; he was lowering himself from the saddle far too stiffly for her taste. Anyone would think he was an old man.

"This isn't just some lordling you've got here," he said. "This is someone far more important."

Dhulyn looked into the boy's face and raised her eyebrows. He licked his lips, but said nothing. She turned back to Parno.

"Another of your High Noble Houses, is it?"

But her Partner was shaking his head. "Better. Or worse, depending on your view of it. Look at the crest on the saddlecloth," he said, "and right there on his breastplate for that matter. This is Lord Prince Edmir himself."

Dhulyn examined the boy again, with more interest. "*Is* he now? Then perhaps you can explain what happened here, Lord Prince Edmir? Where was the power of the Blue Mage that has kept you Tegriani undefeated these last two seasons?"

If possible, the boy became even paler under the blood and dirt. His lips moved, but his eyes rolled up before he could make a sound.

"He's fainted," Parno said.

Dhulyn shrugged. "Good. Easier to take out the arrow."

"You noticed the fletching?"

Dhulyn nodded. "A Tegrian prince, shot by a Tegrian arrow."

Parno squatted down beside her. "Never let it be said that the Mercenary life isn't interesting."

⬩⬩⬩

Dhulyn breathed in deeply through her nose, counted to ten in the old language of the Caids, and released the breath slowly, glancing around at the faces assembled in War Commander Kispeko's tent the next day. Parno, standing to her left, raised his right eyebrow and she raised her own in acknowledgment. Losing her temper would gain nothing. When she was sure her voice would be measured and even, she hooked her thumbs in her sword belt and spoke.

"By contracting with Mercenary Brothers, you accepted our Common Rule. Prisoners taken by us go free, unmolested and unransomed. These are the conditions of your contract with us, you cannot go back on it now."

"Come now, Wolfshead, surely you realize the situation has changed." The lines around War Commander Kispeko's eyes showed how little sleep he'd had the night before.

"No situation changes sufficiently for you to lose your honor by breaking your word." *No point dancing around it,* she thought.

"I wish I had the leisure to think in those terms, Mercenary." Kispeko's voice was colder than it had been a moment before, and his left hand—his sword hand—had tightened into a fist where it lay on maps covering the top of his campaign table. The other people in the command tent, Nisveans for the most part—a few, like the war commander himself, from Noble Houses—all reacted to her words in their own way. Many of the soldiers, even the higher ranks, grimaced, carefully avoiding anyone's eye; but there were a few, among them Squad Leader Jedrick, the one whose cloak she was wearing, whose expressions bordered on smiles of triumph.

"This is no ordinary soldier," Kispeko continued. "Not even a member of a Noble House, such as we might ransom out of hand. This is the heir to the throne of Tegrian."

Dhulyn closed her lips on all the things she *might* have said. She knew that tone, and there was no argument the man would find convincing. "I ask you one final time, Lord Kispeko, to abide by the terms of our contract."

"Wolfshead, I cannot. You must see that I cannot." Kispeko's hand relaxed, but his face was still set firmly. "This is Tegrian we are talking about, and we all know that behind any Tegrian force stands the Blue Mage."

Dhulyn nodded, conscious of the chill that passed through the tent at the war commander's words. "Not behind yesterday's force, surely?" she said. "You cannot claim that there were any magics protecting the prince's troops."

Kispeko shrugged. "Possibly the Lord Prince was acting without the knowledge of his mother the queen, or of the Blue Mage. In any case, in Prince Edmir, I have a bargaining chip that will keep Nisvea safe from invasion—at the very least, a way to turn the Blue Mage's ambitions in another direction."

"No one has succeeded in bargaining with the Blue Mage," Dhulyn pointed out. "He has no interest in treaties and allies."

"But our circumstances are different from any who have tried to treat with the Mage before. Your very presence, for which we thank the Caids, has contributed to this." Kispeko leaned toward her, his eyes fixed intently on hers. "We reorganized our troops as you suggested, holding half our cavalry in reserve, and through this good advice and counsel we have won a battle against the Tegriani—the first such victory since the Blue Mage married their queen." As if he had heard the rising pitch of his voice, Kispeko fell silent and straightened.

"And now," he continued in a milder tone, "not only have we bested his troops, but we have Queen Kedneara's own son and heir."

"Perhaps if Dhulyn Wolfshead had a country of her own, she would not speak so lightly." The voice was quiet, but taut as a bowstring. Dhulyn did not turn her head; she knew who had spoken. She wore his cloak.

"Mercenary Brothers have fought, and killed, to defend the countries of others. As my Brother the Lionsmane and I did yesterday."

"And we were glad to have you," the war commander's sharp tone brought Dhulyn's eyes back to his face. "And we will recompense you in the manner agreed upon. But I will have the prince. With him, I can stop the Blue Mage, and that, let me tell you, Mercenary, supersedes your Common Rule, or my own honor, for that matter."

Dhulyn nodded. There had only been the slimmest of chances that this could have gone any other way. "As Cavalry Leader Jedrick has pointed out, we Mercenaries have only our Common Rule, and our honor." Dhulyn drew her sword and held it, point straight up, and directed her words to the patterned blade. "I am Dhulyn Wolfshead, called the Scholar. I was Schooled by Dorian of the River, the Black Traveler. I have fought at the sea battle of Sadron, at Arcosa in Imrion, and at Bhexyllia in the West. I withdraw my service, and that of my Partner Parno Lionsmane, from the Nisvean force following the battle of Limona."

She sheathed her sword. "You are Oathbreakers, War Commander. No Mercenary Brother will ever fight again at Nisvea's call."

Kispeko's lips thinned until they almost disappeared before he spoke. "So be it."

Dhulyn turned without salute or reverence and left the command tent.

Parno fell into step behind her as they made their way across the camp to where their own much smaller and much plainer tent was set up on the southern verge. He watched the muscle jump next to her mouth and judged it was safe to speak.

"Do you think, one of these days, we might actually get paid for a job?"

"We were paid in Berdana." Dhulyn's voice was quiet, but tight, as if she spoke through her teeth.

"Very well then. Would being paid for two jobs in a row be too much to ask?"

She stopped and faced him, the small scar on her upper lip turning her expression into a snarl. "Blooded, inglera-spawning House lordling—spit on our contract, will he? *Blooded* amateurs."

Parno knew the final remark wasn't aimed at him, but he grimaced just the same.

"What about the Tegriani? What if what Kispeko says about saving his country is true?"

Dhulyn's face was stiff. "Do *you* believe it?"

It took Parno only a moment to consider everything they knew of the Blue Mage. "No, my soul. No. And we would have sold our own honor for nothing."

"Not just our own, but the honor of our whole Brotherhood. 'Trust one, trust all.' If we do not hold to our oaths, if we cannot be trusted, we are not Mercenary Brothers, we are just killers."

Parno nodded. A few of the soldiers nearby had stopped in the middle of afternoon tasks and were looking in their direction.

"Calm down," he said. "You're attracting attention."

She stepped in until her nose was almost touching his.

"Am I not acting naturally, given the circumstances which will, as you well know, be all over the camp in twenty more heartbeats?" Though the corner of her mouth twitched, Parno could see the cold light of rage was still in Dhulyn's eye.

He took his Partner by the elbow and started them back toward their tent.

"You have a plan?" He used the nightwatch whisper, hardly louder than breathing.

"You think I'll let him get away with this?"

"And the Tegrian invasion?"

"What invasion?"

Parno found himself standing still as the full meaning of Dhulyn's question struck him.

"Your Vision said the Nisveans would win. Against all odds they would win," he said, his voice still nightwatch quiet.

"Was that the Tegriani force the world has been led to expect? The troops that never tire? Whom weapons do not touch? Against *that* force we should not have won. Regardless of any advice or help *we* gave, against the army of the Blue Mage, the Nisveans should have lost—" Dhulyn broke off her whisper to nod at the cavalry's head stableman as he passed without stopping. Evidently, news of the events in the war commander's tent hadn't traveled far enough in the camp to reach the old man's ears. "As Balnia lost last season."

"And Demnion and Monara the season before last," Parno agreed, taking Dhulyn once more by the arm. When they were again on their way, he continued. "The Nisveans are being used. The prince was meant to lose, maybe even to be captured or—"

"Or worse," Dhulyn said. "Remember that Tegrian arrow."

Parno gave a silent whistle. "And the commander either knows or doesn't want to know."

Dhulyn was nodding like a Schooler pleased with her student. "Which tells us what?"

Parno grimaced, tasting acid in the back of his throat. "Nothing is as it appears."

"Except our oaths and our honor."

They reached their tent, a gift from their grateful employer in Berdana, and Dhulyn stepped ahead to lift the flap and duck inside. It was larger than they needed, but they'd put it up nonetheless. As the only Mercenary Brothers with this portion of the Nisvean soldiery, they had reputations to maintain, and that could be done as much with a show of wealth as a show of skills.

Once they were inside, the flap down and tied, Parno acknowledged Dhulyn's signal and sat down cross-legged facing her, close enough for their knees to touch. Dhulyn was frowning, her eyes focused on the heavy silk-lined bag that held Parno's pipes. He laid the tips of his fingers on her knee and waited for her to speak.

"Turned your heart a bit, did it, when Kispeko spoke of saving his homeland?" she said, without turning her head. "Took thought for your own House and Imrion there a moment, didn't you?"

Parno smiled, shaking his head. "It was only the once I wanted to visit my home and family. But if you're truly asking me whether I'd put the safety of Nisvea before our Brotherhood . . ." He shrugged. "I'll be honest and say I'm glad that breaking our Common Rule and letting them keep Prince Edmir would change nothing for the Nisveans. It makes what we have to do easier for me." He caught her chin and turned her head until they were eye to eye. "But I would do it, easy or not. Set your mind at rest."

"I believe you." Dhulyn sighed. "But consider this. Kispeko is no fool, when all is said and done. He knows the truth of things as well or better than we do—he's had the Blue Mage on his doorstep all this time, while you and I have been to the East. So he must know that returning the boy will do nothing. And yet he insists on doing so."

"As you say," Parno said. "There is more here than meets the eye."

"Which changes nothing for us." She pressed her lips tight, fingers tapping on her knee. "This is going to take us even farther out of our way."

Parno studied her face, unable to decide whether she was annoyed or merely stating a fact. They had been on their way to Delmara, where a traveler they'd met in Berdana had told them there was a Seer, perhaps even more than one. Seers were the rarest of the Marked, far rarer than Healers, Menders, or Finders. Everyone thought the Mercenaries were going to Delmara to consult the Seer—and they let everyone think so. What they told no one was that Dhulyn was a Seer herself. Since she had lost her Clan before her Mark had shown, however, she'd had no one to train her, and her Visions were erratic and unreliable. Even with the ancient set of vera tiles she'd acquired in Imrion—Seer's tiles used like a Finder's bowl to focus the Mark—she still needed training. They'd been working their way west to Delmara when they'd run into War Commander Kispeko's recruiters.

Dhulyn had turned her eyes away again, and Parno saw that she hadn't been looking at his pipes after all, but at the olive-wood box lying in the center of her bedding. The box that held the vera tiles. She had a way of blaming him for it whenever he suggested she use them. Still . . .

"This might be a good time to try the tiles."

❦

A warm breeze blows from the east, making the banners and pennants flutter, the stiffened cloth rattling softly with a sound like a flock of birds taking flight. There's a mixed crowd of people before her, some wearing the longer gowns of nobility, many in shorter, more workmanlike dress. Most stand, though there are a scattering on horseback, looking over the heads of the rest. Prince Edmir sits on a throne-like chair on a raised platform, the focus of the crowd's attention. He is wearing robes the brilliant blue of the sky in winter, there is a circle of leaves shining gold against his dark hair, and he holds a long two-handed sword across his lap. A fair-haired woman, expensively dressed in a cloth-of-silver gown with a smaller, jeweled circlet around her head stands to Edmir's left, and an armsman in chain mail to his right. Edmir begins to speak and the crowd hushes. . . .

Hands that are her own push back the lid of a plain wood chest small enough to stand on a tabletop. Inside, resting in a bed of pale silk, is a blue crystal as long as her forearm, and perhaps as thick around. It shines blue like the deep ice that has trapped the glow of the stars. Dhulyn reaches down. . . .

At first Dhulyn cannot see what it is that disturbs the forest. Small animals scatter away. A crashing noise to her left and she turns her head, expecting to see perhaps a deer, perhaps even a small bear. There is too much noise for a forest cat, who even in desperate flight makes no more sound than the wind in the branches. Instead, a young boy—younger than the prince, yet taller, thinner, with long hair the color of old blood escaping from his braids—comes stumbling onto the narrow path, almost falling when his feet find the leveled ground. Dhulyn puts her hand up to her own blood-red hair, and her lips part, but she does not speak. The boy, clearly an Espadryni like herself, would not be able to hear her. He looks up then at a noise that only he can hear, whites clearly showing around the sharp blue of his eyes. There is the mark of an old bruise on the left side of his face. He tries to slow his breathing, taking a deep breath, but his diaphragm spasms, and he cannot manage a second one.

His left hand at his side, the boy sketches a complicated sign in the air with his right hand. There is a tug at Dhulyn's memory and she knows that she is frowning now, knowing that something should follow, but cannot think what it might be. Nothing happens, and the boy turns and runs toward her on the path, chest heaving just as Dhulyn catches the sounds of the men hunting him as they too crash through the forest. . . .

❧❦❧

"You sure it was Edmir crowned and on his throne? It wasn't some naming day ceremony?"

Dhulyn stopped rubbing her temples and took the cup

of warm water Parno handed her. "He was older than he is now, that I'm sure of. And he'd have had his naming day already, surely?"

Parno nodded, his eyebrows drawn together as he concentrated. "What about the other boy? Do you think he made it? *Some* other of your kindred must have escaped—you can't be the *only* one."

Dhulyn shrugged and drained her water cup. "That event might be years old, there's no way for me to be sure. Fashions don't change much among Horsemen."

Parno studied her face, but she seemed at peace. "And what he was doing—" Parno mimed the movement Dhulyn had described. "You don't know what that was?"

"It seemed familiar," she said. "Something should have happened, but I don't know what." She looked up, her blood-red brows drawn down in a vee. "And I don't know *why*." She raised her hands to her forehead.

"The prince on his throne, though, that seems pretty clear."

Dhulyn stopped rubbing her temples and looked up at him. "That's what you always say. It never seems so clear afterward."

Parno grinned. She'd *already* found a way to blame him. "So the only question is, do we make a great show of leaving and then sneak back into the camp? Or do we decide to leave in the morning and make off in the middle of the night?"

"That is not the only question, my heart, but it will do to begin with."

Parno returned to the tent some hours later carrying a freshly filled wineskin over his shoulder, bought from their friend the old stableman. As he pushed aside the flap, Dhulyn was setting the bright red cavalry cloak down on the battered, leather-covered chest they used as a table, next to his unwrapped pipes, a bright metal flask, and two Tenezian blue-glass cups.

Parno pursed his lips and looked from one side of the tent to the other. Everything his Partner considered essential—except his pipes—had been packed into two sets of saddlebags, and two largish packs that would ride on their horses' cruppers. That still left a considerable pile of bedding, extra clothing, and weapons, to say nothing of the tent itself.

"I hadn't realized we'd accumulated so much," he said, frowning.

Dhulyn began rolling up a piece of thick canvas sewn with little pockets that held a set of knives. "Lucky for us, as it turns out; it explains the need for the extra horse." Dhulyn eyed both saddlebags before choosing one and stuffing the roll of canvas down one side of it. She hefted it and nodded, satisfied that the weight was balanced.

"Which I've bought." The twist to her mouth told Parno how unhappy she'd been with the bargain she'd made, but an extra horse they had to have. "And I've moved all four of them over to Randle's tether."

"I've gone around telling people we're off in the morning," he said, putting the wineskin down on one of the two large packs. "Anyone asked, I told them we'd be heading down to the Mercenary House in Lesonika to lodge a complaint."

"And they believed it?"

"Why shouldn't they? It's on our way to Delmara, more or less. Most of them think we're complaining of losing our chance at Prince Edmir's ransom. Even those who know the real reason agree with the Commander. It seems when the subject of the Blue Mage enters the discussion, all minds except ours run along the same paths."

"As Jedrick said, it's not our country. There was a time you would have felt the same about the Mage and ridden against him for your House and for Imrion."

"I admit, even now, I wouldn't like my House to fall, nor Imrion either for that matter. But there's little chance of that."

"I'm sure that's what Balnia thought two years ago. How goes their thinking now?"

Parno moved closer to his Partner and dropped his voice to the nightwatch whisper. "They've got him in a tent close to Kispeko's, small enough that there's only the one guard, walking around it."

"*Blooded* amateurs." Any other time Dhulyn's look of disgust would have made him smile.

Parno shrugged. "They don't expect anyone here to let him out, and they don't expect any of his own people to come and rescue him."

"They are right about the second, that's certain."

"Making it all the easier for us, so we won't complain."

She shot him a glance out of the corner of her eye even as she agreed. "Getting out of camp with the prince was never the hard part. It's keeping out of the Nisveans' hands after that will be the trick."

"Then we'll just have to make sure they've no reason to come after us."

"Moon rises at the end of the second watch, sets at the beginning of the fourth. We'll have to be back in our places by then."

Parno jerked his thumb at pipes and wineskin. "I'm ready when you are."

"Then I shall go and find Cavalry Squad Leader Jedrick." She picked up the red cloak and frowned at her hands, lifting them to her nose. "Do I smell of blood?"

Parno reached out and brought her right hand to his lips. Her skin was roughened and cold. "You washed last night, and you smell wonderful. Are you sure you can manage it with Jedrick . . . ?" The words suddenly dried in his throat and he gestured at the red cloak in Dhulyn's long-fingered hands.

"You think I can't?"

"The man makes no attempt to disguise his dislike of you."

She smiled her wolf's smile and Parno found himself smiling back. "You think that means he actually dislikes me? What he can't disguise is his annoyance that I bested him at the knife throw. There's not many see only the woman and not the Mercenary Brother, but he's one of them. And it's for that reason he'll not forgo what he'll see as a kind of triumph," she said. "His ego will play him right into my hands."

"I still think we should switch places. You do the horse trick, and I go for the prince," he said. "An alibi's all very well, but there's no one more recognizable in the whole blooded camp than you."

And there was no arguing with that, he thought. Even if

you set aside her Mercenary's badge, there was still her height, her slimness, to say nothing of her blood-red hair, woven and tied into tiny braids, and her distinctive dress, loose trousers tucked into the knee-high boots of the Western Horsemen, her vest quilted from scraps of leather, bright velvets, silks and ribbons, leaving her arms bare.

"You have it exactly backward," she said to him. "No one will make a wager against me that involves horses— you they're not so sure of. And it's my very distinctiveness will help me vanish in the shadows." She glanced around until her eye fell on the small pile of clothing left unpacked. "Watch." She picked up what he recognized as an old, dull green tunic of his own and slipped it over her vest. She pulled a brown felted hood over her hair and turned back to face him.

"I'll change my trousers and put on a pair of low half boots instead of these Semlorians everyone has seen me in. It will be dusk by the time I try it," she pointed out. "And no one will know me from any other soldier walking through the camp at dusk."

"By the Caids," Parno whispered. He wanted to tell her she was wrong, but the truth was . . . even without the boots and trousers, the bulky tunic alone, the covering of her hair—"I think I'd walk past you myself, without a second look."

"Then it's in Battle?"

"Or in Death," he agreed.

Two

ONCE PARNO HAD GONE, Dhulyn quickly stripped off her disguise; that was for later. She pulled off her vest, practice allowing her not to snag its laces in the braids and loops of her blood-red hair. She quickly unwrapped and discarded the length of silk scarf she used as a breastband before pulling her vest back on, adjusting the ties to push up her breasts and make them seem more round. Parno knew the plan, but there was no point in rubbing his nose in her part.

The cavalry leaders' tents were in the same southern corner of the camp as their own, but Dhulyn took a roundabout route, stopping once or twice to answer questions and taking care to acknowledge the hails and calls of the soldiers she'd been working beside for most of the past moon. She turned down several chances to join celebratory groups anxious to include a Mercenary Brother. Participation was Parno's role; her part of the plan was to be noticed now, and not later.

Her luck was in. Jedrick, his copper hair shining in the late afternoon sun, was sitting on a camp stool between the two squad leaders with whom he shared his tent.

"We hear you're leaving us, Mercenary," the small dark one seated to Jedrick's right called out as she neared them. The dark one's voice was so carefully neutral that even Dhulyn could not be sure of his opinion on the matter of Prince Edmir's captivity.

"We are," she said, coming to a stop just beyond arm's length of the man she'd come to see. "I thought I'd see if you wanted a chance to win your cloak back, Jedrick." She held up the scarlet wool she had over her left arm.

Jedrick was leaning forward, his elbows on his knees, his hands, scarred and callused by the reins, loosely clasped. He glanced at his tent mates before replying, half a grin on his face. "So you admit you cheated?"

Dhulyn shrugged, rolling her shoulders in a way that made her breasts bounce. "If the wind blew in my favor, I hardly think that is accounted cheating."

Jedrick blinked, cleared his throat, and raised his eyes to her face. "What wager do you have in mind?"

"I had in mind we could discuss it in private." She held his eyes a long moment before giving a pointed look at his two companions, showing them her wolf's smile.

Jedrick rose to his feet, smoothing his mustache with his right thumb and forefinger. "Would Parno Lionsmane not object?"

"Parno? Why would he? He's my Partner." Dhulyn had fielded such questions before, so it was easy to look puzzled. Very few outside of the Mercenary Brotherhood—and some within it for that matter—understood what it meant to be Partnered.

"I'll never understand the Mercenary Brotherhood," Jedrick said, shaking his head with a smile.

"And that's how we like it." Dhulyn reached out and gave him the merest nudge on his shoulder.

Not that Jedrick was truly concerned, she thought, as the man gave his fellow officers a mocking half bow and prepared to follow her. Dhulyn wished Parno were here to see how easy it was to seduce a man who claimed to dislike you.

On the other hand, perhaps it was just as well that he was not.

The route she took back to her tent was more direct than the one she used to reach Jedrick, but even so, a good many people saw them together. All part of the plan.

Once in her tent, Dhulyn tossed the cloak down on the bed, and glanced over her shoulder in time to see Jedrick tying down the tent flap. She bit down on her lip to keep from smiling. There were always men who were too sure of themselves.

"This is an interesting flask," he said, coming to stand next to her. He picked it up and hefted it in his hand as if to weigh the contents.

"I was given it in Berdana," she said, taking it from him and letting the tips of her fingers linger on his skin. "It comes from the Tin Isles, and leaves the brandy's taste unchanged."

"Given it? Then you would not wish to trade it for my cloak?"

"I think you mean *my* cloak."

"I thought that was what we were here to . . . discuss?"

Dhulyn had to stop herself from rolling her eyes. Sun and Moon, this was almost too easy. "I've Imrion brandy here," she said, holding up the flask. "Shall we toast our wager? I warn you, though, it's quite strong." She turned her back to fill the blue-glass cups.

"Is it to be a drinking contest, then?" His breath, smelling not unpleasantly of wine, was warm on her cheek, his voice a soft murmur in her ear. But when she looked at him Dhulyn saw the same hard gleam in Jedrick's eyes that was always there. How was it possible that eyes the same clear amber color as Parno's could be so cold?

She handed Jedrick one of the two cups, picked up the other, and tossed its contents down her throat in a single quick swallow. Lowering the cup, she licked her upper lip slowly and smiled. Grinning back at her, Jedrick downed his own brandy just as quickly, smoothing his mustaches as he handed back his cup. Dhulyn raised her brows in a challenge, refilled the cups and, her eyes fixed on his, lifted her own to her lips, taking two long, slow swallows before lowering the cup again. She matched his smile with one of her own, careful to keep the small scar from turning her lip up in a snarl.

Jedrick took three good-sized swallows, and as he lowered his cup from his lips, Dhulyn put her heel behind his, tipped him backward onto the cot, and threw herself down on him slowly enough to let him start twisting out of her way. The trick, she reminded herself, was to dampen her natural reflexes enough that Jedrick actually thought he was besting her. She telegraphed her next move to give him time to grab her wrists—a little too roughly for play, she noted—and flip her over onto her back.

Dhulyn turned her head quickly enough to avoid his chin as he collapsed heavily on her chest.

"Ah, iocain," she whispered as she wriggled out from under the unconscious man. "Works every time."

Dhulyn dug her fingers under Jedrick's jaw and checked his pulse, counting carefully. She'd measured the dose with great accuracy and calculated she had at least two hours before it would begin to wear off. That should give her more than enough time.

She stripped Jedrick and carefully marked his back with several strategically placed scratches. She then sat on her heels and frowned. After a moment's thought, she rolled him over and, using sometimes her closed fist, sometimes the side of her rigid hand, and sometimes the tips of her fingers, made what would later be telltale bruises on Jedrick's torso and limbs. She then bit him once on the neck, and once above the right nipple.

If she knew her man—and she was sure she did—when faced with such evidence, Jedrick would never admit that he had no memory of what had passed between them.

Dhulyn straightened to her feet and took a slow deliberate breath, listening with all her training to the sound of the camp around her. Did she hear the drone of Parno's pipes in the distance, or was it just wishful thinking? She shoved Jedrick's leg aside and sat down to pull off her boots.

Parno tossed back the slightly sour wine in his cup and concentrated on the story the man in front of him was trying to tell around the bellyful of beer he had in him. This particular campfire was well out of sight of their tent, and even if he wanted to keep an eye out for Dhulyn, Parno couldn't see her from here. He'd chosen this particular gathering around this particular fire for that very reason.

Parno distracted the storyteller with another mugful of beer and picked up his pipes, settling them at his side. As they saw what he was about, several others, having lost confidence in the beer drinker's ability to find the end of his tale, began to call out.

"That's it, Lionsmane."

"Give us the one about the Finder's apprentice!"

Parno moistened his lips and tested the bag for air.
"Oh, I know a better one than that."

There. That sound was Parno's piping, no doubt about it.
With tunic, boots, and hood in place, Dhulyn felt for the
ioca leaves she'd tucked into a fold of her sash. Satisfied
they were secure, she rolled under the rear edge of their
tent and stayed crouched, making sure the shadows covered her, before straightening slowly to her feet. Dhulyn
tugged at her hood and set off in the direction of the tent
that held the prince, hunching her shoulders and dragging
her feet a little, in contrast to her usual freely swinging
stride.

She angled her progress through the camp so as to draw
the least possible notice. Her pace was neither purposeful
enough that it drew the questioning eye, nor casual enough
to prompt the friendly invitation. And, further, she'd timed
her approach to Prince Edmir's tent for the middle of the
second watch, when the moon was not yet up. Most of the
host had found their beds, and the few souls hardy enough,
or drunk enough, to be still awake around their small
campfires reliving the unexpected triumph of the day before, paid her no mind.

*Sun and Moon grant you do not find cause to regret your
victory*, she prayed. Considering her present errand was unlikely to bring the Nisveans any good, the least she could
do was wish them luck.

As she drew nearer Prince Edmir's tent, Dhulyn left off
her slouching walk and began the Stalking Cat *Shora*—the
real reason, to her way of thinking, that the rescue of the
Prince was *her* part of tonight's work. Like all Mercenaries,
Parno had been Schooled in the twenty-seven basic *Shora*,
the patterns that made up their intensive training. But
Dhulyn was an Outlander, and the Stalking *Shoras* in particular came as naturally to her as sleep. Now, as her mind
settled into the Stalking Cat, her breathing slowed, her
thoughts focused. The smell of the camp surrounded her.
Unwashed bodies, burning wood and oil, cooking smells—
mostly onions. Behind this she sensed the warm, clean
scent of the horses tethered off to her left, and beyond that,
the smell of old blood and death from the river valley.

Between her and her target, she could smell the beer being drunk by two women around a pinewood fire, hear the murmur of their voices, and the gurgle of the liquid as it poured into their cups. In the near distance she thought she could still hear the melodic drone of Parno's pipes. Ahead and to the right, was the stench of the latrine ditch, unmistakable even under layers of shoveled dirt. She turned her feet toward it.

As she went, her eyes adjusted, making full use of the available light, the campfires, the occasional torch smelling strongly of pine resin and oil. Even the starlight helped her as she slid easily into every shadow large enough to hold her—and one or two which she knew would appear too small to do so—moving only when her senses, heightened by the *Shora*, told her no human eye observed her.

A flicker of movement—and she froze just as she was skirting six sleeping figures rolled in rugs and cloaks with their feet toward the embers of a fire. She turned her head slowly. One of the camp's cats eyed her from the shadows, but the animal recognized the scent and stance of a fellow predator, and allowed her to pass with only a slashing tail as comment.

She froze again as, circling around the back of War Commander Kispeko's tent, she heard voices. No. Only one voice, Kispeko's own.

"I will see to it, my lord."

Dhulyn frowned. The man's voice was oddly flat and toneless, and who could he be calling "my lord"? No one outranked Kispeko here in camp.

"He will die as he tries to escape," Kispeko said. "I will see to it, my lord."

Don't put money on it, she thought. No one else had any need of escape. Kispeko must be speaking of Edmir. But to whom?

Dhulyn waited, but Kispeko made no other sound. She concentrated, letting her awareness float. When she was satisfied that, strange as it was, only one person breathed within the commander's tent, she continued on her way.

Think about it later, the voice in the back of her mind instructed.

Dhulyn finally came to a stop in a patch of shadow

created by an uneven pile of cooking supplies covered over by a canvas tarp, her toe brushing against what felt and smelled like an empty wineskin. If what Parno had told her was correct, the prince was ahead and just to her left, in a plain, square-sided tent about twice the size of their own. Either the prince had no lamp lit, or the tent's canvas was thick enough to show no shadows.

Her awareness increased another notch as her immediate prey, the human guard, walked around the far corner of the tent and came within reach of the Stalking Cat *Shora.* She let him make three circuits around the tent, timing his pacing, matching her breathing to his, before she fell into step behind him, as close as his own shadow.

The guard did not falter, but kept up his steady pace. Dhulyn moved with exactly the same rhythm, imitating even the slight hitch in the guard's right hip, their breathing matched, their hearts beating in time.

As they entered the shadows at the rear of the tent, Dhulyn glanced down at the rope stretched from one of the tent pegs on the short side. Only if you were looking very carefully could you tell that it had been sliced almost through.

Well done, my heart, floated through her thoughts in time with her moving lungs. On one of his ramblings from fire to fire, or perhaps on a visit to the latrine, Parno had managed to pass unnoticed by this spot.

The guard turned the corner, and as soon as he was out of sight Dhulyn dropped to her belly, snapped the cut rope between her hands, and snaked into the tent.

The prince was sitting at a camp table, a shaded lantern casting a shaft of light on the open book in front of him. He had frozen in the act of dipping a pen into a small pot of ink. So, she thought, not a book to read, but one to write in. Dhulyn rolled to her knees and held a finger to her lips, tensed to spring until she saw the young man relax. The tent they'd given him may not have been much, but the accessories—judging by the quality of the carpet she knelt on—were the best the commander could supply. As were Prince Edmir's clothes. His own boots, brushed and polished, lay neatly to one side of the camp bed, but his borrowed nightshirt was fine linen, and the tunic and leggings folded on a small table were likely from Commander Kispeko's own chests.

The prince shifted, and Dhulyn was beside him, her hand over his mouth, while he was still drawing in breath to speak.

"Stay silent," she breathed in the nightwatch whisper. "Dress as quietly as you can. If you need to speak, mouth the words against my hand, slowly, do you understand?" When the prince nodded, Dhulyn relaxed her hold on his face, leaving her fingers lightly in place over his lips.

"The guard?" he asked. Dhulyn had to ask him to repeat it before she understood.

"Will be distracted. Trust me and dress."

Dhulyn had to give the boy credit; he moved as quietly as she'd ever seen a town man do. They had one bad moment when he couldn't bend his injured leg to pull the leggings on, but he let Dhulyn help him without sign of embarrassment. *Probably has a dresser,* she thought. He hissed when her hand brushed against his wound, but stifled it quickly enough that the sound drew no notice. She touched the wound more carefully with the back of her hand, frowning when she found it markedly hotter than the surrounding skin.

"Did they give you nothing for the wound?" she asked, laying her fingers once more against his lips.

"Fens bark tea," he mouthed.

Dhulyn nodded. They had sense enough for that at any rate. Cleaning the wound, plus an infusion to keep the fever down, was the most anyone could do in the absence of a Healer. And she shouldn't be surprised that Kispeko had used his own Knife to attend the prince, rather than asking either of the Mercenaries for help. She smiled in the darkness as a clever thought occurred to her. She could use that in the morning. But for now, she felt for and removed the ioca leaves from her sash. "Chew this," she said, handing him one. "It will dull the pain."

When Edmir pulled the tunic on directly over the nightshirt, Dhulyn shook her head. It was the long formal tunic a noble might wear to dine, not the short surcoat of a commoner. She waved the prince closer to her and pulled out her knife.

"I'll have to cut that short," she said in his ear. "We need to look like a pair of common drunks."

Again Edmir nodded, this time taking her hand and placing it on his mouth.

"Soon?"

"Listen for it, and be ready."

"My Partner, Dhulyn Wolfshead, has never been un-horsed," Parno said, folding his pipes against the now-emptied air bag. "Not even in practice, though I grant you she's 'fallen off on purpose' when she's had to, just to make a point." He paused, furrowed his brow as if a thought had just occurred to him. "'Course, she *is* a Red Horseman."

"I'll concede that, horseman to horseman, the Merce-nary Brotherhood often matches trained cavalry, and might well be able to unhorse almost anyone. But the question was a man afoot, and such an encounter never ends badly for the one ahorse." Nilo was the closest of the five cavalry-men sitting around the fire. He wiped his mouth on his sleeve and offered the wineskin.

Parno shook his head. "I've heard you say this so often, Nilo, you must believe it's true." Two carefully chosen songs and a little subtle prodding had finally led the discussion where he wanted it to go. Not that it usually took much to get professional soldiers to brag about their own special-ties.

Nilo covered a burp with exaggerated care. So exagger-ated that Parno began to wonder if he was the only one more sober than he wanted people to think. "Perhaps," the cavalryman said, "I should say no *true* horseman can be un-seated from the ground—barring archers, of course."

"True horseman be blooded. *I'll* do it." Parno stood and let himself sway ever so slightly, as if he'd actually drunk all the wine that was in the skin at his feet. "Caids, I'll wager that I not only unhorse you, but I do it unarmed."

Nilo also managed to stand, his hand on the shoulder of one of his fellows. "What's the wager, then, Mercenary?"

There it was, the calls in the distance, the flaring up of fresh torches as the word was passed and men and women rose from their sleep in answer to a summons that had them laughing and calling out odds.

"Here it comes," Dhulyn said, barely breathing the words as she drew Edmir toward the place where she'd rolled into the tent. The shadow that was the prince's guard had stopped his steady pacing and seemed to be listening to the din.

"The Lionsmane's going to unhorse Cadet Nilo," called out a woman's voice.

"I'll take a piece of that wager," the guard answered. "Which way?"

With the guard distracted, Dhulyn shoved Edmir through the gap in the tent, following closely behind him. Once outside, she lifted him to his feet and swung her left arm over his shoulders. She was slightly taller, and it was easy for her to take a good grip on the youngster while making it look as though *he* was holding *her* up. She headed him toward the horse lines.

Don't worry, she told herself, *Parno's done this before.* The boy winced and Dhulyn loosened her grip. Apparently, she was doing a poor job of convincing herself. Apparently, it was one thing when Parno was practicing and it was Dhulyn on the horse, and another thing entirely when it was someone else.

Parno stood with one hand held above his head. When he was ready, he would let his arm fall, and Nilo would ride his cavalry horse straight toward him. There was a popular belief among nonsoldiers that horses would not run people down, or even step on them except by accident—but Parno knew that warhorses had been trained to do exactly that, and worse. He had to be careful, the hooves could slash at him from the side, as well as from the front. His arm still raised, he began to slow his breathing in the Python *Shora*, the Wrestler's *Shora*, used for hand-to-hand combat only. *You've done this before,* he told himself. *Do it again now. Just like in practice.*

His awareness narrowed until the tents, the people watching, the flaring torches died away. No sounds, no smells, nothing existed in the world except him and the horse. Time slowed. The horse's breath hung in the air like a cloud.

He let his arm drop.

Through the soles of his feet Parno could feel the ground shudder as the hooves hit. He watched the spurts of dirt jump backward from the slow, regular strikes of the churning hooves on the earth. He bent his knees, allowing the muscles in his legs to coil, to become springs. Focused, counting the time as each hoof fell, he dodged, feeling the horse's breath on his face as he darted to one side, grasped the mane, bounced off the powerful springs of his legs, swinging his body, knees up, under the blow that Nilo was only now bringing down from above. Long seconds too late.

And just as he had done scores of times in practice, he planted both knees in Nilo's midsection and catapulted the cavalryman neatly from the saddle. Parno let momentum continue his movement until he was sitting sideways on the horse, in the spot Nilo had occupied a moment before. As the animal faltered, Parno twisted to lie stomach-down on the saddle, swinging his legs again until he was sitting astride the horse's back.

Suddenly, there was a flash of movement, the yelp of a dog, and the horse twisted violently to one side, almost going down, and only by force of will did Parno manage to stay in his seat.

The cheers and catcalls changed to cries of alarm as the spectators came running up, Nilo first among them, to catch at the bridle of his horse. Parno slid to the ground and joined the man where he was running his hand down the horse's off foreleg. Nilo was frowning, and the horse seemed shy of putting weight down. Parno glanced aside, pressing his eyes shut as the woman crouching over the limp body of the dog shook her head.

Could have been me.

"I don't want to cost you both your money *and* your horse," he said, turning back to Nilo. "Let me take him to my Partner. Dhulyn Wolfshead can tell us what, if anything, is wrong."

As he walked beside the cavalryman, encouraging his horse to walk slowly through the camp, Parno hoped he'd given Dhulyn enough time. He was sorry for the dog, but this couldn't have turned out better if he had planned it. He'd intended to ask Nilo—or whoever made the wager with him—back to the tent for some Imrion brandy. Now it seemed that half the camp would provide Dhulyn with her alibi.

As long as she was back.

The tightness in his chest relaxed as he saw the corner of the tent flap was folded back a scant palm's width. He bent down to toss it back completely, loudly calling out for Dhulyn as he crossed the threshold. Nilo, waiting with his horse, ducked his head to look inside. When he began to laugh, everyone who was close enough crowded forward to get a look. Dhulyn's white southerner's skin glowed in the torchlight as she sat up, yawning and rubbing at her eyes.

"What's all this," she asked in a voice fogged with sleep. "Can't people have a moment's privacy?"

Clear on her skin, and clear on the skin of Squad Leader Jedrick as he, too, sat up, his eyes clouded by what everyone there would take for exhaustion, were telltale bruises and marks of fingernails. As if their nakedness and disheveled hair did not already speak very clearly what they had been doing before they fell asleep.

The cheering and catcalls began again. Clearly, the crowd felt this entertainment was just as good as a horse wager.

⌘

Avylos the Blue Mage let his head fall against the high back of his chair. His eyelids fluttered, and for a moment he struggled against the languor that followed taking power from the Stone. If he slept, he would dream, and it was rarely anything that he wished to see. His lids shut, and the dream began. . . .

"Mama, Mama, look! I can do it, Mama!" And his mother's face was transported by joy, her eyes shining, her mouth in the widest of smiles, as he made the pinecone leap into his hand. Once again, he saw the looks on the faces of the boys he thought of as his friends. They nudged each other and smiled, nodding; his

YOUNGER SELF MISUNDERSTANDING, SAW HAPPINESS NOT MALICE, PLEASURE NOT TWISTED GLEE. HIS MOTHER STROKED HIS HAIR AND KISSED HIM, AND RAN FOR HIS FATHER.

WHEN HIS FATHER CAME, EVERYTHING CHANGED. HIS FATHER PUT A HAND ON AVYLOS' SHOULDER, BUT WHEN AVYLOS OFFERED TO SHOW HIM THE MAGIC HE HAD FINALLY LEARNED TO DO, HIS FATHER HAD LOOKED AROUND HIM, FIXED ON ONE PARTICULAR SMILING FRIEND, AND CLOUTED THE BOY ON THE SIDE OF THE HEAD.

"BEGONE, YOU BRATS! YOUR FATHERS SHALL HEAR OF THIS!"

AND THEY RAN. LOOKING OVER THEIR SHOULDERS, GIGGLING NOW, THOUGH THERE WAS A LITTLE FEAR AS WELL, FEAR OF WHAT HIS FATHER WOULD DO, AND WHAT THEIR OWN FATHERS WOULD SAY.

"BUT, TERAVYL—" HIS MOTHER SAID. "IT WAS A TRICK," HIS FATHER TOLD HER. "THE OTHERS WERE DOING IT, AND LETTING AVI THINK IT WAS HIM. HE IS *SRUSHA*, MY DEAR."

AND HIS MOTHER, CRYING, TURNED HER FACE AWAY FROM HIM, BUT NOT BEFORE HE SAW THE FINAL GRIEF IN HER EYES. HIS FATHER STROKED HIS HAIR, BUT HIS FACE TOO WAS FULL OF PITY, AND REGRET. AVYLOS STARED AT THE PINECONE IN HIS HAND, WISHING THAT IT WAS A KNIFE. . . .

Avylos' consciousness fell back into the living world, his breathing coming fast and sharp as rage coursed hotly through his veins. He ran his hands along the cold stone cylinder he still held, as thick as his wrist, as long as his forearm, and his fingers trembled. He still held the Stone; had he continued taking power from it while in his dream?

Quickly, he spoke the words that closed the ritual, grasped the end, and twisted it to the left. He replaced the Stone in its cherrywood casket on his worktable, and shut the lid. He did not believe he could drain the Stone completely, but he *could* drain that portion of the Stone's power available to him. So far as he could tell, the Stone trapped *all* the power fed to it, but he simply did not know the proper chants or settings that would release that reserve to him.

He looked at the books in his room. One day he would know; one day that power would be his.

Not that he had needed any power to crush his tormentors. They had all been dealt with long ago. Before the power had finally shown itself, before the Stone had come to him and he had begun to understand the truth.

He stood and headed for the door before he could be tempted to use the Stone again. He needed no more dreams today.

He shut the door of his workroom behind him and strode into the corridor, stopping just inside the wide, metal-braced door that closed off his wing from the rest of the Royal House. He straightened his robes until he was sure they fell gracefully from his shoulders. His hair, the color of old blood, had been left loose that morning to dry, and he ran his hands through it, pushing it back from his face. When he was sure he looked presentable, he opened the door, startling the young page who stood outside it into giving him a very awkward bow.

"I will go to my garden, Takian," he said. "See that the queen knows."

"Of course, my lord. At once, my lord." Another short bow, this time more gracefully accomplished.

"My lord *Mage*," Avylos corrected.

The boy's face, flushed with embarrassment a moment before, drained of all color.

Avylos smiled. "It's all right, Takian, you cannot remember everything on the first day."

"Thank you, my lord *Mage*," the boy said carefully, his eyes fixed on his shoes.

"There. You'll soon remember." Avylos waited until the boy had gone on his errand before drawing his robes more closely to him and heading toward the open stairwell to the far left of his door. The stairwell was square, taking up the interior of a small tower in the southern curtain wall of Queen Kedneara's palace. The door at the lower end of the stairs opened into an irregularly-shaped courtyard, once the palace laundry's drying place, but now the private garden of the Blue Mage.

Avylos seated himself on the wide stone edge that surrounded the still pool in the center of his garden and breathed deeply, in and out, three times. Though they were not wet, he rubbed the palms of his hands on his robe. He felt strong, his magic was at its peak. He did not, for the moment, require any more power.

But he wanted it.

He put his hands up to his face and pressed his fingers into the bone above his eyes. "I will find the secret," he promised himself, not for the first time. Taking another deep breath, slowly releasing it, he focused on the still water of the pool. He needed distraction, and the pool could give it to him. With the ease of practice he narrowed his awareness until he saw only the pool. Then he focused his mind and his attention further, until he saw through the pool, to what it could show him.

Night. An army's camp. The moon not yet risen, but enough starlight to see by. A tall slim man, drunk from the look of him, with his arm around the shoulders of a younger, shorter man, who helped him stagger along. The younger man raised his head and the starlight fell on his face.

Edmir.

"Sun burn and blast you." Avylos struck the surface of the water with his closed fist, scattering the image of Edmir's escape into the sudden ripples.

"Something wrong, Avylos?"

Only Kera was allowed to use his private stair, come into his private garden. Kera and the Queen her mother, of course. The princess was standing in the open doorway, her hands tucked into her sleeves, sun on her red-gold hair, her dark brows drawn down, her forehead wrinkled in a frown.

"I'm very much afraid that things have not gone well for your brother, Kerusha. The battle has been lost."

The girl stepped forward, her hands falling free. "Lost? Is Edmir . . . ?"

"I can see no more. But, Kera, I fear you must be prepared for the worst." There, the seed was sown. "You counseled against his going— Oh, do not look so surprised, I knew none of this could be of *your* advising. But I could not foresee . . ."

"But your magic, why did it not work?"

Avylos shrugged and slowly shook his head, as if the weight of the world was on his shoulders. "The magic was prepared, Edmir well instructed. For some reason he did not call upon it—or he was prevented. I have not found all there is to know, but I swear to you, I will."

The girl's face was white, and Avylos stood, putting out his hand. But her chin firmed, and her spine straightened.

"I must tell my mother the queen." Her voice was very small.

"Let me accompany you," Avylos said. "The queen will have questions."

The girl nodded without speaking, thrusting her hands back into the sleeves of her gown.

Three

"NO PRACTICE THIS morning, Mercenaries?"
     She recognized the voice, so without looking up, Dhulyn continued to draw one end of a long strap around the bundle that was the tent. It had been struck and rolled as compactly as she and Parno could manage between them, but it was still bulky.

"Not this morning, nor any other morning," Parno answered, as Dhulyn had known he would. "You slack-wits will have to find someone else to teach you which end of the sword is sharp."

There were disappointed murmurs mixed in with the laughter. She and Parno had been sharing their morning practice with the interested portion of the Nisvean force for the better part of a moon, and there were more than a few who'd miss the benefit of that workout, now that the Mercenaries were going. Dhulyn tossed the loose end of the strap to Parno, who caught it as he straightened to his feet—grimacing as the muscles of his lower back reminded him of his exertions of the night before.

"I'll go for the horses if you like," Dhulyn said, carefully not smiling as Parno arched his body first one way and then the other, bracing both hands on his lower back.

"Oh, Caids," Parno said. "A day in the saddle. That's exactly what my back needs."

"Teach you to get drunk and do acrobatic tricks." Dhulyn easily dodged the half burned stick he tossed at her from the cold embers of their breakfast fire and picked up her sword, thrusting it into her belt and tugging her vest into place.

"Are you Dhulyn Wolfshead?" The voice broke halfway through her name and Dhulyn wasn't surprised that the boy was blushing when she turned.

"I am, and it's pronounced 'Dillin.'"

"Come with me if you please, Mercenary." Embarrassment momentarily making him lose touch with his common sense, the boy spoke more gruffly than many would have considered polite to a Mercenary Brother.

"And if I don't please?" Smiling her wolf's smile, Dhulyn narrowed her eyes and put her hand on her sword hilt, exactly as she would have done to anyone older, and taller, who had spoken to her in that tone. As she had expected, rather than frightening the lad, it only made him clear his throat, and stand on his dignity.

"The Commander Lord Kispeko has sent for you, Dhulyn Wolfshead." This time the tone—and the pronunciation—was perfect. The lad was clearly the younger son of a Noble House, perhaps even Kispeko's own. Dhulyn looked down at her Partner. Parno, in the midst of wrapping the strap once more around the bundle of tent, shrugged one shoulder and winced.

"I would be pleased to accompany you, Camp Messenger." Dhulyn picked up a pair of gloves and began to draw them over her hands.

Parno pushed the end of the strap through the last loop and tied it off. "Has the prince's wound gone bad?"

The boy licked his lips, clearly of two minds as to what he should say. "What makes you ask?"

"I've been expecting Kispeko—your pardon, I meant Commander Lord Kispeko, to send for one of us since last evening. The prince is injured, you have no Healer, and my Partner and I between us have more experience than any of the Knives that ride with your army."

It would be part of the boy's errand to report what they'd said, and he'd say that it was Parno, whom everyone considered "the talkative one" who had asked.

"The commander will explain, I'm sure," the boy said. "If you please, Dhulyn Wolfshead."

"Be so kind as to lead the way." Dhulyn grimaced when the boy's back was turned. She *was* Senior Brother, so it was natural for Kispeko to send for her alone, and in fact he'd done it many times. But she couldn't shake the feeling that she and Parno were being split up because it would make them easier to take. Not that she could do anything but act in the most natural manner herself, and that meant going along with the boy as if she had nothing on her mind but being on their way while there was still good daylight.

Mindful of the part she played, Dhulyn glanced at the position of the sun, sighed, and addressed the arrow-straight back in front of her.

"Will this take very long, do you think, Camp Messenger?"

The boy shot her a look over his shoulder that told her at once how pleased he was at being addressed by his title, and how nervous he was at not being able to tell her what she wanted to know.

"An improper question, and I withdraw it," she said, acknowledging what was no more or less than the truth. "We awoke so late after the excitement of the night that we're setting out much later than I had planned."

A few people called out to her as they walked through the camp—not so many as would have called out to Parno, perhaps, but enough to allow her to answer back in a manner she hoped was relaxed and confident. Not at all the manner of someone who had robbed the Nisvean army of its greatest treasure.

They arrived finally at Kispeko's tent. A few of the lower-ranked officers hovered outside, their faces for the most part hard and unfriendly. Jedrick, wearing his red cloak once more, frowned and raised his eyebrows at her. The edge of a bruise showed where his shirt was open at his throat. Dhulyn gave her head a tiny shake and followed the young boy into Kispeko's tent.

Parno would have said something to the Commander and the two high officers with him. Asked some question or made some polite noise. He'd been the son of a High Noble House himself, in Imrion, before becoming a Mercenary Brother, and still had court manners. Dhulyn merely rested

her crossed wrists on the hilt of her sword and waited for
Kispeko to speak. The commander sat behind his campaign
table, as he had the day before. But this time only his two
subcommanders were with him, two brothers from the Nisvean House of Olesev. As part of the cavalry section, Dhulyn and Parno had reported to the elder, Romenec. He sat
relaxed in his seat to Kispeko's right. The younger brother,
Renic, stood behind the commander's left shoulder, his
brows drawn down in a heavy scowl.

"Would you have any objection to an escort of cavalry
along your way, Dhulyn Wolfshead?"

She let her mouth fall open and her eyes go wide. Then
she smiled her wolf's smile. "You've lost him, haven't you?
Blooded fools and amateurs that you are, you've lost him."
She relaxed her shoulders, shaking her head with a low
whistle. "I should take offense, Kispeko, at what you ask of
me. I should, but it would be mean in me. You may give us
an escort. Sun! You may search our gear and baggage, if
you'd like. Though how you'd think we've hidden the
princeling in amongst our spare boots and extra blades . . ."
She shook her head again.

"You can account for yourself last night, Wolfshead,"
Subcommander Renic spoke up. The harshness of his tone
showed how little amused he was.

Dhulyn grinned. "I can. From the end of the first watch
at least. That is, Cavalry Squad Leader Jedrick can."

Kispeko signaled to the messenger still standing near
the tent entrance and the boy disappeared, returning in
moments with Jedrick. The squad leader did not acknowledge Dhulyn at all, but saluted his commanders and stood
to attention.

"The Mercenary Brother Dhulyn Wolfshead tells us that
you can account for her whereabouts last night, after the
end of the first watch?"

"I can, Commander." Jedrick spoke without emphasis.
"We were in her tent from that time until almost the end of
the fifth watch." His mustache trembled and Dhulyn was
certain Jedrick had almost smiled. "At which time," he continued, "many others can attest that the Wolfshead and I
were both there."

"And half the camp can swear as to where Parno Lionsmane

was and what he was doing the whole of the night, Commander," Romenec said from his seat next to Kispeko. From the dry tone of his voice, it was evident he'd heard nothing new to him. "I tell you there is no point in continuing this line of inquiry."

Dhulyn almost bit her lip. Romenec was a good man, he trusted her, and it went against the grain to trick him. But he had supported his commander against her request that their contract be honored, and that placed him out of the reach of her sympathy.

Kispeko was already nodding. "As you have guessed, the prince has escaped. We can find no trail, no sign. Mercenaries are skilled beyond the usual, will you find him for us?"

Dhulyn lifted one blood-red brow and waited. Apparently, she was the only one to appreciate irony when she heard it.

"Yesterday I called you Oathbreaker," she said finally. "And told you none of my Brotherhood would take service with you again. That was my final word, Commander Kispeko."

Romenec, the brother she'd worked under, showed no surprise at this; the other, Renic, wrinkled his nose in disapproval.

"There is a Finder in Jarasev, at the Royal House. We will be sending for her."

Dhulyn shrugged. "Then you will have no need of us."

Renic leaned on the table to speak again, but Kispeko raised the fingers of his right hand and he fell silent.

"If that is all, Commander, my Partner and I would like to leave today." Dhulyn carefully ignored both subcommanders.

"Very well. Should I decide to lend you an escort," Kispeko said, "they will find you on the north road?"

Dhulyn inclined her head the exact depth courtesy required. "We go to Broduk, to take ship there," she said and turned to go. Jedrick was holding aside the tent's closure for her.

"I would walk with you to your tent, Wolfshead."

She grinned at him, careful not to let her upper lip pull

back. "Sure you don't want to give me that cloak after all?" she asked him. "It looks much better on me."

"It gives a nice color to your skin, when you are lying on it, that much is true. But I must keep it to remember you by."

Dhulyn laughed and tapped the man on his shoulder with her closed fist, lowering her eyes as if embarrassed. *He'll think it's because we* did, she thought, *not because we didn't*. Tricking Jedrick was even more fun than she'd expected.

As they neared her camp space, Dhulyn could see Parno sitting on the large bundle that was their packed tent with a smaller figure next to him looking at something in Parno's hands. He'd sent someone for their horses while she was with Kispeko, or had gone himself, since all four beasts were there, waiting for saddles and packs.

"Wolfshead, a moment."

Sun and Moon, what does he want now? But she turned with a friendly look and raised eyebrows. The camp was alive around them, but no one was near enough to hear what they said to each other. Jedrick was frowning again, and looking at his feet. *Blood.*

"We had no time to take a proper leave of one another," Jedrick said. "We were . . . interrupted. I never had opportunity to ask you if —" He straightened his shoulders and looked her in the eye. "If all went well last night?"

Dhulyn hoped he couldn't hear her heart thumping in her chest. Or perhaps it would be better if he could. "I thought I made that abundantly clear last night," she said. "Come now, Jedrick, I didn't think you were the type who needed to be praised and complimented."

Now Jedrick flushed, and Dhulyn, waiting for the next question, the obvious question, wondered what she would answer.

"No, of course not," was what he finally said. "But with you a Mercenary Brother, and an Outlander . . ."

"Of course," she said, tapping him once again with her fist. "I understand. Let me say then, that I won't soon forget you."

"Nor I you, of course," Jedrick said, a little too quickly, his relief clear. "Nor I you."

"Come, say farewell to Parno Lionsmane."

Jedrick fell into step beside her once more, though it seemed to Dhulyn that his shoulders were lower, and his arms swung with more ease. *Nice enough in his way,* she thought. *But he still has too good an opinion of himself.* After a few more paces she came to an abrupt halt. It was Sjan, the young horse girl who looked after Randle's tether, sharing Parno's seat, but that wasn't what caught Dhulyn's eye and made her press her lips together. The larger horse pack was still open, road rations waiting on the ground beside it. The spare bows lay next to their oiled wrappings, and Parno's pipes—stowed into their special bag with one or two other small valuables before she'd been called to the commander's tent—were out again, as Parno was showing Sjan how to fill the bag of air.

"Sun, Moon, and Stars, didn't you finish?"

Parno looked up. "Back already? Sjan here brought us our horses, so I thought, just to thank her . . ."

Dhulyn rolled her eyes, calling on her gods to witness the nonsense she had to put up with, and sighed elaborately. "Can we finish *now*? I'd like to be on our way sometime today."

"Of course, my soul." Parno sprang to his feet. "What did they want, anyway?"

"The prince has escaped."

Parno was halfway to the bag of pipes that Jedrick was helpfully holding open for him when Dhulyn's words stopped him, and turned him around, eyes wide and mouth open.

Don't overdo it, Dhulyn thought.

"The blooded fools," Parno said.

"That's what I told them." Dhulyn pulled the laces of the large bag shut more sharply than necessary and dragged it over to the new packhorse, clucking at the animal as it rolled its eye at her. "After they'd made sure it wasn't us, Kispeko asked if we'd track the boy."

"*Now* they want our help." Parno stowed his pipes into their bag and nodded his thanks to Jedrick. As Parno dealt with the bag's closures, Jedrick went to help Dhulyn lift the heavy travel pack on to the new horse.

"My thanks, Jedrick," Dhulyn said, tugging the pack forward slightly on the packhorse's back. "Those saddlebags on our mounts, if you would be so kind. Parno will help me with the tent," she added in a voice filled with menace. Jedrick grinned at her, and she winked at him.

The bundle of tent was awkward, but their old packhorse, called Stumpy due to his short legs, had carried much worse and merely snorted at their efforts to balance the bundle on his back. With Sjan's help they had the tent tied securely, and Dhulyn surveyed the rest of the camp. Saddlebags on Bloodbone and Warhammer; tent, extra weapons, clothing and food packs distributed between the two pack animals; finally, she nodded and turned to where Jedrick stood in the empty space where their camp had been. "I believe this is farewell, Squad Leader. Again, I thank you for your assistance."

"It has been a pleasure, Dhulyn Wolfshead. I hope we may meet again." Jedrick gave her a short bow and a wide smile.

Dhulyn swung herself on to Bloodbone's back and settled into her saddle, checking that sword and knives were within reach. "Sun and Moon shine on you. Wind at your back." She nodded, and turned Bloodbone's head away, urging the mare forward with her knees.

Almost at the edge of the camp Dhulyn looked back, catching Parno's eye. She could just see Jedrick in his red cloak, still standing where their tent had been.

"Still there," she said.

"Of course." Parno rolled his right shoulder with a grimace. "He had a good look at everything we'd packed—"

"Which you so cleverly left half-packed for him."

"Just so. And once he'd satisfied himself that I didn't have Prince Edmir in my pipe satchel, he'd want to be sure we were really on our way."

"I hope this is all worth it," Dhulyn said.

Parno raised an eyebrow.

"I really liked that cloak."

The north road to Broduk was well conditioned, and

they rode through the afternoon, stopping twice to check the packs and retie the tent bundle, but eating their road bread and smoked meat while still in the saddle. The horses were fresh and eager for the exercise, and Dhulyn wanted to put as much distance between them and the Nisvean camp as they could.

When the afternoon turned into evening and the first stars began to appear, Parno called a halt, looking up into the heavens.

"If we turn off here, we can pick up the road to the pass and cut off a great deal of the country."

"As well as getting us off the road they'll expect to find us on."

Parno turned in his saddle. "You think they'll send someone after us?"

Dhulyn had been turning that question over and over in her mind, and had an answer. "No, I don't think they will," she said. "That's what Jedrick was watching us for, to make sure we went where we claimed to go. But in two or three days, when their searching proves fruitless, they'll think of us again. By then, we'll be over the border."

The place Dhulyn finally chose for their campsite—she'd learned early in their Partnership not to leave such choices to Parno—was a small clearing in the center of a thicket of young pine trees, with a larger clearing close by to leave the horses. It wasn't a perfect camp. They were closer to the road than Dhulyn would have liked, and there was no nearby supply of water, though they were still carrying plenty. The sky was darkening swiftly, however, and they could not continue much longer. They threw the reins over their horses' heads, hobbled the new packhorse, and went together to take the heavy bundle of tent from Stumpy's back.

They eased it carefully to the ground, untied the lacing, and pulled it open, exposing what they had hidden with such care within the stiff folds of canvas. Dhulyn dug her fingers under the side of Edmir's chin and held her breath, counting.

"Give him an hour," she said, "he'll come to." She peeled down his leggings, knowing from experience that it would be better to inspect his wound while he was still unconscious.

"How's it look?"

"Not as well as I'd like," she said. "Get my kit and I'll clean and redress it now."

⧤⧥

"Slipped it right out from among the Lionsmane's pipes, I tell you. So there's your great Mercenaries for you." At these words Jedrick paused, fully expecting Nilo to make an appreciative remark. Though perhaps that was expecting too much, considering the amount the younger man had lost wagering against Parno Lionsmane. But when Nilo said nothing at all, Jedrick turned from where he stood in the doorway of his tent, ready to make a sharp remark of his own about sore losers.

The remark died on his lips.

"Nilo?" he said instead, taking a step toward where the younger man lay slumped forward over the square chest that stood between the cots and served them as a table.

Jedrick's immediate fear faded. *Dead men don't snore,* he told himself.

Nilo's cup was still rocking on an uneven spot on the carpet that formed the flooring of the tent, where it had fallen from his hand. The cup of Imrion brandy Jedrick had poured out of the Mercenary woman's flask.

"Nilo," Jedrick said, putting his own untouched cup down carefully to one side. "Nilo?"

An hour later he stood in Commander Lord Kispeko's tent, watching the commander's body servant being carried out, not snoring, but just as unconscious as Nilo had been.

"Call in the search parties," the commander said to Subcommander Renic. Kispeko's voice was harsh, as if his throat was tight. "There must be some way to turn this to our advantage." He turned to Romenec as Renic left the tent.

Jedrick kept silent, fearing to be dismissed, as the cavalry subcommander thought for a moment, his teeth worrying at his mustache. "We could send a messenger to Probic," Romenec finally suggested. "To the Blue Mage—no, to Queen Kedneara, at once."

"And how will that advantage us?" Kispeko sat on the edge of his worktable.

"We tell the Tegriani Queen that the Mercenary Brothers have kidnapped their prince."

"No one would believe such a thing of Mercenary Brothers. They are neutral, always have been." Even in his rage, Jedrick knew this much.

Romenec spread his hands, lifting his eyebrows. "We were as surprised as any. All we know is that they took him, and kept him, contrary to what we all understood of their Common Rule."

"It will be enough." Lord Kispeko was nodding. "People in doubt will choose to take no chances and withhold their aid from them. The Mercenary woman is an Outlander, remember. Perhaps blame can be placed on her." He fixed his eye on Jedrick. "It isn't the Brotherhood itself we have to convince, Squad Leader, nor even popular opinion. Only Queen Kedneara. And if we play our tiles carefully, we can make this almost as great an advantage to us as the Prince himself." He turned to Romenec. "There is something else?"

"Commander, it is imperative that ours is the story the queen hears first. I will pick an escort, and go myself." Romenec turned to Jedrick. "They went north, this is assured?"

Jedrick nodded. "As they would, if they were truly heading for Broduk."

Romenec spread his hands and gripped the edge of Commander Lord Kispeko's worktable, leaning forward to better study the map clamped to the table's surface.

"Then they will be heading for the Eagles Pass and from there to the Queen's Royal House at Beolind." He pointed to their own location in the Limona Valley. "We, however, can use the Limona Pass to reach Probic first, and tell our tale to the City Lord there long before the Mercenaries reach anyone of consequence in Tegrian." He tapped the "X" marked "Probic" with his right forefinger. "In the meantime," he continued, "I would suggest that a small party, a select group, be sent after the Mercenaries. Pick from among those who have not fought and trained with them."

The Commander was nodding, but before he could

speak Jedrick was ready. "Permission to go after them myself, Commander," he said.

Kispeko held up his hand. "Romenec, choose your escort and go, lose no time. Jedrick, remain, I wish to speak to you."

Jedrick swallowed. This could not bode well.

Kispeko seated himself once again behind his desk, drumming his fingers on the top.

"She made a fool of you," he said quietly.

Jedrick pressed his lips together. He knew better than to answer.

"You are an ambitious man, Squad Leader. This episode won't do much to further your ambitions, will it?"

"No, Commander."

"No." Kispeko beckoned Jedrick closer. "But there are other ways to gain recognition, Squad Leader. Other ambitions to aspire to. How many men do you think you would need to take these Mercenaries?"

"If I may speak frankly, Commander." Jedrick prudently waited for Kispeko's nod. "I would take archers. It would be easier to kill than to capture them alive."

"And in that case?"

"Five men, counting myself. If they were the right men."

"Choose the right men, then, Squad Leader."

Jedrick drew himself to attention. "Thank you, Commander."

Kispeko did not dismiss him, but leaned on his elbow, tapping his lips with his fingers. "Squad Leader, the prince need not return with you. It will prove to our advantage if the Mercenary Brothers have killed him. Do you, and your ambitions, understand me?"

What he saw in Jedrick's face must have satisfied him.

"You may go, Squad Leader."

❧❧❧

"Dhulyn—"

Dhulyn held up her right forefinger, sipped from the shallow metal ladle in her left hand, swallowed, and nodded before speaking.

"Only my Brothers may call me Dhulyn," she said to the

prince. "To anyone else I am Wolfshead, or Scholar, and my Partner is Lionsmane, or Chanter. And your question?"

Prince Edmir blinked, as though he was unaccustomed to being given instructions, but he swallowed and dropped his eyes in a way Dhulyn didn't like.

"I don't understand how you managed to trick Jedrick into drinking the iocain without drinking any yourself," he said, as he took the cup of rabbit broth she passed him with a nod of thanks. His injured leg, the wound repacked and bound with fresh-boiled cloths, was stretched out straight in front of him. Dhulyn had made a small fire, using the fireproof cloth she and Parno had purchased in Berdana so as to leave no mark on the ground. Even if, at some future time, someone found their campsite and managed to deduce what it was, there would be no way to tell how many of them there had been.

"I didn't trick him," Dhulyn said, ladling a measure of broth with a few chunks of rabbit into a bowl for Parno before she served herself. "I've done three drug *Shoras*, ioca among them, so I could drink the iocain and feel no effects."

"Neither good effects nor bad," Parno added. "Because of the *Shora*, she can't chew the leaves for pain as you did when she brought you out of your tent, nor can she use the drug to sleep through a surgery or recuperation, as you did today."

"Not ever?"

Dhulyn swallowed the bit of rabbit she was chewing on before answering. "Well, no. That's the drawback to the drug *Shoras*."

"And the reason so few of the Brotherhood learn them." Parno took another mouthful of his own stew.

"You needn't look quite so worried, Lord Prince. There are other pain drugs I can use, if I wish to."

"She never wishes to," Parno said. "Don't listen to her."

The young man looked between them, a smile flitted across his face, and then he lowered his eyes again.

Dhulyn knew that look. *Something he's trying not to think about.*

"But *you* may wish to take iocain again tonight," Dhulyn said, as if it was a thing of no consequence. "After sleeping all day you may have trouble falling asleep naturally. A little iocain will help you drop off, and you will awaken in the morning refreshed."

Before Edmir could answer, Parno held up his finger. "Let's see how much there is left before we start dispensing it. There may be a greater need for it later."

They had unpacked very little, merely relieving the horses of their burdens and taking the bare essentials required to make a quick camp. Among those essentials, Parno's pipes had been set down on the bedroll he and Dhulyn would take turns using. Parno set down his stew bowl and dragged the bag closer to him. He undid the closures, slipping his hand past the bulge of the pipes into the bottom of the bag.

"Dhulyn, my heart," he said after a moment. "Did you take out the brandy flask already?"

"No," she said, a note of warning in her voice.

"Well, it isn't here now."

Dhulyn set down her own bowl and took the bag from her Partner. She took out each piece of his pipes, the air bag, the chanter, the drones, and laid them beside her on the ground. There was one of her books, a travel volume, the paper cut and bound between covers. A roll of thick felt proved to contain only the blue-glass cups she expected to find. There was no sign of the flask of iocain-laced brandy.

She looked up at Parno, as a mental picture of Jedrick handing the bag to him flashed through her mind.

"Jedrick," they both said at once.

"He admired the flask," Dhulyn said. "He asked me for it and I said no." She could feel her ears burning. How had she relaxed her guard so much?

"This is my doing." She began replacing the contents of the bag. "I was so sure I was tricking him, I did not watch for his tricking me."

"That may not have been his purpose—the snail dung may simply have wanted a flask from the Tin Isles."

Dhulyn pulled the bag's ties closed once more. The fact that Jedrick might only be a thief would not save them. "It's only a matter of time until he tries the brandy. He may have done so already."

Parno was shaking his head. "The horses are too tired—look who I'm advising about horses! *I'm* too tired; never mind the horses. We can't go on tonight."

"I'll take the first watch." Dhulyn stood, picked up her sword and crossbow, and stepped into the dark beyond the fire's light.

Four

EDMIR WOKE SUDDENLY, a hand over his mouth. For an instant he thought he was back in Commander Lord Kispeko's tent, but the pale dawn light filtering through the trees, and the feel of cool air on his face soon told him where he was—as did the stiffness in his leg. The Mercenary Brothers had wrapped him well, using all their own bedding as well as their cloaks, but after Dhulyn Wolfshead had put out the small campfire by the simple expedient of kicking it apart and then smothering it in the folds of the fire cloth, the night had grown colder and colder.

When he sat up, the Wolfshead spoke in that eerily quiet way they called the nightwatch voice.

"Five horses come down the road. They must have stopped just long enough to rest during the night, and started after us again long before dawn."

"Five? All they sent was five men? Are they mad?" Lionsmane squatted on Edmir's other side.

"Mad or not, they will reach us before the sun clears the trees."

Edmir froze. *How could she know that*?

Lionsmane whistled softly between his teeth.

"Give me up," Edmir said. "Leave me. Don't come to harm because of me." He clamped his mouth shut, glad it was too dark for them to see his chin tremble. He pushed the images of the battlefield, the dead and the dying back into the darkness in his mind. *No more*. No more dead because of him.

"Speak more softly, Lord Prince. You'd be surprised how

far sounds will carry, even here among the trees." The Lionsmane began to unwrap Edmir's bedding, carefully easing the folds of cloth from around his injured leg.

"I say leave me." He took hold of Parno Lionsmane's wrist.

"We will not." The Wolfshead had risen to her feet and her whisper now floated down from above.

"Might they pass us by?" Edmir stifled a gasp as his leg was jarred.

"They might at that," the Lionsmane said. "They might be farmers going to market." He shot a glace at the Wolfshead and flashed her a grin. "Or a flock of sheep and not men on horseback at all, if you really believe my Partner could be mistaken. But do you know what the Mercenary Brotherhood calls those who prepare for what *might* happen, instead of what *can* happen?"

Edmir shook his head.

"We call them the dead. Up you come, Lord Prince."

Edmir looked at Parno Lionsmane's outstretched hand and swallowed. His thoughts seemed to throb in time to the pain in his leg. It shamed him, but he was relieved that the Mercenaries hadn't accepted his offer to leave him. Relieved that his mother wouldn't have to rescue him at the Caids' alone knew what kind of diplomatic price. But he didn't think he'd be walking—let alone fighting—any time soon. Not with his leg.

"I don't think I can," he said, even as he reached up. Parno Lionsmane grasped him by the forearm, and Edmir in turn locked his own hand around the Mercenary's wrist.

"Not to worry," Dhulyn Wolfshead said. "Parno Lionsmane can carry you."

Edmir grimaced. Yes, of course he could. The Wolfshead could probably carry him herself, if she had to. He took firm hold of his lower lip with his teeth as the disappointments of the last three days came crashing down on him. All he'd wanted to do was show his mother that he was as capable as any of her generals. What would she think if she saw him now? Unconsciously, he stood up straighter, choking back a hiss as he put his weight on his injured leg.

But Parno Lionsmane had seen it, and gripped him once

more by the arm, placing his callused hand under Edmir's elbow.

Edmir held up his free hand. "Wait," he said. Even in his own ears, his voice sounded tight and breathless with pain. He took a slow deep breath to steady himself.

"Dhulyn Wolfshead," he said. "Are there more of those ioca leaves? I might be of more use to you if the pain was dulled."

The Wolfshead turned back into the clearing, reaching into the small pouch she kept at her waist and withdrawing a fold of oiled silk. She opened the tiny packet with care, frowning as she exposed the ioca leaves.

"These are the last. Let's hope we find no reason to regret using them now."

Edmir took the two almond-shaped leaves from the woman's long fingers and placed them on his tongue. It seemed that as soon as he tasted their sharp bitterness his leg throbbed less.

"Bring him to the horses." Dhulyn Wolfshead took two steps, and vanished.

Edmir looked at the spot where she'd disappeared. It was darker there, beyond the edge of the clearing, but surely not *that* dark. Edmir glanced at Parno Lionsmane, looked back again, and closed his mouth. The Lionsmane twitched the unrolled bedding off the ground one-handed, slinging it over his shoulder.

"Come," he said, handing Edmir the bag that held his pipes. "We'll want you with the horses."

Once in the thicker part of the trees, the light from the rising sun seemed to make the dark places darker, and the shadows more mobile and deceptive. Edmir had to be careful where he placed his feet, as his leg was apt to turn under him—just because he couldn't feel the pain, didn't mean the injury wasn't there. The Lionsmane, on the other hand, walked as though he was on a city pavement in the full light of the sun. Once Edmir stumbled, and the Mercenary turned back to help, but Edmir waved him on. He'd thought that his own training, supplemented by weeks in the field with the army, had toughened him. But a few hours with the Mercenary Brothers were enough to make him feel he was no soldier, but an actor playing a part. And a poor actor at that.

Well, I am *injured,* he said to himself. *That has to count for something.*

They slowed as they neared the other clearing where the horses had been left, the Lionsmane making comforting sounds under his breath both to warn and reassure the animals. This clearing was larger than the one in which they'd camped, the canopy of the trees thinner, and there was enough light for Edmir to see clearly.

Or maybe my eyes have finally adjusted. When they had camped the night before, the Mercenaries had not unpacked more than the night's bare necessities, though they had unburdened the horses for comfort. Only one, the larger packhorse, was hobbled. Of the other three, Edmir recognized the two cavalry horses, the gray and the spotted mare, from his first encounter with the Mercenaries. The fourth was a sturdy bay beast and looked to be what his mother's stableman called "a horse-of-all-trades," useful for both riding and hauling. Each animal stood near a tidy stack of packs, saddles, and saddlebags, though the gray gelding left his position and came to snuffle at the Lionsmane's hands.

"Hah, Warhammer, no fruit for you, greedy beast," Lionsmane said to the horse, rubbing its nose before he pushed the large head out of his way.

Dhulyn Wolfshead was on her knees, unrolling a long bundle that lay among the packs of the hobbled horse. From it, she extracted two unstrung recurve bows, and two shorter thicker bundles that Edmir recognized as quivers. She tossed one bow to Parno Lionsmane. Could they shoot in this light? He shook his head. They were Mercenaries. They could probably shoot blindfolded.

The Wolfshead gestured with the end of the unstrung bow in her hand. "Edmir can set up over there. Leave the horses where they are."

"I'll come with you and help," Edmir corrected her.

"You'll help best by staying here with both crossbows, Lord Prince," Lionsmane said, unhooking the two crossbows that normally hung from their saddles. "If anyone gets around us, it will be for you to stop them and keep them from the horses. So if you hear someone coming, shoot them."

"What if it's you?"

"I said shoot anyone you *hear*," he said, pushing the bundle that was their tent to one side. "Come, sit here." Edmir obeyed, setting one crossbow on his lap and laying the other down on the ground to his left next to the extra bolts. These were light bows, meant to be fired from horseback, and easily armed by a man sitting down.

"Where will you be?"

"Closer to the road."

Dhulyn Wolfshead had finished stringing her recurve bow and set it down against its quiver on the ground. She then went from horse to horse, catching and holding their heads in her hands, while she breathed into their nostrils, and spoke, murmuring words in a language Edmir had never heard before. The two warhorses quieted instantly, as did the other, smaller horse, but the fourth horse, the hobbled one, took a little longer to soothe. "What is she doing?" Edmir said, as the Lionsmane drew near him.

"Asking the horses to stay quiet and still, no matter what they see, or hear, or smell."

"Will it work?"

"It always has before."

"That's good," Edmir said. *That's good,* he thought again as he watched them disappear into the dark. The Lionsmane was right. They made no noise.

When they were nearly at the wide track that served as the road through this section of the Nisvean West Forest, Dhulyn stopped Parno with a click of her tongue, signaling him with a patting motion of her hand to wait as she stepped out into the road. Holding her bow out to her left, she squatted on her heels, resting her right hand on the track. Her eyes were closed, her head tilted as she listened. The colors of her Mercenary badge were bright in the light of the rising sun.

She straightened, made sure he was looking at her and tapped her ear, silently asking, "Do you hear them?"

Parno pressed his lips together and shook his head, then raised his hand to say, "Stop." There. A muted thunking of horses' hooves on the packed dirt of the road, a murmuring of voices in the still air. Dhulyn rejoined him under the trees. He pointed upward and, when she nodded, made a cup of his hands and braced himself as she placed her foot in it. She disappeared into the branches over his head with no more sound than the wind would have made moving the leaves. After several seconds a silk rope as thick as his thumb fell out of the trees over his head. Parno hung his bow across his shoulders, grasped the rope with both hands and pulled himself upward.

Dhulyn had found a place where a thick limb of the oak tree grew almost parallel to the ground. She pointed at it, then at Parno; pointed at herself, then at another fork just above where they were standing. With the habit of caution, Parno glanced around. From here they had good angle and height on the road. And they could reach the ground quickly if they had to. He beckoned Dhulyn closer and put his lips near her ear.

"Permit me to point out—just this once—that I suggested the sea route," he said. "It was you who insisted on going overland through Nisvea. I won't mention it again," he added. As he leaned away from her, Dhulyn grasped his shoulder and pulled him close again.

"You do, and it will be the last thing you ever mention."

"Now, now, be careful. You know they say Partners don't survive each other."

"It would be worth it."

Parno grinned at her disappearing shadow. "In Battle," he whispered.

"Or in Death," she said.

❧

Avylos the Blue Mage ran his index finger along the spines of the seven books he kept on the high shelves behind his worktable. To the untutored eye, they were unremarkable, three herbal lexicons, two works of early philosophy based on the writings of the Caids, and two books of poetry. Avylos took down the larger of the philosophic works and sat down at his table. He centered the volume carefully on the tabletop, opened it to the middle, exposing the blank center pages. Noticeably different from the other pages of the book, these were folded once from a single piece of parchment made from the skin of a pure white kid goat. Matching pages, cut from the other half of the skin, and as identical as two halves of the same thing can be, occupied the central position in another volume of philosophy. One that did not sit on Avylos' table.

He waited until the rays of the setting sun moved to shine directly upon the blank pages. He made a sign in the air above the book.

"At my command," he said. "Speak to me."

"I am here." As he watched, the words appeared on the page as though they were being written by an unseen hand.

"You have failed me," he said. For a moment it seemed the page trembled.

"Please, my lord," appeared on the page. *"It was the Mercenaries."*

"Tell me."

"Two Mercenaries," appeared on the page. *"A man, Parno Lionsmane, and an Outlander woman, Dhulyn Wolfshead. They discovered and claimed the prince. I refused their claim, but they tricked us and took him. I have sent men after them, trusted men who will follow your instructions."*

"Do they know the instructions are mine?"

"No, my lord."

Avylos straightened, his shoulders pressed against the carved back of his chair. Mercenaries. He had met a Mercenary Brother once, a long time ago. The Brotherhood was ancient, much respected. Followers, some said, of the Sleeping God. He drummed his fingers on the tabletop.

"See that your men are successful," he said. "Make sure of it. In the meantime, send out word that Edmir of Tegrian is dead."

A pause before the words appeared on the page. *"I don't understand, my lord. You mean before we find and deal with them?"*

Avylos cracked the knuckles of his left hand one by one, resisting the desire to look at the casket that held the Stone. "These are Mercenary Brothers," he said dryly. "How would it be if you do not 'find and deal with them'? Let us prepare for the possibility that they might yet escape with their captive. Announce, therefore, that the man

the Mercenaries took is not the prince. Prince Edmir died
on the battlefield, and these rogue Mercenaries play some
trick of their own. Find a suitable corpse, and use the excuse of its return to Tegrian to march on Probic."

*"So the original plan holds? And I am still to have Pro-
bic?"*

"Of course."

Another long pause. Avylos could almost hear the other
man thinking.

Finally. *"Very good, my lord."*

"At my command," Avylos said, and the page turned
blank once more. He shut the book, and sat very still, with
his hand on the cover.

Many spans away, Commander Lord Kispeko looked
down at the blank pages in front of him and let go the
breath he was holding. *So,* that's *the way it will be.* Not exactly the way Avylos had planned it, but this was better for
the Nisveans. Let the Mercenaries be blamed for everything. If anyone could deal with the Mercenary Brotherhood, it was the Blue Mage. Kispeko shut the book and
rose to return it to the chest beside his camp bed.

⚇

Parno was settling into the spot Dhulyn had found for
him—back braced against the trunk, but at an angle to
leave his bow arm free—when he heard the slow notes of
the owl call that was Dhulyn telling him the troop of Nisveans were in sight. He did not see them himself until a few
minutes later. There were five, as Dhulyn had said, and—
what she couldn't have known—one of them was Jedrick.

He must have asked for the privilege, Parno thought, baring his teeth. Though it remained to be seen whether the
man would still think it *was* a privilege in an hour's time.
The trail was wide enough for the Nisveans to ride two
abreast, and Jedrick occupied the leader's position in the
center of the men. The two in front rode as scouts, three or
four horse lengths ahead of their comrades, the two in back
the same distance behind. One of those in the rear guard
was Nilo, Parno realized, and he recognized the others as
well, though he did not know their names. Friends of Jedrick's, without doubt.

The two in front were his. Dhulyn's greater elevation would allow her to reach the two in the rear. As he watched, the forward scouts slowed, finally stopping entirely as they allowed the others to catch up. Parno could almost feel Dhulyn's disapproval at this carelessness wafting down from the branch above him.

"It's along here," the taller of the two forward riders said, pointing into the trees as Jedrick stopped next to him. "If we leave the road here, we'll strike an old hunting trail that will get us to the pass in half the time."

"We'll catch them if we go this way?" Jedrick said.

"We should get ahead of them," the tall man said. "They don't know the country, and they *certainly* won't know the hunting trails. They'll have to stay along this road to the village of Tesnib, where the road to the pass crosses it."

True enough, Parno thought. That was exactly what they would have done, if they hadn't been Mercenary Brothers, for whom the positioning of mountain passes and the maps they appeared on were part of their Schooling.

"Jedrick." That was Nilo. "What made sense last night doesn't make sense this morning. You're right about killing the Mercenaries—we couldn't hope to capture them alive—but the prince is worth any ransom, we could slip him over the border ourselves, none the wiser, and say we got to them too late."

"Do you want to change my orders, Nilo? Is that what you're saying?" The other man stayed silent. "We're to kill them all. Those are our orders. Commander Lord Kispeko has his reasons."

A bit of tree bark struck Parno on the left hand. Without looking, his fingers working automatically, Parno let fly his first arrow, watched it sink into the left eye of the tall man, the one who knew the hunting trails so well. At the same moment, Nilo caught an arrow in *his* left eye. Parno's second arrow caught his other target in the throat as the man spurred his horse into the trees on the far side of the track, the spray of blood showing the man was dying as he went. As fast as he and Dhulyn were, however, Jedrick and the second rear guard managed to turn their horses and take flight down the road, back the way they had come.

Dhulyn's second arrow took the closer man in the small

of the back, just where his armor left a gap as he leaned forward, but Jedrick, his red cloak bright in the light of the rising sun, was racing farther away.

Dhulyn beat Parno to the ground by the simple expedient of stepping off her branch and letting herself fall straight down, meeting the ground with bended knees. She ran quickly into the road, dodged the milling horses with a few quick steps, putting arrow to the string as she went. She still had a clear shot, but there was a bend in the road perhaps ten spans away, and the red cloak was quickly approaching it.

Parno opened his mouth, and shut it again as Dhulyn brought up her bow, released her breath, and let fly. Parno held his own breath. He'd seen her hit targets at greater distances—Caids, he'd done it himself—but that was with the longbow, and a still target. If she missed—he turned to grab the bridles of the two nearest horses.

Then he heard the cry, and saw the red cloak that was Jedrick hit the ground.

Dhulyn dropped her bow and swung herself up on the nearest horse, the animal instantly becoming calm and ready when it felt her in the saddle.

"Demons and perverts," Parno called after her as he struggled onto the back of the other horse. He was a good horseman—he *was,* even by Mercenary standards—but not compared to Dhulyn. Precious time was wasted as he persuaded his new mount that he was going to stay on its back, and that they were both going after the other horse. By the time he caught up with Dhulyn, however, she was already off her horse.

Jedrick must have been turning to look over his shoulder, for Dhulyn's final arrow had caught him in the neck with enough force to knock him off his horse, but it had missed any major arteries. Blood streamed from the wound, and he would die from it if he did not meet with a skilled Knife, but that death was still some time away. Jedrick's foot had caught in the stirrup as he came down. As Parno rode up, the man was trying to keep the horse between himself and Dhulyn at the same time as he remounted.

Dhulyn grabbed the horse's tail, twisted it, sidestepped

the stamping hooves to maneuver herself to Jedrick's side. She caught hold of the arrow shaft that protruded from the side of his neck with her right hand, swept his feet out from under him with her left foot, and pushed the point of the arrow into the ground as he went down. The horse snorted, backed away a few feet and stopped, shaking its head and blowing foam from its mouth.

Dhulyn squatted down on her heels next to the fallen squad leader. Parno swung himself off his own mount, but stayed back.

"Squad Leader," Dhulyn said. "No fear, I will not go without giving you the Final Sword. Though you are no Brother of mine, I won't leave you to die slowly on the road."

"I won't tell you anything." Jedrick's teeth were clenched and there was sweat on his forehead.

"We're to be killed, and the prince with us," Dhulyn said. "You have nothing further to tell us. Kispeko would have told you no more than that."

"I had to follow my orders," Jedrick said then.

Dhulyn nodded, pulling her knife out of its sheath in the small of her back. "You have your orders. We have our Common Rule." She covered Jedrick's eyes with her left hand and cut his throat with her right.

When it was over, Dhulyn wiped the knife off on Jedrick's shirt and straightened to her feet.

"*Blooded* snail dung," she said. "He's gone and bled all over my cloak."

❈❈❈

Avylos the Blue Mage sighed at the muted sound of unexpected voices and put down the book he was reading by the light of the candelabra next to his chair. It was late at night, and only something very momentous would bring even Kedneara's royal pages to make such a noise in the Mage's wing.

"My lord, my lord Mage," called out a voice.

He rose and went into the corridor, pulling the door shut behind him to keep in the warmth of the small charcoal brazier under the table. A glance at the door of his workroom showed the magics intact. When he reached the door to his wing, it was to find two white-faced pages waiting for him.

"The Royal Guard Commander Lord Semlian sends for you, my lord Mage. A horse messenger has arrived from Probic for Kedneara the Queen." The taller page, the queen's page, spoke up before Avylos' attendant could. Avylos frowned, he knew this boy, a Balnian recently come to court, and ready to put himself forward.

"From Probic," he said.

"Yes, my lord Mage, changing horses all the way."

"I will come immediately." There were only two or three pieces of news from Probic that would warrant a horse messenger, and Avylos was curious to know which it would be.

This was one occasion, Avylos thought as he followed the new page through the almost deserted corridors to the stairs which would eventually take them to Kedneara's rooms, in which it might have been handier if he slept in the consort's apartments, rather than in his own wing. But he was more than the consort, more than Kedneara's bedwarmer—much more—and it was vital that people keep that always in mind. Long after Kedneara was no longer queen, he would still be the Blue Mage.

It was certainly not as consort that he was being sent for now, and sent for by Lord Semlian, not the queen. Possibly, Semlian thought Avylos knew something about the news that had arrived, or possibly, the guard commander suspected the news would hit the queen hard. Avylos began to walk a little faster.

One of the first things he had learned about the magic, even before the power finally found him, was that it did not affect women the same way as men. When it affected them at all. He'd asked his father about it, when he was still a small child, before they had all turned their faces away from him, and the old man had laughed, saying, "No power is without limit, Avi, least of all any power over women."

So it was ironic that the one woman it was relatively easy for him to influence and affect with his magics should be Queen Kedneara. Even the armies were almost all male now for that very reason—though he carefully made *that* magic temporary; troops who could never be killed or injured had a way of rebelling against their masters. But the queen's health had begun to fail early, as had her father's before her, and the magics that allowed Avylos to heal her—not *Heal*, as one of the Marked could have done, but better than anything the Royal Knives had ever achieved—also allowed him an access to her mind and spirit he did not have with other women.

Whatever the news was, it had not weakened her. Avylos could hear Kedneara shouting as he turned into the corridor of her rooms. The guards standing at her door looked up in relief when they saw him approaching, and threw open the doors to the anteroom. He nodded them aside and went in, putting his hand to the latch of Kedneara's sitting room door, and hesitated as the thick oak shook under it. Kedneara was throwing things. He must stop her, or she would strain her heart.

"But, my Queen." That was Counselor Csezik's voice. "We can send a complaint to the Mercenary House in Lesonika, and you can confidently expect—"

"What, send a nice, well-mannered clerk to ask them to explain themselves?" There was enough sarcasm in Kedneara's tone to sour milk. "*Complain* that they've kidnapped my son? Are you mad? I want them banished. I want every Mercenary Brother out of my realm by midday tomorrow or I will send you all to the Black Dungeons! I want them GONE. Tegrian is closed to the Brotherhood. Do you hear me? CLOSED."

Everyone in the room found something to look at that wasn't the queen. No one wanted to be the one to explain that midday tomorrow would not be enough time to clear the country of Mercenaries.

Kedneara stalked back and forth over the cold stone tiles like a caged cat. She had thrown on a light robe of fine red wool embroidered with golden dragons, but was barefoot, her waist-length hair—still as dark as Edmir's—flying loose. The robe's trailing sleeves swung as Kedneara paced, and she kicked the train out from under her feet as she turned and saw him.

"Avylos!" She seized him by the front of his tunic. "Find him. Find Edmir!"

"Though I am not a Finder, my Queen, I might—"

"Are you not a Mage? Do something! Where have they taken him?"

Her breath was coming in short gasps, and there were two red spots high on her cheeks. If she did not restrain herself, she might easily have an attack. Almost as if she heard his thought, Kedneara took a deep breath, and then another, though she retained her grip on his tunic.

"Perhaps they only bring him to me? That's possible, isn't it? They are Mercenary Brothers, after all, they are to be trusted, aren't they? Of course they are. Perhaps all is well and Tzanek is an old woman who should be relieved of his post."

Here was the opening Avylos was hoping for.

"Let me sit a moment, my Queen, let me see what I can learn. I was about to say that I am not a Finder, but where your children are concerned I have taken certain other steps, and I may be able to tell you—"

"A chair for the Blue Mage, quickly, quickly, and whatever else he needs."

It was almost pathetically easy to convince them that he was performing a great feat of magic, as he took out his silver dagger, called for new, unlit candles and a bowl of the darkest wine. However, he had faked magics before, long ago, before his power found him, and he'd learned then that a good show would convince its audience of anything. It soured his stomach a little to fall back on those tricks now, when he had real power at his fingertips—but he had no intention of using up real power for this.

After a suitable passage of time, and very visible effort, he set his dagger down, blew out the candles, and took the queen by the hands. "Sit down, my Queen. I must insist."

Kedneara was so white her eyebrows stood out like stains on her face.

"I fear to give you this news, my Queen. You must be strong, for all of us, for Tegrian. For your remaining child."

The screams, Avylos thought with carefully concealed satisfaction, must be audible down in the Great Hall.

Hours later, Avylos shut the door of Kedneara's bed-chamber, letting the latch down slowly until it caught without making a sound. The outer room was now blessedly empty, and Avylos leaned against the doorframe, rubbing his face with his hands. He took a deep breath, tugged his robe straight, smoothed back his hair, and strode across the room to the outer door. The two guards stationed in the anteroom leaped to attention as he came out.

"My lord Mage," they said simultaneously as he emerged.

"Guards." A cool nod to them, another to the pages who stood up from their couches as he passed, and he was at the door to the queen's apartments and through it into the wide corridor beyond.

How fast did horse messengers travel, he wondered as he took the shortest route back to his own rooms. And two Mercenary Brothers? How quickly did they travel, considering they had an injured prince with them? The official proclamation of Edmir's death would be made by the queen from her throne tomorrow, but there were one or two people who needed to know now, tonight. Could he afford the power?

It was late, and even taking into account the news which must be even now spreading through the Royal House on the lips of every servant, page, guard, and noble, Avylos passed only three servants who quickly stepped out of his path as he returned to his own wing. His workroom, when he reached it, was deserted, though the wards he had placed on the door showed what he expected. Two people had attempted to open the door in his absence and been thwarted. He made a mental note of their identities, and the people most likely to have sent them. Princess Kera had also attempted to enter, and had been successful.

He smiled, entered the room, and swung the door shut behind him. Without conscious decision, his feet took him directly to the casket that held the Stone and he had one hand on the lid and the other hunting in his pocket for the key before he caught himself and stopped. He breathed in slowly, lifting both hands and taking a step back. As an added precaution, he clasped his hands behind his back as he considered.

If he used the Stone again now, who did he have to draw upon to refill it? There was the Champion Archer, his talent and art still hot within a body almost too old to pull the bow. The second assistant cook who made those marvelous peach pastries—a pity to use her at all, really. Even though the recipe had been passed on, that particular cook would never again create something so good. There was power and talent left yet in both of those. And, finally, this morning, Lord Semlian had come to him about that ambitious new commander in the Royal Guard. The commander who hadn't yet learned that in order to advance in the Tegrian Guard one must be either talented, *or* ambitious. Not both together.

Avylos thought a moment longer. Yes, that should be enough.

The key was in his hand, the casket was open, and the Stone glowing in response to his touch before the thought was even complete. The Stone had seven symbols etched into its otherwise smooth surface. Four were evenly spaced—like compass points—the width of his smallest finger from one end of the cylinder. A circle with a dot in the middle, a simple straight line, a rectangle, and a long triangle like a spearhead. A finger width farther in was a plain circle, all by itself. Around the other end were only two symbols, though these were larger. One he knew, having drawn it in the air many times, the three-line symbol for "light." The other, using only two lines, he did not know; though he'd tried drawing it, nothing had ever happened.

"You have more power than you are giving me," he told the Stone, stroking the warm, smooth crystal. "And when I have found your secret, then I shall need neither queen nor realm."

"Gehde. Gehde. Monos. Aharneh," he said.

The Stone glowed brighter. He took hold of it by either end, and twisted.

The world disappeared in a blaze of blue light.

When the light had faded, and the world returned, the Stone still glowed faintly but perceptibly. Avylos let out a long sigh. He would leave it set, and ready for the morrow, but in the meantime, the Stone would go back into its box, he would shut the lid, turn the key, and put it away once more.

Temptation behind him, Avylos took one of the two

books of poetry from the shelf behind his worktable and opened it to its central, blank pages. Like the philosophical work he'd used earlier in the day, these pages had been made from half a sheet of parchment, itself the treated skin of a pure white animal, in this case an albino calf. Avylos threw open the tall window shutters and let in the moonlight. The moon was not quite full, but there was more than enough light at this hour to illuminate the surface of the book.

He sat down at the table, placed his hands palm down to each side of the open volume and spoke.

"At my command," he said, and waited. For a long moment nothing happened, and he frowned until he remembered the hour. "At my command," he repeated. This time the answer came.

"I am here, my lord Mage," appeared in script on the page before him.

"I have grave news to tell you, City Lord Tzanek," Avylos said. "Prince Edmir has fallen."

"But, my lord—" the writing broke off, almost as it would if a pen point had broken, before starting again. *"Surely you are mistaken? How is this possible?"*

Avylos bit back his irritation. How dare the man question him like this?

"Do not concern yourself unduly. Kedneara the Queen's Messengers will be sent out tomorrow to inform the country of this tragedy, but there may yet be a service you can perform in the meantime."

"Name it, my lord."

That was better. "It concerns the two Mercenary Brothers who were said to have taken the prince. If they should appear, you will arrest them in the queen's name."

"I do not understand, Lord Mage. If there are any to be trusted out of hand, surely the Brotherhood—I did not understand the Nisveans' declaration, though I passed it along to the queen, of course—and now you say the prince is dead—"

"Enough. The queen has banished the Brotherhood from Tegrian. See that you make this generally known." The man was a chatterer. Not for the first time Avylos thought how lucky it was that the writing did not remain permanently on the pages.

"Of course, my lord Mage." Now the writing appeared hesitant, as if the man on the other end was not very confident in what he was saying.

"My magics tell me there is some deep deceit afoot," Avylos said. "Some plan of which I see only the edges. If you should see the Mercenary Brothers, they may well have a young man with them, a man they will say is the prince, but you will not be deceived." Avylos waited, but again, the reply was slow in coming. He placed the fingertips of his left hand on the edge of the blank page. "I say that you will not be deceived."

"I will not be deceived."

"The young man they have with them is not Edmir."

"The young man they have with them is not Edmir."

Did the writing seem to be in a different, yet very familiar hand? Avylos smiled.

"You know Edmir well, have known him from a child, and you will not be deceived."

"I will not be deceived."

"Mercenaries who have killed a Prince of Tegrian, even accidentally, would wish to make themselves appear innocent. Clearly the person with them is not Edmir."

"Clearly. The young man they have with them is not Edmir. I will not be deceived."

"Excellent. It is a comfort to be counseled by someone so able as yourself. You will inform me, if you have occasion to arrest these people."

"At once, my lord Mage." The subtle difference in the writing was gone.

"At my command," Avylos said, and closed the book.

❧

"We'll saddle these three," Parno said, turning to Edmir and indicating the gelding, the gray mare, and the sturdy bay. The Mercenary had returned alone, silently, and in answer to Edmir's questioning had told him that they could now move on.

Edmir was just tightening the girth on the smaller horse he took to be his own when Dhulyn Wolfshead suddenly materialized on the animal's far side. The horse merely rolled an eye at her, but Edmir had taken a step back and put his hand to his belt before he registered who it was.

The Wolfshead smiled, the small scar making her lip curl. "At least you were going for your weapon, my princeling," she said. Edmir opened his mouth to reply, but she had already turned to the spotted mare, picking up the saddle pad and slinging it over the mare's back with a practiced flick of the wrist.

"I took the horses into the wood on the far side from the bodies, and told them not to worry. They'll work themselves free when they feel like it." Edmir looked from one to the other. Parno Lionsmane had finished with his gray gelding and had turned to sort through the packs that were still on the ground. Apparently, nothing more would be said of the five horsemen on the road. Dhulyn Wolfshead was studying the ground in front of her, frowning, but it was the frown of decision making.

"We were heading for the Eagles Pass," she said, taking up a bit of broken branch lying to one side and beginning to draw on the dirt in front of her. Edmir recognized the curves of the Limona River, and the road they had been following. "The one on the north road from Limona, and the one that would take us most quickly to Beolind, and your mother." She nodded to Edmir. "And that is where they will look for us again. The pass of Limona itself—" she drew in the road that Edmir's army must have followed. "Clearly, we cannot retrace our steps and use it. But there is another." She cast a lightning-quick glance around the clearing. "We won't be able to take everything with us, however. The horses must be lightened."

"There's no other pass," Edmir said. "Not in this part of the border." He hadn't spent all that time with his tutors for nothing.

Dhulyn Wolfshead didn't look up from her drawings. "None on any maps, no. But a pass there is, nonetheless."

Five

EDMIR WINCED, SUCKING IN his breath. When she heard it, Dhulyn Wolfshead called out to her Partner to stop and, scrambling around her mare on the uneven ground, had the back of her hand against his cheek before Edmir could move out of her way.

"Fever, for certain," she said, shifting to touch his forehead with the backs of her long fingers. "How much pain is there?"

"Not much." The next thing Edmir knew his chin was being held in a grip that felt like iron and the Wolfshead's gray eyes were boring into his soul.

"What a liar you are," she said. "Your breath is short, your skin is white around your mouth, and there are lines on your face where there were none before. You are not yet in so much pain that you cannot move, but it grows." She nodded. "And it brings fever." The two Mercenaries exchanged a long look.

"He should not be afoot." Parno Lionsmane said finally from his position in the lead. "It will slow us, but he should mount. And the sooner we find shelter . . ."

"The better it will be," Dhulyn Wolfshead finished.

Any protest that Edmir thought of making died before he could open his mouth. One moment he was standing, the reins of the small horse, Stumpy, in his left hand, the next, Dhulyn Wolfshead had grasped him by knee and elbow and he was in the saddle, Stumpy steady but snorting under him. He still had the reins in his hand.

And the Mercenaries were right. Sore and aching as his

leg now was, the pain was nothing compared to how he'd felt walking on it. He realized, now that his weight was off it, that he could not have gone very much farther.

Dhulyn Wolfshead took Stumpy's reins, and let her own horse, the mare Bloodbone, follow of her own accord. Ahead of them, Parno Lionsmane led both his horse Warhammer and the packhorse, burdened now only with their travel food and what extra weapons the Mercenaries could not do without—which seemed, to Edmir, to be all of them. He would have preferred they pack a few more blankets, but everything else, including the much sighed over tent, had been left hidden—hoisted up into the trees—in the clearing in the woods where the horses had been the night before.

"No way to know if we can ever come back for it," Lionsmane had said as he'd hauled on the rope. "But we've at least a chance that anyone looking for Jedrick and his boys won't find this as well."

The sun had now been up for some hours, and they had been leading their horses up increasingly steep hills, jagged and treeless, since they had left the main trail. The trees had changed from the oaks of the forest below to pines and the occasional aspen. They were still climbing, and as far as Edmir could tell, they'd left any real path behind. Between the trees there was nothing but rocks, tufts of dried grass, and hardly a flat spot at all. His head felt heavy. *There's no pass here,* he thought. Stumpy shifted abruptly to the right, and, jolted, Edmir looked up, aware that he had started to doze in the saddle. Parno Lionsmane had stopped, and was looking upward, as if the rocks around them could speak to him.

"Are you sure of the way?" Edmir asked, unable to keep a note of irritation from his voice. The light seemed much too bright.

Dhulyn Wolfshead pointed. "We are now."

Edmir followed her pointing finger to where the silhouette of a bird hung in the sky far above their heads, the shape of its wings marking it for an eagle of some kind. As he watched, the bird stooped, falling so sharply that Edmir exclaimed, certain that it had miscalculated and would dash itself to pieces on the rocks.

Instead, it pulled up in the last possible second and

landed, talons outstretched, within easy bowshot of where
Parno Lionsmane stood. Warhammer only tossed his head,
backing a pace, but the packhorse shied, its hooves sliding
on a patch of loose earth, and Dhulyn Wolfs head dodged
forward, grabbing its mane and placing her hand over its
eyes as she crooned into its ear. *Thank the Caids,* Edmir
thought, that Stumpy had only wiggled his ears. If the short-
legged beast had so much as tossed its head, Edmir was
sure he'd have fallen straight off.

Instead, Edmir reached for the crossbow that hung from
his saddle, but found his wrist suddenly engulfed in Parno
Lionsmane's rough hand. "Wait," he said. "It's a Racha
bird."

Edmir's mouth fell open and Stumpy took a grudging
step forward before deciding to ignore the involuntary
tightening of his rider's knees. *A Racha.* Edmir had read of
them, companion birds to the Cloud People of the Letanian Peninsula. He had even seen a Racha once, as a child
in the public square in Beolind, his mother's capital, but he
had never seen one so close. If, that is, the Mercenaries
were not mistaken. Though large, this bird seemed very
much like an ordinary eagle to him.

Scrambling around the horses, Dhulyn Wolfshead
reached a rock outcrop about half the distance between
them and the waiting bird. She faced the Racha bird, but
turned slightly, so that Edmir had her in profile. *And so she
can see us in her periphery,* he realized. She was a Mercenary Brother, after all.

"I am Dhulyn Wolfshead," she said, pressing her tongue
to her top lip before continuing. "The Seer."

Fingernails bit into his palms as Edmir tightened his
fists. *A Seer.* By the Caids, was she *really*? Or was she something else? The Marked were rare in this part of the world,
though not unknown. But *Seers* were rarest of all. Edmir
couldn't even think of anyone who'd ever met one, though
there was supposed to be one in Delmara. He shivered,
suddenly feeling cold despite his fever. Why had they not
told him before?

The Wolfshead turned her head as the Racha bird
shifted and the light caught her hair, the color of old blood.

The color of Avylos' hair. And she was pale like Avylos.

And an Outlander, like Avylos. Was Dhulyn Wolfshead also a Red Horseman, or was all this just coincidence?

And was it coincidence, then, that these particular Mercenary Brothers had been among the Nisveans? The only time that Avylos' magic hadn't worked? Coincidence that they were bringing him back to Avylos now? Edmir swallowed past a lump in his throat. He lifted a hand that weighed like lead and rubbed at his damp brow. Why couldn't he *think*?

Surely, he was concerned for nothing? Outlanders were not so very uncommon—nor was red hair. And even if Dhulyn Wolfshead had been a Red Horseman, Mercenary Brothers had no pasts, no lives before the Brotherhood; everyone knew that was their Common Rule. Besides, Edmir rubbed at his face again, he needed them, he could not even get down off this horse without help. He *had* to trust them. He had no choice.

But his brain kept arguing. What other magics were they hiding? He squeezed his eyes shut.

"I was Schooled by Dorian the Black Traveler," Dhulyn said to the waiting bird. "And I have fought with my Brothers at Sadron, at Arcosa, where I found my Partner, Parno Lionsmane, and with the armies of the Great King at Bhexyllia. We have come from the battle of Limona, where the forces of Nisvea have triumphed over the invaders of Tegrian. We have with us a charge of honor, and we seek help, shelter, and passage."

The Racha had watched her while she spoke, turning its head from side to side as it looked first from one bright golden eye and then the other. When she fell silent, the bird waited a moment, as if to be sure she had finished, before bobbing its head, shaking out its wings, and launching itself into the sky. It did not fly immediately away, however, but hovered and beat its wings once, twice, three times, and was gone.

Dhulyn turned, feeling two days without sleep in every tired muscle, and in the grit in her eyes. "Clearly, we are to wait."

"Wait for what?" The words were bitten off and spit out of a tight mouth.

Dhulyn glanced at Parno, but her Partner only raised his eyebrows. She turned to the prince, schooling her face to serenity, her lips to a smile.

"The Cloud People, of course."

"Cloud People? There are no Clouds in Tegrian." The prince's voice shook.

"Is your pain worse?" Dhulyn took a step toward him.

He shook his head, leaning away from her. "There are no Clouds here. What really comes?" Dhulyn would not have thought it possible that a person could sound both angry and resigned, but somehow Prince Edmir was managing it. She rubbed at her face, but the gritty feeling never left her eyes. She rubbed at the pain in her lower back and stretched, ex-aggerating the movement as much as she could, loosening the muscles in her shoulders, before looking around her, and finally sitting down on a nearby outcropping of rock.

Prince Edmir yawned, his body responding to the mes-sages of fatigue and exhaustion hers had sent it.

What was biting the boy? He was looking at her as if she'd threatened to kill his dog. Parno looped the pack-horse's lead around his wrist and, as if aping her, rubbed at his own eyes, and in that gesture, she understood. Had it frightened the boy to know she was a Seer? Was that it? True, the Marked were rarer as you went farther west, but their skills were valued the more for it—any Mender, Finder, or Healer could set their own prices, though most followed the rules of their Guild. She had never heard that there was any particular prejudice against the Marked in Tegrian. She glanced at Parno, scratching her nose using the fourth finger of her left hand. Let him be wary.

"There are no Cloud villages here, truly." She answered the prince's declaration as if she had not seen the sullen look that made him seem so much younger than he was. "No settlements as there are in the Antedichas Mountains between Imrion and Navra. But there *is* a small colony of Racha birds here, and where there are Rachas, Clouds will always come for their Life Passage, to attempt to bond with the infant birds."

"And that is all that comes now? No squad of the Teg-rian Guard? Not . . . not my stepfather?"

"Your stepfather?" Parno straightened from securing

hobbles to the new packhorse against the return of the Racha, and stepped forward so that he stood between her and Prince Edmir. "Are you expecting him?"

The prince wrinkled his nose and looked away. *Sun and Moon.* Dhulyn narrowed her eyes. That had not been the look of a young man, a commander of an army. That had been the look of a frightened child, a child whose world had changed under his feet, and not for the better.

She sighed. "The Racha bond only with Clouds, Lord Prince, as apparently you do not know. I had not heard that the Blue Mage was a Cloud, or had any Clouds among his followers. Am I incorrect?"

The prince now looked at her with narrowed eyes. "No."

"Then I do not know who, or what it is *you* expect," she continued. "But the Lionsmane and I expect Clouds."

"And a good thing that is, yes? Since that's what you're getting."

Dhulyn had not heard the woman approach, but iron discipline kept her from showing any surprise.

"I greet you, Seer." The raven-haired woman stepped lightly from rock to rock as she came down the slope toward them, the seven gold feathers tattooed on the left side of her face clear in the afternoon sunshine. "I am Ayania, once of Pompano, yes? And now of Hrylesh."

"My Partner, Parno Lionsmane the Chanter, and our charge of honor, Edmir of Tegrian."

"*The* Edmir of Tegrian?" Ayania had reached their level finally and, her eyes on Edmir, had tentatively stretched out her hand. Dhulyn touched her own fingers to the Cloudwoman's.

"According to my Partner, and to the prince himself, yes."

"Who was it you *were* expecting then, Lord Prince of Tegrian, if not a Cloud?"

Edmir studied his hands, clasped together on the pommel of his saddle, and did not speak. Dhulyn shrugged and answered the Cloud herself. "He seems to think his stepfather has something to do with us."

"No room for the Blue Mage in our caves, that's certain, yes? Room for the three of you, however, since it's not the season for young birds. So long as you don't mind close quarters, yes? Ho! What's to do with him?"

Parno had moved fast enough to catch Edmir before he'd done more than tilt slightly out of the saddle, helped by Stumpy's shifting over. The beast was well-trained.

"He's had an arrow through the leg, followed by hard usage. You won't have a Healer with you?"

"Too right, we won't," Ayania said. "But we've herbs and medicines. Between us and two Mercenary Brothers, we'll have enough experience to keep him alive and on both feet, yes?" She raised her head and smiled at the bird that hovered high over their heads, almost too far away to see. "We can leave him on the horse if we go 'round the long way. Once we're in the caves, we'll see to his leg, yes? And what else did you need?"

"Sleep." Dhulyn said. Sleep where it was safe, where there was no need for either of them to keep watch. It wasn't every Mercenary Brother who could get those things from Clouds. But as a Seer, she could.

The Cloudwoman smiled. "This way, Seer, if you please."

Dhulyn blinked. By the angle of the moonlight coming through the smoke hole in the roof of the cave, she'd been asleep several hours. She could hear three people breathing, Parno right behind her on the soft mass made of their combined bedrolls, Edmir a few feet away on one of the cots, Ayania nearby on the other. The sleeping chamber was otherwise still and silent, with Ayania's two apprentice Racha Clouds sharing the watch with their birds in the outer cave. Dhulyn shifted, checked that there were several layers of cloth between them before pushing her back firmly against Parno. She shut her eyes again.

By the time they had reached the caves the evening before, the spasms that had started in Dhulyn's lower back had moved to her abdomen, and she was certain the pain from her woman's time would keep her from sleep. But her inability to take the major drugs for pain—and to have them used against her—did not prevent her use of minor drugs and remedies. While Parno and Ayania had tended to Edmir, Ilyan, the older of the Cloud's two young apprentices, with five feathers tattooed on the left side of his face, had heated stones for Dhulyn, while his fellow apprentice warmed water with valerian in it. Both had watched her out of the corners of their eyes, even the Clouds' legendary reserve insufficient to stifle their curiosity.

They would have helped her with the stones, too, anxious to perform a service for a Seer, had not Parno shooed them away. "Best you don't touch her skin to skin," he'd told them. "Her Visions come more often and stronger with her woman's time, and you don't want her to See anything about you, now do you?"

From what Dhulyn had seen in their faces, she rather thought they did. And it seemed that Parno had seen the same expressions.

"Better you shouldn't know, believe me," he'd told them. "If it's good, it makes your delight in it smaller, and if it's bad, you'll only feel your pain and your fear for that much longer."

"We could avoid it, though, couldn't we? The thing that would cause the pain and fear?" The younger apprentice, with two feathers tattooed on her left cheek, showing that she'd had her Racha only two months, had said before Ayania had cuffed her quiet.

"You might, if Dhulyn Wolfshead's Visions were clear, complete, and either you or she could understand them," Parno said. "When I say it's better you shouldn't know, I speak from knowledge."

"Leave the Seer be," Ayania said. "She's not here to help us, yes? We are here to help her." An attitude that Dhulyn had been counting on. She rarely revealed her Sight, but the Cloud People considered themselves the ancient and traditional protectors of the Marked, and she was as safe with them as she would have been with her own Brotherhood.

Dhulyn shifted, trying for a position that would relieve the pain in her back. What Parno had said was true, her Visions *were* often incomplete, and for that reason misleading. All the same, she thought now, as she drifted off to sleep, she should try to See in the morning. Her Visions were stronger, clearer, at her woman's time, as if the blood brought them. And sometimes a partial glimpse of the future was better than none.

When Dhulyn woke again, daylight was coming in through the hole in the cave's roof, and her stomach was

rumbling from the smell of cooking meat. She was alone in
the bedding—in fact, alone in the sleeping cave but for the
prince in his cot.

The stone against her belly had gone cold, but it seemed
the worst of her pains had gone with the heat, as was often
the way. Dhulyn tossed back the coverings Parno had
heaped on her and rolled to her knees, automatically making mental note of the location of her boots, her sword
belts, gloves, and weapons. All close at hand. She got to her
feet and stretched, holding each position until the stiffness
in the muscle slowly loosened. She squatted by the prince.

They had unwrapped and cleaned the wound, packing
it with herbs they had brought with them to draw out the
poisons. The Clouds had no iocain, but poppy syrup they
did have, laced with fens bark tea, and Edmir still slept,
his breathing heavy under its influence. His black hair,
thick and curly, had fallen back from his face, and only his
scanty beard stubble betrayed his age. Otherwise, his face
in repose was as unlined and innocent as that of a young
child.

He had one hand tucked under his chin. Lower lip between her teeth, Dhulyn wrapped her fingers around his
exposed wrist.

Edmir's hair is still curly, but the black shows streaks of steel,
and his face is more oval, now that he has a grown man's
forehead. There's a straight scar on his left cheek. And his
hair is shorter now, much shorter, the close-cropped head of
a man who regularly wears a helm. He is wearing a heavy
wool tunic, finely woven and warm, with a dark red lining
thrown over his shoulders. It is night, and Edmir is alone.

This is a tent. There is torchlight shining faintly through
the canvas behind him. He is sitting at a camp table, like the
one Commander Kispeko had, like many Dhulyn has seen.
Edmir is writing; his ink, in a ceramic bowl, is kept warm
over a small burner that provides both heat and light. The
point of his pen splits. Cursing, his breath making small
clouds in the cold air, Edmir searches the tabletop before

rising and fetching a knife from the belt pouch that hangs on a tent support.

He lives, Dhulyn thinks. *And he keeps the leg. . . .*

A tall woman with hair the color of old blood hanging in a thick braid down the center of her back strides along a path in a small formal garden. Dhulyn has Seen this woman before, and knows this Vision is of the past, and not the future. But what would bring her mother into a formal garden? When and why? Is it before Dhulyn herself was born? Her mother looks younger than the last time Dhulyn has Seen her, and she wears a pale blue gown, embroidered with vines and leaves in darker blue lines. She turns, and Dhulyn prepares to be greeted. She know, this much about the Sight, that if she can See her mother, her mother can also See her. But the expected smile does not come, instead, her mother's brow furrows, her smile fades, and she reaches for the weapon that does not hang from her belt. . . .

A hawk-faced woman with hair the color of summer wheat sits at a narrow table polishing something in a dark blue cloth. Dhulyn's heart skips a beat, she has *SEEN* this coloring before. A lamp like nothing Dhulyn has ever come across is attached by a metal bracket to the side of the narrow table, and light shines straight down on the woman's hands, and reflects upward to harshen the bladelike planes of her face. She peels back the polishing cloth, revealing a blue crystal rod. She smiles, satisfied, and fits a jeweler's lens to her left eye. She picks up a carving tool, so fine Dhulyn can hardly glimpse the tip of the blade, and begins to work close to the edge of the cylinder . . .

The vibration of sword blade striking sword blade shivers through the hilt she holds in her right hand. Another thrust—the man whips his blade around hers, but he's not fast enough to disarm her. She leaps back, dodges forward with her blade, avoids the parry, and draws blood from her opponent's arm. A lunge to the right, followed by two steps back, he jumps on a bench and begins to rain blows on her from above—she *knows* this *Shora,* but if this is practice, why, then, has blood been drawn? The next blow comes from . . . there, and can by countered with—a gasp of indrawn breath as her sword enters her opponent's side. But it is Parno who falls to his knees as she withdraws the blade from between his ribs. She puts out her hand to touch his face.

Wait, this is wrong. This is not how Parno dies—she wills herself to wake, the Vision to clear, before the decks slant, and the wall of water comes to wash Parno overboard into the churning sea . . .

⬦⬦⬦

Dhulyn sat back on her heels, lifting her hand from Edmir's wrist. Her heart was racing and there were tears in her eyes.

⬦⬦⬦

"Never seen the *Shora* before?" Parno dropped down next to Edmir on the rock shelf that served the Clouds as an outdoor bench. He had a fold of soft leather in his hands, along with a few knives that needed cleaning.

The prince turned toward him, wincing as his body began to follow the turn and his leg moved. Parno knew the arrow wound had much improved in the two days since they'd come into the Clouds' mountain stronghold, but a little more time would be needed to be sure all the heat was gone from the wound. The Racha woman, Ayania, was very pleased with the healing, and none of them were in any mind to undo her good work. Before going off into the hills in the early morning light with her apprentices and their Racha birds, Ayania had handed Edmir a walking staff, with the warning not to press himself too far.

"Lionsmane." Edmir acknowledged Parno's question with a nod. "I've seen my mother's Guard practice what they call *Shora*. But though there have been Mercenary Brothers at her court from time to time, I have never seen . . ." At a loss for words, the prince gestured toward Dhulyn. "She doesn't even look down."

"That is the Mountain Goat *Shora*," Parno said, putting down the bundle of knives between them. He turned his own eyes to where Dhulyn Wolfshead moved as surefooted as the *Shora* she was practicing. *About two thirds of the way through,* he noted. "It's specially designed to perfect your technique on rocky terrain. If you'd been up earlier, you'd have had a chance to watch me."

"Can you do that?"

Parno nodded. "The Mountain Goat's one of the twenty-seven basic *Shora* all Mercenary Brothers must learn to be considered Schooled. There's eighty-one all told, some with more moves, some with less. I know a few more than the basics," he shrugged, unrolling the bundle and laying out on the wide strip of soft leather five knives of differing lengths, along with the honing stone. "Not as many as Dhulyn Wolfshead, she must know close to sixty now. But then it is her ambition to be a Schooler herself one day, if she lives. If we both do." Parno fell silent, picking up the honing stone in his left hand and a long straight dagger in his right. *We'll live,* he thought. He caught Edmir's worried look and raised his eyebrows at the boy. But the prince turned away before speaking.

"Will she not use her magic to stay alive?"

Parno fell silent again, automatically finishing the stroke on the blade before he let his hands relax into his lap, and looked at the prince with new eyes. There was a tension to him, a staring to his eyes, that had nothing to do with pain from his wound.

"What has my Partner done to you to deserve that tone, besides rescue you from an embarrassing captivity?"

That drew Edmir's head around. He tried to draw himself upright, difficult to do on the uneven seat of the stone. "I may use what tone I wish," he said. "I am the Lord Prince of Tegrian."

Parno blinked, but even the long-practiced habits of courtesy could only do so much. Dropping the stone, he slapped his knee, and laughed out loud. Dhulyn froze in her *Shora* and looked their way.

Color flooded the prince's face. He began to stand, but Parno took his elbow in an iron grip before he got very far.

"Sit down, you blooded brat." The words were harsh, but Parno was still half laughing. He released Edmir's arm and the boy sank down until he had perched himself on the edge of the bench. Parno picked up the stone, and ran it once more down the long blade.

"You speak to a Mercenary Brother," he said, keeping

his eyes on his work. "Not to one of your Tegrian Houses— though the Caids know, if it comes to that, I left behind me a more noble House even than yours when I became a Mercenary Brother.

"But I did leave it behind me, so I'll say no more of it. Courtesy is something you owe all men, Lord Prince, even those you intend to kill—and even those who have rescued you," Parno continued. "And it's for the sake of that courtesy I'll explain to you now."

He glanced up. Edmir was watching him out of the corner of his eye, but his mouth was twisted to one side in what was clearly a sheepish apology.

Parno smiled, put down the cleaned weapon, and picked up the next, a wrist knife. "Dhulyn Wolfshead is no Mage. First and last, she is a Mercenary Brother, and my Partner. Though she is the younger, she is Senior Brother, having been a Mercenary longer than I. She is also Marked—you know the Marked?"

Edmir nodded. "I've seen some, a Mender and two Finders, though no Healer has ever come to be licensed at my mother's court."

"Licensed?"

"They say that in my father's time there was a rash of fakery in the country, a group of people claiming to be Marked, and cozening all who came to them for aid. My father arranged for anyone claiming to be Marked, or claiming any other kind of magic, to be brought to the capital to be examined and licensed. It's gone on ever since, but fewer and fewer come now."

When Parno glanced at him, Edmir was looking to where Dhulyn Wolfshead once more fought her invisible foe. The boy licked his lips. "And there's never been a Seer."

"Not surprising, they're so rare. What have you heard of the Seer at Delmara?"

"Only that there is one again, after so many years that the Seers' Sanctuary stood empty. And that news came fairly recently."

"If there are Marks living in Tegrian, licensed, why do their numbers grow fewer?"

Once more, Edmir nodded, as if it was a question he'd thought of himself. "We have no Guild here, so most of the newly Marked go elsewhere to be trained, to Imrion for the most part, or Berdana. They rarely come back." Edmir shifted in his seat until he was facing Parno more directly. "That's one of the plans we have," he said. "My sister and I. We want to send to the Tarkin of Imrion for help to establish a Guild here in Tegrian, so that Marks can be trained here, and stay to help the people as they do in the lands to the east."

Parno blew out a sigh. "There's fewer Marked even in the east these days, though your plan is a good one, for all that. You're the elder child, correct? And it's your mother who's the queen? Not your father who was the king?"

"That's right. He was the consort, just as Avylos . . . as the Blue Mage is now." The boy looked down and away, but Parno took note of his stumbling over the Mage's name.

"And is the Blue Mage licensed?"

Edmir squirmed on the hard seat. The last thing he wanted to talk about right now was Avylos. But he'd taken heart at what Parno Lions mane had said about putting his own past behind him. And the man was right, he owed the Mercenary Brothers for saving his life, and rescuing him from the Nisveans. And if information was what they wanted from him . . .

"He's the only Mage, so far as I know. Certainly I don't remember any others. Though he wasn't the Blue Mage when he first came. He called himself that, but he had only small magics." Edmir looked at Lionsmane out of the corner of his eye. "Real, mind you, not the tricks of the stage magicians. He could light candles, cause small objects to come to him. Sometimes he could tell you what people were doing in other rooms. Such things. He was very kind to us when we were children, my sister Kera and I. He and my father were friends, and my father gave him a place among his retinue, and helped him in his studies." Edmir swallowed and fell silent.

"Lord Prince. Clearly there is some heavy matter between you and the Blue Mage. That was not *all* fever talking the other day, nor is it fever that makes you avoid speaking of him now. Consider what I'm telling you." The Lionsmane waited until Edmir raised his head and looked him in the eye. "Either my Partner and I are in league with the Mage, in which case we already know what you are keeping to yourself. Or, we are what we seem to be, your friends and rescuers, and what you know may be vital to keep us all alive."

What Parno Lionsmane said made sense, and Edmir's instinct was to trust the man, not that either his instincts or his judgment had been very good of late. Why hadn't he listened to Kera? She'd warned him nothing good was going to come of this.

"I wanted to show my mother the queen I could be a good commander, as my father was." Edmir licked his lips and swallowed. "I planned a small foray over the border—just a display of tactics and strategy—"

The Lionsmane coughed. "You mean something your mother could explain away as youthful high spirits, something that didn't violate the treaty that exists between Tegrian and Nisvea?"

Edmir felt the heat rise into his face. "Something like that, yes. But somehow the Blue Mage learned of it, and instead of forbidding it, somehow it became, because of his backing, a true test of Nisvea's defenses, not just—as you call it—youthful high spirits, but something that could be useful in the future. Still, we'd keep it secret, so that my mother the queen could deny any knowledge of it diplomatically."

"So the Blue Mage *was* supporting you, and your forces should *not* have lost."

Edmir rubbed at his eyes. "The magic didn't work. There's a . . . a ceremony, a ritual that the Blue Mage gave me and I swear I did it properly, just as I had practiced it."

"But it did not work."

Edmir shook his head.

"So perhaps he isn't as friendly to you now, as he has been in the past." The Lionsmane set down the dagger he was working on and stood, stretched by putting his fists in the small of his back and leaning into them before sitting down again. "And so they've prospered, these studies of his?"

Edmir blinked at the change of subject. "He's had books and scrolls brought from everywhere, and Scholars are always coming with more. He's commissioned copies of many." Edmir frowned as he considered the full depth of the Mercenary's question. He hadn't really thought about it until this moment, but there were so many magics Avylos could do now, that he couldn't do before. "Yes. I'd have to say his studies have prospered."

"Dhulyn Wolfshead is called Scholar, but she's not that kind. And though she's Marked, you understand that the Mark's not magic, it comes down from the Caids."

"A gift from the gods isn't magic?"

Lionsmane picked up another, shorter dagger and examined one edge of the blade with a critical eye. "The Caids weren't gods, however much they might seem that way. Go to any Scholars' Library and they can tell you, show you the old books. They were people just like us, very long ago." He squinted along the other edge and rubbed at an invisible spot. "True, they knew more, could build better, but they were people just the same. There were Marked among them, and so the Mark's passed down to our time."

"Like curly hair or blue eyes?" Edmir smiled, sure the man must be joking.

"Well, yes. Though I think of it more like a good singing voice, or a good eye and hand for knife work." He gestured with the blade in his hand.

"The Scholars who taught me said nothing of all this."

The Lionsmane put down the dagger and picked up the last weapon, another short knife with an almost triangular blade. "Scholars have a way of teaching you what you've asked to be taught. And their knowledge of the Caids is not complete; they don't like to admit such things outside their own Libraries. But if you went to them, and asked, they would tell you."

"How do you know all of this?" The man was not as old as he sounded, Edmir realized, looking at him more closely, only about as old as Edmir's mother the queen pretended still to be. Easy to see that his name "Lionsmane" came from his coloring, skin and hair both a golden brown, the hair showing no gray.

"Dhulyn Wolfshead spent a year in a Scholars' Library before she took her final vows to the Brotherhood, and she's never lost the habit of reading. She can tell you that

there's a link between us, that is, the Mercenary Brotherhood, the Scholars, and the Jaldean priests of the Sleeping
God. The writings say we were all charged with keeping the
knowledge of the Caids. The Brotherhood, their physical
and fighting skills; the Scholars, their acquired knowledge—
whatever *that* might mean— and the Jaldeans, the secrets
of the Sleeping God."

"So there *are* gods? The Sleeping God?"

The Lionsmane was silent for so long, his hands unmov-
ing, that Edmir glanced up. The man was looking at his
Partner, who had fallen still as a statue, her blades catching
fire from the angle of the sun.

"Yes," the man said, his voice quiet. "The God's real."
He blinked, took in a deep breath and turned to Edmir.
"But the Wolfshead is no Mage. And as for what lies between you and your stepfather? You should know that the
arrow we pulled from your leg was a Tegrian arrow."

The wound in Edmir's thigh throbbed.

They had needed the rest, and the time to let the prince's
leg heal, but Dhulyn was glad, three days later, to be back
on her horse, with the hills, the Clouds, and the Racha behind them. And the walls of Probic a dark mark on the
horizon ahead.

"Once we're in the city," Edmir was saying, "I can give
you an official welcome, and I'll be able to repay your hospitality, and your aid, in a proper fashion."

It was obvious that the rest had done the prince good.
There was less of the injured boy in the way he sat the saddle, and more of the thoughtful prince. Not that she cared
either way, Dhulyn reminded herself. She might well be reluctant to return Edmir to his people, considering what
Parno'd had to tell her of the Blue Mage, but it was the
boy's decision. However much it went against the grain to
rescue him and see him back to health, only to then turn
him over to the very people who had let him get that way in
the first place, they could hardly force themselves on the
boy.

And just to add more water to wine that wasn't very
good to start with, so far, this engagement was a net loss.

As they neared the gates of Probic, Dhulyn automatically scanned the walls, mentally counting the bastions and calculating the number of guards it would take to man them fully. As the town closest to the Nisvean border, Probic was most at risk from invasion—if any Tegrian town could be considered at risk from invasion since the Blue Mage seemed to know when any sizable band of men, or pack of dogs, crossed the border. Still, for so small a place, Probic's walls were impressive, and Dhulyn would wager that the number of guards would be the same.

Whether it was the time of day, or because this gate was closest to the border, they were the only party approaching. The gate stood open, and as they drew nearer, Dhulyn made out the passage through the walls, a dark and invitingly cool tunnel, at least six horse-lengths deep. Any other town of this size, and Dhulyn would consider the walls to be unusually thick, but again, this was a border city.

There would be archers in the bastions, though she could not see them, and likely holes in the passage itself to allow defenders to either shoot or pour boiling water and oil on any invader who managed to pass through the gate.

Just stepping out from the opening itself were three guards in deep blue tunics, showing them to be part of the Royal Army. Dhulyn frowned.

"Two of the guards have crossbows, cocked and with bolts ready to fly," she said. "Unusual, surely, even for a border town?"

"If any of those who escaped from Limona made it this far," Parno said, "I'm not surprised the guards come armed."

"I should think they would keep the gates shut in that case."

"They can see we're only three—" Whatever else Parno might have said was lost as Edmir spurred his horse forward, heading straight for the waiting guards. Dhulyn hissed, gave Bloodbone her head and dashed after him, calling out to Stumpy and leaning far out from the saddle, reaching out for the smaller horse's bridle.

Stumpy was fighting his reins as Dhulyn came alongside the prince, using Bloodbone's greater height and weight to nudge Stumpy aside just as the crossbow bolt passed harmlessly to their left.

"Are you insane? Did you not hear me say they were armed and waiting to shoot?"

"But I'm the Lord Prince, I . . ." The boy was white with shock.

"And how are they to know that? Where's your escort? Where's your horse of state? Where are your blooded clean clothes for that matter?"

Edmir looked down, but his nostrils were flared, and Dhulyn knew that was the only acknowledgment she'd get that she was right. The boy wasn't stupid, it just hadn't occurred to him that his own people wouldn't know him.

She shook her head in disgust. What were his people thinking to let him grow up this way? Were they *trying* to get him killed?

"Easy, Lord Prince," she said. "I know you are anxious to be finally at home, but we go carefully, even here."

He took a deep breath and nodded. Dhulyn released Stumpy's bridle as Parno joined them.

"They're watching us now," he said, his arm lifted in salute to the waiting guards. "Slow and easy should keep us with whole skins."

Slow and easy was the pace they set, riding in a line, Edmir between her and Parno, the extra packhorse trailing behind them. As they reached the three waiting guards, she let Edmir move slightly into the lead, so that it was he who spoke to them.

"I am Edmir of Tegrian," he said, his clear, educated voice raised enough to be heard by any unseen but listening guards on the walls.

"Prince Edmir's dead, you lying weasel." The young guard on the left took a step forward, and the officer in the center jerked him back into his place and cuffed him with his open hand.

Edmir sat openmouthed and frozen. Dhulyn's blood suddenly sang, and she could feel Parno become alert on the prince's other side.

"Four archers watch us," the officer said, ignoring Edmir, his eyes going first to Parno, then to Dhulyn. "I see by your badges that you are Mercenary Brothers. Can I rely on you to act sensibly?"

"So long as we *all* act sensibly," Dhulyn gave a hard look

to the young man who had spoken out of turn. "I am Dhulyn Wolfshead, called the Scholar," she said. "I was Schooled by Dorian the Black Traveler, and I fight with my Brother, Parno Lionsmane."

"And I am Parno Lionsmane, the Chanter. Schooled by Nerysa Warhammer."

"I assure you I *am* Edmir," the prince said. Dhulyn smiled. His voice was steady and showed only a very little of the strain he must be feeling. "You and I have not met, Watch Leader, but there are others in the city who know me. City Lord Tzanek for one. Perhaps you would be so good as to send for him."

"We'll take you to him—under escort, with no offense intended," the watch leader added to Dhulyn.

Dhulyn composed her features, eyed the crossbowmen, then shrugged. No one was going to say aloud that the Guard wouldn't send for the City Lord at the request of a boy in torn and dirty clothing who claimed to be a dead prince.

"That seems *sensible*," she said. "I hope it's the custom in the City House to offer ganje to guests," she added. "I could use a cup."

There was ganje in the room they were asked to wait in when they reached City House, hot and strong the way Dhulyn liked it, but she was ready for a second cup long before Lord Tzanek arrived. Everyone they'd met with was being very careful. In case Edmir spoke the truth, the House pages had put them into a small but comfortable waiting room, and seen that ganje was served promptly. In case Edmir was lying, there were two guards on the outside of the unlocked door. Parno appeared to be taking advantage of the delay to take a nap in one of the padded chairs, his hands folded on his chest, but Edmir couldn't sit still. He kept getting to his feet and pacing across the small carpet that covered the polished oak floor, only to sit down again as his leg bothered him.

"You'll see," he told them more than once as they waited. "This is some misunderstanding. Old Tzanek's known me since he was a senior adviser in Beolind—he was a friend of my father's. He'll clear this up."

"And then it's hot baths and soft beds?" Parno said, his eyes still closed.

"Well, yes, among other things."

A bustle of footsteps and voices at the door signaled the arrival of Lord Tzanek. Parno stood and put his hand on the back of the chair he'd been using. Dhulyn stayed leaning against the small table that held their ganje cups; Edmir surged to his feet and strode closer to the door.

The man who came in, short beard well sprinkled with gray, was dressed for the court or the audience chamber. His half boots were low-heeled and sueded, his tunic a fine wool, ankle-length and belted with a wide embroidered sash. There was an ink stain on his left hand. He stopped short just inside the door.

"You did not take their weapons?"

The watch leader's wide eyes showed his surprise. "But, my lord, they're Mercenary Brothers, why would we disarm them?"

"The Mercenary Brotherhood has been banished from Tegrian."

Dhulyn's mouth dropped open in shock. *Banished.* It was like stepping onto a staircase in the dark and finding it gone.

"And as for this boy, I know Edmir well, since he was a child, and I will not be deceived," Tzanek said. "The young man they have with them is not Edmir."

"Tzanek." Edmir's voice was disbelieving. He took two further steps forward, with his hands outstretched. "It's me, it's Edmir."

But the man's face did not change. He turned back to the watch leader.

"I will not be deceived. This is not Edmir. Seize them."

Six

FOR A MOMENT, NO ONE moved. The watch leader cleared his throat.

"My lord," he began.

Dhulyn gave herself a mental shake. Whatever the City Lord meant, banished or not, they were here, and had more pressing problems. She measured the distance between herself and the three guards. Parno had his right hand on the back of his chair, ready to knock down the City Lord with it—the man wasn't armed, so that would take him out. Edmir was on his feet, but he was white with shock, and unlikely to be of any help. Only one of the guards had even put hand to weapon, and she was the farthest away. Once Lord Tzanek was down, Parno would deal with the two closest to him, and Dhulyn would take the third one herself.

"What are you waiting for? He is an imposter, I tell you. Seize them all!"

The watch leader looked from Tzanek to Dhulyn and back again, clearly weighing the possibilities in his mind.

"Come," Parno said, beckoning the guards forward with his empty left hand. "See if *we're* impostors."

Noises at the door spoke of reinforcements, and Dhulyn drew her sword left-handed, but the page that burst in was alone.

"Lord Tzanek," he gasped. "Nisveans . . . already in the gates . . ."

Dhulyn shot a glance at Parno, and found him looking at her, eyebrows raised. How had the Nisveans managed to overpower the gates? How had guards so careful to inspect the three of them before they were even close to the gates overlooked an invading force of the Nisvean army?

"How . . . ?"

Apparently, she wasn't the only one to wonder.

"They said they were returning Edmir's body." The page was now in better control of his lungs. "By the time we realized they lied—"

Lord Tzanek turned back to face them. "This is your doing," he said. "While you distracted us, your fellows have invaded."

Dhulyn did not even bother to shake her head; the man was clearly deranged. What he said made no sense whatsoever. Not that any of this was making any sense. *Banished.* She held out her right hand, index finger extended.

Parno threw the chair. Lord Tzanek went down and Parno leaped over him, elbowing the first guard in the face while drawing his sword and giving the second man a sharp rap on the side of the head with the pommel. Dhulyn slid into the gap, knocked the remaining guard's weapon up with a twist of her own blade, and struck the woman between the eyes with the heel of her right hand.

The page, evidently no fool, turned and ran. Parno followed him as far as the doorway where he stopped and looked both ways before beckoning them forward. Dhulyn grabbed Edmir by the upper arm and pulled him away from the prone City Lord.

"He should have known me," Edmir said, twisting his head to look back at Lord Tzanek even as Dhulyn tugged on his arm.

"How long since you were here?"

"You don't understand," Edmir said. "I didn't just meet him a few weeks ago. I've known Tzanek my whole life."

They stepped out into the corridor. Parno had gone right, to retrace their route from the entrance, and was waving them on where this passage met another, clearly impatient at their delay.

"He has no reason to dislike you personally?" Dhulyn said, more to keep Edmir moving than because she thought it important.

"He taught me to throw darts," Edmir said. "One night when I'd been allowed to stay up with my father, after Kera

had been sent to bed. Of all my father's friends, he had the
best eye, no one could beat him." Edmir looked behind him
again, as if part of him still wanted to turn back.

If he had no personal reason, Dhulyn thought, then he
must have had a political one. Either way, dangerous.

When they reached Parno he led them around the corner to the left. They'd only gone a few more paces when he
signaled and Dhulyn pulled Edmir into a doorway, glancing
at him as she did. The whiteness around his mouth had not
lessened. She thought she knew exactly how he felt.

There were people ahead in this larger passageway, but
the chaos and confusion with which they moved was ample
evidence that all was not well in Probic. As Dhulyn waited
for Parno's signal to continue, guards in uniform, some only
half dressed and scantily armed, ran past them, followed by
pages with white faces, most—but not all—heading for the
gates of the House.

Parno moved them onward with a jerk of his head, leading them away from the main gates and toward what should
be the kitchen wing of the House. Just as Dhulyn thought
they would be able to leave unremarked, they were challenged by three guards with weapons at the ready. Dhulyn
pushed Edmir behind her and pulled her dagger out of her
boot, tossing it up until she held it by the blade.

"I assume you want them left alive?" she asked.

"I . . . yes." Edmir stuttered.

Dhulyn shrugged. "Takes longer," she said as she dove
forward on her knees under Parno's left arm and knocked
two of the guards sprawling. Once they were down, she
used the heavy handle of her dagger to knock them out,
while Parno dealt with the remaining guard.

"Here." Parno hustled them around another corner and
into an empty room. This had the look of a pantry, with
stone floors, and two plain trestle tables for the preparation
of plates.

"Let's give everyone some time to return to their posts,"
Parno said. "When there are fewer people in the halls, we'll
only have the regular patrols to deal with, rather than every
guard we come across."

Edmir was rubbing at his leg, and Dhulyn made him sit
on one of the tables. She wasn't afraid for the wound, but

she knew that it was still all too easy for Edmir to overtax the damaged muscles. She needed to distract him.

"How did Tzanek become City Lord here?" she asked.

"When my mother the queen remarried, and the Blue Mage became consort, she rewarded and recognized many of my father's friends. Tzanek was one of the first."

"Getting the old husband's friends out from under the new husband's feet," Parno said. Dhulyn nodded.

"So he might want to get back to the capital," she said. "He might be sick and tired of being City Lord out here in rustic Probic."

"And how could denying the prince get him that?" Parno had the door cracked just slightly open, and he turned his face away from it to speak.

Dhulyn leaned her hips against the other table. "You said the Blue Mage found out about your expedition. Who might have told him?"

"My sister told me not to accept his help, but the others were so enthusiastic . . ." Edmir's voice faded into nothing.

Without turning, Parno made a chopping motion with his hand, but Dhulyn hadn't moved toward the prince. She knew that the least show of sympathy would only make the boy feel worse.

"One or two of the younger Houses were with me—we knew my mother the queen would be turning her eyes to Nisvea soon enough, the treaty is over next year. We thought just a quick strike across the border, something to show her that men were willing to follow me—" He stopped. His voice had quavered on the last few words, and his jaw trembled until he clamped it shut. After a few seconds he continued. "We wanted to know what it was like, to be invulnerable, even if it was only for a few hours."

"Look me in the eye," Dhulyn said, with enough command that even Lord Prince Edmir of Tegrian blinked twice and met her eyes. "What happened was *not* your fault, do you understand?"

Dhulyn expected some reaction from the boy, but the change which came over Edmir's face was all out of proportion to her words.

"What is it?" she asked, beginning to look behind her.

"Wait," Edmir said, grabbing at Dhulyn's arm in his turn. "There's something wrong."

Parno put up his hand like a junior Scholar in a Library. "I know," he said. "We're trapped inside a fortress and the city's under attack."

Dhulyn rolled her eyes, but Edmir ignored them both.

"No. I mean Tzanek. I was looking right at him, straight into his eyes, as I looked into yours just now, and I saw nothing. Do you understand? No hidden message. No recognition. It isn't just that Tzanek *said* he didn't know me. He *didn't* know me."

"Can you be sure?"

Edmir nodded. "My sister and I used to play at disguises, and see who we could fool among the court people and the servers. I know what it looks like when people know me and when they don't." He rubbed at his forehead. "And what it looks like when they know me and are pretending they don't. Tzanek doesn't know me."

"And who do we know that might be able to do that?"

"The Blue Mage," Dhulyn said. She exchanged a glance with Parno behind Edmir's head. She could see that they shared the same thought. Was the Mage working alone, or was the sister in it as well?

⊱⊰⊱⊰

"If you will take these to the House Seamstress, that will be all for today."

Princess Kera indicated a bundle of Edmir's cloaks and watched Metrick the page gather them up and make his way slowly to the door of Edmir's quarters. She wondered if he would have been so ready to help her if her brother wasn't dead. Metrick was one of the new pages, from a High Noble House in Balnia—not that she could remember which one just at the moment. There, the Noble Houses had long had the custom of sending their children for a final polish of manners and service to their Tarkin's House, and since Tegrian had conquered them, and their Tarkins were no more, those sons and daughters came to Queen Kedneara instead.

"Be careful what you say in front of that one, Lady

Prince." Sharian Tzeczova, Kera's own senior lady page was taking folded shirts out of Edmir's clothespress. "The other pages are already saying that he's too ready to run with tales to others."

"He's like a badly trained dog," Kera agreed. "He goes begging to everyone in the room, and performs his tricks for everyone."

"Well, to be fair," Sharian said. "He's just a House page at the moment, and doesn't really have a master yet. Though it seems to me, since your brother's death, he's thinking you'll do."

"I'll have to be careful, then."

"Do so. His House is a good one, and he might fancy himself at your side. You're Lady Prince now, remember."

Kera turned her face away so Sharian wouldn't see her grit her teeth. As if she could forget. As if she wasn't here, right now, in Edmir's room, going through his things because Edmir was dead.

"Sharian, would you mind leaving me here a while?"

The lady page couldn't really mind, whatever she might think, and however often she might serve as an informal tutor.

And besides, it would seem natural to anyone that she would like to sit a while in her late brother's room, by herself, where she might think about him, and what his absence now meant to her.

Sharian picked up the shirts she'd been sorting and headed for the door, bestowing an understanding smile that put Kera's teeth on edge. As soon as the door shut behind the older woman, Kera jumped to her feet and went to it, pressing her ear against the opening. Sharian's house shoes made no noise on the smooth wooden floors of the passage outside Edmir's rooms, so Kera counted to twenty before looking to assure herself that the passage was empty. She shut the door, latched it from the inside, and threw the bolts. The outer room secure, Kera went into Edmir's bedroom, directly to the fireplace that took up much of the far side of the room.

The hearth was surrounded by an elaborate mantel built up of several different kinds of dark wood, and large pieces of stone on which the faces of animals had been carved. It took only a few seconds for Kera to find the face of a fox on the left-hand side of the fireplace and press its nose with her thumbs. The stone gave under the pressure and a square of wood lower on the right-hand side popped soundlessly open.

Kera knelt and stuck her hand into the opening, smiling as her fingers brushed against a leather corner. Just as she'd thought, Edmir had *not* found a new hiding place for his journals. She pulled them out one by one. Altogether there were seven books, all showing wear and one a chewed corner where a favored puppy had once got hold of it. The two most recent were made from the newer, lighter-weight paper, cut and bound with the pages sewn together, and stiff covers made from leather. She opened them, and found both were filled from cover to cover with Edmir's neat handwriting.

Of course. She sat back on her heels. The latest one, the one he was writing in now, must have gone with him to Nisvea. Kera tilted her head back, taking a deep breath and blinking to forestall the tears. Where would it be now, her brother's last journal? On the battlefield somewhere, soaked in Edmir's blood? Did the Nisveans have it? Or the Mercenaries who were said to have taken him — might they have kept it?

She hadn't really thought he'd leave it. Edmir was always writing in his journal. But she'd hoped to be wrong. She'd hoped to have this chance to find out why Edmir had ignored her advice. Without his journal, she would never know what possessed him to change his plans, to listen to the Mage.

She gathered together the hem of her gown, making a pouch in which she could stash the journals. There was a satchel in Edmir's clothespress that would hold them all, and she could use that to transport them unseen to her own secret hiding place. As she reached into the hole, making sure that she hadn't left a journal behind, one slipped out of the fold in her skirt and fell open onto the floor. Kera caught sight of her own name in Edmir's handwriting.

Princess Kera and the Seven Suitors, were the words at the top of the page. *There are seven silver fish in the garden pond of the Queen of Tegrian,* the story began. Kera sat heavily on the floor and touched the ink with her fingertip. Edmir had once made up a story that the fish in her mother's pond were really princes who had been turned into fish when they'd come, one by one, to beg for her hand. One had been a pirate prince, she remembered, who'd tried to steal her away. She'd never known that Edmir had written the story down.

This time, she could not stop the tears.

✧✧✧

"Troop of six pikemen just ran by," Dhulyn said. They had made it past the kitchens, and were at a scullery door that would take them out into the courtyard and stables. "They're joining others leaving by the gate into the city." She turned back to the door crack in time to see another small group, this time armed with swords and small round shields, heading in the same direction as the first. She needn't have bothered being careful; none of the soldiers were looking her way.

"They'll be coming from the guardhouse, at the other end of the courtyard." Edmir tried to see around her, but Dhulyn kept her elbows out.

"And heading for the walls, though from the sounds of things, those are already breached."

"How is any of this possible? The strength of Probic's walls is legendary . . ." Edmir shook his head.

"All it takes is one man to open a door," Dhulyn said. "And if they tricked their way in, as that page said . . ." She shrugged.

"But who would do such a thing?"

Dhulyn just stopped herself from sighing aloud. The lad would have to get more cynical than this if he expected to be king one day. "The same person who doesn't seem to know you any longer, I would judge. Or someone that he sent."

"But the Blue Mage . . ." Edmir's voice died away, and he drew down his brows as he processed the idea that Dhulyn had lent him.

She knew what he would have said. That fear of the Blue Mage—or respect for his powers, which amounted to much the same thing—had kept Tegrian free of invasion for the last three seasons at least. Why and how had that changed now?

And what other change had resulted in the banishment of Mercenaries from Tegrian?

"Edmir. Can the Blue Mage communicate with others over long distances?" Racha Clouds could with their birds, she knew, but she had never heard such a thing about the Blue Mage.

"Now is not the time for such questions, my heart." Parno gestured Dhulyn forward with a tip of his head. She shrugged and turned back to the door. Her Partner was right. She hovered in the doorway for another few heartbeats, shaking her shoulders loose, moving her head from one side to the other, as she began the Stalking Cat *Shora*. Her breathing slowed, her heartbeat slowed. Her hearing grew more acute. She toned down her awareness of Parno and the prince so that their breathing and their heartbeats would not distract her.

She tilted her head to one side. She held up her left hand, pointed to the open doorway of the stables, and held up one finger. From the corner of her eyes she saw Parno nod. She moved out of the scullery and over to the stable door, noting the shifting of air as Parno and Edmir fell in behind her. The prince was very quiet, but she could hear both his breathing and his footfalls. She pointed downward with the index finger of her left hand and they stayed back, allowing her to approach the stable alone. She paced to the left, staying out of line of sight for the single person she knew to be inside. When she reached a point to the left of the opening, she squatted on her heels and took a quick glance inside the building, her mind and eye automatically registering all within.

She beckoned the others forward, easing back from the edge of the opening. "A table between us and him. Some bowls, tack, and harness on it. Stool on our side," she said, using the nightwatch voice. She looked at Parno. "I went last time."

Parno shrugged. "True." He sheathed his sword, pushed his hands through his hair, and sauntered loose-footed into the open doorway so naturally and so casually that he had the tall, three-legged stool in his hands before the man shutting the stall gate on the opposite side of the table even felt his presence as a threat. The stableman was no amateur, however, and was turned around in one heartbeat, an ax in his hand the next.

The prince pushed against Dhulyn's arm. "He's got an ax."

"And Parno has a stool. Calm down. This will only take a moment."

As if prompted by her words, Parno smashed the stool down on the tabletop, breaking off the seat and leaving himself with two of the stool's stout legs, each as thick as three of Dhulyn's fingers, and as long as Parno's forearm and hand.

She drummed her fingers on the doorframe and blew out a breath.

Parno tossed the hair out of his eyes, and leaped onto the table, kicking horse brushes and pots of liniment at the stableman. The man's eyes widened at the sight of Parno's Mercenary badge, but almost without hesitation he took a step back, lessening the advantage of Parno's elevation, and swung the ax in a controlled sweep at Parno's legs. Without taking his eyes off the man's face, Parno jumped over the moving blade and moved the chair legs once—a blow numbing the stableman's arm with a swing of his left hand—and twice—clubbing him to the ground with a swing of his right.

"They don't pay this man enough," he said, as he jumped back to the ground and held his fingers at the man's throat.

"Will he be able to collect more pay in the future?" Now that she was in the stable, Dhulyn whistled and saw three heads pop out over stall doors along the left-hand side of the stable: Bloodbone, Warhammer, and Stumpy.

"Of course, what do you take me for?"

"I thought you might have been a bit rushed." Dhulyn pushed past him and ran down to Bloodbone. The horses she'd known would be here. What she hadn't expected was to find their own packs and saddlebags sitting in each stall, at the horses' feet.

"Not even opened," she said. Their extra weapons, even the crossbow Parno had hooked on his saddle, were lying untouched on top of the packs.

"Our reputation precedes us," Parno said, as he stepped past her and opened Warhammer's stall. Edmir looked between them frowning, clearly bewildered. Parno indicated the unopened packs. "Not a buckle, not a flap, not even the knots in the laces have been disturbed. Someone's told them we booby trap our packs, that's why they've not been opened."

As they spoke, Dhulyn opened the pack at her feet, slipping the buckles loose and pulling the ties open with one practiced flick of her wrist. If you knew your knots and ties—and there were *Shora* for ropes and bindings—a bundle you had tied shut yourself was as good as open, however confounding it might have been for someone else.

She reached inside, took out the two leather gauntlets she'd packed on top, and pulled them on, settling the knives they held along the inside of her forearms. She bit her lip. Her other throwing knives were in their roll in the saddlebags, no time to fetch them out now. But the small hatchet slipped easily into its place down the back of her vest, and two more daggers went into the tops of her boots, along with a moon razor.

There, now she felt properly dressed.

"We leave the packhorse," Dhulyn said. She picked up Bloodbone's saddle pad and threw it over the mare's back. "Saddlebags, weapons, and camp gear only, and then what food we have room for."

"We don't take everything?"

"We must travel faster now," Parno said. "And the packhorse will slow us down. As for food, unlike an army, we can feed ourselves as we go."

"Hunting won't slow us down?" He might be questioning them, but Edmir was already moving to open Stumpy's stall.

"Not the way we hunt," Dhulyn said.

The prince hesitated, his hand on Stumpy's saddle pad. "Can't I take one of the better horses?"

Dhulyn continued saddling Bloodbone. "Better how, Lord Prince? Stumpy's trained to our ways, and we've no time to train any of these."

"And besides," Parno added, "at the moment we want to

get away unseen, and unnoticed. Old Stumpy here draws no one's eye, and you've more chance to be recognized on a good horse."

And judging from the look on Edmir's face, it could go unsaid that recognition, with invaders already inside the gates, was the last thing they wanted right now. The prince was not stupid, Dhulyn thanked Sun and Moon, just inexperienced.

They left City House finally by the simple expedient of joining the tail end of a small contingent of guards and riding out of the gate after them. It appeared that the banishment Tzanek had spoken of was not widely known.

"Don't skulk, Edmir," Parno said in an undertone. "Shoulders back, chin up, ride as though you belong here."

Edmir straightened his shoulders and lifted his chin as he followed Dhulyn through the gate. His grip on Stumpy's reins was too tight, he could feel the tension in his forearms already, but he didn't seem to be able to relax. No one took notice of them, however. Once outside into the city proper there was so much else to notice. More noise, for one thing, the unmistakable sound of steel striking steel in the distance, cries and shouts, and the smell of burning. Edmir gritted his teeth and tried to push the images of the battle of Limona out of his head.

They took the first turning they came to, and found themselves suddenly alone in a small square with a stone pillory in its center, raised above the cobbles of the square itself on three granite steps. The iron arms, with their hooked ends for tying off ropes and prisoners, looked innocent enough, but Edmir licked his suddenly dry lips when he saw the stains on the pillar, on the granite steps, and on the flagstones immediately around them. The pillory's long shadow stretched almost the length of the square. The late afternoon sun cast their own shadows before them.

Dhulyn Wolfshead touched him on the elbow and Edmir jumped.

"This way."

Seven

THEY LEFT THE SQUARE just in time to avoid a small group of four mounted guards wearing Probic's town colors of green and rust, their uniform tunics torn, their weapons bloodied, one being steadied on his horse by a comrade. Even in these smaller streets and alleys Parno could hear the sounds of fighting, the clash of metal, the far-off yells, and even the occasional blast of trumpet or horn as signals were given to troops too spread out to hear their orders.

And there was the smell of fire as the poorer, wooden quarters of the town were set ablaze.

Dhulyn stopped, holding up her right hand. Three men in dark blue tunics—wall guards—crossed the alley in front of them without even so much as looking their way.

"It goes against the grain to leave the fight behind us," Parno said, as Edmir caught his eye. "But we have nothing but enemies here."

The prince nodded, his teeth clenched, and at Parno's gesture, fell back into position between him and Dhulyn. She set a steady but unremarkable pace, neither chasing nor running from, the best way to avoid unwelcome attention. As they got farther away from the City House, the streets became quieter, deserted, and doors were clearly bolted. Dhulyn stopped once more, tilted her head like a Racha bird catching its partner's thoughts. Then she relaxed, glancing at Parno and indicating upward with her eyes. *Yes,* he thought, following her glance, there *was* someone watching them from behind a third-floor shutter. He touched his fingertips to his forehead in the Mercenary salute to the silent watcher. Banished or not, it seemed not *everyone* here was their enemy, after all.

Two men wearing the long leather aprons of smiths, dragging a corpse in Nisvean colors by the heels, turned into their path and stopped abruptly—looking first at them, down at the corpse, and back at them again. Parno tried hard not to smile as, without speaking, Dhulyn turned her head and tapped the side of her face, indicating her Mercenary badge. The two smiths stood aside then, dragging the corpse out of their path, and watched as they passed by. Once again, Parno touched his forehead to them.

They hadn't gone much farther along, and Dhulyn was signaling a turn to the left as their alley approached the square in front of a Jaldean Shrine, when the unmistakable sound of a woman screaming brought Dhulyn up short.

Out in the late afternoon sunlight that filled the square, a young woman hung between two men, not much bigger than she was herself, who were twisting her arms up behind her back. Her spangled head scarf lay on the ground at her feet, and the taller, wider man in front of her had hold of her white-blonde hair in his right fist, his left cocked back to hit her again. Her face showed signs that she'd been punched at least once already, but she was still screaming, and kicked out—a well-placed blow that had her attacker bent over and bellowing as she caught him squarely in the groin. The man holding her left arm laughed, but the man holding her on the right pulled his knife from his belt and held it to her throat, yelling something in her ear. The girl stopped squirming, her eyes almost crossing in her attempt to look simultaneously at both the man and his knife.

Dhulyn finished her turn into the new alley, but Edmir stopped, hauling back on his reins as Stumpy tried to follow Bloodbone.

"Wait! Aren't we going to stop them?"

The Wolfshead reined in and looked over her shoulder at the prince with a frown. "Why?" she said.

Edmir looked from Dhulyn to Parno and back—his head whipped round again at the sound of tearing cloth.

"I'll go."

Parno grabbed Stumpy's reins just in time. The boy didn't even have a weapon out.

"I've no stomach to leave her, my heart," he said. "It's not an act I'd find easy to live with."

Dhulyn turned Bloodbone back to face the opening to the square. "*Blooded* nobles. We'll be food for crows ourselves if there are archers in the square. Oh, but we'll be able to live with ourselves—no, wait, we'll be dead." She unhooked the small crossbow from her saddle harness. "Come on, then."

Dhulyn dug her heels into Bloodbone's sides and shot straight into the square, screaming out a challenge as she went. As soon as she cleared the buildings, she ducked, leaning far enough out of the saddle that anyone who didn't know her would think for certain she'd fall off. Parno, riding Warhammer into the square at an angle to Dhulyn's left, did not see her fire, but the man holding the knife to the young woman's throat went down with a crossbow bolt through his eye, just as Parno fired and the man on her left caught a bolt of his own. The girl immediately crouched, holding the front of her dress together with one hand, and retrieving the knife from her dead attacker's grip with the other.

The taller, heavier man still stood, having recovered sufficiently from the kick to the groin to have struck the girl again and torn her gown. He whirled around at the sound of hooves but when he saw Parno bearing down on him from his right, and Dhulyn Wolfshead, standing now in her saddle and howling, waving her long sword in her hand as she flanked him on his left, he turned and ran.

"He's getting away!" Edmir spurred Stumpy forward but the horse pulled up at Dhulyn's whistle, almost dumping the prince out of his saddle.

"So would the others have done if they'd been smart enough to drop the girl and go," Parno said. "As it is, to save one we've killed two."

"But they were going to rape her, perhaps kill her." Edmir urged Stumpy closer to Warhammer. "We did the right thing."

"No argument," Parno said. "I've never cared for rapists. I merely point out the cost of doing the right thing."

Dhulyn had reached the girl and dropped down from Bloodbone's back to land at her side. With the bruising and swelling already distorting her features, it was hard to tell what expression she had on her face, but she was holding the knife up, ready to defend herself.

"There now, little Cat, sheathe your claw. I am Dhulyn Wolfshead, called the Scholar," the Mercenary woman said, crouching on her heels just out of striking distance. "That's my Partner, Parno Lionsmane, the Chanter, and our charge of honor. Where are your people?"

The girl lowered the knife, grimacing as her swollen lip interfered with her smile. "I greet you, Dhulyn Wolfshead, and I thank you for your timely rescue. I am Zania Tzadeyeu. My troupe and family has our caravan in the Pine Tree Hostel two streets closer to the gate."

"Dancers?"

"Players, dancers, and musicians, Lady Wolfshead. If you would accompany me, my father will amply repay you for my rescue." The top layer of her voice held the cool graciousness of an imperial princess talking to some member of her court who had done her a favor. But under it was the same shock that whitened her lips and made her hands tremble.

Dhulyn helped the little Cat—Zania—to her feet, blood-red brows drawn down. "We are leaving the town, Zania Tzadeyeu, but I thank you for the offer."

"You are leaving Probic? We could all leave together; there's safety in numbers." With a complicated motion of her shoulders Zania shifted her clothing around until she was decently, if somewhat raggedly, covered. Standing at her full height, Parno noted, the girl was rather shorter than his Partner, and more rounded.

"There's ample space for you to ride on Edmir's horse," Dhulyn was saying, but Zania was already shaking her head.

"Please, Lady Wolfshead, with you." Her voice was steady and clear, but the whites showed around her eyes.

Dhulyn flicked a glance at Parno before she nodded, her mouth twisted to one side. Parno stifled a smile. His Partner always made a large task out of helping someone. She turned and mounted Bloodbone, arranged her weapons behind her, and reached down a hand toward the younger woman.

"Do I look diseased?" Edmir asked Parno out of the corner of his mouth.

"You look like a man, as do I. And you may have noticed that the people who bruised her face and tore her dress—and planned to do considerably more, as we think—were also men. I think you'll find Zania Tzadeyeu will be wary of all such creatures for the next while."

Edmir took his lower lip between his teeth. Evidently, that hadn't occurred to him. He glanced toward the two women, and his lips parted.

Parno rolled his eyes—hadn't there been any women in his mother's court? "What do you think, Edmir?"

Edmir flushed red and turned away from watching Zania's legs as she climbed up onto Dhulyn's saddle.

"Sorry, Lionsmane, I wasn't listening."

"At least you admit it. Are you for traveling with the troupe?"

"There's sense in what she said, about traveling in numbers," Edmir said, his eyes returning to Zania.

"I thought you'd say that. Still, it's for Dhulyn as Senior to decide, so don't hope too much."

❁

Tzanek shut the door of his workroom with more force than he intended, and ran to his worktable, holding his temples as he went. His head was throbbing in a most fearsome headache, and any quick movement seemed likely to make it break completely off. He sat down in the chair next to the table and, reaching into the front of his gown, pulled out a key hanging under his clothes by a small chain. He unlocked the oak box that sat to one side on the table and took out the book of poetry the Blue Mage had given him.

Tzanek took a deep breath, and then another. His head pounded with the beating of his heart. His hands trembled as he fumbled the book open to the blank central pages, careful to touch only the very edges of the parchment. He hoped this would work. The Blue Mage had told him the magic was in the book, not in the user, so it should work even though Tzanek was not a Mage, but he'd never had to do this before. And now his head ached so much.

"Lord Mage." Tzanek cleared his throat and began again. "Lord Mage."

Avylos looked up from the scroll he was reading, certain that someone had called him. He went to the workroom door, but when he looked out, he could see that the metal-bound door closing off this wing of Royal House was shut. No page was there calling him.

There it was again.

Avylos lifted his eyebrows, tapping his upper lip with his tongue. Was it possible?

He went behind his worktable and reached up to the books on the shelf, hesitating only a heartbeat before selecting the book of poetry with the central pages of albino calfskin. He laid the book down on the table, and as soon as he opened it, writing appeared on the right-hand page.

"My lord Mage. Thank the Caids! You must send help, immediately. The Nisveans are here, they are within the walls already, and the city is aflame—"

Avylos smiled. After all, Tzanek couldn't see him. "And the Mercenaries, with the imposter they protect, no word of them?"

"It was they who distracted us while the Nisveans attacked, we were—"

"You have them?"

"No, I'm sorry, my lord Mage, they escaped—at least, they must still be within City House. They could not have gone far."

"Just a moment, Tzanek. Do not go away, but stay silent until I speak." Avylos' fingernails were biting into his palms, and he forced himself to relax, to breathe deeply, to ride the waves of his rage, rather than to let them overwhelm and drown him. Edmir kept slipping through every trap he set for him—Sun *blast* those Mercenaries. This was intolerable. If only he were there, but Probic was five days' ride . . . he rubbed his fingers across his lips. If he could transport himself there—how could he be sure of having enough power left to do what must be done?

There had to be a way. He drummed his fingers on the tabletop, glanced at the window. He could see Probic through the medium of the pond, but seeing it was not enough. He needed a channel through which power could flow. He looked down at the open book before him, where Tzanek still waited for him. *That* channel already existed.

He could do this. He *knew* it. And it would ultimately serve his purpose very well. Still, it would take much, if not all his present power. He looked quickly around the room. There were magics here he could undo, freeing the power for his own use. The other books he should leave, the pond likewise. They were his lines of communication, using little power to maintain, but a great deal to recreate. The Stone also, ready with a single word to trigger it. But the casket. He pulled it toward him. Locked *and* magicked. He traced a design on the lid and sucked in his breath as the lines of fire lifted and flew into his hand. The lock alone would suffice, so long as he left the door to his workroom magicked. Kera could enter, but then she could not unlock the casket, could she?

But the magic that told him who had come to the door, *that* he could remove and regain. The magic that kept the floor warm, and likewise the one that guarded the door to his sleeping chambers. All these could be renewed when he returned and restored himself. He had used up the talents he still had in Royal House, but there was one he'd been saving for an emergency such as this, a carpenter's apprentice who was far too lucky with dice.

He sat back down at the book. "I will come myself," he said. "Place your left hand on the right-hand leaf of the book."

"But, my lord Mage, your instructions—"

"Are superseded. Do it at once!"

A moment passed, and then the outline of a man's left hand appeared on the page. Avylos placed his own right hand on it.

A pulling at his skin, a twist of the guts, dizziness and nausea. For a moment he was sure his heart had stopped.

He coughed, and lifted his left hand from the page. He looked around at the unfamiliar room. Stone walls and floor. A truly horrible tapestry evidently created by a right-handed person using his or her left hand. Avylos stood and steadied himself on the back of the heavy, leather-covered chair. He'd forgotten how much shorter Tzanek was.

And the man hadn't mentioned the towering headache he had. Avylos hated to use any magic to relieve the pain, but he could not afford the distraction. He went to the door of Tzanek's workroom and looked around. He needed the tallest tower, and it would be . . . he rummaged through the mind he was wearing. This way.

On his way to the tower Avylos met only one guard, whom he dismissed with a short, economic gesture that left the woman unconscious and bleeding from the nose and ears. He had to slow down as he took the stairs to the top of the tower; his breath came short and his heart pounded. Tzanek was heavier and older, and Avylos could not spare any further power to improve the older man's body. *Get me to the top and back down again,* he told it. *That's all I need.*

The air was cool on his face when he pushed open the door at the top of the tower. Here, five days' ride from Beolind, the sun was lower in the sky to the west, but Avylos could clearly make out the edges of the battlements, and the colors of the Nisvean soldiers as they took strategic positions in the streets below. He used his Mage's sight to probe the city, noting where the largest gatherings of soldiers were, the wooden buildings, storage houses full of grains, hay, firewood, oil. Of the city's four gates, two were closed and barred, but there were still Nisveans entering by the other two.

Avylos drew a symbol in the air, the same one he would have used over the pond in his garden. Without the medium of the magicked pond, he could see Edmir, but very little of his immediate surroundings. The boy was on horseback, and the angle of his shadows showed in which direction he must be.

And close. Very close. He could feel it.

When he was sure where he wished to strike, Avylos raised his arms and sketched green fire across the sky.

The wind rose, and the lightning began to fall.

"I must get some damp cloths for my face as quickly as possible—do I look very bad?" the girl said over her shoulder as they turned another corner. "We've a performance to give tomorrow in a country holding, and I can't go on with my face all swollen. Paints can only do so much."

Since the little Cat couldn't see her, Dhulyn let her lip curl back over her teeth. Didn't it occur to the child that with the invasion there very likely wouldn't be any performance? Dhulyn was already wishing she'd insisted Zania ride with Edmir. The girl's hostel *was* closer to the gate, but it wasn't just two streets over. Either the little Cat couldn't count, or she simply wasn't an accurate observer. And she wouldn't stop talking.

"Here we are."

Finally. Dhulyn slowed to a stop. The hostel itself was a modest one, as befitted a company of strolling players who had their own caravan. They'd want comfortable beds as a change from traveling, and someone else's cooking, but they wouldn't be inclined to pay much for it. It was not the size of the establishment that made the hairs on Dhulyn's neck rise.

"The gates to the stable yard are open," she said, as Parno came up on her left side.

"Any other day, I'd expect it," Parno said in a voice that indicated he shared her thoughts. "But this would be the only open doorway we've seen since leaving City House."

Dhulyn tilted her head back and widened her nostrils.

"Smells wrong," she said. "Get down, little Cat, and stay back."

For all her chattering, Zania must have been welltrained, probably by her actor parents. She caught Dhulyn's tone and obeyed, swinging her leg nimbly over Bloodbone's head and sliding to the ground without argument or questions.

Dhulyn caught Parno's eye and jerked her head toward the open gateway. He winked his left eye, dismounted, and took up his stance at the left of the gate.

"Edmir," she said, as she pulled her sword from its scabbard across her back. "Stay with the dancer." She turned and rode through the gate.

Edmir dismounted and concentrated on looking as innocent and harmless as he knew how. He needn't have bothered. Zania, lower lip sucked into her mouth, had her eyes fixed on the gateway.

"What are they doing?" She took a determined step forward, and Edmir swung in front of her with his hands raised, palms outward, resisting the urge to grab her by the arm.

"They said to wait, we'd best wait."

"You're not a Mercenary Brother." She looked at him, meeting his eyes for just a second before glancing away. Her eyes were a startling violet color, all the clearer for the darkening around the left side of her face.

"No, I . . ." For some reason his tongue felt thick. "No, they're my bodyguards. It, uh, it was my idea to stop and help you."

"I thank you, good sir, for your courtesy." But she had turned her eyes back to the gateway, and her words sounded rehearsed. In fact, Edmir thought with a twist to his lips, they probably came from some play she had acted in.

Even Edmir was beginning to wonder whether they should go in when Wolfshead and Lionsmane finally came out of the stable yard on foot. The Lionsmane's face was impassive as he picked up Warhammer's reins, except for a tightening around his mouth. His Partner was smiling her wolf's smile, lip curled back from her teeth. Seeing their faces, Zania cried out—the sound strangely natural and real after her affected tones. Edmir took a step toward her and stopped, not knowing what he meant to say.

Dhulyn Wolfshead caught Zania by the arms as the girl tried to run through the gates. "How many in your troupe? Zania!" She shook her until Zania blinked and focused on her. "How many?"

"Seven—six and me."

"There are eleven dead. One is wearing a Nisvean tunic, and four look like they belong to the hostel. You had better come and look, we have covered the worst of it."

What they'd left uncovered was quite bad enough, Edmir thought as he followed the Mercenaries and the girl into the stable yard and the smell hit him full force. For a moment he was back in the battlefield, he swore he could hear the same flies. His stomach sank under a wave of guilt and fear. Then Parno coughed, and Edmir was back in the yard of the hostel.

The stable yard had not been purpose-built, but was formed by the walls of the surrounding buildings. There was no entrance to the hostel at the ground level, though a set of rough wooden stairs led to an upper balcony. A handful of rough stalls lay along one side, and the stable yard was made tiny by the presence of a gaily painted caravan, built like an elongated coach. The coppery smell of blood was everywhere, and the iron smell of burning was following drifts of smoke from the open windows on the second floor.

The Mercenaries had laid out the bodies roughly where they'd found them. The Nisvean and two others in the back rooms of the hostel they'd left inside; of the rest, three were in the public room and five on the cobblestones of the stable yard. Heads and faces were covered with scraps of blankets and other cloths. Six were dressed in the same bright colors and flowing style that Zania herself wore; except for the Nisvean, the rest were in plain dull homespun.

As soon as they cleared the gate, Zania ran to the body that lay nearest the tall wheel of the caravan, and this time Dhulyn Wolfshead did not stop her. Zania knelt and, picking up the corpse's hand, laid her face against it and began to wail, her voice rising higher and higher. Edmir stepped forward, biting on the inside of his cheek as he fought tears.

Movement caught Dhulyn's eye and she turned toward Parno, who gestured her toward the sobbing girl. She raised her eyebrows at him. He rolled his eyes, pointed at Dhulyn, pointed at the girl, and made shooing motions with both hands. Her stomach sank. The girl would have to be cuddled and quieted, and Parno could not do it. Not now, not with the attack in the square so fresh in the little Cat's mind. *It will have to be me.* Was that a grin her blooded Partner was hiding? She gave him a look that told him it better not be, and went to comfort the weeping girl.

I'm no blooded good at this, she thought, as she wrapped her right arm around Zania's shoulders, drew the girl into the circle of her arms, and covered her mouth with her free hand.

"Stop crying, or I'll have to kill you," she murmured in the girl's ear.

Zania stiffened, flashed Dhulyn a disbelieving look, but fell silent, pushing herself free of the Mercenary's arms, and drying her tears with the trailing end of her sleeve.

"Get your things together," Dhulyn told the girl. "We must be gone."

The little Cat straightened to her feet, smoothing her hair back from her face and automatically adjusting her clothing. She looked around her, eyes blinking and mouth twisting in the effort to keep from crying. She coughed, took in a deep breath, and released it.

"I want the caravan." The girl looked from Dhulyn to Parno and back again, her jaw firm with determination, her voice steadying as she spoke. "*My* caravan, *your* horses. We should manage very well together."

"No offense," Parno spoke up before Dhulyn could. "I see the advantage to you, but what's the advantage to us?"

"Because no one looks at a troupe of traveling players and sees Mercenaries."

"And why should that concern us?"

"*He* says you're his bodyguards." Dhulyn wondered what the Prince of Tegrian thought of being referred to with a hooked thumb. "If that were true," the little Cat continued, "you wouldn't be going so quietly, and watching around every corner. The Nisveans and the Tegriani have been squabbling over the border for generations. Why would you need to hide from either side? Why would they interfere with Brothers going about their legitimate employment? Therefore, either you, or the one you guard, must be kept hidden from the Nisveans, or the Tegriani, or both. I can help you do that."

Dhulyn turned to Parno and punched him lightly in the shoulder. "You see? I told you that reading poetry and plays was not a waste of time." She turned back to the girl. "How?"

Zania gestured at the wagon. "In there I have all the disguises and costumes we could need. By sunrise tomorrow, even your own Brothers wouldn't recognize you. As an acting troupe, we can go anywhere unquestioned." She took a deep breath. "And we already have an engagement."

Warhammer and Bloodbone were not cart horses, but this was not the first time they had been used as such. Though they snorted a bit at first, they gave no real trouble, and with Zania's help Dhulyn had them harnessed in very short order. Parno got Edmir to help him move the bodies farther out of the way, and stow their gear into the caravan itself. Dhulyn's Mercenary badge was covered with one of Zania's colorful head scarves and his own with a peaked hood. He and his Partner had armed themselves only with axes and stout sticks, the weapons generally used by travelers such as Zania and her family. Edmir had wanted a crossbow, but Zania insisted that no player would ever expect to use such a thing, except as a prop on stage.

"We're like Scholars that way," she said. "No one bothers us. Or at least, nothing that sweet words or a little money can't turn away."

"That what happened here?" Edmir said.

Zania pressed her lips together and looked at the Mercenaries.

"Likely they were trying to help their friends and got caught up in the frenzy," Parno said when the silence grew strained. "Once killing begins, it's hard to stop."

"And once the dying begins, that's hard to stop as well," Dhulyn said. "Go," she said to Zania, "say your farewells." She turned back to Parno and Edmir. "Is Stumpy tied on?"

"Why not use the packhorse, rather than one of your own?" Edmir said, as he tied Stumpy's reins to the hook near the caravan's rear door.

"What is it you have against Stumpy?" Parno asked. "That's the second time you've spoken against him. He's too small to be paired with either Warhammer or Bloodbone. Those two are closer in size, and that makes a difference. That's the real reason coach horses are matched as closely as possible, not to make things pretty."

Parno was looking up at an ominously darkening sky when Dhulyn stuck her head around the corner of the caravan.

"We go," she said.

"Have you Seen something?" Parno hoped his tone made it clear what he meant.

"Just a bad feeling," his Partner replied, shaking her head. "I'll get the little Cat."

Zania Tzadeyeu returned from saying farewell to her family with her face as stony as bruising and swelling would allow. She joined Edmir on the driver's seat with Parno. It was a tight fit, but he'd rather they were with him than floating about loose where he couldn't see them.

"I'm sorry we can't give them any better rites than this," Dhulyn called to Zania from her position at the horses' heads. "But they'd want you safe more than anything else."

"They're in the hands of the Caids now," the girl said.

They had no more than cleared the gate of the inn, with Dhulyn jogging ahead with the horses, when a bolt of lightning struck the gatepost. In moments the entire front of the inn—old timbers and plaster—was engulfed by flames.

"Dhulyn!" Parno called, but she was already in motion. Their horses were too well-trained to bolt even at this, but Dhulyn had swung herself onto Bloodbone's back, to help calm them even more. Parno let the reins go slack, she would do the guiding for the present. From the stable yard to the north gate was only a matter of turning the right corner and negotiating a few spans of mostly deserted streets.

The ground rumbled and another bolt of lightning fell. Stumpy squealed, but when Parno looked around, he saw the packhorse running alongside the caravan, eyes wide and neck at its full extent. A building ahead of them was already on fire, with people running into the streets from suddenly unbolted doors.

"Dhulyn!" he called again. This time all she did was point to the left.

"Grab hold of something and get ready to lean all your weight to the left, as soon as we turn the corner," Parno told the two youngsters. He wrapped the reins around the cleat in the center of the footboard in front of him and took hold of it himself, his eyes glued to his Partner.

Dhulyn led the horses around the next corner at a speed even Parno found unbelievable. At the very last instant she pointed again.

"Now!" Parno yelled, leaning all his weight to the left as the caravan careened around the corner. Zania fell against him, gripping Edmir's arm with both her hands.

The caravan righted itself, and Dhulyn was already pointing to the left again.

The entire right side of this narrow street was in flames, but Dhulyn kept the horses galloping, and suddenly they found themselves in the small open space in front of Probic's north gate. The gates were open, the portcullis raised, and bodies of guards in dark blue showed how that had happened. Even here the smoke was thick enough to make them cough, and the ground was trembling once more. A ball of flame leaped from the nearest building to the gate itself, and the ropes that connected parts of the mechanisms began to smolder.

Dhulyn spoke to the horses, patted them both wherever she could reach them. Stumpy would not have her presence to calm him, but he was the most phlegmatic of the three in any case—she would just have to hope for the best. None of them could keep up this pace for long, but they had to get as far away from Probic as quickly as they could. Bracing herself with her hands, Dhulyn kicked up until she was standing crouched on Bloodbone's back. The rhythm of the horse's movement was as natural to her as the beating of her own heart, so she wasted no time in turning to face her Partner.

Parno grinned at her, and touched his forehead with his fingertips. She laughed, and did the same.

"That was not natural," she called out.

"The Mage," Parno answered. She should have known he would be thinking along with her.

"Take up the reins," she said. "I'll slow them very soon."

When she saw him comply, she turned back again to face the road, letting herself down once more to a sitting position astride Bloodbone's back. She began to sing, and the horses pricked their ears, waiting for the chorus, when they knew they should begin to slow.

"Sun blast, Moon drown you!" Avylos put Tzanek's left hand on Tzanek's chest, feeling the heart pound like a fast drum, the breath short. He had missed them. Missed them! His right hand formed a fist and brought it down again and again before he turned and started down the stairs that would take him back to Tzanek's chamber.

This time he leaned heavily against the wall as he went.

❈❈❈

With Parno on the reins, and Dhulyn to encourage the horses, they continued traveling well into the night, having turned off the main road out of Probic on the first track leading toward the Household where Zania's family had their next engagement.

"Even if we don't perform, we'll be welcome for the news we bring and we'll be that much farther along our road," the white-faced girl had pointed out.

"At the moment, any road that takes us from Probic is a good one, but first chance we get, we decide where our final road must be," Dhulyn said. All four of them were on foot to spare the horses as much as possible, with the two youngsters taking it in turns to ride up on the driver's seat. Hardy as both of them might normally be, they were not Mercenaries, and it was all they could do to keep up with the horses for even a short while.

"Somewhere safe, is my suggestion," Parno said. When Dhulyn glanced over to him, he winked at her. It was his job to play the prosy oldster when they had to deal with outsiders. Especially young outsiders.

"Well if that *was* the Mage in Probic, he's stopped now," Dhulyn said. "And we've no way of knowing whether it was us he was after." Once again, Dhulyn caught his eye and he knew that her thoughts on that matched his own. Too much coincidence, he thought, that they, and the Nisveans, and a freak storm with fire falling from the sky should all arrive in Probic on the same day.

Parno hated coincidence. It wasn't natural.

He was more than ready to stop by the time Dhulyn called a halt, leading them into a clear spot off the track just large enough to squeeze the caravan through the trees. They could not have gone much farther in any case, the waning moon had set and taken what little light there was with it. Parno let the caravan pass into the trees and looked back in the direction they had come. The moon might have set, but there was a glow to the southeast.

"Probic." Dhulyn's voice at his left elbow.

"Nothing else it could be," he agreed. "Amazing there's still something left to burn."

"Mage fire," Dhulyn said.

"I did not think the Mage had such power."

"I don't think anyone did."

Eight

AVYLOS' FOREHEAD SLAMMED down on the tabletop and he groaned. Somehow he had managed to bring Tzanek's headache back with him. He tried to push himself up, but his head was too heavy; he ended by having to lift it with his hands. Once upright, he could, with great care, balance his head on the top of his neck. It felt like trying to balance an apple on the tip of his finger. Fortunately, he had once been very good at that kind of trick.

He did nothing for several minutes but breathe deeply and try to still the pounding in his head. When he thought he could manage it, he reached to his left and put his hand on the casket that held the Stone. Getting the key out of the pocket of his gown almost defeated him, but after several tries his trembling fingers managed to fit it into the lock. With the casket open, the Stone in his hands, he already felt much better, just knowing that restoration was so close.

"*Aharneh.*" His throat was so dry, his voice so weak, that had there been others in the room with him, they would not have heard the word. But the Stone heard. His teeth closed on the inside of his lip as his head fell back. The power washed through him, the headache vanished, and his feeling of fragility lightened but did not disappear entirely. Avylos drew a symbol in the air. It appeared, wavered a moment, and faded away.

Avylos tasted the blood from his lip. He had used too much power in Probic, enough that the magics had drawn on the strength of his own blood and bones. His rage had consumed him in more ways than one. Instead of filling him once more, restoring his Magehood, the power he could tap from the Stone had only restored him to normal humanity.

And that was a *lie*. His right hand closed into a fist. He was *not* a normal man, without magic and without power. That was the lie his family, his *Tribe*—his lip curled back and he resisted the urge to spit—had tricked him with for so long. But he had punished them for that, and when he mastered the secrets of the Stone, that lie would be banished forever.

There would be a page standing his post at the entrance to this wing. Avylos stood, dusted down his gown, made sure that the folds of his cloak fell straight, and headed for the door. The page would fetch him Olecz the guard. And the guard would fetch him the dice boy.

❊❊❊

"The Wolfshead says we'll stop here," Zania was saying to Edmir, with the unnecessary precision of the exhausted. It was Edmir's turn on the caravan's high seat, and the girl's face, ghostly pale in the darkness under the trees, was peering upward at him from the ground.

"Be careful getting down, Edmir," Parno said as he neared the front of the caravan. "Your leg may have stiffened." He needn't have bothered warning him, the boy lowered himself from the seat with the movements of a man twice Parno's age. And a sick man at that.

"Get inside, you two," Dhulyn said, leaving off stroking and praising the horses to join them. "Find us something to eat and drink—and for the Moon's sake, don't wait for us, eat something yourselves."

She beckoned to him and Parno joined her at the horses, first rubbing Warhammer's nose and praising him before beginning to undo the harness attaching him to the caravan's central shaft. Dhulyn was doing the same to Bloodbone, crooning to her in the language of the Red Horsemen. Like anyone from a Noble House with country Holdings, Parno had been taught to take care of his animals. Dhulyn's approach made even Parno's training look like neglect, but he had to admit, time-consuming as it was, the results made it worthwhile.

"At least we won't need a fire for warmth, not tonight at any rate," Dhulyn said, as she tugged at a stiff knot on Bloodbone's harness.

Parno nodded. "The bunks are large enough for two to sleep, if they're friendly."

"We'll see how friendly the prince feels."

It wasn't quite a smile Parno could hear in his Partner's voice, but it was close. "What about you?"

"I'm far enough away from my woman's time to share a bed, if that is what you ask." The last bit of harness undone, Bloodbone moved free of her own accord, and Dhulyn coiled up the trailing ends of leather harness and hung them in their places before coming to help Parno.

"Any wagers on which one wants to sleep with you?" he asked, moving aside for her.

"My wager is neither," Dhulyn said. "Since we met with the Clouds, the prince looks at me with eyes that see something uncanny, and the dancer girl is still not comfortable enough in her skin to be close to anyone."

"Don't fret, my heart, that still leaves me."

"We should be so lucky. We'll have to take watch turn-about. Neither of *them* will know what to watch for."

"Do we?" Without meaning to, Parno had glanced back over his shoulder to where the glow from the destruction of Probic could still be seen in the sky. "What did City Lord Tzanek mean when he said that the Brotherhood was banished from Tegrian? The wall guards certainly seemed to know nothing of it."

"Today's trouble today." Dhulyn put her hand on his arm. "We've seen worse than this," she said. "And we are still here to talk about it."

"In Battle," he said.

"Or in Death," she answered.

Free, the horses shook themselves and immediately went to investigate the tufts of grass by the side of the clearing away from the road. Parno unhooked a bucket from the caravan's side and filled it with water from the barrel fastened next to it, as Dhulyn rounded the caravan to untie Stumpy.

"Why do you call her dancer?"

"That's what her name means in the old tongue, the language of the Caids."

"Tzadeyeu?"

Dhulyn slapped Stumpy on the rump and nodded. "The word has changed a bit in the passage of time, as our old friend Gundaron the Scholar would tell us, but it's the same word." Dhulyn joined him at the water barrel. "Did you see their faces?"

Parno shrugged. "They'll be twitching for hours."

"A long day, and a bad one. For them both." Her fingers felt rough and cold on his wrist. "Play for them. Play them to sleep."

The interior of the caravan was as compact and well-arranged as a ship captain's cabin. Two benches—wide enough, as Parno had said, to hold two people who were friendly—ran lengthwise down each side, and the netting above them held all manner of parcels and packages—and would hold people, too, Dhulyn thought, if the packages were on the floor, and more beds were needed. Cupboard doors under the benches showed where more supplies, and probably the bedding, could be stowed.

Dhulyn left the door of the caravan open behind her as she and Parno climbed in. The two youngsters sat on opposite benches, eyeing each other over the caravan's table, a flap of time-darkened wood that had been let down from where it attached to the wall at the front end. A candle set into a silvered holder reflected light into the space, and illuminated a platter on which rested a partially eaten loaf—yesterday's bread, Dhulyn thought, eyeing it with sudden interest, half a dozen cold potatoes, and a handful of sticks of dried meat.

Parno rubbed his hands together and slid in next to Edmir, leaving Zania's side of the table to Dhulyn.

"And to drink?" Parno said.

Zania lifted a clay jug from the floor at her feet and passed it over the table. Parno pulled the stopper, smelled the jug, and frowned.

"I'll fetch water," he said, and started to rise to his feet.

"There's water here also," Zania said, reaching down for another jug. "I didn't think you'd want it."

"We're Mercenary Brothers," Dhulyn told her. "Not soldiers, not guards. We don't go off duty at the end of the watch."

"And in any case, our watch lasts until Edmir here gets home safely," Parno added, wiping off his mouth with the back of his hand and passing the water jug to Dhulyn. She stifled a smile as she accepted the jug. As Parno had told the prince, he came from a House fully as noble as the prince's own—perhaps more so—and yet here he was pouring water directly into his mouth without touching the jug to his lips as handily as any country man. There was no bumpkin in the man—country or otherwise—and yet Parno liked to play the part. She looked at the faces of the prince and the dancer. Parno's little act did help to set people at ease, she thought. It did that.

"Then the sooner I get home, the better for all of us," Edmir said. "We must get to Beolind as quickly as we can, we must reach my mother."

Parno caught Dhulyn's eye and scratched his nose with his left forefinger. She blinked, and gave herself time to swallow the bread she'd been chewing. "Let us not be hasty, *Edmir*," she said, emphasizing the prince's name ever so slightly. Let him hear her use his name without a title, let him remember, she hoped, that Zania did not know who he was. "It's no return for you if it's not a return to *safety*."

"I know he's Lord Prince Edmir, if that's what you're being so careful about." The girl's tone was at once crisp and smug, like a student who had all the right answers and was ready to show off.

Edmir coughed on the water he was drinking. Dhulyn looked at Parno and saw the twinkle in his eyes. When she smiled back, her Partner broke into laughter. Still smiling, she shook her head at him.

"I didn't tell her." Edmir was indignant.

"No need to tell me." The smugness was now clearly to the fore. "You were declared dead almost four days ago, time enough for likenesses to be made and put up around the town. I saw one in front of the Jaldean Shrine, as well as at the prayer stations for the other gods. They made you look younger and more innocent, of course, but it was you all right."

Parno sat back against the cushions. "Well, this will make things more comfortable."

"For you maybe," Edmir muttered.

"We, at least, can stop watching our tongues when we are in private," Dhulyn said, letting a touch of frost enter her voice. "And you can stop pretending to be an ordinary person."

"And doing a poor job of it." The two women gave each other brisk nods. Parno grinned broadly, took the last piece of bread, broke it, and gave half to her. She took it with a shrug. No point in doing without, it wouldn't last another day.

"Zania's brought up a good point," Parno began.

"What, that he's no actor?"

"Enough, little Cat. I meant that if Edmir's been declared dead, and the country is in mourning, we can't merely turn up at the Queen's Court with him and ask for breakfast."

This time it was the two young people who looked at each other, shared ignorance bringing them together until they noticed what they were doing and looked away.

"Why? If it's not a stupid question?" the girl said.

"There are no stupid questions," Dhulyn said. She sat forward, her elbows on the tabletop. "The prince isn't dead, but someone wants him to be, and going straight to the capital doesn't seem the best method to keep him alive. There are too many questions with no clear answers."

"Who warned the Nisveans you were coming? Because they knew, no doubt there," Parno put in, looking at Edmir.

"Why didn't the Blue Mage's magic work? And why were the Nisveans so adamant about keeping you?" Dhulyn added.

"And why have you been so quickly declared dead, since you obviously aren't?" Zania blinked and lifted her chin to return Edmir's stare.

"And why," Parno said in the tone of someone being careful not to hurt, "did a man who has known and loved you all your life not recognize you, when recognizing you would mean that all the country—including your mother and sister—would rejoice?"

"Meaning that until we find out who wouldn't be rejoicing, it's best we stay hidden." Dhulyn gently tapped the table with her index finger.

"And not just for the prince's sake," Parno said. "If what Lord Tzanek was saying is true, the Mercenary Brotherhood has been asked to leave Tegrian—" He caught Dhulyn's eyes with the look that said, *We'll talk of this later.* "And since we have no intention of leaving Tegrian at the moment, where can we go to both learn things and stay hidden?" Parno asked.

"I still say here's the best place to hide." Zania rapped the table in front of her hard. "The last place anyone will look for you, prince or Mercenary Brother, is performing on a public stage. And we can learn things, too. People are used to passing the news, even letters, along with travelers like us . . ." Her voice faltered. "Like me."

"Agreed," Dhulyn said. "But even players have a destination, a route. And so should we." She bit off the end of a twist of dried meat.

"We can go to Jarlkevo," Edmir said.

Dhulyn, her mouth full, raised her eyebrows at Parno.

"And what's in Jarlkevo?" he asked.

"My aunt Valaika."

"And we can know that she's not part of this—whatever this is?"

Edmir shook his head. His lips were pressed into a thin line. "She's my father's sister. She came with him from Hellik when he married my mother. They had some kind of falling out when I was a child—" Edmir shrugged. No need to say, Dhulyn thought, that he hadn't been interested, or perhaps old enough at the time to remember the details now.

"She wanted to marry someone unsuitable, something like that," he continued. "She left the Royal House, and the Holding at Jarlkevo, part of my father's marriage gift, was elevated to a House and given to her. I don't think she's been back at court since my father's funeral. She didn't come for Kera's naming day, just sent her a nice horse." From the change in his voice, Dhulyn thought Edmir would have liked a nice horse from his aunt as well.

"And will she be disposed to help you now?" Dhulyn asked.

Edmir shrugged, every line in his face turning downward. "I can be sure she had no part in my present circumstances," he said. "That, at least, I can say."

"Jarlkevo it is, then," Dhulyn said.

"Parno," Dhulyn said, once the platters had been cleared away and the tabletop folded to its upright position. "Get your pipes, my soul. Some music will soothe us."

Parno met her glance and made the smallest shrugging motion with his shoulders. Edmir was staring into space again, looking at the Moon and Stars knew what ghastly sight, and Zania's eyes had taken on that hollow look which said "my people are all gone, and I'm still alive." It was a look Dhulyn herself was well familiar with. The girl would be feeling some guilt now, and would feel it again and again, as even planning what she should do next would seem selfish and a betrayal in the light of what had happened to her family. It would be a long process, coming to terms with the events of the past day, but what the girl needed right now was sleep, to give her thoughts at least one night's distance from the events of the day.

And Edmir—how must he feel? *Someone* had betrayed him, the question was, who?

The bag holding Parno's pipes was one of the first things they had brought into the caravan, and it was a matter of moments for him to unfasten the heavy silk cords of the bag's opening. As he set the drones to one side, and took out just the chanter, Dhulyn helped the little Cat bring out the bedding and unfold it along the benches. Edmir lay down without hesitation, his eyes still focused on the middle distance, but Zania shook her head.

"I can't sleep," she said. "There's too much to think about, plans to make." Her chin trembled for a moment, but she soon had it under control again. "There's things that won't wait until tomorrow, now that my uncle is dead—" Abruptly, she stopped and clamped her jaw. Dhulyn guessed that she was seeing once more the blood-drained face, the staring eyes.

Sitting in the open doorway, Parno began to play softly, a simple tune that made Dhulyn smile. It was a variation on a well-known children's song, a game which often involved a blindfold, but played at a tempo that made it a lullaby.

"Tell me your ideas," Dhulyn said, drawing the girl's attention. "What should you be planning? Do you have other family? Another troupe, perhaps, with whom you have ties?"

The little Cat was shaking her head, but her color was better, and her trembling had stopped. "There *is* a meeting place, after the Harvest Fairs have run their course and the Midwinter Festivals have yet to begin, but before that I must finish—If you are going to Beolind, that will suit me perfectly. I can begin there."

"Begin what?" Edmir was not asleep yet, after all. His dark eyes looked even darker in the shadows cast by the oil lamp.

"Your pardon, Lord Prince," Zania said, lowering her eyes. "But my business is my own."

"Fair enough, for now, little Cat," Dhulyn said. "But our road will lie together, and we have pledged to help each other, keep that to mind."

The girl straightened her shoulders. "In part, that's what has been pulling at my thoughts," she said. "Most of our pieces—the ones I know by heart anyway—use my . . . use the whole troupe. But there are others, smaller plays, pieces that would need only two or three players."

"Best think of something for two." Dhulyn patted the bedclothes on the bench and stood up. "Think lying down. Let Parno's music guide your thoughts."

The little Cat drew in her brows and nodded as she obeyed, tucking up her feet and letting Dhulyn cover her.

"I remember we did all manner of things before the troupe split up, when my mother still lived. There are books and scrolls . . ."

"To be looked at in the morning's light," murmured Dhulyn. "Come, just rest your eyes for a moment. Is it not a beautiful tune my Partner plays?"

Still frowning, Zania closed her eyes. Dhulyn waited, letting the familiar music wash over her as well, loosening the tensions of the day. She glanced at Parno, but his eyes were closed in concentration. Dhulyn let herself out past his sprawling feet and settled on the step outside. She let her head fall back against his thigh and her own eyes closed.

❈

It's summer, late in the day, but the sun still shines, and it is warm enough that the boys all have their blood-red hair braided and one or two are shirtless. They sit on the ground, cross-legged, in a circle, taking turns making gestures in the air, as if they are drawing. One or two are quickly successful, a symbol in light hovering in front of them for a few moments before disappearing. One boy forgets a part of the symbol he is drawing, and it collapses; the other boys laugh. There is one who does not laugh. Only Dhulyn can see him, hiding, watching from behind the hanging awning of a nearby tent. This is not a child, excluded because of age from the business of those who are almost men. He is the same age as the others; his hair is braided, down is forming on his cheeks. Something else keeps him hiding, watching, his hands in fists, with a look of dark hatred on his face . . .

Parno is sitting at a small table, an oil lamp with a curious glass shade illuminating the page on which he is writing. Dhulyn frowns. Usually, when there is any writing to be done, she does it. Parno is literate, and in the manner of the sons of Noble Houses in Imrion, well-educated, particularly in history, politics, and economics. But she is the one who has spent a year in a Scholars' Library, while she learned the life was not for her, and it is she who writes a better hand. He frowns, crosses out a short word, and writes something else.

This is an older Parno, Parno-to-come, Dhulyn realizes. The familiar dark red and deep yellow of his Mercenary badge is clear in the lamplight. The lines in his face are more pronounced, his hair is cut much shorter than he wears it now, and there seems to be gray under the gold. Parno lays down his pen and rubs at the wristband on his left wrist. Dhulyn recognizes it. She wears it on her own wrist now. The now of the real world, not the now of the Vision.

Where is she? . . .

Moonlight washes all the color from what must be a beautiful garden surrounded by high walls. A slim man is seated on the edge of a pool of water. He looks down at the surface with great concentration. Perhaps he is a Finder, using the pool as a scrying bowl. Dhulyn can't get close enough

to him to see his face, which is turned away and obscured in
the faulty light. Nor can she see what it is that so absorbs
him in the water. A movement to one side reveals there is a
girl sitting on a rough part of the wall, watching the man. He
doesn't know she's there. . . .

A redheaded man on horseback, his fur-lined cloak
pushed back to free his arms, makes a curiously familiar gesture, drawing in the air in front of him. A blue line of light
follows the end of his finger, lingering in the air a moment
before it fades. The trail of hoofprints in the snow behind
him disappears.

When she woke up, Zania thought for one blessed moment
that all the horror—the blood on her aunt's face, her cousin's limp hand—had been a nightmare, and the voices she
heard coming from outside were her uncle Jovan and her
aunt Ester. But then she remembered. They both were
dead, lying in a row, wrapped in blankets in the stable yard
of the hostel, and she would never hear their voices again.
As the tears began, she turned over to face the caravan's
wall, covering her face with her hands to stifle any sound
she might make. She couldn't let anyone see her crying.
They would lose respect for her, think her no more than an
untried child.

When she could finally take a deep breath without sobbing, Zania sat up, throwing off the rugs she didn't remember pulling over her. Everything in the caravan was now
hers. Everything. Including the troupe's charter from the
old Galan of Cabrea, an age-yellowed bit of parchment
that at least in theory gave them free passage wherever
they might choose to go. These important documents were
here, inside, where her elder relatives normally slept while
she, Jovana, and the twins slept under the caravan. But
Prince Edmir was asleep in her great-uncle's place, and she
couldn't light a lamp now. There were more papers, books
and scrolls, performance pieces for the most part, wrapped
in oiled cloth and stored in an old chest that was rarely
opened, and therefore, was kept up top, under the flat
pieces of scenery.

But *that* wasn't what she wanted just now. Zania swung her feet off the bench and padded silently to the door, letting herself out before she could change her mind. The cool night air made her shiver, but she didn't expect to be out very long. She heard a horse snort over to her left, but though she waited, holding her breath, she heard nothing else. They were silent sleepers, then, these Mercenaries.

The moon had set, and even the stars had been obscured by clouds. But this caravan had been Zania's home her whole life; she didn't need light to find her away around it. She crept forward along one side, trailing her fingers across the painted surface until she felt the hard edge of the ladder that gave access to the driver's seat. Zania hitched up her skirt, pulled herself up the three short steps, and swung into the seat. She ran her fingers over the bits of decorative wooden trim that formed geometric shapes on the front of the caravan. She'd never actually done this herself, but she and her cousin had watched Great-Uncle Therin many times, when they were supposed to be asleep under the wagon.

There. The bottom piece on the left shifted down under her prodding, swung to one side and exposed a flat opening panel about the size of her hand. Zania hesitated, hand lifted, tongue pressing on her upper lip. This was Great-Uncle Therin's secret hiding place, never even to be spoken of. If she had needed any proof that life as she'd known it had ended, and that things would never be the same again, she had it now. She took a deep breath, slipped her hand into the space, and brought out her great-uncle's journal. She lifted it to her face. It smelled like him, of the garlic he loved in all his food, of the herbal rub he used on his lower back and arthritic knees.

She tucked the journal into the front of her gown, returned the piece of wood trim to its original position, feeling the slight "click" through her fingers. She let herself down the short ladder and felt her heart leap as a long-fingered hand closed over her left biceps.

"Stay quiet, there are others who wish to sleep, though you've finished."

The Wolfshead. Though her breath still came short, Zania relaxed. Intellectually, she knew—she'd been warned by her aunt—that women could be just as dangerous to a young person as men, but the bare truth was that predatory women were rare, and if she was safe with anyone, it would be Dhulyn Wolfshead.

"There's a chest up top I wanted to check," she said, trying to match the Mercenary woman's whisper-quiet voice.

"In the dark?"

When Zania didn't answer, the Wolfshead gave a short laugh.

"But then, you did not need any light to find what you were looking for in that hiding place, did you? Go back to bed," she said. "I will wake you when there's enough light to see anything."

Zania waited, but it seemed that Dhulyn Wolfshead was not going to ask her anything more about what she'd found.

"I don't know if I can sleep inside," Zania said, closing her mouth abruptly. It was true, she realized, but it hadn't been what she'd meant to say. "That's . . . that *was* the elders' place and I . . ."

"You thought you'd be there one day, but not so soon."

A statement, not a question. A tug on her wrist, and Zania followed the older woman as she led her away from the caravan, under a willow tree whose overhanging branches provided them some cover from the cool breeze. Dhulyn Wolfshead leaned her back against the trunk of the tree. Zania glanced around. *Of course,* she thought. *From here she can see the whole clearing, moonlight or no moonlight.*

"What will be the first thing we need to do, Zania Tzadeyeu, if our disguise is to work? People have only to look at Parno Lionsmane and myself to know that we are Mercenary Brothers."

"I have an idea for that, but we should also see what talents we have among us," Zania said. "The Lionsmane can play, for example. Can he make songs as well? There's money to be made bringing new music to people. Can we all sing, dance? And we must find scenes and plays we can perform with so few players. Not that Great-Uncle Therin takes . . . took so very many parts, I suppose." With the darkness to cover her, Zania tried to imitate the Mercenary woman's stance, chin up, head slightly tilted on an angle like a bird listening, feet shoulder-width apart, knees a little bent, shoulders squared to the torso and arms hanging loosely from the shoulders.

"What did he do, then?"

Zania thought she heard a whisper of amusement in the Wolfshead's voice, as if she'd seen what Zania was doing, and what's more, had understood *why* she'd been doing it. Zania shook herself. "Why ask me all this about the past? We have to plan where we go from here."

"To know where we go, I must know where we have been," Dhulyn Wolfshead said. Her voice was the merest thread of sound in the darkness. "I am the strategist of my Partnership. Let me see how things *were* done, and I can help you to see how things *will* be done."

Zania found herself nodding. That made sense.

"Well, Therin took the parts of the older men, you know, kings, counselors, old Jaldean priests full of advice, and the like. My cousin Jovana and I would take all the younger parts between us, pages, young sons or daughters, sometimes the young lovers, if the story called for such."

"Played both parts, did you?" Though the Mercenary woman was close enough to her that Zania could feel the warmth from her body, her voice seemed to come from some distance away.

"Female and male, you mean? Yes, it's easy enough. We were on the lookout for a boy to join us, but all we found were the acrobats. Twins, Nik and Sari. They'd do for spear carriers, but neither of them could act." Zania sat down cross-legged at the Wolfshead's feet. "My aunt Ester played the more important lovers or princesses or pirate queens." Zania was dismayed to hear the note of discontent and envy that had crept into her voice and hurried on. "My uncle Jovan partnered her, taking the man's roles, lords or lovers, the parts Great-Uncle Therin was too old to play."

"And soon you would have taken your aunt's roles?"

"Yes. Well, either Jovana or I would. Depending. It was Great-Uncle Therin decided who played what, and what story it was we acted, for that matter."

"We must all serve an apprenticeship," Dhulyn Wolfshead said. "Mercenaries in our Schools, Scholars in their Libraries, even the Marked in their Guilds. We cannot all begin by playing Nor-iRon Tarkina."

"You know that play?"

"There's a reason I'm called the Scholar," the Mercenary said, "and you have just learned what it is."

"Do you know the play well? We have enough people to do the first act. Parno Lionsmane could play the old Tarkin on his deathbed. You could play the Marked counselor, the Seer Estavia. I'd be Nor-iRon as Heir, and the prince could play . . ." Zania became aware that Dhulyn Wolfshead had stiffened, and fell quiet. The Mercenary was silent for a long time, long enough that Zania's heart began to thump uncomfortably.

"We should leave talk of performances for when the others are with us," she said.

Zania relaxed. "Of course."

Nine

"I SWEAR TO YOU, LORD MAGE, the dice are not weighted, I'm not cheating, I swear it." His hands shaking, Zel-Nobic took the cup of brandy-laced wine the Blue Mage gave him and held it, too frightened to actually lift it to his mouth and take a drink.

"I never thought you were, Zel-Nobic. If I thought you were a mere cheat, I would be very disappointed." The tall Mage's voice was mellow as warm honey, and Zel-Nobic's hands stopped shaking.

"Disappointed, Lord Mage?"

The Blue Mage sat back and rested his elbows on the arms of the chair on the far side of the worktable. "I am not concerned with cheating at dice—that carries punishments, certainly, but not from me. I am looking for something else, something much more important. When I realized that I would not find a teacher, I began looking for an apprentice," he said. "If my own experiences have taught me anything, it is that knowledge is a fragile thing, and we must all do what we can to preserve it."

"Yes, my lord Mage." Zel wasn't sure exactly what the Blue Mage meant, but he nodded, and raised the cup to his lips. The wine was smooth and sweet. The Blue Mage was proving to be very friendly. Really, much friendlier than people here in Beolind had led him to believe.

"Do you think you might be willing to help me in this, my friend? You might become the first pupil in my Academy. Do you think you could try?"

Friend, Zel thought. *The Blue Mage of Tegrian, consort of the queen, has called me friend.* "Yes, my lord Mage."

"Call my Avylos when we are alone together."

"Yes, my . . . yes, Avylos."

"That's better." Avylos smiled, and Zel realized the man was younger than he appeared. "Come, stand by me here."

Zel obeyed Avylos' gesture and came round the end of the worktable to stand at the Mage's side. The top had been cleared of everything except a small wooden chest, plainly carved of a fine-grained wood. Avylos placed a pair of blue-glass dice with white pips on the table in front of him. *Not blue glass.* Zel didn't know how he knew, but he knew he was right. *Not glass at all. Sapphire, maybe?*

"Now, roll these dice for me, Zel-Nobic."

For the next hour Zel did just that, rolling dice over and over. At one point Avylos gave him a different set of dice, green instead of blue, and Zel went on rolling the numbers the Mage asked for. Then Avylos gave him the blue set back again, and Zel rolled all four. Then six, red ones; then eight, another blue pair, but these with red pips. When the Mage gave him yet another pair, however, this time smoky topazes, they fell randomly. Zel couldn't even manage to get eight out of ten to fall correctly, getting only three dice to turn up the number Avylos called out.

"No, no, that's fine," Avylos said, patting him on the arm as Zel apologized. "Naturally, there's a limit to what the untrained skill can do. We'll take that as our starting point, and work forward from there. How do you feel?"

Zel shrugged. He often played for longer than this. "My wrist aches a little, but otherwise fine."

Zel almost stepped back when Avylos took him by the shoulders, but managed to stay still when the Mage clasped him to his chest, and kissed him on both cheeks.

"Finally." Avylos' voice resounded in his chest. "An apprentice. A brother." The Mage stepped back until Zel could look him once more in the face, his hand still on Zel's shoulders. Avylos smiled, his lips twisted to one side, his eyebrows raised. "That is, if you want it?"

"Oh, yes, my lord—I mean, yes, Avylos." Zel could barely speak around the lump in his throat, the pounding in his ears. He would be a Mage, he would be Avylos' brother. And to think his mother had been worried about him coming to the capital.

"You won't mind, will you, if I ask you to bind yourself formally to the apprenticeship."

Zel almost fell over himself agreeing that no, he wouldn't mind. He'd have to let the man he was working for know, of course, but no one was going to deny the Blue Mage. Already, Zel could see himself in a soft linen robe, like the one Avylos was wearing—a different color of course, there couldn't be *two* Blue Mages. And perhaps he could get his sister brought to the Queen's Court. Zelniana couldn't manage the dice as well as he could, but if there was to be training, perhaps she, too, could improve.

Avylos had opened the wooden chest on his worktable, exposing a blue crystal rod, resting in a bed of dark silk.

"What is it?" he asked, regretting his question as soon as it left his lips; in that instant, Avylos' eyes shuttered. But then the Mage smiled and all was well once more.

"It shows well that you are curious," Avylos said. "This is an artifact of the Caids. It will change color if one of us swears falsely, and so it will give us the Caids' blessing on our contract. Lay your hand here, alongside mine, and repeat after me."

Zel put his hand down on the blue crystal, finding it oddly warm and almost soft under his fingertips. *What's it made out of?* he wondered, but stopped himself from asking. Even the most patient teacher, even his *brother* the Blue Mage, wouldn't like to be interrupted too many times. He would have all the time he wanted for questions once his apprenticeship began.

When Zel awoke some hours later, he was behind a table in the taproom of the Archer's Rest Hostel. He licked his lips and blinked. Had he been dreaming? His head felt strangely hollow. Zel cleared his throat, casting his eyes around the room and feeling for his money purse, and his dice bag. All that about the Blue Mage and the apprenticeship, had it been a dream? How long had he been asleep? Had anyone noticed?

To cover and explain the motions of his hands, Zel drew out a pair of dice and idly threw them on the table. Fours.

He blinked, and tried again, saying "sixes" to himself as his hand moved. The dice showed a three and a five. "Fours" he said to himself. A two and a three.

No change with a different pair of dice. Nor did tossing with the other hand help. Nor did waiting and trying again. Nor did a cup of ale. Nor two.

Hand shaking, Zel rubbed at his upper lip. *Not a dream,* he thought. There *was* a hollow inside him, an emptiness that used to be filled. The Caids-cursed Mage had done this to him. Couldn't have another magic man in the place, oh, no, not even a poor boy trying to make his living with dice. No apprenticeship, no brotherhood. Zel had his hands on the table, braced to stand up, before he thought better of it and sat again. What could he do? Who could he go to and say "I used to be able to control the movement of the dice, and the Blue Mage took that power from me?"

Thank the Caids he hadn't mentioned his sister, Zel thought. At least *she* was safe.

❧

"Sun, Moon, and Stars, I tell you. I am not a player, nor do I dance or sing." Dhulyn looked up from where she squatted by the fire, poking the glowing embers back to life. She smiled her wolf's smile, and Parno laughed as the two young people leaned away from her as far as they could without falling off the rocks they were using as seats next to the cook fire.

"That's not strictly true," he said, still grinning as Dhulyn turned her fierce look to where he leaned against the side of the caravan. "You dance very nicely with a sword in your hands, and you have a pleasant singing voice, but nothing, I agree, that people would normally pay to hear."

"All of this is beside the point," Dhulyn said. "Until the little Cat explains how we will not be known for Mercenaries, the singing and dancing are irrelevant."

"Wait." Zania leaped to her feet and dove into the caravan where they could hear her burrowing among the boxes and bags stowed in the overhanging net. Dhulyn shrugged and rolled eyes, letting her hands fall on her knees.

When Zania came back out, she dangled six or seven small linen bags from their drawstrings. She deposited them on the ground, tossed one to Parno and another to Dhulyn before she knelt down and began to work at the strings of a third. It took both fingertips and teeth to loosen the mouth of the bag, but finally she had it open, and took from it a long fall of dark hair. She shook it out, and fitted it over her own short white-blonde hair. Instantly, as the dark hair blended with her sun-darkened skin, she became a Berdanan.

"There are maybe twenty of these wigs," she said, indicating the bags Parno and Dhulyn had in their laps. "All kinds of colors, and lengths. Made over the years from human hair, and sewn onto caps."

Dhulyn had her own bag open and was turning the gray wig it held over in her hands, examining the tiny stitches that attached the hair to the cap. The caps themselves had been made from strips of leather, very supple, and likely able to fit more than one person.

"I thought if you shaved your heads—or at least cut your hair very close like mine," Zania was saying, "you could wear one of these wigs. No one would think it odd if they noticed it. Players must be ready at all times to look like someone else. People would expect us to wear wigs and even costumes to draw attention to ourselves." She indicated her own brightly colored skirts.

Dhulyn sighed noisily, ran her fingers over her hair and tugged on one of her braids. Parno nodded. If she was already thinking about her wires and picklocks, and where she would hide them if her hair was cut, then she was already in agreement. One thing to be said for Mercenary Schooling, he thought. It cured you of useless modesty, and of vanity as well.

"I thought that tonight, at the Vednerysh Holding, Parno Lionsmane could play, and I could dance. And then, you two could give a fighting demonstration—what did I say?"

Dhulyn was shaking her head. "Then we might as well leave our badges showing. Anyone who has ever seen a Mercenary fight, even just a *Shora*, will know us for what we are. The last thing we can do is give such a demonstration."

"But you *can* fake one." Edmir had been silent for so long, Parno had almost forgotten he was there.

Dhulyn froze, her hands in the act of pulling the strings on the wig bag closed again.

"Perhaps you should explain," Parno said.

"You know what I mean," Edmir insisted. "You see performers and stage magicians do things all the time and you know they must be faking it, somehow, even if you can't figure out how. Swallowing swords, making eggs appear out of nowhere. We could do something like that. Make a large show of how difficult it is to do something that is actually very easy for you. Easy for Mercenaries, I mean," he said. Parno looked at Dhulyn, but she seemed just as puzzled as he felt, and Edmir went on. "Do you know the knife-throwing trick? Acrobats and jugglers do it sometimes in the market squares. A person stands against a target and someone else throws knives at them—"

"Sometimes blindfolded," Zania cut in.

"That's right. Or standing with their back to the target. And they make an outline of the person's body with the knives, without ever hitting the person. Or not often, anyway."

"But we don't know the trick," Zania pointed out. "We don't know how it's done."

"We don't need to know," Edmir said. "*They* can do it without trickery, can't you?" He looked first at Parno, then at Dhulyn, waiting until they nodded.

"It's not unlike a game we play in the Mercenary Schools called Coward's Knife," Parno said. "Two players throw knives at each other, getting closer and closer. You lost points if you flinched, or if you drew blood."

"As long as no one thinks you're Mercenary Brothers," Edmir said, "everyone will be sure it's a trick. Only we will know it's real."

"I don't know," Zania said. "Oh, I believe you can do it," she added quickly. Dhulyn lifted her hand to rub her mouth, and Parno stifled his own smile. The poor girl actually thought they needed her reassurance. "But this is still Troupe Tzadeyeu, and people will expect plays, not juggling and trickery. I think we must try."

Dhulyn shook her head. "I'm very sorry, but I can't do this. All our Schooling, our *Shora*, teach us to be truer, not to pretend."

Parno frowned and leaned forward, his elbows on his knees. "Dhulyn, my heart. You know how sometimes, when swords are out, it seems that you—" he lifted his shoulders and let them drop. "That you *charm* a man onto your blade?" *Or into your bed,* he didn't say aloud, though he knew from the quirk of her eyebrow and the start of her grin that she'd heard him say it nonetheless.

"The Two Hearts *Shora*?"

Parno nodded. "Try it on Edmir here, but without the sword."

Dhulyn turned to Edmir, looked him up and down. "It would only work standing up."

They all stood, and Dhulyn stepped a few paces away, rubbing her temples and breathing deeply. Parno cut off Edmir's questions.

"Better you don't know what to expect," he said. "Then it will be a true test."

As they watched, Dhulyn lowered her hands from her face and adjusted her feet. Though her hands were at her sides, her feet were placed as though she were holding a sword in her right hand, and was about to use it. Used against a single opponent, the Two Hearts *Shora* had been known to work even on a Mercenary Brother, as it wasn't one of the basic training *Shoras*. Parno knew it, he'd made sure Dhulyn taught it to him, but he wasn't as good at it as she was.

Parno waved Edmir into place in front of his Partner. The prince hesitated, looked once at Parno, once at Zania, before he moved into the opponent's space in front of Dhulyn. The boy was more frightened than he should be, Parno thought.

It was only seconds more until Dhulyn's respiration stilled, coming slower and the breaths themselves deeper. Color rose into her cheeks until she looked flushed. Her lips parted. After a moment, his eyes locked on Dhulyn's, Edmir also stilled. His breathing slowed, until his chest rose and fell in time with hers. Suddenly, his color changed, he grew pale, and his breathing quickened, growing loud in the still morning air. He took a step toward Dhulyn, reaching out, and Parno CRACKED his hands together.

Edmir stopped, blinking, and flushed red.

"If you can do that with an audience," Zania said, her voice tight, "we'll be rich."

❧❧❧

Kera tugged at the laces on the front of her shirt as she took the chair on her mother the queen's right. She'd come flushed and sweating from her swordplay lesson with Megz Primeau, the current holder of the Queen's White Blade, but from the look on her mother's face, it was lucky she hadn't taken the time to change out of her trousers and boots before answering the summons. Kedneara was seated in the thronelike chair in her anteroom, dressed formally in dark blue robes with white trim, her hair dressed high, with a circle of gold leaves to bind it.

Rage had brought unusual color to her mother's face, but the queen was still a great beauty, Kera thought, taller than both her children, her hair still raven-black. *She's only forty-seven,* Kera reminded herself, though Kedneara had been queen for more than thirty years. *At my age, she was already the ruler of Tegrian.* And at forty-seven, Kedneara's father had been dead already, as Kedneara herself would be, if it were not for Avylos. Kera wasn't sure quite when it was she'd realized that the Blue Mage was keeping the queen alive; it seemed that she'd always known it.

The problem was that Avylos wasn't a Healer, nor had there been one in Tegrian for as long as Kera could remember, and though he didn't like it spoken of, there were limits to Avylos' magic. All Kera knew for certain was that his attempts to magic women were chancy —either the magic didn't take at all, or it didn't last as long as it did on a man.

As if called by her thought, Avylos entered the room, going directly to the queen, bowing low over her extended hand, and kissing it. He took a step back and bowed again— not quite as low—to Kera herself.

"My Queen," he said, in his melodious voice. "Lady Prince."

Kera clenched her teeth. Would she ever get used to being called that?

"Another messenger has come from Probic. The city has been destroyed by fires from the heavens. Is this your doing?" The last words were bitten off. Her mother's breath was short, her hands trembling. Kera almost put out her hand, but stopped—they were not in private, and her mother the queen would not appreciate any signs of concern or even of affection now.

"Please, my Queen, compose yourself. You must be calm, you are putting too much strain on your heart."

At first, there was nothing but silence from the queen. Kera risked a glance at her mother out of the corner of her eye.

"Do not take that tone with me, little Mage. I am queen, and you are not Karyli."

Avylos turned so white his eyebrows stood out on his face like slashes of blood. His hands closed into fists. Kera wondered whether she could draw her sword fast enough, or whether it would make any difference if she could.

But Avylos only took a deep breath, and flexed his hands. It seemed the Mage would follow his own advice and remain calm. Kera relaxed back into her seat, though the tension did not completely leave her body.

"It was the Nisveans, my Queen. They were to bring the body of Prince Edmir to Probic, and they . . . they *used* him, Keda." Kera blushed at the Mage's use of her mother's pet name. "*Used* the noble gesture of returning his body to violate the treaty and attack Probic. They spit on his nobility, and on yours. They had to be punished, my love. They had to be destroyed."

"You acted without consulting me." The words were harshly spoken, but Kera could tell the fire was gone from her mother's anger.

"There was no time to call the Houses," Avylos said. "No time to prepare the armies. I needed a faster solution. Quick, deadly, and final.

"I had to punish them."

"And the people of Probic, *my* people?" Kedneara's only movement was the quick rising and falling of her breast as she breathed. Again Kera risked a glance sideways; her mother's face was as cold and hard as the profile on Kedneara's coins.

"I could not pick and choose, my Queen. My magics do not work in that fashion. I had to act quickly. But only think! It will send a message of warning to the Nisveans—to anyone!—showing what will happen if they dare to invade your lands. As for your people, I am certain they would rather die and be held in the hands of the gods than be slaves in Nisvea."

Kera wasn't so sure of that herself, but it seemed that the queen found Avylos' argument persuasive. She was nodding.

"So be it. They are in the hands of the Caids, and let the Caids sort them out."

Avylos looked squarely into the queen's deep blue eyes and bowed. At the very last moment Kera saw a flash of satisfaction pass over the Mage's face.

Kera gripped the arms of her chair, and she was speaking before she was even aware of her intentions.

"How was it your magics prevailed in Probic, when they failed in the Limona Valley?" There. That should upset some of his smugness.

Her mother the queen's face changed, her eyes narrowed in speculation. She reached out for Avylos' forearm, and Kera saw the strong fingers dig in.

"You *knew*? You knew Edmir went to Nisvea and you did not tell me? You failed to either stop or aid him?"

Slowly, reluctantly it seemed, Avylos came to his knees before the queen. "Most assuredly I did not. My magics cannot fail, as you know. But they must be *used*. Edmir was misled somehow, tricked or prevented from calling upon me. The battle was done before I knew of it. Tzanek in Probic was the last to see him, to counsel him. Who knows what may have passed between them?"

"But you did not tell me of his intentions. Who else knew of them? Did *you* counsel Edmir to go to Nisvea? The Houses whose sons went with him—Avros and Redni—they have returned, ransomed. Was this their idea?"

Avylos was still on his knees, his head lowered, but he turned his eyes to Kera and a trickle of cold ran down her spine. Would he speak? Tell her mother the queen that Kera herself had known of Edmir's plan and said nothing? She sat up straight. Well, she'd started this herself by exposing Avylos. She might as well keep control of the tiles in her own hands.

And out of the Mage's.

"Edmir didn't want you to know, Mother." She'd be safe enough, she hoped. Kera was now her mother the queen's only child. Never the favorite, but given the choice, Kedneara would choose her own blood, every time. "This was Edmir's own plan. He shared it with me, and later with the Blue Mage, but I did not counsel him against it. At least, not at first."

"Oh, Edmir." The queen rubbed at her eyes with her fingertips. "He was always so impetuous, so eager. He should have waited for the treaty to be finished."

Kera stifled a sigh. "He wished for your approval," she said. "He wanted to show you he could lead your armies."

Kedneara waved this away. "Of course I approved of him, he was my son. How could he be so foolish?" Kedneara took Kera's hand in both of hers.

From his position still on his knees, Avylos placed his hand atop both of theirs. "Calmness still, my Queen."

"But, Mother, you see, don't you, that Avros and Redni have no blame in this."

Kedneara nodded, and patted Kera's hand.

"Who else knows of the Lady Prince's involvement, my queen?"

Kera was momentarily speechless. She had not thought of what she'd done to help Edmir in quite those terms.

"What do you mean, Avylos?" the queen asked.

"Who knows that the Lady Prince advised her brother in his plans? Wait, hear me out. We had the same motives, Kera and I, to aid our Lord Prince, to enhance his reputation and gain him a greater following among the younger House lords. But—" he turned to Kera. "It could also be said that you deliberately urged him to go, and secretly advised him to reject my aid, knowing that he would very likely meet his death."

There was a sudden buzzing in Kera's ears. "But I would have no motive . . . ." Her voice died away. Of course she had a motive. Of course she did.

"Exactly." Avylos was nodding. "You would have your brother's power for yourself. You would have the throne." He turned back to the queen. "And people would believe it, Keda. She is, after all, so much better suited to rule."

Kera thought she couldn't register any more surprises, but she was shocked speechless when her mother merely pursed her lips and nodded at this.

"If it had been Lady Prince Kera at Limona, rather than Edmir," Avylos was still speaking. "She would not have failed. She would have carried the day, magic or no, and we would even now be marching on their capital in her train. Edmir was a fine young man, but Kera will make the better queen, and all know it."

"But people didn't think Edmir was such a fool," Kera said, "or why would anyone have followed him?"

"You are right, Kera. They thought him courageous, and were proud to be among his friends. Still, they will be happier to follow you."

Kera wanted to deny what Avylos was saying. But she knew when she'd been outmaneuvered. Anything she could say now would only sound like false modesty—something her mother the queen would not appreciate.

And besides, her mother was satisfied now, and nothing Kera could say would change that.

"If you have no further need of me." Avylos raised the queen's hand to his lips, lowered it gently, then moved toward the door.

"Avylos."

The Mage stopped with his hand on the door.

"We will not speak of this further, since it could do Kera harm. But you will not act in such a manner again without my orders. *I* am Queen in Tegrian."

Kera made sure to keep her face straight.

Avylos kept his face impassive and his pace steady as far as the door to the consort's apartment. He could not contain himself enough to make it back to his own apartments in the Mage's wing. Rage burned through him like fire through a dry field of grass. He'd come within a breath of reaching out and snapping her neck. The cow. That she would speak to him in such a way—as if his magics were of no account. As if they were not all that kept her alive and on her throne.

She would not speak to him like this if she knew what had really happened to her precious Karyli whom she'd loved so much. She was no different, to dismiss all he had done for her, the conquests he had made possible once Karyli and his foolish scruples were out of the way.

He rubbed his lips with his hand, pushed his fingers through his hair. He could not be seen like this. He must calm himself. He could not afford to treat them as they deserved—both of them!—until he had the full power of the Stone in his hands.

Kedneara he'd expected to have to soothe and explain—she was easy, he understood her. Any explanation that praised her, or her children, would persuade. But Kera! She had been such a pleasant child. She would often come to play in his garden, and he had thought of her—when he thought of her at all—as a sweet child, even his friend. And perhaps she had been, once. Now that she had the throne within her grasp she was just like her mother. They saw him only as a tool, a servant, useful for what they could get from him.

All of them, sneaking, conspiring she-cats. All the women in his life, none of them to be trusted. First his mother—

He rested his forehead against the pane of glass. It was cool, soothing. He needed to calm down, not enrage himself further. And besides, it wasn't true. Not all the women in his life had turned on him, though it had certainly felt that way at the time. . . .

At first, he hadn't even been able to identify the feeling, it was so strange to him. He could never remember feeling content, let alone happy. But the troupe had welcomed him, had been impressed by his talents—not only as a magician, but as a mechanic. Inventing the mechanisms to help him in performing his magic tricks had given him several useful ideas that could be used in staging plays as well. When they saw that he was ready to help them and share his expertise, their respect grew.

And there was Marika. No older than himself, but wise beyond his understanding, already a widow with a small child. Matters between them proceeded rapidly, adding to his sense of well-being and contentment.

"For the first time I feel as if I belong," he said to her one night, rolling up on his elbow. He brushed her hair back from her face and kissed her eyes, her cheekbones, her lips. She laughed and rolled up to meet him, pressing her cool forehead against his own, giving him the courage to go on, to say aloud what he'd been thinking of for days.

"Marika, I could not bear to leave you. I would like to stay with you, to become a permanent member of the troupe. Marry me?"

Marika consulted her father, and the others of the troupe, and they had all agreed. He would join them. They would become his family, his Clan, his Tribe. He would not be alone again. Not excluded, not laughed at. Not hunted down.

Three nights later, they welcomed him into their ceremony, allowed him, as part of their family, to pray with their household spirits. They showed him the Stone.

And he learned what the Stone could do.

He learned he wasn't *srusha*, wasn't barren, and everything in his world changed, even his history, even his past, now that he understood what had really been happening, and just how badly his own people had betrayed him—before he betrayed them and escaped.

All that he had been, all that he had done, had occurred in order to bring him to the moment when he had first touched the Stone, and had felt the magic within him rise.

He lifted his forehead from the window and sighed. All that was years behind him. He would think of it no more.

When he was calm enough to control his face, and the way he held his body as he walked, Avylos headed back to his own wing. Almost unnoticed around him were the usual activities of the Royal House, the stewards on their rounds, pages, guards, and kitchen servants already beginning the preparations for the evening meal. In a shaft of sunlight from one of the upper windows in the Great Hall, a Knife sat beside her patient as the man—injured by a fall from a ladder while working on the roof tiles of the Westwind Tower—snored under the influence of the poppy she'd given him.

Avylos' steps slowed as he considered taking the Knife, but his pace soon quickened again. She was too useful, even though she could not help the queen. Without the Knife, he might be called upon to waste his magics on just such injuries as she tended now. Instead, he would hold her in reserve; the time might very well come when he would need her. Ordinary skills, talents, and abilities such as the Knife's were useful to him—even if not as useful as the talents of another Mage.

And he might need to feed the Stone even the Knife's meager talents sooner than he'd like.

Kedneara would not be useful to him for very much longer. And Kera . . . Kera would take handling of a different kind. Perhaps everything would need to be handled differently from now on.

Typically, Kedneara had seen the destruction of Probic only as it affected her personally. The woman thought the sun rose and set for her. *Her* message, what happened to people who invaded *her* Tegrian. But Probic's fate carried another message, one Kedneara had not considered. With Probic in ruins, and the army of Nisvea destroyed, Avylos had told the world that the Blue Mage did not need an army.

Ten

IN THE END, they did not do a performance at Vednerysh Holding after all. At least, not a proper performance, not to Zania's way of thinking. So much time had
been spent earlier in the day making sure the Mercenary
Brothers no longer looked like Mercenary Brothers that
there had been no time left for learning parts. Neither of
them had hesitated for a moment to cut their hair quite
short, and the Wolfshead had even insisted on having hers
shaved completely.

"It's the color," she explained. "The one thing everyone
knows about the Red Horsemen is the color of our hair."
She accepted a dark blonde wig which Zania had passed
over with reluctance, her fingers suddenly clumsy, and tangling in the long tresses.

"It's my mother's hair, from when she was a young girl,"
Zania said, when her hesitation became apparent. "It's
been worn since of course, many times, but never . . ." She
fought to bring her trembling chin under control. "Never
by someone outside the family. Please be very careful with
it, Wolfshead."

"And speaking of being careful," the Lionsmane inter-
jected. "We must be Dhulyn and Parno to you both from
now on, even in your thoughts. Our other names will give
us away as quickly as our badges, to those who know the
Brotherhood."

Zania considered, her head on one side. That made
sense. "If we think of you by your public names, we'll slip
up, for certain." She turned to Edmir. "We do the same

when we rehearse a new play. We make sure never to think of the other actors by their real names, lest we use them on stage."

Zania had the paste ready, and with a few practiced strokes of the brush applied it to the Wolfshead's—*Dhulyn's*, Zania corrected, *Dhulyn's* head along the front edge of her hairline and over her temples. A very small part of the Mercenary badge still showed, but Zania knew she could cover that with stage paint in an instant. Deftly, she moved the wig into place and pressed firmly along the glued edge.

"You can lift it off from the back if you have to," she told the Mercenary woman. "But the glue should hold for several days unless it becomes wet."

"Keep the beard, do you think?" Parno was saying. "I haven't shaved since Limona."

"Why not? If you're normally clean shaven, the beard will be a decent disguise in itself," Edmir answered. "I wish mine would grow in so well."

"As for you, *Edmir*," Zania said, making sure she emphasized his name. "There's no point in hiding Parno and Dhulyn if *you're* left undisguised. What do you think? I've a powder here that will lighten your hair."

"I could pierce my ears," Edmir said. He took the packet of powder from her, wrinkling his nose as he took a sniff. "I've always refused to do it because everyone at court had it done—Kera thought it would seem ordinary. So if I did it now . . ."

"People would feel sure it wasn't you, though they might not know why. Yes, that's a good idea." Zania's smile felt forced and hollow. She had always thought she'd make a good planner, but to have these people go along with her ideas and suggestions felt . . . She'd often imagined herself in charge of her own troupe, but not at this price. Not at the price of everything—and everyone—else that mattered to her. Belatedly, she realized the expression on Edmir's face had changed. She spun around . . . and froze.

Dhulyn, a slight frown on her face, had gone to inspect the clothing Zania had left out for her. After sorting through each piece she had turned her back and pulled her tunic off over her head. Her shirt had come with it, leaving her in just the wrap of silk she used as a breastband.

And a crisscross patterning of scars across her back.

Edmir made a sound in his throat. "The Mercenary Schools are much stricter than I'd thought," he said.

They both stood watching as the scars were covered by a short sleeved blouse with a tight, low-cut bodice, blue as a meadow flower. Dhulyn then stepped into a bright saffron-colored skirt, full and reaching almost to the ankles, covered over with embroidery: black, green, and a blue that matched the blouse. The wig she had caught up carelessly into a knot, letting it frame her face softly.

"Do we have to wear skirts all the time?" she asked, lifting the offending item out from under her feet as she rejoined them.

"It's a wonderful disguise for you," Parno said. "Better even than the wig."

"How beautiful you are." Zania stepped forward, surprise leading her to speak more bluntly than she normally would have.

"Thank the Moon and Stars, my lifelong ambition has been fulfilled." Dhulyn Wolfshead put the back of her hand to her forehead and sighed. Then she dropped the hand and smiled at Zania, letting the small scar curl her lip back. She laughed aloud when Zania took a step back.

"I shall have to be careful, with that, won't I," she said. "It would completely undo the effect of the Two Hearts *Shora*."

Flustered at having shown her fear so plainly, Zania had stepped in closer than courtesy usually allowed and peered at the scar. "Was it from a knife?" she asked.

"Oh, no," Dhulyn said, laughing. "The tip of a whip flicked 'round and caught me—luckily as it happened. It spoiled my looks for my owner and he sold me. It was while I was in the hands of the slavers that Dorian the Black took their ship and rescued me."

"You don't normally think of it as a 'rescue' when you're taken by pirates," Edmir said.

"You do when the pirates are Mercenary Brothers."

"You'll have to use some of Edmir's powder on your eyebrows." Parno frowned, scrutinizing Dhulyn's face. "Lighten them up a bit."

Slavers? Pirates? Zania looked from one to the other,

but there was nothing on their faces to show that they were joking. And Dhulyn *did* have those scars.

It didn't taken long to find clothing distinctive enough to make Parno and Edmir look less like soldiers and more like a couple of traveling players, but the last thing they'd done before repacking and hitching up the horses had been to pierce Edmir's ears. Dhulyn produced two silver-colored wires from the small braids she'd cut off before shaving her head.

"Let me just heat these in the fire and let them cool," she'd said.

"Whatever for?" Edmir said.

"It will help the wounds keep clean and heal faster," Parno said. "All the Knives in the Mercenary Brotherhood do their surgeries with tools heated this way."

"Or soaked in very strong spirits." Dhulyn cut the wires to the length of her forefingers and stood up. "Ready when you are."

The two Mercenaries made Edmir sit down on one of their saddlebags and Dhulyn brushed the curls—not so black now that Zania's powders had been used—back from his face to expose his ears.

"You'll want to wear your hair brushed back now," she said. "No point in wearing earrings that no one can see."

"I haven't any earrings—ow!" Edmir snatched his hand back from Parno. While Dhulyn had been fussing with Edmir's hair, her Partner had taken the prince's right hand and folded his fingers sharply in toward the palm.

"That hurt," Edmir said, shaking out his hand. "What did you do that for?"

"So that you wouldn't notice your ear being pierced." Dhulyn produced a small pair of metal pincers. "Now hold still while I bend the wire."

"You didn't need to hurt my hand," Edmir grumbled as Parno held the prince's tilted head and Dhulyn worked the wire around into a circle.

"Oh, yes, we did."

"Tell you what," Parno had said, releasing Edmir's head. "I'll let her do the other one without distracting you, and then you can tell us which you prefer."

"That won't be much use—ow!"

"There, all done."

Dhulyn took the first turn at the reins with Zania to tell her the way, while Edmir spent the first hour or so they were on the road whistling a new tune until Parno was satisfied he had it. When they'd stopped to eat, Edmir had taught Zania herself the dance that went with it.

"It's the latest at the Queen's Court," he said. "Usually, it would take months for it to filter down to these country Holdings. They'll love it."

And he was right, Zania had to acknowledge. She'd half expected their performance to be canceled, but the Vedneryshi had very quickly overcome the shock of the news from Probic.

"How can they be so calm," Zania had asked Dhulyn Wolfshead, even as she mentally stored the expressions on the faces of the Vednerysho and his spouse.

"So near the border," Dhulyn had replied, speaking in that most quiet of whispers. "They become accustomed to this type of news and alarm. And let's not forget the Blue Mage; since his coming, everyone in Tegrian is less fearful and less cautious than they once were. As for what we've told them of Probic's destruction, I would wager my second-best sword that they think our account greatly exaggerated."

Now, as Zania sat down with Edmir after performing the dance, the family seemed completely recovered from the news. The son of the Holding, whose naming day was the reason for the performance, made the Lionsmane —Parno, Zania reminded herself—made Parno promise to teach him the tune, and Zania could see that the Lady Vednerysh was already imagining herself leading the way in the next Harvest Festival.

Once the young lordling was able to whistle the entire tune himself, Parno had taken the drones off his pipes and accompanied with chanter only the three songs Zania knew best, the ones that really showed off her range and breath control. Dhulyn had joined them for one song by clapping her hands in a complicated rhythm that somehow made the song more exciting, and set toes tapping.

Now, Dhulyn herself was rounding up the evening's entertainment by reciting an old poem she said had been written by Tarlyn. She wore her blonde wig loose, and dressed in a simple dark gown that had been Aunt Ester's, with a chain metal belt painted gold. The cut of the gown made her seem much more shapely than her old clothes had. Her voice was good, Zania thought, and her gestures well-timed, if a little wooden. The Vedneryshi would think well enough of the performance, but Dhulyn would have to do better than this if they were to have any real acting in a more discerning House.

The material itself helped, of course. Zania knew Tarlyn as a playwright, but this poem was a wonderful one about a soldier king coming home after long years away at a war, only to find himself declared dead, and his house full of suitors trying to marry his queen and become guardian of his young children.

"You're sure Tarlyn didn't do this as a play?" Edmir whispered to her, as they joined in Dhulyn's applause. His breath made the curls of her chestnut wig tickle her neck.

Zania had been surprised that of the three outsiders, Edmir had turned out to be the most comfortable in front of an audience. *On the other hand, he's probably used to people staring at him,* she thought now, watching him out of the corner of her eye. *He'd have no fear of it, that's for certain.* But how was it he should be so ready to pretend to be someone else? Usually, the rich and important were quite happy to be who they were.

"Don't you see Dhulyn as the queen, Parno as the returning soldier king? You and I could, in turn, play the suitors, the children, or the servants, as we were needed."

Zania raised her eyebrows in a conscious effort not to frown where it could be taken as a comment on the performance. But why would he see *Dhulyn* as queen?

"Wouldn't the audience have to know the whole story?" she whispered back. Though Dhulyn was not up to the role, it *was* a good idea—one she should have thought of herself. *She* was the leader of this troupe. Once again, her heart caught in her chest. *Not this way,* she pushed the thought away. *I didn't want it this way.* She cleared her throat. "Because for a play," she continued, "we would have to begin as the soldier king arrives home. That's where the action begins."

Edmir waved away this objection. "We could tell them the first part of the story in a prologue." His eyes grew distant. "We'd have to change it a bit, I think. If we made the wife queen, the children could be older and still not inherit. It would give us more opportunities with the characters of the suitors. Some of the suitors would want her only for her position."

"But some would want her for her beauty." Even to her own ears Zania's voice sounded flat.

"Oh, yes, some would."

Zania pressed her lips together and stifled a snort. Fortunately, with the applause finishing, she could step forward to join Dhulyn and Parno on the cleared floor space serving as their stage, not caring whether the prince joined them for their bows or not. Edmir's eyes had been fixed on Dhulyn when he spoke, just as if she was the only woman in the world. He'd been mooning at her like that since Dhulyn had mesmerized him that morning. Who would have thought it took so little to impress the Lord Prince of Tegrian? Or perhaps he was the kind who liked women who could kill him?

After all, his mother was queen.

❧❧❧

The Blue Mage's garden was still cool, the sky just beginning to lighten. Dew was forming, settling onto Kera's clothing as she sat on her perch in the hollow made by a forsythia bush and the rough portion of the wall where the repair had been made. This had been a favorite spot of hers when she was a little girl—and still was, though she barely fit into the space any longer. The perch was sheltered, and raised enough above the ground that she could look down on almost the whole garden without being seen.

Even Kera's new awareness of the caution she had to take with Avylos could not change the feelings of peace and calm that the garden still gave her. Strange that she felt closer to Edmir here than she did anywhere else, even his own chambers—or perhaps it wasn't so strange. They'd played here as children, accompanying their father as he helped Avylos plan the garden, turning an old, disused laundry space into the Blue Mage's private retreat.

Kera hadn't thought of those times for a long while, but reading Edmir's journals was bringing so much of her childhood back to her—though, of course, Edmir didn't remember *everything* in precisely the same way Kera did herself. There was that time he'd had three of her gowns shortened, switched them while she slept, and made her think she'd grown a handspan overnight. She didn't remember it as quite so funny.

But what Kera valued most in Edmir's journals was his stories. Many of them were ones she remembered him telling, like the one about the seven enchanted princes. Some she'd forgotten, and only reading them now had brought them back to her. She'd never known that Edmir had been writing his stories down. She wondered now why he'd never told her.

At the noise of the door opening, Kera pressed back against the cold stone and froze to the spot. Footsteps crunched on the gravel of the paths and Avylos brushed past the taller plants, making his way to the edge of the pool. He stopped by the topiary, the one that needed trimming, the mountain cat almost shaggy enough to qualify as a northern lion. It needed seeing to, but Kera knew that Avylos was reluctant to let anyone into the garden to do it. Absently, his eyes still focused on the pond, he moved his hand in the air as he always did when he performed one of his magics, and the ends of the branches shivered, shrinking. He startled, as if just realizing what he'd done, and made a gesture of impatience, but Kera was no longer watching him.

The mountain cat was perfect, its haunches smooth. The branches were not merely trimmed shorter, she realized—he had actually reversed the growth. The plant was now as it had been some weeks before.

"*Blooded* fool," Avylos cursed, as he sat down on the rim of the pool. It took a moment for Kera to realize he wasn't speaking to her, and for her heart to resume beating. Her hands were pressed over her mouth, stifling the cry that had almost escaped when she saw what had happened to the topiary. Could he do that to her? Turn her back into a young child? A baby?

Was that what he was doing to her mother?

Avylos drew another symbol in the air, above the surface

of the pool, and it sank into the water, making the smooth surface glow a dull orange. Kera licked her lips. It was more than curiosity that kept her quiet and still as a mouse watching a cat. She *was* allowed here, but she had never come here alone in the night before, and possibly her allowance did not extend to the dark hours. And she should have spoken as soon as Avylos had come into the garden, *before* he'd fixed the topiary, *before* he sat down at the edge of the pool.

If she moved now, he would think himself spied on. She would have to stay quiet, hoping he never became aware of her. Because now Kera *was* curious. What was it Avylos was doing with the pool at daybreak?

At that moment the glow left the surface of the water, and Kera saw a room filled with candles and torches and people dressed for supper. She started to stand up, her mouth open, her brain rejecting what her eyes saw, but she sank down again before she made a sound.

Avylos didn't seem surprised.

At first, she didn't recognize the young man she saw wearing the fine brocaded tunic, dancing with a lithe young woman, her chestnut hair an elaborate creation of curls piled high on her head. There were thick silver hoops in his ears, giving him the rakish look of a court dandy, and his hair, an odd shade of light brown, was brushed straight back in the fashion of Imrion. And then he took a turn in the dance, kicked up his foot in a particular way, and she knew.

It was *Edmir*.

She couldn't be mistaken. Kera's hands closed tightly on the folds of her gown. She'd seen him move this way and dance a hundred times. In fact, *she'd* taught him that dance herself. And that little skip he'd added to the turn was a flourish of his own. Edmir, without doubt.

She waited until the pool was dark again, though she would have liked to go on watching her brother dance. She waited until Avylos left the garden. She waited until the sun was up before she finally allowed herself to move, stiff and chilled, from her perch against the garden's inner wall.

Her brother was alive. And Avylos knew it.

Parno opened the second saddlebag and began lifting its contents onto the blanket he'd spread on the ground. He was positive he'd seen Dhulyn stash her roll of throwing knives in a saddlebag back in the Nisvean camp, and if he didn't find them here, he had nowhere else to look.

"Once more, Dhulyn, please, and look up when you speak."

Parno looked up himself. In the two weeks since they'd left Vednerysh Holding, Edmir had been working on a dramatic version of the poem of the soldier king. He was walking Dhulyn through one of the earlier scenes now.

Their progress toward Jarlkevo was not as quick as any of them would have liked, but unlike real players, they had to spend time perfecting their disguises—and also unlike real players, they had no store of plays or scenes already learned. Both he and Dhulyn had excellent memories, and had been able to learn the lines of three short plays just from hearing Zania read them, but rehearsing the action meant stopping the caravan, and that slowed them down.

"Blessed Caids, I can't believe it." Zania appeared at his elbow, brows drawn down, mouth pressed to a thin line. "Her voice is so good, and her delivery is so nearly perfect, but she stands like a stick and moves like a broken frog."

Parno mentally sighed. Much could be forgiven in someone who had recently lost their whole family, but Zania's behavior since leaving Vednerysh Holding had become increasing difficult for him to tolerate. The little Cat seemed to alternate between treating Dhulyn Wolfshead as a long lost sister, and treating her like a useless apprentice wished on her by a doting patron.

He eyed Zania now, his hands still inside the saddlebag, and registered the look on the girl's face. *Ah. That's where the problem is.* He pursed his lips in a silent whistle.

"I would have thought your training would make it easier for her to learn new things, but it seems I'm mistaken."

Parno put down the well-wrapped packet of road bread he had fished out of the saddlebag and gave her a hard look. "We're not 'trained,' Zania Tzadeyeu. Soldiers are trained. Acrobats are trained. Dogs are trained. Mercenaries are *Schooled*." He took a deep breath. "And besides, Dhulyn meant what she said before." His hand closed on a bundle with a familiar feel and he pulled out the set of throwing knives with a satisfied grunt. "She has a natural inclination to be truthful, born into her. Slavery did not beat it out of her, and our Schooling simply reinforced it."

"So she *was* a slave? She did not jest?"

"You saw the scarring on her back. Did that look like a jest? Her people were killed and she was taken for a slave when she was a small child. The way her people count their ages, she'd only seen the Hawk Moon eleven times when Dorian the Black Traveler captured the slave ship she was on and offered her a chance to be Schooled as a Mercenary Brother."

He glanced up at his Partner, and his voice softened. "Seeing what she had been, and the use that is made of slave children, it was an offer she accepted gladly."

Zania knelt down next to Parno and began handing him the items that had come out of the saddlebag. "What use is made of slave children, then?"

Parno sighed. He'd no wish to broaden the girl's horizons in this way, but truth was truth, and warnings made good armor. "For the most part," he told her, "children don't make good servants; they're not strong enough for labor, and not yet skilled enough for anything else. People who buy slave children use them as bed partners."

Zania's hand froze with a second packet of road bread halfway to the saddlebag. He'd shocked her, sure enough, if her white face and wide eyes were anything to go by. As good an actress as she was, she couldn't control the movement of the blood under the skin. But she was, as she'd said so many times, a player. She shook herself and rallied, pasting an almost natural smile on her face. After taking a good deep breath she sat back on her heels and pitched her voice in the coy manner of a lady engaged in flirtatious concerns.

"And you, Parno? What is *your* story?" She laid her hand on his arm and stroked his skin ever so lightly with the tips of her fingers.

"Oh, I'm the natural son of the Great King of the West," he said. He looked down at her hand. "And you can stop touching me like that. Even if you actually meant it, you're too young for me."

"You're just teasing about the Great King." She did drop

her hand, however. "I could tell you were from a Noble House. *She's* an Outlander. So cold. Can't even express a true feeling. You have more culture and learning than she."

"It's Dhulyn who's the Scholar. And the fact that she expresses her truest feelings with a weapon means I've seen plenty of them." He put the last of the bundles back into the saddlebag and drew the laces shut once more. The girl was still far too close to him. He turned to face her.

"Zania, listen to me. I've not seen so many performances as you, but I know an act when I see one. Do you think no paid companion has ever approached me in a tavern? I'm not sure what your goal is, but it's a mistake to play this game. You can't come between Dhulyn and me. We're Partnered. There is no 'between' where you can fit. You've called her cold. Well, if she's cold, I am her ice."

The girl blushed a deep red, and then paled again just as suddenly. "I don't know what you mean, I wasn't trying to come between you."

"That was clumsily said; no audience would believe it. Zania." Parno sat back on his heels. "Let me tell you what I see. First, you're not truly interested in me as a man—much as it hurts my ego to admit it. Second, you're not as worried by Dhulyn's acting as you claim, or you would be helping her to better it, instead of leaving it up to Edmir. Third, it's Edmir you actually want, and you think my Partner is standing in your way."

Zania stared back at him, her mouth open, but without giving her a chance to answer, Parno called out to the two rehearsing on the far side of the clearing.

"Dhulyn, my soul, I've found the throwing daggers and Zania wants to see a demonstration."

A piece of scenery that was normally stored against the bottom of the caravan was judged suitable for the trial, and Parno stood it upright against the rear steps. Edmir looked ready to offer himself as the test subject, but Parno stepped in before the boy could speak.

"No offense, Edmir, my lad," he said, putting out a hand to hold the boy back. "But the audience will care far more about it if a beautiful young woman is at risk than a young man, however handsome. Go ahead, Zania. Take your place against the board."

With a very firm jaw—no doubt clenched to show she wasn't afraid—Zania pressed her back against the board and held her arms out, away from her body.

"Where do you want my arms—"

THUCK THUCK THUCK THUCK THUCK THUCK-THUCKTHUCKTHUCK *THUNK*

Zania froze, her words still hovering in the air, the blood draining from her face, leaving two red spots isolated on her cheeks. She looked to one side, then the other, saw the handles of the knives protruding scant fingerwidths from her skin. She took a single, measured step away from the board, turned to look at her silhouette outlined in knives. She touched one with the tip of her finger.

"It's like magic," she breathed.

"Don't think that because you've seen her clumsy and inept in one thing, you'll find her clumsy and inept in all things," Parno said. "You players have your skills, and we Mercenaries have ours."

But it was clear Zania was no longer listening to him. Her eyes were opened wide now, and the smile on her lips was pure pleasure as she turned to Dhulyn, her hands outstretched.

"We'll announce you as a royal assassin," she said, taking Dhulyn's hands and tapping out a few dance steps. "Exiled from the Great King's court. You'll wear a black wig and we'll paint your eyes in the western fashion."

Edmir wrinkled his brow. "But they'll know she's not from the Great King's Court, they'll have seen her already, wig or no wig."

"Of course they will, lad," Parno said. "It's because they'll *know* she's not from the Great King's court that they'll *know* it must be a trick. It won't occur to them it's skill and skill alone."

Zania nodded. "They'll be wondering how we're faking it. We can ask for volunteers from the audience, as 'proof' that we're not."

"And that will convince them all the more." Now it was Edmir's turn to nod.

"The cleverer they think us, the less likely they'll think we're actually doing it."

Zania still held Dhulyn's hands. "Do you think you can

fumble a bit? Make it look as though it's much harder for you? Squint at the target? We'll need to stretch the action out a bit, at the very least, to increase the drama."

"Certainly, my little Cat. This is the kind of drama I understand."

The smile vanished from Dhulyn's face just as Parno caught the sound himself. They both turned at the same time, Dhulyn dropping Zania's hands and Parno reaching for his sword before he remembered he wasn't wearing one. He slapped the dust off his leggings in an effort to cover the movement and didn't look up until the soldiers who were entering the clearing spoke.

"Don't tell me what you're doing," the woman in the old-fashioned helmet said. "I don't think I want to know."

Eleven

"THE BRIGHTEST OF GOOD days to you armsmen, and welcome!" Zania bounced over to the woman who was obviously in charge of the unit of six soldiers and gave her a deep and showy curtsy. Out of the corner of her eye she saw Dhulyn sweep forward, hips swaying in a most obvious manner, to give a curtsy of her own. Parno and Edmir stayed back, though Parno stepped away from the board that held the knives, and both gave good stage bows, sweeping the ground with their hands.

Dhulyn linked her arm through Zania's—and calm swept over her as her hands stopped trembling and her smile became relaxed. *How does she do that?* Zania thought, unaware until that moment that she'd even been frightened.

Dhulyn lifted her free hand to shade her eyes from the sun. "Welcome, indeed. Will you share our camp, Commander? We've no fresh meat, but there's water, dried fruit, and road bread to share."

The woman lifted off her leather helmet and hung it by its strap from the pommel of her saddle, revealing a grinning face and gray-streaked, sweat soaked hair. "I'm no commander, thank the Caids. Just a simple unit leader. Thanks for your offer, but we've no time to stop, worse luck. That was a fine trick you were doing just now, and I wouldn't mind seeing it again." She looked with interest at the knives stuck into the board at the foot of the caravan.

"Don't spoil it for us, Mira!" one of the other soldiers called out, and the unit leader—Mira—laughed.

"Not such a fool. Players, are you? Been camped here long?"

Obeying a slight pressure from Dhulyn's arm, Zania winked at the woman and spoke up. "As you can see, Unit Leader Mira. We're Troupe Tzadeyeu—players, singers, and dancers—at your service. My Uncle Parryn, my Aunt Dilla, my husband Edan, and myself."

As if they had been rehearsing this all morning, Dhulyn chimed in. "Camped here since yesterday evening, practicing away from the prying eyes of our public."

"Heading where?"

"To Jarlkevo, my dear Unit Leader. Sure we can't interest you in a shared meal? We don't have time for a full performance, but we could sing and play. You won't hear finer this side of Beolind." Dhulyn's voice was full of sunshine, and her smile was just as warm. *Why can't she do this on stage?* Zania thought.

One or two of the soldiers had perked up at this renewed offer and even Unit Leader Mira hesitated before slowly shaking her head.

"I believe you, Dilla Tzadeyeu, but we'll have to take our chance that you'll still be in Jarlkevo when our patrol is over. We're due back to our guard tower tonight, like it or not."

"Is the House in residence, then?"

"She is," the unit leader said. "You won't find Valaika Jarlkevoso off in Beolind like many of your fine Houses, with the Steward of Keys left in charge. And good thing for her people, seeing what's happened in Probic—and for you as well, seeing as she's very fond of plays and music."

"What's your errand, if you don't mind my asking?" Parno had come forward and slipped his arm around Dhulyn's waist.

The unit leader's face turned sour for a moment, but her displeasure was not, Zania was sure, aimed at them. When she heard the woman's answer, however, she was glad of Dhulyn's warm arm through hers.

"You'll have heard of the devastation of Probic?"

"It *is* true, then?" Parno said. "We were told, but we found it hard to believe."

"It's true enough, some of us have been there. The very

stones are melted in the streets. But some few escaped the
Blue Mage's fires, and we're looking for two Mercenary
Brothers. Have you seen any such at your performances, or
encountered them on the road?"

"Mercenary Brothers?" Dhulyn's voice had just the
right hint of confused curiosity. "We understood the Brotherhood was banished—why, almost a moon ago now. Are
these stragglers, then, you look for?"

"I wish that's all it was, Lady." The unit leader shook her
head. "A bad business. Word came from Beolind these two
in particular are wanted for questioning in the death of
Lord Prince Edmir. Them and a young man they might
have with them."

Perfectly all right to look shocked and dismayed, Zania
thought. *Perfectly normal.* She glanced at Dhulyn and saw
her lick her lips.

Parno shifted to his left, until he had his arms around
both of them, squeezing their shoulders. "What's unexplained about a death in battle, even at the hands of Mercenaries?"

"Ah, but it's said this wasn't such a death, but rather a
case of kidnap and murder by a pair of Mercenaries gone
rogue."

"Rogue Mercenaries? Is that even possible? By the
Caids, what's becoming of the world?" Parno shook his
head, but the hand on Zania's shoulder tightened enough
to hurt.

Dhulyn patted Parno's arm. "There, there, my dearest,
I'm sure there's some simpler explanation than the end of
the world. Should we be worried?" she added, turning to
the unit leader. "Is there news of them, hereabouts?"

"No, there isn't, for which we're thanking the Sleeping
God, I can tell you." There were shrugs of agreement from
among the soldiers at her back. "But formal complaint and
a request for outlawry's gone from Kedneara the Queen to
the Mercenary House in Lesonika, that's for certain, with
banishment for all in the meantime." A grumble came
from the soldier who'd spoken up before and there were
sidelong looks. Zania had the feeling none of them were
looking forward to finding or detaining any Mercenary
Brothers.

"Well, best of luck to you, Unit Leader. The Caids bless you, and the Sleeping God keep you in his dreams."

"And the same to you, players."

"Oh, Unit Leader," Dhulyn piped up just as the woman was turning her horse aside to lead the way through the south side of the clearing. "What should we do if we run into these Mercenaries?"

The unit leader frowned, suddenly looking much older. "Do the same you did with us," she said. "Offer to feed them and sing them a song. With luck, you'll get the same answer. In the meantime, if you head southwest from here, you should reach the village of Luk before nightfall, if you'd rather not camp alone." With that, she put her helm back on. The others in the unit nodded as they went past, the second to last one giving Zania an appreciative look as he went by.

"Well." When the sounds of movement through the trees had died away, Parno hugged them closer for a moment before stepping back, his hand still on Dhulyn's shoulder. "The banishment's real, then, for all that not everyone we've met has heard of it. But outlawry? *Sons of blooded demons and perverts*. Has there ever been a Mercenary Brother outlawed?"

Dhulyn rubbed her face, let her hands fall back to her sides. "I believe so. Long ago, perhaps even before Pasillon, the scroll I read was unclear on that point. The Common Rule's supposed to prevent it."

"Wonderful. Blooded Common Rule's what's got us into it this time." Parno strode over to the board and pulled a knife free. Edmir looked up as Parno passed him, a furrow between his eyes, his lips pressed tightly together.

Too many hard faces, Zania thought. *Let's have a change of subject.* She turned to Dhulyn and confronted the older woman, hands placed firmly on her hips.

"And how was it you found it so easy to put on an act for those soldiers? You who can barely walk across the stage without tripping over your own feet?"

Dhulyn raised her bleached eyebrows. "But they were soldiers. I understand them and what it takes to . . ." her voice trailed away.

"They were *people*," Zania spread her hands. "And so

are the audiences who come to see us every day." Dhulyn gave a slow whistle. "*That's* it, my dear 'Aunt Dilla,' *now* you're beginning to understand. You'll be a fine actress yet, if you stop thinking and just *be*."

Smiling, Dhulyn shook her head at Zania's words, and joined Parno at the knives. "To think it's come to this," she murmured. "My head turned by a few scraps of praise from a half-fledged girl. And this time last year, I was a god."

Parno snorted. "Don't get above yourself. You were only part of a god." He raised his voice so the others could hear. "Zania, what would your people have done, if they'd heard the soldier's news?"

"We'd have gone to the village," Zania answered. "Though to be honest, we probably would have gone anyway, business being business."

"Then let's get packed up. We'll be off to Luk as soon as we've eaten."

Parno waited until Zania had turned away before pulling out another knife. He glanced at his Partner's face as she knelt and unrolled the heavy canvas pouch, ready to slip the knives back into their sleeves. For all of her joking a moment before, now that no one was looking at her, Dhulyn's face was set like stone. She was younger than he, but she'd been longer in the Brotherhood. That made her Senior Brother, and that was all it meant, most of the time. But every now and then, and this seemed to be one of those times, something happened to remind him that for Dhulyn, there had been nothing outside the Brotherhood but loss and slavery.

"I've been Cast Out," he reminded her. "It *is* possible to survive it."

"Your Noble House didn't come looking for you, nor was every hand turned against you," she said, mildly enough.

"We're not outlawed yet, my heart. You won't get careless, will you?"

She fixed him with a sharp look from her steel-gray eyes. "And why should I be careless?"

"My heart, it's one thing to know that the Nisveans are accusing us of murder, it's another thing entirely to know that we've been denounced to our own House, and that we stand in danger of being Outlawed."

"And as you said yourself, we're a long way from that yet." Dhulyn returned the throwing knife he handed her to its pocket in the canvas pouch. "This whole thing started as a way for us to hold by our Common Rule, to keep our honor, and the honor of our Brotherhood. Though, it's true, we don't look very honorable now."

"There's an easy way for us to clear our names."

"And what is that?"

"Show that Edmir's still alive."

Dhulyn sat back on her heels. "So far, that's got him denied by one who's known him since childhood, and on the run for his life."

"I was afraid you were going to say that."

"Parno, my soul. I'm very much afraid there's no easy way out of this. Any and all might give us the same reaction we had from Tzanek in Probic. They won't know him."

"I don't like what you're saying." Parno pulled out the last knife with more force than necessary.

"It's no longer merely a question of restoring Edmir safely to his home—which the Common Rule still requires of us—now we must clear ourselves as well." She held out her hands for the last of the knives. "There might be only the one way to do both."

"The Blue Mage."

She nodded. "The Blue Mage. My soul—"

He held up his hands. "I'm not arguing, I just don't like what you're saying . . ."

But she'd stopped listening. And she'd stopped putting away knives. Instead, Dhulyn was looking at Edmir and Zania.

"You were very quiet when the soldiers were here."

Edmir shook himself and blinked. "It's one thing to know that you've been declared dead," he said. "You can persuade yourself it's some kind of mistake. But when soldiers come looking for you . . ." His lips were a thin, tight line. "The Mercenaries were right. This *must* be Avylos."

Zania stiffened. "Did you say *Avylos?* Who is Avylos?"

This time Edmir roused himself enough to look at her. "The Blue Mage, of course—ah, I'd forgotten. He doesn't like people to use his name. There's only my sister and I, and my mother the queen, who use it now my father's dead."

"Avylos is the Blue Mage?" Zania swallowed. Her voice sounded far away.

"What of it?"

"Wait." Her heart pounded in her ears so strongly she felt like the skin of a drum. Her hand shook as she thrust it into the pocket of her skirt where she had hidden Great-Uncle Therin's journal. She tore the pocket's edge, getting the journal free. She turned the pages until she found the one she was looking for. "Have you ever seen something like this?"

Edmir's eyes narrowed; he took the book from her and his brows pulled down as he tilted the page until the light fell fully on it. After a moment his brows lifted.

"Where did you get this?" he said. "Avylos has a small casket just like this one on his workroom table." He tapped the drawing of the open casket. "I've never seen inside it, but the clasps, and the handle, are identical. How can you know about this?"

"What is it has you both looking so serious?"

The Mercenaries had approached so quietly that both Zania and Edmir jumped.

"Zania has a drawing of something that belongs to the Blue Mage," Edmir said before Zania could speak up.

"Does she?" Dhulyn Wolfshead looked not at the book Edmir was handing to her, but at Zania. *I must look very odd,* Zania thought. She felt Dhulyn take her firmly by the elbow, and she heard the older woman's voice from far away.

"Parno, my soul, leave the packing. Bring food and strong spirits."

"His name when he was with us was Avylyn," the little Cat said. She held the piece of road bread Parno had given her as if she wasn't aware of it. Parno had found some brandy, and a few swallows had restored most of the color to Zania's face and something of the sparkle to her eye. "If it's the same man," she added.

Dhulyn sipped at her mug of water and swallowed. "Well, we can't know how likely that is until you tell us the full tale. You say the man was part of your troupe?"

Zania nodded. "When the troupe was bigger, the whole family together, and we had other acts—dancers, jugglers, acrobats." She looked around at them. "Shows of magic."

"And this Avylyn was your magician?"

"I don't think I really remember *him*," Zania said. "I was little more than a baby when he left us, walking perhaps, no more. But people spoke of the magic. Small things. He could light a fire even in the rain. He could call a light to sit on the palm of his hand. He could make small objects appear and disappear. I don't know if it was real."

"If it was Avylos, then it *was* real." Edmir sat across from Zania, turning his food over and over in his fingers. His eyes did not sparkle, but burned, cold and dark.

"Or it was the Muse Stone." Zania put her hand on the book in her lap.

Dhulyn put down the strip of dried meat she'd been worrying between her teeth and took another sip of water. Now they were getting to the interesting part.

"This is a drawing of it?" Parno had put out his hand for Zania's book.

"My Great-Uncle Therin said so—but we'd had it, my family I mean, forever, since there was a troupe. It was a relic of the blessed Caids . . ."

Edmir opened his mouth to speak, but Dhulyn silenced him with a negative motion of her head. Time enough later to explain the Caids were no more blessed than anyone else.

"The Ritual of the Stone was what united us as a troupe," Zania said, her voice taking on the singsong cadence of words oft repeated. "What gave us our luck and our prowess, what made us better and more successful than ordinary traveling players. Than what we are now. Until it was stolen from us. We've looked for it since I can remember. All our journeyings have been following news of it." She held out her hand for the book. "There are closer drawings of it on the next pages, and writing, but nothing that I can read."

Dhulyn waited until Zania had found the pages she wanted before reaching out herself. "May I?" she said. "There are only nine written languages," she added, as

Zania hesitated. "And three of those are found only in the Scholars' Libraries. I cannot read them all, but even if all I can do is recognize which one this is, it may be a help."

"Come," Parno said. "We know what we are all thinking. This Avylyn of yours and the Blue Mage may be the same person. If so, we are all on the same trail here, and can help one another."

Zania's smile when she finally nodded and handed Dhulyn the book was strained. *And why not?* Dhulyn thought. What a great triumph to find the thing her family had been searching for her whole life—what a tragedy that she would find it alone.

And finding was still not the same thing as having.

Dhulyn took the book and turned it over between her hands, examining it as she'd been taught during her year in the Scholars' Library. There were things to be learned from the whole of the book, not just what was found on the pages themselves. The color and feel of the cow's hide binding told her the book was old, much older than she was herself. The pages were made from very fine paper, such as was found beyond the country of the Great King in the West. It hadn't been so very long—perhaps two generations—that pages were cut and sewn into bindings like this, for easy traveling and storage. This must have been a very early example of such work. The stitches were firm, even, and small, but not in the pattern of any Library she had ever seen. This book had likely been made privately, by some early practitioner of the art.

Finally, she opened it. Unlike a copy of a work which already existed, the paper in this book had been bound blank, so it was created to be a journal, or a traveling record book. It was only about two thirds full, the final portion still blank. The same hand appeared throughout, the lettering uniformly even and neat, though larger as it neared the end, as if the sight of the person writing grew longer with age. Still, a practiced hand.

As for the language, Dhulyn smiled. Finally, Sun, Moon, and Stars were smiling on them.

"Were there Scholars in your family? Did anyone, your great-uncle perhaps, ever spend time in a Scholars' Library?"

Zania leaned forward, squinting to see what Dhulyn was looking at.

"Not that I know of," she said, looking at the book as if for the first time. "We can most of us read, but we were taught by the older ones, as we in our turn taught the younger ones."

"This is the common tongue," Dhulyn said, tapping at the words on the page. "Though it will take me some time to read it. It's a Scholar's quick way to take notes, they call it a 'shorthand.' It isn't normally found in any book, just on wax tablets and such that Scholars use to prepare longer pieces and remind themselves of stray thoughts."

"But you can read it, my heart?"

"Not so easily as I once could, it has been a long time, and it will cost me some effort, but yes, I think so." Dhulyn turned to the pages that held the drawings of the Muse Stone. "It may be smart to start here, since the writing will have some reference to the drawing."

At first glance the object Zania had called the Muse Stone appeared to be a fashioned cylinder—most unlikely that it was formed naturally in that shape. Tiny figures gave the dimensions . . . "Is this stone *blue,* by any chance?"

"I believe so, do you read that there?"

Dhulyn kept silent. Clearly, this was the same blue crystal cylinder she'd Seen in her Visions, but whether saying so would get them any further just now . . . a detail on the side of the page showed symbols carved near one end.

Four symbols Dhulyn knew very well.

※※※

A hawk-faced woman. A blue crystal. A jeweler's lens. A carving tool so fine the point of it seems like a wire.

※※※

"Dhulyn?"

"It is nothing, I am well." She swallowed, and touched the drawing again. *This,* this is what that long-ago woman—for though she could not say why, Dhulyn was sure the woman did live long ago—what she had been making.

Parno closed his hand on her wrist. "You see something," he said, the double meaning intended. "Tell us."

"The Stone may or may not be a relic of the Caids, but if your great-uncle has drawn accurately, it *is* a thing of the Marked. You said there were no Scholars in your family or troupe. What of the Marked?"

Zania shook her head while she finished chewing. "How does it concern the Marked?"

"You see these symbols?" Dhulyn tapped the detail with her index finger. "The circle with a dot in the middle stands for a Seer. This straight line for a Finder. This long triangle? Like a spearhead? That's a Mender. And this rectangle is a Healer."

"How do you know this?"

"She's Marked herself," Edmir said. "A Seer."

"But then you can—" Zania fell silent in the face of Dhulyn's raised hand.

"Wait. What I can do may be very little. And the more of the tale I have, the more I can do. Tell me," she said. "What do *you* know of how the stone was used?"

"There was a ritual." Zania looked for someplace to put down the last of the road bread she was holding, and, finally, Parno took it from her. "I should say, there *is* a ritual. Even though the Stone was gone, we still completed it before every performance, against the day the Stone would be returned. We would take hands and stand in a circle . . ."

Dhulyn caught Parno's eye and twitched her left eyebrow. This was beginning to sound familiar.

". . . and we would recite the words of the ritual, as Great-Uncle Therin had taught us. But, of course, without the Stone, nothing would happen."

"And *with* the Stone?" Dhulyn said.

The girl looked from one face to another, teeth holding her lower lip. Finally, she shrugged. "One night, Great-Uncle got drunk, and he started talking about the 'days before,' the days when we still had the Muse Stone. He said that the ritual filled them with fire, with the spirit of the Muse, the god of players. He talked about how, in those days, you could hear the audience holding their breath during Nor-iRon Tarkina's duel. He said that when he recited the storm clouds speech from *The Mad King*, the heavens answered him with thunder."

The little Cat's mouth had turned down, her eyes had lost their sparkle. "Aunt Ester started to cry, and Uncle Jovan told Great-Uncle to go to bed."

"An enhancer," Parno said. Edmir sat up straighter, his eyebrows raised.

"There are certain drugs that will improve performance . . ." Parno looked at Dhulyn. "Certain *Shora* do the same, though it's thought through focus and concentration, rather than by calling on the gods."

"Finders use their scrying bowls," Dhulyn said. "Seers vera tiles." Her brows knitted in thought. "*Whose* performance was enhanced by this ritual with the Muse Stone?"

"Everyone's. Everyone who participated in the ritual." Zania looked from one face to another. "At least, that's what I always understood. That's why we were so successful. *All* of the acts were improved."

"And it was this Avylyn who took the Muse Stone?"

"My cousin told me that her mother, my aunt Ester, said that when he first came to us, the tricks he did were just that, tricks. He claimed not to believe in any magics, questioned even the actions of the Marked, which no sensible person doubts. He said he would show anyone who cared to see how the tricks were done. Grandfather Devin was troupe master then, and he told him to keep the tricks secret, that it made a better show if the audience thought the tricks were real."

"There's irony for you," Dhulyn said, slapping her hands lightly down on her knees. "Our knife throwing is real, and here we are trying to convince our audiences that it is just a trick."

Zania smiled, but her heart wasn't in it. "You know what I mean," she said.

"I do indeed," Dhulyn said. "What's real is a trick, and the tricks are real. That's theater for you."

For a moment Zania looked as though she would argue, but then the light faded out of her face.

"Let me see if I can shorten this tale," Edmir said. "This Avylyn learned of the Muse Stone, learned how to use it, and one day he was gone, and the Stone also."

"And the troupe broke up, first the smaller acts drifting away, the acrobats, jugglers, and jesters. Then the family split up and we have been looking for him and for the Stone ever since." Zania looked around at them, her face set and determined. "I must go to Beolind."

"So must we all. These revelations change nothing for us," Parno said. "If anything, it just makes plainer what our task will be once we are in the Royal House. Confront Avylos, restore Edmir, and regain the Stone."

"Jarlkevo still gives us our best odds of doing that," Edmir said.

Dhulyn shook her head. "I must have time to read the book first," she said. "Who knows what there may be in it that will help us defeat the Mage?"

"But in Jarlkevo—"

"Certainly, if your aunt knows you, and will support you, hide you," Parno said. "But that is a great many 'ifs,' perhaps too many. Dhulyn is right, we need to do this *before* we reach Jarlkevo, in case we do not find an ally there."

"What of this Luk the unit leader spoke of?" Zania said. "It's not uncommon for a troupe of players to stay in one such village several days while they try out a new play. We could be doing both."

Dhulyn looked up from the book. "Did your troupe initiate all its members to the use of the Stone?"

Zania's brows drew down in a sharp vee. "They had to show some talent, I think. Sometimes Great-Uncle would say we were 'ready for the Stone' when we'd done something particularly well." She looked up. "And they could not be people who had joined us for a season. Only firm members of the troupe would be taught the ritual."

"And Avylos did this?" Was it a question, Dhulyn thought, when you knew the answer? "He became a firm member of the troupe?"

"He became my mother's man. He took part in the ritual with the rest."

"And likely found his powers enhanced, and his magics real instead of tricks."

"All this happened when you were still a babe—he's not your father, is he?"

The color drained completely from the little Cat's face. She got to her feet and backed away from them, shaking her head. Before Dhulyn could retract her words, Zania turned and ran, pushing her way through the low bushes into the deeper forest. At a gesture from Parno, Edmir took off after her.

"Ah," Parno said, as Edmir disappeared into the wood. "That went well."

Dhulyn looked sidewise at him and smiled her wolf's smile.

"Zania, Zania stop."

Edmir had caught hold of her sleeve and Zania, out of breath, her heart pounding in her ears, wasn't strong enough to jerk it from his grasp. He took her by her upper arms and shook her until she grabbed the front of his shirt.

"He can't be your father, do you hear me? You don't look like him, nothing like him at all. His coloring's completely different, he's very pale, with dark red hair and very blue eyes. Even if you took after your mother, there'd be *something* in you of him, and I tell you there isn't."

"I just thought . . ." she swallowed and tried to make her fingers loosen their grip on his shirt. "Sometimes it seemed that they treated me with extra care, my family, as if they were watching me. I told myself it was because my mother died when I was still so young. . . ."

"Of course it was that," he said. But Zania shook her head, her eyes squeezed shut.

"Look at me, you half-wit." Shock opened her eyes again.

"Were you a normal girl?"

"What?"

"You're not a blessed Caid, are you? Incapable of doing wrong? Because you could have fooled me. Did you never behave so badly that you made your aunt or uncle—or more likely your cousin, furious with you?"

Heat flushed her face. "Let go of me!"

"They would have said something then, don't you see? If he had been your father, they would have thrown that in your face when you angered them. Any normal person would. People say things they regret when they're angry." As Zania stopped struggling, Edmir lowered his voice.

"They'd have told you if Avylos was your father, to punish you—and to explain to themselves why you were bad.

Don't you see, he can't be your father. They would have said."

Her heart resumed beating. "He's not my father. He's not." She rested her head on Edmir's shoulder. He smelled of woodsmoke.

"Zania."

She felt his breath against her ear and lifted her head. His lips felt very soft and warm on hers.

Twelve

AVYLOS SLID THE THICK glass lens off the map he'd been scrutinizing and let the parchment roll closed. He rubbed at his eyes, and straightened, stretching out his back. He selected the next scroll and unrolled it, using small carved stone weights to hold down the corners. Like the others, this map showed a section of northwest Tegrian, on a scale large enough to display roads and tracks, Houses, Holdings, and even certain Households. The lens revealed tiny drawings, and notations in a neat hand. Avylos moved the lens over to the area he wanted to examine, and blew out his breath in frustration.

When he'd seen Edmir in the pool, he'd seen a clearing in a wood with a fire laid and burning. A sword resting against a rock showed the Mercenaries were still with him, though the magic of the pool did not show any other people. The trouble was that there were so many wooded areas in Tegrian where the particular combination of trees—pine, ash, and birch—could be found. Even supposing that Edmir would choose one of the most direct routes to Beolind from Probic, Avylos had still found four different spots his camp could be in.

And patrols were already in these areas, and none of them had found Edmir, or the two Mercenary Brothers with him. Was it possible that they had left the country after Probic? And gone where?

Avylos tapped his lips with his fingers. Perhaps he should also look at routes to Hellik. It would not be beyond the possible that Edmir would try to reach his relative, the Tarkin.

His eye was caught by his own name magnified by the lens.

"Avylos." The Lady Prince Kera stood in the doorway. "I was told you were here."

And Avylos could guess who had told her. He'd passed that new Balnian page in the corridor. Evidently, the blooded boy would babble about anything and everything.

As Kera came no farther into the room, Avylos glanced up again. She must have come from attending her first Royal audience as Lady Prince. She was wearing her brother's coronet, the circlet of twisted gold-and-silver wires almost disappearing in her red-gold hair. Avylos was surprised to note that Kera looked younger than usual, like a child dressed in grownup's clothing. Was she finding it lonely, to be in her brother's place? Could he turn that to his advantage?

"Come," he said, rising and moving one of the other chairs closer to his own seat. "Sit by me. There is something here I would like you to see."

He waited until Kera had sat down next to him before moving the lens once more over the place on the map he'd noted.

"Do you see this writing?"

Kera leaned forward. "It's so tiny."

"It was made using a lens—no, not this one, another, suspended in a stand. This is your father's writing."

Kera leaned still farther forward, this time with interest, not mere politeness, and touched the miniscule letters with her fingertip.

"Your father was my best friend," Avylos said. Kera looked up, blinking, as if seeing him for the first time. Avylos smiled inwardly.

"People forget that, you know." He frowned down at the map in front of them, and then glanced at her from under his brows. "My best friend. I was still a young man when I came here, unsure of my powers and untaught. Pursued by those who would use me for their own ends. Your father's friendship and protection changed all that. He gave me a home, a place to belong, a quiet and safe place to study my art."

Avylos took a deep breath, and tapped the place on the right side of his blue tunic where the consort's coronet was embroidered. "Now everyone sees this and forgets I was your father's friend. No—" Kera had opened her mouth to speak, but Avylos held up his hand. "Even you and your brother forgot. Perhaps especially your brother. It occurs to no one that when your father died, my sanctuary died with my friend."

And so it had, in a way. Karyli had been the brother— the family—he should have had. Avylos had even come to feel that Karyli actually did not care whether he had power or not, whether his magics worked or not. The first person since . . . who had loved him for himself. Who took him seriously, trusted and understood him. Avylos came to feel that he, too, could trust his friend. So much so, that a desire began to form in Avylos' heart, a desire to tell his friend, his brother, what it was he had done. Karyli would understand, Avylos had told himself. Karyli would agree that in the face of the resentment and oppression Avylos had suffered at the hands of his own people, Avylos had done the right thing, the only thing. Karyli would forgive him.

Kera had lowered her eyes, her brow furrowing in thought. Her coloring was so much like her father's. His eyebrow had wrinkled in just that way. Avylos risked a smile. It was working. She was considering what he'd said— what he'd lost, as well as what he'd gained. Kedneara's affections were real, but they were volatile, capricious, especially since Karyli's death—who would know that better than Kera herself? So perhaps Avylos' gain wasn't, after all, as great as it might appear. Kera was considering, perhaps for the first time, that he had pursued her mother the queen not for power, but for the protection of being the consort.

Avylos took another deep breath, letting it out in a shaky sigh. "What I tell you now," he said, "no one else knows. It was not only for myself that I became the consort. After all, I am the Blue Mage, and while my powers were not as great then as they are now . . ." He shrugged. "But your father's last words to me were 'Watch for Kera and Edmir, swear to me you will watch for the children.'

"I know both you and your brother blamed me for marrying your mother. And Edmir blamed her as well, I know this. But I assure you, Kera my Lady Prince I swear to you, I married your mother in order to fulfill my vow to your father. I could not risk that she would marry someone else, get other children, send me away from you as she sent so many others of your father's circle." He reached out with his left hand, stopping just short of touching her sleeve.

Kera, her eyes still on her father's handwriting, reached out her own hand with the Lady Prince's seal ring on it, and patted Avylos'. There was compassion in her face.

Again, he risked a smile. Kera was a good child, with a kind heart. She would take her father's place and become his friend. And he would never make the mistake of telling her that his family, his Clan and Tribe, had betrayed him out of jealousy and greed, hiding his magic from him. Never tell her how he'd punished them by betraying them in turn to their enemies. That he'd watched them killed down to the last child, their tents burned, their herds taken or scattered.

He would never have to tell Kera how her father Karyli had reacted not with love and understanding, but with horror and disgust. And had died, moments later, gasping for air.

As he watched Lady Prince Kera leave the map room, Avylos trusted that she would never force him to deal with her as he had dealt with her father.

Kera waited until she was well down the corridor, and even around a turn, before she wiped her hand off on the skirt of her overgown.

⚛

"It's not *my* guesthouse, you'll understand." Farmer Bar Wilseyeu, prosperous if her inglera wool tunic was anything to go by, opened the wooden door of the single-story stone structure that made up one of the four sides of the village square. On the other three sides were the farmer's own house—two-storied—the mill, and a Jaldean Shrine featuring the sigils of the Three Planting Gods along with the more customary sign of the Sleeping God.

"I keep it ready in the name of House Jarlkevo, for guests who might need it. Players are always welcome, of course, especially if, well, if there's any chance of a performance." She looked up from under the edge of her leather cap, a tentative smile on her face. Her rough palms rasped as she rubbed them together. "There's time to send word to those who live nearby."

"Send it, my good lady, send it," Parno said, with an actorly flourish of his embroidered gloves. "Give us a chance to wash off the dust of the road, and take a bite of supper, and we'll be at your service."

"Well, as for that, it's late to roast anything, but we've a goodly supply of sausages still, both kinds, and some of the winter hams are just now ready for trial. And there's bacon, which I smoked myself. We'd be happy to have you join us."

"And we'd be happy to come," Parno said. "And perhaps we've news to exchange as well."

"We've heard about Lord Prince Edmir." The farmer's face lost its jovial expression. "All the more need for us to find cheer where we can. The Sleeping God curse those blooded Nisveans—and those Mercenaries, too, if it's true what's being said, and they're involved. Hard to believe it, but there it is. These are hard times." She turned and spit on the ground, saluting the Planting Gods in the farmers' way.

"A true word, my friend, a true word. Has the news of Probic preceded us as well?"

Farmer Wilseyeu turned back, her mouth hanging open a second before she shut it with a snap. "It's not good news, that much I can see from your face. Save it, will you? Tell it but once. Come up to the house when you're ready, and I'll send round to the outliers to come in."

After more than half a moon on the road, even Edmir, not used to fending for himself, was finding the routine of unpacking familiar, and it took them much less time to sort themselves out, choose what they would perform for the local people, and put their hands on scenery and costumes than it had done when they were only a few days out of Probic.

"If it's cheering up they want, I'd say the comic scene from *The Barber's Wife*," Zania said, once they had carried their choices into the guesthouse. Dhulyn thought her voice sounded distant, and the girl was careful to direct her words and attention to Parno—as Edmir was careful to offer his help to Dhulyn.

What has happened between these two? From the stiffness of her smile, and the way she kept her eyes lowered, Zania seemed about ready to cry. And she wasn't the type to cry because Edmir had made advances —more likely, Dhulyn was careful to hide her smile, because he *hadn't*. But now it seemed that something had made these two uncomfortable with each other—unless it was something else entirely. Zania could be excused almost any emotional behavior. Had she not lost all her family and Clan? It had been only, what . . . a moon? A few days more? Dhulyn's own experience told her that these thoughts could never be far from the surface for Zania.

"What about this?" Parno picked up the thick parchment scroll Edmir had just rolled shut, tying it tightly with a loop of leather, and tossed it into the air. He quickly followed it with a painted crown from the open property box in front of him, one of last year's apples plucked from the bowl on the table next to the property box, and the knife he pulled from his own belt. His juggling was clumsy for the first few passes, as each item, different in shape and weight, fell and resisted the push of the air in a different way. In moments he had the feel of it, however, and the items flowed in a smooth stream.

"Here," Dhulyn called and tossed him a thick bracelet to add to the mix.

"I didn't know he could do that," Zania said, her face brightening.

"I'd forgotten myself," Dhulyn said. "I think he once had younger siblings to amuse."

"You *think?*"

Dhulyn turned to her, smiling. "Mercenary Brothers do not have lives before our Schooling began. We leave all that behind us."

For the first time, the little Cat did not flinch from Dhulyn's wolf smile. "And does that work well?"

"Sometimes better than others, but that is the Common Rule."

Parno tossed the bracelet back to Dhulyn, replaced the painted crown, tossed Edwin back his scroll, and with a flourish impaled the apple on his knife, taking a bite out of it before giving them a deep bow. "What do you think," he said to Zania. "Start with a little juggling, *The Barber's Wife*, and music for the rest?"

"Nothing that would weigh too heavy on the heart. A sad song or two, just for flavoring," Zania agreed. "Give them an opening for their grief to leave them. But for the most part, light and happy."

"But not the knife throwing, my little Cat." Dhulyn made it a statement and not a question.

The girl nodded, looking into the middle distance. "Too soon, I think," she said. "We need to work out the patter a bit more."

"Dhulyn, what's Pasillon?"

Thank the Caids, Dhulyn thought. She preferred always to take care of the horses herself, and had sent away the boy the farmer had lent them. Edmir had followed her out and she'd been very much afraid that the prince would use this chance to unburden his soul about whatever had passed between him and the little Cat. Perhaps there had been nothing, after all.

"Where did you hear about it?" She watched him over Warhammer's back. Edmir had gone straight to untie Stumpy, without being asked. For a Lord Prince, Dhulyn thought, he made a decent stableman, which was more than she could say for many a son of a Noble House.

"This morning, after the soldiers were gone, you said that there might have been Mercenary Brothers outlawed before Pasillon. I meant to ask you then, but," he shrugged, "there were other things to think about."

Dhulyn ran her hand along Warhammer's neck and flanks, taking comfort from the horse's quiet strength. "Long ago," she began, "after the time of the Caids, but long ago for all that, two city-states fought, and Mercenary Brothers carried arms on both sides."

"Fought against each other?" Edmir paused, his fingers on the buckles of the long traces.

Dhulyn looked at him sideways. "'In Battle or in Death,' it is our greeting and farewell. We are all of us, all living things, walking on a path toward our deaths, and for a Mercenary Brother, to die at the hand of one of our own . . ."

She shrugged. "What better way?" She led Warhammer out of the traces and into the first stall. "In any case, one party was victorious," she said. "But at the cost of their prince's life, and so, in their anger, and their grief, they spared no enemy soldier, cutting them down as they fled, killing them as they lay wounded in the field."

"Like at Limona." Edmir's voice was hollow.

"At Limona they took prisoners for slaves. At Pasillon there was not even that cold hope." Dhulyn turned her attention to Bloodbone, caressing the mare's long nose. "This would have had nothing to do with the Brotherhood, except that in their fury, and the heat of their blood, the victors saw no reason why a Mercenary badge should free anyone of the price they wished to take, and so they began to kill Mercenary Brothers as well."

"Oh, no."

"I see you know enough of our Common Rule to anticipate my story." Dhulyn waited, her fingers working on a knot in Bloodbone's mane. "Those of the Brotherhood who were of the winning faction ran to the aid of their Brothers, but they were outnumbered, and so they died."

"But not all?"

"So the story goes. Against fearful numbers, they held their ground until nightfall, allowing three Brothers to escape. And after that night the victors began to die. Not everyone. Just those who had killed Mercenaries that day. The officers. The lords who gave the orders." She accepted the coil of harness from Edmir and took it into the stable, the boy close on her heels.

"So that's why a request to outlaw a Mercenary Brother has to go through your own House."

"We take care of our own." There was a flaw in the reins, as if the edge of a knife had scored it. She rubbed at it with her thumb. "Defend one another if we are in the right, punish one another if we are in the wrong. We cannot allow others to do it."

"But you *can* be outlawed."

Dhulyn nodded.

"What a play it would make." Whatever Dhulyn expected him to say, it wasn't this. "The leader of the winning side—do you know which it was? His great grief, stained with his arrogance, bringing about his downfall. His growing awareness of the march of his own doom."

Edmir's eyes had taken on that faraway look, the look that meant he was seeing the actors on the stage, hearing the words leaving their mouths. Dhulyn shook her head and left him there, going to join the others.

The evening's performance seemed at least to have restored some of the youngsters' good spirits. Parno's juggling had been warmly appreciated, with contributions from everyone in the audience, especially the children, and the comic scene from *The Barber's Wife,* good physical humor, seemed to have helped release the tension she'd earlier sensed between Edmir and Zania. They came back into the travelers' quarters still buoyant and smiling, even taking hands and dancing a short measure across the guesthouse's dressed stone floor. This had been an audience of farmers and the like, and so the performance had been over earlier than it would have been at a House or even a Holding, where some at least would have stayed up reveling longer into the night. Dhulyn leaned back against the edge of the table and watched, wondering whether the twinges she was feeling in her lower back signaled the approach of her woman's time, or just the unfamiliar exercise of dancing.

"That was well done, very well done, all," Zania said, spinning around to bless them all with her smile. "Only one thing I would say to be careful of and that's for you, Parno." She stepped toward him and put her hand on his arm. "That place where you have delivered your speech to the Barber and you must step to the side, you were supposed to wait, and move at the same time Dhulyn did, so that her movement covered yours. You moved after her, during her speech, and so the audience's eye stayed upon you, and so you drew off some of the effect of her speech. In the future, remember to wait, and move as she does, and you'll be a help instead."

"Like an army in the field," Parno said. "Each doing their part in support of the whole."

"We should have a signal," Dhulyn said, trying to stretch out the muscles of her back, "as we do in the field, to set us right again when we stray. Something the audience will likely not know or recognize."

"Pasillon." They all looked at Edmir. "Something to remind us that we work as a team, and not in conflict with one another."

Parno looked at Dhulyn and raised his right eyebrow. She smiled and shrugged. "Why not? In this endeavor, at least, we are as Brothers."

"Dhulyn, my Dhulyn," Zania sang, dancing up to her and taking her hands. "I have had a great thought, a brilliant thought. I just can't imagine why none of us have thought of this already. You're a Seer, yes? So why don't you See for us? See what we must do next?"

Edmir looked back and forth between the two women. Satisfaction warred with curiosity on his face. Parno caught Dhulyn's eye, his lips pursed in a silent whistle. Dreading the disappointed expectations, her immediate response was to refuse. It was one thing to See for herself and Parno, they both understood the limitations of her Mark. But when she looked at the eager faces of Zania, and Edmir . . .

Had she not just said that they were as Brothers?

"Not a bad idea in itself," Dhulyn said, managing to release her hands from Zania's without hurting the girl. "But let me warn you. Do not expect too much. The Visions are never clear, and even when I think I am directing them, they do not always show me what I ask to See."

Parno ducked into the room he and Dhulyn had chosen for their own and came out carrying the olive-wood box that held her vera tiles. Edmir cleared the tray holding a jug of cider and clean clay cups from the sturdy square table, as Dhulyn took the box and seated herself on one side. The others took the other seats, watching her as she spilled the tiles out on the table's worn surface.

"But these are vera tiles," Zania said.

"A little more than that." Dhulyn picked up the tiny moleskin bag that held the one unique tile in the set, the Lens tile which was the focus of all Seeing. "You see these tiles here? They're not found in the ordinary sets of vera tiles. You'll recognize these symbols from the drawings of your Muse Stone, the symbols of the Mark. The eye, the line, the rectangle, and the triangle. Seer, Finder, Healer, and Mender, four of each."

Parno sat in the chair next to her and began turning tiles face up, and she slapped his knuckles. "Each of you find a tile to represent yourself. One of the major tiles, Tarkin, Tarkina, Mercenary, Scholar, or Priest, and pay attention also to the suit, Coins, Cups, Swords or Spears. Whichever one feels right to you. Hold it a moment in your hand and give them to me as I ask you for them."

Dhulyn set the Lens tile in the center of the space she had cleared by pushing the tiles to one side. She placed her own tile, the Mercenary of Swords, just above it, and a Seer's tile above that. Edmir chose the Scholar of Cups, she noted with an inward smile. So the Lord Prince of Tegrian did not see himself as a Tarkin, or even as a Mercenary. And he did not see himself as Sword or Spear. As she expected, Parno chose the Mercenary of Spears, and Zania the Tarkina of Coins. Trying to make no conscious decision, letting her own internal Sight make the decision for her, Dhulyn placed Parno's tile below the Lens, opposite her own, Zania's to the right, and Edmir's to the left. Next to Parno's she placed a Mender's tile, with its spearhead symbol. Next to Zania's the straight line of the Finder, next to Edmir's the rectangle of the Healer.

She studied the cross formed by the tiles for the space of three heartbeats before nodding, and pushing the remaining tiles back into their box. Keeping her eyes on the tiles in front of her, she reached into the box and pulled out the first tile, setting it on top of her own. Six of Cups. For Edmir, the four of Swords; for Parno, the nine of Swords; for Zania, the three of Coins. For all of them, a Finder, the two of Spears, the seven of Spears, the Priest of Spears. No, the Mage.

The high walls of the garden hold the moonlight like a deep bowl holds water, washing all color from the trees and flowers. The pond is a black diamond held within the setting of its stone rim. For a moment Dhulyn thinks there is someone seated on this stone edge, but it must have been a trick of the light. There is nothing there. She looks up, and there is the girl sitting in a niche created by a rough section of the garden wall and thick piece of hedge almost as tall as the wall itself. Dhulyn waves her arms; sometimes she can be seen by the others who inhabit the Visions, but not this time. The girl watches the pond, as if someone is there, but when Dhulyn looks again, there is no one.

But there *is* an image in the water. Dhulyn moves closer, and the image is clearer, though still without color. It is Edmir, asleep, dreaming. He frowns and rolls over on the bed, his arm sweeping up to cover his eyes. The shadow on his palm created by his curled fingers looks like a curl of hair. . . .

There is Edmir, again on his throne. His robes are the brilliant blue of the sky in winter, there is a circle of leaves shining gold against his dark hair. He puts aside the long two-handed sword he is holding across his lap, handing it to the armsman who stands to his right. Edmir stands and approaches the front of the dais. He raises his hands to speak, and the crowd hushes. . . .

This is her mother, again. Her mother as a young woman, who never had the opportunity to be an old woman. She is in the garden again, dressed in her lady's gown, her hair bound and swinging down her back. She swings a sword . . . a stave. No, it is a sword. And she fights a slim-hipped, dark-haired man who wields a very familiar sword.

It is Parno. When she looks closely at him, the dark wig disappears and she sees his red-and-gold Mercenary badge, with the black line of Partnership threaded through the pattern. In what possible past can this be? In what possible future? Dhulyn looks more closely at the woman she takes for her mother. No, the features are clear. Whoever this person is really, for the purposes of the Vision, she is Dhulyn's mother. Parno is armed with his second-best sword, the one with the nick in the guard, and he is using it to defend himself against the blows of the Espadryni woman. But all he does is defend, and this makes him slow and weak. He will lose if he does not attack. He does not want to kill this woman, but she wants to kill him.

Fight, my soul, she tries to say. *Don't let her kill you. Fight and return to me.*

In Battle, or in Death. . . .

Zania holds a blue crystal cylinder between her hands, thick as a man's wrist, as long as Dhulyn's forearm. Shining blue like the deep ice that traps the glow of the stars. The Muse Stone. A drop of blood falls from Zania's nose to the Stone. There is movement in the room behind her, but Dhulyn cannot make it out in the bright blaze of light that comes from the stone.

Dhulyn pushed back from the table. "Hard to say whether there was anything helpful," she said, her voice coming dry and creaking from her throat. She took the cup of water Parno gave her with a nod of thanks.

"I Saw you on your throne, Edmir, something I've Seen before. And you, Zania, you were holding what appeared to be the Muse Stone in your hands, though I could not see around you."

"But that's good. That means we'll find it." Zania's smile was enough to add light to the room.

"That is one of the possible futures, yes," Dhulyn croaked. "But now you see the limitations of my Sight. *How* will we find it? How can we ensure that is the future we attain? What must we do—and leave undone—for that future to arrive?"

"And are they things we *can* do, or are willing to do?" Parno added.

"But we do know that it's *possible,*" Edmir said. "Even if we don't know how *likely* it is."

"True, and so we go ahead." Dhulyn massaged the muscles around her eyes with her fingertips, lowered her hands, and looked around at them. "Perhaps there is something in your book, Zania, that may help make my Visions clearer. It has happened so in the past."

When they were alone in their own room, Dhulyn sat flipping through the pages of Zania's book.

"I Saw you fighting someone," she said, without looking up. "It seemed to be my mother."

"Which is why you didn't mention it to the youngsters."

She nodded. "This is becoming a nightmare," she said, not meaning her Vision.

"Yes, it is," Parno agreed.

"Sleep my soul. I will read."

Several hours later, her eyes gritty with her effort to concentrate on the Scholar's shorthand in Zania's book, Dhulyn got up, stretched the kinks out of her back, and put out the lamp she'd been reading by. In the morning she would have to find paper, something on which to make her own notes. When her eyes adjusted, she made rounds through the other rooms, checking that Zania and Edmir both were asleep and undisturbed. Edmir moved as she started to close the door of his chamber and she froze, but he only rolled over, his arm sweeping up to cover his eyes. He had left the shutter open, and there was enough moonlight to make a shadow on his palm, created by his curled fingers. It looked like a lock of hair. *"Blood,"* Dhulyn said.

Thirteen

"WHY SHOULD AN IMAGE OF Edmir appear in a pool in a garden?"

Parno rolled over. The open shutter let in enough light to show him Dhulyn standing, fully dressed in her player's clothing, by the window. He propped himself up on his elbow.

"Is that what's kept you restless all night?"

She nodded.

"What else was in the image?"

She turned and moved toward him, silent as a shadow. "At first, I thought I saw someone else there, seated by the side of the pool. But I looked again, and nothing. There was, however, a young girl, hiding, watching from some distance away."

Parno scratched at his mustache. "Is someone watching Edmir? I would hate to see the fires that destroyed Probic come to Luk," he said finally.

"By someone, you mean the Mage? All I know for certain is that I saw no one else but the girl. The image was of Edmir asleep in his bed. . . ."

"And possibly his location cannot be discovered from that."

"Possibly."

Parno looked at her. She knew as well as he did how many people could be killed with only a "possibly" to lead the way.

"How long will it take you to read the book?"

"I must have paper."

Parno swung his legs out from under the covers and reached for his leggings. "The Jaldeans will have some."

It was quiet on the steps of the caravan. Zania had been sitting out here long enough to watch the hamlet come to life for the new day. The sun was barely up, but a young girl had come from Farmer Bar's already to bring them breakfast and see to their horses; others had gone out to the fields, and somewhere the milking was being done. This time of year, there would be hay to bring in, if nothing else. But the square itself was quiet.

Zania had woken up sometime before dawn, and finding herself unable to go back to sleep, she'd hoped that coming out to sit somewhere familiar would help to still her racing thoughts. Last night when they'd gone to bed, everything had seemed possible. Dhulyn had Seen the Muse Stone, and even the question of how they were to achieve what the Vision had shown them—well, as Dhulyn had said to her last night, "today's troubles today, tomorrow's for tomorrow."

Somehow, when she woke alone in the dark, the questions had all come flooding back. And now it *was* tomorrow. Zania realized that she hadn't really given much thought to what it meant, getting the Muse Stone back. It had been something Great-Uncle Therin was going to do, with Uncle Jovan. When she'd thought about it at all, she'd imagined a dramatic confrontation, with perhaps herself and her cousin Jovana—Jo in a minor role, of course—a denunciation of the thief, a restoration of their rightful property to enthusiastic applause. To find out now that it was the Blue Mage himself who had the Stone. *The Blue Mage.* Had Great-Uncle Therin suspected anything of the kind? What was she to do now? She was the only one left. . . .

"Where is everyone?" Edmir startled her. He had a meat pastry in his hand, taken from the dish the farmer's girl had brought them. There had been a jug of water as well as the makings for ganje.

"If you mean Dhulyn and Parno, I saw them going across to the Jaldean Shrine a while ago."

"The shrine?" Edmir looked over his shoulder to where the facade of the other building caught the light from the morning sun. "Of course," he added, nodding. "They *are* Mercenaries, they're probably followers of the Sleeping God."

When Edmir turned back, their eyes met, and he blushed.

Zania looked down at her hands, clasped between her knees, hoping she looked relaxed and uncaring. There *had* been one other subject on her mind, other thoughts that had chased themselves around her brain all night. Edmir had said nothing about kissing her. Unless, she eyed him sidewise, unless he'd been waiting for them to be alone.

Though it seemed Edmir wasn't going to say anything after all. He leaned against the corner of the caravan, which put them more or less at the same height, but he was staring off to one side, frowning as if he'd heard Parno play a bad note. Zania cleared her throat.

"Do you think Dhulyn will be able to read my book?"

"Hmm?"

Nervousness changed to irritation. He wasn't even thinking about her.

"You're supposed to lift your left index finger if you're writing in your head," she said in her crispest voice. "If you've lost some precious words of *The Soldier King*, you've only yourself to blame."

Edmir turned to her and smiled. Zania felt her ears grow warm.

"Zania," he said.

Something in his tone made her glance quickly away. *Here it comes,* she thought, her heart speeding up. *Now we'll talk about the kiss.*

"Zania, is the play good?"

"What?" The buzzing in her ears faded, leaving a cold quiet behind it.

"*The Soldier King,* is it a good play?"

Zania was so surprised, she forgot her shyness and turned on the step to face Edmir fully and frankly. His eyes were lowered again, and she could see the wrinkle in his forehead, between his bleached brows, the set look to his lips, as he braced himself for her reply. She could make an easy answer—either the quick, cutting slap down or the smooth reassurance—but neither felt right, somehow.

Parno had said that she wanted Edmir. Zania had thought about that, and before their kiss she'd almost persuaded herself that it just wasn't so—that she wasn't interested in Edmir in the way a woman was interested in a man. But if she was going to be honest, there *was* something about him, something she'd never noticed in any other young man. *Of course, he is a Lord Prince; that will set him apart from the others.* But she didn't think it was only that.

Maybe her interest *had* started off that way—many a traveling troupe was sponsored by a House lord or lady who had a lover among the troupe, and what better sponsor than a Lord Prince? If anything, the kisses they had shared yesterday had shown her how easy that could be for them. But they had also shown her something else. Kisses were easy, knowledge was harder. She knew him now, and liked him for himself. Which meant she had to set aside her wounded pride and answer his question truthfully, seriously.

"It is a good play," she said finally. "Among the best I've heard, and I've heard many." She took a deep breath. "But you know this, you've looked through the ones we have in the chest, you've heard enough of the pieces we've been practicing. You know it's good."

"I'm just using Tarlyn's poem."

"No. What you're making is a good deal more than Tarlyn's poem ever was. That's just a story—a good one, maybe, but a story just the same. Your play is different, it's more *real* somehow."

"Thank you. It's not often you say something that doesn't sound as though you were quoting a line."

Zania opened her mouth and shut it again. There was really nothing to say to that. She eyed him more closely. There was a different kind of frown on his face now.

"There's something else worrying you, isn't there?"

"When I think about everything that's waiting for me when we reach Aunt Valaika's House . . ." He shook his head, lips a thin line. He looked at her and tried to smile. "We'll sort it out somehow. My sister says that when she's worried about how something will turn out, she thinks about how things will be afterward, when the worrisome event is long over. What will *you* do when it's all over? Take your Stone and lead your own company?"

"Of course, I—" The words stuck in her throat. The troupe she had wanted to lead was dead in the hostel courtyard in Probic. Weeks dead. And she would never rise to be their leader. They would never vote for her in the fullness of time. That was over. Gone.

Her breath caught in her throat.

"They're all gone," she whispered, sobs rising. "They're all gone, and I don't *know* what to do."

Edmir was appalled, frozen with horror as the girl he'd privately thought so strong and practical, rather hard, really, even if the idea of Avylos as a father had frightened her—the girl he couldn't believe he'd had the nerve to kiss—bent over, face buried in her hands, and broke into wrenching sobs. He reached out a tentative hand to her shaking shoulder, and drew it back. What was the right thing to do? Nothing growing up in the Royal House had prepared him for anything like this. There, the girls took care that he never saw them blotchy-faced and weeping.

He chewed on his lower lip. What would he do if this was his sister, Kera? That thought released him. Gently, careful not to startle her, he put his arms around Zania, stroking her on the back and making every soothing and sympathetic noise he could think of.

"We'll think of something, you'll see," he said as the sobs finally began to die down. *She hasn't cried at all,* he realized. *Not at all since it happened.* This reaction was long overdue, and all the stronger for being repressed. "Look at everything we've thought of already. A knife throwing act, a new play. Having the Muse Stone back will change everything. Who knows, maybe the Mercenaries will stay with you."

"You don't really believe that," she said, lifting her head but remaining within the circle of his arms. Her voice was a croaking echo of its normal self. She dabbed at her eyes and nose with the wide sleeve of her blouse. "They're Mercenary Brothers, not players."

"And I'm a prince, not a playwright." Edmir blinked. Those words had come out sounding much more bitter than he'd intended.

Zania moved away enough that Edmir had to lower his arms or look like a fool. "And you'll go back to being a prince," she said, dabbing again at her eyes. Was it his imagination, or did she sound regretful?

For a moment he imagined himself beside her like this for the rest of his life. Writing plays, watching her act in them. Watching their children act. Then he pulled himself together.

"We must deal with Avylos." His voice sounded harsh even in his own ears. How could he tell her that he had to steel himself to push her away?

"Of course," she said. "No use casting the parts before the play is written."

Edmir licked his lips. There was something else he'd like to say. . . .

Dhulyn Wolfshead came around the corner of the caravan, her arms full.

"We've found paper," she said. "The Jaldeans had a supply they were willing to sell us—whatever is the matter? You two look as though someone has killed your pony."

Dhulyn set out her pens, her small bottle of ink, and the paper she'd purchased from the Jaldeans to her right, opened Zania's book, and placed it to her left. The muscles in her lower back spasmed, but the pains had not yet moved around to her belly. They would come soon, she judged, but perhaps they would not be too bad this time.

"Is there anything you need?" Zania was in the doorway. Her voice sounded thick. Obviously, the little Cat had been crying, but Dhulyn judged it was not trouble with Edmir. The two had been upset when she'd come upon them at the caravan, but the way they stood with one another showed the problem did not lie between them. The kind of crying that left those signs on a woman's face—Dhulyn recognized those feelings, and knew there was nothing to be done. It was hard to be the only one left, to have no one of your blood, kin or Tribe. Hard not to hate yourself for rejoicing in your own life. Good that the girl had cried, finally.

In the meantime, the little Cat needed something else to occupy her thoughts. And to keep her out of Dhulyn's way.

"I have an idea, little Cat," Dhulyn said. "Do you re-

member we spoke of *Nor -iRon Tarkina*? While I am reading your book, why should Parno not teach you a *Shora*
that you could use in the dueling scene? Slowed well down,
it will show very nicely on stage."

Zania gave a dim but genuine echo of her usual smile.
"We'll make a player of you yet," she said.

Dhulyn went out with her and caught Parno's eye. They
went through possible *Shoras* while Edmir helped Zania
pull out the stage swords from their storage spot on top of
the caravan.

"Rutting Ram *Shora* it is, then," Parno said. "Two people, one sword each, a series of strong attacks—perfect for
the purpose, if I make them clash enough."

"Make up a different name for it," Dhulyn said. "Something grows between these two, and it would embarrass
them."

Parno shrugged. "They're of an age. Together all day, every day, with similar tastes and goals—for the moment at
least. Of course they're falling in love."

About to head back to the guesthouse, Dhulyn turned
to look at her Partner. "This is just a camp romance, then?
It will fade away when the campaign is over?"

"Haven't you ever fallen in love?" Parno looked at her
sideways.

Dhulyn smiled the smile she gave only him. "No."

"Get to your reading, woman."

"There, that's enough for now. We'll try it again tomorrow, and next day and the next, until I know you won't forget it."

Edmir nodded, breathing deeply, his hands on his knees.
Even slowed down, the Mountain Ram *Shora* took strength,
concentration, and skill. It had been almost a moon since
he'd last held a sword in his hand with any intent, and he
was embarrassed to see how out of condition he was. It
helped that Zania was also blowing and out of breath, but
not much.

"I'm for the bathhouse," Zania said, handing Edmir her
sword. "I'll see if Dhulyn is ready for a break from her labors."

Edmir climbed up to the top of the caravan, and Parno
passed him up the swords. "Thank you for showing us that."

"It will be useful to Zania to know how this type of thing is done—and good training for you, once you return to your own station in life."

Edmir licked his lips as he slid the swords back into the pack they'd come from and began retying the cords.

"How is it that you came to leave *your* station in life?"

The silence lasted long enough that Edmir became afraid he had somehow stepped over a line. But when he jumped down once more to the ground, he saw that Parno was merely considering his answer.

"You know that the Common Rule holds that we put aside what life we had before the Brotherhood?"

"I know that you've already mentioned your House was nobler than mine," Edmir pointed out a little sourly.

Parno laughed and clapped him on the shoulder. "True, so no reason not to answer your question." Parno continued smiling, but his eyes grew serious. Edmir had a strange feeling that the Mercenary Brother knew exactly what had prompted the question. Which was strange, seeing that Edmir wasn't sure himself.

"I didn't leave my House," Parno said, serious now. "I was Cast Out."

Edmir felt suddenly cold. The man he'd been trusting all this time, admiring, respecting . . . an outlaw?

"Don't look at me like that, lad. Are we not even now, ourselves, being looked for by soldiers and guards?"

Edmir felt his face grow hot. "I beg your pardon," he said. "I didn't think."

"No, well." Parno shrugged. "A kinsman insulted my sister," he said. "The Kir of my House—do you understand? Do you use the term here?"

Edmir nodded. The Kir was the heir of a House.

"Good. I struck the Kir of my House, and . . . disfigured him. He insisted on my being Cast Out. My father had to obey, or he would have lost everything, and my sisters as well. As it was, the eldest of my two sisters inherited."

"And the Kir? Is he now the House?"

"Alas, no."

Edmir answered Parno's grin with one of his own.

But the humor faded from the older man's face, and Parno's eyes narrowed.

"Edmir, listen to me. I thank the gods every day that I am where I am. I *did* choose to become a Mercenary Brother, but my House was already behind me. I would no more have chosen to leave my House than I would choose to leave the Brotherhood now, or break my Partnership—supposing such choice were given me. I cannot break these bonds, these oaths. Nor could I have left my House. My oaths and my bonds to them were just as strong. I would never have *chosen* to break them. Do you understand?"

"Yes, I think so."

"Do you? I would not have left my father, my mother, and sisters in danger if I had not been forced to go."

Edmir's nod was very slow; his head felt so heavy, and his ears were hot with shame. He *did* understand. He knew what Parno Lionsmane the Chanter, Mercenary Brother, was telling him, Lord Prince Edmir of Tegrian. He, too, had oaths and bonds, responsibilities and obligations. He could not choose to break them. Lord Prince Edmir could not leave his sister, nor his mother the queen, in the hands of the Blue Mage.

He would think of such things no more.

Dhulyn studied the page in front of her. The ends of the Stone *twisted,* but according to the notes, they did not stop in any particular place, even though indicator marks suggested they would. She looked more closely. Yes. The indicator symbol on the one end *was* the concentric circles of the Lens, while the symbol on the other end was a crescent moon. Interesting.

She lifted her hands and mimed holding the Muse Stone. *"Gehde. Gehde. Mones. Aharneh."*

"No, it's 'aHARneh,'" said Zania's voice from the doorway.

Dhulyn looked up, and slowly straightened her back. She should know better than to sit so long in one position, but it had been years since she'd studied anything with so much concentration. The feeling that she could not let time slip away was nagging at her.

"That's the Chant of Opening," the little Cat said, as she came into the room.

"Then I would take it that 'Ahar Ahar Mones GeDERneh'

is the Chant of Closing." Dhulyn frowned down at the book in front of her and made a notation on the paper to her right.

"So we always practiced it." Zania took a seat at the table, pulled a sheet of paper covered with Dhulyn's neat handwriting toward her. "You can read the Scholar's code, then?"

"It's not a code, exactly, just a way to write things quickly. To take notes at lectures, for example."

"And does my great-uncle say where he learned such a thing?"

"Not directly. But he does mention a trip to the Library of Ishkanbar. Apparently, when he was himself a young man, his grandfather took the Muse Stone to the Scholars there, to see what they could tell him of it."

"And what did they say?"

"A relic of the Caids," Dhulyn thought, thinking of that fair-haired woman with the long-fingered hands she'd Seen in her Vision. Had she been a Caid, then? For what purpose had she made the Stone?

"According to your great-uncle, at the time it took much persuading to get it back out of the hands of the Scholars." Dhulyn sighed. "If I had time, my little Cat, I would translate the whole of the book for you. There is much here that would be of use and interest, much that has nothing to do with the Stone. It was only when your great-uncle began to feel the first twinges of age—and that was astonishingly recently—that he thought to write down what he knew of the Stone." A movement made Dhulyn glance over. "I know. Why use the Scholar's shorthand if he meant this as a record anyone could use?"

"Do you think Uncle Jovan would have known the shorthand, too?"

Dhulyn nodded. "If, as you say, reading and writing were taught to you by your elders. Your great-uncle would have taught his son and heir, never thinking they would both be carried off at once."

Dhulyn grimaced as the light went out of Zania's face. *That* had been entirely the wrong thing to say. A distraction was needed. She put out her hand for the page Zania had taken.

"There appears to be at least three other chants," she said. "And there are symbols on both ends of the Stone."

"So you've told us, the symbols of the Marked."

Dhulyn shook her head. "That is just the one end. On the other are symbols I do not recognize, though for some reason I feel I should. See here, I've drawn them larger, do you know them?"

Zania drew down her brows, then her face cleared. "There's a tunic with these symbols embroidered into it, do you think that's where you've seen them?"

"I haven't seen a tunic such as you describe," Dhulyn said. Now it was her turn to frown. "In fact, I know that I haven't seen these particular symbols before, only that they seem familiar."

"What of the other chants? The opening and the closing are the only ones I've ever heard."

"Your uncle calls the others 'Null Chants.' He says that the Stone glows when they are spoken, and the ends turn, but nothing happens."

"I wonder if Avylos the Blue Mage has found a way to make something happen?"

"That is a most unpleasant thought." Dhulyn drew her finger down the list of symbols she had drawn. A crescent moon. Three geometric patterns—not unlike a Mercenary badge, she thought—a Healer, a Mender, a Finder, a Seer. And finally a Lens.

❧❧❧

This is the boy in the woods again, the red-haired Espadryni boy. Younger, unbruised, unbloodied. But still in the woods. He is drawing in the air, very slowly at first, and then faster and faster. But nothing happens. Something should happen, Dhulyn realizes. Colored light should follow the path of his finger, leaving a symbol drawn upon the air. How does she know this? The boy draws more symbols. Nothing. Nothing. He pounds the ground before him with his fists, grunting in frustration and rage. She takes a step forward and he looks in her direction. But he frowns, chest heaving, tears streaming down his red face, puzzlement coming to replace the rage. . . .

***

Complete darkness. So dark, so heavy, for a moment Dhulyn imagines she cannot breathe.

Edmir?

❊❊❊

"Dhulyn?" There was worry in Zania's voice.

"I think I've read enough," Dhulyn said. Her own voice sounded hollow in her ears. "Tell the others, we eat, then we ride."

Fourteen

"YOU ARE SOONER THAN I expected you, Squad Leader Olecz." Avylos set aside the ancient scroll he had been studying when the squad leader had been announced.

"We completed our first search very quickly, my lord Mage, and were on our way to the second village when we encountered a patrol sent out from Tsarin with the same errand as ourselves. You did not tell me, my lord Mage, that there would be others."

"No, I did not." Avylos stared until the other man lowered his eyes.

"Of course, my lord Mage." Olecz licked at his lips. Good. Let him remember to whom he was speaking. In the sweat beading on Olecz's forehead was the knowledge of what had been done in Probic.

"Continue," Avylos said.

"Yes, my lord Mage. We found no signs of the persons we were looking for, nor did the other patrol. The only persons of interest encountered were a team of inglera shearers on their way home after their circuit, a troupe of players, five men hiring out for work in the hay fields, and three bandits living in the forest east of Luk."

"Players." A cold grip on his heart. "A large group?"

"No, my lord Mage. One small caravan, with four people. We were told three women and an older man, if memory serves."

"And the bandits?"

"I saw them myself, my lord Mage. A man and two

young boys, one of those a runaway servant. Not the people we were sent to find."

Avylos leaned back in his chair, let his hands rest along the arms. "Very well," he said. "Return to your regular duties. Await my future instructions."

The bow Olecz gave him was fully as deep as the one he would have given to Kedneara the Queen. That almost made Avylos feel a little better. Almost. He tapped the arm of his chair with the side of his right fist. He couldn't spare any more magic to keep looking for Edmir in this way. If he kept this up, he would have to recharge the pool in the garden, and he did not have enough power left for something like that. Not unless he could find someone else to tap, someone who had the same level of power as that dice boy.

He would have to follow the trail in a more ordinary way.

He realized that he had placed his left hand on the casket that held the Stone, and pulled the hand back again. No help there, no help until he unlocked the secret of its stored power.

He reached for his maps of Tegrian.

❧❧❧

Valaika Jarlkevo pushed the lists in front of her farther away. She clasped her hands at the back of her neck and pushed her head back against them, trying to loosen the tight muscles of her shoulders.

"That bad, is it?"

Valaika looked up, a smile coming automatically to her lips. Only Sylria would come in without knocking, and only Sylria would ask such a question so bluntly. Valaika released her hands and leaned back in her chair. Any interruption was welcome, but this was better than most.

"Anyone who can read a balance sheet can see we've no more people to spare for Kedneara's armies."

"You mean to say 'Kedneara the Queen.'"

"I mean Kedneara my blooded sister-in-law the Queen, yes." Valaika pulled one of the sheets of paper closer. "As if farming isn't hard enough in these mountain valleys, I sent her every able body *last* season, and we were promised no more would be needed *this* season."

Sylria crossed the room from the door, her house slippers noiseless on the rugs, and seated herself in the wide, padded chair on the other side of the table. Like Valaika, the other woman was dressed entirely in dark blue, the queen's colors, to remind all who saw them that they were directly related to the Royal House, and in mourning. Instead of the usual badge in the Jarlkevo House colors of orange and black, both women followed the custom of Hellik, Valaika's homeland, and wore an embroidered crest, in the shape of a bear's head, on the left side of their tunics.

"I would have thought, after Probic, that Nisvea would have been the last of our worries, but no, Kedneara wants another levy of soldiers."

"What possessed poor Edmir to break the treaty? *That* war should have been at least two years away." Sylria took up the jug of watered wine that sat on the table and poured herself a cup. "And what possessed him to take so few with him. And what, for that matter, possessed the poor child to get himself killed?"

"I should have stayed in Hellik." Valaika addressed her inkpot. "Failing that, I should have stayed in Beolind." She looked up at Sylria. "All right, so I would have killed somebody out of sheer boredom, or been killed myself. How bad could that have been?"

"You've said that many times, and let me remind you of what I've told you, each and every time. If you'd done any of that you wouldn't be House Jarlkevo, important in your own right and not just as the consort's sister. You wouldn't have the land, and the people, and yes, the responsibility. And you wouldn't have Janek to become the House after you, and take the responsibility from you, and, not least I think, you wouldn't have me."

With a grunt, Valaika rubbed her face vigorously in both hands. "You're right, of course."

Sylria leaned forward again and pulled a large sheet of parchment toward her, studying the figures, crossed out and rewritten, and the notation on the bottom of the page. Her brows raised.

"Here I'd been thanking the Caids that spring was early and mild this year, but if your figures are correct, we won't have enough ice in the cellars to keep the stored meat from thawing."

"Of course my figures are correct." Valaika poured a glass of wine for herself. "The question is, should we let it thaw, and salt what we can to send to Kedneara in place of the soldiers we don't have? Or should we cook it all, give the Valley a feast, and tell Kedneara's Steward of War that we have nothing to give?"

Sylria twisted a lock of hair around her finger as she considered. "That would work. So long as the Blue Mage doesn't take occasion to look in this direction. He has uncanny ways of finding things out."

"He's no reason to look this way," Valaika said.

"True." Sylria put the sheet of parchment down. "Don't we have stewards for this work?"

"They're out bringing me more information."

Which Sylria well knew, Valaika thought, eyeing her consort with a frown. Valaika liked to go her own way in more than just the crests they wore on their clothing. Here in Jarlkevo she'd insisted on breaking that ridiculous custom that had spread from the Letanian Peninsula which kept the Steward of Keys confined to the House proper for life, and the Steward of Walls confined within the fortified walls of the town. Hard enough to do in a large House such as was found in the capital. Barbarous to impose here, where winter weather was often bad enough, for long enough, to set the occupants of a House gritting their teeth at each other.

Valaika tapped her lower lip with the feathery end of her pen.

"Is everything all right, Syl? I know you didn't come here to go over the accounts with me."

Sylria roused herself from whatever thoughts had put that frown on her face and smiled. "There's a troupe of players come to town," she said. "A small one, but new faces, and maybe new songs, who knows? Janek would love it, and he deserves a treat after the hard work he's put in this winter. Or is a moon not considered mourning enough?" she added, when Val didn't speak.

Valaika leaned back, her elbows on the arms of her chair, and rested her folded hands on her belt buckle. "I hadn't even seen Edmir for six—no, perhaps it's seven years," she finally said. "It would have been at his father's burial ceremonies. Janek was only five, I think, wasn't he? And formal mourning doesn't forbid theater, in any case. Where are these players?"

"Their caravan's in the courtyard of the Hostel Plazan. The players themselves are walking through town singing for business."

"What odds do you give me they won't know any Hellish songs?"

"Is that any reason to go without entertainment?"

Valaika grinned. "Go ahead, invite them up here and send word around the town that as many as can fit into the courtyard will be welcome. Let Janek know he'll be allowed to stay up."

❧❧❧

"So, this is Jarlkevo?" Zania said the next afternoon, as they stepped out into the street from the courtyard of Hostel Plazan. They'd changed into their brightest clothing, the better to catch the eyes of their potential audience. Parno walked ahead with his pipes, playing familiar country dances, interwoven with the songs children use in their games. Already they were being followed by a few children, escaped from their lessons and chores, and even one or two idling adults.

A familiar series of notes made Dhulyn glance ahead at Parno. Since they had been in Imrion last year he had added that particular children's rhyming song to his store of music, embellishing it as he did everything that touched his ear.

"Technically, House Jarlkevo is the whole of the territory, and we've been in it since the day after we left Luk."

"And 'House' is also the title of the person to whom the land belongs," Edmir added from Zania's other side.

"And who belongs to the land, in the old way of thinking," Dhulyn said. "The House *is* the House. The territory is the person, and the person the territory. Now Jarlkevo House, on the other hand, is the residence of House Jarlkevo. The Jarlkevoso, she'd be called in Imrion, though I don't know whether that's the practice here."

"How do you know all these things," Edmir said.

Dhulyn tapped her temple, where the wig hid her Mercenary badge. "It's our business to know these things." She turned to call out a greeting, blowing a kiss to a smith looking up from his forge, a horseshoe glowing brightly in his tongs. "The town looks prosperous enough, though it's larger than I would have expected in a newly created House."

"It used to be a Holding of the Royal Family," Edmir said. "A performance, good sir," he called out at an elderly man who had paused to watch them and their trail of children. "At dusk in the courtyard of the Hostel Plazan."

"Is there good hunting in the area?" Dhulyn asked.

"According to my mother, Jarlkevo was used as a summer Court, and I do vaguely remember coming here as a child—at least I think it was here—before it was made into a High Noble House, and given to my Aunt Valaika."

Dhulyn nodded.

"Yes, madam, yes, good sir, a performance this very night, a small taste only of what we can do, to whet your appetites against the morrow." Zania had stepped ahead of them, holding out her arms and pirouetting down the narrow street.

"Which explains the size of the town," Dhulyn said, as she smiled and blew a kiss at a young man with a wheel of cheese on his shoulder. "Good hunting or not," she continued as Edmir raised his eyebrows at her, "this town is too large for a place visited for just a few weeks out of the year. But as a summer retreat, and now the seat of a Noble House, and at that of the late consort's sister, a woman who is still the niece of the Tarkin of Hellik—or do they call him King there?" Dhulyn shrugged. "In any case. With your Aunt Valaika in permanent residence here as House Jarlkevo, the town had reason to grow."

Just at that moment a young woman in the long vest of a House servant—orange and black with a narrow dark blue band around the bottom edge—stopped Parno where he was playing several spans ahead of them. He listened to what the servant had to say, and turned toward them, a smile on his face.

"We're invited to the House this evening, isn't that lucky?"

"And as much of the town as can make it," the messenger said, loud enough for the townspeople around them to hear.

Dhulyn glanced at Edmir, but other than a slight tightening of his lips, there was no reaction to the invitation at all. *The boy's learning,* she thought. She nodded to Zania.

"Return our most grateful acknowledgment and respectful greetings to House Jarlkevo. We will await her summons after the midday meal."

"We should do *The Soldier King*," Dhulyn said. She turned to Zania. "If you think I'm ready to perform it."

Parno smiled. A capable expert in her own field, Dhulyn had no difficulty bowing to the expertise of another, even if that other was so much younger than herself. They had set up their small table in the hostel's courtyard and were eating a light meal of rabbit stew and dried apples in preparation for the message that would summon them to the House.

"You're ready, though a week ago I wouldn't have believed it possible. That's not what makes me hesitate," Zania said. "It's a long play, and fairly serious . . ."

"The Jarlkevoso would be in mourning, though, wouldn't she?" Dhulyn turned to Edmir. Parno thought the boy looked paler than usual, and he'd been quiet and more thoughtful since the talk they'd had in Luk. Judging by the way he was getting through his bowl of stew, however, his appetite was fine. Edmir nodded in answer to Dhulyn's query, but his eyes remained hooded.

"She'd be expected to mourn six moons at least, though she's not known for her conservative approach to social things," he said. He looked up. "Theater's allowed during mourning, but something serious *would* be more suitable."

Parno smiled at the boy's querying tone. Edmir wanted to see his play performed, but he didn't want to seem to be suggesting it.

"Listen." Dhulyn leaned forward and tapped the tabletop with the end of her spoon. "This may be our only chance to perform it —certainly Edmir's only chance to perform in it himself. After tonight, he will be the prince again, and he will have walked on the stage for the last time."

Edmir's hand stopped halfway to his mouth, the piece of bread he'd been using to sop up the stew's gravy dripping on the table until Zania's nudge brought him back to himself. He smiled guiltily and wiped up the mess with the cloth that had been used as a potholder when the dish was brought out to them. Parno glanced at Dhulyn and saw that she, too, was watching Edmir. So, he wasn't the only one who thought the boy didn't seem as happy as he should be, considering they were taking the first step along the road that would restore him to his birthright.

"There's another consideration," Parno said, and waited until they were all looking at him. "The play's about a king who comes home from the wars after everyone believes him dead, correct? No one recognizes him, and he has to trick his way into his own home before he can reveal himself to his family?" Zania was nodding, and Dhulyn smiling. "Under the circumstances, what better play *could* we put on?"

⊱⊰

Jarlkevo House was an old-fashioned, square-towered fortress, standing at the highest point of land within the walled town. What had once been a lonely crag of rock with strategic command of an entire valley was now a steep hillside lined with narrow streets and the openings of houses and buildings that appeared to be hanging from the face of the rock itself. Clearly, space was at a premium.

"I've seen larger courtyards at some country inns," Edmir whispered to Parno, as the Mercenary stopped to try the tautness of the rope securing the screen in front of them.

"You'll not find the rooms within to be very spacious either, I'd wager," Parno agreed as he turned away to check the next rope.

Edmir looked out from behind the screens he, Parno, and Dhulyn had earlier set up across the short end of the courtyard. There were a great many more people out there than the murmuring voices and sounds of movement had led him to expect. A raised platform had been set up perhaps halfway between their stage and the far end of the courtyard. This platform had seats for several people—and children had already taken up places on the front edge, following a bold, brown-haired child in deep blue—but there were two padded chairs covered with a canopy which were obviously intended for his aunt and her consort, Sylria.

Edmir frowned. He remembered their son, his cousin Janek, as a rather sickly child, coughing and pale, though letters from his aunt had reported the boy much improved in the last few years. Apparently, however, he was not improved enough to attend this evening's performance since there was no chair of state put out for him. Too bad, Edmir thought, remembering the boy's trusting brown eyes as he'd stood next to Edmir at his father Karyli's burial ceremonies. Later, in his mother the queen's private sitting room, they had played a game of tiles while the grown-ups talked. He'd taught Janek and Kera both to play the Sparrow game. He hoped the boy was all right. Janek was his only cousin, and besides Kera, the only living relative of his own generation.

Edmir's stomach clenched suddenly and he tasted acid in the back of his throat. He was beginning to regret having eaten anything at all; even the half bowl of stew and few mouthfuls of dried apples he'd managed to wash down with watered cider felt like lumps of stone in his belly. Dancing in public was easy, even speaking—he'd done as much before his parents and their Noble Houses since he was a child, to say nothing of functioning as his mother the queen's representative. And he'd thought the half dozen parts he'd done in the last moon or so had accustomed him to acting and the stage. Tonight felt entirely different. This was *his* play, these were *his* lines, *his* words. Even before the battle in the Limona Valley his stomach hadn't felt this queasy. Soon he'd have to step out to give the Prologue—Dhulyn had insisted he should do it—but right now he savored the comfort and safety he felt behind the scenes.

The screens themselves were canvas stretched over light frames of wood, painted on both sides to make the most use of them. Like much of the troupe's properties and costumes, the scenery was normally laid flat on top of the caravan, covered over in heavier canvas against the weather. These particular screens were painted to look like a garden or perhaps a wood on the side currently facing the audience, and like a stone wall on this side. The play opened with the Soldier King coming through the forest where he had hunted as a young man, and the meeting with the old huntsman who would be the only character who recognized him right away. When they were ready, he and Parno would swing the screens around and they would end the play in front of the painted stone walls that represented the castle. Zania, in her costume as the old huntsman, came up on his left side; he grinned at her, glad of the distraction.

"There were more of these when I was a child," she said, running her fingers lightly along the crosspiece of the screen of scenery. "I remember one in particular that was a lady's private bedchamber, with tapestries painted on the walls. I remember my mother standing in front of it. I don't know who has it now." Her voice was wistful.

"This was before the troupe spilt up to look for Avylos?"

She nodded, and then pointed with her chin in the direction of the unseen audience. "Is *she* out there? The House?" On the Mercenary's orders, they'd all been careful to refer to Edmir's aunt by her title only, in case anyone should overhear them, and wonder at their use of her personal name.

"I thought I saw her walking into one of the doorways on the far side of the courtyard, but I'm not sure." He scratched at the pointed chin beard that Zania had carefully glued to his face for his appearance as the Prologue. That, along with the long formal robe he was wearing, was meant to make him unrecognizable to anyone who may have seen him in the Queen's Court. Or on the funeral coins that were already circulating.

So far, at least, it seemed to be working.

Parno rejoined them and put his hand on Edmir's shoulder, giving him a little shake.

"Ready? The House and her consort have just come in and taken their seats."

Edmir, clenching his teeth, shot another quick glance at the audience and nodded. Parno patted him on the shoulder, and Zania squeezed his arm. They each took careful hold of the handles on the screens in front of them and pulled them aside just enough to give Edmir an entrance.

He swallowed again and stepped through. The crowd noticed him and hushed.

"Long ago, and far off," he began. "Among the lands of the Great King . . ."

Valaika leaned forward, chin on hand, elbow on knee, when the Prologue stepped out from behind the screens. He was a tall young man with sun-streaked curly brown hair, wearing a short, pointed beard slightly darker in shade. He was richly dressed, like a courtier at a formal audience, and, unexpectedly, his accent was Tegriani. There were not so very many players in Tegrian, and Valaika thought she knew them all. And she was certain that Sylria had said these came from elsewhere.

But the play was beginning now, and she turned her attention to the action.

When she saw the Prologue again, in the second act, it was as one of the suitors of the widowed queen. He wore the same formal tunic, though now he was beardless, and his hair had been brushed straight back from his face, revealing his jeweled earrings. He walked with the kind of swagger that made Valaika hope that, at the very least, this character would not end up winning the queen's hand. He was making the queen—a striking woman indeed with eyes like gray pools in her white face—a very pretty speech, which somehow had an iron threat in the back of it.

"Mother." Janek had come up from where he sat in the front with his friends to whisper in her ear.

"Not just now, my heart, if you please. It's rude to speak during a performance."

"But, Mother, that's Edmir."

"What?" The boy was addled. "Janek, mind your tongue. That can't be. Edmir is—"

"Mother, please. Look at him carefully."

Janek was so insistent, so serious, that Valaika swallowed the reprimand that was rising to her lips and looked back at the stage.

A maidservant—Valaika swore she'd seen her earlier as the aged huntsman—had come on stage to offer the queen and her suitor refreshment in the form of goblets of wine. The queen took her goblet, but the suitor waved his away with a lifted shoulder and a short chopping movement of his hand.

Valaika sat up so abruptly that she banged her elbow on the arm of her chair. She'd seen that movement before. That *exact* movement. The question was, where had this actor seen it?

"See! See!"

"Hush, Janek."

Sylria laid a hand on her knee. "What is it?"

Valaika leaned over so as to whisper in Sylria's ear. "We must invite them to stay after the play. Ask them for music, anything."

Sylria frowned, shrugging her right shoulder in question, but Valaika shook her head and indicated the stage. No point in ruining the show for the rest.

And it was a testament to the play itself, and how well it was acted, that Valaika didn't remember her request until she was standing with the rest of the audience at the end of the play, clapping and shouting.

Fifteen

"WHERE ARE YOUR PIPES?" Dhulyn felt along the edges of her wig. She'd sweated so much under the torches kindled for the final scene—but it seemed the glue still held. She knew she should be pleased at this summons to meet with the Jarl kevoso and her family. They had been wondering how to get a private audience with the woman since they'd received their invitation to play in the courtyard, but this felt a little too pat, a little too easy. It seemed that since picking Edmir up out of the battlefield, everything that should have gone easily, hadn't. Dhulyn did not think of herself as a superstitious type—like all Red Horsemen, she believed that humans made their own luck, since the gods of Sun, Moon, and Stars had larger things to occupy them—but the fact remained that when it looked as though some god was helping you, that was the time to be most wary.

"Relax," Parno addressed her feelings rather than her question. "What's the worst that can happen?"

She stopped tightening the ribbon laces in her bodice and looked at him. "Oh, very funny."

He put his hand around her wrist, the palm warm and callused against her skin. "Seriously, what is the worst that can happen?"

"We die separately."

His hand tightened. "We are always together," he reminded her. "In Battle."

"Or in Death." And she felt better.

As they followed the two pages who served as their

escort through the narrow halls and steep staircases of the House, Dhulyn took automatic note of bottlenecks and potential escape routes. The prince was silent, pale, and tense, as she would have expected. For him the next few hours—even the next few minutes, could mean everything. Zania walked beside him whenever she could, at one point reaching over and straightening the cuff of his sleeve. Dhulyn smiled and looked away.

It wasn't long before the pages were ushering them up a short circular stone stair on the western side of the fortress, through a thick wooden door padded with blue leather and into what was clearly the family's private chamber. In addition to the door from the stairway, there were three windows with shutters in the wall opposite, and a smaller, lighter door to the left, in the far wall of the rectangular room. Dhulyn saw no fireplace, though an unlit brazier stood off to one side of the chairs gathered in the center of the room. Obviously, the family's summer sitting room, Dhulyn thought, and even now there was a chill in the air that made her glad of the thick rugs still on the floor.

There were three people waiting for them, Dhulyn saw with interest, as she made her formal bow from the doorway. Their hostesses were seated with their backs to the windows in large chairs upholstered on arms and seats with brocaded cloth. But beside them, clinging to the arm of Valaika's chair and fidgeting with excitement, stood a slim, young boy who had seen his birth moon perhaps ten times. This brown-haired, ruddy youngster would be the son and heir, she thought, Edmir's cousin, Janek. There was a smudge of dirt on the boy's cheek, which told Dhulyn much that she liked about his parents. All three were dressed in loose trousers, long-sleeved tunics, and half boots, though there was no mistaking which one was the House, Edmir's Aunt Valaika. She had the same strong features, though her nose was considerably more prominent. Her hair was much fairer than Dhulyn would have expected, with silver threads among the gold, her eyes a piercing blue, and her skin a golden brown not unlike Parno's natural coloring. The consort, Sylria Jarlkevo, was taller, slimmer, with chestnut hair and ruddy skin. Valaika Jarlkevoso had a sword within reach of her hand; both her consort and her son carried only the knives at their belts.

"Here they are, my House," the page said when they were all in the room.

"Thank you, Rudian. Welcome, Troupe Tzadeyeu. Before you sit down," Valaika said, with a smile for her guests, "let me present my consort, Sylria, and our son, Janek Jarlkevo. He's been dying to meet you since he heard there were players in the town." The Jarlkevoso's voice was very rough and low, with a Hellish accent buried deep beneath a few decades of living in Tegrian. So deep, Dhulyn thought, that perhaps she wouldn't have noticed it if she hadn't known the woman was Hellish.

"And threatening to run off with you when you go," the consort said. *There* was the educated Tegrian accent Dhulyn was used to hearing from Edmir.

"We never take people from their homes, young man, until they've reached the age to be apprenticed," Parno said with a smile as they all bowed their heads in acknowledgment of the introduction.

"Please, seat yourselves."

Drawn up to face the two seated women was one backless armed chair with a cushion on the seat, and next to it a small wooden bench with a thin pad made of embroidered cloth. Dhulyn lengthened her stride slightly, to put herself in front, and took the chair for herself, seeing out of the corner of her eye that Parno had claimed the far end of the bench, leaving Edmir and Zania between them. Dhulyn did not have a sword with her—there would have been no manner of way to explain that—but she was more than armed enough, she thought, to deal with either or both of these women, and that included the remaining page, who was no doubt doubling as a guard.

There were no refreshments on the table beyond a jug of water and a single clay cup. None of the cakes or pastries that Dhulyn would have expected, if they had really been invited to sing. She sat forward in her chair, adjusting her center of gravity to make it easier to lunge forward. She'd take the consort, she thought, and leave Valaika Jarl kevoso for Parno.

"We did not know whether you took refreshment after performing," the House said. "May we send to the kitchen?"

"Something light, House Jarlkevo, would suit us perfectly."

Dhulyn suppressed a smile. She'd heard that courtly tone from Parno before. These were manners he'd learned from his own parents, in his own House.

The House glanced up at the page who stood to one side of the door.

"Rudian, fetch ganje for our guests, and jeresh, if you please," she said. "And some of Cook's cheese pastries, and apple tarts." She waited for the door to close behind the page and, turning to Parno, spoke in an entirely different tone. "Would you be kind enough to check that Rudian has actually gone? Occasionally, he oversteps."

Parno glanced at Dhulyn, his right eyebrow raised. She gave him the tiniest of nods, and he rose, and went to the door to listen.

"All clear," he said, remaining by the door. "He's gone."

Suddenly, the boy Janek shot forward, holding out his hands to Edmir.

"Edmir! It *is* you."

Dhulyn was on her feet, but Sylria had caught hold of the boy's tunic and was hauling him backward. Edmir had also stood, his hands half raised, a look of luminous joy on his face.

That's how afraid he was, Dhulyn thought.

"Just a moment, everyone. Janek, stand back, please." Valaika Jarlkevoso narrowed her eyes and leaned forward. "Tell me, young man," she said. "Where did you learn that gesture of shrugging off the servant?" And she made it, the half shrug, half wave that Dhulyn had seen Edmir make a dozen times.

Edmir licked his lips. "Aunt Valaika, I *am* Edmir."

The taller, younger Sylria lifted one hand to her mouth. Valaika Jarlkevoso, sister to the late consort, cousin to the Tarkin of Hellik, moved not one muscle, except to blink, slowly, like an owl. Dhulyn almost smiled. She could like this woman, she could like her very much.

"You see? I told you!" Janek strained against Sylria's hold on his arm.

Finally Valaika unclasped her hands and placed them on the arms of her chair.

"Turn around," she said to Edmir. "Take off your shirt. Show me your back."

Edmir licked his lips again, and turned.

There was no shock, no disbelief, or anger or even hope on the older woman's face. Just a blank and careful mask.

They had all changed out of their stage costumes before answering the summons of the House, and Edmir was dressed simply in woolen trousers, a linen shirt with three-quarter-length sleeves, and a leather vest laced up the front. Standing, he loosened the lacing of the vest and pulled it off over his head. The linen shirt he merely took by the lower edge and lifted as he turned to present his back to his aunt.

"Come a little closer to me, you are out of the light there."

Edmir obliged by taking two short steps back.

As Dhulyn watched, the older woman narrowed her eyes, focusing on the right side of Edmir's back. After a long moment she made a noise in her throat, and, lifting her right hand, traced her finger in a short line just below Edmir's right shoulder blade.

"Embrace your cousin, Janek. Embrace the Lord Prince Edmir of Tegrian."

Now the boy launched himself forward, almost pushing Edmir off his feet with the force of his hug. Edmir laughed, taking his young cousin by the shoulders and holding him a little farther away.

"Let me see you, Janek. However did you know it was me? I wouldn't have known you, you're so much taller." There was great pleasure in Edmir's voice.

"We thought we had disguised him very well," Parno said, still at his post by the door.

"His face is the same," the boy said, as the adults exchanged glances. "His face hasn't changed at all."

"Valaika?" Sylria's voice was a soft croak. The consort was clearly of two minds about what was going on in her sitting room.

"Do you see this scar, my love?" Valaika's voice was tight, and yet there was some triumph in it. She gestured Edmir forward and had him pull up his shirt again. Dhulyn's feet twitched and she had to hold herself back from getting up and looking for herself.

"I know this scar, know it well. And so I should, seeing as I'm the one who put it there. And I'm the one who sewed it up and swore you to secrecy, didn't I?"

"You thought my mother the queen wouldn't approve of your cutting me during fencing practice," Edmir said, smiling.

"And I was right, she didn't approve. How did she find out?" The question was clearly intended as a test, but the tone made it clear that Valaika was already satisfied.

"Kera told her, not knowing it was supposed to be a secret. But it had almost healed by then, you'd taken the stitches out, so we didn't get into too much trouble."

"Speak for yourself, boy, I was almost exiled."

Sylria held up her hands. "Stop. Janek, Valaika, stop a moment. Do you mean to tell me that *this* is *Edmir?* Your nephew Edmir who is declared dead?"

"Edmir that we're all in mourning for, yes." Valaika stood. "Edmir." She lifted her arms, hesitantly, as any aunt might do, Dhulyn thought, when confronted with a nephew she had not seen in years. As if the boy might have grown too big for an embrace.

But no. Edmir immediately stepped forward into his aunt's arms. The two clung closely together, and Dhulyn thought she saw Edmir's shoulders shake. Only at that moment did she understand how afraid Edmir must have been, afraid of the possibility that his aunt, too, might no longer know him.

Now Sylria stood also, but only to lower herself to one knee. To her, this was no mere nephew, but the Lord Prince of Tegrian.

"You're so much like your father . . ." Valaika's voice faded. "But what did you do to your hair, you miserable brat." Valaika put her fists on her hips. The tension broke. Both aunt and nephew began to laugh, Edmir brushing at his eyes with the back of his hand.

Out of the corner of her eye Dhulyn saw Zania watching everyone closely, as if memorizing what they did, and how they looked when they did it. *Actors,* Dhulyn thought.

"Stand up, Consort Sylria," Parno said from the door. "The servants return. And you do not kneel to players."

"But Val . . ." The woman was already rising to her feet as she spoke.

"In a moment, Syl, they'll have their reasons." The House turned to Dhulyn, "which I'm sure they'll tell us."

As Parno walked back to his seat, filling the air bag of his pipes as he came, Edmir and the Jarlkevo women sat down. Zania hopped to her feet and took up a position to one side of the company, where she would be seen immediately by anyone coming in the door. With a nod to Dhulyn, Zania started singing the "Spring Enchantress," beginning in the middle of a verse, and gesturing to Dhulyn to clap. When the servants entered a few moments later, one carrying a large tray, they were just reaching the rousing finish of the song, and Valaika was clapping along in counterpoint to Dhulyn.

"But do you know any Hellish music?" Valaika said, once Zania had taken her bows and sat down again.

"Why do you suppose I've brought my pipes, House Jarlkevo," Parno said. "It's the best accompaniment for Hellish songs."

"I'm not so sure I agree," Valaika said, waving the servants forward. "But take some refreshment first, and then show me."

The second servant fetched another low table from under the middle window and set it between the seats. From the tray they took a jug of ganje, still steaming from the kitchen fire, and a small stone bottle well-corked, two cups made from the rare and expensive Tenezian glass, and four ceramic mugs. When all had been set out on the table, the servants stood back.

"I thank you, and send my compliments to the kitchen. Hellish music is not to everyone's taste, I know," Valaika said. "So you have my leave to be elsewhere." She laughed at the evident disappointment on their faces. "Go on now, I hope to persuade the troupe to favor us with an evening of music, perhaps a dance —" she snapped her fingers. "In fact, prepare chambers for them — you'll stay the night at least — the small suite in the north wing."

"But House Jarlkevo, our caravan—"

Valaika raised her hand. "Can be moved here in the morning. No, I won't hear it. I'll keep you until I've heard every Hellish song you know, and taught you a few of mine."

"Perhaps Janek . . ." began Sylria.

"Sylria, no!" said the boy.

"If you're to stay, young man, it must be quietly," Valaika said. "The first sign of yawns or sleepiness and you're off to bed."

The consort made room for their son on her own chair. It occurred to Dhulyn that she herself must be occupying the boy's usual seat.

The servants grinned and bowed, leaving easily enough now. Valaika was by no means the first Noble House Dhulyn had met, but she was the first to speak to her servants in this free and easy manner. Was it all the Hellish who were like this, or was it just Valaika herself? If the latter, it was easy to see why she had left her sister-in-law's court. Queen Kedneara had the reputation of being a tyrant when it came to protocol. Among other things.

When the door had closed once again behind the servants, Valaika turned back to her nephew.

"Not the best rooms, I'm afraid, Lord Prince, but if you must keep up this masquerade, anything else would give you away. I can't give you better than I would normally give to traveling players."

Parno got back to his feet. "I'll play as softly as I can," he said, as he headed to the door."

"Oh, come now," Valaika said, her brow furrowed. "We have more important things to do than indulge my taste for the music of my homeland."

"Certainly," Parno said. "But don't think for a moment that the servants have gone far, or that others won't be along shortly—curiosity if nothing else will bring them. Best they hear music coming from this room. At least for now."

Valaika pushed her hands through her graying hair and took the glass of steaming ganje her consort was holding out for her. "Forgive me," she said. "I am not thinking clearly." She paused as Parno took up his position at the door and began to play softly, having removed the drones from the pipes.

"It's not every evening the nephew I thought was dead is returned to me alive," Valaika continued under the cover of the music. She turned to Edmir. "But now, how is it we were told you were dead? How did you escape from the Mercenary Brothers?"

Edmir pressed his lips together, wagging his head from side to side. "It isn't just one thing they've lied about, Aunt, it's everything." He looked at Dhulyn. "Shall I . . . ?"

"Allow me," Dhulyn said. For her role as the queen in Edmir's play, Dhulyn had worn the long blonde wig that had been made from Zania's mother's hair. She pushed her fingers under the lower edge, at the back of her neck where the wig had not been glued, and began to loosen and dislodge the glued edges above her ears. In a moment, the wig was free and she pulled it carefully off, revealing her shaven scalp, and what was more to the moment, the blue-and-green tattoo of her Mercenary badge.

"Caids bless us," Sylria whispered.

"I am Dhulyn Wolfshead, called the Scholar," she said. "Schooled by Dorian the Black. There by the door is my Partner, Parno Lionsmane, called the Chanter, for reasons which are obvious. Schooled by Nerysa Warhammer."

"Was *nothing* we were told the truth, then?" Valaika's words were bitten off, and she looked from Dhulyn to Parno and back again as if she would demand answers.

"My turn," Edmir said. Dhulyn nodded, giving him a stage flourish with her hand that Zania had taught her. This was not a report being made to a Senior Brother, and over the last moon Edmir had shown himself more than skilled at telling a tale. She settled back in her chair, rubbing off the residue of the glue that still clung to her temples and forehead before she replaced the wig.

With the accompaniment of the softly playing music, Edmir began.

"We lost the battle at Limona."

Parno had run out of Hellish tunes and was enjoying a cup of jeresh by the time Edmir finished telling the tale of the last moon's adventures. There had been no chance of Janek falling asleep, the boy had been spellbound by his cousin's adventures. Dhulyn had to admit, Edmir had left nothing pertinent out, though he'd glossed over the part involving the Muse Stone, and had made things sound far more interesting than they had seemed at the time.

Valaika had remained quiet throughout the narrative, the narrowing of her eyes and clenching of her jaw her only reactions to what she was hearing. Sylria had exclaimed once or twice, notably at the point where Tzanek, Lord of Probic, had not recognized Edmir.

"I couldn't think of anywhere else to go," Edmir said, as he reached the end of the story. "And so I came to you."

Valaika pounded the arm of her chair with her closed fist. "And you say this is Avylos?" she questioned, through gritted teeth.

"Who else?" Dhulyn said. "A magic that has never been known to fail, fails the only time the Lord Prince calls upon it? Nisveans refuse to release him, when letting us return him would achieve the same results as returning him themselves? An old childhood friend genuinely fails to recognize him? The whole country knows he's dead within days—when does news travel that quickly? If this is not the Blue Mage, what is it?"

"And let's not forget Probic," Parno said.

A short silence fell over the room, even Janek holding perfectly still, though his eyes were alive and round with excitement.

"The queen . . ." Sylria looked around. "I may be prejudiced, but surely she wouldn't countenance this strike against one of her own children."

"If she needed an excuse to invade Nisvea . . ." Edmir fell silent, his eyes bleak.

"Nonsense. Any excuse would do for that. I don't like the woman, never have, but nothing will persuade me that she would put one of her children in harm's way, let alone connive at his murder."

Dhulyn was looking at Edmir and from the expression on his face, his aunt's words did not convince him.

Evidently, Valaika saw it, too. "I know what you are thinking, Nephew. Your mother the queen is a self-absorbed, arrogant woman, the more so since your father is no longer here to laugh her out of her natural tendencies. But you forget that she sees you and your sister as part of herself. Less than herself, without doubt—she would never put your needs before her own—but you would still come before anyone else in the world. Anyone."

"Even if we found an ally in the queen—and there's no way to know that she hasn't been magicked in the same way old Tzanek was in Probic . . ." Parno began.

"She would be a most volatile ally at the best of times—to be handled carefully. She'd find it difficult to believe that Avylos either could or would do anything against her, but once convinced, she would confront him in a rage, without fear or subtlety, and . . ."

"And that might not be the best way to confront the person who destroyed Probic," Dhulyn said.

"Better we should approach him ourselves," Parno said.

"How, precisely, are we to do that?"

Zania leaned forward eagerly, but hesitated as Dhulyn raised her hand, and murmured, "Pasillon."

"We have reason to believe," she said, giving Zania a small smile, "that the Mage's magic is not a natural part of him, like the Mark of a Finder or a Healer. Rather, it has an outside source, and we believe we know what that source is. If we can remove it, we remove his power."

Valaika looked at each of their faces in turn. "And you have a plan for this?"

"You can get us into the Royal House, can you not?"

Zania shivered suddenly, and hugged herself, cupping her elbows in her hands.

"I'll light the brazier," Sylria said, getting to her feet.

"Wait." Parno put out his hand. "It's late already, and it's not likely that you'd sit up so long with players you've given houseroom to. Someone will wonder why we've not been dismissed."

"Oh, but surely there's no need to keep up your disguise now?" Sylria said.

"Better cautious than cursing," Dhulyn said. "Can we be certain of everyone in the House? Or the town for that matter? The return of a dead prince is too good a tale for anyone to keep to themselves."

"They're right, Syl. And this is for you, too, Janek. Nothing of what you've heard here tonight can be spoken of—it might very well kill your cousin."

"I was the only one who knew him," the boy replied. "And I told no one but you."

Dhulyn smiled, finding herself well satisfied with the boy's answer. From Valaika's nod, it seemed his mother was as well.

"Come," Valaika got to her feet. "I'll show you to your rooms—I often do so," she said, answering their protests. "No one will think it strange."

❧❧❧

"Let's see this famous scar, Edmir."

The rooms they'd been given consisted of two tiny bedchambers which shared a small sitting room, furnished with three short benches, a single armed chair, and a low table on which the servants had placed a stone lamp now almost out of oil, and a triple-branched candelabra with the candles left unlit. Late as it was, they all drifted back into the sitting room after checking their rooms. At Dhulyn's words Zania turned from her inspection of the stars outside the window. Parno had taken the large chair and Dhulyn perched on the arm.

Edmir obeyed her request by stripping off his shirt and presenting his back. Dhulyn took up and lit one of the candles and held it above the prince's shoulder.

"Careful you don't burn him," Parno said.

"Teach your grandmother," Dhulyn answered. She found the scar quite easily. It was, as Valaika had said, a shallow cut made with the edge of an almost dull blade. She could easily imagine the stroke that caused it, an accident pure and simple. She saw another discolored mark lower still, below the kidney, and crouched on her heels to examine it more closely.

"Is that another scar?" Zania peered over Dhulyn's shoulder.

Dhulyn shook her head. The mark was too dark to be a scar, and too well-shaped. "A tattoo perhaps," she said.

"I don't have any tattoos." Edmir tried to twist around to see the thing everyone else was looking at.

"There's a mirror in my side bag," Zania said. "Let me fetch it."

The mirror was brought, and held up at the right angle to permit Edmir to see what everyone else could see, a dull reddish mark like an oval with a smudge in the center of it.

"You're not holding it right," Edmir said. "I still can't see it."

"We are holding it right," Dhulyn said. She caught Parno's eye and summoned him with a jerk of her head.

"Why can't I see it, then?"

"It doesn't show in the mirror, lad. It casts no reflection." Parno looked over Dhulyn's head, first at Edmir's back, then at the mirror.

Dhulyn stepped back, her hand rising to her throat, her fingers seeking out a spot on her breastbone, just below the points of her collarbones. "It's not a scar," she said. "It's a . . ." She hesitated, groping for the right word. "It's a ghost eye."

"A type of birthmark?" Zania said.

"I don't have any birthmarks." Edmir jerked down his shirt and turned to face them, his brows drawn down in a sharp vee. "And that wouldn't explain why the thing doesn't show up in a mirror." He reached behind as if to rub the spot and then lowered his hand, thinking better of it. "And how is it you know about them?"

"I had one myself, as a child." Again, Dhulyn touched the spot on her breastbone where the ghost eye had been. "Eventually, it wore off."

Zania gasped. "A slaver's mark? But how did Edmir get one? The Nisveans—"

"It was not a slaver's mark, no," Dhulyn said. "I had it before the slavers took me. I had it . . ." she took a deep breath. "Among my people—among the Red Horsemen," Dhulyn corrected. "Children bore these sigils. So we could not be lost." She frowned, concentrating on a wisp of memory that hovered just out of her grasp. Grasp. A memory that involved a rough, callused hand grasping her by the shoulder. "My father used it." She looked up. "It was for my father to find me."

"Your *father*? Was your father a Finder, then?" Parno said.

Dhulyn shook her head, frowning. "You know the Mark doesn't work like this. Finders Find. They don't need to draw signs on things, they just Find. Use a tool, maybe, like a bowl of water, to focus . . . But *this* sigil, the ghost eye, *was* for my father to use. I don't think there were Finders among us, it was . . ."

"We'd better find some way to get this off," Parno said. He looked around at them. "If it's some kind of Outlander magic, and it can be used to find people—if your father used one to find you, than someone can use it to find Edmir."

"I'll wager my second-best sword we know who the someone is," Dhulyn said, the image of Edmir in the pool clear in her mind.

Sixteen

ARLY AS IT WAS WHEN Dhulyn returned from accompanying Valaika's grooms to the Hostel Plazan—knowing that Bloodbone and Warhammer would not allow someone else to harness them—when she returned with the caravan to Jarlkevo House she found the Jarlkevoso already up, dressed for hawking, and with Parno at the breakfast table.

"I've asked that hunting birds be brought out for us," Valaika Jarl kevoso said. "We won't have a quiet moment to talk once the day starts. There's not a room, including my own study, that someone might not walk into. If we're to talk privately without causing remark, we'll have to do it on horseback."

"Nothing would suit me better," Dhulyn said. A morning in the saddle, with well-trained birds, would make a nice change from walking across a stage pretending to be someone else. Parno could do most of the talking—he was good with Noble Houses. "Are the youngsters up and ready?"

Valaika considered this a moment while she chewed. "Leave them here with Sylria," she said after she'd swallowed. "There were Mercenary Brothers at my cousin's court when I was a girl, and I still remember how he relied upon them. Edmir is a grand boy, but I'd rather hear your assessment of events than his."

Back in their rooms, Zania seemed oddly indifferent to their plans, merely shrugging and agreeing with a small smile. Edmir would have liked to go hawking, but saw the sense of his and Zania's staying behind. He closed the journal he'd been writing in and reached for the scrolls of *The Soldier King.* "I can work on that part in act four that feels so flat," he said, eyes already looking into the middle distance.

Dhulyn rolled her eyes to the heavens. His color was better than it had been the day before, and there were fewer lines of worry in his face, but otherwise, Edmir was taking his return to his family very quietly. Shaking her head, she changed into her own boots and leggings, topped them with one of Parno's smaller tunics, and joined Valaika in the courtyard.

"First, let me tell you now what I did not wish to say in front of Edmir," Valaika said, once they were well out into the fields south of the town. The hawk on her wrist bobbed as she turned in her saddle to speak over her shoulder. "It would take a great deal to make Kedneara turn on Avylos. She will not believe that the man does not love her. And she will not believe that he has killed Edmir, or ordered him killed—else she'd have to admit that she herself made a grave error in judgment. An impossibility in her mind. While she would move the heavens and the earth to keep her children safe, she will do little to revenge them once they are dead, if it means admitting any such unwelcome truths."

"Do you mean she will *not* invade Nisvea?"

Valaika waved that away with her free hand. "She was planning to do that anyway. Though after Probic, does anyone really think an invasion necessary? Say, rather, she would not change a plan she already had in mind. She has no sentiment. Once the child is dead, he's dead. Look at how quickly she married Avylos, and she genuinely loved my brother, insofar as she is able to love anyone. When the children were small, and Karyli still alive, then Kedneara was at her best. Since then . . . she has been queen, with no one to remind her she is also a woman and a mother, for a *very* long time. Any plan we make that includes her must take this into account."

Dhulyn exchanged a glance with her Partner. They had spent two seasons in the Great King's Court, far to the west. Ruthlessness on the part of a country's ruler was something with which they were well familiar.

"This source of Avylos' power, what can you tell me of it?" Valaika said.

They had two beaters with them, but on foot and positioned well away from the mounted hunters, they were easily out of earshot of those who knew how to speak without letting their voices carry.

The older woman's eyes narrowed, her lips thinning, as Dhulyn told her Zania's history.

"The girl believes the Blue Mage is this same Avylyn that her family has been tracing the last fifteen years," Dhulyn concluded. "And that the secret to his magics is this Stone that belonged to her people."

A rabbit dashed out into the field ahead of them, and Valaika loosed her hawk.

"And this book you speak of, it tells you how to control the Stone?"

"I would not go so far as that," Dhulyn said. "It is rather a description of how Zania's family used it, and some speculations on its origins and true purpose." Dhulyn hesitated. How much did she want to reveal to this woman? "But as for any help in getting it away from Avylos —nothing I have read so far gives me any clues."

"I remember when Avylos first came," Valaika said, her eyes following the progress of her bird as it swung and stooped on the moving air. "He had perhaps twenty summers then, not many more. A dark-haired young man, thin as a reed, but very striking, very handsome. The timing fits with the girl's story."

"And has he grown in his powers, as Edmir believes?"

Valaika tapped her upper lip with her tongue, shaking her head before answering. "That I cannot say. I have not lived in the Royal House for more than fifteen summers. I've only met the Blue Mage twice—no, three times since he first came, and not at all since my brother died." She turned again to look them in the face. "But there is no doubt that until Limona, no Tegriani force has lost a battle, and that is the Mage's doing."

They had reached the place where the hawk still crouched over the body of the rabbit. Valaika called out to the grooms and dismounted, swinging off her horse with the agility of a woman half her age.

"Shhhh, come, Tera, come." She enticed her hawk off the prey, offering her wrist and as a reward, a pellet of specially prepared food. When the hawk was restored to her wrist and hooded, Valaika stepped nimbly back into her saddle.

"Oh, well done," Dhulyn said. "Most people cannot remount without disturbing the bird."

At Valaika's signal, the beaters spread out once more, and they were once again advancing, this time with Parno's bird unhooded.

"What is your plan?" Valaika asked.

Dhulyn was pleased that Parno kept his eyes on the beaters as he answered. A certain amount of clumsiness would be excused, since the servants thought them to be merely players, but it wouldn't do for them to pay no attention whatsoever.

"We saw in Probic," he said, "what could happen if we simply appear, claiming we have Edmir. In coming to you, Edmir thought that with your backing, he could be restored to the Royal House, and we could gain entry ourselves." His eyes narrowed. Dhulyn looked ahead and saw the beaters were moving in on a clump of long grass.

"Once guests in the Royal House," she said, taking up the thread of Parno's explanation, "we would have access to the Mage, and the Stone."

"You say you *wanted* this," Valaika said. "What has changed your minds?"

"Last night we learned something more," Dhulyn said. "Edmir bears a sigil on his lower back, called a 'ghost eye' among the Red Horsemen, used to see or watch the person who bears it."

"Avylos again," Valaika said, in the same bitter tone she'd used the night before. "Can we remove this sigil?"

"The one I bore as a child wore off with time," Dhulyn said. "But perhaps the process can be speeded up. Soap and water, obviously, is not the answer—at least, I would suppose a prince is bathed more often and more thoroughly than a Red Horse child."

A covey of what looked like grouse broke from the long grass between the beaters and Parno loosed his hawk.

"Distilled spirits," Parno said, while his eye followed the flight of the hawk. When it struck, calling out its success, he kneed Warhammer forward, saying over his shoulder as he advanced, "I seem to remember my mother removing a stain from a favorite gown with clear distilled spirits."

"We will try it," Valaika said. "But how will this affect your original plan? Even if you suspect the sigil is Avylos', there has been a general order to be on the lookout for two Mercenary Brothers and a young man, but no one has been sent to any particular place."

"That we know of." Dhulyn shrugged, causing the falcon on her wrist to spread its wings to balance itself. "Your pardon," she said to the bird mechanically. "I do not know for certain what the ghost eye reveals, but my guess is the Mage sees only Edmir and his immediate surroundings. One forest clearing looks much like another, and the same can be said for a village green—or a House's courtyard for that matter. So long as he does not see anyone in House colors, or any recognizable building, there is no way he can tell where Edmir is."

"That's why you agreed to leave him indoors just now."

Dhulyn nodded. "But I tell you, as we approach Beolind there are landmarks, well-known stretches of road; Avylos *will* recognize what he sees, and he will have time to prepare for our arrival. If the Mage has not already bewitched the queen and others to make sure Edmir will not be recognized, he'll have time to do so—and we will lose potential allies."

Valaika nodded. "So Edmir must remain here—or better, our gamekeeper's lodge lies vacant just now. It's not far from here, and there is nothing to show the place is Jarlkevo. Like the rooms we gave you last night, it is exactly the type of place we would lend to traveling players who needed privacy and time to rehearse."

Parno returned, the body of a plump grouse hanging from his pommel.

"Then our first task when we return to the House is to see about removing this sigil. All our planning rests upon that."

Distilled spirits did not remove the ghost eye from Edmir's lower back. Nor did animal fat, nor olive oil. Nor hot water and horse brushes.

"I don't suppose you'll consider having it cut out," Parno

said as he threw the stiff-bristled horse brush down in disgust.

Edmir spun to face him, hands grabbing protectively at the spot on his back where the sigil was.

"No, I didn't think so." Parno smiled.

"We have no way of knowing whether it *can* be cut off, my soul," Dhulyn pointed out. She eyed Edmir's back from where she leaned against the wall. "There's only one way to find out, and perhaps we should save that as a last resort." She turned to Valaika. "It's as I've said; for now Edmir must remain behind."

"But how is it safer for me to stay here?" Edmir said. "If he *can* see me, Avylos will see me here as well as anywhere else."

"The Blue Mage has never been to Jarlkevo, to my knowledge," Valaika said. "If he has looked this way since your arrival, we must hope he recognized nothing. And to be certain, we are moving you now to another place. As Dhulyn Wolfshead has said, one set of stone walls looks much like any other." Valaika thought, lips pursed. "I can get the two of you into the Royal House," she said to Dhulyn. "After that, it will be up to you."

"How will you explain *your* appearance, Aunt Valaika?" Edmir pulled his shirt on. "It's well known how much you dislike Beolind."

Valaika blew out her breath. "If I come to see my sister-in-law, Queen Kedneara, to offer her my support at the death of her son, my brother's child—I could not have come for anything less, but this, this I think they will believe."

⋙⋘

Janek was the first stumbling block. It was Edmir who finally convinced him.

"It's like a play—or a battle," he told the boy, when nothing either of his mothers said would change his mind. "Everyone has to do his part. I don't want to go and hide any more than you want to stay here with Sylria, but those are our orders. You wouldn't be allowed to go with us if we were really just players—and you wouldn't go with your mother Valaika to her hunting lodge as she's pretending to do, not if she were really only going for overnight. You'd have to stay here and attend to your studies and other duties. And so you will now."

"It is your carrying on as usual that will provide the rest of us the cover we need," Dhulyn added.

Almost as hard to convince had been Valaika's Steward of Walls.

Sylria had laughed. "Valaika managed to convince him that a caravan load of players was escort enough—he knew better than to argue; old soldier as she is, Valaika avoids an escort whenever she can. It's easier in the last few years, of course. Tegrian has never been so safe for travelers. We have the Blue Mage to thank for that much, at the very least."

There's irony, Parno thought. It was only the work of the Blue Mage that made Tegrian so safe, and here they were on their way to put a stop to him.

"That's the third time you've moved those slippers from one box to the other and back again." Edmir looked up from the entry he was making in his journal.

"I should be with them," Zania said, not for the first time, as she sat back on her heels and looked from one open chest to the other. "It's *my* Stone."

Edmir understood her frustration—after all, as she'd pointed out, *she* didn't have a ghost eye on *her* back—but he was very glad the Mercenaries had insisted on leaving Zania behind, though he wasn't sure if he should tell her so. The idea that she would be anywhere near Avylos, that Zania might look at Edmir and in that dead voice say that she didn't know him. He shivered and bent back over his journal.

Zania's frustration had taken the form of fussy activity. She'd decided to reorganize her props and costumes, now that there were so few players to use them, and in the absence of any eyes to oversee them here at the gamekeeper's lodge, Edmir had helped her drag the costume trunks into the lodge's large common room from where they normally rode under the caravan. The lodge itself consisted of this large room, with its cooking hearth, oak plank table, carved stools and uneven stone floor, and a single windowless inner room which Edmir had insisted Zania take as her bedchamber. There was nothing in either room to tell the Blue Mage where he was, no clue to give them away.

Edmir glanced up at her again. She certainly seemed to be making very little progress with her organizing.

Could he tell her how happy he had been with the decision to leave them together? He wanted to, that he was sure of, but from the tight look on the girl's face, he knew it would be unwise. It was so much easier to write these things down. On the page in front of him he had sketched in the outline of a short tale, just a few lines detailing a love story. Here, in the pages of his journal, was the one place—the only place—a life with Zania would ever exist.

His talk with Parno Lionsmane had made that very clear.

Best he not say anything to Zania. He sighed and applied himself once more to his story. He had just reached the point where the young prince declares his love to the beautiful lady player when Zania spoke again.

"The Muse Stone *is* mine," she said addressing a pair of boots with turned-down tops. "It belongs to my family." The muscles in her jaw moved as she gritted her teeth. "And Dhulyn took my great-uncle's book as well. They're all I have left."

Edmir swallowed. "Zania, if anything should happen . . . I mean. I want you to know that this past moon has been . . ."

Zania looked up, and her lips twisted to one side in a wry smile. "Better than life at court?"

"That's easily answered. How happy are the nobles in the plays you know?"

"In the comedies, very happy." She tossed the boots back into the chest and stood up, crossing over to lean against the table where he sat. "But your family, you must miss them?"

"I miss Kera, but even with her, lately . . . it's different when you'll be king someday. That sets you apart even from your brothers and sisters." He put the quill he'd been using to one side. "But I have to say, at least *part* of what's made the last few weeks so pleasurable is not being around my mother." He thrust his hands through his hair. "Since my father died— *Caids,* it's like putting down a weight."

Zania moved the inkwell Edmir had been using and perched on the side of the table, doing her best not to look down at what Edmir had been writing. "What weight?" *Part,* her heart said. *Part of what's given him pleasure.*

"The weight of her disapproval, the weight of not meeting her standards. She expects you to be perfect the first time, without giving you a chance to practice. You tell her you've done your best and she tells you to try harder next time, not to be so lazy." He smiled, but to Zania's practiced eye, it looked forced. "She was different when we were younger."

"So *that's* why you're always asking whether the play is good. I was thinking that for a prince, you needed an awful lot of reassurance."

"None of *you* seems to think that there's anything wrong with praise—Dhulyn acts like she thinks praise will make you try harder."

Zania drew up her feet until her heels were on the edge of the table, and she could wrap her arms around her knees. "And so it should, if it's earned. Then you'll do as well or better the next time, in order to be praised again."

"Do you think you should have your feet on the table?"

"What, are you turning into your mother?" She smiled when she said it, but she lowered her eyes. Edmir picked up his pen.

"With the Stone," she said. "I could start a new troupe."

"Well, fresh material—new plays, I mean—that might help you attract some new actors." She looked up then and met his eye.

Only part *of what's made him so happy,* she thought.

I don't want to go back, he thought.

❧❧❧

Sylria waited for the moon to rise before leaving her bed. She and Valaika were not in the habit of having pages sleep in the anteroom, something she was very glad of now. No questions to answer as she lit the lamp standing on the table in her chamber, drew on a dressing robe over her nightgown, and stepped into the corridor. A right turn and a short flight of stone steps brought her to her own workroom.

Sylria liked having her own room, where she could close the door behind her and look around with the satisfaction she always felt when she saw the orderly papers, inkpots well-stoppered, pens carefully cleaned and laid out in a neat row.

"You should have been a Scholar," Valaika had always said to tease her. Well, her father had been one, and Sylria had always wanted a home life, not a life spent chasing down a new theory, a just-discovered scrap of the Caids' writings, an untranslated poem in some unpleasant ancient tongue.

She took a book of poetry from her shelf, threw open the shutter of the narrow window, and set the book down on the ledge, where the moon would shine directly on it. She turned to blow out the lamp, and when her eyes had adjusted to the darkness, she opened the book to the central, blank, pages. She laid her index fingers on the lower corners of the open pages and spoke.

"My lord Mage," she said. She had time to wish she'd thought to bring a cup of water to the window with her—time enough for second thoughts, time to wonder whether she should just shut the book before any writing appeared. . . .

"Tell me."

And then it was too late.

"I keep our bargain," she said, whispering the words into the cool night air.

"Tell me."

"This will be the last time. With this, I pay my debt in full." She hadn't meant it to sound like a question, but she was fairly sure how it would appear in the book that was a twin to hers.

"Tell me."

"The Lord Prince is here, in Jarlkevo, near at hand." In the gamekeeper's lodge, where whatever the Blue Mage visited on him would be far from Janek.

"The Mercenary Brothers?"

Sylria's mouth was too dry to swallow. She'd been right to call him, she thought. He knew so much already, really, it was impossible to hide anything from him.

"They have gone, with my House, to Beolind. Here is only myself, and the prince."

"Kill him."

Sylria fumbled with the book, in her shock she nearly let it fall to the floor from the stone window ledge. "You cannot ask this of me," she said, when she had her voice again. "You wanted only news of him, you never said—"

"Does your son walk? Does he take food? Does he breathe the air? Grow? Laugh? Do you wish this to continue?"

Sylria sank to her knees, her hands still carefully maintaining the position of the book in the moonlight. *Janek, oh, sweet Caids, not Janek.* And yet she saw, with a sickening coldness in her belly, that this was exactly what she should have expected. Valaika was the one who had brought the child to term, for the House could only pass to blood, but Janek was Sylria's —*she* had nursed him, *she* had held him, rocked him, dealt with his fevers, coaxed him to eat, and watched him grow, but thin, hollow-eyed, and weak. Not thriving as other children did. And there would be no other. Valaika had waited too long; she could not have another child.

Sylria had watched as Janek's illness took its price from Valaika as well, making her thin, her hair dull, the bones of her face showing like a skull.

When she could not find a Healer, Sylria had gone to Avylos. And the Blue Mage had helped her. And she had promised him anything, *anything* to save their child.

And now she knew what *anything* was.

"I cannot," she whispered, and then roused herself. What was she saying? "I cannot promise," she said. "What if I am not successful?"

"I will help you. Put the palm of your left hand down on the right-hand page."

❈❈❈

When Valaika Jarlkevoso had said that Beolind was a day and a half's ride from the gamekeeper's lodge, if both weather and horse were good, Parno had given Dhulyn the look that meant "we'll laugh about this in private." He remembered that look when, almost exactly a day and half later, they entered the city of Beolind. Valaika was greeted with salutes and attention, and a runner was sent ahead of them to inform the Royal House of their approach.

"Are you all right?"

Dhulyn nodded, but Parno thought she looked pale. "This is the first time I've passed through city gates without declaring myself a Mercenary Brother," she replied, using the nightwatch voice. "Let's hope we never have to do so again."

He and Dhulyn, both in short, dark wigs, wore tunics in the same orange and black as the cloak Valaika wore, the better to disguise them as retainers of Jarlkevo. Parno moved his shoulders. The tunic was a good fit, but he was getting awfully tired of wearing borrowed clothes. He looked at Dhulyn as she swung herself onto Bloodbone's back. If *he* was getting tired of it, he could only imagine how Dhulyn felt.

Warm, he thought, as she rolled back her sleeves. After all these years, she still found it too warm here in the north.

"This way," Valaika said once they had passed through the lengthy gate passage that led through the walls of the city. "I have my own suite in the western wing of the Royal House, and we can go straight there."

As they followed Valaika through the city, Parno noticed Dhulyn looking around, frown lines between her brows. He knew that look. She was remembering something she had Seen in a Vision, and comparing it to what she saw now.

A man on horseback came along, calling out to make way for the Royal Guard. Valaika could have stood on rank herself, but instead, she moved to one side.

There were only five people in the party, two nobles on horseback, and three in the dark blue tunics of the Royal Guard walking along with them. As the group drew abreast of them, Dhulyn suddenly stiffened and called out in a language Parno had never heard her use.

The taller of the two on horseback turned around at her call, and Parno saw what Dhulyn had seen. The man had the distinctive blood-red hair of the Red Horsemen. Now the two Outlanders were calling to each other, Dhulyn smiling and excited as she pushed through the crowd to the man. As Parno started to follow, Valaika grabbed him by the arm.

"Don't," she said. "Don't move. That's Avylos."

Seventeen

"COUSIN!"

Dhulyn spoke without thinking. When the men rode out of the shadow of a Jaldean Shrine into the sunshine, and Dhulyn saw the taller man's face clearly, and his hair—blowing back from that remembered face and red like old blood—the greeting had burst from her. She had spoken in the old tongue, the language of the Espadryni, that she hadn't used since her Schooler, Dorian the Black, had found her in the slaver's ship.

She was urging Bloodbone forward even as the man stopped and looked at her. It *was* the boy, the one her Vision had shown her being hunted in the woods, much older, but still recognizable as the prey running in the forest of her Vision. So it was the past she'd Seen.

"How can we be kin?" he answered her, also in the old tongue. His deep blue eyes were narrowed, calculating. The foot guards with him exchanged glances, round-eyed, but they stayed silent. He looked over behind her, his eyes narrowed still further, and he inclined his head—not a bow, but as someone who acknowledges an acquaintance. He had seen and recognized Valaika, Dhulyn thought, so this was evidently someone from the Royal House.

"We are the same Tribe, if not the same Clan," she said, willing his attention back to her. Now that she *had* spoken, and drawn his notice, she'd better make the best she could out of this. "What does that make us, in this city of northerners, if not kin?"

He tilted his head. "You speak the old tongue. The Hunter Moon has passed more times than I wish to remember, since I have heard it last. You have the voice, but not the look of an Espadryni."

"It is easy to change the color of one's hair," Dhulyn said. "I will be pleased to prove our kinship, but not here, in the street. I was Dhulyn of the Darklin Plain Clan. My mother Asmodhul and my father Fentlyn."

"You say you *were?*"

"The Darklin Plain is empty. The horses and cattle run wild. You know this as well as I."

"I do. I was Avylyn of Forest Plain Clan. My father Teravyl and my mother Werlyn. Come with me now, and if what you say of yourself is true, you shall be welcomed here as though we were of one blood." He put out his hand, palm down, in the manner of their Tribe.

A cold knot formed in the back of her throat and Dhulyn cursed herself—she was even more a blooded fool than she'd thought. She recognized the name. She knew what his next words would be.

"Here I am known as Avylos, the Blue Mage."

She took his hand, palm to palm, turned their wrists until her hand was uppermost and released him. She let Bloodbone fall into step beside his horse. What else could she do, but find some way to salvage this? As she rode away from her Partner, she stretched up her right arm, as if adjusting the fall of her cloak. First, she extended her thumb and index finger only. *Follow and watch.* And then, she closed her fist. *In Battle.*

"And in Death." Parno mouthed the response from where he sat on Warhammer, pushed up against Valaika's horse, automatically giving the open hand signal as he did. Then both his own hands closed into fists, and he forced them to relax.

"I thought you said he had dark hair?"

"He did when I knew him." Valaika said. "What now?"

"Follow and watch," Parno said.

The older woman took a deep breath and let it out slowly. "Then it's a lucky thing we're all going to the Royal House."

Parno hoped the smile he gave her was more confident than the feeling behind it. "We wanted to get into the Mage's quarters. Well, now we're in."

❧❧❧

Avylos' hand trembled slightly as he adjusted the magic that locked his workroom door. A woman of his tribe. What if she was? How much did she know, and how many others had survived? He would have to kill her—it was the only way to be sure, to be safe. But she was younger, what if she knew nothing? What if she *was* the last?

And there was more to consider than her parentage. He had never felt such a strong manifestation of power as he had when the woman, Dhulyn, had taken his hand. Espadryni or not, she was Marked. That was beyond doubt. When he was young, he no more thought the women of the Espadryni were Seers than he'd believed the men were Mages. Tricks and illusion—that's what he'd told himself before the Stone had shown him that magic truly existed. But now, with the power of the Stone pulsing through his veins, he could see the Mark for himself, a glow somewhat like the young dice boy's, only . . . thicker. *Could* he feed it to the Stone, even if he wanted to?

An Espadryni. A Seer. The use he could make of her—what if she was of more value to him alive? Would it be a waste to feed her power into the Stone?

"All the rooms in this wing are mine," he told her as he pushed open the door and led the way in. "But this is my workroom, where I conduct my private business."

"Your pardon, Lord Avylos, but you are the consort, are you not? Do you have any private business?"

Avylos pressed his lips together, glad that his back was turned as he opened the shutters to let in the afternoon light. He could not let her see how her casual disrespect had cut through him like a knife.

"As consort, perhaps not, but as the Blue Mage, much of my business is private," he said through gritted teeth. Perhaps he should show her the Stone after all, and sooner rather than later.

He turned back toward her and found her standing, perfectly relaxed, looking around the room with an expression of polite interest. Her face was a long oval, her skin coloring naturally pale, like his own, showing little or no darkening from the sun. Her eyes large, a steel gray in color. Her mouth was full, but there was a small scar on her upper lip. As if she felt his eyes on her, she looked at him and smiled. For a moment, the scar caught at her lip and made her seem about to snarl, but then her mouth softened again, and her smile was gentle.

"Of course," she said. "You must excuse my ignorance. I know nothing of Mages and their responsibilities, but surely they must be heavy. In my excitement at finding a kinsman, I may speak too familiarly. Pray believe that I do not wish to offend."

Avylos found himself smiling. He'd forgotten what the Espadryni were like. This Dhulyn was plainspoken, not disrespectful. Open and straightforward, nothing sycophantic in her tone or carriage. But he remembered, and sobered again. How much did she know?

"What do you remember of your time among the tribes?"

She shrugged. "I was so young when the tribes were broken, that I remember very little about the life. I have learned some things since through study—I can read—but I was not sure . . . were there many Mages among the Espadryni?"

"No," he said, and then smiled to soften the bluntness of his answer. She *didn't* know. If she didn't know that, she wouldn't know that he'd been *srusha*. "But I did not start to come into my powers until after the tribes were broken. No doubt, as a child, much was hidden from me."

"No doubt."

"But please, seat yourself, let me offer you some jeresh." When she nodded, he unstoppered the bottle sitting on the table to his right and poured out two portions into the waiting glass cups. He handed her one, and raised his own in salute.

"To proofs," he said.

The woman raised her own cup, took a sip, and lowered it again. She looked at him steadily for a long moment, as if she were considering something of great weight. Finally, her lips formed the smallest of smiles.

"I am ready," she said. She set her glass down and lifted her hands to the back of her head. She pushed her fingers into the dark brown curls on her neck and her hair moved. The hairs on Avylos' own neck shivered for an instant until he realized she was wearing a wig, and was lifting it off. She pushed her hands forward until her fingers were scraping at the hairline around her face, and in a few moments more the wig was lying in her lap.

She rubbed her hands quickly over her scalp, brushing off loose bits of the glue that had held on the wig. There was stubble exposed on her shapely skull, perhaps three days' worth, a deep red, a blood color almost identical to his own. But something else was exposed as well. Something that cast all his half-formed plans into the fire.

"You are a Mercenary Brother." He tapped his upper lip with his fingers. Edmir at Jarlkevo, and now this? He was wary of coincidences.

"I am. I am Dhulyn Wolfshead, called the Scholar. I was Schooled by Dorian, the Black Traveler. I have fought with my brothers at Sadron, Arcosa, and Bhexyllia."

He waited, but it seemed Dhulyn Wolfshead had finished. "You had better stay in my rooms until I can find you another wig, Dhulyn Wolfshead—a red one by preference, though I do not know where I will find one so fine as yours. Kedneara the Queen does not feel well-disposed toward Mercenaries, just now."

"The very reason for this." She picked up the dark brown wig and laid it aside on the table. "As you see from my colors, I am employed as a House Guard for Valaika Jarlkevoso, and have been for six or seven moons now. When we heard what was being said about the Lord Prince's death, and the banishment, the Jarlkevoso advised me to cover my Badge and wait."

"Do you believe what is being said?" *Can I believe what's being said?* Had she been all this time with Valaika? Or had she come more recently? And with a princely companion?

"No," she said, looking directly at him with her steel-gray eyes. For a moment he believed she had read his thoughts. "The Brotherhood does not murder—but the Queen of Tegrian will not be the first grief-stricken person who puts blame in the wrong place."

Avylos leaned against the edge of the table, propping his elbow in his free hand. "Do you know why the Jarlkevoso has chosen to come to Beolind just now?"

Dhulyn Wolfshead shrugged, but seemed to give his question some thought. "A group of players came to Jarlkevo. They did a play where a king returns from war to his family. Perhaps the story reminded the Jarlkevoso that her nephew would not be returning from his battle, and that her sister-by-marriage, Kedneara the Queen, might be bereft." Again, she shrugged. "I was not told anything of the matter."

Avylos nodded. It *could* be. It *was* possible. The players he had already heard about, and if she was merely a guard— however valued, as a Mercenary Brother would be—she might know nothing of the arrival of Edmir. Valaika would bring her to Beolind to keep her from finding out . . . And whatever else she might be, she *was* Espadryni, and Marked. So long as he had her here, in his hands, surely she was more asset than liability. "However did you become a Mercenary Brother?"

"I had seen the Hawk Moon perhaps five or six times when the Espadryni were overrun. My parents were killed, and I was sold to slavers. Sold several times, in fact—I don't believe we make good slaves, we Espadryni. When I had seen the Hawk moon eleven times, the slave ship I was on was taken by Dorian the Black, the Mercenary Schooler. He said he would teach me to kill my enemies, an offer I was happy to take."

Slavers. Avylos hoped she did not see him shiver. "I was luckier than you, I think," he told her. "My Clan was near the forest that is found at the western end of the plains and I escaped into the wood when we were overrun. I was found and hidden by farmers—folk we'd often traded with. They would have made a home for me, gladly, for their family was not so numerous, but I could not settle to that kind of life. And then my powers began to come, and the news out of Tegrian spoke of the Consort Karyli's gathering of the gifted and Marked to be licensed. So to Tegrian I came, and to Beolind. And I have been here ever since."

"Are you happy here?" There was something different in the tone Dhulyn Wolfshead used to ask this question, and to his surprise, Avylos answered honestly.

"I have been glad of the time to study, to increase my powers. I have done much here in Tegrian, and will have a chance to do more, as Kedneara the Queen extends her rule. But tell me, what brings you to Beolind?"

Not for the first time, Dhulyn wished she had Edmir's gift for telling tales. Already she was losing track of what she *had* told him, and she was keenly aware that she was taking too long to answer now. But she was just as certain that she had to tread carefully. Avylos reminded her of Delmarin Hammerfist who had been Schooled with her, a person quick to feel slighted, and who needed frequent reassurance. Parno was better at handling this kind of person than she was.

"I might easily say that you are yourself my reason to be in Beolind, Lord Avylos. There was talk of you in Monara, and someone who claimed to have seen you, described you in such a way that I thought you might be Espadryni, and so I came to see. I had been, as I said, six moons or more with House Jarlkevo, working my way here, when the news came of the Lord Prince's murder and the banishment of the Brotherhood. House Jarlkevo, knowing of my intention to seek you out, in her generosity chose me to be one of her guard when she came to see the queen." She picked up her glass and took another sip of jeresh. "I did not dream I would be so lucky as to see you on the street. Will you speak for me to the queen? Ask her to exempt me from her order of banishment?"

Avylos leaned back again in his chair and Dhulyn breathed more easily. If he was relaxing, perhaps he believed her.

"I will be happy to speak to her," he said. "But if you take my counsel, we will wait. Give her more time. My assurances will help her to act justly, but you will not gain her favor unless we wait. And I wish you to gain that favor. You may stay here as long as you desire—as you said, we are each of us the closest thing to kin that either of us has left in the world." Avylos hesitated, as if these words had stopped his throat. "I must ask that you remain here in my apartments for now," he continued. ", if you will resume your wig, in my garden. Others cannot enter here without my knowing. Give your own hair time to grow out more. If I can claim you as kin, our assurances to the queen will be stronger."

"What of your escort? Will they not speak of me?"

Avylos shook his head. "I will tell everyone that you are ill, and that you must stay in my care until there is no danger."

Suddenly, he came around the table and took her hands in his. They were cool, and strangely rough as if his calluses were in the wrong places. There was a softness in his eyes, and for a moment Dhulyn thought he was going to kiss her hands. She widened her eyes and lifted her brows.

He smiled and the moment passed. "I am expected to join my wife the queen for supper, so I must leave you. Let me show you into the garden, you will be safe there. If you can be patient and wait, I will bring you a meal myself later in the evening."

"I am used to going without food," she said. "It is part of our training." She picked up the wig and pulled it on. It fit well enough, even without the glue, to fool anyone who would only see her in a garden.

As soon as she was alone, Dhulyn made her way back to the Blue Mage's workroom. Once there, however, she stood outside the door tapping her upper lip with her tongue. The door was now a plain, smooth expanse of painted wood. There was no door latch, no sign of hinges. It could be a decorative piece of paneling, for any evidence to the contrary. Knowing it to be a waste of time, she nevertheless, felt over the smooth surface, paying particular attention to the spot where she had seen the latch when Avylos had used it.

Still nothing. She blew out her breath in a noiseless whistle and turned back to the garden. So much for sneaking into the room, grabbing the Muse Stone, retrieving Bloodbone and the bulk of her weapons from the stables, and riding away while the Mage was elsewhere. She would have to think of a new plan.

Dhulyn expected to find the garden familiar, even though this would be the first time she had seen it directly, and in the clear light of day. There was no mistaking the pool, for example, in which she'd seen Edmir's reflection. She sat down on the poolwide stone edge and trailed her hand in the water. Too bad she couldn't use the Mage's ghost eye to see Edmir for herself. Though if she was wishing things, she'd prefer to see Parno.

Escaped into the woods, she thought. *I wish I could believe him.* But she couldn't, not really. In her Visions, Avylos had been terrified, granted, but there had been no sign of what he'd been running from. And while Avylos had been young, he was old enough to hold a sword and die beside his family—or at the very least old enough to lead other, younger children away into the woods, to escape as he had himself. Why hadn't he done so?

Why would he have run without even trying to help? Dhulyn rubbed her hands dry on her leggings. Were her questions reasonable? Or did her thinking reflect that of a Mercenary Brother, and not that of a young Espadryni boy? She'd always assumed that what had made the Mercenary School feel so right for her was that it had provided the same sense of unity she remembered feeling as a child, riding behind her father on his horse. The unity that would keep one Mercenary standing over an injured Brother until the fight—or their lives—ended. In Battle, or in Death.

If Avylos had not felt this, was the fault in him, or in her own memories?

Even if she were willing to believe that part of his story, what of the things he *hadn't* mentioned? There could be no doubting now that he was the same Avylyn who had been a member of Troupe Tzadeyeu. Even if the names had not agreed, there was that plain wooden casket she'd been so careful to ignore, sitting on the end of his worktable, that matched so perfectly the drawing in Zania's book. Dhulyn put her hand where she could feel the edge of the book under her tunic. She stood up once more and followed the path on the far side of the pond. It led to a section of wall that had obviously been rebuilt at one time. In this light, and from this angle, it seemed likely she could climb the wall, when the opportunity presented itself.

"Oh, yes," she muttered, still in her mother's tongue. "I'm *sure* he spent ten summers living on a farm, *that's* likely." But a short time on a farm, and then a second escape to the players troupe? That was far more likely. And if the Stone enhanced what powers he did possess—or somehow triggered powers which had been latent? *That* would explain a great deal. It seemed likelier still that he had taken it and fled for the greater protection of the Royal House of Tegrian.

She stepped back from the wall, propped her left hand on her hip, and tilted her head to one side.

"Aren't you going to miss your supper, loitering about here?" she asked.

After a long moment, the girl Dhulyn had sensed sitting behind a flowering bush on a rough protruding stone in the rebuilt section of wall stood up and picked her way down to the ground level.

Dhulyn's face relaxed into a smile. She knew who this girl must be. Her hair was the same red gold as Valaika Jarlkevoso's, though obviously without the gray. And while her face was more oval, she had her brother Edmir's strong nose. Dhulyn raised her hand—

⋙⋘

Older. Perhaps ten years older. On horseback, a white horse with deep blue saddlecloth, crested. Her light red hair clubbed back away from her face, smoothed down to take the helm. Her deep blue shirt and cotte covered by a hammered silver cuirass, worked around the edges with lapis lazuli inlay, and crested with the crowned mark of the princes of Tegrian. The soldiers around her, clearly awaiting her orders.

⋙⋘

And just that suddenly the Vision was over.

"Avylos can't tell when I'm there," the girl said, half question, half statement.

"I'm not Avylos," Dhulyn said. But the girl's observation was interesting. "Are you often in his garden unknown to him?"

The girl shrugged, and in that movement Dhulyn saw Edmir again. What was the name? Kera, that was it.

"You are wearing Jarlkevo colors," the princess said. "Did you bring the Mage some news?"

"I may have news for you, Princess Kera."

"I'm called Lady Prince now," the girl said, looking away. The corners of her mouth turned down.

"That may be," Dhulyn said. "But you have no right to the title. Your brother is alive, Princess. He misses you, and thinks of you often."

The girl took a step back. Suspicion and anger fought each other on her face. "How do you know?"

To answer, Dhulyn once again pulled off her wig.

"Don't point, don't even look," Parno said, walking just behind Valaika's shoulder, where a good personal guard would naturally be. "When we're looking in some other direction, tell me relative to *that* where our objective is."

"The trouble with you Mercenaries is that you think no one but yourselves knows how to do anything." There was amusement in Valaika's voice. "Believe it or not, I was practicing this kind of misdirection before you were born."

Parno grinned. That was exactly the reaction he'd expected. It had been only a few hours since they'd arrived in the rooms permanently set aside for Valaika and her family in the Royal House—rooms within the Royal compound, but actually in a separate building from the queen's own residence. Valaika had sent word to the woman who had been her sister-in-law as soon as they'd arrived, but it seemed the queen was in no hurry to acknowledge Valaika's presence.

"From here you can see the road we used to come into the city," Valaika said, coming to a standstill at the top of a short flight of stairs that raised them to the level of a small square tower which would provide shelter to the night guard in bad weather. "The wing we want is behind us, and slightly to our left. When we turn to go back, look for where a section of wall has been repaired with lighter stone. Behind that section is his garden."

Another thing Parno hadn't needed to tell her was not to say the words "Mage" or "Avylos" aloud, lest they catch the wrong ear.

When they reached the doorway into the square tower, Valaika turned and they began to retrace their steps. As the personal guard he was pretending to be, it was natural for him to scan their perimeter, easy to look in the right direction. The repaired wall stood out, just as Valaika had said it would. Apparently, the Mage took as his apartments the very end of a long ell built against the outer wall of the Royal House. It would have windows giving on both the courtyard and the outer world.

The young man with a Balnian accent who had escorted them to Valaika's apartments had already told them of the gossip that was circulating, that a cousin of the Blue Mage had arrived and was recovering in his apartments from the crying fever. A young woman whom he was isolating for fear she would spread the infection. But she was alive, and she was expected to appear in public as soon as her recovery was complete.

Parno concentrated, fixing the image of the Mage's wing in his mind for later consideration, even as every muscle in his body wanted to launch himself across the distance separating him from his Partner. *Now*. He wanted to go *now*. See her with his own eyes, touch her with his own hands. Make sure she was not looking at Avylos with a heart that said, "Cousin."

Just as they were nearing the stone stairway that would return them to the grounds and the path that would take them back to Valaika's wing, a page with a crown embroidered on the left side of her deep blue tunic came toward them with a determined step.

Valaika stopped and signaled the young girl to approach.

"Good morning, House Jarlkevo. I bring greetings from Kedneara the Queen. She welcomes you to Royal House, and looks forward to seeing you the second morning from now, at her audience."

"I thank you, Page. Tell my sister, Kedneara the Queen, that I anticipate with great satisfaction seeing her, and my niece, the Lady Prince Kera."

"I will tell her so." The page gave an abrupt nod that set her dark curls bouncing and turned on her heel. Parno watched which way she went. Her errand accomplished, she was headed back to the pages' room where she would wait until sent on another.

"Well, only a three-day wait altogether. The Great King's been known to keep even his own mother waiting for longer than that."

Valaika shrugged and turned once more to the entrance of her suite. "It's not as though I'd asked to see her with any urgency. I may be aunt to the next ruler, but since my brother died, there are Noble Houses closer to the throne than I."

"And related to the Tarkin of Hellik?"

They had reached Valaika's door, and she paused, hand on the door's handle.

"That is why I'll be kept waiting only three days."

"All to the good, then," Parno said, following her in. "Any particular reason to invite you only to this audience and not a more private meeting?"

"Oh, yes," she said, her smile twisted to one side. "There's reason."

Eighteen

CROSS THE PASSAGE AND down three paces from
the magicked door to the Blue Mage's workroom,
was another door, this one with a plain wooden latch
clearly in view. It opened, Dhulyn found, into what appeared to be a more personal sitting room. Here, in addition to a wide wooden bench covered with bright cushions
under the narrow window, there was a small round table
with the shelf for a brazier pan between the legs, a short
cabinet of the type used to hold plates and cups, several
large, well-padded chairs, and niches holding oil lamps decorated with the patterned glass shades for which the city-
state of Tenezia was well known. As in the other rooms,
winter rugs had been removed, revealing a tiled blue-and-
green floor.

It was here, Dhulyn imagined, that Avylos received social guests—if he had any, for she noticed that only one
chair showed signs of repeated use—and took his meals
away from his workroom, where all his focus and concentration was needed for his magical pursuits. During the
year she had spent in the Scholars' Library before taking
her final oaths as a Mercenary Brother, Dhulyn had been
taught that, wherever possible, Scholars should keep their
workrooms separate from their living quarters. It appeared
that the Blue Mage had been given the same advice.

Since there was no magic on the door, Dhulyn did not
hesitate to enter the room. She checked the cupboard—
plates and eating utensils as she had expected—lit two of
the lamps, and, wrinkling her nose at the honeyed smell of

the scented oil, pulled one of the unused chairs over to the table. She angled herself so that the light would fall into her lap, and sat down to read, leaving the door to the hall standing open. It was some hours later that she heard footsteps slow as they approached the open doorway. She closed Zania's book, pushed it into her tunic just above her waist, and pulled the laces shut, tying them where they would support the book without outlining it. She crossed her ankles, resting her feet on the brazier shelf under the table and folded her hands on her belly, as if she'd been taking a nap.

As Dhulyn expected, it was Avylos himself who appeared in the doorway, the brilliant blue of his overrobe catching the light from the oil lamps. He was carrying a tray on which rested bread, a large piece of game pie, the meat layered with slices of dried fruit, and a pottery flask of what smelled like spiced crab apple wine, sweeter than she would normally drink.

"Here, let me," she said, getting to her feet and taking the tray from him. "You should be better served than this. Or is it that you're hiding me even from your servants and pages?"

He smiled as though something had mightily pleased him. "Indeed, I've let it be known that you have the crying fever."

Dhulyn raised her eyebrows. "That will be sure to keep away all but the desperately curious."

"Even the desperately curious usually know better than to explore my rooms uninvited."

"I will be sure to remember that."

She set the tray on the table and sat down herself. The portions were generous, but even so, there was only enough food for one. As a Mercenary Brother, held captive however comfortably by an enemy, she should not touch it. But that was not the role she was playing here. If Edmir were writing her lines, and Zania directing her movements, what would they be telling her? If she and Avylos were truly what they claimed to be, the last of their tribe, the only Espadryni either of them had ever met since the Tribes were broken—how would Avylos expect her to act? What would be natural under the circumstances? Dhulyn thought of the surge of emotion she had felt on seeing and recognizing

Avylos as an Espadryni. *I would want to trust him,* she thought. Though it went against her Schooling, and the Common Rule of the Brotherhood, she would want her kin to be worthy of her trust. And that gave her a way to turn the Common Rule to her advantage.

"Is the food not to your liking?"

"I was just thinking that if I were anywhere else, or if you were anyone else, I would have to find a way to refuse the food, or to trick you somehow into sharing it with me. It is our Common Rule," she added, "to aid us against eating poisoned or drugged food."

He reached for the plate.

Before he touched it, she laid two fingers on the back of his hand. "I said, 'if I were anywhere else.'" She pulled the plate toward her, took her knife from her belt and cut herself off a bite-sized piece of pie. Avylos smiled and poured her out a glass of the wine, pleased, as she'd thought, that she trusted him.

Sun and Stars—if it is drugged, I hope it's one I've been Schooled against, she thought.

Avylos got up and went to the cabinet to the right of the door. He selected for his own use a stemmed blue glass and brought it back to the table, filling it with wine before sitting down across from her once again. "Tomorrow, I must leave you for the morning," he said. "I will have food left in the corridor where this part of the House joins the main section. I advise you to be sure no one sees you fetch it. Can you do that?"

"It is another of the things I have been Schooled to, yes," she said.

He nodded, and took a careful sip of the wine before setting it down once more on the table. "I know enough about the Mercenary Brotherhood to know that your commitment there is for life. I cannot—I must not—ask you to abandon the Brotherhood, but would you take work here?"

"In Beolind?"

"In the Royal House. We are kin, as you said. Perhaps the only Espadryni left in the whole world. Certainly, you are the only one I have ever seen." He lifted his eyes to her face for just a moment before lowering them again to the glass he was turning in his fingers.

Stick to your role, Dhulyn told herself. What would she say if she were just a lone Mercenary Brother, made such an offer? "The Brotherhood *is* a life tie." That, at least, was no more than the truth, the Common Rule. "We have no pasts once we are Schooled."

"Yet you came looking for me here, thinking that I might be one of the Espadryni. When you saw me, you called me cousin."

She had. Dhulyn tore off a piece of bread and put it into her mouth, buying herself time to think. Despite the Common Rule, despite what she may have thought, when she had seen a Tribesman her heart *had* lifted and she *had* called out to him, instinctively, without conscious decision. As though a part of her had, after all, wanted more than the Brotherhood had given her. She'd often been impatient with other Brothers, who found it hard to put aside the years before they came to the Brotherhood. With Parno, especially, she had been short. Now, she recognized that it had been very easy for her to follow the Common Rule and put her past behind her. Until she'd met with Avylos the Blue Mage, she'd had no past.

Blooded fool, she said to herself. Whatever he might make her feel, this man was *not* her past, this was the Blue Mage.

"I will be guided by you," she said finally. "But perhaps I should make no plans until you have spoken with the queen."

He leaned back, smiling. Dhulyn wished she was as satisfied with her answer as Avylos appeared to be.

"While we wait for the time to be right, will you do something for me?"

Dhulyn, her mouth once more full, raised her eyebrows as she chewed.

"Will you See for me?"

Dhulyn let herself fall back against her chair, laid her knife down on the table, and allowed herself to blink and appear startled. No matter what he knew, or how he knew it, that would be the safest reaction to Avylos' question. Stay in character. She could almost hear Zania's scolding her. The sharp spike of fear that shot through her she pushed away, and kept well hidden.

She swallowed. "What do you mean?"

He smiled, and in that indulgent smile she saw the smugness, the arrogance which was what *he* tried to keep hidden.

"As you were so young at the breaking of the Tribes, you may not realize that the Sight was a common thing among our women. But even if I had not known this, I *am* a Mage. Your Mark is as clear to me as the color of your eyes."

Dhulyn picked up the cloth napkin that still lay on the tray and began to wipe her trembling hands. She could do nothing that might betray her excitement. She and Parno had been following the rumors that said there was a Seer once more in Delmara, in the hope that Dhulyn could learn from her. But if Avylos knew the women of the Espadryni were Seers . . . He *was* older. He remembered his life among the Tribes. *Here* might be the source of what she needed most to know.

Even so, she was not here to learn from him, but to stop him. Perhaps, if she were very careful, and played her part well, she could do both.

"A Sight of the future would be of great use to me," he said, as the silence grew.

She leaned forward. "I would do everything within my power to help you," she said. "But how much help you'll find me . . ." She lifted her shoulders and let them drop.

"Now it is my turn to ask what you mean."

How much to tell him? If she were to learn anything useful, she must be as truthful as possible. There was no way to know what detail was important.

"I have long hidden my Mark, and not simply because it would complicate the life of a Mercenary Brother," she said. "It did not come to me until after the breaking of the Tribes, when I had seen the Hawk Moon perhaps twelve times. It terrified me, for I had no one to train me or explain. Seers are so rare, that even the Guildhalls of the Marked have little or no information to help me. So my Visions remain erratic, they do not always come when I summon them, nor can I control what I will see. They are strongest during my woman's time, as though the blood calls them, but few other things have any effect. I was hoping to reach the Shrine of Delmara, where they say a Seer sits once more, to ask for training, but I have my living to make, and even for a Mercenary Brother, that's not so easy.

"You are older than I," she added, placing her hands on the edge of the table and leaning forward. "Did you have sisters? Do you remember any ritual they performed? Any tool they used?" If he knew about the vera tiles, that would tell her whether there was anything to learn from him.

He was nodding. "My magic also came late to me, after I'd left the Tribes. Like your Mark, it was limited and erratic at first. I could magic only myself, or my immediate surroundings." Avylos gestured, and suddenly he was a brown-haired man, with Edmir's dark eyes, then his hair returned to its normal blood red, his eyes their vivid blue. He held out a hand and a tiny blue flame appeared on his palm.

"Then, as I practiced and studied, I could send the magic farther from me." He drew a small circle of light in the air with his right index finger and a flame appeared in one of the oil lamps Dhulyn had left dark. The surprise she did not trouble to hide was not a reaction to the lighting of the lamp, however. She had recognized the gesture he'd used painting the streaks of light in the air. She had seen it, or something very like it, before. She had seen Avylos himself gesturing in the air, but without any light following his finger. And she had seen an older Espadryni man do exactly what the Mage was doing now. Avylos painted another symbol and the shutters opened; yet another, and a small scroll flew in the window and came to rest on his open hand.

"But surely you can magic things even farther away?" Dhulyn said. "Unless you travel with the armies . . . ?"

"I have ways of sending the magic farther afield, yes, but nothing I can show you now." He laid the scroll to one side. "And you, Cousin, what can you show me?"

Dhulyn nodded smartly, as if she were only making her decision as they spoke. "If you like, I will try, but you may prefer to wait until my woman's time comes again."

"You asked what I remembered of the women of the Tribes," he said. Dhulyn noticed that he did not say whether any of these women were his sisters. "Sometimes they chanted, or hummed the same tune, over and over, until it seemed they fell into a light trance, and it was then the Visions came. The chants I do not remember, but the trance I can give you myself."

It should work, Dhulyn thought, even as she desperately wanted to say no. The Visions often came as she dropped off to sleep, while her mind was loose and drifting. She knew that certain drugs, those which relaxed and freed the mind, could make the Visions clearer—but a trance would mean being unconscious, and vulnerable, in front of him. Still, there was no way she could refuse without making it plain she did not trust him. And always before her hung the possibility that she might learn something.

"I will try," she said.

❧❧❧

An Avylos much younger than the man she knows sits back on his heels. He is in a small tent, just large enough to allow two people to stand upright, though at the moment he is alone and kneeling on a cushion. As she has seen him do when a child, he is drawing figures in the air, but this time lines of light trail after his moving finger. His face is split in a wide smile, as he draws faster and faster. *"Ne foromat srusha,"* he is saying over and over again in the tongue of the Espadryni. "I am not barren." . . .

The room has a floor of polished oak, inlaid with a fine banding of a much darker color near the walls, almost like the edging on a carpet. There are shelves and cubbies for books and scrolls. The large worktable is to her left, placed where it will receive the light from one of two tall, narrow windows, under which a bench has been built. There are cushions on the bench, and a three-legged stool lying on its side. She has seen this room before, but this time the door is closed, the tabletop is empty except for the plain casket. No unrolled scrolls, no open books. The room is empty . . . .

It is night. The moon shines through the narrow windows, illuminating the worktable, casting shadows from the bars across the wood floor. She walks into the room and approaches the desk. Her field of vision takes in the room's far corner, beyond the windows, to her left as she approaches the worktable. Something is wrong. She has Seen this before, she has Seen herself walk into this room, over to the worktable, her hands outstretched to the casket that sits there. She should be able to See her other self, her *Seeing* self, but the corner of the room is empty, she's not there . . . .

Zania is wearing a winter cloak, the throat well closed with elaborate frogging, the hood pulled up close around her face. Her cheeks glow and her eyes dance. She is singing, and looking down at a bar of blue crystal which she holds in her bare hands. As she sings, she turns the bar first one way, then another, first by the middle, then by each end in turn. Finally, she holds the bar between the flat palms of her two hands, and shuts her eyes. . . .

Avylos is made of light. Beams of light pour from his fingers' ends, from his eyes, from his open mouth, from the ends of his hair. He walks toward her, his hands stretched out and she feels herself stepping forward, even as she wills herself back.

❋

Her eyes snapped open and he was kneeling in front of her, his face white, his eyes focused on her, searching, as if her features would tell him something.

"What did you See?"

"You were full of light, lord Mage. Full of light."

❋

"More jam?"

"Mmm." Dhulyn accepted the small ceramic pot of nellberry jam Princess Kera handed her and spooned some onto her biscuit while she swallowed what she already had in her mouth. She'd never eaten nellberries before, and was beginning to be afraid that she'd never get another chance. She'd gone down to the castle end of the corridor that morning as Avylos had instructed her, and hadn't been altogether surprised to find the princess had brought breakfast herself. Like anyone of her age, the princess was curious, and as Dhulyn expected, she had many questions.

Dhulyn returned the spoon to the tabletop, where it had been representing the Limona River. "Your strategy was a good one," she said, pointing to the battleground she'd created using the saltcellar, spoons, jam pots, and dried fruit that had accompanied the biscuits and bite-sized meat tartlets that made up their breakfast. "You made good use of the terrain, very good use of your cavalry. Your archers, perhaps, could have been in a better position." She tapped a spot that had been left blank before looking up at the princess. "Your brother had no hand in this plan?"

Kera shook her head without lifting her eyes from the tabletop. "Edmir has no head for strategy. The plan was all mine. Why did it fail?"

Dhulyn held up a finger. Frowned. Licked the jam off it and held it up again. "First, you expected to be outnumbered, but not as greatly as you were." She held up another finger. "Second, you did not know that Parno and I had changed the usual strategy and formation of the Nisvean forces." Another finger. "Third, you expected the magic that has protected the Tegrian armies for the last two campaigning seasons to work this time as well."

"So it really wasn't my fault?"

Dhulyn raised her eyebrows. "Come. You knew as soon as you'd seen Edmir's image in the pool what had really happened."

Kera looked up from the representation of the battle of Limona. "I know. It *had* to be Avylos. Yet, somehow, I couldn't feel *sure*."

"And you are sure now?"

The girl nodded. "Avylos tried to kill my brother."

"And he is still trying."

"Why are you helping us?"

Dhulyn shrugged. "It began as a way to follow our Common Rule. We don't hold for ransom, and your brother was ours to decide upon, no one else's. Then, things grew more complicated. With respect to your mother, an ambitious and predatory queen is a worry for her neighbors, if for no one else. Such a queen with a tame Mage can be a larger worry, then." She fell silent as images passed through her mind. "If you had seen what he did to Probic, you would not need to ask me why we are here. We have had some experience, my Partner and I, of Mages and the like who become ambitious for themselves. It is not a problem from which you can walk away. It will follow."

"But he is powerful—" Kera stopped and turned abruptly to face Dhulyn. "Can you call upon others of your Brotherhood? Can you oppose him?"

Dhulyn leaned forward, scanning the youthful face in front of her. The princess returned her look steadily, even raising one eyebrow a fraction. Edmir would already have been fidgeting; the girl was much cooler than her brother, more direct and less dreamy. She would make a better ruler than Edmir, Dhulyn thought, and wondered if the girl herself realized it.

"The short answer to your question is 'no,'" she said. "Even setting aside the banishment, the Brotherhood is not a standing army, not a force that can be called upon. Once, long ago, perhaps, close to the time of the Caids, we were more numerous, but in recent years our numbers have dwindled. Many cities, like Beolind, no longer have a Mercenary House. I would not be surprised to learn that Parno and I were the only Mercenary Brothers now in Tegrian. But—" Dhulyn lifted her hand as the princess opened her mouth to speak. "We *are* here, Parno and I, and we will do what we can to stop him.

"We have reason to believe that the source of his power is a blue Stone, a crystal as long as my forearm, and perhaps as thick around as this." Dhulyn held up her hands to demonstrate the dimensions. "He may have some latent power or abilities of his own, but the crystal fuels them, gives them power and force."

"And if you remove this Stone, you remove his powers?"

"Yes."

"And that's why you are here."

"Yes."

"But he's the consort, he's been helping . . ." Kera's voice died away.

"He's been helping your mother the queen," Dhulyn finished Kera's thought for her. "Do you think your mother wanted Edmir dead?"

Kera shook her head slowly, her eyes unfocused.

"What will he do next that she does not want? Comes a time, when you must ask yourself, do you wield the sword, or does the sword wield you?"

Kera's eyes narrowed. "Is removing the Stone enough? Will Avylos not try to recapture it?"

Dhulyn smiled. The girl was definitely worth two of her brother; this question had not occurred to Edmir. "We may have to destroy it," she said. "But it may be possible to simply neutralize it. His powers may then return to their latent condition."

"How can I help?"

"I need to get into his workroom. When I tried last night, I could not even find the latch; it was as if the door was simply a solid piece of wood."

"He magics it when he leaves the wing," Kera said, nodding. "But unless he has used something new, I should be able to open it."

"How so?"

Kera shrugged. "Edmir and I discovered this when our father was still alive. When Avylos works a magic on a woman, or against a woman, sometimes it does not work at all, and if it does, it will eventually wear off, and must be reworked. On a man, it seems to last for always—that is, if Avylos wants it to. He *can* magic a man temporarily if he chooses to, as he does with the armies, for example. But with a woman, the magic *always* fades by itself. That's why there are so few women in our armies, and why, I suspect, Avylos won't have female pages nor allów my mother to have them," Kera added, in a tone that showed this had just occurred to her. "I don't know if any one else has noticed this, but Edmir and I did. Also—" She hesitated as if choosing her words carefully. "It seems that there are times when he doesn't . . . when he *conserves* his magic."

"Again, how so?"

"Well, take his workroom as an example. At times we've noticed he uses what Edmir called magics of concealment, where a thing is simply not visible, like the latch on his door. Other times, there might be magics of avoidance, where you approach his door, or the shelves behind his worktable say, and then find yourself in another part of the corridor entirely, or on the other side of the room, looking out the window." Kera straightened the spoon next to her plate. "Sometimes all these magics are in effect. But there are times when there is no magic of concealment, if an avoidance magic would serve the purpose just as well, or where there's no avoidance magics if a lock would do."

Dhulyn whistled silently. "So there are times when the door is magicked, but the things inside the room are not?"

Kera nodded.

Dhulyn would wager her second-best sword that it was Kera herself who noticed this and told Edmir. "And if the magic on the door is an old one, one which has been there a while, you should be able to see the latch, and open the door?"

"I've done it before." Kera studied the jam pot with great concentration.

"Will he know you've helped me?"

Kera spoke without raising her eyes from the empty jam pot. "From what Avylos has said before, he can tell *that* I've been somewhere, like his workroom or the garden. But he can't tell *when* it was, or for how long."

"Nor, from what you said in the garden yesterday, can he always tell when you are actually present, but hiding." Dhulyn drew away from the table. It seemed, then, that she was not the only one whose control over their gift was less than perfect. Perhaps Avylos depended too much on his magics, and that might provide them with an opening. "So, his magics can tell him certain things, but not *all* things."

"He learns new magics all the time, though," Kera said. "When we were small, he couldn't tell that we'd been in his room. Then he could tell that someone had been, but not who. Now he call tell who." The girl frowned. "Dhulyn Wolfshead, if Avylos gets his power from this Stone, where does the Stone get its power?"

As her hand strayed to brush against the book under her tunic, Dhulyn scanned the table once more for any food she'd missed before answering. "The Stone is like a well," she said. "You draw power from it, as you would water from the well, and then it must be replenished, as the well is replenished by an underground stream or lake."

"But how is the Stone replenished?"

Dhulyn knew from Zania's book how the players had refilled the Stone. After every performance, they had returned to it the power they took. Old Therin had believed that their own skill, and the heightened energies created by the performance itself, had enabled them always to return at least as much as they had used, if not a little more.

"Avylos is the one who checks new Mages and the Marked, isn't he? For licensing?"

Kera pushed her empty plate away. "Yes."

"And has he issued any new licenses?"

"I wouldn't necessarily know," Kera said. "There have been a few of the Marked, a Finder, I think, and a Mender. Edmir was trying to work out a scheme to get them to return here after they'd been sent to the Guilds in Imrion for training. But if the ones here are already licensed . . ."

"You say the Marked, but what about Mages? How many of them have been found and licensed?"

"Mages?" Kera looked puzzled, her brow furrowed and her lips parted. "None," she said finally. "None that I've heard of, anyway."

"I'd wager that's how he is powering the Stone, then." Dhulyn rubbed at her forehead with her fingertips. "Anyone who has magic within them comes to be examined and licensed. And then he takes their power, and feeds it to the Stone."

"Maybe not just Mages." Kera had turned very white, and her eyes stared into the distance. "There was a harper used to live here at Royal House. She would make new songs for my mother's birthday, and other songs, all kinds, great stirring ballads and light funny tunes. She fell ill, and Avylos tended to her—we have no Healer here, not since before my grandfather's time. When her illness was gone, she couldn't make new songs anymore. She could still sing the old ones, but there were no more new songs."

Dhulyn shivered. No more new songs. That would also fit what Therin had described. The Stone could take in talent of every kind.

"Even if I get you into the workroom," Kera said finally. "What if there are other avoidance magics in the room itself?"

"What are the areas he makes you avoid?" Dhulyn said.

"The shelves behind his worktable. There's mostly books, a couple of other things. And the small casket on the table itself. To the left, if you're sitting in his chair, on the right if you're facing the table."

Dhulyn nodded, she'd seen the casket, and the bookshelf for that matter. "The casket holds the Stone," she said. "We'll just have to try and see." Another thought occurred to her. "Are Avylos' enchantments just against people? Could I reach the Stone with a weapon? A fire arrow, for example?"

Kera leaned forward, her brows drawn down in a vee. "I've never tried throwing anything into the magicked area." Her brows lifted. "A fire arrow might be very interesting indeed."

"How soon can you get me into the room?"

Kera thought, turning her spoon over and over on the tablecloth. "Tonight," she said. "There's to be a banquet. Avylos will attend with my mother the queen, and won't come back to his rooms until late. If at all."

❦

Edmir sank to his knees, let his face fall forward into Zania's hands, and crushed his lips against her palm.

The audience—four herd children, a dog, and nine of their flock—was silent for two heartbeats before breaking into thunderous whistling, clapping, and stamping of bare feet. The dog barked, and the sheep shied away a few paces before settling once more to their cropping of the clumps of grass.

"I thought there might be too much kissing," the tallest boy said, his fair hair tied back in a tail. "But there wasn't. It was just right."

"High praise, indeed," Edmir said, and swept the boy another bow. When the children had gone their way up the hillside with promises of more dramatics the next day, Edmir turned to Zania. She had taken off the cloak she'd been wearing to rehearse the part of the queen and spread it on the ground before sitting down.

Edmir sat down next to her, feeling light as a feather. He turned his face up to the warmth of the sun. He couldn't stop smiling, and his lips could still feel Zania's skin.

"You don't think you could write me a half dozen more of these before you go back to your real life, do you? This one pleases all who've seen it, but I can't make a living with just *The Soldier King*." Zania ran her hands through her short hair and leaned back on her elbows.

Edmir came down to earth with a thump that almost stopped his heart.

"That's all you have to say," he said, finally, when he could trust his voice—and his breathing—to sound normal. "You didn't feel anything just now?"

Zania sat up, her eyes turned away. "Of course I did, I was supposed to." She glanced at him, her green eyes dark. "It's the play, Edmir."

He spread his hands, shaking his head. "I must be a great writer, then."

Zania took hold of his sleeve between her thumb and forefinger and gave it a little tug. "You are. And I understand how you feel. It's one of the reasons that actors so frequently marry other actors. Let's see how you feel when you're Prince Edmir once again."

"You could come with me," he said. The words were out before he knew it, but once out, he was certain he wouldn't take them back.

"You don't mean it."

"I do."

Zania took in a deep breath through her nose. "Your mother the queen would let us marry?"

Edmir didn't speak, he knew the answer was on his face.

"That's what I thought. You'll be Lord Prince, and then King. What will I be?" Zania stood up and tugged on the edge of the cloak. Edmir waited long enough to be sure she wasn't running away before he stood up also, holding the edge closest to him in his hands. Zania dropped the edge she was holding and started to walk down the hill toward the track that led to the gamekeeper's lodge.

But she *was* walking, not running.

"You could have a theater in Beolind," he said, trying to keep his voice neutral as he hurried to catch up with her.

"Or in Gotterang, or Lesonika or Tenezia. Any city large enough to have the business. Why should I stay in Beolind?"

Because I would be there. But he couldn't say it aloud,

couldn't bare his need so plainly. "Because I would ask you to," he said instead. That was as close as he could come.

She looked back at him then and stopped, her feet carefully braced on the uneven dirt of the track. She smiled, but it was a stage smile; her eyes were still hooded and dark. "Yes," she said. "And you could write me plays in your copious free time, between ruling the country, going to war, and making a good political marriage. As for me, I would never know whether my audiences loved my work, or whether they applauded because I was the king's woman."

It was true, what she was saying, they both knew it.

And that's *why she pushes me away,* he thought. Because he would be going back to his own life, and because, when he became Lord Prince Edmir once again, he would have to put his feelings for her aside.

But not because she doesn't feel the same way. She'd been speaking plainly, out here with only the rocks and grass to hear them, and if she didn't care for him, she would have said so. If she did not ask him to stay with her, it was only because she knew what his answer must be.

There was a strange horse tied up outside the lodge, which drove all other thoughts away.

"We're just players," Zania reminded him under her breath. "Nothing to worry about."

"Where are the others?" he murmured.

"Fishing."

But acting turned out not to be necessary, as it was the Consort Sylria who greeted them when they reached the door.

"There you are, I was just coming out to see to the horse. You had me worried a moment, though I could see all was well." She gestured at the orderly room around her. "I have news, we leave for Beolind tomorrow, can you be ready?"

"Tomorrow?"

The older woman nodded. "A messenger came from Valaika. We're to leave for Beolind tomorrow."

"Have they spoken to my mother?" Edmir was afraid to look at Zania.

Sylria came closer to them and lowered her voice. "I would think she had to be careful how much to entrust to a messenger. All I know is we're to go to Beolind." She smiled and patted them both on the shoulder. "Tomorrow."

"Shouldn't we be leaving right away?" Did Zania have to sound so eager?

"It's already late to begin the journey today," Sylria said. "Though I came as quickly as I could." She went to the doorway and clucked at her horse. "My instructions were quite clear. We're to leave for Beolind tomorrow." Sylria smiled again, and disappeared through the doorway.

Edmir shared a look with Zania, their earlier awkwardness forgotten.

"That still doesn't leave us much time," Zania said. "Lucky thing I've repacked almost everything already."

Edmir looked back at the doorway. "Something's wrong," he said, when he judged Sylria was far enough away. "Something in the tone of her voice . . ."

"You think you know her tones so well?" Zania sat down on the bench along one side of the table.

Edmir sat down next to her, taking care to leave space between them. "'We're to leave for Beolind tomorrow,'" he said. "I know *that* tone—Caids know you've made us all so sensitive to intonation and syllable stress and what all in the last moon. I know I've heard that tone before." He reached for the knife at his belt, suddenly wishing for his sword instead, as the hairs on the back of his neck rose. "And I know where."

He turned to face Zania. "In Probic, that's how Tzanek sounded when he said, 'The young man they have with them is not Edmir, I will not be deceived.' I'll never forget it, never."

"You sounded just like her."

"So you see?"

Zania looked at the doorway, gnawing on her lower lip. "It's like sleep suggestion," she said finally.

"What?"

"It's a stage show trick—or not a trick exactly, but it doesn't need real magic. At least—well, I think Avylos used to do it, but I've seen it done by others I know are not Mages."

Edmir wanted to take her by the shoulders and shake it out of her. "Explain," he said through clenched teeth.

"You focus someone's attention in such a way that they appear to fall asleep, but they can still hear you. Then you tell them to do something, dance, or sing, or beg some stranger to marry them, something to make the audience laugh."

"And they do it?" Edmir had a cold feeling in his stomach.

"Usually, yes, but it's meant to be funny. Or sometimes you give them a command to follow after they've woken up and when the cue comes, they'll do it, even though they're awake. Oh—"

His face must have shown what he was thinking because Zania broke off, shaking her head and hunching up her shoulders.

"I don't know *how* it works, exactly, but it *does* work. And that's what Sylria makes me think of."

"And Avylos can do this." Edmir looked down at his hands. "I don't think we should go anywhere with Sylria. Dhulyn and Parno haven't sent for us, I'm sure of it."

"But we *want* to go to Beolind. If we can't trust Sylria any longer . . ." Zania shrugged. "The only people we *can* trust are there."

"So we go along with her, and look for our best chance to escape?"

"Now you're thinking."

Nineteen

DHULYN WOLFSHEAD FINGERED the edge of the short, blood-red wig Avylos had found for her. He'd been right; it wasn't as good a quality as the one she'd been wearing, the one she'd had from Zania's stock. Nor was the fit as secure without the paste from Zania's well-sealed jars. And, if anything, it had been *more* disconcerting to catch sight of herself in the small mirror that hung in her chamber with hair the right color, but no Mercenary badge. She lowered her hand and brought her attention back to what she was supposed to be doing, waiting for Princess Kera.

Dhulyn had earlier made note of the spot where the corridor of dressed stone widened as it approached the doorway of Avylos' workroom, and made a small corner. It wouldn't appear possible, but at night, with only the light from the sconces in the main hallway, that small corner created just enough shadow for a slim person to stand unseen. Provided that person was using one of the Stalking *Shoras*. Dhulyn pressed her shoulder blades against the cold stone and breathed shallowly. She'd arrived early, but just as she'd expected, she hadn't been able to open the door to the Blue Mage's workroom. Once again, there was neither latch nor lock, just the plain, unbroken expanse of wood.

She had only been waiting for a few minutes when the rustle of stiff silks warned her that Kera was coming. *Loud enough for three people,* she thought. *Good thing I'm the only one here.* And a good thing that she wasn't wearing formal court clothes herself—even her breathing would have been too loud for caution.

"Kera," she whispered as the girl passed her.

The princess squeaked and brought her hands up in self-defense, almost taking off the end of her sleeve with the sword held in her right hand. Squeak or no, Dhulyn noted, the girl held her sword steady, and she'd turned in the right direction, *toward* what had frightened her. Kera lowered her left hand slowly, and peered into the shadow.

"Dhulyn Wolfshead?"

Dhulyn stepped out of the narrow shadow and carefully took the blade out of Kera's hand.

"How much time have you?"

"Not long. I said I was going to the water closet, and then I had to stop in my room for the sword." She looked at it, lower lip between her teeth. "It was my father's," she said.

Dhulyn had already noticed it was a soldier's blade, plain with only a single rough stone in the pommel.

"Best that you don't come in with me, then." *Not that I would have let you, but there's no need for you to know that.* "The door will not open for me," she added.

"Unless he's renewed it . . ." Kera stood in front of the door and slowed her breathing. She lifted her hand to a spot rather higher than Dhulyn would have expected a door latch to be, and an elaborately wrought metal handle appeared just as Kera's fingers closed on it. The door swung open the width of a hand.

"Either he has no secrets from you," Dhulyn said. "Or he thinks there's nothing in there you can discover by yourself."

"I used to think it was the first one." Kera shrugged. "But what need to spell the door against me if I can't open anything once I'm inside?"

"I'll see what *I* can do," Dhulyn said. "Best you be off before you're missed."

Kera looked once more into the room, indecision plain on her face. Finally, she took a step back. "Caids smile on you," she said, and ran back down the hallway toward the main part of the Royal House.

Dhulyn waited until the sound of rustling silk died away,

and she could both hear herself think, and hear anyone else who might be coming. Standing to one side, she pushed the door farther open with the tip of the sword blade, and listened.

She took four measured strides into the room and stopped, looked about, and took one more step. What she now saw matched what she had Seen in her Vision. There was the angle of dim light from a moon only half full slanting in the narrow window, casting the shadows of the bars across the polished oak floor, with its band of dark inlay around the edges. There were the softer shadows cast by the chairs, the piece of rug that seemed, in this light, to have no pattern and no color. The worktable and the plain casket that stood upon it. And the darkness in the far corner. Where, in her Vision, she was standing with a full view of the room.

But sometimes, in her Visions, the room had been empty. She hadn't always Seen herself.

Out of habit and training Dhulyn moved slowly, her feet making no sound. As she advanced toward the worktable, she felt along the left seam of the shirt she was wearing and finally pulled out a steel wire as long as her hand. She'd bought it off a jeweler in Cabrea, a long time ago, and it was still her best lockpick, though usually she wore it woven into the braids of her hair. She put the lockpick between her teeth, and pulled a soft silk scarf out of the front of her shirt. Among its many qualities, silk was thought to insulate and cleanse. Finders, she knew, often used silk to wrap and store their scrying bowls, and the ancient box that held her vera tiles was lined with it. She wrapped the scarf carefully around the hilt of the sword and, taking it in her left hand, approached the worktable with its small casket.

She was alert for the phenomenon Kera had described, of heading toward the casket and finding herself suddenly on the far side of the room. Dhulyn slowed her breathing, let herself fall into a Hunter's *Shora*, senses alert, focused on her prey, the plain wooden box. The box filled her mind, her vision narrowed. Almost, she could taste it.

Turning her body sideways to present the smallest target, Dhulyn struck with the blade in her left hand, making flashing touches on the casket's lid, then on the right, left, and front sides.

Nothing. No resistance, no flash of light, no shimmer such as Finders or Menders had described to her sometimes happened when they used their Mark.

Dhulyn took two steps closer, still focusing her senses on the casket. She laid the sword on the tabletop and wrapped the silk around her left hand, lowering it slowly, alert for any change in either the box or herself. But she felt no reluctance—nor did she suddenly find herself at the other end of the desk, unaware of her intention of moving. Even through the silk, the wood was cool and smooth under her fingers. She could clearly see the faceplate of the locking mechanism, a fine Balnian lock after the old pattern—just as Therin had described it in the journal still tucked into her shirt. It seemed there was no avoidance magic on the box itself, that Avylos was relying solely on the magicked door. It struck Dhulyn as a strange economy of magic, to use both spells and physical deterrents. Was there some strategy she did not see, or was Avylos only conserving power?

Still, the box would not open.

Dhulyn rolled her eyes as she pulled the lockpick from between her teeth. Balnian locks, though good, could be mastered with sufficient practice. The pick went in easily, and after a few tense moments of careful prodding, Dhulyn felt through her fingers the 'click' that signified the lock was open.

She licked suddenly dry lips, picked up the sword once more, and backed away from the table. Using the tip of the blade, she flicked the lid open with a twist of her wrist.

Inside the box, nestled in what looked to be layers of dark red velvet cloth, was the Muse Stone. Even if she had not already Seen it in her Visions, she would have recognized it from the meticulous drawings in Therin's journal. A cylinder as long as her forearm, the dark blue of a Berdanan ice sapphire, though the moonlight was not bright enough to make it sparkle. There were lamplighters in a bowl, and Dhulyn used one to light the squat oil lamp on a nearby shelf. The crystal remained dark, as the journal had led her to expect. She frowned, peering more closely. She could not quite make out the markings that should be around the end of the Stone.

Dhulyn took a deep breath and let it out slowly. Both the journal and Zania herself had said that the older members of the troupe had handled the Stone many times and had taken no harm from it. Still, it was as well to be careful. Dhulyn shifted the sword to her right hand, reached out with her left, and picked up the Stone.

It was warm. There was no vibration, no noise, but it was warm, like a grindstone recently in use, or a stone crock kept close to the kitchen fires. And now she could see the symbols the journal had described. The *Marks,* circle around a dot, rectangle—though here it was closer to a square—long triangle, and straight line. Each Mark clear, the carving deep, and set at the four compass points within a bowstring's width of the end of the Muse Stone. A finger width farther in, Dhulyn found the fifth Mark, the Lens, three concentric circles. As Therin's journal had indicated, the Lens was placed exactly between two of the Marks, at present, between the triangle of the Mender and the dotted circle of the Seer.

And there were the symbols on the other end. Dhulyn's eyebrows arched as high as they would go. She knew these symbols now, though she hadn't when she'd first seen them in the book. They were like the signs that Avylos had drawn in the air. Like the signs she'd Seen him, and one other, draw in her Visions.

So one end for the Marked, and one for Mages?

She tried to turn the bottom, twisting it as the journal described, but it stood fast, as if in one solid piece. There was no feeling of either resistance or give. In fact, Dhulyn had no sense of a mechanism at all, as she'd had with the lock.

She checked the tightness of her belt preparatory to slipping the Muse Stone into the front of her shirt. With her shirt collar in one hand, she paused, thinking.

A few moments ago, she'd questioned Avylos' strategy. A magical lock on the door that at least one person could get through, at least some of the time. No other magics, nothing but mundane locks and bars. She held the Stone out in the light again. Was it all too easy?

A false Stone, set to trap the ignorant? If *she* could think of this idea, *he* could think of it. But unlike any other who might come into the room, she was not entirely ignorant. She tapped the book hidden in her shirt with her fingertips. She could test the Stone. She wanted neither to receive power nor to bestow it, but surely what Therin had called the Null Chant, the empty words which drew no response from the Stone other than to turn the cylinder, *they* would be safe.

> *Elis elis tanton neel;*
> *Dor la sinquin so la dele.*
> *Kos noforlin sik ek aye,*
> *Kik shon te ounte gesserae.*

The Stone grew marginally warmer, as if the stone crock had been moved closer to the flames. Careful not to put her fingers on any of the symbols, Dhulyn tried again to turn the end of the Stone, and this time it moved. Repeating the lines, she kept turning until the Mark of the Seer lined up with the Mark of the Lens.

The room disappeared. A great light filled her eyes. A bell began to ring.

⚬⚬⚬

A snowstorm, a voice calls from somewhere to her left . . .

A man with hair the color of wheat sits behind a desk reading a massive book in an unknown tongue. A large round mirror stands to his right . . .

A stocky, fair-haired boy looks down into a bowl . . .

The deck slants almost vertical and water pours off in sheets; a man with a red-and-gold Mercenary badge goes over the side into the churning waves . . .

The body of a Cloud falls from a great height, his Racha bird keeping pace with him, keening . . .

An older Kera walks toward a throne. A circle of women across a room . . .

***

A one-eyed man peers into her face, asking a question . . .

A smiling man with hair the color of old blood matching his huge mustache offers her a ball of light in the palm of his hand . . .

A horde of cavalry rides over the ridge and darkens the valley below . . .

A red-haired woman pushes a sword through Parno's heart . . .

Water seeps up through pale gray sand, forming a pool as wide as her spread hands . . .

She stands in the dark corner of Avylos' workroom and takes a step toward herself . . .

Avylos runs through the woods, falls, gets up and runs again, looking back over his shoulder. Far down the trail, two men with hair the color of old blood give chase . . .

Three sisters hold hands, beckoning toward her, and holding out their free hands for her to join their circle. Each has the Mark of the Seer tattooed on her forehead.

A strange sensation. Her cheek on something cool. Tiles? Floor tiles? She set the palm of her hand down flat. Oak. Hard wood. She thought about pushing herself upright. But her head was so heavy.

A sharp crackling sound, and there was light on the other side of her eyelids.

Footsteps. Feet. Black house shoes with a dark blue trim. Satin? Velvet? Hands on her arms, in her armpits, dragging her upright. How could her head possibly be so heavy? Had she been ill? What was she doing on the floor? Where was she?

Who was she?

Strong fingers on her chin, holding her head steady and upright. She blinked. A long face, pale. Blue eyes. Hair a very dark red. Blue eyes narrowed, dark red brows drawn down in a vee over a long, thin nose. Lips pressed tight together.

She tried to speak, but her throat was thick. She licked her lips, cleared her throat, and tried again.

"Where am I?" she said, finding she could not bring herself to ask the more important question, "who?" "Who are you?"

The man's face relaxed, though his eyes were still narrowed. The hand on her chin became a caress, and the muscles in her neck and shoulders which had been very tight a moment before loosened. Her head still throbbed.

"Don't you know me, my dearest? Has your fever become worse?"

She took his hand and struggled to sit up. Something hard poked painfully into her ribs and she winced, her hand going automatically to the spot. There seemed to be something . . .

"Here, let me help you." The man helped loosen the ties of her shirt and drew a slim book out from under her clothing. He raised his eyebrows, but did not seem in any way surprised or upset. He reached up and put the book on the tabletop above her head.

A sound made them both look to the door.

❧❧❧

Kera went directly to Dhulyn Wolfshead's room when she was finally excused from the banquet. She'd never realized, when Edmir was alive—when Edmir was at court, she corrected, Edmir was *still* alive. She hadn't realized, in any case, just how much of his time was taken up with being the Lord Prince, meeting the right people at the right times, attending functions that until now she'd mostly been excused from. Which probably explained why he'd been so much more tense and abrupt in the last few years, without time to play with her. Even his journal entries, she now knew, had been shorter, with fewer of the stories he used to make up for her.

Now that she was Lady Prince, and the heir to the

throne, it seemed there were not enough hours in the day. Her feet slowed. If she was being honest, she would have to admit that *she* didn't feel at all tense or abrupt. Even her mother the queen was easier to handle, now that all their contact was strictly formal. And the servants were definitely easier to deal with. Now, when she told them to leave her, they stopped cooing over her and patting her on the head. They actually went. Well, most of them.

Kera turned from the main hallway just before she reached the passage which held Avylos' study, into a much shorter passage which had only one door at the end of it. Kera lifted the latch and stepped inside. The Wolfshead's room was very simply furnished, like that of an upper servant. A bed, a table with a single chair. A brazier under the table, empty, and unlit now in the warm weather of summer. Three wooden pegs attached to the dressed stone wall to hold clothing, also empty. There was enough clothing tossed over the furniture, however, to make it difficult to be sure what Dhulyn Wolfshead was wearing. The bed was rumpled, the pillow showed the indentation of a head.

Had the Mercenary woman returned to this room, then? Or was all this a stage setting, so that if the Wolfshead was found up and wandering around she could claim to have just left her bed?

Kera took her lower lip between her teeth. The room was telling her nothing. The Wolfshead was not here; could she be still in the workroom?

She retraced her steps back along the passage to the main corridor, turned left, carefully eyed the patch of shadow where it widened to assure herself that the Mercenary was not in it, and stopped at the door to Avylos' workroom. The thinnest line of light showed in the opening. She waited, straining forward. Was that voices? She tilted her head closer to the door, and held her breath. Voices, for certain, though she couldn't hear any words. She touched the door with her fingertips, meaning just to open it slightly, but misjudged the pressure, and, dry mouthed, watched it swing fully open.

Kera stood dead still, her fingertips still on the door. Dhulyn Wolfshead was on the floor, propped against the table leg. Avylos had his hand on her face, holding her by the chin, the way a Knife might when he wanted you to stay still for an examination. His head was tilted forward at such an angle that Kera was certain he had been about to kiss her.

Avylos dropped his hand when he saw her, but he did not move away from Dhulyn Wolfshead. Kera saw she had hold of Avylos' sleeve.

Kera stepped forward, speaking before anyone could ask her questions.

"I saw the light," she said, "I thought you were still with my mother the queen."

"Avylos, who is this child?" A thread of accent heavier than Kera had heard from Dhulyn Wolfshead before.

Kera stepped forward with more confidence. Dhulyn Wolfshead would not be speaking in that tone, and asking that question, if there was any trouble. She was letting Kera know that their acquaintance was still a secret from Avylos. But as she got nearer to the two at the table, Kera's step faltered. She expected Dhulyn Wolfshead to pretend not to know her, but that wide-eyed stare, that hint of tension — even fear — that was no pretense. When they were younger, she and Edmir used to disguise themselves and wander through the public portions of the Royal House, and even into the nearby streets when they could manage to get out the gates. They learned very early to tell the difference between people who genuinely didn't recognize them and people who were just playing along with the Royal children's game.

And Dhulyn Wolfshead was not faking. She no longer knew her. Kera's heart pounded in her ears. Think, *think*. What would be the natural thing for her to say?

"Is this your kinswoman, Avylos?" Kera hoped her smile didn't look as fake as it felt.

"It is, Lady Prince, my cousin. Dhulyn, my dear, this is the Lady Prince Kera, the heir to the throne of Tegrian."

Avylos helped her to her feet, and the woman looked down at Kera with a grave face and nodded her head once.

"I thank you, Lady Prince, and your mother the queen, for your hospitality. I am Dhulyn of . . ." She looked at Avylos, lips beginning to tremble before she clamped her mouth shut firmly enough that a muscle twitched at the hinge of her jaw.

"Of the Forest Plain Clan," the Mage finished for her, and Dhulyn Wolfshead nodded.

Had she been about to say something else, Kera wondered. Was there anything of Dhulyn Wolfshead left? How had Avylos done this?

※※※

The evening meal, a simple one of rewarmed rabbit pie, fresh water from the lodge's well, and a few dried apples found in a stone crock near the door, went smoothly enough, with Sylria telling stories of how she and Valaika had met, and Zania telling of how her uncle had once performed *The Galan of Illrya* without the false nose the part required, and how he had done it.

It had been a long, tiring day, so Zania's suggestion of an early night was welcomed. Sylria was surprised when Edmir insisted she use the bedchamber, and tried to defer to his rank.

"I've been sleeping rough the last moon," he'd told her. "Plenty of time for beds when we're back in Beolind."

When the large shutter that was the bedchamber's door was closed, Edmir left the soft pile of sheep and inglera skins that made up his bed and crept across the floor to Zania.

"Shall we keep watch?" he said in as close an approximation of the Mercenary nightwatch voice as he could manage.

"Dhulyn and Parno—" Edmir put his finger on Zania's lips. Trained to project her voice over an area the size of a market square, even her whispers were too loud. Too bad he couldn't read her lips against the palm of his hand, as Dhulyn had done in Nisvea.

"They would say we should keep watch," Zania said.

Edmir nodded. "Sylria sounded her normal self at supper, but I thought she was looking at us . . ." He shrugged. Had he actually seen anything? Or were all his fears the result of too easy an imagination?

But Zania was nodding again, and patting his arm. *Take*

the precautions anyway, he thought. What was it Dhulyn was always saying? Prepare for what *can* happen, not for what *might* happen.

"I'll take the first watch."

Edmir crept back to his own bed and watched the shadowy form of Zania lie down again and pull a blanket over her head to block what little light from the half full moon came in with the breeze through the open windows. He left the bulk of his bedding where it was, taking only an inglera hide thick with wool. He shifted over against the wall, made a pad for his back, and sat braced against the stone.

Caids grant I don't fall asleep.

Whether it was the spirits of the Caids or not, Edmir was wide awake when the shutter of Sylria's bedchamber swung noiselessly open, and the older woman, her pale sleeping shift making her stand out in the gloom, padded out into the main room on bare feet. The figure hesitated, looking between the two piles of bedding. Edmir held his breath and shifted his weight forward, prepared to spring to his feet.

Sylria turned to Edmir's bedroll and squatted down on her heels—an unattractive position, Edmir felt sure, that no woman of her age and rank would take voluntarily. She raised one hand above her head, and Edmir was already rolling forward onto his feet when he saw the blade flash in moonlight as it plunged down into the blankets of his bed.

Edmir continued the roll that brought him to his feet, turning it into a dive that took him across the short stretch of floor and into Sylria's left side. He landed on top of her, trapping her blade hand, and, half winded himself, hoping even after what he'd seen that he hadn't injured the woman under him.

"Zania. Some light."

But she was already throwing off blankets and running to the table. When she turned with the oil lamp in her hand, her eyes went first to him, her eyebrows crawling almost to her hairline when she saw where he was, and who he had under him. A sound, quickly stifled, escaped her lips when she saw the weapon.

"Get the knife, quickly."

Zania darted forward, her eyes huge and dark, took the

knife from Sylria's slack hand and jumped back. Edmir scuttled backward, heels and hands, until he was brought up short by the wall. His mouth was dry, and his heart thundered in his ears.

"Something to tie her with," he managed to say. As Zania disappeared into the bedchamber, returning with Sylria's sashes and scarves, Edmir crept forward and held his fingers under Sylria's jaw. His hands were shaking so badly he had to take a deep breath and try again. Sylria's heart beat steadily, but her eyes were shut.

"She must have hit her head against the edge of the bench," Zania said, kneeling down next to them. It made Edmir feel less of a coward to see her hands were shaking as well. "Let's get her bound before she wakes up."

Edmir sat quiet, holding a long orange sash between his hands. "*If* she wakes up." He licked his lips.

"Edmir, she tried to kill you."

He looked up, blinking. "Maybe she didn't. Sylria wouldn't want to kill me." He sat back on his heels. "What if it was sleep suggestion? What if it was Avylos?" Not that that changed anything. It didn't make him feel any better about leaving Sylria unconscious. She was still his aunt's consort. Oh, Caids, his aunt. What was he going to tell Valaika?

"Edmir." Zania's voice a mere thread of sound.

Sylria's eyelids were fluttering.

"Move the light away," he said. The sound of his voice brought Sylria's eyes wide open.

"Are they dead?"

The hairs rose on the back of Edmir's neck and cold sweat trickled down his back. He realized that with the dim lamp behind him, Sylria saw only his silhouette.

"Yes," he said.

A look of pain crossed Sylria's face. "I had to kill them," she said. "He would have magicked our Janek, made him waste away. Kill them," she repeated. "Or Janek will waste away. Kill them. Or Janek will waste away."

Edmir caught Zania's eye. She had her bottom lip between her teeth and her eyes were huge in the lamplight.

"They're dead, so you can rest now," he said to Sylria. "Come." He helped her to her feet and guided her back to her bed. She crept in like a small child, and Edmir was reminded of putting his sister to bed when they had both been much younger, and Kera wouldn't sleep unless he tucked her in. He pulled up Sylria's covers and smoothed them over her with the same gentle gestures he'd used then.

"Close your eyes and sleep now," he said. "We're going to —" he cleared his throat. "We're going to take the bodies away with us, so no one will know. Janek will be safe."

"I must go to him."

"No." Edmir glanced at Zania, at a loss of what to do or say next. She moved closer and put her hand on Sylria's shoulder.

"You must wait here," she said, her tone calm and authoritative. "Wait until your servants come."

"I must wait until my servants come."

"If they ask, tell them the players have gone to Beolind."

"The players have gone to Beolind."

"Tell the Blue Mage the one he wanted killed is dead."

"The one he wanted killed is dead."

"That's right. Sleep now." Zania backed away, and Edmir swung the shutter closed again. He listened for the sound of the latch on the inside, but when he did not hear it, he wedged it shut with the blade of Sylria's dagger.

"She'll be all right," he whispered, more to convince himself than Zania. "Someone will come within a day or so."

"He threatened their child," Zania said. "The sleep suggestion alone was not enough to persuade her to kill you, the Mage had to threaten their child as well."

"Zania, we should go now. We can't risk being here when she wakes up."

"Of course." She got to her feet with a shadow of her usual briskness. "I'll harness the horses, I'll be faster."

"Zania, we can't take the caravan."

She stiffened, and turned to look at him.

"Zania, even with both Stumpy *and* Sylria's horse, the caravan would slow us down too much. We'd be easy targets. As it is . . . If all goes well, we can retrieve it—look, I know how much it means to you, what it holds of all your family and your life, but it isn't worth *risking* your life for! Everything you are, your family, it's in here." He touched her on the forehead. "And in here." A light touch just above the collar of her gown. "The rest . . . it's just things."

She bristled, and for a long moment he braced to continue the argument, wondering how far he would take it before he gave in. Finally, her eyes dropped, and her shoulders lowered as she nodded her agreement.

Twenty

"THIS THING IS VERY HOT." Dhulyn's fingers strayed to the edge of the new wig Avylos had found for her. Somehow, she looked more natural with longer hair, though why he should think so Avylos didn't know; he'd never seen her with long hair.

"Nevertheless, you must leave it on, my dear," Avylos said as he sat down in the chair next to where Dhulyn had been served her breakfast in the garden. "The scarring from your head injury will cause too much remark. Town people are suspicious and untrustworthy enough, as I've told you already, without giving them something to worry about."

Dhulyn nodded. "And it is that injury which has affected my memory?"

"Not precisely." Avylos wondered how much it would be useful to tell her at this point. His excitement at finding what was clearly a manual for the Stone kept him fidgeting with his cup of ganje, and pushing his breakfast away. He had spent most of the night in study of the book she'd had hidden in her tunic, but the language in it was like nothing he had ever seen. If Dhulyn Wolfshead was able to read it—and she *must* have been, she had changed the setting of the Stone—she was more valuable to him than ever. And it was safe to keep her now. *Safe*. She remembered nothing of her former life. He could tell her whatever he chose, and with the sleep suggestion, he could control what she remembered. It would be worth it. He took hold of her hand, and held it, rubbing the back of it with his thumb. "I am doing everything I can to restore you completely, but I am a Mage, not a Healer."

"And *are* you my cousin?"

He hesitated. What to say? What might prove most useful in the long run? If she believed they were blood, well, no tie was greater to an Espadryni—but he should not make it too close a tie, he thought, looking at her hand in his, there were other considerations after all.

"A distant cousin, yes," he said finally. "However, there may be no others of our Tribe, and that makes us closer." He squeezed her hand and replaced it on her lap, sitting back in his own chair. A bird landed on the back of a nearby branch, looking with a hopeful eye at the remains of Dhulyn's breakfast on the low table beside her. Dhulyn's hand flashed out, and the bird was caught.

"I'm not finished yet, little cousin," she said, holding the bird close to her face. She blew into its beak and tossed it into the air, where it flew off, clearly more annoyed than frightened.

Avylos smiled. As events were unfolding, how right he'd been to put off killing her. It had *not* been sentimental weakness in him, not at all, but strength, and shrewdness. Events were unfolding better than if he had planned them. Not that he'd ever before felt any lack of family. His own siblings, his two brothers, and their sisters, had never looked at him the way Dhulyn did now. On him, she smiled, her gray eyes warm, showing stony only to the pages who had brought their food.

She did not treat him with exaggerated patience, she did not dismiss him as of no value. She did not look on him with pity, when she thought he did not see. He could keep her. He *must* keep her.

And, he thought, looking around for the bird she had released, Dhulyn clearly still retained the physical skills she'd spent a lifetime developing. His hand strayed back to the book that now rested in the pocket of his robe. Had someone sent her after the Stone, or had she come on her own, having learned of its existence from Edmir? Where had the book come from, and *could* she read it? Surely she would not have had the book with her if she had merely been sent by another?

"Tell me, Dhulyn, do you recall what you were doing with the Blue Stone in my workroom?" It had been on the floor when he'd entered and found her there.

"That cylinder of crystal?" She frowned, her eyebrows, growing blood red once more with the removal of the dye, drawn into a vee above her gray eyes. "I'm not sure. Judging from where it was lying, I would say that I had it in my hand when I fell. But I don't remember." She looked up at him. "Is it important? Did I damage it?"

"No, no. It's come to no harm. But it is a very powerful magical artifact, and touching it may have contributed to your memory loss. I must ask you not to touch it again."

The Blue Stone had come to no harm, that was true, but something *had* happened to it—though what he didn't know. The setting was definitely changed, and it seemed active, alive in a way he had not seen before. But its power level appeared the same, neither higher nor lower. Perhaps the Stone worked differently on the Marked? Perhaps the talent was stored in a different way?

Or perhaps it had not drained Dhulyn Wolfshead of her Mark, just her knowledge of who she was. What irony, if it had also drained the knowledge that would help him finally achieve his goal. Now, with the book and this woman of his own blood who could read it, now, he was the closest he had ever been to having total control over the power of the Stone.

Dhulyn cleared her throat and he looked over at her once more. Her brow was furrowed, her breath came short, and she clutched at the edge of the table with both hands.

⊗⊗⊗

A golden-haired man with tattoos on his temples laughs and holds out a peach . . .

A woman with hair the color of wheat and a jeweler's lens in her eye carves on a length of blue crystal . . .

An older, red-haired man draws pictures of light in the air while she laughs and claps her hands . . .

***

She stands in the dark corner of Avylos' workroom and takes a step toward herself . . .

She lunges with her sword at the tattooed man . . .

Water crashes across the deck of a ship . . .

She has the blue crystal in her own hands, she is speaking, and turning the ends . . .

Avylos holds the blue crystal in his hands, light streams from it . . .

⊗⊗⊗

"Dhulyn? My dear?"

She blinked and looked into Avylos' face. What had just happened to her? What did it mean? She swallowed and licked her lips. Better she should say nothing just now. Her cousin thought she was getting better, and she wanted to do nothing that would upset him.

"A momentary dizziness," she said, smiling as naturally as she could.

He got to his feet and held out his hand. "Come, then. Kedneara the Queen has graciously invited you to this morning's audience."

⊗⊗⊗

In this informal audience chamber, the dais was only two steps up from the floor, but from her seat next to the queen, Kera could clearly see everyone as they entered the room. This was not a public audience where anyone could come to petition the Royal House for judgment or favor, but rather a private gathering of people invited expressly by Queen Kedneara. Petitions would be made here, yes, favors granted and accepted, but there was a pretense of informality and intimacy to the gathering. Servants circulated with cups of ganje, jeresh, and wine, and others with small bite-sized nibbles from the kitchen.

"Be careful not to fall for any of these boys, my lamb," her mother said, just loudly enough to be overheard by the people standing nearest the throne. "Trifle with them if you like—experience is always a good thing, but go no further than trifling."

There *were* High Noble Houses present, and some *had* brought younger kin with them—for the most part unmarried kin, and male. Kera nodded at her mother the queen, and put on her most careful smile. Now that she was Lady Prince, and not to be sent away to seal some foreign alliance, every High Noble House saw profit in dangling their sons before her.

"I'll be careful, Mother." And she would be, too, if not for the reason her mother expected. The throne was not to be hers, no matter what all these people might think. *And no matter what I might think,* said a traitorous inner voice. Edmir would be back. She would not wish her brother dead, not for all the thrones in the world.

As if in response to the sound of her voice —*blessed Caids, let it not be my thoughts he heard*—Avylos turned to smile at her from his position to the left of the dais. He also had his seat, on the other side of the queen's throne, but at these affairs he liked to stay on his feet, and watch those who approached his queen from their own level.

And today, of course, he had Dhulyn Wolfshead with him. Though she still seemed not to know who she really was.

"There is your Aunt Valaika, Kera my sweet, do you see her? The golden-haired woman coming in the door."

As if Kera wouldn't remember her aunt perfectly well from her father's burial ceremonies. Valaika had taken her out hawking, a pastime she still loved, and had sent her a horse for her naming day only last year.

"Though she's getting gray I see, and a little stouter than when I saw her last. Her consort's a woman, you know. Ran off and married her when I married your father, her brother, so you know what *that* means."

Kera managed to refrain from shutting her eyes and sighing. She'd heard the story a thousand times. How Aunt Valaika had fallen in love with her mother, and, of course, how her mother had wanted her father and how Aunt Valaika had been persuaded to go away, and "stop mooning around me" as Kera's mother had always put it, by the granting of Jarlkevo House.

Her aunt had eventually married, Kera knew, and had produced an heir—though no one knew who the father had been. It was not her consort with her today, Kera saw, as she watched her aunt stroll through the room, heading steadily, if not particularly directly, to the throne. Valaika was a High Noble House, and as such had taken her privilege to bring her own retainer with her.

The man who kept correctly just behind Aunt Valaika's left shoulder would make a fine father of anyone's children, Kera thought. On the tall side of average, muscular but lean, the sun had toasted him a golden brown, his skin just a shade lighter than his hair, and two shades lighter than his short beard. As his eyes scanned the room, he seemed to be on the verge of smiling, and he padded along at Valaika's heels with the smooth movement of one of her mother's hunting cats.

Kera had expected to recognize her aunt, but there was something familiar about her aunt's servant as well, something she couldn't quite—

The man suddenly became alert, eyes brighter, focused. Kera shifted her own eyes to see what the man looked at—of course. Dhulyn Wolfshead had appeared almost four days ago, the day after the message had come announcing the imminent arrival of Aunt Valaika. They had arrived in the city at the same time, the man with Valaika walked with the same catlike smoothness as Dhulyn Wolfshead, and he was looking at the Mercenary woman with an expression that made Kera's breath grow short.

And then his eyes met hers, and his expression cleared, becoming again the correct, bland politeness of a personal guard.

I must speak privately with Aunt Valaika.

The princess was not quite so much the stiffly dressed girl child that she looked, Parno Lionsmane thought. Conscious that what *her* eyes could see, others could see also, he dragged his own gaze away from where Dhulyn stood next to Avylos the Blue Mage. He had seen her for the last moon with her Mercenary badge covered, but not with hair her natural color. This is what she might have looked like if she'd grown up in her own Tribe, if she'd never become a Mercenary Brother. What her mother must have looked like, according to Dhulyn's descriptions of the Visions in which her mother had appeared.

She didn't look all that much like the Blue Mage, beyond the superficial similarity of their coloring. But Parno didn't like how closely together they were standing.

He was certain she'd looked at him, but there had been no change of expression on her face. Of course there wouldn't be, he thought, with a mental sigh. His Partner schooled her features better than anyone he'd ever met— even if she *was* an Outlander. She looked calm but watchful, like a person somewhere for the first time. Or like a personal guard.

But she should have acknowledged his signal.

He followed Valaika up to the throne, and when Avylos, too, stepped up onto the dais to greet the woman who was still, to a degree, part of the Royal House, Parno took advantage of everyone's attention being elsewhere to shift over next to Dhulyn. He pretended to stumble and took hold of her arm.

His own arm was instantly in a grip like a Racha bird's talons and he was roughly pushed away.

"Take your hands from me, town man."

In an instant Avylos was beside them, taking Dhulyn's elbow and turning her away.

"Your pardon, Lord Mage, Lady." Parno spoke in the exaggerated Imrion accent he'd practiced for the stage. "New boots have made me clumsy." He peered at Dhulyn as if seeing her for the first time. "Do I not know you? Have we not met?"

"No." Her voice was very cold, very final. "I do not know you." She turned away from him to the Blue Mage.

Valaika appeared as Avylos was murmuring to Dhulyn. "Any trouble?"

"Not at all, House Jarlkevo." Avylos turned to face them, keeping Dhulyn behind him. "My ward was startled, that's all. She has only recently recovered enough from her illness to rise from her bed."

"I'll see it doesn't happen again. You." She turned to Parno. "Back to our rooms, now."

It was the only thing Valaika could have done, the only order that would make sense to the audience watching them out of the corners of their eyes. Parno didn't like it, but he had to leave the audience chamber.

He blew out each breath slowly and completely as he went, consciously forcing the muscles in his shoulders, arms, and hands to relax. He would kill that Mage with his own hands. He didn't know when, or even how, but if it took him the rest of his life, he would kill that Mage. Now he knew how Edmir had felt, back in Probic, when that City Lord hadn't known him.

Dhulyn's reaction had been no act. She hadn't known him. His Brother, his Partner, hadn't known him.

Sylria woke with a dry mouth and a head that felt strangely light and empty, as if she'd had a fever and had taken too much fens bark tea. At first, the door to the tiny bedchamber seemed to be stuck, but with repeated jiggling and shoving she eventually had it open. Her foot kicked something almost as soon as she entered the main room, and sent it skittering a short way across the cold stone floor.

A dagger.

And then the whole of the previous night came sweeping over her, and Sylria had to sit down, and hold her now too full head in her hands.

"I did it," she said aloud. "I killed him." And not just Edmir, Sylria realized, as she looked around her. She'd killed them both, the young girl as well.

She barely made it as far as the door before she threw up.

When she was finally able to turn back into the room, she was struck by how clean and tidy it was. She must have cleaned up, removed the bodies. Of course. She must have. She fetched herself a cup of water from the bucket that sat next to the fireplace, rinsed out her mouth, spat, and sat down again.

She knew absolutely that she had killed Edmir. But now that she thought about it, she could not remember the actual act. She knew the bodies had been removed, and the players' caravan hidden. She could not remember doing it.

It *had* been done. All of it, of that she was certain. What did it matter that she could not remember the details?

"This comes of Avylos' 'help,'" she said aloud. Even her voice sounded sour. Her stomach threatened to rebel again and she sipped at the cup of water. She simply could not bear to recall what she had done, and so her mind rejected it. There had been a guardsman once, who had lost his wife, but he simply could not retain the fact of her death, and so he had eventually gone mad. Would that happen to her now? Would she lose her sanity? She took in a deep breath, released it slowly. Better that, better anything, than losing Janek.

One thing did remain to be done. Carefully, feeling unsteady on her feet, Sylria went into the bedchamber and came out with her saddlebags. From an inner pocket she took out the book of poetry she'd brought with her from Jarlkevo House. She set it down on the table, in the full light of the sun, and opened it to the middle pages.

Avylos snapped the book shut with a snort of pleasure. It was done. Finally, Edmir was really dead. Finally, everything was falling into place.

⚜

The grounds of the Royal House of Tegrian resembled a small park, with sections for fruit and shade trees, and stretches of formal garden with white-pebbled paths. Like all such places, and at this time of the morning, it was busy, with messengers and guards in livery walking to and from the gates, servants on errands to the stables at the southern end, or to the kitchen gardens. No one took special note of Parno Lionsmane as he strolled through, his chanter to his lips, warming up by playing parts and snippets of tunes and runs of notes. In no time, as he'd fully expected and counted on, a group of children were following him, begging for tunes and songs. Anyone who was within the grounds had been passed through the gate, and was safe to play with.

By allowing the children to think they were chasing him, Parno led them close to the repaired wall that marked the

Blue Mage's wing. He noticed that the children were not afraid to approach it—and that there seemed to be no special guards or watchfulness on the wing itself. He went so far as to lean his shoulders against the repaired part of the wall, hiking up one knee and making himself comfortable. He began to play an old tune, a familiar tune, one that he'd both heard and played many times himself, and the children clapped their hands and whistled, beginning to bounce up and down in time with the music. In a moment, they had chosen one of the smaller boys to be the Blind Man, and an older girl pulled off her neck scarf and bound his eyes as the rest organized themselves in a circle around him, joining hands.

One eye on the children—it wouldn't do to outstay their pleasure—Parno settled in to accompany them for as long as he could. He was playing not for them, but for his Partner, and the longer he played, the greater the chance that Dhulyn would come into the garden on the other side of the wall and hear him. Would she recognize the tune? He hoped so; she'd been studying this child's game, and the tune that came with it, when they'd been in Imrion the year before, and she had special reason to remember it. Of all the tunes that he could play, he wagered this would be the one to catch at her mind and memory.

Whether the magic of the music would be enough to undo what the Mage had done to her—that was what he couldn't know.

He wasn't sure exactly how long he'd been playing, long enough for the shadows to move a finger's breadth perhaps, but not long enough to dry his mouth unduly, when he saw a page whose colors marked him as one on loan to Valaika, coming toward them down one of the nearby paths. Parno waited until the page was almost standing next to him before lowering the chanter from his mouth. Immediately, the children who were waiting their turns to play surrounded him, calling out for him to continue.

"Off with you, fiends and torments! I'm summoned and that's the end of it. Off now, enjoy your freedom while you can." He turned to the page even as he began the walk back across the grounds to Valaika's suite. "I *am* summoned, I take it? Not that I could have played much longer, mind."

"If you please, sir. The Lady Prince Kera has announced her intention to visit her aunt, and our House wishes you to be present."

"Lead on, youngster." Parno was happy to get another look at Edmir's sister. And he was interested in what made Valaika think she needed a Mercenary Brother with her when her niece visited.

❧

Dhulyn was humming along with the tune she heard rising and falling on the other side of the garden wall, and soon found herself on her feet, stepping two paces to the left, to the right, forward and back, turning and offering her hand to someone who wasn't there. She faltered.

Surely there was a song as well. The words were on the tip of her tongue. She could almost see them—

"What are you doing?"

She turned, smiling, and ran to Avylyn—no, she corrected herself, he was called Avylos here. The Blue Mage. He was smiling, as if he'd had some very good news.

"Did you hear that music? Come, I remember the steps to the dance. Come dance with me."

"Men do not dance." Avylos actually put his hands behind his back, as if he feared she would catch them and pull him forward. "Not our men, anyway, not Espadryni."

She stood still, something throbbed behind her left eye. Was that right? "Do they not? I remember . . . no, I suppose I don't. For a moment there I thought—but perhaps you're right, perhaps it is only women who dance." She shrugged and stepped away from him again. "Then I shall dance by myself." Three steps to the right, two steps to the left. A spin with the arms wide open.

❧

A circle of women, their hair the red of old blood, holding hands, eyes closed, feet moving in rhythmic pacing . . .

An old crone, a young woman with dark hair and a heart-shaped face, a stocky blond man in a Scholar's tunic, and a young boy, thin and round-eyed, holding hands, singing, feet moving in rhythmic pacing . . .

The golden-haired, tattooed man, with pipes in his hands . . .

Water crashes over the deck of a ship . . .

A golden-haired man with tattoos . . .

Avylos with the Blue Stone in his hands, light burning through him . . .

❧❧❧

She was standing still.

"Could you dance later, my dear one? Would you come with me, now? I would like you to try something."

"Something to eat, I hope?"

He smiled, but stiffly now, his good humor already faded. *Sun and Moon,* what was wrong with the man? No humor, no fun, stiff as a bow that was never bent. She stopped spinning. That was an odd simile to think of. Perhaps she'd been a hunter?

"Very well, then, Avylos my brother—" The words stuck in her throat, and she had to cough. Odd. "I'll be as serious as a Scholar, nay, as serious as a Mage." She dusted off the skirts of her gown and joined him, linking her arm through his.

Twenty-one

KERA'S MOUTH WAS AS DRY as winter sand. She held herself stiffly as she walked, her hands folded at her waist since her awareness of the need for caution was giving them a tendency to tremble. She had dressed carefully, had a lady page at her elbow, and she'd rehearsed her speeches to Aunt Valaika until she felt she could recite them without hesitation or sign of how nervous she really felt. She put on the face that she'd been taught to use in public. Formality, Edmir had always told her, was a tool to fall back on when fear or uncertainty nipped at your composure. Informally, she would have walked directly across the grounds to the section of rooms set aside for the use of House Jarlkevo. As it was, she and her escort were walking sedately around the long way, through the buildings, Kera pausing where appropriate to let her lady page open and close doors for her.

As she walked along, she used the time to consider—yet again—what she was doing. Logic said that Aunt Valaika, by virtue of her long estrangement from the Royal House, and her subsequent isolation in her mountain fortress, had few ties, if any, that would make her an ally of the Blue Mage.

But logic made for poor signposts on the road of human nature. Just because Valaika had no particular friends at court didn't mean she wanted to make an enemy.

After what seemed like hours, Kera's lady page opened the door to her aunt's suite and announced her. Kera signaled that the woman should remain outside, and walked in. Her first thought on entering her aunt's receiving room was relief that the tall, golden-haired personal guard was already there. Now she wouldn't have to make up some excuse to ask for him.

Very correctly, Valaika stood as Kera entered, and waited for the door to be shut behind her. Kera stopped just inside the door and let her aunt come to her. Now that she was Lady Prince, she took precedence over even an older blood relative. Over everyone except the queen, herself. As a close blood relative, however, Valaika did not kneel, but took Kera's hand and bowed over it. When she straightened, and would have stepped away, Kera found herself clinging to the hand, warm and rough, in hers. She looked into her aunt's face, and Valaika met her eyes steadily. Her aunt's eyes were the same dark blue as her father's, full of warmth. The same warmth, the same welcome, as the day they had buried her father.

Kera's lower lip trembled, her determination to remain formal crumbled, and she took another step forward into her aunt's arms.

"There, my little one. I'm here. Whatever it is, I'll help you." Even the voice, with its Hellish accent, reminded Kera of her father.

Strong arms around her, hands patting her back. Valaika *would* help her, Kera was certain, though she didn't know how she knew it. These weren't just words. But much as she would have liked to go on clinging to this woman who reminded her so much of her father, there was someone else in the room, and pride made Kera straighten her shoulders and take a step back, clearing her throat and adjusting her brocaded sleeves, trying to regain the composure she'd had when she'd come in the door.

"I thank you," she said in as steady a voice as she could manage. Pride told her to say no more, but curiosity was stronger. "What makes you think I need help?"

"No one stands near the throne and doesn't," Valaika said, smiling to take the sting of cynicism from the words. "I knew that when I was younger than you are now, and farther from a throne."

Kera swallowed. "You're right, of course," she said. "I have come looking for an ally, though to be honest, I'm not sure what any of us can do."

"Start at the beginning."

The deep, unexpected voice made Kera jump just a little, and she brushed a bit of fluff from her skirt to cover the movement. If he were just a personal guard, he wouldn't have spoken, and that meant her thinking was correct. Time to set formalities aside.

"Do you know a Mercenary Brother called Dhulyn Wolfshead?" she said. Her breath caught. "I see from your face that you do."

The man stepped forward until he was almost too close for protocol, and Kera found herself leaning very slightly away from him.

"My name is Parno Lionsmane, called the Chanter. I was schooled by Nerysa of Tourin, the Warhammer. I fight with my Brother, Dhulyn Wolfshead, she is my Partner. Do you know what has happened to her?"

Valaika drew Kera to a seat at the small table, waving to Parno Lionsmane to bring up another chair. There was a plate of small poppy seed cakes and ganje in a glazed jug being kept warm on a metal stand over a small oil lamp.

Kera lowered herself into the seat and rested her hands along the arms of the chair; nodded her thanks as Valaika poured her a cup of ganje. "Five or six days ago, the Blue Mage returned from one of his tours with a woman who claimed to be of his Tribe, the Red Horsemen. Avylos let it be known that she was ill—the crying fever was mentioned—or perhaps injured, and that he was tending her in his wing. But she wasn't sick at all, and she caught me spying on her in the garden." Kera paused, checking their faces. The Lionsmane looked solemn, except for his shining eyes, and Valaika seemed about to smile. Kera took a deep breath.

"She told me that Edmir was still alive." A lifted eyebrow was the only reaction to her statement. "It's true, then?" She hadn't really doubted it—it was impossible to look Dhulyn Wolfshead in the face and doubt her—but Kera's heart gave a little skip when both Valaika and the Lionsmane nodded.

"She told me about the Blue Stone," Kera continued, "and together we formed the plan of stealing it." As quickly as she could, she outlined what had happened three nights before—and how Dhulyn Wolfshead had been behaving ever since.

"Did Avylos do this?" The Lionsmane's voice was a low growl.

Kera shook her head. "He seemed just as surprised as I was. The look on his face was almost frightened before he regained command of himself. I wondered—I have heard that if a person takes a blow to the head . . ."

The Lionsmane was nodding. "Certainly. That is possible, though I've only seen memory loss on this scale once, and I've seen many thousands of blows to the head."

"What was done in that case?" Valaika asked.

"A Finder and a Healer combined their talents to restore the lost memory. But that is not an option we have here."

"Could it be the Stone?" Valaika drummed on the polished wood with her fingers.

Parno shrugged, blowing out a lungful of air. "If we had the journal, and we could read it, perhaps there would be something there that would tell us. Zania certainly never mentioned such a possibility. As it is . . . Can you get me into the Mage's wing?"

Kera blew out a long breath, shaking her head. "Something prevents it. My mother or I can enter whenever we wish. But no one else, not even Edmir. We've tried disguising him," she added, as the Lionsmane opened his mouth to speak. "It doesn't work. Besides, what can you do? Dhulyn Wolfshead doesn't remember you."

He fell quiet, his eyes narrow, his lips pressed tight. "We're Partnered," he said finally. "She will remember." He looked up again. "Did you ever try getting someone over the wall?"

"It's impossible to climb over . . ." Kera leaned forward, the heels of her hands on the table's edge. If Avylos was conserving magic, as it seemed he was, would he have bothered to magic a wall everyone considered impossible to climb? She looked Parno Lionsmane over, taking in the hardness of the muscle under the golden hair on his arms.

If he could move the way Dhulyn Wolfshead could . . . Mercenary Brothers were *supposed* to be able to do impossible things.

"If you can get over the wall," she said. "I will bring Dhulyn Wolfshead to the garden."

⁓⁓⁓

Parno had looked the wall over fairly thoroughly when he'd been leaning against it, playing for the children as they skipped and danced through their game of Blind Man. Old as it was, the stones of the original wall were still smooth and beautifully fitted. He suspected the lower courses had been laid without mortar, probably by some long-dead craftsman who had studied the technique of the Caids. It was hard to tell from below, but Parno was sure the individual stones had been placed in such a way that the wall actually leaned out slightly from the bottom. At one time, this must have been part of the outer wall of the Royal House. Climbing it might well be as impossible as Kera thought.

The repaired portion, now that was a different tale. Clearly, the repair had been made after the courtyard had been created, and this had become an interior wall, no longer exposed to the possibility of an enemy attack. It was not merely the newer, unaged stone that made the repair stand out. It was good, sturdy work, and the unpracticed eye would see no difference other than color from the original wall. But Parno could tell that the newer portion had been created by a much less skilled craftsman than the old. There was more mortar, for one thing, which meant greater possibilities for finger- and toeholds. And he was virtually certain that the wall did not lean outward, toward the climber. If he was right, then all he had to deal with here was an ordinary wall. A little taller than the ones he'd climbed before, perhaps, but still, only an ordinary wall.

Parno and Valaika arrived at the spot Parno picked out as the most climbable while there was still light in the sky. It had to be late enough in the day that the grounds were as good as deserted, but early enough that Parno could take advantage of the minute shadows created by the slanting rays of the sun to find purchase as he climbed. A torch would flicker too much to help him, and would undoubtedly draw far too much attention. As it was, even the torches that burned nightly in the entrances to the main section of the citadel had not yet been lit.

Valaika eyed the wall as Parno shifted his sword around to hang down his back.

"You sure about this?" she said. "It looks too high."

"They all do, from the bottom," he said. "But I was Schooled in the mountains, I won't even need a Climbing *Shora* for this," he added. Climbing was, in fact, one of the few things he did better than Dhulyn, though it was she who had taught him the Sable Monkey *Shora*. However, Parno suspected he knew what Valaika was really asking. If Dhulyn had not known him in the audience hall, why would she know him now?

Because she had to. That was why. Because they were Partnered, and apart they were incomplete. That was why.

He bent down to pull off his boots and folded the tops into his belt. He had taken off the wig covering his Mercenary badge, and replaced it with a knitted hood that fit closely around his face. If Dhulyn was in the garden, he could push the hood off. In the meantime, he still looked like an ordinary retainer of House Jarlkevo.

"I'll hold those for you," Valaika said, pointing to his boots.

"If my Partner is not in the garden," he said, "I may want to look around a little. If I'm fully dressed, I can claim to be lost, but if I'm missing my boots, that might be a little harder to explain."

Parno turned once more to the wall, took several deep breaths, put his hands on the cool stones, and looked up. The top seemed much farther away than it had a few moments before.

"Is it too difficult?" Valaika asked. "Perhaps I can get you in, if I asked to visit Avylos . . . ?"

"A moment, if you will," he said.

He rubbed his palms together, dried them on the front of his tunic. He looked up and saw his path, laid out as if drawn on a sheet of paper. There were his first fingerholds, and there the first spots where he could brace his toes. From there he would veer slightly to the left and then . . . He launched himself upward, sliding his fingertips into two uneven spots in the mortar around a stone and pulled himself up.

✖

The last of the sunlight still glowed in the windows of the upper stories, but here in the garden torches had been lit. Dhulyn shifted in her seat, wincing and rubbing her lower back. She set down the tile she had just removed from the board.

"When is this drug supposed to start working?" she asked.

"My mother says in a short span of minutes." The Lady Prince Kera concentrated on the board. "I don't get the birthing pains when my woman's time comes, so I've never needed it."

"Pray Sun and Moon you never do." Dhulyn twisted from side to side. Was the pain subsiding, or was it wishful thinking?

"My old nurse used to say that bad pains every moon meant that real births would come easier."

"It's hard to be glad of that just at the moment."

Dhulyn tried to refocus her attention on the game in front of her. Strange that she could remember perfectly well how to play Two-handed Tailor with the vera tiles, and yet nothing much else from the time before her memory loss wanted to come to the surface. Her hand went once more to her head, as if this time she would feel something different. There was still some pain, and when she moved her head quickly lines of light and color seemed to trail after things, but she could find no sore or tender spots anywhere. She had not, apparently, struck her head. Was it indeed this Stone that Avylos made so much fuss about which had robbed her of her past?

If she touched the Stone again, could she get her past back? And what of those odd visions with their confusing cascade of images? Should she tell Avylos that they were still troubling her?

Princess Kera finally made her move and Dhulyn kept her face carefully still. The princess had discarded the precise tile Dhulyn needed to complete her hand. As she reached for it, she heard the unmistakable sound of feet hitting the ground behind her.

In the time it took for the intruder to circle the pond and close on them, Dhulyn snatched up the only weapons to hand, the jug of iced lemon laced with pain drugs that Kera had brought with her from the Royal kitchens, and the silver tray on which it sat. She whirled, threw the contents of the jug first, followed immediately by the jug itself. But the man, moving in a golden-brown blur, dodged both drink and jug.

"Kera, run for Avylos—now!"

But the man didn't follow Kera, not even with his eyes. Not an assassin after the Lady Prince, then. She must herself be the target. But why would anyone want to kill *her?* To strike at Avylos? Or was this still another thing from her past she couldn't remember?

The man stepped forward again, and Dhulyn hurled the tray like a disk, aiming for the side of his head. Cursing— that wiped off his smile!—he barely got his forearm up in time to keep the tray from striking him.

Without waiting, Dhulyn ran to a row of climbing flowers and wrenched up a wooden stake from out of the garden fencing. It was as thick, though not as long, as a quarterstaff. It felt awkward in her hand, no proper hilt, badly balanced, but as long as she avoided meeting the edge of his sword directly, she could use it. She took up a defensive position, and began circling to the man's right. Perhaps she could angle him so as to get the light of the torch in his eyes.

Dhulyn blinked, even as she kept her own eyes on the intruder. *What is this?* How did she know these things? Why should this knowledge just come to her? What *was* she?

The man drew the sword that hung down his back, and stood ready for her, sword up, knees bent. Dhulyn felt her body automatically imitating his stance and she faltered.

"Dhulyn Wolfshead," the man said. "You don't want to hurt me."

"Will you cut me with words, or do you plan to use that blade?" She leaped forward, feinted a blow to his head, dropped the point of her stake, intending to jab him in the groin—only to be met by the flat side of the man's blade, deflecting her blow and almost knocking the unwieldy thing out of her hand. She brought up her left hand to steady it, and dodged to her right, making the man take two steps to her one in order to keep his sword between them.

But he didn't cross his feet when he moved, didn't drop his guard; and the torchlight wasn't enough to dazzle him.

"Dhulyn Wolfshead," he said. "You were Schooled by Dorian the Black Traveler. You fought at Sadron, Arcosa, and Bhexyllia, where you slapped the Great King's face. You must remember?"

"Blooded nonsense," she said. She leaped up on the white boulder that marked the corner of the rock garden. He was not that much taller, but this would remove even that advantage from him. She struck again, bearing down on the stave, but he blocked her, once more with the flat of his sword so that her wooden stake remained intact.

"I'm your Partner," he said stepping back to avoid a rapid series of blows she aimed at his sword arm, his ribs, and his groin. "Parno Lionsmane, called the Chanter. We met at Arcosa, fighting for the old Tarkin of Imrion, remember? I saved your life."

As he said this he swung at her legs, and Dhulyn was forced to leap up and to the left to avoid his blade. Landing once more on the pebbles of the garden path, she had lost the advantage of height the boulder gave her, but his back was now to the door. When Avylos came, the man would be finished.

"If you aren't who I say you are," he said, warding off her next strike, "how is it you can fight me? How is it you can hold me off?"

The truth was, her body seemed to move by itself, as if it remembered things she did not.

"I'm a Red Horseman," she said aloud, grasping at the only idea she could think of. "We are formidable warriors."

In answer, the man reached up and pushed back the hood he was wearing. His close-cropped hair was the same amber gold as his eyes, but had been removed above the ears and along the temples. In its place was a dark red-and-gold tattoo with a black line tracing through it.

"Formidable enough to hold your own against a Mercenary Brother?"

Sun, Moon, and *Stars*, she cursed under her breath. A Mercenary Brother. She felt she should know something about them, but what? A town man, though. He was a town man just the same, Mercenary or not. Town men were liars and brigands, and Avylos had told her it was town men who had injured her and brought on the fever. Without the hood it was easier to see his face . . .

"Sun burn you! You're the blooded spawn of a snail who bumped into me in the audience room. You're nothing to me, or my kinsman would know you."

"He's no kinsman of yours! Listen to me, you have a tattoo just like mine under that wig of yours. How else could you know what you know?"

She feinted again with the stake, but this time let it drop from her right hand to her left, and lunged at his heart.

Or where his heart should have been. He knocked the stake flying out of her hand, but did not attack again. Rather, he dropped back two steps, his point up, his eyes fixed on hers.

"How is it you knew how to do that? And how is it I knew what you were going to do? That was the Mirror *Shora* for two-handed swordplay. Where did you learn it if you are not a Mercenary?"

Could he be telling her the truth? She glanced toward her weapon.

"Dhulyn, my soul, *think*. If you don't remember me . . . where is your horse? Where is Bloodbone? What has happened to her?"

Dhulyn stayed crouched, knees slightly bent. Her horse? She was Espadryni, what the world called the Red Horsemen. So where, indeed, was her horse?

The man smiled. No! He was trying to trick her, take her from her kin. Not again. She could not lose her Tribe again. She threw back her head and as she gave the snow heron's cry . . .

❊❊❊

Sword in hand, she fights a one-eyed man in a room with a round mirror . . .

***

Sword in hand, she fights the golden-haired tattooed man, but she is laughing, pleased . . .

Her own hands lay out vera tiles in a pattern she does not recognize from any game. The floor under her is moving like the deck of a ship . . .

A young woman with almost white hair holds the Blue Stone in her hands . . .

Avylos as a young man, running through a forest; the hunters behind him are Espadryni . . .

※

With the weird howling still echoing in his ears Parno landed heavily on the courtyard side of the wall. Valaika was there in an instant, pulling up his hood and drawing her own sword. Calls, running footsteps, and torches were heading in their direction.

"Guards, quickly, this way," Valaika called out. "What happened?" she said in a quiet aside.

"Dhulyn almost killed me." His hands were still trembling, muscles twitching. He could not tell her what the worst cut had been. That Dhulyn should cry out for Avylos the second she laid eyes on him—he pushed the thought away. That wasn't the real Dhulyn. It *wasn't.* "If she'd had a sword instead of a garden stake—" he shook his head as two guards in the queen's colors ran up to them, swords out, torches to the fore.

"It came from the other side of this wall," Valaika said, pointing upward with a gesture that both took her sword point away from them, and showed her own Royal colors to good advantage. "The weirdest howling noise."

Both guards grinned and lowered their own weapons, the shorter one going so far as to sheathe his sword as he stepped forward.

"You're the Jarlkevoso, aren't you, Lady? What brings you out this way?"

"Trying to settle my supper with a bit of a walk. Not

used to the rich fare at my sister the queen's table. For the Caids sake, what was that noise?"

"Don't you worry, Jarlkevoso, this is the Blue Mage's wing. Whatever it was, it's no concern of ours, nor yours either, with respect. The Blue Mage will manage it, whatever it was."

"Of course." Valaika backed a few paces from the wall, looking upward, and letting Parno trail a little behind her. "I'd forgotten Avylos had this end of the old keep for his use. I'm sorry to have disturbed you."

The guards walked them back to the entrance of the building that housed Valaika's suite of rooms, and bade them good night. By this time the trembling had stopped, and the sweat on his face had dried. But Parno's mind was no further settled.

"She was thinking too much," he said, as they walked into Valaika's private sitting room and shut the door. "That's the only thing that kept her from killing me—and I made sure she thought too much, asked her questions, kept her consciously aware of what she was doing—I'm blooded lucky she didn't break something."

"Are you all right?"

He looked up, blinking. "I'll be all right when I get my Partner back."

❧❧❧

"You say he came over the wall?" Avylos sat behind his worktable and pulled at his lower lip.

"He did."

"And what did young Kera do then?"

"I sent her to fetch you."

"Which she manifestly did not do, as this is the first I'm hearing of it."

Red spots appeared in the sudden pallor of his cheeks, and Dhulyn found her muscles readying themselves for action in response to Avylos' anger. Then his gaze shifted from the book he had open in front of him to the small casket to his left, and she relaxed. It looked out of place here—old, plain, and unadorned where everything else was of the first quality. Inside it, Dhulyn knew, was the Blue

Stone. Dhulyn waited until he was looking at her once more.

"Perhaps she could not find you," she said.

Avylos' expression told her how much he believed that. She shrugged, for some reason finding herself reluctant to think ill of the Lady Prince. But Avylos knew these town people so much better than she did herself. She must trust in his knowledge of them.

"Is it possible what he said was true? Could I have been a Mercenary Brother?"

"He is a town man, you say?"

"From his accent and speech, I would say so, yes." Dhulyn frowned, rubbing her forehead. "Though how it is I know this, *that* I cannot tell you." She looked up again. "But you know him, you have seen him yourself. It was that man who jostled me in the queen's audience. The retainer of House Jarlkevo." Avylos' eyes narrowed and the corners of his mouth turned down. Dhulyn felt a trickle of fear run up her spine. Her muscles tensed as she prepared to either flee or defend herself.

"Are you certain?" Whatever it was that had disturbed him, his anger was not aimed at her. Dhulyn allowed herself to relax.

"Of course. *That* I remember perfectly."

Avylos came out from behind his table and took her hands in his, squatting so that she looked directly into his eyes. They were a brilliant blue, and kind in a way that made her draw in a deep breath.

"Are there any other signs of your memory returning?" When she shook her head, he continued. "Can you guess why this man should be so interested in you? No? Nothing comes to mind?" Rising, Avylos released her left hand, and stroked her cheek with the back of his fingers. "Rest easy, my dearest cousin. I will help you, I promise."

"Have there been others like me? Others who have lost their memories to the Stone?"

Avylos hesitated, his fingers still caressing her face, and then seemed to come to a decision. "I will not lie to you," he said. "There have been others. But they regained their memories within hours of touching the Stone. But again, I promise you—" here his hand tightened on hers. "I swear that I will not abandon you, I *will* help you."

Without meaning to, Dhulyn squirmed, lowering her eyes.

"What is it? I cannot help you, if you do not tell me everything."

"I have told you—" She began again. "Once or twice I have spoken of feeling dizzy . . ."

"But there was more?"

There was a hardness under his words that made Dhulyn hesitate. But once begun . . . "I see images, rapidly, one after another. Sometimes things I recognize—you, the Blue Stone, myself fighting the Mercenary—but often people I don't know, places I have never, to my knowledge, seen. I thought at first it would pass, and so I did not mention it." She let her hand fall into her lap and raised her eyes to his. "But it is not passing. Is this the Stone? Can you help me?"

Avylos did not answer her immediately, and Dhulyn felt a tremor of worry pass through her. Still holding her hand, he straightened. He was thinking, and from his face it seemed as though he debated what to tell her. Finally, he spoke.

"Very likely. These may be some form of waking dreams. It may be that proximity to the Stone has brought out some latent power in you, as it did once with me. You must tell me if it happens again, and what you see. I have promised to help you, and I will help you in this as well."

He kissed her hand. "And to start that help, let me assure you, I have known you your whole life and you were never a Mercenary Brother. It's as you said to him, the Espadryni are formidably skilled, that is all. You were injured, suffered a fever, and have lost your memory, but you are my cousin. You were never a Mercenary Brother."

He paused, and obediently Dhulyn repeated the phrase.

"I was never a Mercenary Brother. I have been injured and lost my memory, but I am your cousin."

"There you are."

Dhulyn waited until Avylos had left her before throwing herself backward into her chair, with a huff of breath. "I was never a Mercenary Brother," she said in the tones of gravest solemnity that Avylos seemed to require. "I have been injured and lost my memory." She leaned back in the chair and rolled her eyes to the heavens. Sun, Moon, and Stars, but grown-ups thought the silliest things were important.

Twenty-two

LATE AS IT WAS, AVYLOS found the Lady Prince Kera coming up the Great West Stair, as if she was heading to his apartments, rather than toward her own. He gestured her into a nearby alcove, empty since the removal of a bust of Kedneara's grandfather.

"But I met a messenger from my mother the queen—I *had* to go to her. I came back to find you as soon as I could," Kera said in answer to his query.

It was a good lie. One that on any other day he might have believed. Had he not been returning from the queen himself, he might very well have believed it. As it was, he fought to keep his face serene against the rage that swept through him, hot as fired metal. Fought to keep his hand at his side when it itched to lift up, draw a symbol in the air, and watch her try to breathe through a closed throat.

How dare she. How *dare* she lie to him. Just like her mother, using him, treating him with smiles and now lying to him, turning her back. After all he had done, and was doing, to ensure that the throne would come to her. Well, that was at an end. He saw clearly now. Very clearly. Edmir was already gone, he had accomplished that through Sylria. He had Dhulyn, and she had Seen him full of light. Full of power. What did this mean but that together they would unlock the Stone and he would have all the power he wanted. He no longer needed to bring Kera to the throne. With Dhulyn, and the book, he could bring himself there. He could be Mage King, not over the Espadryni, not over a mere ragtag band of nomads as his father had been, but over the whole of Tegrian and its territories. Over the whole world.

A shifted foot, a cleared throat, returned Avylos' attention to the girl in front of him. However compelling, he must set his vision of the future aside for now. There were still items in the present which required his attention.

"Did you not tell them you were looking for me?" His voice was mild. "That it was urgent?"

"I did." Kera's cheeks flushed. "But it was Lady Mora who came for me, and she refused to listen." Again, on any other day Avylos might have taken her flushed cheeks and trembling lips for embarrassment and frustration at having been thwarted by her old nurse. But today, he knew it for a liar's agitation.

"If there is nothing else, Avylos, and your cousin is safe, then I must return to my mother the queen."

"Of course, my Lady Prince."

As he watched her go, walking as fast as dignity and formal gown would allow her, he lifted his hand again, index finger extended, thumb out in the proper position . . .

Avylos let his hand fall. Not yet. Soon, but now was not the time. He should have realized that the other Mercenary would come looking for his Brother. He and Valaika were as yet unaware that Edmir was dead, and their involvement in these events was now at an end. But if Avylos wanted to keep Dhulyn Wolfshead, and he did, he would have to find a way to deal with the other Mercenary—and perhaps Valaika as well. But it was already late, and there was little he could accomplish now that could not wait until morning.

Wait. He had already taken a few paces down the corridor toward his wing when a thought occurred to him. There *was* something he could do, and now was the best time. He descended the West Stair into the Great Hall, but instead of heading toward the East Stair that would bring him eventually to the queen's rooms, he set out across the hall toward the outer doors. The evening meal was long over, and the extra wall sconces were starting to be doused for the night.

Avylos was aware that his anger still burned, a small flame like those in the sconces, deep inside him. Not yet, but very soon he would deal with Princess Kera, and the queen, as he had dealt with Edmir. Soon, he would have no further use for the Royal House of Tegrian. He had thought—even hoped—that Kera was malleable, but he now knew she also would lie to him, hide things from him, treat him as though he was a person of no consequence. Avylos took a deep breath, and unclenched his fists. Only Dhulyn repaid his attentions with trust, only she came to him for help, came to him as one does to family.

And her trust of him did not come about through magic. *He* had not removed her memory, nor tampered with her feelings in any way. What he was experiencing—what *she* was experiencing, must be Dhulyn's own natural reaction to him.

Avylos had never thought to see another of his Tribe, of his race. He'd long ago convinced himself he never *wished* to see one, not after all the tricks and lies they had shown him, making him believe he was *srusha*. Once he had encountered the Stone, and it had unlocked the powers those jealous of him had blocked—yes, even his own father, making him believe he was barren and empty of magic—he no longer feared the appearance of an Espadryni. But Dhulyn was different. She was too young to remember what he had done to revenge himself. If he could see to it that she now regained only *parts* of her memory . . . surely it could not be dangerous to keep her, once he'd dealt with the people who had come to take her away.

And her Mark? If it was truly returning, he had only to tell her what she'd told him herself. That it was erratic, and not to be trusted. He could still use it.

The guards at the entrance to the Great Hall saluted him and sprang to swing open the heavy doors.

The main entrance of the citadel of Royal House was raised above the level of the grounds by five stone steps, each wide enough to be almost a platform in itself. Avylos paused on the top step, letting his eyes adjust until they could see into the darkness beyond the torches that bracketed the doors. A breeze had sprung up with the sun's setting and pulled at his hair and the edges of his cloak, bringing the scent of flowers and greenery with it.

And if her Mark made Dhulyn herself unreliable— Avylos pushed that thought away. He would not think it.

He *would not*. She was his kin, something he never thought to want again. But now that he had her, she was his. He would not lose her. He started down the steps.

Avylos did not need light to find the portion of the wall he was looking for. He laid his hands on the stones. The avoidance magic he'd laid on it two moons ago was gone, he could feel no trace of it. The stones were rough here where the repair had been made, and he had noticed before that the better a thing was made, the longer it would hold a magic. Magic or no, however, he hadn't been overly concerned with anyone obtaining entrance from this quarter. The wall was rougher here, but not so rough that it was easily scaled. It would take an accomplished climber to do so. Apparently, the Mercenaries Schooled their Brotherhood in more than force of arms. He hadn't been concerned when Dhulyn had managed to get into his workroom. As his father had told him so long ago, women were difficult to magic, and Espadryni women even more so. But if the Mercenary Brother could climb this wall . . .

With his right hand he drew a pattern on the stones. It glowed blue, and held. With his left hand he drew another, a different pattern over the first. It glowed gold, and where the line of one pattern touched another, the colors began to run, twisting and twining.

"You cannot be climbed," he told the wall in the language of the Espadryni. "You have no handholds, no toeholds. You are as smooth as blown glass."

There, let the Mercenary try to climb that.

Sword in hand, she duels with the golden-haired, tattooed man, the mercenary brother . . .

Two men trot down a narrow path in heavy woods. It is early morning, and the sun is just penetrating the canopy of trees. The pines are ancient, so thick that there is little underbrush, and the snow that shows on upper branches has managed to fall to the ground only on the path. This is a wild place. One man has a cloth tied over the right side of his

face, and from the blood on it, Dhulyn would guess that he
has lost the eye. The other man has his left arm tied closely
to his body. His right arm is out for balance as he runs, the
hilt of his sword shows over his right shoulder, where it is
slung down his back. Both men have hair the color of old
blood; both men show other wounds sketchily cared for;
both men have the flushed cheeks and bright eyes of fever.
The one-eyed man grunts out something Dhulyn cannot
catch, pointing ahead. The other man draws his sword and
they break into a run . . .

She fights a one-eyed man . . . the mercenary brother . . .
a tall black man stripped to the waist . . . a thickset woman
with green eyes . . .

Avylos is on his knees, laughing. He spreads his arms
wide, and beams of light pour from his fingers' ends, from his
eyes, from his open mouth, from the ends of his hair. And he
laughs . . .

A storm rages, pushing walls of water over the rails of the
ship washing over the decks. There is so much water it is
almost impossible to breathe, one could drown standing upright, clinging to the sheets. She looks down to the deck in
time to see a man, his golden hair darkened by the wet,
swept off the pitching side of the deck by a wave taller than
two men. She wails, her heart breaking, and lets go of the
rope she clings to . . .

⊗⊗⊗

Dhulyn woke up tasting tears, her chest heaving. What
strange nightmares. She sat up, swung her legs over the side
of the bed, taking deep breaths to slow down the thumping
of her heart. That golden-haired man, that was the Mercenary Brother. Why should his loss, even in a dream, affect
her so? She went to push her hands through her hair and
felt the wig. In a daze, almost as though she were still
dreaming, she threw off her coverings and went to the
round mirror that hung on one wall. The moon was down
and it was too dark to see any reflection. She used the

sparker laying to one side on the table and lit the oil lamp, carrying it over to the mirror.

With her free hand she pulled off the wig.

Scars covered the sides of her head above her ears. There was no tattoo. The man *had* been lying, then.

The morning's rain made it seem much later, but the sun was only just up when the Lady Prince Kera joined Dhulyn for breakfast in Avylos' sitting room. Dhulyn put her hand out for the crockery pot of nellberry jam the princess was passing her and froze, blinking, her hand suspended in the air. She had the strangest feeling that she had lived through these actions before. What was it that was familiar? Breakfast? Nellberry jam? She groped after the memory, but nothing came.

Twice she had opened her mouth, about to ask Kera why she had not gone to fetch Avylos to the garden. Both times she'd filled her mouth with jam-covered biscuit instead. Her instincts were telling her to trust the girl—but she didn't know whether she could trust her instincts. For now, she would have to rely on Avylos' judgment.

"I woke up wondering about what that man told me, night thoughts, I suppose," she said instead. "I wondered whether I might have been a Mercenary Brother. So I looked."

"You looked?"

Dhulyn nodded, waving her free hand at her wig. "But it was as Avylos had told me, only scars."

"Do you think the scars might have been caused by removing a Mercenary's badge?" Kera waited, a cup of ganje halfway to her mouth. "Perhaps I should take a look."

Dhulyn held up a finger, turned her head, and a moment later, Avylos entered the room. Dhulyn smiled. Now that the Mage was here, Kera did not repeat her offer to examine Dhulyn's scars. The girl *did* have secrets, that was clear. But were they dangerous ones?

"I had a most curious dream last night," she said, reaching toward Avylos. "I dreamed I saw you full of light."

The sun was just up, but the rain was making everyone at Beolind's west gate grumpy and querulous. Not that there were many people here, Edmir noticed, just those few like themselves, travelers already out when the rain began. Anyone else with business in the city was doubtless taking shelter, waiting for the rain to stop.

"Members of House Jarlkevo with a report for our House."

Caids, Edmir thought, Zania even *sounded* more like a soldier than he did. He kept his focus on the gate guard's chin strap in an effort to pretend that he was looking the man boldly in the face. Though he doubted that many among the guard at the west gate had any clear idea of what their late Lord Prince looked like, Edmir still felt as though anyone and everyone in Beolind would recognize him.

Or maybe I'm hoping *they recognize me.* Surely Avylos couldn't have magicked the whole city?

Zania flirted a bit more with the guard before they were passed through. Once they had emerged on the far side of the long tunnel that led under the city walls, Zania cuffed him on the shoulder and pointed up the street. Edmir looked, but could see nothing of consequence.

"Try to put an awed look on your face," she hissed through a strained smile. "We're plain country soldiers on our first trip to the capital. Try to look as though everything's new to you. Gawk, you idiot. Gawk."

Edmir did the best he could to follow Zania's direction, smiling and nodding like a fool as she pointed and gasped. She was right, he knew she was. They'd talked about it on the way here, and had decided on this as the safest way for them to behave, as if they were merely plain country folk who had never seen a city the size of Beolind before. Trouble was, Zania was a much better actor than he would ever be. In fact, it was some help to Edmir that he'd rarely, if ever, come into the city through this particular gate, though that hadn't been the reason they'd picked it. His mother the queen always used the north gate, as it would accommodate both carriages and people on horseback, which she felt made a much better entrance. It was far more likely he'd be recognized by the guards there.

The rain did help them by emptying the streets and making their passage much faster than it would have been on a bright day. Still, last night's hasty biscuits and cheese felt a long time ago, and his stomach was growling by the time they led their horses up the final slope toward the sheer stone walls of his home.

Zania touched his elbow and they stopped in an alley just before reaching the immediate precincts of Royal House. He pushed back his hood while Zania reached into her waist pouch for the makeup she had there, leaning forward to touch his face with a few streaks of shading, making his cheekbones seem flatter, and giving his jaw a contour it did not naturally have. This gate would be the real test. The Royal House Guard had seen Edmir every day, though perhaps not from very close up. This was where his lightened hair, brushed back so uncharacteristically from his face, his earrings, and the fact that both he and Zania were dressed in Jarlkevo colors, would be put to the test. He scratched his chin. Along with everything else, he was letting his beard grow in, though it was much sparser than Parno's.

"Perhaps I should cough when we get to the gate," he suggested. "That way I can cover my face."

"Haven't you learned anything? Coughing will only make everyone look at you. I'm telling you, *soldier*—" Zania was careful not to say his name, "Just act as naturally as you can. Look around you, be respectful, let me do the talking."

Just like rehearsal, he thought.

The walls of the Royal House were not as thick as those of the city itself, but thick enough to provide for two offset pairs of gates. Even this early in the morning, even in the rain, these *were* public gates, and he and Zania found them standing wide open. But there were armed guards on watch, and everyone passing through here, even those wearing the Royal dark blue, would have to stop and account for themselves.

Ahead of them were a farmer and his son with a donkey cart, obviously delivering their load of lettuces to the kitchens. Sitting quietly on his horse as they waited their turn was the hardest thing Edmir had ever done. The last time he'd passed through was only two moons ago, he realized with a sense of shock. He'd been on his way to Probic, riding at the head of his escort of twenty handpicked soldiers, most from High Noble Houses with only a handful of the lesser nobility, followed by wagons carrying provisions for the journey, changes of clothing, tents, even musical instruments. His friends, Jenshan of Toron House and SuRohl of Kinton House, had been riding beside him that day. Had either of them made it back to Beolind?

And would they know me, if they had?

He and Zania dismounted, and Edmir saw that both the guards there were strangers to him. He began to relax.

"Members of House Jarlkevo with a report for our House," Zania said again as they drew level with the guards.

"How go things in your mountains, then, Jarlkevos?" the guard asked, as he took in their colors, the Jarlkevo brands on at least one of their horses, and the Jarlkevo bear heads stamped into the leather of their saddles.

"Well enough," Zania was answering with a grin. "More to see here, though, that's for certain, even in this rain."

Just as Edmir was sure the man was going to pass them through without further hindrance, a guard officer stepped into the gate area and approached them. Though wearing the same uniform as the two guards already at the gate, the officer's shirtsleeves showed the shine of silk, and there was gold braiding edging her tunic, not just turned cloth.

"Did I hear you say Jarlkevo?" she said as she came nearer.

Edmir knew her, and he tightened his grip on his reins, to keep from lifting his hand to cover his face. Section Leader Megz Primeau, champion swordplayer, and the current holder of the Queen's White Blade. She had once shown Edmir how to parry her secret thrust, and he had promised never to show it to anyone else.

"Yes, my lady," Zania said, ducking her head.

"I'm section leader, not 'my lady,'" Megz said, her eyes taking in every detail of their clothing and crests. She looked at their faces, and Edmir hastily lowered his eyes. That would be what a young guard would do when faced with authority, he thought. It was what young guards had usually done when he looked at them.

"Well, it seems your House was telling the truth when she said she'd sent all her best people to the queen's armies already. You two look as though you've hardly spent three weeks between you holding a sword." The first guard laughed, but not unkindly.

Edmir judged it was safe to lower his head entirely.

"Do you know your way?"

"Yes, we do, my—I mean, yes, Section Leader."

"Pass them in," Megz said. "Give my regards to your House," she added as she stepped out of their way.

"We will, and thank you," Zania said. She led her horse forward and Edmir was quick to follow her. As they remounted and walked their horses into the clear area of the courtyard beyond the gate, heading to the right toward House Jarlkevo's rooms, he risked a look back over his shoulder. Section Leader Megz was still standing under the arch watching them, her fists on her hips.

Valaika Jarlkevo was gray-faced. Her hand kept rising to her trembling lips and sinking again into her lap, as if she didn't have the strength to hold it up. She had aged twenty years, Parno thought, in less than twenty minutes.

"My Lord Prince." She kept repeating it, over and over, her voice drained of all life and substance. Finally, she struggled to her feet. Edmir moved forward, but Parno gave the older woman his arm, indicating to Edmir with a twist of his head that the boy should step back. Shaking, Valaika went to her knees before her nephew and, taking his hand, pressed her forehead to it in submission.

"My Lord Prince," she began again. "I beg you, hold your hand back from my consort. Do not tell your mother the queen. Let me—give me a chance to—"

"But, Valaika." Edmir was white under the tan that a moon of traveling had given him. "Jarlkevoso," he corrected when Parno coughed. His aunt *had* addressed the boy with his formal title. "It wasn't Sylria —that is, she was tricked. But no harm was done, at least not to us. This may even work in our favor. She believes we're dead, and she'll report that to Avylos."

These words didn't seem to help. Valaika shook her head from side to side as if she would never be able to stop.

"She'll report it to Avylos. *My* consort. *My* love. And she'll report to Avylos."

"He threatened her, Valaika." Now it was Zania's turn to speak up. "Threatened your child."

Parno had taken a step back, and leaned against the wall with his arms crossed, the only way he could keep still. This was getting them nowhere.

"Listen to me, all of you." The ring of command in his voice made everyone, even Valaika, even Edmir, turn to him. "Of course it was not Sylria. Avylos magicked her somehow, as we know he's magicked others. She'll be as horrified when she learns of it as you are now, Valaika. *But—*" And here he waited, making sure he had their absolute attention. He must give no one the chance to raise the question of whether the Consort Jarlkevo would put the life of her prince before the life of her son. Let them not think of that. "Sylria won't have a chance to *be* horrified if we don't deal with Avylos. This time, Edmir and Zania were able to turn his trickery to our advantage. As Edmir said, Avylos won't bother watching a dead man, so we now have reinforcements we didn't have yesterday. Get up, Valaika. I grieve for you, but we cannot allow your private grief to slow us, or change our course. We cannot let him win."

This time it was Edmir who offered his arm, and Parno did not interfere. When Valaika had regained her feet, Edmir embraced her. Zania stood watching, tapping her lips with the fingers of her clasped hands.

Parno turned toward the door. "Stand away, Edmir," he said. "Someone comes and we could not explain what a common guard is doing embracing his House."

Edmir did step back, but it was not until Zania took hold of his sleeve and pulled him away that he really took note of what he was doing and where he was standing. They had taken up reasonable positions to the right and left of the doorway, and Parno had seated Valaika once more in her chair when the expected knock came at the door.

"Come." Valaika almost managed to sound like her old self.

The door opened inward, hiding Edmir behind it. A voice announced, "The Lady Prince Kera," and she walked into the room.

Parno kept his hand pressed down on Valaika's shoulder, holding her in her seat. The last thing they needed was for the older woman to rise up and fall flat on her face. Her color was only now returning, and she still looked very pinched about the mouth.

Kera came all the way into the room and waited until the door had been pulled shut behind her. As soon as she heard the click of the latch she ran forward, her hands held out to her aunt.

"What is it?" she said. "What's happened. Is it Edmir?"

"It *is* Edmir," the boy said, striding forward from his place by the door.

At the sound of her brother's voice Kera spun around so quickly the skirt of her stiffened gown swung like a bell.

Well, Parno thought. *He hasn't spent the better part of a moon pretending to be an actor without learning a thing or two about theatrics.*

For a moment Kera did not move, and Parno thought with a sudden sickening drop to his stomach that she, too, had been magicked in the way of the City Lord in Probic, in the way Sylria Consort Jarlkevo had been magicked. And from the look in Edmir's eyes, he, too, feared that his sister would not know him. But then the girl made a noise in her throat that turned Parno's heart over and ran forward.

"Quietly, children. Quietly," he said. "We don't know who is on the other side of the door."

His words checked the brother and sister just as they reached each other. They gripped arms for a moment before embracing fully, Kera with her face buried in her brother's shoulder.

Let this be an omen, Parno pleaded. *So may I be reunited with my Brother.*

Kera stepped back, wiping at her eyes. She reached out and ran her hands over his dyed hair, her fingers resting for a moment on the rings in his ears. "How are you here? When did you come? How . . . ? Oh, Ed, I thought you were dead, I read your journals, I'm so sorry."

That brought a smile to Edmir's lips. "It's all right, Kera. Everything's all right."

That was an overstatement, if anything was, but Parno held his tongue.

A small cough reminded him that Edmir had not arrived alone. Zania, her cheeks flushed and the corners of her mouth turned slightly down, stepped forward.

"Your pardon, Princess, Jarlkevoso," she said. "But we've had no food today. Before we do anything else—"

"Of course." Valaika looked up at Parno.

"Princess," he said, as he held out a chair for Kera. He jerked his head at Edmir and the prince returned to his position to one side of the door.

Motioning Zania to stay still, Parno opened the door just enough to let the lady page who was waiting there see Kera seated behind him.

"The Lady Prince begs you will see that refreshments are brought," he murmured. The young woman's eyes brightened and her smile spread. Evidently, the idea of a trip down to the busy kitchens pleased her more than standing in silent attendance in a doorway. She bobbed her head and went off practically dancing.

Parno turned back into the room to find Edmir setting chairs around the table and Zania at the window shutters.

"Leave them," he told her. "The rain falls in the other direction, and as warm as it is, someone will notice if they are closed."

There was not really enough room around the small table for all five of them to sit comfortably, but the very closeness meant they could speak softly and lessen their chance of being overheard. Parno was about to take what would have been Dhulyn's favorite spot—against the wall between the two windows—when Kera settled the problem by sitting on the arm of Edmir's chair.

"Princess Kera, please." Zania, still on her feet, indicated one of the chairs. "I can stand."

"And eat standing up? I don't think so, you've had hardships enough from the look of my brother." Kera patted Edmir on the head as if he had been a huge dog. She was smiling as she spoke, but the sparkle had gone from her eyes. Parno could see that somehow, there was a shadow on the young girl's happiness. Well, and why not? She might have her brother back, alive and well, but they still had to deal with the Blue Mage.

"Princess," Parno said. "What occurred after my entry into the garden?"

Kera's narrative was interrupted only by the arrival of servants carrying trays of tarts, some berry, some cheese, and others of spiced meat, and a jug each of water and cider. Edmir and Zania listened to the rest of Kera's story with mouths full.

"I don't know that we accomplished anything, except perhaps to make Avylos suspicious of me," Kera concluded.

"We must kill Avylos, or else destroy the Stone." Edmir was quiet, but forceful.

"Both, if we can manage it." Kera seemed as determined as her brother.

Lips parted, Zania looked from one face to another. "I think you forget," she said. "The Muse Stone is my property, mine and my family's. You can't just destroy it, I need it."

"I may need it myself, for that matter," Parno said, before anyone else could answer her. "If it is the Stone that has taken Dhulyn Wolfshead's memories, then it may be needed to restore her."

"You would risk everything on that chance?" Kera asked not as though she would disagree, but as if she actually wanted to know. Dhulyn must somehow have made an impression on the girl, either before, or after her memory loss.

"She's my Partner. In Battle or in Death." *She is my world,* he refused to say aloud. *If I have lost her . . .*

"Does she still have my great-uncle's book?" Zania asked. "Surely, with both the Stone *and* the book, we can find another Scholar, we can learn how the Stone works, and . . ." Her voice trailed away at the look on Parno's face.

"Does Dhulyn remember the book? Or how to read it?" he asked. Zania subsided, pushing her cup away from her. From the look on her face, Parno thought, she would not agree to a plan that meant destroying the Stone. Any more than he would agree to a plan that meant leaving Dhulyn.

Kera's brow was furrowed. She looked down into the cup of cider she held in her free hand. "It would be best if we could simply put an end to Avylos. But how likely is that, here in his stronghold, with his source of power at hand? And if we fail? We must secure the Stone, not only for your sake, Zania Tzadeyeu, nor for Dhulyn Wolfshead's, but because it is the source of Avylos' power. One of two things will happen if we have the Stone. Either Avylos' powers will eventually wane to the point where we *can* deal with him, or, we can learn how to use the Stone to neutralize him. So, first the Stone, then Avylos."

Parno smiled. He would wager his pipes that Kera was the thinker in the family. Edmir had better not marry her off too far away, she might very well be his best counselor. It took the others a few minutes longer, but soon enough they were all nodding in agreement. Zania, in particular, was all smiles.

"We can get in over the wall," Parno said. "Zania, Edmir, and I."

Kera made a sharp movement that had them all looking at her again. She flushed, almost as though she were guilty of something. "Not Edmir. The one thing we can be sure of is that Avylos wants him dead. He can't walk into danger like that. From here, he could still manage to escape."

"Escape to what?" Edmir said.

Zania put her hand on his arm. "Better a live playwright than a dead prince."

From his angle to one side of them, Parno was the only one who could see the look Edmir gave Zania. It was the look of a man tempted almost beyond his ability to withstand. But perhaps he wasn't the only one who saw something pass between them, Parno thought. Kera was looking at her brother as if seeing him for the first time.

"There would be no point in my escaping without you," he said to Zania. "What use is a playwright without a troupe?"

"Then I will go," Kera put in. "Edmir, we can't risk everyone. One of us must remain alive to keep fighting if we're not successful—"

"Or to tell our tale, if that's what's left to us," Zania added.

"Stop." When he was sure he had their full attention, he continued.

"The one who has the best chance of getting out alive will go in. That would be me. The only other one who can contribute something to the fight will go in. That would be Zania with her knowledge of the Stone."

Kera was nodding her agreement. "I will get Avylos away by telling him that my mother wants to see him. There are often delays in getting to the queen, even for Avylos, and I can make sure there are more than usual. By the time he gets to her presence, you'll have ample time to get to the Stone, and get out again. And then we all escape."

"I will not leave without my Partner." Let them make of that what they'd like.

"But, Parno . . ."

He raised his hand, palm out. "I cannot. It is our Common Rule. Even if Dhulyn Wolfshead was not my Partner, I could not leave a Mercenary Brother behind me in such a condition. I must either persuade her, or bring her with us by force." *Or kill her.*

Parno stopped Kera as she reached the door.

"Did she say anything of me?" No need to say who "she" was.

"She's troubled, that's clear. At times she looks at me almost like her old self, or she seems about to speak and then it fades again, and she falls silent." Kera shot a glance back at the others around the table and then faced him again. "She said she looked for the Mercenary badge and all she saw was scarring."

A cold hand clutched at his heart and stopped his breath. "And is it gone?"

"I don't know, I asked to see for myself, but we were interrupted by Avylos. Could it be a magic? Are they easy to remove?"

"I would not have thought so."

Twenty-three

THIS WAS AN EXCEPTIONALLY good idea. Dhulyn stretched out in the hot water until her toes touched the far end of the bath. The water was scented somehow with pine, and she took a deep restful breath, letting it out slowly. She'd turned the servants out, not because she preferred to bathe herself, but because of their obvious discomfort at the scarring on her back. Or perhaps it was her own inability to explain where the scars had come from that made the bath attendants uncomfortable. Since Avylos had judged her well enough to take part in one of the queen's audiences, Dhulyn had asked to be given more freedom around the Royal House. Her kinsman had not agreed entirely, but he could hardly deny her a trip to the bathhouse.

According to what Lady Prince Kera had told her while bringing her here after breakfast, the Royal Baths had been built years before over a hot spring. Though from the smooth perfection of the stone floors Dhulyn suspected that this was the site of an ancient Caid building, and that certainly the Royal House, and perhaps the city of Beolind itself rested on an old Caid settlement—

She opened her eyes. That seemed like a Scholar's thought. But surely, if she were a Scholar, Avylos would have told her so. And her clothing, she eyed the carefully folded gown and overtunic on the bench against the warm inner wall. That was not the blue tunic and brown leggings of a Scholar. She sighed, closed her eyes, purposefully letting her muscles relax again.

The scent of pine was very soothing. And were the candles not beeswax? The heat was so pleasant.

There is smoke and screaming, the wild flickering of fires, and running shadows. A woman bends over her, though her arms are bare, her face is wrapped in scarves as though against the winter's cold; only her gray eyes show above the folds of material. She is tying similar scarves around Dhulyn's face, and as if that realization frees something in her mind, Dhulyn knows this is her mother, and the scarves are to keep her from choking on the smoke. Her mother speaks, and Dhulyn strains to hear her, trying to force the dream to give up her mother's voice. She fears that, as often happens in dreams (and how does she know this?) she will hear the voice clearly within the dream itself, but will have lost the precise sound of it when she awakens. . . .

A circle of women, their hair the color of old blood . . . Her own hands lay out vera tiles in a pattern she does not recognize from any game. . . . The Mercenary Brother with pipes in his hands. . . .

She is in the garden again, dressed in her lady's gown, her hair bound and swinging down her back. She swings a sword . . . a stave. No, it is a sword. She is in Avylos' workroom, and she fights a slim-hipped, dark-haired man. When she looks closely at him the dark wig disappears and she sees his Mercenary badge, with a black line threaded through the red-and-gold pattern. The steel rings, and rings again, the vibration of sword blade striking sword blade shivering in the hilt she grips in her left hand. There is blood dripping from her right hand, which she holds high to give her balance. Another thrust—she whips her blade around the other, keeping the point away from her skin, though she doesn't manage to disarm her opponent. Another thrust, this time at her belly, another parry, a thrust of her own that draws blood from her opponent's forearm; her satisfaction is short-lived as he changes hands and begins to fight left-handed as well. A lunge to the right, followed by two steps back—this is the Knife-Maker's *Shora*, but why then has blood been drawn? The next blow comes from . . . there, and can be countered with—a gasp of indrawn breath as her sword enters her opponent's side. He falls to his knees as she withdraws the blade from between his ribs. She puts out her hand to touch his face. . . .

A circle of women, their hair the color of old blood . . . Her own hands lay out vera tiles in a pattern she does not recognize from any game . . . The Mercenary Brother with pipes in his hands. . . .

Again, the smell of burning. Blood. Now she stands to one side and watches herself watching her mother. She has never Seen herself with her mother before, never from this perspective (what does that mean? *Before what?*) Her mother turns toward her and *sees* her, within the dream itself, as if they were both really there. Even though she can't see her mother's face, Dhulyn knows that she is smiling. She turns the head of the child so that she is looking at herself. She blinks, seeing a tall, slim woman with short red hair and tattoos above her ears. She blinks and sees her mother and the small child who is herself. She puts out a hand, but there is nothing to steady herself against.

"Go," her mother tells her. "Oh, my soul, do not watch. Find your own soul and save yourself. Go now, go."

But she does not go. She sees her mother tell her to hide in a nearby tree. "You'll be found in the morning," she hears her mother tell her. "When they have tired of killing us."

Why did I not remember this? she thinks, as the Vision fades. *Why have I never Seen this before?"*

And what do I mean by before?

She tried to follow that thought, but as she does. . . .

A circle of women, their hair the color of old blood . . . Her own hands lay out vera tiles in a pattern she does not recognize from any game . . . The Mercenary Brother with pipes in his hands. . . .

⬤⬤⬤

Dhulyn jolted awake just as her nose was about to slide under the surface of the water.

⧉

"My lord Mage."

Avylos kept his eyes focused on the book in front of him, as if by concentrating on the symbols he would be able to force his brain to understand them. When Dhulyn returned from her bath, he resolved, he would show her the book and see if she remembered how to read it. There was a chance, of course, that in doing so the rest of her memory might be triggered, but Avylos thought he had found a solution to that in one of his old texts. A light sleeping trance should do the trick. . . .

The page was still standing in the doorway and Avylos finally raised his head. Though he could not recall the name, he recognized the young man. This was that son of one of the Balnian Houses, recently come to Beolind to give his service to Kedneara. The talebearer and gossip. Though from the shrewd hardness of the eyes above the pleasant smile, there was more to him than a flapping tongue. Perhaps he was more astute than he seemed, astute enough to know that the way to advancement lay through Avylos.

For a moment, Avylos considered simply sending him away. Whatever it was he had come to report, it could not be more important than the study of the book. But the young man *was* astute, and only a very good reason would have brought him into the Mage's wing at this hour, when breakfast was over, and no other service would be required for some time.

"Yes?"

"My lord Mage," the young Balnian began again. "The Lady Prince Kera has gone to visit Jarlkevo House."

Avylos closed the book with a snap and leaned forward. Emboldened, the young Balnian came two steps into the room. Avylos had fully expected Kera to remain in the bathhouse with Dhulyn, in a futile attempt to interrogate her.

"The Lady Prince may certainly visit her aunt Jarlkevo if she chooses."

"Of course, Lord Mage. But two newcomers arrived this morning, and must have ridden through the rain to arrive so early. Young guards from Jarlkevo, it is said, with a report for their House."

Yes, the boy *was* astute. The guards must be bringing the news that Edmir was dead. And Kera, no doubt hurrying for a counsel with her aunt and the Mercenary Brother following the unsuccessful attempt of the night before, would learn that her brother was definitely dead.

And Edmir's body? Where would it be now? Sylria, showing good sense, had buried it without mention to anyone. Better he should know where it was, however, in case Valaika was thinking of doing anything with it. He could send Olecz and a few carefully chosen others.

"Come with me."

The Balnian page stood to one side and followed Avylos out of his sitting room, along the corridor and down the steps to the garden doorway. Here Avylos hesitated. It was unlikely that the boy could see anything in the pool, but it was best to be cautious.

"Wait here," he said. The boy took up his post next to the open door and Avylos strode down the path, white pebbles crunching under his house shoes, until he reached the pool. He sat on the wide stone ledge, leaned forward, and with his left hand drew a symbol, about a handbreadth above the surface of the still water, as though he were writing on an invisible tablet. When he withdrew his hand, the symbol remained, drawn in light, and the water began to darken.

As the water cleared, Avylos sat up straight, drawing in a sharp breath. He had expected to see first the darkness of earth, and then some hidden forest clearing where the angle of light would tell him in which direction from Jarlkevo lay this gamekeeper's lodge. This was no grave site, however, but the shadowy darkness of a shuttered room, the flickering light of candles. A sitting room. A fireplace freshly cleaned and laid with kindling. The bear's head emblem of Jarlkevo House carved into the thick oak beam of the mantel.

Avylos clenched his teeth. It had not been guards bringing news of Edmir's death who had arrived this morning, but Edmir himself. How was this possible? How had Sylria managed to lie to him?

Rising to his feet, he headed for the door, calling out to the still waiting Balnian page. "Fetch Royal Guard Commander Lord Semlian to the queen's apartments. Run."

Avylos waited until the boy was out of sight before returning inside. He checked his workroom door before following, keeping his pace brisk but controlled. Even now, he could not afford to look as though he were in any way perturbed. Meeting him, no one would be able to guess how loudly the blood pounded in his ears.

Edmir, the Mercenaries who had rescued him, Valaika. All here. Now. His plans unraveling. His pace slowed as his thoughts moved furiously fast. There *was* a way he could turn this to his advantage. A very clever way. A way that might very well solve more than one problem, and speed his plans.

He walked faster.

When he arrived at the double doors leading to the queen's private rooms, Royal Guard Commander Semlian was already waiting for him. The Balnian page was nowhere in sight, but the guard commander was accompanied by Megz Primeau, one of the section leaders. All the better. Nodding to them, Avylos threw open the doors, waved aside the startled pages who sat ready for orders in Kedneara's anteroom. He had never done this, never just charged his way into the queen's presence. Until now, he had always observed protocols scrupulously in approaching the queen, and it was obvious that none of her pages knew quite what to do. The old consort, Karyli, yes, *he'd* been allowed to flaunt protocol, but never Avylos. It was with unexpected relish that, Lord Semlian at his heels, Avylos pulled open the inner doors and found Kedneara on her feet, her shocked face turned toward the sounds of intrusion.

He went directly to her, taking her right hand in his and going to his knees. "Forgive me, my love, my Queen. I bring news of traitors to your rule."

"Traitors?"

Avylos rose to his feet and slipped his free arm around Kedneara's waist. "Sit, please, my Queen. You must be strong." The lady page who had been pinning the sleeves of her new gown pushed her abandoned chair closer and Avylos lowered the queen into it.

"Tell me." Her face was flushed with anger.

Smiling on the inside, Avylos knelt again and pressed her hand to his forehead. "I grieve to be the one who brings—"

"Tell me."

"It is House Jarlkevo, my Queen."

"Valaika?"

He raised his eyes to her face. "Yes, my Queen. My magic tells me that in her apartments she has an impostor, a young man she plans to claim is Edmir." Out of the corner of his eye, Avylos saw Section Leader Megz put her hand on her sword hilt.

"This is how she repays me." Kedneara's whisper was harsh. "This is what comes of spurning her love, all those years ago."

Avylos blinked, but kept his face steady. Was it possible that all Kedneara saw here was the revenge of unrequited love? Could even Kedneara be this self-absorbed? She gripped the arms of her chair.

"How can she do this?"

"There is a resemblance. I can only guess that he must be a child of the Jarlkevoso's own, a puppet she has been hiding, holding in reserve against a bid on your throne."

"And are you sure . . . ?"

"There speaks a mother's heart." Avylos kissed the back of the hand he still held. "But you know it cannot be. You know he is dead. This is not and cannot be Edmir."

"This cannot be Edmir."

He felt her pulse slow under his fingers. Much as he would have preferred it, it would be dangerous to have Kedneara repeat his words in front of these people.

"Is it Valaika then who is behind all this? Nisvea's invasion? Edmir's death?"

Good. She clearly believed in Edmir's death. "That I cannot know, my Queen. But it seems likely."

Kedneara's face hardened, and Avylos felt her pulse increase. She turned her stony face to the guard leader. "Bring them here."

"My Queen, you distress yourself too much. Let me spare you. Would it not be better—let me go with Guard Leader Semlian. Think of the scandal. Let *me* deal with the traitors. If necessary, it can be made to look like an accident."

"I thank you for your advice," Kedneara said in a voice that meant the opposite. "But I would speak with this woman and with those she uses against me. Bring them here. *Now.*"

As Avylos led Lord Semlian and Section Leader Megz Primeau toward the Great West Stairs, his face was hidden from them and he was able to smile. Kedneara was so easily manipulated, he thought. All he had to do was suggest that he wished to spare her, that something might be too much for her, and Kedneara would insist on seeing the traitors for herself. And if her health was completely undermined by the depth and deviousness of the treachery—one which might even involve the Princess Kera, if she were still in Valaika's rooms—well, who would be surprised?

❧❦❧

Parno came out of the room Valaika had given him tugging on the sleeves of his shirt. It was now of fine silk, with wide sleeves and buttons rather than simple lacing, and over it he wore a long formal velvet overgown, open in the front and edged with marten fur. If his trousers were cut more loosely than was the strict court fashion of the moment, he trusted that no one would be looking at him closely enough to notice. He would have preferred to keep his own boots, with their hidden knives and his lockpicks sewn into the trim, but in order to pass as a minor House member, he had to settle for leather half boots.

With her lifetime of practice, Zania had taken less time than he had to change her costume, and was already dressed in a heavily brocaded gown, tightly laced, which left her neck and the upper part of her shoulders exposed, but whose long sleeves reached almost to her feet.

"The laces can be cut," Zania said, "and then the whole gown just falls to the ground."

"Undoubtedly, exactly what the designer had in mind," Parno said. "Though I would imagine for a different purpose than the one we have." Zania curtsied, fluttering her eyes before she started to laugh.

"Guess where she has the rope," Edmir said from his perch on the edge of the table. Valaika was still sitting in her chair on the other side, frowning at her own thoughts.

Parno looked Zania up and down, taking two paces around her to be sure. "Around her hips. Oh, don't worry," he smiled, seeing the look of annoyance on Zania's face. "I'd give odds that no one else will notice it, and if they do, no one will remark on it. They'll just think you feel yourself too thin." He was pleased that Zania had come up with this solution. His sword he'd be able to carry openly, but the climbing rope they needed to get Zania up the wall wasn't something they could simply carry through the grounds.

Parno cocked his head, turning toward the door. He automatically moved to place himself between it and the others in the room.

"Someone's coming," he said. "Valaika, any legitimate reasons for guards to be coming to your door?"

The Jarlkevo roused herself. "None," she said, crisply enough.

"Well, judging by the sound of their footsteps, guards are coming now." Parno crossed quickly to the door and made sure the latch and locking mechanisms were secure. Not that that gave them much security. The lock was impressive in looks only, meant to give a feeling of security to what should, after all, be a perfectly secure place already. One well-placed kick and the door would open.

As if in answer to his thoughts, the door shivered under a pounding fist. "Open in the name of Kedneara the Queen."

"Quick, the window." At this time of the morning, it was unlikely that anyone would notice their descent. They were only one story up, and the window opened directly onto the wide cobblestone path that skirted the inner wall of the grounds. A short hedge of flowering bushes edged the pathway at this point, enclosing a small orchard of carefully pruned apple and pear trees. The trees wouldn't provide much in the way of cover, but they would at least slow down pursuit.

And if they were very lucky, the guards were all at the door, and none had been left to watch the windows.

"Edmir." Parno caught the prince's eye and jerked his head toward the open casement.

"No," Valaika strode forward, taking hold of Edmir's sleeve and addressing herself to Parno. "You and Zania go first. Edmir and I are the least at risk if it transpires that we cannot follow. Whatever else may happen, you must get to the Stone, that is the most important thing."

Parno hesitated, surely Edmir was the most at risk, but there was no longer any time to argue. "Zania, follow me. Edmir, you're next lightest, and lastly, Valaika." He caught the older woman's eye. "I expect you to follow, Jarlkevoso," he told her, with as much meaning as he could force into his tone. He thought he recognized the look on Valaika's face. Defeat, and despair. Now that the planning was over, and she'd been given time to brood, her shock over what Sylria had done had once more taken possession of her mind.

The pounding on the door renewed. With a nod at Valaika, Parno crossed back to the window, drew his sword to keep it from getting in his way should he fall, sat down on the windowsill, and swung his legs over. He let himself drop straight down, knees slightly bent, ankles flexed, mindful that he might have to correct for the roughness of the cobbles below. He landed cleanly, and a quick look to the right and left assured him that he'd landed unobserved as well. He sheathed his sword and looked up in time to see Zania's face in the window. He beckoned with his hands, and held up his arms to catch her.

She must have learned something from the tumblers who had been with her troupe, for she twisted quickly in the air and landed in his arms as if she were throwing herself backward into a feather bed. He tipped her to her feet and looked up again. Edmir had one leg over the windowsill, but he was looking back into the room, not down at Parno and Zania.

"Come on, boy, come on," Parno muttered under his breath. As if he'd heard him, Edmir looked down and his lips moved silently, but almost immediately he looked away again. He dropped the hand that was hidden by his body from those within below the level of his waist, and waved them away, already withdrawing his leg.

"What's he doing?" Zania said. "What did he say?"

"Guards must be in the room," Parno said. "He's waving us off before anyone can look out the window. Come on." He took Zania by the elbow and pushed through the hedge beside them. If it had been more than waist high it might have been of some use as cover, but as it was, Parno needed to get them past at least two rows of fruit trees before the foliage, thick as it was at this time of the season, could adequately cover them from anyone looking out the window.

"But what did he say?"

"He said, 'the Mage,'" Parno said. "Avylos must be with them. No, don't look." Parno took her by the elbow and urged her forward.

The orchard turned out to be only three rows deep, but the hedge on the far side was as tall as Parno's shoulder. They burst out onto yet another white pebbled path and just to their left was a stone bench, shaded at this hour of the day. Parno hooked Zania's hand through his bent elbow and led her to the bench.

"Sit." He suited action to word.

"But—"

"We're on a stage," he told her, and felt her immediately relax at this bit of direction. "We're noble lovers in a garden. And that is what anyone who may be looking out a window just now will see."

"Parno, what's happening to them?"

"Nothing we can do anything about. And Valaika was quite right, nothing very serious *can* happen to them, not being who they are—or, at least, who Valaika is. It's not so easy to dispose of a High Noble House, let alone the cousin of the Tarkin of Hellik. It will take time, and in this, time is on our side."

"Surely Edmir will tell them who he is."

"The moment he thinks it will do any good."

"And for us? What now?" She looked up at him and

smiled, just as if they were merely a courting couple taking advantage of a shady nook.

He smiled down at her and patted her hand. "We take advantage of the absence of the Mage to get to the Stone."

"How will we get into Avylos' workroom without Kera?"

"We'll worry about that when we get there. Today's problems today. In a few minutes we'll get up, and we'll start off in that direction." Parno nodded to the right. "We'll be strolling, just a couple taking advantage of the rain having stopped, and the sun coming out to dry the paths.

"And if we turn away from others, seeking out the darker and more secluded parts of the queen's gardens and grounds, well, no one seeing a courting couple sauntering about is going to find that unusual."

Avylos leaned against the doorframe, arms crossed, fingers tapping. Lord Semlian had managed to get himself slashed across the arm. Whatever could be said of Valaika, Avylos eyed her, she could still fight. Edmir —*no*, Avylos corrected himself, *I must not even* think *of him as Edmir*. Not that he was very likely to slip up. The young man had fought defensively, clearly reluctant to hurt anyone, let alone kill them. Not an unexpected attitude given who he was —*but don't say it, don't even think it*—typical really, avoid the unpleasant, even when it was necessary. Kera would have done what she needed to do, however much it might have pained her. In that, as in so many things, she was stronger than her brother. All this young man had achieved with his sensibilities was a bloody nose and a relatively quick disarming. Section Leader Megz had him bent over a chair as she bound his wrists behind him. He was smart enough to stay quiet at least.

The two extra guards with them returned from their search of the inner rooms, shaking their heads.

"This is everyone, my lord Mage, Guard Commander," the shorter one said with a nod to each captive.

"There should be at least one other," Avylos told them. He crossed to the window and looked out. What he could see of the grounds looked normal for this time of the morning. The watch was changing, and guards walking in pairs were coming and going from stations around the perimeter wall of Royal House. On a short stretch of lawn toward the western part of the grounds a huntswoman was training a dog. Avylos lifted his head and narrowed his eyes. Near the barracks, someone was setting up butts for archery practice. There were scattered people strolling through the grounds, fewer than normal given that the rain had stopped recently, though there were even a few couples sitting on benches.

No sign of anyone running. Nothing out of place.

Avylos turned back into the room. "Where have you sent him this time?" Valaika did not even raise her head. Avylos wrinkled his nose. "You have seen him," he said to the waiting guards. "The bodyguard who follows Valaika Jarlkevo. As tall as I am but thicker about the body. His dark hair is a wig, remove it and you will see a Mercenary badge." The guards in the room exchanged glances. "If you fear to engage with him, shoot him from a distance," Avylos told them, careful to keep the sneer from his voice. "An arrow will kill a man no matter where he has been Schooled.

"Guard Commander, you will see to your wound and the search. Assign Section Leader Olecz. You others will bring these traitors to Kedneara the Queen."

❧❧❧

Kera turned out of the corridor which led to Avylos' wing and started back toward the Great Hall. She ducked into the alcove just before the Great West Stairs that until this winter had held the bust of her grandfather. Her lower lip was caught tight between her teeth, and in her hands was a broken strand of Tenezian glass beads, ready to spill on the floor if she had a sudden need to explain what she was doing standing in such an out of the way place.

Though it was cool here in the alcove, Kera felt a drop of sweat trickle its way down her back. Avylos had not been in his rooms for her to lure away with a false summons to her mother the queen. What should she do now? Find him and make sure—somehow—that he stayed away? Or trust that whatever occupied him at the moment would hold his attention long enough for Parno and Zania to steal the Stone? They could not possibly have reached Avylos' garden yet; she still had some time to decide what to do.

She heard the sound of footsteps coming up the staircase to her left. Kera knelt, tossed the beads on the floor, and bent down to pick them up. It did not sound like Avylos, but . . .

"Allow me, Lady Prince."

Kera looked up. Metrick. Metrick the Balnian. Metrick the gossip.

"I would not keep you from your errand, Metrick."

"I have no errand, Lady Prince, but to find you."

Kera's hands froze for one second before she forced her fingers to continue picking up beads. "Who sent you?"

"No one, my Prince, only, I have noticed that you are frequently in this part of the House, and when I wished to find you . . ."

"*You* wished to find me?" Kera sat back on her heels, not knowing whether to feel flattered or skeptical. She *was* Lady Prince. Metrick of Balnia might very well feel his path to advancement lay through her. Or indeed, more than advancement. How important *was* his family in Balnia? Was he one of the people her mother the queen had warned her against? She realized that he had gone on speaking, and that she'd missed the first part of what he'd said.

"I'm sorry, could you repeat that?"

"You may well be shocked, Lady Prince. I'm sorry to be the one to bring you this news."

But he wasn't sorry, Kera could tell. He was pleased, not at the news, but at the importance it gave him in bringing it.

"Valaika Jarlkevoso has been arrested, along with an impostor she had in her rooms and planned to pass off as Prince Edmir, your brother."

"Where are they now?"

"The Blue Mage has taken them to Kedneara the Queen."

Kera thought quickly. Valaika and Edmir. That meant Parno and Zania were still free. Could they have been already on their way to the Mage's wing when the guards had come? What had brought the guards to Valaika? Not that there was time to think about that now.

And what should she do? If Parno and Zania *were* free, then they would be coming to the Mage's garden. And that's where she should be. She would simply have to trust that her mother would not act so quickly that Valaika and Edmir would be in danger. And surely, surely, her mother would recognize her own son?

"Metrick, go now and fetch—no," she interrupted herself as if she was having a change of thought. "Please take these beads to my apartments and give them to Sharian, my lady page. Explain to her what has occurred." He'd like that, he evidently liked being the bearer of news. "I will go myself to tell the Blue Mage's cousin what delays him, as she may not trust another. Tell Sharian to go to my mother the queen's apartments and await me there."

"At once, Lady Prince."

Kera waited until Metrick was part of the way down the Great West Stairs before turning and running back into Avylos' wing.

❧❧❧

As they walked, Parno steered them farther away from Valaika's rooms, seemingly taking paths at random, so anyone watching them would not even believe they had a destination, let alone guess what it might be.

"I think this is the first thing I've ever done where my goal was *not* to attract attention." Zania's voice was calm and measured, but Parno could feel her arm trembling ever so slightly in his.

"Not true," he said. "Remember how and why we started using the code word 'Pasillon'? To remind us that we are not the only people on stage, and that sometimes we must efface ourselves to let others shine, or to let the story unfold of itself? What is that if not a need to deflect the audience's eyes?"

The farther they got from the gardens closest to Valaika's rooms the greater the urge to walk faster. It seemed that every corner they turned led to yet another piece of statuary, yet another formally laid out bed of flowers or ornamental trees. Finally, the paths began to widen, and Parno knew that they approached the edge of the garden plantings closest to the section of repaired wall.

Parno slowed down even more; the only person within eyeshot was a kitchen boy passing with a basket of eggs hanging from one arm, and the instant the turnings of the path faced him away from them, Parno pulled Zania into the nearest shrubbery. In a moment, Parno had discarded his formal overgown, and had cut Zania's laces, allowing her to drop her own gown and step out of it. She pulled up the shoulders of the simple vest she had been wearing under the gown. At a distance, with her tousled hair and leggings, she could pass for any lower servant. Only the rope wound around her hips was out of place. A wriggle, and that too was on the ground. Parno picked up the coil of rope and slung it over his shoulder.

A trumpet call from toward the front gate—and the guard barracks —made Zania look around and grab Parno's arm.

"Ignore it," he told her. "They call the guard to assemble a search party. By the time they reach us down here, we'll be in the Mage's garden." As he spoke, he took sights from the top of two battlements, and the flagstaff on a tower he knew lay to the north. The repaired part of the wall was to their left.

"Just ahead there," he said. "Follow me." The distance they had to cross was short, and in a moment Parno had his hand on the surface of the wall. He frowned. The wall was smoother than he remembered, much smoother.

"What is it?"

"I may have cut the angle a little short after all, coming through the garden. Wait here." He took three paces to the right, but the wall was equally smooth there. He returned to where Zania marked the spot he'd started from, took three paces to the left . . . and found nothing but smooth wall.

"Zania, you did not move?" He hardly needed her indignant response to tell him that she hadn't. He checked his position again against the closest guard tower, the edges of the garden, and the distant murmur of noise that would be the guard barracks. He had not made a mistake. They were in the right place.

Parno's skin crawled with a sudden chill.

"The wall's been magicked," he said. "He must have been told. Avylos must have been told that I came over the wall."

Zania's face fell. "We'll get our court clothes back on,"

she said. "We'll have to try bluffing our way in the front doors."

"With everyone now looking for us? No disrespect intended to your ability to bluff anyone into anything, we would still have to find our way through the entire House, to say nothing of the magic that would keep me at least out of the Mage's wing once we got there."

Parno eyed the wall again. Demons and perverts, he needed to *think*. Kera had said that Avylos used as little magic as he could in any given situation—he would not use both an avoidance *and* a locking magic, where he could simply use a lock. That had made sense, given that Avylos' power source constantly had to be renewed. Would it follow that he would be equally parsimonious when it came to placing a magic on the wall? Parno put his hand on the stone and rubbed it back and forth. Smooth, but smooth like a polished stone floor, not like glass or the glazing on a pot. So Avylos had not changed the nature of the wall itself. He tapped his fingertips on the stone as though on the airholes of his pipes. That wasn't exactly the right sound.

"A surface as smooth as this one appears to be should make a cleaner sound," he said aloud.

"It doesn't seem so very smooth to me," Zania said, looking up and squinting.

"Doesn't it? Touch it, would you, and tell me what you feel."

Zania lifted her hand slowly, glancing at him sideways to see if she was doing what he wanted. She laid her palm flat on the wall.

"Move it back and forth a little."

"What am I trying to find?" she asked.

"Can you feel the individual stones, the mortar?"

"Y–yes."

That hesitation told Parno everything he wanted to know. Avylos would not waste his power. He would magic the wall against those, such as Parno, who intended to climb it. Zania, in truth, would be doing no climbing, it was Parno who would bring her up once he had reached the top himself. Evidently, that slight difference between them was enough to make them experience the wall differently.

So the magic didn't make the wall impossible to climb, it just made the wall *seem* impossible to climb.

"Parno?" Zania was still standing with her hand on the wall.

"Give me a moment," he said. "I need to try something." He shook out his hands. The Sable Monkey *Shora*. That's what was needed here. Used for climbing trees, rock faces and yes, stone walls, the *Shora* trained the eye to see and recognize holds that would support weight. Dhulyn had taught him the principles, not that there had been many opportunities for him to practice.

Climb, he told himself. *You're a Sable Monkey and you're going to climb this wall.* Nothing. He waited a handful of heartbeats longer and touched the wall again. Still nothing. Was it that he didn't know the *Shora* well enough? Or was it that it would not work?

Sun and Moon. He heard Dhulyn's voice in his head as he'd heard it so many times during practice. *The Shora* always *works. Pattern is always pattern.* Tradition said the *Shoras* came from the Caids. Was that enough for them to counteract the Mage's magics?

Parno settled the coil of rope over his shoulder and took a deep breath, releasing it slowly. This time he concentrated on relaxing his muscles, regularizing his breathing. He repeated seven times the three words that were his own personal *Shora* triggers allowing him to concentrate his focus and draw upon the *Shoras* that he knew. And he *did* know the Sable Monkey *Shora*, Dhulyn had taught it to him only last year, and he'd practiced it since. And he *did* know this wall. It was climbable. He'd already climbed it. His hands and feet knew the pattern. *And pattern is always pattern.* He flexed his fingers in the pattern prescribed by the Sable Monkey *Shora. I am climbing, I will reach the top. I cannot fall.*

Parno put up his hands, found the first fingerholds, and pulled himself up. There were the toeholds he had used before. He did not rest or pause, but put out his hands for the next holds, and then the next. He was more than halfway to the top when his hands felt only smooth stone. For a heartbeat his belly turned to ice, and the muscles in his calves began to tremble. How long until his toes felt nothing but smooth stone? How long before he fell?

Parno laid his cheek flat against the stone, eyes squeezed shut, and whispered his triggers, whispered them seven times seven times.

"I am the Sable Monkey," he said aloud. "I will not fall." He opened his eyes, and continued climbing.

Twenty-four

IT WAS HARD TO GAUGE the passage of time, since the water in these baths grew no colder, and Dhulyn had sent the attendants away. She found, however, that she could not recapture the languor she'd felt before falling asleep; just as she felt herself relaxing once more, she was disturbed by the nagging feeling that she had forgotten something. Her laugh echoed sharply in the tiled room. She hadn't just forgotten *something,* she'd forgotten *everything.*

Except she hadn't, not really. Life with Avylos would be considerably easier if she really had forgotten everything. If she didn't have these constant reminders, these surfacing thoughts, these *dreams.* The dreams felt real to her, solid, full of color, sound, and feeling. Her life with Avylos, on the other hand, felt empty and flat, as if it had left no footprints in the pathways of her brain.

There. That kind of thinking. What kind of person had thoughts like those? Footprints. Paths. Arrows. Swords. Surely not someone who had spent her whole life in the Tegrian Queen's Royal House.

Dhulyn rolled her shoulders and flexed her feet. She should try to relax, take advantage of this wonderful bath. It was seldom she ever got the chance for a long soak in a place like this one. In fact, she couldn't remember when—

"*Blooded* Stars," she said aloud, her voice echoing once more off the walls. She sat up and looked around for the towels the attendants had left. There was certainly no point in remaining here any longer, chasing the same thoughts around and around. Surely there must be something Avylos could do. Find a Healer, use a magic on her. *Something*.

And what was she doing wearing this ridiculous wig in the baths? It itched, and there were no servants here to whisper behind their hands at the scarring on her head. Besides, they'd seen enough of the scars on her back to give them plenty to whisper about. She gathered her feet under her and stood, wiping the water off her body with the edges of her hands before reaching for a towel. After wrapping a large sheet of toweling around herself, she sat down on the bench next to the bath and inserted her fingers around the edges of the wig. She would have it off, if only for a few minutes.

She peeled the wig off gently and spread it out along the bench. It would have to be brushed out, in any case, she thought. Dhulyn knelt by the side of the bath and stuck her head under the warm water to loosen and remove the last of the sticky paste that had held on the wig. Her head felt so much lighter now, and so much cooler. She eyed the wig, twisting her mouth to one side. If only she could go without it. What about when her own hair grew out, could it be combed in such a way that it would cover the scarring on her head?

Dhulyn put her hands to her temples . . . and froze. She felt the skin more carefully with the sensitive tips of her fingers. Nothing. No roughness. She trailed her fingertips over her cheeks and forehead, and back to her temples.

It all felt the same. No scarring.

Dhulyn lowered her hands, and pursed her lips in a silent whistle. She tucked the towel around her more tightly and proceeded to the outer room, where clean clothes had been left out for her away from the moist air of the bathing chamber. As she had requested, she'd been left trousers, a shirt, and a short-waisted tunic to replace the gown she'd been wearing. She frowned. The shirt was long sleeved, and the shoes house slippers instead of boots. Why *that* should trouble her was just another thing she didn't know.

She had buckled the sword belt around her hips and was attaching the sword to it before she was aware what she was doing. She lifted her hands away and took a few steps.

It felt right. Natural. As if she had often had a sword there. She found herself nodding. *This* was why she'd fought so well against the Mercenary. She *was* skilled as a warrior. It must be common among the women of the Tribes.

She drew the blade and weighed it in her hand, admiring its balance.

"Is this your doing, Avylos? Did you hope to trigger my memory?"

Dhulyn resheathed the sword. She needed a mirror. She needed answers. And she would find neither of those things here.

❈❈❈

Strange how different even your own home can look, when your hands are bound behind your back and you're being marched along as a prisoner by the very guards who are supposed to be protecting you. On the other hand, Edmir thought, perhaps it was lucky he *was* bound. This way no one could see how badly he was shaking. His mother the queen was never an easy person to contend with, and they had not planned on having to deal with her until after Avylos had been neutralized. His stomach clenched and he licked a drop of sweat from his upper lip.

Do I want her to know me, he thought, *or* not *know me*?

And that thought made him pause. Staying alive was his worry at the moment, and he needed to focus his attention on that. What would happen with the rest of his life was only important if he lived.

"Lord Mage," came the voice of Section Leader Megz Primeau from behind him as they neared the doorway which would let them out into the grounds. She tightened her grip on his right arm and gave him a shake. "This one does look most remarkably like Prince Edmir." Her hand clamped down painfully when she said his name, and Edmir winced. "May I," another painful *squeeze*, "suggest that we cover their heads, lest the whole House know," *squeeze*, "of this imposture? I do not offend you," *squeeze*, "I trust." *Squeeze*.

Edmir heard enough of Avylos' answer to know that it was in the negative, but his attention was focused elsewhere. Whether it was his recent training at catching cues on the stage, or that his present predicament sharpened his wits, Edmir couldn't know, but he thought he understood Megz Primeau's message. His arm would be badly bruised, the section leader had fingers like metal pincers, but her squeezing had not been random.

Edmir. I. Know. You. . . . Trust.

In that moment, Edmir's perception shifted. With Megz's words, what happened in the audience with his mother the queen—what she believed, and what she would say to him—became less important. Getting through the interview —*that* was now the goal. Section Leader Megz was the senior guard present, and would undoubtedly be put in charge of them when they were dismissed from his mother the queen's presence. All he and Valaika had to do was hold out until then.

That, and do everything they could to buy time for Parno and Zania.

Now Edmir lifted his head and looked around him. They were almost across the corner of the grounds between Valaika's rooms and the main citadel of Royal House. From what he could see, they were heading for the entrance known as the consort's door, not the main entrance and the more direct route that would take them through the Great Hall. So Avylos was taking no chances. The fewer people who saw them, the fewer there would be to ask questions and delay them. But just the same, Royal House was full of people, personal servants, cleaners, kitchen staff, pages, and guards on normal patrols. It was impossible for them to march through even the lesser-used corridors without being seen and remarked on.

Avylos said nothing, his set stare was enough to clear their way of anyone they encountered. The other guards were not so quiet, however, and Avylos did nothing to stop their murmurs of "traitors to the queen" and "an impostor."

What Edmir saw when they finally entered his mother the queen's private sitting room made his heart sink. She wasn't stalking back and forth, her long strides making the skirt and sleeves of her gown flutter. That would have meant she was angry. She wasn't standing by her window, leaning on the ledge and looking out into her private garden. That would have meant she was seriously annoyed.

No. Kedneara the Queen was sitting in her large chair, the one that most resembled her throne, gripping its arms so tightly that her knuckles were white.

She was in a flying fury. They would be very lucky if blood was not shed.

Edmir lowered his eyes and tried to make his breathing as shallow as possible. It was cowardly of him, he knew, but he did not want to do anything that would bring the full force of that fury down on him.

"Get out," the queen said. Her voice was still musical, but it was as if someone plucked the strings of a harp with a dagger. The three pages who had been waiting with her looked at each other out of the corners of their eyes, but they did so as they were moving to the door. Even the guards holding Valaika shuffled their feet, falling still only when Avylos raised his hand to them. Edmir risked a glance upward, but his mother was looking at Valaika.

"Valaika, you Hellish cow," she spat, as the door was closing behind the last page. "Have you always hated me this much?"

Edmir knew a sudden, though not unfamiliar, pang. Once his mother would have looked at him first, asked about him, even if she thought he was only an impostor. Those days were long gone.

"I never hated you, Kedneara," Valaika was saying. The guards had forced her to her knees. "You loved my brother, you chose him. You were happy, Kedneara, and Karyli was happy with you. That was enough for me."

"You don't hate me?" Kedneara, hands still gripping the arms of her chair, leaned forward as though she would spit in Valaika's face. "You say you don't hate me? Why else would you do this? Join with my enemies to conspire against me, kill my child, come here with an imp—"

Edmir pulled against Megz's grip as his mother's face darkened, suffused with blood. Her mouth was open, but it seemed she could neither speak nor breathe. Her grip on the arms of her chair became, if possible, even tighter, but her body began to heave and jerk. Megz let go of his arm and moved forward, but Avylos reached the queen's side before anyone, holding the others back with a short chop of his hand.

"Kedneara, my Queen, look at me."

It seemed that his mother couldn't raise her head, but she managed to twist it enough that she could look sideways at Avylos through slitted eyes. Froth tinged with blood formed on her lips. Holding her gaze with his own, Avylos took hold of the queen's wrist in his right hand. With his left, he began to sketch in the air. Edmir was not surprised when lines of light flowed from the end of Avylos' finger, and a symbol formed in the air, but the guards, who perhaps had never seen the Blue Mage actually perform from this close a distance, drew their breaths in sharply and took a pace back, leaving Valaika alone on her knees. She watched, tight-lipped, as the symbol glowed first blue, then gold.

"Inhale, my Queen. Inhale." As if Avylos' words were themselves a magic, Edmir's mother suddenly inhaled. The gold symbol flew in between her parted lips and almost immediately, the dark color faded from her face, leaving her pale except for a slight blush on her cheeks. Her breathing regularized, she blinked, and sat back in her chair, holding both hands against her heart.

Edmir's own heart felt cold in his chest. This was what they had not known, he and Kera. They had not known how sick their mother was, and how dependent on Avylos' magic. Of course, Kedneara was a woman, the Mage's magic would not cure her once and for all. He would need to renew the magic regularly, perhaps even find new magics when the old ones failed to serve. If he and his friends succeeded in what they were trying to do, if they succeeded in taking and destroying the Stone and Avylos' magic faded away, so would his mother the queen. She would die, if they stopped Avylos.

Finally, she looked up, right into Edmir's eyes.

"Edmir," she said, but her voice was so flat, it was impossible to know what she meant, impossible to be sure that she knew him.

"That is not Edmir, my dear one, my Queen, do not let your illness trick you." Avylos was already drawing in the air again, this time in the open space before the queen, short, chopping lines, a symbol harsh with corners. "This is an impostor, my Queen, Edmir is dead. This is not Edmir."

Edmir watched as his mother dragged her eyes from his to focus on the Mage and his symbol. She began slowly to nod.

"Mother," he cried, pushing forward. If only he could get her to look at him again.

But Section Leader Megz Primeau's steely hand on his arm pulled him back. "Edmir is dead," Megz said. "This is not Edmir."

"Valaika, close your eyes," he cried out. "Valaika!" Megz raised her fist to strike at him, but when he lowered his head and turned away, she let her hand fall open again.

"Edmir is dead. This is not Edmir."

His mother the queen, Megz, and the two other guards had spoken in unison. Without looking up, Edmir couldn't be certain whether Valaika had also spoken, or whether she remained unaffected by Avylos' magic.

Two at least of the people affected were women, which meant that eventually both his mother and Megz Primeau would recognize him again—but that eventuality was very small comfort to him now.

"My Queen, do not hesitate, do not let your kind heart lead you astray." Avylos was still standing next to the queen's chair. "You see how insidious they are, what havoc they could cause, do not hesitate I beg you, send them to the Black Dungeons now."

"But the other Houses—"

"Do you believe that any of them will speak for Jarlkevo? Outsider as she is? If you feel the need to tell them, do it after the fact, when the imposter is dead and the danger is past."

At these words Edmir looked up, unable to believe that Avylos gave this advice seriously. Jarlkevo *was* a new House, as these things were counted, but a High Noble House it was, and the idea that the other Houses—so jealous of their rights and privileges as they had always been —would stand meekly and nod agreement when one of their own, even a relative newcomer and outsider, was put to death without trial or hearing . . . No. What was done to Valaika Jarlkevo could be done to any of them, and they would know it, and their reaction would be swift and dangerous.

Regardless of the consequences to himself, Edmir had opened his mouth to say so, but Avylos pointed at him, a flicker like the flame of a candle appearing on his fingertip. The flame flew to Edmir's mouth, and he found he could not speak.

"I will see to it that the other Houses are informed," he told the queen. "Trust me, this you must do, for your own protection."

Edmir looked on, astonished, as his mother the queen nodded, and waved her hand. "Take them away," she said. She had not looked at him again.

"To the Black Dungeons?" It seemed even the other guards could not believe what they'd been told.

"Yes," said the queen. "Take them, now."

It was not until he felt the pain in his throat that Edmir realized he was trying to scream.

❧❧❧

Parno sat astride the top of the garden wall, his hands shaking, and the sweat drying on his face. He could taste blood; he must have bitten the inside of his lip on his way up. The Sable Monkey *Shora* controlled his breathing and heart rate while he was using it, but now he felt the exertions in the burning of his muscles, and the pounding of his heart.

He spat to one side as he uncoiled the rope and tied one end around his waist before tossing the loose end down to where Zania stood waiting, her arms already raised to catch it. As soon as it reached her, Zania created a loop in the rope, using the knots he'd shown her, and pushed her head and arms through it. When she was ready, she tugged on the rope. Parno swung both legs over to the garden side of the wall, and began to walk down, taking it nice and slow. With his weight to counterbalance hers, Zania would be lifted up the outer side of the wall at a pace which would let her use her hands and feet to prevent scraping or bumping against the wall. This was a trick taught in the Mercenary Schools, and Parno had practiced it many times before, both as anchor and counterweight.

Just as his feet touched the ground on the garden side of the wall, Zania's head popped up over the top. She swung her legs to the garden side of the wall, and, in answer to

Parno's waving hands, maneuvered herself over a half a span to her right, where she could use the limbs of a tree to help lower herself to the ground.

"What now?" Zania said as he freed her from the rope and began coiling it again. "Kera is not expecting us until nightfall."

"Can't be any harm in looking around a bit. Who knows, maybe Avylos has left his workroom open."

When he straightened from hiding the rope under the nearest flowering bush, Zania was looking at him with her brows drawn down. "Are you sure it won't be safer to hide somewhere in here? Those hedges against the wall over there would give us plenty of cover."

Parno found his hands had clenched into fists and forced them open, spreading his fingers as far as they would go. It went against the grain to tell his true feelings—his true *worries* was more the point, to anyone except his own Partner. Even to Zania, even after spending all this time on the road with her. But his own Partner had not known him the last time they spoke, she had fought with him, tried to kill him. In fact, the last time the real Dhulyn had said anything to him had been her signaled "In Battle" as she rode away. She had not even seen his response "In Death." He filled his lungs with air, and let it out slowly. They were not dead yet, and if this wasn't a battle, he'd like to know what it was.

"Dhulyn may be inside," he said finally. "I cannot wait here, hiding, knowing that. I must at least try to find her."

Zania was silent for so long Parno turned to look at her. Except for the tiny wrinkle between her brows, her face was expressionless. She glanced up at him, just a flash of her green eyes before she looked away again. "I understand," she said. "Lead the way."

Parno patted her shoulder. He should have known Zania would understand. He imagined that she would like to know where Edmir was just now. "The door's this way," he said.

The Mage's garden was like a miniature of the grounds outside, but the pathways and plantings were not so numerous that Parno could not remember the layout. He followed one narrow path and came, as he expected, to the small pool. Just beyond it, near the rock garden, was the table and two sturdy wooden chairs where Dhulyn and Kera had been sitting. He stopped and picked up the garden stake Dhulyn had used against him. He put it back down and looked around, mentally counting the paths leading from this spot. When Dhulyn had sent her for Avylos, Kera had run in that direction, he decided, choosing the central pathway. That way lay the door. He gestured to Zania to follow him.

"Will the door be magicked?" she asked, as they drew closer to it.

"Unlikely. But then again, I didn't expect the wall to be magicked." Standing as far back as he could and still retain leverage, Parno reached out with his sword, positioned the point under the metal latch, and lifted. The door swung open outward. Neither locked nor magicked by the look of it.

"Avylos must have thought putting a magic on the wall was enough to keep people out."

"It's as Kera told us," Parno agreed, "he does not waste his power."

The door opened on a small stone landing. Three steps led upward to another, smaller landing where an arched doorway opened onto a corridor. Parno signaled Zania to stand back, went down on one knee, and shot a quick look down each arm of the corridor from a spot just below the height of his own waist. Empty, and, except for three closed, doors, featureless.

"Which way?" Zania breathed.

Parno held up his hand, listening. He would swear he could hear a distant but rhythmic tapping. He nodded. Running footsteps. For a moment his heart leaped, only to subside again. It was not Dhulyn, he knew every sound she could make, and this was not her.

"This way," he said, turning toward the sound.

Zania took a pinch of his sleeve between her thumb and forefinger. "How do you know?"

"Someone is running toward us, it's only courteous that we go to meet them."

"Shouldn't we avoid whoever it is?" Zania's tone was sour, but she followed.

"From the lightness of the sound, and swiftness of the

footsteps, this is a young, slim person wearing lady's house shoes. The only person I can think of who would match that description, and who would be running in this direction, is Princess Kera. But just in case I'm wrong—" he grinned at her to show how unlikely *that* was. "Take this." He pulled his spare dagger from his sleeve and handed it to her. Better careful than cursing, was what Dhulyn would have said.

Parno set a cautious pace, and they had advanced only a few spans down the hall when Zania stopped him with a whisper.

"Parno, this must be the door."

Still with his eyes on the end of the corridor he backed up two steps to come even with her.

"The other two have latches," Zania said. "But look, this one's just plain, no latch, no hinges showing, nothing."

"That's it, then," Parno agreed. "But finding it doesn't get us much further. What is it?" Zania had gone close enough to almost press her nose against the polished wood. She squinted, wrinkling up her nose.

"There's a shadow here," she said, "like a bunch of cobwebs, but if I move, the shadow doesn't change." She waved her hand up and down.

"I see no shadow at all, except your own."

"If only I see it . . . do you think it might be the latch?"

"It's placed higher on the door than these others," Parno said, pointing at the closest door with the point of his sword. "But who knows, that might help the magic." He turned to look down the corridor. The footsteps were getting closer. "Behind me," he whispered, gesturing with his head.

But it was indeed Princess Kera who turned into the far end of the corridor and slid to a halt at the sight of them, her hand pressed tightly to her waist, and her breath coming short and fast.

"Parno Lionsmane," she said, as soon as she had caught her breath and drawn closer to them. "Do you know? Avylos has arrested Valaika and Edmir."

Parno looked past her, but no one was following Kera from the main part of the citadel. "We know," he said. "If Avylos is occupied with them, we must use this time to get the Stone. Do you know where Dhulyn Wolfshead is?"

Kera gave a short nod. "Still in the baths, I should think."

Parno grinned despite himself. "She's always loved baths, that's for certain. We should have time enough, then, so long as we can get to the Stone."

"Have you tried the door?" she asked, stepping around him.

Zania tapped the spot where she'd seen the shadow. "Is this the latch?"

Kera nodded and put out her hand. As her fingers closed on the spot Zania had indicated, an intricate iron latch took form under her hand. She lifted it and the door swung silently open.

Avylos' working chamber was a large rectangular room with two windows equipped with both shutters and bars. The shutters were open, and Parno could see dust motes floating in the sunlight that shone across the Mage's worktable and the dark oak floor. There were shelves and cabinets against the walls of the room, including some behind the table itself, but Parno's eyes went almost immediately to the wooden casket that sat to the right on the table.

"Zania?" he said.

"I think so," she said. "It looks like the drawing, don't you think?"

"You never saw it, not even as a small child?"

"I don't remember." Zania walked over to the casket and put her hand on it. It was locked.

"Well, your touching it doesn't prove there's no magic on it, just that whatever there is, doesn't affect women. Let's see what happens . . ." He stood at Zania's side and put his own hand where hers had been on the casket's lid. The wood felt warm. Warmer than it should have felt, even with the sun upon it. Parno frowned.

"What is it?" Kera had crept up beside them.

"It's a Balnian lock," he said. "I *have* opened Balnian locks, but not many, and not recently."

"Dhulyn Wolfshead must have opened it," Kera said. "I saw the Stone that night."

"My Partner has a better hand with locks than I do," Parno said. But all the while he was speaking his hands were busy feeling along the inner seam of his sword sheath, where his lockpick was hidden. The fold of leather was stiff, but he pried it open with his thumbnail and the thin, flat, metal rod popped out into his hand. Dhulyn had found this for him, and had an old smith in Cabrea fashion it to her specifications. Half of Parno's trouble with locks had disappeared once he had a proper tool.

Half his trouble. Not all.

He took a deep breath and looked around. He found himself reluctant to sit in the Mage's chair. "Zania, pull that chair closer, would you?" He indicated where he wanted it to be placed, but the moment he sat down, he wondered if he had made a mistake. The muscles in his legs burned now that he was no longer standing, and he felt a tiny tremor in his hands that did not bode well for the picking of the lock. Since early morning he'd jumped out a window, run across half the grounds of the Royal House, used the *Shoras* to help him climb a magicked wall, and pulled Zania up behind him. He risked a glance at her. Her lips had no color, and there were dark smudges under her eyes.

We're a fine pair, he thought. He had reserves of strength the girl did not have, and she was neither complaining nor trembling. He smiled at her, and was comforted to see her smile back.

No point in putting this off any longer, he was not going to get less tired. There was no *Shora* for picking locks, more was the pity. If they lived through this, he would help Dhulyn make one. He put the lockpick between his teeth, flexed his fingers, and rubbed his hands together before taking hold of the pick once more and lowering his eyes to the level of the lock. One end of the lockpick was formed like a squared-off hook, the metal bent at right angles. That end he inserted into the lock and moved it to feel gingerly to the right and left. Nothing. Up. Nothing. Down. Ah, there was the first catch of the locking mechanism.

He had reached the fifth catch when he slipped, and lost his place. He sat back and took two deep breaths, rolling his shoulders. He would have to release the first four catches again, but having done it once, it would be much easier the second time. So he told himself, and so it proved, as he was soon unlocking the fifth catch and moving along to what he hoped was the sixth, and final catch. There were more complicated Balnian locks, he knew, but he had to hope this was not one of them. Any more catches and he would need a second lockpick, and that he did not have.

The final catch moved with a click he felt more in his fingers than heard with his ears and he was just leaning back to share his satisfied smile with Zania and Kera when a sound made them all turn to look at the door.

It had swung open and standing in the doorway was his Partner, Dhulyn Wolfshead.

Twenty-five

THE WAY TO THE BLACK DUNGEONS was not entirely dark, contrary to what Edmir had always been told. He'd known that the stories told around the fire in the Royal Guardroom couldn't all be true, seeing as how so many contradicted each other. But as children, he and Kera had loved to be frightened by rumors and gossip, and with wondering which tales *were* true. According to one source, the Black Guards never came up out of the dungeons, once their time of service there began. Another said the Guard was a secret duty, and that its members walked about mixing with the House Guard unknown to anyone but themselves. You might sit down next to one at the meal table, and never know.

Some stories maintained the Black Guards were blind from birth, carefully selected and trained, and that the hoods and masks tradition said they wore were used only at the delivery of prisoners, to preserve anonymity. Other stories said they were sighted people, but bred—or helped by magic—to see in the dark. Most stories claimed that once Black Guards accepted their positions, the hoods and masks never came off, and hid their identities not just from guards delivering prisoners, but even from each other.

The only thing all the stories agreed on was that the work of the Black Guards was done in the dark, "neither in sunlight, nor moonlight, nor light of flame." That's how Edmir had heard it. Wisdom that came down from the Caids warned against the witnessing of torture and executions. While such actions might be deemed necessary, those who watched them were in danger of developing a taste for such things. Hence the stories that even the Black Guards themselves were blind, not just dark-adapted.

Edmir did not find it reassuring that the reality was more prosaic than the rumors. He'd been familiar with the entrance to the Black Dungeons his whole life; the circular stone stairwell was in his mother the queen's apartments, and as Lord Prince he'd known that one day he would make the journey down into the foundations of the Royal House to visit the Black Dungeons, as his mother had done before him. No one could rule in Tegrian without knowing what sending someone to the dungeons meant.

Truth to tell, a part of Edmir, *the playwright part,* he was now aware, had been looking forward to that visit, to finally learning for himself which of the stories were true, and which false. *I just never thought I'd find out* this *way,* he thought. *Not as a prisoner.*

When his mother the queen had passed her sentence on them, Edmir expected other guards to be sent for, but it seemed that Avylos had thought of that as well, and Megz Primeau and her companions were senior enough for this duty. At the top of the circular staircase Edmir tried to make them stop, but he still couldn't speak, and when he dug in his heels and pulled away, one of the two guards with Megz Primeau simply tripped him, and toppled him down the stone steps.

"We can roll you all the way down, if you'd like." Megz's voice actually showed some pity. "You could break your neck, but you might prefer that to what you'll find at the bottom."

Edmir shook his head and staggered to his feet, pressing his right shoulder against the stone wall of the stairwell. Whatever it was he needed to face, he'd do it better unbruised, and unbattered. He stood still, therefore, and allowed Megz to take hold of him once more by the upper arm. The larger of the two guards had four short torches in his belt. At Megz's nod, he lit one and began the descent. He was soon lost to sight as the turnings of the stairs carried him away, but the light continued; he used the torch to ignite the evenly spaced wall sconces as he passed them by.

Four torches, Edmir thought. *Two to get us there, and two to lead them back again?*

By the time they stepped off the final stair Edmir's legs were trembling with the strain of keeping his balance with his hands tied behind his back. Megz did not pause, however, but set off along the wide passage. After so many turns on the staircase, Edmir found he could not even guess in what direction they were now heading. The row of wall sconces continued, and in their flickering light Valaika looked gray and stunned, her lower lip trembling as she shuffled in the grip of her guard. She was in no danger of falling, or stumbling, however, as the floors and walls of the passage were clean, neither dusty nor damp, and even the stones underfoot were beautifully fitted and smooth.

Work of the Caids, Edmir thought, remembering what the Mercenaries had told them, him and Zania. The Royal House must have been built on ruins dating from the time of the Caids themselves. These stones were older than his family, older than Tegrian, older, perhaps, than the gods. For a moment, his awe at that immeasurable, unthinkable expanse of time was enough to distract him from his own present. But only for a moment.

The temperature increased, and Edmir realized that, dry as this passage was, they were passing close by the hot springs that surfaced in the Royal Baths. Before he could think about what that meant, the corridor ended abruptly in what was obviously a much more recent addition, a heavy oak door with metal banding, and a thickly barred grate at the height of an average man's head. Above the door, a shaded lantern with a fat candle inside replaced the wall sconces that had lined the passage. The larger guard was there, the candle was lit, and the stubs of the first two torches lay extinguished on the floor. A rope bell pull, stout and tarred such as might be found outside the night door of any respectable inn, hung to one side.

At a nod from Megz, the large guard put his hand on the rope.

"It's not like they couldn't hear us coming," he said.

"Just ring the bell, Tzen."

The sound the bell made was very pure, very sweet, like the bells that hung on the trees in the queen's private garden. Edmir swallowed and blinked away sudden tears.

Tzen must have been right, the Black Guards *had* heard

them coming, because the gate was swinging silently inward even as the last notes of the bell faded away.

The man who stepped forward into the opening, and the two others who kept their places behind him, *were* masked, *and* hooded, as tradition had it, but there were eyeholes in the masks, something that would not have been necessary if they were blind. But their eyes *were* huge and dark, with no color showing around the pupils. They were squinting, as if even the shaded light from the lantern was more than they could tolerate comfortably. The Black Guard in the doorway looked at Megz, and said nothing.

The section leader cleared her throat. "Two for the dungeons," she said.

"Are there questions?"

Edmir expected the voice to be rusty from disuse, but on the contrary, it was smooth and warm, even pleasant.

"No," Megz said. "Death only."

Edmir shivered. He had not considered the possibility that there might be torture waiting for them, but his sense of relief was so great that it restored his courage. Everything, even death, took time. He did not wait for the House Guards to push him, but stepped forward, turning to face Megz and the other guards. When he was sure that she was looking at him, he took two quick, short steps to his right, and one back, almost dancing steps, and then twisted, dropping his left shoulder. If only his hands were not bound, but maybe this would be enough to remind Megz, to make her think about the block to her secret thrust—and who she'd shown it to. Who knew? At this point, anything was worth trying.

His heart sank as Megz only looked at him with impatience before spinning him around again to face the Black Guards.

Edmir cleared his throat and opened his mouth, the words that would give him a good exit already on his tongue.

But a soft moan was all the sound he made.

"A mute?" the Black Guard in the doorway said.

"The Blue Mage took his voice," Megz said.

The Black Guard shook his head. "A shame. Often there is much they wish to say before they die." He gestured, and Edmir stepped past him into the dark hallway beyond.

⋇⋇⋇

"It's them trying to pass that lout off as Lord Prince Edmir that burns the worst," Tzen said.

Megz Primeau let them talk. All they'd done in leaving the traitors in the hands of the masked and hooded guards of the Black Dungeon was their plain duty. But they were forbidden to talk to anyone else about it outside of this underground passage. Let them have their say here and now, get things off their chests where no one else could hear them.

"There wasn't a member of the family better liked," Granz the other guard said. "Best noble in the Royal House, he was. Even the chamber servants had good words for Prince Edmir." Unspoken was the knowledge that the same most emphatically could not be said for Kedneara the Queen.

"Best noble in Beolind, comes to that," Tzen agreed. "Too good to be king, that's certain."

"And that's why the Caids took him," Granz said. "To save him from that path, poor lad." Again, the three guards shared the unspoken awareness of what every soldier in the Royal House knew: well-liked as Edmir had been, even loved, the Princess Kera would make the better ruler.

"Black Dungeons' too good for those two," Megz said, making her own contribution to the purging of fury and sadness that threatened to rise in her own throat as she thought about Edmir's loss. Why it had been only this morning she'd seen him riding in the west gate . . . She stopped dead in the center of the dark hallway. The other two guards, wrapped in their own grieving, continued several paces before noticing that they were alone. They stopped, turning back toward her. She waved at them to continue.

"I've dropped a buckle," she said, holding her hand over the left side of her harness. "You two go on, I'll check down here first while the light lasts."

Megz waited until the other two had reached the far end of the corridor. She needed to think, and their chattering wasn't helping her. On the one hand, the prince was dead, had been for more than a moon, though no one had seen his corpse thanks to those Caids-cursed Nisveans. But on the other hand—

Two steps to the right, a step back, drop the left shoulder to twist the torso to . . . allow for the block to her secret thrust —*EDMIR*. Megz *had* seen Edmir this morning. She knew she had. She'd recognized the one thing it was impossible to copy or disguise—the way he sat his horse. Maybe she hadn't put her finger on it right at that moment, but when she'd seen him in the Jarlkevoso's rooms, she'd known. She didn't know how or why, but that young man, the young man she'd just left with the Black Guards, *was* Edmir.

"Oh, Caids. What have I done?"

And what could she do about it now?

She looked back in the direction from which they'd come. What could *she* do to get the Black Guard to release the prince and the Jarlkevoso? Had she ever heard of anyone being released from the Black Dungeons? She tapped her sword hilt with her fingers. Surely there must be a way. She started running back, back toward the heavy oak door, back to the candle lantern. There in the darkness were three masked and hooded people who could answer her question.

❧❧❧

Parno's heart leaped in his chest. For a fleeting instant he thought the woman in the doorway was *his* Dhulyn, the Wolfshead, his Partner. Her lip was even curled back in that familiar wolf's smile, though it had been years since she had shown that smile to him. Her hair was uncovered, growing in blood red, and her Mercenary badge was perfect and unscarred. Parno had sheathed his sword and taken three steps toward her before he registered what that wolf's smile meant. He halted and put his hand back on the hilt of his sword.

"Dhulyn."

"Thief."

Parno stood still and spread his hands wide. "Now I'm no thief, and you know it."

"I do beg your pardon. You are not a thief until you leave here with something that does not belong to you. So, you are a would-be thief, since you will not be leaving here." She took a pace forward and the door swung shut behind her.

"I disagree. I *will* be leaving, but only with something that *does* belong to me. You."

"You were looking for me in that box?"

Parno drew his sword, turned back to the casket, and flipped open the lid to expose the Stone. "This is the source of the Mage's power," he told her. "But it belongs to this young lady, making Avylos the thief, and his powers stolen. We came here," he pointed first to Dhulyn and then back to himself, "to restore the Stone to its proper place and function. So again, we'll be taking it with us when we go."

Dhulyn's eyes narrowed, and her brow wrinkled in a frown. For a moment, Parno thought she might be remembering. But then she turned sideways, kicked at the door where the metal tongue of the latch protruded. Her heel hit the latch just right, bending the tongue, and effectively locking the door. Parno had to shake his head in admiration. Dhulyn could now ignore the girls entirely, seeing that they could not get out of the room without his help. Habit made him glance at the open windows, even though he remembered the bars. What Dhulyn couldn't know is that none of them actually wanted to leave the room—at least not yet.

Parno moved to his left, keeping his feet shoulder width apart and his weight evenly distributed. Dhulyn would shift to follow him—she would correctly assess that he was the danger, not the two young women—and that would give Zania a chance to reach the Stone. What the girl would do with it once she had the chance, he couldn't be sure, but he had to give her that chance. As he moved, he whistled through his teeth, the same tune he'd played for the children under the wall, the same tune Dhulyn, his Dhulyn, knew so well. She frowned, but continued her own even pacing, as she waited for the inevitable moment when they would be close enough to engage.

"I am Parno Lionsmane," he said, keeping his eyes on hers and his voice even and smooth. "Called the Chanter. I was schooled by Nerysa the Warhammer. I came late to the Mercenary Brotherhood and my first battle was in the vale of Arcosa. That is where you and I first met, fighting for old Nyl-aLyn, the Tarkin of Imrion. We became Partners then. Last year we were in Imrion again, and you sang to this tune, do you remember?"

He began whistling again, and again, her wolf's smile faltered. But she pressed her lips together and shook her head, moving it just once to the left, and back again. Her cold gray eyes never moved from his face. All the while he was speaking, he kept circling to the left, and he and Dhulyn drew slowly closer to one another.

"You have told me this tale before," she said. "Why should I believe you?"

"What do I gain by such a lie? Look in a glass, your own Mercenary badge supports my tale."

Her left hand floated to her temple, her fingers stroked her badge. She was frowning again. "Tell me what you see."

"A Mercenary badge, like this one," he gestured to his own temples. "Yours is blue and green, the colors of Dorian the Black Traveler, who Schooled you. But the Partner's Line is identical to mine." He traced the black line going through his badge with the tip of his index finger. "You are Dhulyn Wolfshead, called the Scholar. Dorian Schooled you on his ship, called, like him, the *Black Traveler*. He took you from the hold of a slaver's ship when you had seen the Hawk Moon eleven times."

"You tell a fine story, Mercenary, but I think I know a better one."

She moved so fast that only Parno's own finely Schooled reflexes saved him. He arched his body away while at the same moment sweeping her sword down with his own, knocking her point aside when it was only a fingerwidth from his guts. She had moved on the word "think," he realized, and he could not keep the smile from his face.

It was as he suspected. He parried a blow to his head, flicking her blade up and to one side. Dhulyn might not remember herself, but her body remembered her Schooling, whether she was aware of it or not. He feinted to his right and she followed, but not enough to put her off-balance. "To think is to move, to move is to think" was a saying in the Common Rule of Mercenary training. After being Schooled a Mercenary no longer needed to plan out the steps and moves of a fight, for them there was no longer any difference between thinking and moving.

Dhulyn's blade sliced through his left sleeve and he jumped back.

When Dhulyn had attacked on the saying of the word "think," it was in unconscious reflection of the Common Rule. He had noticed this in her strategy before, though he could not recall whether he had ever mentioned it.

"You're always doing that," he told her. He swept aside her blade with his left hand, followed through with the thrust he would normally execute into that opening, but slowly enough that she could easily parry him in return. So easily in fact that she wrapped her blade around his and came within a hairsbreadth of snaking it out of his hand.

"You mean I'm always almost killing you?"

He grinned. He could give her no quarter, he realized, or she *would* kill him. Without her memories, she had no reason not to. "Always moving in one of the *Shora*." To illustrate his point he executed an attack in three moves to her throat, which she parried brilliantly. "That was part of the Desert Snake *Shora*," he said. "Your body remembers who you are, even if you do not." *But I'll* make *you remember*, he thought. *I'll keep you thinking, keep you aware.*

Parno saw movement out of the corner of his eye as Zania took advantage of their position to slip behind the Mage's worktable. When Dhulyn's eye flickered in that direction he lunged in, striking like the desert snake. She blocked his sword with the palm of her hand against the flat of the blade, pushing it out to her left and simultaneously stepping in to thrust at his neck. Parno twisted out of the way and took another step to gain himself some breathing room.

He blinked as sweat dripped into his eye. The long muscles of his thighs burned, and he could feel the corded tendons in his wrists and elbows. What else could he do to bring her back to herself?

It was hard to think and plan while keeping her blade from his guts and blood. Switching to the left hand would not help him in this fight, as Dhulyn would simply do the same. He was in the same predicament as he'd been when he fought her in the garden—he couldn't keep up a defense only. Tired as he was, she would kill him. Even in top condition, Parno needed all his speed and all his wits to stay even with her, they were so perfectly matched. As for now, he could feel exhaustion not so very far away, in the burning of his muscles.

As if to illustrate his thought, Parno felt the cold edge of her blade slide through the skin on the upper part of his left arm, as his block was seconds too slow. He had no reserves left after climbing the wall, after fighting his way through Avylos' magic—

The *Shora* had led him through the magic. Without the Sable Monkey *Shora* showing him the path, he and Zania would still be standing at the bottom of the wall, or, more likely, in the hands of the Royal House's Guard. Was he going about this the wrong way? Interrupting Dhulyn, breaking into her unconscious movements, *did* slow her down a bit, but it didn't seem to be bringing her any recognition, it did not seem to be triggering any memories for her.

Should he let the *Shora* have her? If a *Shora* could show him a pathway through Avylos' magic, could one also show Dhulyn the path back to herself?

He blocked a thrust to his groin, and another to his throat, stepping back each time.

What did he have to lose?

Rapidly, he ran through the basic *Shora* for right-handed swordplay, instinctively discarding each one as too simple or too short to engage the level of concentration he thought would be required.

Another thrust, again he stepped back, only to feel against his calves the edge of the bench that ran along the wall. Dhulyn's smile widened, her lip curling back. Parno could not back away any farther, and she would not let him move to the side.

But now he had an idea. He swept his blade at her face, and leaped backward onto the bench as she flinched away. Then, bringing his sword straight down toward Dhulyn's head, Parno began the first movements of what she had once called the Older Brother *Shora*. Parno did not know what its real name was—or even if it had one. Older Brother was not one of the Mercenary Brotherhood's basic twenty-seven *Shora*, though it had been the first Dorian the Black had taught to Dhulyn as a child. A specialty of Dorian the Black's, Older Brother was designed for use against an opponent much taller than oneself, and as such, an ideal *Shora* for children.

It meant a great deal to Dhulyn, and she had once taught it to Parno on a whim. Though taller than Dhulyn, he was not really tall enough for her to use the Older Brother *Shora* against him. So long as he stayed on the bench, it would work, he could keep it up, but if she managed to force him down, he knew he would not have the strength to keep his arms lifted, trying his best to mimic the angles of a taller person.

This would have to work. He had no more ideas, and no more strength. *She will remember herself, or she will kill me.*

"In Battle," he told her. "Or in Death."

Dhulyn and Parno moved so fast that Zania couldn't even distinguish the individual movements of their blades. This was nothing like what she had seen done, and done herself for that matter, on stage.

"Come on, Dhulyn," she muttered under her breath as if they *were* on stage and she was giving the Mercenary woman a cue. "Come back to us, come back." She shivered as the tiny hairs on the back of her neck stood straight. It was one thing to be told that Dhulyn had lost her memories, it was another thing entirely to see her look at Parno with that snarling smile.

Zania sucked in her breath. Blood darkened Parno's sleeve, though she hadn't seen the touch that caused it.

A movement at the periphery of her vision. Princess Kera was waving her hand down almost behind the skirt of her gown, and angling her head toward the worktable, and the open casket. Parno and Dhulyn were along the side wall now, Dhulyn forcing Parno back against the bench. The path to the worktable was clear. Her eyes on the two combatants, Zania began sliding her feet sideways toward the Stone. She had her hand out when she saw another flower of blood blossom, this time on Parno's right sleeve.

Section Leader Megz Primeau was panting by the time she reached the top of the circular staircase. She had run the last few spans in the dark, as the sconces they had lit on their way down to the Black Dungeon had burned out. The Black Guards had been very helpful. It had rarely happened, but as Megz had suspected, there *was* a way to bring prisoners out again. She had to reach Kedneara the Queen, and persuade her to come. Only the physical presence of the queen herself would stop the Black Guards.

❦

The Black Guards were firm but not cruel. They placed Edmir and Valaika into a cell almost as gently as Edmir's own nurse had moved him when, as a child, he resisted going to bed. As the cell door closed with an ominously quiet thud, Valaika seemed to awaken from the stupor that had held her since they left the queen. She turned toward the faint glow of the tiny candle that burned in the corridor, and seized the bars of the grating in the door.

"Wait," she called. "You don't understand. I would *never* do this. I would never bring an impostor to Kedneara . . . this doesn't make sense." The last few words were almost too faint to hear, but a soft musical voice answered from beyond the door.

"We will give you some time to compose yourselves. There is water to the right of the door. You need fear no pain, or horrors. Since there are no questions for you, your deaths will be quick and painless."

"Why? Why are there no questions? Why aren't you going to ask us to betray the rest of this conspiracy?" Valaika seemed to become aware that there was no longer anyone at the door. "Why," Valaika said, as if to herself. "Unless it is because there is no conspiracy."

Blinking, Edmir could make out his aunt as a darker shape among the shadows around the door.

"I don't know who you are, young man; I don't understand what's going on, what's happening. I—you're an impostor, you're not Edmir—"

At this, Edmir tried again to speak, but all he could manage was a coughing croak that hurt his throat, making him swallow. He could not bear for Valaika to die like this, not knowing him, thinking him an impostor, not understanding why she should have to die. He knew the magic would wear off, as it wore off all women, but would it be soon enough?

"I brought you to Beolind. *I* brought *you* to Kedneara. But I would not bring an impostor to the queen, try to take her from her place on the throne. What do I care about her throne? She was my brother's wife, he loved her, and I was content. I would not bring her an impostor."

Edmir wished there was light enough for him to show her the scar on his back. It had been the proof that convinced her, back in Jarlkevo, it might have been enough to jog her real memory of him loose. But in this darkness, he might just as well wish to be out and free, sitting next to Zania on the driver's seat of the caravan, arguing about stagecraft.

Still, he had to try something. Reaching out with his hands, he edged closer to where he could just make out her shape. When he touched her, she flinched away, and Edmir braced himself, expecting a blow. But Valaika relaxed, and let him take her hand. Holding her hand in his, he turned his back on her, and pulled her hand toward his back.

Her arm and hand were tense, but Valaika did not pull away. Edmir thought her resistance stemmed from caution, not knowing what he wanted her to touch, rather than fear.

"What is it? What—oh, that's right, you can't speak. Show me, then." Her arm relaxed more. "Your back?" She snatched her hand away. "What could there possibly be about . . . the scar," she said, her voice hollow and cold in the darkness. "You had the scar, I remember. And if you had the scar, then you *are* Edmir. But how? Why did I stop thinking so? Why do I not believe it now, even when logic tells me it must be so? You are not Edmir," she repeated in that dead voice Edmir knew so well. "You are an impostor." But now her voice was rising high and tight. He had to do something more, not leave her in this state of confusion.

After all that she had done for him, risked for him, this is not how his aunt Valaika should spend her final moments.

If only this was Dhulyn Wolfshead, he could speak against the palm of her hand, as he had done back in the tent of the Nisveans. Edmir clapped his hands. If Valaika could not read lips with her hands, perhaps there was something she *could* read.

He felt more than saw Valaika turn toward him, and took her hand once more in his, opening it to expose her palm. Using the tip of his finger, he wrote, "A." She did not react and he tried it again.

"What are you doing, boy, what is it? I don't understand." She pulled her hand away and Edmir let it go. No use upsetting her further if she didn't understand. He rubbed at his face in frustration. If only there was more light. He could do it if he were on stage. Zania had showed him all the tricks for making light appear. Or if he could make a flame appear in the palm of his hand, like Avylos used to do . . .

He grabbed Valaika by the shoulder and turned her toward the door edging her backward until she was the right distance from the opening in the door. Between his teeth he whistled a tune he was sure she would recognize, the traditional bit of music that would accompany the appearance of a Mage or Mark in a play. The sound he could make was faint, his mouth was so dry, but he thought that Valaika heard and understood.

Still whistling, he held up his left hand, palm upward. He snapped the fingers of his right hand, and pointed to his left.

"What? I don't see . . ."

Edmir snapped his fingers again and again pointed to his left hand. If he had positioned it correctly, and if Valaika was standing the right distance away, it would seem as though the glow of the candle in the corridor rested on his open palm.

"Oh, Caids. Avylos. The Blue Mage. This is Avylos' work. Avylos and his blooded magic." The change in Valaika's voice told him that the magic was broken. "Then you *are* Edmir, after all."

Edmir stepped into her open arms.

"Oh, my Prince," Valaika whispered. "How I have failed you, and failed myself. Over and over again. My own consort, my Sylria, keeping her debt to Avylos from me all these years, and paying it back in this way. How can I face your father, if he waits for me at the side of the Sleeping God, knowing what I have done. I would rather I had died beforehand, than to bring you to this."

But I wouldn't, Edmir thought. He shook his head, and to be sure she understood him, he took her right hand, brought it to his face, and shook his head again. Holding her right hand still to his face, he took her left hand, tapped himself on the chest, then tapped Valaika, and moved her hand to touch her lower abdomen.

"You would give your life for me?" she said. "Edmir, no."

He shook his head again, touched her belly again.

"For Janek? For my son?" Valaika's breath hitched, as if she were trying to stop crying. "Not my life," she said. "Not Sylria's. It is Janek's life that is purchased with yours."

This time he nodded. In his mind's eye he could see the smiling face of the boy who had been the only one to recognize him. And this time, Valaika stayed quiet. Edmir understood. When it came to herself, or to Sylria, Valaika was his aunt, his father's sister, one of the High Noble Houses of Tegrian and the cousin of the Tarkin of Hellik. She knew where her duty lay, and she would die to save him, Edmir had no doubt. But when it came to Janek, she was a mother first, and she could not bring herself to say that she would trade her son's life for his. Not even here, where a gesture was all it would be.

He patted her cheek, and kissed her. For a long moment, they clung to each other in the dark.

"We are ready now."

Both Edmir and his aunt jerked and jumped away from the door. How long had the Black Guard been standing there?

"One of you will come with us," the Black Guard said. "Do you prefer to choose, or shall we?"

Edmir tried to put himself forward, but Valaika was closer to the door, and she could speak.

"Take me," she said. "No," she added to Edmir as he clutched her arm. "However long it takes for me to die, I would buy you that time."

"Your death *can* be slower," came the voice of the Black Guard. "But there is more pain."

"Make it as slow as you can," she said. "Goodbye, my Prince, my nephew. May the Sleeping God keep us both, and may I meet you at his side."

Goodbye, he said, kissing her again on the cheek. This silent goodbye was the only one he would make, he realized, as he strained to watch them disappear into the shadows. He would never take his leave of Dhulyn and Parno, never thank them for all they had done, and tried to do.

They might yet succeed, even now, and he would never know.

And then Kera will be king. His sister would make a better king than he would have, he told himself, wishing that he had the chance to tell her as well. *My best kings would have been on the stage.*

And he would never be able to tell Zania that he was a fool ever to have put his throne before her. Never be able to tell her that he loved her. He would ask for the slow death, he thought. He would find a way to make them understand. He would like to think of Zania as long as he could, and the plays he would have written for her.

Twenty-six

DHULYN SAW THE SECOND WOUND begin to bleed and laughed aloud. Her body moved like oiled silk sliding across skin, as if she knew where the Mercenary's sword would be before he did himself. As if she was Marked, and had the Sight. She felt her smile falter, but her body still moved automatically, parrying each blow as it fell on her from above. He should have picked a different *Shora*, she thought with a frown, he wasn't really tall enough for this one, though the bench did help him there. Still, he was tiring, and she knew this *Shora* so much better than he did, it was almost the first one she'd been taught . . .

She hesitated, blade hovering in the air. Where had those thoughts come from? Just in time, she saw his sword coming down upon her, stepped half a pace closer and blocked it, blade against blade. He bore down on her, taking advantage of his height and weight, and she pushed back—give her an inch or two, and she could twist away. He grunted, and Dhulyn looked up into his amber eyes, so close she could see the individual lashes. As their gazes locked over the crossed swords, he whistled four notes, and something within her loosened, and gave way.

Her own hands lay out the vera tiles, but not for any Solitary game that she recognizes. She chooses one tile, the Mercenary of Swords, covers it with another tile, a circle.

Lays out the rectangle, the triangle, the straight line, the circle with a dot in the center. She draws out more tiles and begins to lay them down . . .

The smell of burning, and blood. she stands to one side, watching herself and her mother. Her mother turns toward her and *sees* her. Her mother is smiling as she turns the head of the child. Dhulyn blinks, and with her child's eyes sees herself, a tall, slim woman with short red hair and tattoos above her ears. She blinks and sees her mother and the small child who is herself. She puts out a hand, but there is nothing to steady herself against.

"Go," her mother tells her. "Oh, my soul, do not watch. Find your own soul and save yourself. Go now, go. . . ."

The redheaded boy she has Seen before is squatting next to a map drawn on the ground. The map shows passes, game trails, a wide expanse of plain, the juncture of two rivers. Where the herds will be, and how many will be guarding them . . .

And then the boy is running through the woods, running from the sound of screaming and the smell of smoke. His eyes are wide and frightened, but his lips are pulled back from his teeth in a grimace. Or a smile . . .

A tall black man, the tallest she has ever seen, a triangular scar along the orbit of his left eye. A dead man with a sword in his gut lies between them. The black man pulls the sword free, wipes the blade clean on the corpse's clothing and holds it out to her, hilt first. "Come with me," he says, "and I will teach you to kill your enemies." . . .

She runs along a ship's rail as the motion of the sea causes it to rise and fall beneath her bare feet. Her breath comes short with the effort of speed and balance . . .

A golden-haired man with eyes like melting amber stands over a map on a table. There is something lionlike about him. He looks up at her and smiles. His Mercenary Badge is dark red and gold. There is something missing. There should be a black line through it. Parno? . . .

Zania holds a blue crystal cylinder between her hands, thick as a man's wrist, as long as Dhulyn's forearm. Shining blue like the deep ice that has trapped the glow of the stars. The Muse Stone. A drop of blood falls from Zania's nose to the Stone. There is movement in the rooms behind her and Dhulyn sees herself, her hair far too short, her Mercenary badge blue and green showing smooth and unscarred, leaping back out of the path of a sword, dashing forward again just as Parno brings up his sword again and running herself full onto his blade . . .

Dashing forward again with her own blade perfectly positioned to pass between his ribs and through his heart . . .

Her Mercenary badge. Blue and green for Dorian the Black Traveler. The black line of partnership running through it . . .

Herself.

An old crone, a young woman with dark hair and a heart-shaped face, a stocky blond man in a Scholar's tunic, and a young boy, thin and round-eyed, and herself. They hold hands in an intricate pattern, ready for the dance. . . .

Herself.
Avylos is standing in the doorway of his workroom, raising his hands to work his magic . . .

❧❧❧

A crash, and the workroom door sprang open to reveal Avylos standing in the doorway of his workroom, his hands raised.
Did I not just see that, she thought. No, she realized. She had *Seen* it. Her own hands, she found, were raised, sword pointing straight to the ceiling. The point of Parno's sword rested on the skin above her heart.

"Dhulyn," Parno said. He eased his sword back.

"My soul," Dhulyn answered. Parno grinned back at her, and her heart turned over. He jumped down off the bench. "Zania," he called out to the girl, "Quickly, it's—"

Avylos drew a symbol in light and with a hard gesture flung it toward them. Dhulyn was slammed back, as if a huge wave of water crashed her against the wall, forcing the breath from her body. She slid down, the bench catching her painfully in the small of her back, and tried to get her frozen lungs to pull in a breath of air. Her whole arm would be bruised, if she lived through this, but she had kept hold of her sword. Parno, a shadow on his face like the symbol the Mage had thrown, fell to his knees beside her, and pitched forward, getting his hands out in front of himself just in time to keep from crashing onto his face.

Dhulyn began to cough and choke, her lungs resisting her efforts to breathe. She tried to stand, but her legs were so rubbery they would not support her. Avylos, she saw, had turned to look her way. Could she trick him somehow? She could not draw in sufficient air to speak, but she held out her arms to him, as if begging for his help. Let him just get within reach of her hands . . .

Dhulyn saw a fleeting shadow of doubt fly across his face. Then his blue eyes hardened.

"Wait, my dear," he said, in the language of the Tribes. "I will be but a moment. Kera," he said, turning back to the others. "Get the Stone and bring it to me."

No, don't do it. Still, the words would not come, though Dhulyn's breathing was beginning to ease.

Painfully, Dhulyn turned her head enough to see the other end of the room. Zania and Kera were at opposite ends of the worktable. Zania had the Stone and was murmuring under her breath. Ignoring both Kera and the Mage, she was twisting the ends of the Stone as she muttered, but nothing was coming of it.

"Why should I help you?" Kera was looking from the Mage to Zania and back again, her lower lip caught between her teeth. "So you can treat me as you did Edmir?"

"But now *you* will be king, Kera. You will rule. That is what all this is for, everything I have done is to bring you to the throne. All you need do now is bring me the Stone."

"No." Dhulyn coughed. A sound made her turn to Parno. He was still on his knees, holding himself up with his hands. His lips were turning blue, and he did not appear to be breathing. Dhulyn pulled at one of his wrists until she toppled him over. Sucking in as much air as she could, she held his mouth open and breathed into it. His chest moved as his lungs expanded. But not by very much. And not on their own.

Dhulyn looked back to the Mage. And across to the girl holding the Stone. Had Kera answered him?

Zania had stopped trying to manipulate the Stone. Her face was white, and she looked not far from tears. Finally, she looked up. "I will give you the Stone for Edmir," she said. Princess Kera gasped, turning abruptly toward the other girl, but shut her mouth on what she would have said.

"It is already too late for that, I'm afraid." The Mage was shaking his head. "Come, give me the Stone, and I will let you at least go free."

Dhulyn forced another breath into Parno and touched his face. "Hold," she said, and levered herself to her feet. She could not see which end of the Stone Zania was trying to turn, but the chants the girl was using were not working. There was only one thing left to try. "Throw *me* the Stone," she said. She cleared her throat, drew in a deeper lungful of air and repeated herself.

"Zania, throw me the Stone."

The young girl's face, still white as snow, hardened. Her grip on the Stone shifted, and she glanced around her quickly, as if she was looking for something hard enough to smash it on. Finding nothing, she took a step back, looking between Dhulyn and Avylos.

"Don't let her trick you," Kera said, her voice hoarse with unshed tears. "She heard Parno say your name. How is she better than the Mage?"

Dhulyn breathed in deeply and took two paces closer.

"Listen to me, Zania," she said, and held out her hands. "Pasillon," she said. "Pasillon, Zania. Give me the Stone."

For a moment Zania stood frozen, as if she were turned to stone herself, and Dhulyn's heart sank. If Zania did not believe her . . . Then Dhulyn saw the sudden blaze of understanding and relief ignite across Zania's face, as the girl realized that only the real Dhulyn, the one who remembered, would know that code word. The code word they'd all agreed on. Work as a team. Do not draw the eye of the audience upon yourself. Let others do their work, and have their moments.

Zania gave a quick nod, and tossed Dhulyn the Stone.

While it was still in the air, Avylos flung another symbol of light across the intervening space, but Dhulyn threw herself forward, snatching the Stone out of the air, and rolled with it to the other side of the room.

"Dhulyn, my dear one," Avylos said coming toward her with his hands outstretched.

Parno shifted, slowly, so that his knife was closer to his hand. Dhulyn could not tell whether he had begun to breathe properly, but she forced her attention back to the warm bar of crystal in her hands. She could only hope that what she was going to try would work. She *had* to concentrate, to remember, without the book to refer to. Parno would die if his breathing was not restored, but if she failed in what she was about to try, they were all dead.

"I am not your dear, and never was," she said, turning the Stone over in her hands feeling for the places where her fingers should go. It would have to be the Null Chant again, she would have to hope it worked the same way on both ends of the Stone. Because this time she would not use the end she had tried before, not the symbols of the Marked. The *other* end. The symbol she had seen in the book, the ones she had finally recognized from her Visions.

"Give it to me, my own one, my cousin, my kin. We are the only two, the last. Do not forsake me." He took a step toward her, his voice a charm of music, alluring and pure.

But the music Dhulyn heard was a simple tune, that could be whistled or played on the pipes. The children's song she knew so well.

Perhaps because of the song, or perhaps because she was holding the Stone, running over the chant in her head, Dhulyn had a sudden flash of the Visions she had just Seen, and others she had Seen before. The young Avylos drawing the map in the dirt, consulting with men who were not Espadryni. Those same men running through the camp as her mother told her to hide. Avylos hunted, not—as she now realized —by those who had broken the Tribes, but by two dying Espadryni, who hunted their betrayer with their last breaths.

"We may be the last," she agreed. "And who is to blame?"

Avylos went chalk white, but whether with fear or anger Dhulyn could not tell.

"That was why you kept asking me what I remembered of the Tribes," she said. "That was what you were afraid I knew, what you were afraid I would remember. *You* broke the Tribes. *You* sold us to the Bascani. You."

"No. You are wrong. You said yourself you were too young to remember."

"I have *Seen* it," she said. "Did *you* forget? I bear the Mark of the Seer. Did you not know how the Mark works? I *See* both the future and the past."

Her fingers slid into place on the Stone.

"Elis elis tanton neel," she said to Avylos.

"They kept the power from me," he said. "They told me I was *srusha*, barren, without magic. They did that to me, their own child. Excluded me, shut me out."

"What?" Her voice dripping with disbelief, only Kera, only a princess, would have thought to interrupt Avylos at such a moment. "The whole Tribe in agreement, every man, woman, and child, every new babe taught an elaborate pretense, to trick *you?* Why were *you* so important?"

"Because they would keep from me my rightful rule. Because I was to be stronger than all of them. Because in me the power will be greatest." Avylos was almost spitting.

"Not without the Stone. You are nothing without the Stone," Zania said.

"Dor la sinquin so la dele," Dhulyn said. Let the others keep Avylos occupied. The end of the stone began to turn in her fingers. *"Kos noforlin sik ek aye."*

As if he knew how close she was, Avylos threw both hands into the air, fingers flashing symbol after symbol. The furniture in the room trembled, and then jumped into the air, even the worktable, even Parno's sword where he had dropped it. The bench behind Dhulyn rose up and struck her down—only her Mercenary training allowed her to retain her grip of the Stone as she hit the floor. She heard

Zania scream, but put it out of her mind as she said the final chant.

"Kik shon te ounte gesserae."

She felt the end of the Stone "click." Felt the power surging like an underground river, felt her own bones begin to tremble. The Stone became a bar of bright light.

Now, she thought. She could wait no longer.

"Avylos," she called. And tossed him the Stone.

"No!" Both girls cried out together, Zania from under the table that held her pinned to the floor, with Kera on her knees beside her. Their faces were stained white with the shock of betrayal.

"Watch. *Watch!*" Dhulyn called out to them, but she was already turning away, crawling to where Parno lay on his side. Did his chest move? From this angle she could not tell. "In Battle," she called to him. Saw his hand move as he opened his fist. *In Death.* Her own breathing eased as she kept crawling. If she was wrong in what she had done, if this was the end, Dhulyn knew where she wanted to be. It was not until she had her hand on Parno's back that she turned once more to watch Avylos herself.

The Mage stood tall, drawn up to his full height. He held the Stone between his hands, his face alight with joy as the blue crystal light washed over him.

Dhulyn's heart sank. She had made a mistake after all. Surely when she had used the Stone herself, it had knocked her out before this much time had passed. But Avylos showed no signs of any adverse effect. On the contrary, his eyes were bright and glowing, his lips split in a huge smile. As she watched, the Mage's head fell back, his eyelids fluttered, his nostrils flared, and a look of blissful contentment crossed his features. But even as Dhulyn gathered her feet under her and reached for Parno's dagger, Avylos' skin paled, his smile became a rigid grin. A wrinkle formed between his brows.

The Mage fell to his knees.

He made a motion as if to drop the Stone, or at least to put it down. His arms curled toward his chest, and began to tremble. The crystal blue light intensified until it seemed to burst from him, from his eyes, his ears, and mouth. Cracks appeared in the skin of his face and head, his shoulders, his elbows, and wrists, and light poured out, filling the room. Suddenly, the blue light became crimson, and then a yellow so bright, that Dhulyn shut her eyes and turned away, burying her head in Parno's shoulder.

∞∞∞

"Zania." Edmir was so startled by the sound of his own voice that for a moment, he was not sure he had actually spoken aloud. "Zania," he said again. Realization brought him to his feet, his hands to the bars of the door. "Valaika," he called out as loudly as he could. "Wait! Valaika, hold on!"

∞∞∞

"I assure you, Kedneara the Queen will wish to speak to me." Section Leader Megz Primeau was holding onto her temper by main force of will. She knew the door page was only doing his duty, and that she had to be patient. It was hard, though, considering what was resting on the passing of even minutes.

"Kedneara the Queen has retired for the night," the page was saying. "We cannot disturb her, even for you, Section Leader."

Megz thought quickly. The guard commander had been injured and taken to the infirmary; where would his deputy be? And would she be able to convince him in time? As she was having this thought, noises and a sharp cry from within caused the door page to turn his head. Megz took advantage of this momentary lapse of discipline to push her way past him. Once she was actually in the anteroom, the page made only a token effort to stop her, and settled for preceding her into the inner chamber.

There they found the queen fallen to the floor beside her couch, her chamber pages trying to support her head and shoulders as she coughed and gasped for air. There were horrible wet sounds coming from her lungs, and Megz grimaced. She'd heard just such sounds coming from soldiers whose lungs had been pierced by arrow or blade.

"Sit her up, quickly," she said, striding forward and drawing off her gloves.

"I'll send for the Mage," the door page said.

"No!" Kedneara the Queen coughed more violently after the exertion of speaking that single word. She waved her hand to emphasize her point.

"Whisper, my Queen," Megz said. She lowered herself to her knees, slipped her arm around the queen's waist, and put her own shoulder behind the queen's.

"Edmir. Section Leader, it *was* Edmir." There was blood on the queen's lips. "His hair dyed and rings in his ears, foolish boy. But it was Edmir."

"Yes, my Queen." The three pages looked at one another, mouths agape, fear and confusion on their faces.

"You are my White Sword," rasped Kedneara the Queen.

"I am, my Queen."

"That stinking piece of Red Horse *dung.*" More coughing.

"Yes, my Queen." No one could say that Kedneara the Queen was not quick to see the point.

"I must go, Section Leader, I must go in person."

"I know, my Queen, the Black Guards told me." Megz looked up. "You heard her, she must go down to the Black Dungeon."

"But we cannot move her," the young man who was evidently the senior page was shocked, his fear showing in the trembling of his voice.

"We must," Megz said. "Only Kedneara the Queen herself can stop the executions."

"But, Section Leader—"

"Now!" The effort made the queen start coughing again, and Megz gritted her teeth as precious minutes were lost.

"Bring that chair," Megz said, nodding at one of the guest chairs next to the table at which Kedneara the Queen was accustomed to break her fast. The queen's taller, heavier chair would tire them out before they even reached the dungeons. As soon as the chair was close enough, Megz assisted Kedneara to her feet, and settled her in.

"You two." Megz pointed to the two huskier pages. "Pick up the queen and follow me. You, fetch four torches and bring them immediately to the Black Stairs." Megz knew where the torches were kept, ready at all times, and knew that as slowly as they could move, carrying the queen, the third page could quickly catch them up. She would have been better off with guards, even ones unfamiliar with the path to the dungeons, but there was no time. No time.

It was tricky to maneuver the chair on the circular stairs, and only hoarsely whispered orders from the queen herself kept the pages moving. Once at the bottom, another coughing fit forced them to stop completely while the queen recovered. With a whispered apology, Megz placed the first two fingers of her left hand under Kedneara the Queen's jaw, and felt her heart beat, thready and irregular. Megz pulled her lower lip through her teeth. Where did her duty lie strongest, with keeping the queen alive, or with saving Prince Edmir?

"My Queen," she said finally. "I fear you should rest."

"No." The once vibrant voice was whisper thin, but unmistakable in the eerie quiet of the corridor. No one was in any doubt of what Kedneara wanted.

"I will go before you," Megz said. "And light the sconces. The rest of you, bring the queen as quickly as you possibly can." Red splotches in otherwise white faces already showed the pages' unaccustomed exertion. But there was also some curiosity in their rounded eyes.

She raced down the corridor, pausing only to light the sconces as quickly as she could, and reached the door while the sounds of the queen advancing behind her grew faint. She did not wait, however, but tugged fiercely on the bell pull as soon as she reached it.

"Please wait," she said, as soon as the notes of the bell died away. Though she could not see beyond the bars of the gate, Megz knew at least one Black Guard was there. "Kedneara the Queen comes, please proceed no further."

"We cannot stop without word from the queen herself." It was the same soft voice Megz had heard before. "The first of the prisoners is already being bled."

"Will you tell me which it is?"

"It is the woman."

Megz turned and ran back to where the two pages, now red-faced and short of breath, still struggled with the queen's chair.

"My Queen," she said. "They have not begun on the prince, we are in time for him at least, but you must hurry."

Kedneara the Queen signaled that the pages put her down, which they did with relieved grunts.

"I can go faster on my own feet," she said. "There is not so much farther to go. My son." She swallowed. "Give me your shoulder, White Sword." Megz knew she should protest, that she should protect the woman who was the queen from the impulsiveness of the woman who was the mother. But she could not bring herself to argue. They were already too late to save the Jarlkevoso, if they stood here arguing, they would lose their chance to save the prince. And saving Edmir felt like the right thing to do, however much damage it might do to the queen. Though it seemed that at the moment she was not so much the queen, as she was Edmir's mother.

So Megz bent forward, helped the queen put her arms around her neck, and straightened, lifting the other woman to her feet. With one arm around the queen's waist, and the other hand keeping the queen's arm around her own shoulders, Megz set off down the corridor toward the barred door of the Black Dungeon as quickly as she could.

"Shallow breaths, my Queen," Megz murmured as they reached the door.

Kedneara turned to the door, and with an effort that Megz felt tremble through her own body, raised her hand to clutch one of the bars in the door.

"Open for me," she said. "I am Kedneara of Tegrian, and I would have my prisoners back." The queen's voice bubbled unpleasantly, and Megz's stomach chilled.

The door opened without a sound, and a Black Guard stepped back to allow the queen to enter.

"My prisoners," she whispered.

"The younger one is still whole and will be brought immediately, Kedneara the Queen." The Black Guard bowed his head. "But the older prisoner has already been cut."

"Can you stop the bleeding?"

Megz looked sideways at the queen's face, so close to her own. Evidently, Kedneara knew exactly what was done here in the Black Dungeon. Then Megz took a closer look. That was not a shadow on the queen's face, but blood dripping from the corner of her mouth.

"A chair for the queen, quickly," Megz said. "And bring

more light." But the Black Guard did not move until Kedneara herself waved her hand.

"Look at me, my Queen." Megz dared to give Kedneara a shake. "Stay with us. It won't be much longer."

The arm around Megz's shoulder tightened, and Kedneara the Queen lifted her head. Megz held the queen's gaze with her own. What she saw there made her hiss in her breath.

Edmir could hear footsteps, and a confused murmuring of half-recognized voices. Shadows formed and retreated at the far end of the corridor outside his cell, as lights were struck and carried away. A Black Guard carrying a stool with a low back appeared out of the darkness, and ran down the corridor toward what Edmir judged was the entrance to the dungeons.

"Stop!" he called. "Wait! What is going on? Where is Valaika Jarlkevo?"

Finally, a Black Guard came running back to his cell, his feet making no more sound than a cat's. "Come with me, young man," the man said as he unlocked the door.

Edmir tried to dash past, but the Black Guard grabbed his upper arm in both hands and hung on. "Slowly," the man said. "Do not startle her."

Edmir allowed himself to be led, hoping from the Black Guard's words that he was being taken to Valaika. But when they reached the end of the corridor, they turned right, toward the doorway to the upper world.

There, in the light of three candle lanterns, their pierced metal doors wide open, Kedneara of Tegrian sat on a simple stool, held upright by Megz Primeau. Three of her chamber pages stood in the outside passage, gawking through the open doorway. His mother the queen raised her head, and Edmir saw recognition in her eyes.

"Mother," he said, coming to his knees at Kedneara's side. "They have taken Valaika."

A look of inquiry passed over his mother's face, and the Black Guard behind Edmir spoke.

"She is gone, my Queen."

Edmir took his mother's hand and pressed it to his forehead. His shoulders shook, but he said nothing. He felt his mother's hand, light as a breath of wind, stroke his hair. A spot of blood fell on his cheek.

"My son. Oh, my son."

The hand on his hair fell away.

Edmir glanced up, but his mother's eyes were closed now, her breathing stilled. "Caids take you," he said automatically, laying her lifeless hand at her side. He could feel the cold stone under his knees, but nothing else.

Then a hand on his shoulder, Megz's voice above his head.

"What now, my King?"

I'm King, he thought, grinding his teeth together.

❧❧❧

Parno turned until he had Dhulyn's face pressed into the curve of his neck, rather than on his shoulder. His chest and throat no longer felt tight, and the air moved smoothly through his lungs. He blinked, trying to clear the after-images of brightness that still half-blinded him, though he'd had his eyes shut tight. The furniture was back on the floor, much of it broken and tumbled about. At first he thought his ears had been as badly affected as his eyes, but he swallowed, moved his jaw, and slowly he registered the sound of crying.

"Dhulyn, my heart," he said, squeezing her on the shoulder. She pushed herself upright, blinked at him, and, frowning slightly, touched his face with her fingertips. Parno felt himself relax, and despite everything, he smiled. Dhulyn nodded, and turned away, getting to her feet.

Kera was on her knees beside Zania. The player's face was a circle of pain, though it was Kera who was wiping away tears with her free hand. Parno rolled to his feet, ignoring Dhulyn's offer of her hand. So far as he could see, they were alone in the room, except for the girls. There was nothing here large enough for Avylos to hide behind, and the possibility of a trapdoor could wait until they had seen to Zania.

"I can't move the table," Kera said. "She's hurt."

Leaving Dhulyn to check the rest of the room, Parno went directly to the injured girl. The table he lifted off in a moment, and he breathed more easily when he saw that both Zania's legs were straight, and moving. Her arm told another story, however.

"Hold still, little Cat," he told her. "It's just the smaller, outer bone, the best kind of break you could have." He smiled at her. "I've broken my own arm that way several times, and so has Dhulyn Wolfshead. It will hurt to set it properly, but not more than it hurts already. We're not Healers, nor even Knives, but we've done this many times before, and we know what we're doing. All we must do is get the arm straight, and bind it well."

"It *is* Dhulyn Wolfshead, then?" Kera asked.

"Oh, yes, don't doubt it."

"What happened? All I saw was a bright light."

"Time for that soon. We're alive, and that's all we need to know just now. Dhulyn! Can you find something to splint the little Cat's arm? A leg from that stool might do."

Dhulyn bent quickly and picked something off the floor.

"Parno," she said, and something in the quality of her voice made them all turn to look at her.

She held a dull blue cylinder by the very tips of her fingers. It was dirty, and stained along one side, the exposed side, with a pale pink mist, damp and slightly greasy.

But it was the Muse Stone.

"Be careful." The words were out of his mouth before he could stop them. He felt he more than deserved the look Dhulyn gave him. "He must have got past us somehow, got to the door."

"You think he's running about somewhere in Royal House unaware of who he is?" Dhulyn asked. "That's the only way he would have left without it, that's certain." She looked at the Stone again.

"Oh, Sun and the *blooded* Moon." Dhulyn was rubbing the tips of her fingers together, then she lifted her fingers to her nose and sniffed. Her lip wrinkled back to show her teeth in a parody of her wolf's smile. She turned her head and spat on the floor over and over. She looked around her, but finding no cleaner surface, wiped off the Stone on the front of her shirt.

Dawning realization made Parno's stomach churn and his eyebrows crawl up his forehead. Dhulyn had turned away from Avylos, turned her back to him and hidden her face. Her face, and the front of her shirt were clean, but the back of her shirt, much of the floor, and the sides of the girls' faces, their sleeves and hands, were marked by the same residue as the Stone.

"Princess Kera," he said. "Have you an underskirt? Would you remove it please, and use it to wipe off your mouths and faces. Quick as you can."

"What is it?" Kera immediately lifted the skirt of her gown and pulled off her underskirt. Gathering a soft fold of it, she wiped Zania's face before doing the same for herself.

"It's Avylos."

Twenty-seven

"I THINK THAT, IN MY case, the force of the power only pushed me aside." Dhulyn put down the leg of roasted duck she'd been chewing on and picked up a cloth to wipe her hands. She tapped herself on her chest. "*I* was still there, my Visions still came, though I thought they were dreams. And I think that even without my Mercenary Schooling—even without the *Shora*—I would have found my way back, perhaps through the Visions themselves, if no other way."

"And is that what you expected to happen with Avy-los?" Edmir spread a coating of nellberry jam on a slice of breast meat, rolled it up, and inserted it into his mouth. They were using Avylos' sitting room, the first chance they'd had in days to sit down together. Parno, Dhulyn, and Edmir had kept to the Mage's wing, sorting out his books and devices, in part to learn what they could, in part to make sure nothing remained that could cause any harm. Princess Kera, using Megz Primeau and Zania to help her, had been dealing with the upheaval caused by the sudden death of Kedneara the Queen.

Kedneara's body had been retrieved from the Black Dungeon and was lying in state in the Great Hall as her pyre was being built in the center of the Royal Courtyard. High Noble Houses were coming from all of Tegrian and the subject lands to attend her burning, and the ceremonial burial of the ashes. No one disputed that Kedneara had very obviously died from the same ailment that had plagued her father, brought on by the shock and stress of recent events, and particularly the disappearance of the Blue Mage.

"It's what I hoped would happen, yes," Dhulyn said in answer to Edmir's question. "I hoped that the wave of power released from the Stone would overwhelm and drown him, as it had done to me."

"And so we'd have a different man entirely to deal with," Kera said, nodding.

"It was a rough chance to take, just the same," Parno said. "If you could find your way back, so could he, and he'd have all that power in him."

"Would he? I don't think so." Dhulyn shook her head. "According to what Zania had told us, Avylos had no power when he first came to her family's group of traveling players. Avylos himself told me that his power had grown little by little, which fit with what Valaika remembered of his first coming to Tegrian. I think he had no magic himself."

Zania was nodding. "That's what I remember my uncle telling us. He did stage magic only when he first joined the troupe, tricks that anyone could do, if they had talent and were taught the method. It was only after he learned about the Stone, and how we used it, that . . . he changed."

"He was *srusha*," Dhulyn said. "In the tongue of the Espadryni it means 'barren,' or 'empty,' though I have never heard it used in connection with people. We surmised that all the men of the Espadryni were Mages, as all the women were Marked with the Sight. But the truth must be that not all had the same degree of power, just as we have all seen different strengths in those who bear a Mark."

"So it would follow that from time to time one would be born with a power greater than others . . ." Edmir said, following the thread of the tale, as Dhulyn had known he would.

"And from time to time, one without power at all," she said. "Oh, he knew the methods—" She drew a symbol in the air. "He'd seen it done hundreds of times, knew what to do and what to say. But until he felt the residual power that the Stone generated even while it slept . . . until then, no magic had ever worked for him. In me, the Stone found a Mark untrained, and so the power it gave me overwhelmed me. But in Avylos it found a broken vessel, cracked and unglazed, which could not hold the power at all."

"And is that why his power did not affect women so well? Because it was borrowed?"

"Can you see the women of the Red Horsemen letting the men have magics which could be used against them? And those women all Seers? I can't, not if they were anything like Dhulyn Wolfshead." Parno laughed.

"It seems that some of his magics disappeared with him," Zania said. "As if, like his powers, they had no permanence."

"Not long-standing magics," Kera said. "There are soldiers that he magicked who are still whole and healthy, so it seems likely that Valaika's son will keep *his* health. It does appear, however, that some of Avylos' most recent magics *have* died with him. His cure of my mother the queen. His curse on Parno Lionsmane. But other things are still with us—"

"We've had to prop open the workroom door," Parno said, "otherwise the latch keeps disappearing."

"The ghost eye on my back is still there," Edmir said. He shivered, and Zania put her hand over his. He smiled at her, but the smile was strained, and both lowered their eyes as Zania withdrew her hand.

Kera saw this, and her glance went back and forth between the two. There was something bothering the young princess, Dhulyn thought. Something she was hesitating to say.

"Will you want the Stone?" Dhulyn asked, when no one else seemed ready to speak. "It is drained now, but I can finish translating the book, and . . ."

Zania was shaking her head. "I don't think so. Not after what I've seen. I'd rather rely on my own talents, and my own powers."

"Then, Lord and Lady Princes, I'd suggest the Stone, and the book for that matter, should be sent to the Scholars' Library of Valdomar for study. They know much of the Caids there, and this will be a find of great importance for them."

"Speaking of powers." Kera sat up straight and turned to Edmir.

Here it comes, Dhulyn thought. *Whatever it is that's been biting the girl.*

"There's a different power altogether that we have to settle," Kera said. "Edmir, you have kept yourself in the shadows these last few days, and I have not argued with you."

The corners of Edmir's mouth tightened, as if he had clenched his teeth. "I'm sorry, Kera," he said. "I thought it would be less confusing this way, with everything else that's happened. I'm ready to lift the burden from your shoulders if you think the time has come."

"Please believe there is no one more loyal to you than I—well, perhaps there is one other," Kera nodded across the table at Zania. "But, Edmir, I have given the events of the past moon much thought, and I believe—whatever *I* might want, whatever *you* might want, you cannot be king."

Edmir sat back in his chair as if he'd been pushed. But the color had come up in his cheeks, his eyes widened. He looked, Dhulyn thought, for all the world like a tired horse seeing the open door of its own stable, but who fears it may be only an illusion.

"Kera." Edmir cleared his throat and started again. "Kera . . . what are you saying? I have not come all this way, they—" He gestured at where Dhulyn and Parno sat next to each other. "—have not done all they have, in order for me not to be king."

"Edmir, please listen. The country believes you are dead. Many who have seen you alive here in the Royal House were told you are an imposter. We know the truth, and those who have known you your whole life will know you and believe, but what about the rest of the country? Ordinary people who have never seen you? With Kedneara dead and Avylos gone, we cannot afford more cause for insecurity and doubt. And as for the subject lands, what will the Noble Houses of Balnia, or Demnion, or—" Kera threw up her hands. "Edmir, I swear to you, if I saw any way for you to keep the throne, safely, and without danger to the country, I would say so."

And it was that last point, Dhulyn saw, that convinced him.

"I will be an excuse for war," Edmir said. "And not just now, but always. Whenever there is discontent, a bad harvest, a long winter, there will be someone ready to challenge my right to the throne," he said. "Someone who will say I am not Edmir, son of Kedneara."

Dhulyn watched. From where she sat, she could see Edmir's hands under the edge of the table, clenching and unclenching. He was not stupid, and his imagination was such that he could always clearly see that all actions and events had a number of possible consequences. Edmir glanced up, and she caught his eye.

"Prepare for what *can* happen," she told him. "That is the Common Rule. I have Seen Visions of you as King, Edmir," she added. He frowned. "But Zania was always with you. I think perhaps you were on a stage, not on this throne. I have Seen you late at night, in a tent, writing. I have also seen your sister, in armor, leading troops into battle, the royal crest of Tegrian on her breastplate."

"Of course," Edmir said. He turned to Kera. "I wanted to be a soldier, like our father. But you were always better at it than I was. It was always you who came up with the plans, the strategies. It was never me, Kera, always you. *You* were the soldier. *You* will be Queen."

❦❦❦

Dhulyn folded up the sleeves of her shirt, uncomfortable with being so much covered in the summer heat. She resisted the urge to scratch, for the fifth time, at her wig, but not quickly enough that Parno had not seen the beginnings of the movement.

"We're only a week out of Lesonika," Parno said. "It won't be that much longer. We'll present our documents from Queen Kera to the Senior Brother at our House there, and we won't have to disguise ourselves any longer."

Dhulyn tried to smile without snarling. "It seems that in the last month everyone's lives but ours have been settled. The player Zania Tzadeyeu and her new husband, the soon-to-be famous playwright of *The Solder King*, have left Beolind well laden with gifts from the new Queen of Tegrian, to return to Jarlkevo to collect their caravan."

"And the Stone and the book, together with your letters, have gone off to Valdomar in the capable hands of Megz Primeau."

"Who, on her return, will also go to Jarlkevo, to become

Steward of the House, until Janek Jarlkevoso is old enough to hold the House himself." Dhulyn blew out a short breath.

"As for us, how settled do you want us to be? We're finally back on the road to Delmara after that little detour to earn some money from the Nisveans."

Dhulyn pressed her lips together and shifted in her saddle. Her back was sore, and the muscles in her belly and thighs were cramping.

"Separate beds tonight, my soul," she said, in as pleasant a voice as she could manage. "And *that* means more money spent."

"Ah, but look on the sunny side," Parno said. "Evil Mage destroyed, princes and princesses all where they want to be— and out of our hands, let me point out. As for us, we've got our horses, all our weapons, food for the journey, money for inns. What more could we ask for?"

Despite herself, Dhulyn found the corner of her mouth turning up. Still . . .

"Those Sun-burnt, Moon-drowned Nisveans never paid us."

Parno laughed. "There is one thing you haven't explained, my heart," he said. "It was Avylos who broke the Tribes, or so your Visions tell you . . ."

"But how is it that the women of the Espadryni— Marked Seers as we know them to have been—how is it that they did not See him, and stop it?"

"Exactly."

Dhulyn shook her head. "My mother did not seem surprised, or afraid. She acted as though she were putting into effect long-planned events."

"Do you think we'll ever know?"

Dhulyn put her heels to Bloodbone's sides. "I know we won't make the next inn if we stand about talking."

Barbara Ashford

Spells at the Crossroads

A brand new omnibus edition of *Spellcast* and
Spellcrossed, together in one volume for the first time!

"[A] novel about the transformative power of the theater...a
woman with an unsettled past...and the intersecting coincidences that move her toward the future. Maggie is relatable
and her journey compelling. Four stars."

—*RT Book Reviews*

"*Spellcast* had me spellbound, and *Spellcrossed* was no
different. [It] moved me to tears more than a few times, and
was equally heartwarming and heartbreaking.... Magic and
the magic of musical theatre intertwine seamlessly to create
a read worth savoring. I can't recommend this series highly
enough!"

—My Bookish Ways

ISBN: 978-0-7564-1021-6

To Order Call: 1-800-788-6262
www.dawbooks.com

DAW 204

S.L. Farrell

The Nessantico Cycle

"[Farrell's] best yet, a delicious melange of politics, war,
sorcery, and religion in a richly imagined world."
—George R. R. Martin,
#1 *New York Times* bestselling author

"Readers who appreciate intricate world building,
intrigue, and action will immerse themselves effortlessly
in this rich and complex story."
—*Publishers Weekly*

A MAGIC OF TWILIGHT
978-0-7564-0536-6

A MAGIC OF NIGHTFALL
978-0-7564-0599-1

A MAGIC OF DAWN
978-0-7564-0646-2

To Order Call: 1-800-788-6262
www.dawbooks.com

DAW 119

Tanya Huff

"The Gales are an amazing family, the aunts will strike fear into your heart, and the characters Allie meets are both charming and terrifying."
  —#1 *New York Times* bestselling author
    Charlaine Harris

"Thoughtful and leisurely, this fresh urban fantasy from Canadian author Huff features an ensemble cast of nuanced characters in Calgary, Alberta.... Fantasy buffs will find plenty of humor, thrills and original mythology to chew on, along with refreshingly three-dimensional women in an original, fully realized world." —*Publishers Weekly*

The Enchantment Emporium
978-0-7564-0605-9

The Wild Ways
978-0-7564-0763-6

and now...
The Future Falls
978-0-7564-0753-7

To Order Call: 1-800-788-6262
www.dawbooks.com

Seanan McGuire
The October Daye Novels

"...will surely appeal to readers who enjoy my books, or those of Patricia Briggs." —*Charlaine Harris*

"I am so invested in the world building and the characters now.... Of all the 'Faerie' urban fantasy series out there, I enjoy this one the most."—*Felicia Day*

To Order Call: 1-800-788-6262
www.dawbooks.com

DAW 142